Jeffrey Archer is a master storyteller, the author of ten novels which have all been worldwide bestsellers. *Not a Penny More, Not a Penny Less* was his first book, and it achieved instant success. Next came the tense and terrifying thriller *Shall We Tell the President?*, followed by his triumphant bestseller *Kane and Abel*. His first collection of short stories, *A Quiver Full of Arrows*, came next, and then *The Prodigal Daughter*, the superb sequel to *Kane and Abel*. This was followed by *First Among Equals*, considered by the *Scotsman* to be the finest novel about parliament since Trollope, the thrilling chase story *A Matter of Honour*, his second collection of stories, *A Twist in the Tale*, and the novels *As the Crow Flies* and *Honour Among Thieves*. *Twelve Red Herrings*, his third collection of stories, was followed by the novels *The Fourth Estate* and *The Eleventh Commandment*. A collected edition of his short stories was published in 1997, followed by a new selection, *To Cut a Long Story Short*.

Jeffrey Archer was born in 1940 and educated at Wellington School, Somerset and Brasenose College, Oxford. He represented Great Britain in the 100 metres in the early sixties, and entered the House of Commons when he won the by-election at Louth in 1969. He wrote his first novel, *Not a Penny More, Not a Penny Less*, in 1974. From September 1985 to October 1986 he was Deputy Chairman of the Conservative Party, and he was created a Life Peer in the Queen's Birthday Honours of 1992.

D1054348

By the same author

Novels

NOT A PENNY MORE, NOT A PENNY LESS
SHALL WE TELL THE PRESIDENT?
KANE AND ABEL
THE PRODIGAL DAUGHTER
FIRST AMONG EQUALS
AS THE CROW FLIES
HONOUR AMONG THIEVES
THE FOURTH ESTATE
THE ELEVENTH COMMANDMENT

Short Stories

A QUIVER FULL OF ARROWS
A TWIST IN THE TALE
THE COLLECTED SHORT STORIES
TO CUT A LONG STORY SHORT

Plays

BEYOND REASONABLE DOUBT
EXCLUSIVE

JEFFREY ARCHER

A MATTER OF HONOUR

TWELVE RED HERRINGS

Grafton

This omnibus edition published in 2003 by
HarperCollins*Publishers*
77-85 Fulham Palace Road,
Hammersmith, London W6 8JB

www.**fire**and**water**.com

A Matter of Honour
Copyright © Jeffrey Archer 1986

Twelve Red Herrings
Copyright © Jeffrey Archer 1994

The Author asserts the moral right to
be identified as the author of this work

This novel is entirely a work of fiction. The names,
characters and incidents portrayed within it are the work of
the author's imagination. Any resemblance to actual persons,
living or dead, events or localitites is entirely coincidental

ISBN 0 00 768306 5

Set in Baskerville

Printed and bound in Great Britain by
Mackays of Chatham Ltd, Chatham, Kent

All rights reserved. No part of this publication may be
reproduced, stored in a retrieval system, or transmitted,
in any form or by any means, electronic, mechanical,
photocopying, recording or otherwise, without the prior
permission of the publishers.

This book is sold subject to the condition that it shall not,
by way of trade or otherwise, be lent, re-sold, hired out or
otherwise circulated without the publisher's prior consent
in any form of binding or cover other than that in which it
is published and without a similar condition including this
condition being imposed on the subsequent purchaser.

A MATTER OF HONOUR

To Will

PART ONE

THE KREMLIN
MOSCOW

May 19, 1966

CHAPTER ONE

THE KREMLIN, MOSCOW
May 19, 1966

"It's a fake," said the Russian leader, staring down at the small exquisite painting he held in his hands.

"That isn't possible," replied his Politburo colleague. "The Tsar's icon of St George and the Dragon has been in the Winter Palace at Leningrad under heavy guard for over fifty years."

"True, Comrade Zaborski," said the old man, "but for fifty years we've been guarding a fake. The Tsar must have removed the original some time before the Red Army entered St Petersburg and overran the Winter Palace."

The head of State Security moved restlessly in his chair as the cat and mouse game continued. Zaborski knew, after years of running the KGB, who had been cast as the mouse the moment his phone had rung at four that morning to say that the General Secretary required him to report to the Kremlin – immediately.

"How can you be so sure it's a fake, Leonid Ilyich?" the diminutive figure enquired.

"Because, my dear Zaborski, during the past eighteen months, the age of all the treasures in the Winter

3

Palace has been tested by carbon-dating, the modern scientific process that does not call for a second opinion," said Brezhnev, displaying his new-found knowledge. "And what we have always thought to be one of the nation's masterpieces," he continued, "turns out to have been painted five hundred years after Rublev's original."

"But by whom and for what purpose?" asked the Chairman of State Security, incredulous.

"The experts tell me it was probably a court painter," replied the Russian leader, "who must have been commissioned to execute the copy only months before the Revolution took place. It has always worried the curator at the Winter Palace that the Tsar's traditional silver crown was not attached to the back of the frame, as it was to all his other masterpieces," added Brezhnev.

"But I always thought that the silver crown had been removed by a souvenir hunter even before we had entered St Petersburg."

"No," said the General Secretary drily, his bushy eyebrows rising every time he had completed a statement. "It wasn't the Tsar's silver crown that had been removed, but the painting itself."

"Then what can the Tsar have done with the original?" the Chairman said, almost as if he were asking himself the question.

"That is exactly what I want to know, Comrade," said Brezhnev, resting his hands each side of the little painting that remained in front of him. "And you are the one who has been chosen to come up with the answer," he added.

For the first time the Chairman of the KGB looked unsure of himself.

"But do you have anything for me to go on?"

"Very little," admitted the General Secretary, flicking open a file that he removed from the top drawer of his desk. He stared down at the closely typed notes headed 'The Significance of the Icon in Russian History'. Someone had been up all through the night preparing a ten-page report that the leader had only found time to scan. Brezhnev's real interest began on page four. He quickly turned over the first three pages before reading aloud: "'At the time of the Revolution, Tsar Nicholas II obviously saw Rublev's masterpiece as his passport to freedom in the West. He must have had a copy made which he then left on his study wall where the original had previously hung.'" The Russian leader looked up. "Beyond that we have little to go on."

The head of the KGB looked perplexed. He remained puzzled as to why Brezhnev should want State Security involved in the theft of a minor masterpiece. "And how important is it that we find the original?" he asked, trying to pick up a further clue.

Leonid Brezhnev stared down at his Kremlin colleague.

"Nothing could be more important, Comrade," came back the unexpected reply. "And I shall grant you any resources you may consider necessary in terms of people and finance to discover the whereabouts of the Tsar's icon."

"But if I were to take you at your word, Comrade General Secretary," said the head of the KGB, trying to disguise his disbelief, "I could so easily end up spending far more than the painting is worth."

"That would not be possible," said Brezhnev, pausing for effect, "because it's not the icon itself that I'm after." He turned his back on the Chairman of State Security and stared out of the window. He had always

5

disliked not being able to see over the Kremlin wall and into Red Square. He waited for some moments before he proclaimed, "The money the Tsar might have raised from selling such a masterpiece would only have kept Nicholas in his accustomed lifestyle for a matter of months, perhaps a year at the most. No, it's what we believe the Tsar had secreted *inside* the icon that would have guaranteed security for himself and his family for the rest of their days."

A little circle of condensation formed on the window pane in front of the General Secretary.

"What could possibly be that valuable?" asked the Chairman.

"Do you remember, Comrade, what the Tsar promised Lenin in exchange for his life?"

"Yes, but it turned out to be a bluff because no such document was hidden . . ." He stopped himself just before saying "in the icon".

Zaborski stood silently, unable to witness Brezhnev's triumphant smile.

"You have caught up with me at last, Comrade. You see, the document was hidden in the icon all the time. We just had the wrong icon."

The Russian leader waited for some time before he turned back and passed over to his colleague a single sheet of paper. "This is the Tsar's testimony indicating what we would find hidden in the icon of St George and the Dragon. At the time, nothing was discovered in the icon, which only convinced Lenin that it had been a pathetic bluff by the Tsar to save his family from execution."

Zaborski slowly read the hand-written testimony that had been signed by the Tsar hours before his execution. Zaborski's hands began to tremble and a bead of sweat appeared on his forehead long before he had reached the last paragraph. He looked across at the tiny painting, no larger than a book, that remained in the centre of the Chairman's desk.

"Not since the death of Lenin," continued Brezhnev, "has anyone believed the Tsar's claim. But now, there can be little doubt that if we are able to locate the genuine masterpiece, we will undoubtedly also be in possession of the promised document."

"And with the authority of those who signed that document, no one could question our legal claim," said Zaborski.

"That would undoubtedly prove to be the case, Comrade Chairman," replied the Russian leader. "And I also feel confident that we would receive the backing of the United Nations and the World Court if the Americans tried to deny us our right. But I fear time is now against us."

"Why?" asked the Chairman of State Security.

"Look at the completion date in the Tsar's testimony and you will see how much time we have left to honour our part of the agreement," said Brezhnev.

Zaborski stared down at the date scrawled in the hand of the Tsar – June 20, 1966. He handed back the testimony as he considered the enormity of the task with which his leader had entrusted him. Leonid Ilyich Brezhnev continued his monologue.

"So, as you can see, Comrade Zaborski, we have only one month left before the deadline, but if you can discover the whereabouts of the original icon, President Johnson's defence strategy would be rendered virtually useless, and the United States would then become a pawn on the Russian chessboard."

CHAPTER TWO

APPLESHAW, ENGLAND
June 1966

"And to my dearly beloved and only son, Captain Adam Scott, MC, I bequeath the sum of five hundred pounds."

Although Adam had anticipated the amount would be pitiful, he nevertheless remained bolt upright in his chair as the solicitor glanced over his half-moon spectacles.

The old lawyer who was seated behind the large partners' desk raised his head and blinked at the handsome young man before him. Adam put a hand nervously through his thick black hair, suddenly conscious of the lawyer's stare. Then Mr Holbrooke's eyes returned to the papers in front of him.

"And to my dearly beloved daughter, Margaret Scott, I bequeath the sum of four hundred pounds." Adam was unable to prevent a small grin spreading across his face. Even in the minutiae of his final act, father had remained a chauvinist.

"To the Hampshire County Cricket Club," droned on Mr Holbrooke, unperturbed by Miss Scott's relative misfortunes, "twenty-five pounds, life membership."

Finally paid up, thought Adam. "To the Old Contemptibles, fifteen pounds. And to the Appleshaw Parish Church, ten pounds." Death membership, Adam mused. "To Wilf Proudfoot, our loyal gardener part time, ten pounds, and to Mrs Mavis Cox, our daily help, five pounds."

"And finally, to my dearly beloved wife Susan, our marital home, and the remainder of my estate."

This pronouncement made Adam want to laugh out loud because he doubted if the remainder of Pa's estate, even if they sold his premium bonds and the pre-war golf clubs, amounted to more than another thousand pounds.

But mother was a daughter of the Regiment and wouldn't complain, she never did. If God ever announced the saints, as opposed to some Pope in Rome, Saint Susan of Appleshaw would be up there with Mary and Elizabeth. All through his life 'Pa', as Adam always thought of him, had set such high standards for the family to live up to. Perhaps that was why Adam continued to admire him above all men. Sometimes the very thought made him feel strangely out of place in the swinging sixties.

Adam began to move restlessly in his chair, assuming that the proceedings were now drawing to a close. The sooner they were all out of this cold, drab little office the better, he felt.

Mr Holbrooke looked up once more and cleared his throat, as if he were about to announce who was to be left the Goya or the Hapsburg diamonds. He pushed his half-moon spectacles further up the bridge of his nose and stared back down at the last paragraphs of his late client's testament. The three surviving members of the Scott family sat in silence. What could he have to add? thought Adam.

Whatever it was, the solicitor had obviously pondered the final bequest several times, because he delivered the words like a well-versed actor, his eyes returning to the script only once.

"And I also leave to my son," Mr Holbrooke paused, "the enclosed envelope," he said, holding it up, "which I can only hope will bring him greater happiness than it did me. Should he decide to open the envelope it must be on the condition that he will never divulge its contents to any other living person." Adam caught his sister's eye but she only shook her head slightly, obviously as puzzled as he was. He glanced towards his mother who looked shocked. Was it fear or was it distress? Adam couldn't decide. Without another word, Mr Holbrooke passed the yellowed envelope over to the Colonel's only son.

Everyone in the room remained seated, not quite sure what to do next. Mr Holbrooke finally closed the thin file marked Colonel Gerald Scott, DSO, OBE, MC, pushed back his chair and walked slowly over to the widow. They shook hands and she said, "Thank you," a faintly ridiculous courtesy, Adam felt, as the only person in the room who had made any sort of profit on this particular transaction had been Mr Holbrooke, and that on behalf of Holbrooke, Holbrooke and Gascoigne.

He rose and went quickly to his mother's side.

"You'll join us for tea, Mr Holbrooke?" she was asking.

"I fear not, dear lady," the lawyer began, but Adam didn't bother to listen further. Obviously the fee hadn't been large enough to cover Holbrooke taking time off for tea.

Once they had left the office and Adam had ensured his mother and sister were seated comfortably in the back of the family Morris Minor, he took his place behind the steering wheel. He had parked outside Mr Holbrooke's office in the middle of the High Street. No yellow lines in the streets of Appleshaw – yet, he thought. Even before he had switched on the ignition his mother had offered matter-of-factly, "We'll have to get rid of this, you know. I can't afford to run it now, not with petrol at six shillings a gallon."

"Don't let's worry about that today," said Margaret consolingly, but in a voice that accepted that her mother was right. "I wonder what can be in that envelope, Adam," she added, wanting to change the subject.

"Detailed instructions on how to invest my five hundred pounds, no doubt," said her brother, attempting to lighten their mood.

"Don't be disrespectful of the dead," said his mother, the same look of fear returning to her face. "I begged your father to destroy that envelope," she added, in a voice that was barely a whisper.

Adam's lips pursed when he realised this must be *the* envelope his father had referred to all those years ago when he had witnessed the one row between his parents that he had ever experienced. Adam still remembered his father's raised voice and angry words just a few days after he had returned from Germany.

"I have to open it, don't you understand?" Pa had insisted.

"Never," his mother had replied. "After all the sacrifices I have made, you at least owe me that."

Over twenty years had passed since that confrontation and he had never heard the subject referred to again. The only time Adam ever mentioned it to his sister she could throw no light on what the dispute might have been over.

Adam put his foot on the brake as they reached a T-junction at the end of the High Street.

He turned right and continued to drive out of the village for a mile or so down a winding country lane before bringing the old Morris Minor to a halt. Adam leapt out and opened the trellised gate whose path led through a neat lawn to a little thatched cottage.

"I'm sure you ought to be getting back to London," were his mother's first words as she entered the drawing room.

"I'm in no hurry, mother. There's nothing that can't wait until tomorrow."

"Just as you wish, my dear, but you don't have to worry yourself over me," his mother continued. She stared up at the tall young man who reminded her so much of Gerald. He would have been as good-looking as her husband if it wasn't for the slight break in his nose. The same dark hair and deep brown eyes, the same open, honest face, even the same gentle approach to everyone he came across. But most of all the same high standards of morality that had brought them to their present sad state. "And in any case I've always got Margaret to take care of me," she added. Adam looked across at his sister and wondered how she would now cope with Saint Susan of Appleshaw.

Margaret had recently become engaged to a City stockbroker, and although the marriage had been postponed, she would soon be wanting to start a life of her own. Thank God her fiancé had already put a down-payment on a little house only fourteen miles away.

After tea and a sad uninterrupted monologue from his mother on the virtues and misfortunes of their father, Margaret cleared away and left the two of them alone. They had both loved him in such different ways

13

although Adam felt that he had never let Pa really know how much he respected him.

"Now that you're no longer in the army, my dear, I do hope you'll be able to find a worthwhile job," his mother said uneasily, as she recalled how difficult that had proved to be for his father.

"I'm sure everything will be just fine, mother," he replied. "The Foreign Office have asked to see me again," he added, hoping to reassure her.

"Still, now that you've got five hundred pounds of your own," she said, "that should make things a little easier for you." Adam smiled fondly at his mother, wondering when she had last spent a day in London. His share of the Chelsea flat alone was four pounds a week and he still had to eat occasionally. She raised her eyes and, looking up at the clock on the mantelpiece, said, "You'd better be getting along, my dear, I don't like the thought of you on that motorbike after dark."

Adam bent down to kiss her on the cheek. "I'll give you a call tomorrow," he said. On his way out he stuck his head around the kitchen door and shouted to his sister, "I'm off and I'll be sending you a cheque for fifty pounds."

"Why?" asked Margaret, looking up from the sink.

"Just let's say it's my blow for women's rights." He shut the kitchen door smartly to avoid the dishcloth that was hurled in his direction. Adam revved up his BSA and drove down the A303 through Andover and on towards London. As most of the traffic was coming west out of the city, he was able to make good time on his way back to the flat in Ifield Road.

Adam had decided to wait until he had reached the privacy of his own room before he opened the envelope. Lately the excitement in his life had not been such that he felt he could be blasé about the little ceremony. After all, in a way, he had waited most of his life to discover what could possibly be in the envelope he had now inherited.

Adam had been told the story of the family tragedy by his father a thousand times – "It's all a matter of honour, old chap," his father would repeat, lifting his chin and squaring his shoulders. Adam's father had not realised that he had spent a lifetime overhearing the snide comments of lesser men and suffering the side-long glances from those officers who had made sure they were not seen too regularly in his company. Petty men with petty minds. Adam knew his father far too well to believe, even for a moment, that he could have been involved in such treachery as was whispered. Adam took one hand off the handlebars and fingered the envelope in his inside pocket like a schoolboy the day before his birthday feeling the shape of a present in the hope of discovering some clue as to its contents. He felt certain that whatever it contained would not be to anyone's advantage now his father was dead, but it did not lessen his curiosity.

He tried to piece together the few facts he had been told over the years. In 1946, within a year of his fiftieth birthday, his father had resigned his commission from the army. *The Times* had described Pa as a brilliant tactical officer with a courageous war record. His resignation had been a decision that had surprised *The Times* correspondent, astonished his immediate family and shocked his regiment, as it had been assumed by all who knew him that it was only a matter of months before crossed swords and a baton would have been sewn on to his epaulette.

Because of the colonel's sudden and unexplained departure from the regiment, fact was augmented by fiction. When asked, all the colonel would offer was that he had had enough of war, and felt the time had come to make a little money on which Susan and he could retire before it was too late. Even at the time, few people found his story credible, and that credibility was not helped when the only job the colonel managed to secure for himself was as secretary of the local golf club.

It was only through the generosity of Adam's late grandfather, General Sir Pelham Westlake, that he had been able to remain at Wellington College, and thereby be given the opportunity to continue the family tradition and pursue a military career.

After leaving school, Adam was offered a place at the Royal Military Academy, Sandhurst. During his days at the RMA, Adam was to be found diligently studying military history, tactics, and battle procedure while at weekends he concentrated on rugby and squash, although his greatest success came whenever he completed the different cross-country courses he encountered. For two years, panting cadets from Cranwell and Dartmouth only saw his mud-spattered back as Adam went on to become the Inter-Services champion. He also became the middleweight boxing champion despite a Nigerian cadet breaking his nose in the first round of the final. The Nigerian made the mistake of assuming the fight was already over.

When Adam passed out of Sandhurst in August 1956, he managed ninth place in the academic order of merit, but his leadership and example outside the classroom was such that no one was surprised when he was awarded the Sword of Honour. Adam never doubted from that moment he would now follow his father and command the regiment.

The Royal Wessex Regiment accepted the colonel's

son soon after he had been awarded his regular commission. Adam quickly gained the respect of the soldiers and popularity with those officers whose currency was not to deal in rumour. As a tactical officer in the field he had no equal, and when it came to combat duty it was clear he had inherited his father's courage. Yet, when six years later the War Office published in the *London Gazette* the names of those subalterns who had been made up to Captain, Lieutenant Adam Scott was not to be found on the list. His contemporaries were genuinely surprised, while senior officers of the regiment remained tight-lipped. To Adam it was becoming abundantly clear that he was not to be allowed to atone for whatever it was his father was thought to have done.

Eventually Adam was made up to captain, but not before he had distinguished himself in the Malayan jungle in hand-to-hand fighting against the never-ending waves of Chinese soldiers. Having been captured and held prisoner by the Communists, he endured solitude and torture of the kind that no amount of training could have prepared him for. He escaped eight months after his incarceration only to discover on returning to the front line that he had been awarded a posthumous Military Cross. When, at the age of twenty-nine, Captain Scott passed his staff exam but still failed to be offered a regimental place at the staff college, he finally accepted he could never hope to command the regiment. He resigned his commission a few weeks later; there was no need to suggest that the reason he had done so was because he needed to earn more money.

While he was serving out his last few months with the regiment, Adam learned from his mother that Pa only had weeks to live. Adam made the decision not to inform his father of his resignation. He knew Pa would only blame himself and he was at least thankful that he had died without being aware of the stigma that had become part of his son's daily life.

When Adam reached the outskirts of London his mind returned, as it had so often lately, to the pressing problem of finding himself gainful employment. In the seven weeks he had been out of work Adam had already had more interviews with his bank manager than with prospective employers. It was true that he had another meeting lined up with the Foreign Office, but he had been impressed by the standard of the other candidates he had encountered on the way, and was only too aware of his lack of a university qualification. However, he felt the first interview had gone well and he had been quickly made aware of how many ex-officers had joined the service. When he discovered that the chairman of the selection board had a Military Cross, Adam assumed he wasn't being considered for desk work.

As he swung the motorbike into the King's Road Adam once again fingered the envelope in his inside jacket pocket hoping, uncharitably, that Lawrence would not yet have returned from the bank. Not that he could complain: his old school friend had been extremely generous in offering him such a pleasant room in his spacious flat for only four pounds a week.

"You can start paying more when they make you an ambassador," Lawrence had told him.

"You're beginning to sound like Rachmann," Adam had retorted, grinning at the man he had so admired during their days at Wellington. For Lawrence – in direct contrast to Adam – everything seemed to come so easily – exams, jobs, sport and women, especially women. When he had won his place at Balliol and gone on to take a first in PPE, no one was surprised. But when Lawrence chose banking as a profession, his contemporaries were unable to hide their disbelief. It seemed to be the first time he had embarked on anything that might be described as mundane.

Adam parked his motorbike just off Ifield Road, aware that, like his mother's old Morris Minor, it would have to be sold if the Foreign Office job didn't materialise. As he strolled towards the flat a girl who passed gave him a second look: he didn't notice. He took the stairs in threes and had reached the fifth floor, and was pushing his Yale key into the lock when a voice from inside shouted, "It's on the latch."

"Damn," said Adam under his breath.

"How did it go?" were Lawrence's first words as he entered the drawing room.

"Very well, considering," Adam replied, not quite sure what else he could say as he smiled at his flatmate. Lawrence had already changed from his City clothes into a blazer and grey flannels. He was slightly shorter and stockier than Adam with a head of wiry fair hair, a massive forehead and grey thoughtful eyes that always seemed to be enquiring.

"I admired your father so much," he added. "He always assumed one had the same standards as he did." Adam could still remember nervously introducing Lawrence to his father one Speech Day. They had become friends immediately. But then Lawrence was not a man who dealt in rumours.

"Able to retire on the family fortune, are we?" asked Lawrence in a lighter vein.

"Only if that dubious bank you work for has found a way of converting five hundred pounds into five thousand in a matter of days."

"Can't manage it at the present time, old chum –

not now Harold Wilson has announced a standstill in wages and prices."

Adam smiled as he looked across at his friend. Although taller than him now, he could still recall those days when Lawrence seemed to him like a giant. "Late again, Scott," he would say as Adam scampered past him in the corridor. Adam had looked forward to the day when he could do everything in the same relaxed, superior style. Or was it just that Lawrence was superior? His suits always seemed to be well-pressed, his shoes always shone and he never had a hair out of place. Adam still hadn't fathomed out how he did it all so effortlessly.

Adam heard the bathroom door open. He glanced interrogatively towards Lawrence.

"It's Carolyn," whispered Lawrence. "She'll be staying the night . . . I think."

When Carolyn entered the room Adam smiled shyly at the tall, beautiful woman. Her long, blonde hair bounced on her shoulders as she walked towards them, but it was the faultless figure that most men couldn't take their eyes off. How did Lawrence manage it?

"Care to join us for a meal?" asked Lawrence, putting his arm round Carolyn's shoulder, his voice suddenly sounding a little *too* enthusiastic. "I've discovered this Italian restaurant that's just opened in the Fulham Road."

"I might join you later," said Adam, "but I still have one or two papers left over from this afternoon that I ought to check through."

"Forget the finer details of your inheritance, my boy. Why not join us and spend the entire windfall in one wild spaghetti fling?"

"Oh, have you been left lots of lovely lolly?" asked Carolyn, in a voice so shrill and high-pitched nobody would have been surprised to learn that she had recently been Deb of the Year.

"Not," said Adam, "when considered against my present overdraft."

Lawrence laughed. "Well, come along later if you discover there's enough over for a plate of pasta." He winked at Adam – his customary sign for "Be sure you're out of the flat by the time we get back. Or at least stay in your own room and pretend to be asleep."

"Yes, do come," cooed Carolyn, sounding as if she meant it – her hazel eyes remained fixed on Adam as Lawrence guided her firmly towards the door.

Adam didn't move until he was sure he could no longer hear her penetrating voice echoing on the staircase. Satisfied, he retreated to his bedroom and locked himself in. Adam sat down on the one comfortable chair he possessed and pulled his father's envelope out of his inside pocket. It was the heavy, expensive type of stationery Pa had always used, purchasing it at Smythson of Bond Street at almost twice the price he could have obtained it at the local W. H. Smith's. 'Captain Adam Scott, MC' was written in his father's neat copperplate hand.

Adam opened the envelope carefully, his hand shaking slightly, and extracted the contents: a letter in his father's unmistakable hand and a smaller envelope which was clearly old as it was faded with time. Written on the old envelope in an unfamiliar hand were the words 'Colonel Gerald Scott' in faded ink of indeterminate colour. Adam placed the old envelope on the little table by his side and, unfolding his father's letter, began to read. It was undated.

My dear Adam,
Over the years, you will have heard many expla-

nations for my sudden departure from the regiment. Most of them will have been farcical, and a few of them slanderous, but I always considered it better for all concerned to keep my own counsel. I feel, however, that I owe you a fuller explanation, and that is what this letter will set out to do.

As you know, my last posting before I resigned my commission was at Nuremberg from November 1945 to October 1946. After four years of almost continuous action in the field, I was given the task of commanding the British section which had responsibility for those senior ranking Nazis who were awaiting trial for war crimes. Although the Americans had overall responsibility, I came to know the imprisoned officers quite well and after a year or so I had even grown to tolerate some of them – Hess, Doenitz and Speer in particular – and I often wondered how the Germans would have treated us had the situation been reversed. Such views were considered unacceptable at the time. 'Fraternisation' was often on the lips of those men who are never given to second thoughts.

Among the senior Nazis with whom I came into daily contact was Reichsmarshal Hermann Goering, but unlike the three other officers I have previously mentioned, here was a man I detested from the first moment I came across him. I found him arrogant, overbearing and totally without shame about the barbaric acts he had carried out in the name of war. And I never once found any reason to change my opinion of him. In fact, I sometimes wondered how I controlled my temper when I was in his presence.

The night before Goering was due to be executed, he requested a private meeting with me. It was a Monday, and I can still recall every detail of that encounter as if it were only yesterday. I received the request when I took over the Russian watch from Major Vladimir Kosky. In fact Kosky personally handed me the written request. As soon as I had inspected the guard and dealt with the usual paperwork, I went along with the duty corporal to see the Reichsmarshal in his cell. Goering stood to attention by his small low bed and saluted as I entered the room. The sparse, grey-painted, brick cell always made me shudder.

"You asked to see me?" I said. I never could get myself to address him by his name or rank.

"Yes," he replied. "It was kind of you to come in person, Colonel. I simply wish to make the last request of a man condemned to death. Would it be possible for the corporal to leave us?"

Imagining it was something highly personal I asked the corporal to wait outside. I confess I had no idea what could be so private when the man only had hours to live but as the door closed he saluted again and then passed over the envelope you now have in your possession. As I took it, all he said was, "Would you be good enough not to open this until after my execution tomorrow." He then added, "I can only hope it will compensate for any blame that might later be placed on your shoulders." I had no idea what he could be alluding to at the time and presumed some form of mental instability had overtaken him. Many of the prisoners confided in me during their last few days, and towards the end, some of them were undoubtedly on the verge of madness.

Adam stopped to consider what he would have done in the same circumstances, and decided to read on to discover if father and son would have taken the same course.

However, Goering's final words to me as I left his cell seemed hardly those of a madman. He said quite simply: "Be assured. It is a masterpiece; do not underestimate its value." Then he lit up a cigar as if he was relaxing at his club after a rather good dinner. We all had different theories as to who smuggled the cigars in for him, and equally wondered what might also have been smuggled out from time to time.

I placed the envelope in my jacket pocket and left him to join the corporal in the corridor. We then checked the other cells to see that all the prisoners were locked up for the night. The inspection completed, I returned to my office. As I was satisfied that there were no more immediate duties I settled down to make out my report. I left the envelope in the jacket pocket of my uniform with every intention of opening it immediately after Goering's execution had been carried out the following morning. I was checking over the orders of the day when the corporal rushed into my office without knocking. "It's Goering, sir, it's Goering," he said, frantically. From the panic on the man's face, I didn't need to ask for any details. We both ran all the way back to the Reichsmarshal's cell.

I found Goering lying face downwards on his bunk. I turned him over to find he was already dead. In the commotion that immediately followed I quite forgot Goering's letter. An autopsy a few days later showed that he had died from poisoning; the court came to the conclusion that the cyanide capsule that had been found in his body must have been implanted in one of his cigars.

As I had been the last to see him alone and privately, it took only a few whispers before my name was linked with his death. There was, of course, no truth in the accusation. Indeed I never doubted for one moment that the court had delivered the correct verdict in his case and that he justly deserved to be hanged for the part he had played in the war.

So stung was I by the continual behind-the-back accusations that I might have helped Goering to an easy death by smuggling in the cigars that I felt the only honourable thing to do in the circumstances was to resign my commission immediately for fear of bringing further dishonour to the regiment. When I returned to England later that year, and finally decided to throw out my old uniform, I came across the envelope again. When I explained to your mother the details of the incident she begged me to destroy the envelope as she considered it had brought enough dishonour to our family already, and even if it did point to whoever had been responsible for helping Goering to his suicide, in her opinion such knowledge could no longer do anyone any good. I agreed to comply with her wishes and although I never opened the envelope I could never get myself to destroy it, remembering the last sentence Goering had uttered about it being a masterpiece. And so finally I hid it among my personal papers.

However, since the imagined sins of the father are inevitably visited upon the next generation, I feel no such qualms should influence you. If there is therefore anything to be gained from the contents of this envelope I make only one request, namely that your mother should be the first to benefit from it without ever being allowed to know how such good fortune came about.

Over the years, I have watched your progress with considerable pride and feel confident that I can leave you to make the correct decision.

If you are left in any doubt about opening the envelope yourself, destroy it without further consideration. But if you open it only to discover its purpose is to involve you in some dishonourable enterprise, be rid of it without a second thought.

> May God be with you.
> Your loving father,
>
> Gerald Scott

Adam read the letter over once again, realising how much trust his father had placed in him. His heart thumped in his chest as he considered how Pa's life had been wasted by the murmurings and innuendoes of lesser men – the same men who had also succeeded in bringing his own career to a premature halt. When he had finished reading the missive for a third time he folded it up neatly and slipped it back into its envelope.

He then picked up the second envelope from the side table. The words 'Colonel Gerald Scott' were written in a faded bold script across it.

Adam removed a comb from his inside pocket and wedged it into the corner of the envelope. Slowly he began to slit it open. He hesitated for a moment before extracting two pieces of paper, both yellowed with age. One appeared to be a letter while the other seemed to be a document of some sort. The crest of the Third Reich was embossed at the head of the letterpaper above the printed name of Reichsmarshal Hermann Goering. Adam's hands began to tremble as he read the first line.

It began, *Sehr geehrter Herr Oberst Scott:*

CHAPTER THREE

As the black Chaika limousine drove out under the Spasskaya Bashnya and on to Red Square, two Kremlin guards in khaki uniforms sprang to attention and presented arms. A shrill whistle sounded which ensured that Yuri Efimovich Zaborski would experience no delays on his route back to Dzerzhinsky Square.

Zaborski touched the corner of his black felt hat in automatic acknowledgment of the salute although his thoughts were elsewhere. As the car rumbled over the cobbled stones, he didn't even glance at the long snake-like queue that stretched from Lenin's Tomb to the edge of Red Square. The first decision he had to make would undoubtedly be the most important: which of his senior operatives should be charged with the task of heading the team to find the Tsar's icon? He continued to ponder the problem as his driver took him across Red Square, passing the grey façade of the GUM department store away to his left before driving along Neitsa Kuibysheva.

Within moments of leaving his leader, the Chairman of State Security had formed in his own mind a shortlist of two. Which of those two, Valchek or Romanov, should be given the nod still taxed him. In normal circumstances he would have spent at least a week making such a decision but the General Secretary's deadline of June 20 left him with no such freedom. He knew he would have to make the choice even before he reached his office. The driver cruised through another green light past the Ministry of Culture and into Cherkasskiy Bolshoy Pereulok lined with its imposing block-like, grey buildings. The car remained in the special inside lane that could be used only by senior Party officials. In England, he was amused to learn that they had plans for such a traffic lane – but it would only be for the use of buses.

The car came to an abrupt halt outside KGB headquarters. It hadn't helped that they had been able to cover the three kilometre journey in less than four minutes. The driver ran round and opened the back door to allow his master to step out but Zaborski didn't move. The man who rarely changed his mind had already done so twice on the route back to Dzerzhinsky Square. He knew he could call on any number of bureaucrats and academics to do the spade work but someone with flair was going to have to lead them and be responsible for reporting back to him.

His professional intuition told him to select Yuri Valchek, who had proved over the years to be a trusty and reliable servant of the State. He was also one of the Chairman's longest serving heads of department. Slow methodical and reliable, he had completed a full ten years as an agent in the field before confining himself to a desk job.

In contrast, Alex Romanov, who had only recently become head of his own section, had shown flashes of brilliance in the field but they had been so often outweighed by a lack of personal judgment. At twenty-nine, he was the youngest and, without question, the most ambitious of the Chairman's select team.

Zaborski stepped out on to the pavement and walked towards another door held open for him. He strode across the marble floor and stopped only when he reached the lift gates. Several silent men and women had also been waiting for the lift but when it returned to the ground floor and the Chairman stepped into the little cage, none of them made any attempt to join him. Zaborski travelled slowly up towards his office, never failing to compare it unfavourably with the speed of the one American elevator he had experienced. They could launch their rockets before you could get to your office, his predecessor had warned him. By the time Zaborski had reached the top floor and the gates had been pulled back for him, he had made up his mind. It would be Valchek.

A secretary helped him off with his long black coat and took his hat. Zaborski walked quickly to his desk. The two files he had asked for were awaiting him. He sat down and began to pore over Valchek's file. When he had completed it, he barked out an order to his hovering secretary: "Find Romanov."

Comrade Romanov lay flat on his back, his left arm behind his head and his opponent's right over his throat preparing for a double knee-thrust. The coach executed it perfectly and Romanov groaned as he hit the floor with a thud.

An attendant came rushing over to them and bent down to whisper in the coach's ear. The coach reluctantly released his pupil who rose slowly as if in a daze, bowed to the coach and then in one movement of right arm and left leg took the legs from under him and left him flat on the gymnasium floor before making his way quickly to the off-the-hook phone in the office.

Romanov didn't notice the girl who handed him the

phone. "I'll be with him as soon as I have had a shower," was all she heard him say. The girl who had taken the call had often wondered what Romanov looked like in the shower. She, like all the other girls in the office, had seen him in the gymnasium a hundred times. Six foot tall with that long, flowing blond hair – he resembled a Western film star. And those eyes, 'piercing blue' the friend who shared her desk described them.

"He's got a scar on his . . ." the friend confided.

"How do you know that?" she had asked, but her friend had only giggled in reply.

The Chairman meanwhile had opened Romanov's personal file for a second time, and was still perusing the details. He began to read the different entries that made up a candid character assessment which Romanov would never see unless he became Chairman:

Alexander Petrovich Romanov. Born Leningrad, March 12, 1937. Elected full Party member 1958.
Father: Peter Nicholevich Romanov, served on the Eastern Front in 1942. On returning to Russia in 1945 refused to join Communist Party. After several reports of anti-State activities supplied by his son he was sentenced to ten years in prison. Died in jail October 20, 1948.

Zaborski looked up and smiled – a child of the State.

Grandfather: Nicholai Alexandrovich Romanov, merchant, and one of the wealthiest landowners in Petrograd. Shot and killed on May 11, 1918, while attempting to escape from the forces of the Red Army.

The Revolution had taken place between the princely grandfather and the reluctant comrade father.

Alex, as he preferred to be known, had nevertheless inherited the Romanov ambition so he enrolled for the Party's Pioneer organisation at the age of nine. By the age of eleven, he had been offered a place at a special school at Smolensk – to the disgust of some of the lesser Party workers who considered such privileges should be reserved for the sons of loyal Party officials, not the sons of those in jail. Romanov immediately excelled in the classroom, much to the dismay of the Director who had been hoping to disprove any Darwinian theories. And at fourteen he was selected as one of the Party's élite and made a member of the Komsomol.

By the age of sixteen, Romanov had won the Lenin language medal and the junior gymnastics prize and despite the Director's attempts to undermine young Alex's achievements, most members of the school board recognised Romanov's potential and ensured that he was still allowed to take up a place at university. As an undergraduate he continued to excel in languages, specialising in English, French and German. Natural flair and hard work kept him near the top of every subject he specialised in.

Zaborski picked up the phone by his side. "I asked to see Romanov," he said curtly.

"He was completing his morning work-out at the gymnasium, Chairman," replied the secretary. "But he left to change the moment he heard you wanted to see him."

The Chairman replaced the phone and his eyes returned to the file in front of him. That Romanov could be found in the gymnasium at all hours came as no surprise: the man's athletic prowess had been acknowledged far beyond the service.

During his first year as a student, Romanov had continued diligently with his gymnastics and even gone on to represent the State side until the university coach had written in bold letters across one of his reports, "This student is too tall to be considered for serious Olympic competition." Romanov heeded the coach's advice and took up judo. Within two years, he had been selected for the 1958 Eastern Bloc games in Budapest and within a further two years found other competitors preferred not to be drawn against him on his inevitable route to the final. After his victory at the Soviet games in Moscow the Western press crudely described him as 'The Axe'. Those who were already planning his long-term future felt it prudent not to enter him for the Olympics.

Once Romanov had completed his fifth year at the university and obtained his diploma (with distinction), he remained in Moscow and joined the diplomatic service.

Zaborski had now reached the point in the file at which he had first come across the self-confident young man. Each year the KGB were able to second from the diplomatic service any person they considered to be of exceptional talent. Romanov was an obvious candidate. Zaborski's rule, however, was not to enlist anyone who didn't consider the KGB to be the élite. Unwilling candidates never made good operatives and sometimes even ended up working for the other side. Romanov showed no such doubt. He had always wanted to be an officer of the KGB. During the next six years he carried out tours at their embassies in Paris, London, Prague and Lagos. By the time he had returned to

Moscow to join the headquarters staff he was a sophisticated operative who was as relaxed at an ambassadorial cocktail party as he was in the gymnasium.

Zaborski began to read some of the comments he himself had added to the report during the last four years – in particular how much Romanov had changed during his time on the Chairman's personal staff. As an operative, he had reached the rank of major, having served successfully in the field before being appointed head of a department. Two red dots were placed by his name indicating successful missions. A defecting violinist attempting to leave Prague and a general who had thought he was going to be the next head of a small African state. What impressed Zaborski most about his protégé's efforts was that the Western press thought the Czechs were responsible for the first and the Americans for the second. Romanov's most significant achievement, however, had been the recruitment of an agent from the British Foreign Office whose parallel rise had only assisted Romanov's career. Romanov's appointment as head of a department had surprised no one, himself included, although it soon became clear to Zaborski that he missed the raw excitement of field work.

The Chairman turned to the last page, a character assessment, in which the majority of contributors were in accord: ambitious, sophisticated, ruthless, arrogant but not always reliable were the words that appeared with regularity in almost every summation.

There was an assertive rap on the door. Zaborski closed the file and pressed a button under his desk. The doors clicked open to allow Alexander Petrovich Romanov to enter the room.

"Good morning, Comrade Chairman," said the elegant young man who now stood to attention in front of him. Zaborski looked up at the man he had selected and felt a little envy that the gods had bestowed so much on one so young. Still, it was he who understood how to use such a man to the State's best advantage.

He continued to stare into those clear blue eyes and considered that if Romanov had been born in Hollywood he would not have found it hard to make a living. His suit looked as if it had been tailored in Savile Row – and probably had been. Zaborski chose to ignore such irregularities although he was tempted to ask the young man where he had his shirts made.

"You called for me," said Romanov.

The Chairman nodded. "I have just returned from the Kremlin," he said. "The General Secretary has entrusted us with a particularly sensitive project of great importance to the State." Zaborski paused. "So sensitive in fact that you will report only to me. You can hand-select your own team and no resources will be denied you."

"I am honoured," said Romanov, sounding unusually sincere.

"You will be," replied the Chairman, "if you succeed in discovering the whereabouts of the Tsar's icon."

"But I thought . . ." began Romanov.

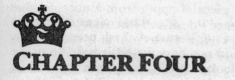

CHAPTER FOUR

Adam walked over to the side of his bed and removed from the bookshelf the Bible his mother had given him as a Confirmation present. As he opened it a layer of dust rose from the top of the gold-leaf-edged pages. He placed the envelope in Revelation and returned the Bible to the shelf.

Adam strolled through to the kitchen, fried himself an egg and warmed up the other half of the previous day's tinned beans. He placed the unwholesome meal on the kitchen table, unable to put out of his mind the slap-up meal Lawrence and Carolyn must now be enjoying at the new Italian restaurant. After Adam had finished and cleared his plate away, he returned to his room and lay on the bed thinking. Would the contents of the faded envelope finally prove his father's innocence? A plan began to form in his mind.

When the grandfather clock in the hall chimed ten times, Adam lifted his long legs over the end of the bed and pulled the Bible back out of the bookshelf. With some apprehension Adam removed the envelope. Next, he switched on the reading light by the side of the small writing desk, unfolded the two pieces of paper and placed them in front of him.

One appeared to be a personal letter from Goering

to Adam's father, while the other had the look of an older, more official document. Adam placed this second document to one side and began to go over the letter line by line. It didn't help.

He tore a blank piece of paper from a notepad that he found on Lawrence's desk and started to copy down the text of Goering's letter. He left out only the greeting and what he assumed to be a valediction – '*hochachtungsvoll*' – followed by the Reichsmarshal's large, bold signature. He checked over the copy carefully before replacing the original in its faded envelope. He had just begun the same process with the official document, using a separate sheet of paper, when he heard a key turning, followed by voices at the front door. Both Lawrence and Carolyn sounded as if they had drunk more than the promised bottle of wine, and Carolyn's voice in particular had ascended into little more than a series of high-pitched giggles.

Adam sighed and switched off the light by the side of the desk so they wouldn't know he was still awake. In the darkness he became more sensitive to their every sound. One of them headed towards the kitchen, because he heard the fridge door squelch closed and, a few seconds later, the sound of a cork being extracted – he presumed from his last bottle of white wine, as they were unlikely to be so drunk that they had started on the vinegar.

Reluctantly he rose from his chair, and circling his arms in front of him, he made his way back to the bed. He touched the corner of the bedstead and quietly lowered himself on to the mattress, then waited impatiently for Lawrence's bedroom door to close.

He must have fallen asleep because the next thing he remembered was the tick of the hall clock. Adam licked his fingers and rubbed them over his eyes as he tried to get accustomed to the dark. He checked the little luminous dial on his alarm clock: ten past three. He eased himself off the bed gingerly, feeling more than a little crumpled and weary. Slowly he groped his way back towards the desk, banging his knee on the corner of a chest of drawers during his travels. He couldn't stop himself cursing. He fumbled for the light switch, and when the bulb first glowed it made him blink several times. The faded envelope looked so insignificant – and perhaps it was. The official document was still laid out on the centre of the table alongside the first few lines of his handwritten duplicate.

Adam yawned as he began to study the words once more. The document was not as simple to copy out as the letter had been, because this time the hand was spidery and cramped, as if the writer had considered paper an expensive commodity. Adam left out the address on the top right hand corner and reversed the eight digit number underlined at the head of the text, otherwise what he ended up with was a faithful transcript of the original.

The work was painstaking, and took a surprisingly long time. He wrote out each word in block capitals, and when he wasn't certain of the spelling he put down the possible alternative letters below; he wanted to be sure of any translation the first time.

"My, you do work late," whispered a voice from behind him.

Adam spun round, feeling like a burglar who had been caught with his hands on the family silver.

"You needn't look so nervous. It's only me," said Carolyn, standing by the bedroom door.

Adam stared up at the tall blonde who was even more attractive clad only in Lawrence's large unbuttoned pyjamas and floppy slippers than she had been when he had seen her fully dressed. Her long, fair hair now dropped untidily over her shoulders and he began to understand what Lawrence had meant when he had once described her as someone who could turn a matchstick into a Cuban cigar.

"The bathroom is at the end of the corridor," said Adam, a little feebly.

"It wasn't the bathroom I was looking for, silly," she giggled. "I don't seem able to wake Lawrence. After all that wine he's passed out like a defeated heavyweight boxer." She sighed. "And long before round fifteen. I don't think anything will rouse him again until morning." She took a step towards him.

Adam stammered something about feeling rather whacked himself. He made sure his back shielded her from any sight of the papers on the desk.

"Oh, God," said Carolyn, "you're not queer, are you?"

"Certainly not," said Adam, a little pompously.

"Just don't fancy me?" she asked.

"Not that exactly," said Adam.

"But Lawrence is your chum," she said. Adam didn't reply.

"My God this is the sixties, Adam. Share and share alike."

"It's just that . . ." began Adam.

"What a waste," said Carolyn, "perhaps another time." She tiptoed to the door, and slipped back out into the corridor, unaware of her German rival.

The first action Romanov took on leaving the Chairman's office that morning was to return to his *alma mater* and hand-pick a team of twelve researchers. From the moment they had been briefed they proceeded to study in pairs on four-hour shifts, so that the work could continue night and day.

The early information had come in almost by the hour and the researchers had quickly been able to establish that the Tsar's icon had remained in his private quarters at the Winter Palace at Petrograd until as late as December 1914. Romanov studied religiously a photo of the small delicate painting of St George and the Dragon. St George in tiny mosaic patterns of blue and gold while the dragon was in fiery red and yellow. Although he had never shown any interest in art, Romanov could well understand why people could be moved by the little masterpiece. He continued to read details of the icon's history, but still couldn't work out why it was so important to the State. He wondered if even Zaborski knew the reason.

A royal servant who had testified before the People's Court a year after the Revolution claimed that the Tsar's icon had disappeared for a few days in 1915 after the visit of Ernst Ludwig, Grand Duke of Hesse. At the time, the inquisitors had taken scant interest in the misplaced icon because it was still on the wall of the Tsar's study when they had stormed the Winter Palace. What concerned the court more was why, in the middle of a fierce war with the Kaiser's Germany, the Grand Duke of Hesse should want to visit the Tsar at all.

The Professor of History at the university had immediately been asked for his opinion. The great academic was puzzled by the request, as the KGB had never shown any interest in the nation's past history before. Nevertheless, he briefed Romanov on everything that was known of the incident. Romanov pored over his report once again. The Grand Duke, it was thought, had been on a secret visit to his sister Alexandra, the Tsarina. Historians now believed that it had been his intention to secure a cease-fire between Germany and Russia, in the hope that Germany could then concentrate her war efforts on the British and the French.

There was no proof that the Tsar made any promises on behalf of his people but the Grand Duke, it seemed, did not return to Germany empty-handed. As the reports of the proceedings of the People's Court showed, another palace servant had been instructed to wrap up the Tsar's icon and pack it with the Grand Duke's belongings. However, no one on the palace staff could properly explain to the court how a few days later the icon reappeared in its rightful place on the wall of the Tsar's private study.

Romanov's chief researcher, Professor Oleg Konstantinov, having studied the professor's notes and the other researchers' contributions, had underlined his own conclusion in red ink.

"The Tsar must have replaced the original painting with a brilliant copy, having handed over the real icon for safe-keeping to his brother-in-law, the Grand Duke."

"But why," asked Romanov, "when the Tsar had a palace full of Goyas, El Grecos, Titians and Rubens did he bother to smuggle out one icon and why does Brezhnev want it back so badly?"

Romanov instructed the professor and his twenty-four researchers to turn their talents to the Royal House of Hesse in the hope of tracing what had then happened to the Tsar's icon. Within ten days, they possessed between them more information about the Grand Duke and his family than any professor at any university had managed to gather in a lifetime. As each file appeared on his desk Romanov laboured through the night, checking every scrap of information that might give him a lead to the whereabouts of the original painting. He came to a dead end when, after the Grand Duke's death, the painting had been left to his son who was tragically killed in a plane crash. Nothing had been seen or heard of the icon after that day.

By the beginning of the third week, Romanov had reached the reluctant conclusion that there was nothing new on the whereabouts of the icon to be discovered. He was preparing his final report for the Chairman of the KGB when one researcher, Comrade Petrova, whose mind did not work in parallel lines, stumbled across an article in the London *Times* of Wednesday, November 17, 1937. Petrova bypassed the research leader and handed the relevant photocopy to Romanov personally, who, over the next few hours, read the news item so often that he came to know it off by heart.

In keeping with the Thunderer's tradition, the foreign correspondent remained anonymous. The article carried the dateline 'Ostend, November 16, 1937'.

It read:

Grand Duke George of Hesse and four members of his family were tragically killed this morning when a Sabena aircraft carrying them from Frankfurt to London crashed in thick fog over the Belgian countryside.

The Grand Duke had been on his way to England to attend the wedding of his younger brother, Prince Louis, to the Hon. Joanna Geddes. The young prince had been waiting at Croydon Airport to greet his family when the news was broken to him. He immediately cancelled his original wedding plans and announced they would be rescheduled with a small private service in the Chapel at Windsor.

The Times went on:

Prince Louis, who succeeds his brother as the Grand Duke of Hesse, will leave for Ostend with his bride later today in order that they can accompany the five coffins on their journey back to Germany. The funerals will all take place in Darmstadt on November 23.

It was the next paragraph that the researcher had circled boldly.

Some of the late Grand Duke's personal belongings, including several wedding presents for Prince Louis and his bride, were scattered for miles in the vicinity of the crashed aircraft. The German Government announced this morning that a senior German general has been appointed to lead a team of salvage experts to ensure the recovery of any family possessions that still belong to the Grand Duke's successor.

Romanov immediately called for the young researcher. When Anna Petrova arrived a few minutes later she gave no impression of being overawed by her head of department. She accepted that it would be hard to make any impression on him with the clothes she could afford. However, she had put on the prettiest outfit she possessed and cut her hair in the style of an American actress called Mia Farrow whom she had seen in one of the few films not banned by the authorities. She hoped Romanov would notice.

"I want you to scour *The Times* every day from November 17, 1937 for six months, and also check the German and Belgian press during the same period in case you come across anything that would show what the salvage experts had discovered." He dismissed her with a smile.

Within twenty-four hours Comrade Petrova barged back into Romanov's office without even bothering to knock. Romanov merely raised his eyebrows at the discourtesy before devouring an article she had discovered in the Berlin *die Zeit* of Saturday, January 19, 1938.

"The investigation into the crash last November of the Sabena aircraft that was carrying the Hesse royal family to London has now been concluded. All personal possessions belonging to the family that were discovered in the vicinity of the wreckage have been returned to the Grand Duke, Prince Louis, who, it is understood, was particularly saddened by the loss of a family heirloom that was to have been a wedding gift from his brother, the late Grand Duke. The gift, a painting known as the 'Tsar's Icon', had once belonged to his uncle, Tsar Nicholas II. The icon of St George and the Dragon, although only a copy of Rublev's masterpiece, was considered to be one of the finest examples of early twentieth-century craftsmanship to come out of Russia since the Revolution."

Romanov looked up at the researcher. "Twentieth-century copy be damned," he said. "It was the fifteenth-century original and none of them realised it at the time – perhaps not even the old Grand Duke himself. No doubt the Tsar had other plans for the icon had he managed to escape."

Romanov dreaded having to tell Zaborski that he could now prove conclusively that the original Tsar's icon had been destroyed in a plane crash some thirty years before. Such news would not ensure promotion for its messenger, as he remained convinced that there was something far more important than the icon at stake for Zaborski to be so involved.

He stared down at the photograph above the *Zeitung* report. The young Grand Duke was shaking hands with the general in charge of the salvage team which had been successful in returning so many of the Prince's family possessions. "But did he return them all?" Romanov said out loud.

"What do you mean?" asked the young researcher. Romanov waved his hand as he continued to stare at the pre-war, faded photograph of the two men. Although the general was unnamed, every schoolboy in Germany would have recognised the large, impassive, heavy-jowled face with the chilling eyes which had become infamous to the Allied powers.

Romanov looked up at the researcher. "You can forget the Grand Duke from now on, Comrade Petrova. Concentrate your efforts on Reichsmarshal Hermann Goering."

When Adam woke his first thoughts were of Carolyn. His yawn turned into a grin as he considered her invitation of the night before. Then he remembered. He jumped out of bed and walked over to his desk: everything was in place exactly as he had left it. He yawned for a second time.

It was ten to seven. Although he felt as fit as he had been the day he left the army some seven weeks before, he still completed a punishing routine of exercise every morning. He intended to be at his peak when the Foreign Office put him through a physical. In moments he was kitted out in a singlet and a pair of running shorts. He pulled on an old army tracksuit and finally tied up his gym shoes.

Adam tiptoed out of the flat, not wanting to wake Lawrence or Carolyn – although he suspected she was wide awake, waiting impatiently. For the next thirty-four minutes he pounded the pavement down to the Embankment, across Albert Bridge, through Battersea Park to return by way of Chelsea Bridge. Only one thought was going through his mind. After twenty years of gossip and innuendo was this going to be the one chance to clear his father's name? The moment he arrived back at the flat, Adam checked his pulse: 150 beats a minute. Sixty seconds later it was down to 100, another minute 70, and before the fourth minute was up it was back to a steady 58. It's the recovery that proves fitness, not your speed, his old Physical Training Instructor at Aldershot had drummed into him.

As Adam walked back through to his room there was still no sign of Carolyn. Lawrence, smart in a grey pinstripe suit, was preparing breakfast in the kitchen while glancing at the sports pages of the *Daily Telegraph*.

"The West Indies made 526," he informed Adam forlornly.

"Have we begun our innings?" shouted Adam from the bathroom.

"No, bad light stopped play."

Adam groaned as he stripped for the shower. He was ready for his morning game of finding out how long he could last under the freezing jets. The forty-eight needles of ice cold water beat down on his back and chest, which made him take several deep intakes of breath. Once you survive the first thirty seconds you could stay under for ever, the instructor had assured them. Adam emerged three minutes later, satisfied but still damning the PTI from whose influence he felt he would never escape.

Once he had towelled himself down Adam walked back to his bedroom. A moment later he had thrown on his dressing-gown and joined his friend in the kitchen for breakfast. Lawrence was now seated at the kitchen table concentrating hard on a bowl of cornflakes, while running a finger down the Foreign Exchange rates in the *Financial Times*.

Adam checked his watch: already ten past eight. "Won't you be late for the office?" he asked.

"Dear boy," said Lawrence, "I am not a lackey who works at the kind of bank where the customers keep shop hours."

Adam laughed. "But I will, however, have to be shackled to my desk in the City by nine thirty," Lawrence admitted. "They don't send a driver for me nowadays," he explained. "In this traffic, I told them, it's so much quicker by tube."

Adam started to make himself breakfast.

"I could give you a lift on my motorbike."

"Can you imagine a man in my position arriving at the headquarters of Barclays Bank on a motorbike? The Chairman would have a fit," he added, as he folded the *Financial Times*.

Adam cracked a second egg into the frying pan.

"See you tonight then, glorious, unwashed and unemployed," jeered Lawrence as he collected his rolled umbrella from the hat stand.

Adam cleared away and washed up, happy to act as housewife while he was still unemployed. Despite years of being taken care of by a batman he knew exactly what was expected of him. All he had planned before his interview with the Foreign Office that afternoon was a long bath and a slow shave. Then he remembered that Reichsmarshal Goering was still resting on the table in the bedroom.

"Have you come up with anything that would indicate Goering might have kept the icon for himself?" asked Romanov, turning hopefully to the researcher.

"Only the obvious," Anna Petrova replied in an offhand manner.

Romanov considered reprimanding the young girl for such insolence, but said nothing on this occasion. After all, Comrade Petrova had proved to be far the most innovative of his team of researchers.

"And what was so obvious?" enquired Romanov.

"It's common knowledge that Hitler put Goering in charge of all the art treasures captured on behalf of the Third Reich. But as the Führer had such fixed personal opinions as to what constituted quality, many of the world's masterpieces were judged as 'depraved' and therefore unworthy to be put on public view for the delectation of the master race."

"So what happened to them?"

"Hitler ordered them to be destroyed. Among those works condemned to death by burning were such masters as Van Gogh, Manet, Monet – and especially the young Picasso who was considered unworthy of the blue-blooded Aryan race Hitler was grooming to rule the world."

"You are not suggesting Goering could have stolen the Tsar's icon," asked Romanov, staring up at the ceiling, "only then to burn it?"

"No, no. Goering was not that stupid. As we now know, he didn't always obey the Führer's every word."

"Goering failed to carry out Hitler's orders?" said Romanov in disbelief.

"Depends from which standpoint you view it,"

Petrova replied. "Was he to behave as his lunatic master demanded or turn a blind eye and use his common sense?"

"Stick to the facts," said Romanov, his voice suddenly sharp.

"Yes, Comrade Major," said the young researcher in a tone that suggested she believed herself to be indispensable, at least for the time being.

"When it came to it," Petrova continued, "Goering did not destroy any of the denounced masterpieces. He held some public burnings in Berlin and Düsseldorf of lesser known German artists, who would never have fetched more than a few hundred marks on the open market in the first place. But the masterpieces, the real works of genius, were moved discreetly over the border and deposited in the vaults of Swiss banks."

"So there's still an outside chance that having found the icon . . ."

"He then had it placed in a Swiss bank," added Petrova. "I wish it were that simple, Comrade Major," said the researcher, "but unfortunately Goering wasn't quite as naïve as the newspaper cartoonists of the time made him out to be. I think he deposited the paintings and antiques in several Swiss banks and to date no one has ever been able to discover which banks or the aliases he used."

"Then *we* shall have to do so," said Romanov. "Where do you suggest we start?"

"Well, since the end of the war many of the paintings have been found and restored to their rightful owners, including the galleries of the German Democratic Republic. Others, however, have appeared on walls as far-flung as the Getty Museum in California and the Gotoh in Tokyo, sometimes without a fully satisfactory explanation. In fact, one of Renoir's major works can currently be seen hanging on the walls of the Metropolitan Museum in New York. It undoubtedly passed through Goering's hands although the curator of the museum has never been willing to explain how the gallery came into possession of it."

"Have all the missing pictures now been found?" asked Romanov anxiously.

"Over seventy per cent, but there are still many more to be accounted for. Some may even have been lost or destroyed, but my guess is that there are still a large number that remain lodged in Swiss banks."

"How can you be so certain?" demanded Romanov, fearful that his last avenue might be closing.

"Because the Swiss banks always return valuables when they can be certain of a nation's or individual's right of possession. In the case of the Grand Duke of Hesse and the Tsar's icon there was no proof of ownership, as the last official owner was Tsar Nicholas II and he, as every good Russian knows, Comrade, had no successors."

"Then I must do exactly what Goering did and retrace his steps by going direct to the banks. What has been their policy to date?" asked Romanov.

"That differs from establishment to establishment," said Petrova. "Some banks wait for twenty years or more and then try either by extensive research or advertising to contact the owner or their next of kin. In the case of the Jews who lost their lives under the Nazi regime, it has often proved impossible to trace a legitimate owner. Although I have been unable to prove it, I suspect they kept the rewards and split the proceeds among themselves," said Petrova. "Typical capitalists."

"That is neither fair nor accurate, Comrade," said Romanov, glad to show that he had also been doing some research. "Because that is another of the great myths perpetrated by the poor. In fact, when the banks have been unable to discover the rightful owner of any treasure left with them they have handed it over to the Swiss Red Cross to auction."

"But if the Tsar's icon had ever been auctioned we would have heard about it by now through one of our agents?"

"Precisely," said Romanov. "And I've already checked through the inventory of the Red Cross: four icons have been disposed of during the last twenty years and none of them was St George and the Dragon."

"Then that can only mean some unscrupulous bankers have disposed of the icon privately once they felt sure no one was going to make a claim."

"Another false premise, I suspect, Comrade Petrova."

"How can you be so certain?" the young researcher asked.

"For one simple reason, Comrade. The Swiss banking families all know each other intimately and have never in the past shown any propensity for breaking the law. Swiss justice, in our experience, is as tough on corrupt bankers as it is on murderers, which is precisely why the Mafia was never happy about laundering its money through the established banks. The truth is that Swiss bankers make so much money dealing with honest people that it has never been in their best interests to become involved with crooks. There are remarkably few exceptions to this rule, which is the reason so many people are willing to do business with the Swiss."

"So, if Goering stole the Tsar's icon and deposited it in a Swiss bank vault, it could be anywhere in the world by now?" said Petrova.

"I doubt it."

"Why?" sighed Petrova, a little peeved that her deductions were now proving wide of the mark.

"Because for the past three weeks I have had heaven knows how many operatives combing Europe for the Tsar's icon. They have spoken to nearly every major curator, keeper, dealer and crook in the art world and yet they still haven't come up with a single lead. And why not? Because the only people who have seen the icon since 1917 were the Hesses and Goering, which leaves me with only one hope if it was not destroyed when the Grand Duke's plane crashed," said Romanov.

"Namely?" asked Petrova.

"That while the rest of the world is under the illusion that the original still hangs in the Winter Palace, it has, for the past twenty years, been lodged in a Swiss bank waiting for someone to claim it."

"A long shot," said the researcher.

"I am quite aware of that," said Romanov sharply, "but don't forget that many Swiss banks have a twenty-five-year rule before disclosure, some even thirty. One or two even have no deadline at all as long as enough money has been deposited to cover the housing of the treasure."

"Heaven knows how many banks there might be who fall into that category," sighed Petrova.

"Heaven knows," agreed Romanov, "and so might you by nine o'clock tomorrow morning. And then it will be necessary for me to pay a visit to the one man in this country who knows everything about banking."

"Am I expected to start straight away, Comrade Major?" the researcher asked coyly.

Romanov smiled and looked down into the girl's green eyes. Dressed in the dull grey uniform of her trade, no one would have given her a second look. But in the nude she was quite magnificent. He leaned over until their lips nearly met.

"You'll have to rise very early, Anna, but for now just turn out the light."

CHAPTER FIVE

It took Adam only a few more minutes before he had checked over both documents again. He put the original back in the faded envelope and replaced it in the Bible on his bookshelf. Finally he folded his duplicated copy of Goering's letter into three horizontal pieces and cut it carefully along the folds into strips which he placed in a clean envelope and left on his bedside table. Adam's next problem was how to obtain a translation of the document and Goering's letter without arousing unnecessary curiosity. Years of army training had taught him to be cautious when faced with an unknown situation. He quickly dismissed the German Embassy, the German Tourist Board and the German Press Agency as all three were too official, and therefore likely to ask unwanted questions. Once he was dressed he went to the hall and began to flick through the pages in the London E–K Directory until his finger reached the column he had been searching for.

German Broadcasting
German Cultural Institute
German Federal Railway
German Hospital
German Old People's Home

His eye passed over 'German Technical Translations' and stopped at a more promising entry. The address was given as Bayswater House, 35 Craven Terrace, W2. He checked his watch.

Adam left the flat a few minutes before ten, the three pieces of the letter now safely lodged in the inside pocket of his blazer. He strolled down Edith Grove and into the King's Road, enjoying the morning sun. The street had been transformed from the one he had known as a young subaltern. Boutiques had taken the place of antiquarian bookshops. Record shops had replaced the local cobbler, and Dolcis had given way to Mary Quant. Take a fortnight's holiday, and you couldn't be sure anything would still be there when you returned, he reflected ruefully.

Crowds of people spilled out from the pavement on to the road, staring or hoping to be stared at, according to their age. As Adam passed the first of the record shops he had no choice but to listen to 'I Want to Hold Your Hand' as it blared into the ears of everyone within shouting distance.

By the time Adam reached Sloane Square the world had almost returned to normal – Peter Jones, W. H. Smith's and the London Underground. The words his mother sang so often over the kitchen sink came back to him every time he walked into the square.

> And you're giving a treat (penny ice and cold meat)
> To a party of friends and relations,
> They're a ravenous horde, and they all came aboard
> At Sloane Square and South Kensington stations.

He paid a shilling for a ticket to Paddington and, installed in a half-empty carriage, once again went over his plan. When he emerged into the open air at

Paddington he checked the street name and, once he was sure of his bearings, walked out on to Craven Road until he came to the first available newsagent and then asked the directions for Craven Terrace.

"Fourth road on the left, mate," said the shopkeeper, not bothering to look up from a pile of *Radio Times* on which he was pencilling names. Adam thanked him and a few minutes later found himself standing at the end of a short drive, looking up at the bold green and yellow sign: The German Young Men's Christian Association.

He opened the gate, walked up the drive and strode confidently through the front door. He was stopped by a porter standing in the hallway.

"Can I help you, guv'nor?"

Adam put on an exaggerated military accent and explained that he was looking for a young man called Hans Kramer.

"Never 'eard of 'im, sir," said the porter, almost standing to attention when he recognised the regimental tie. He turned to a book that lay open on the desk. "'E isn't registered," he added, a Woodbine-stained thumb running down the list of names in front of him. "Why don't you try the lounge or the games room?" he suggested, gesturing with the thumb to a door on the right.

"Thank you," said Adam, not dropping the plummy tones. He walked smartly across the hall and through the swing doors – which, judging from the lack of paint on the base, looked as if they had been kicked open more often than they had been pushed. He glanced around the room. Several students were lounging about reading German papers and magazines. He wasn't sure where to start, until he spotted a studious-looking girl on her own in a corner, poring over a copy of *Time* magazine. Brezhnev's face stared out from the cover. Adam strolled over and took the empty seat beside her. She glanced sideways at him and couldn't hide her surprise at his formal dress. He waited for her to put the paper down before asking, "I wonder if you could assist me?"

"How?" enquired the girl, sounding a little apprehensive.

"I just need something translated."

She looked relieved. "I will see if I can help. Have you brought something with you?"

"Yes I have, I hope it isn't too difficult," Adam said. He took the envelope from his inside pocket and extracted the first paragraph of Goering's letter.

Then he put the envelope back in his pocket, took out a little notebook and waited expectantly. He felt like a cub reporter.

She read the paragraph over two or three times, then seemed to hesitate.

"Is anything wrong?"

"Not exactly," she replied, still concentrating on the words in front of her. "It's just that it's a little bit old-fashioned so that I might not be able to give you the exact sense."

Adam breathed a sigh of relief.

She repeated each sentence slowly, first in German and then in English as if wanting to feel the meaning as well as just translating the words.

"Over the last . . . past year we have come to know . . . each other somewhat . . . no, no," she said, "quite well." Adam wrote each word down as the girl translated them.

"You have never disguised — perhaps a better meaning is 'hidden' —" she added, "your distaste for the National Socialist Party."

She raised her head and stared at Adam. "It's only out of a book," he assured her. She didn't look convinced but nevertheless continued. "But you have at every time . . . no, at all times, behaved with the courtesy of an officer and a gentleman."

The girl looked up, even more puzzled, as she had now reached the last word.

"Is that all?" she asked. "It doesn't make sense. There has to be more."

"No, that's it," said Adam, quickly taking back the sheet of paper. "Thank you," he added. "It was most kind of you to help."

He left the girl and was relieved to see her shrug resignedly and return to her copy of *Time*. Adam went in search of the games room.

When he swung the door open he found a young man in a World Cup T-shirt and brown suede shorts. He was tapping a table tennis ball up and down listlessly.

"Care for a game?" said the boy, not looking at all hopeful.

"Sure," said Adam, removing his jacket and picking up the table tennis bat at his end of the table. For twenty minutes Adam had to play flat out to make sure he lost 18–21, 21–12, 17–21. As he replaced his jacket and congratulated his opponent he felt sure he had gained the young man's confidence.

"You put up good fight," said the German. "Give me good game."

Adam joined him at his end of the table. "I wonder if you could help me with something?" he said.

"Your backhand?" said the young man.

"No, thank you," said Adam, "I just need a paragraph of German translated." He handed over the middle paragraph of the letter. Once again, the would-be translator looked puzzled.

"It's from a book, so it may seem a little out of context," Adam said, unconvincingly.

"Okay, I try." As the boy began to study the paragraph, the girl who had already translated the first section came into the games room. She made her way towards them.

"This hard to make out, I am not good translation for," the young man said. "My girlfriend better, I think. I ask her. *Liebling, kannst Du dies für den Herrn ins Englische?*" Without looking at Adam he passed the second paragraph over to the girl who immediately said, "I knew there was more."

"No, no, don't bother," said Adam, and grabbed the piece of paper away from the girl. He turned back to the boy and said, "Thank you for the game. Sorry to have bothered you," and walked hurriedly out into the corridor, heading for the front door.

"Did you find 'im, sir?"

"Find him?" said Adam.

"Hans Kramer," said the porter.

"Oh, yes, thank you," said Adam. As he turned to leave he saw the young boy and his girlfriend were following close behind.

Adam ran down the drive and hailed a passing taxi.

"Where to?" said the cabbie.

"The Royal Cleveland Hotel."

"But that's only just round the corner."

"I know," said Adam, "but I'm already late."

"Suit yourself, guv," said the cabbie, "it's your money."

As the cab moved off Adam peered out of the back window to see his table-tennis opponent in conversation with the porter. The girl stood alongside them, pointing to the taxi.

Adam only relaxed when the cab turned the corner and they were out of sight.

In less than a minute the taxi had drawn up outside the Royal Cleveland. Adam handed the cabbie half a crown and waited for the change. Then he pushed through the revolving doors of the hotel and hung around in the foyer for a few moments before returning to the pavement again. He checked his watch: twelve thirty. Easily enough time for lunch, he thought, before going on to his interview with the Foreign Office. He headed across the Bayswater Road into the park at a brisk pace, knowing he couldn't hope to find a pub until he reached Knightsbridge.

Adam recalled the table tennis match. Damn, he thought. I should have thrashed him. At least that would have given him something else to think about.

Romanov's eye ran down the list of the fourteen banks. There was still an outside chance that one of them might be in possession of the Tsar's icon, but the names meant nothing to him. It was another world, and he knew he would now have to seek advice from an expert.

He unlocked the top drawer of his desk and flicked through the red book held only by the most senior ranking officers in the KGB. Many names had been scratched out or overwritten as regimes came and went but Aleksei Andreovich Poskonov had remained in his present position as Chairman of the National Bank for nearly a decade, and only Gromyko the Foreign Secretary had served in any office longer. Romanov dialled a number on his private line and asked to be put through to the Chairman of Gosbank. It was some considerable time before another voice came on the line.

"Comrade Romanov, what can I do for you?"

"I urgently need to see you," said Romanov.

"Really." The gravelly tones that came from the other end of the line sounded distinctly unimpressed. Romanov could hear pages being flicked over. "I could manage Tuesday, say eleven thirty?"

"I said it was urgent," repeated Romanov. "It concerns a State matter that can't wait."

"We are the nation's bankers and do have one or two problems of our own, you might be surprised to hear," came back the unrepentant voice. Romanov checked himself and waited. There was more flicking of pages. "Well, I suppose I could fit you in at three forty-five today, for fifteen minutes," said the banker. "But I must warn you that I have a long-standing engagement at four."

"Three forty-five it is then," said Romanov.

"In my office," said Poskonov. The phone went dead.

Romanov cursed out loud. Why did everyone feel obliged to prove their manhood with the KGB? He began to write down the questions he needed answered in order to put his plan into operation. He couldn't afford to waste even a minute of his allocated fifteen. An hour later he asked to see the Chairman of the KGB. This time he was not kept waiting.

"Trying to play the capitalists at their own game, are we?" said Zaborski, once Romanov had outlined his intentions. "Be careful. They've been at it a lot longer than we have."

"I realise that," said Romanov. "But if the icon is in the West I'm left with little choice but to use their methods to get my hands on it."

"Perhaps," said the Chairman. "But with your name such an approach could be misunderstood."

Romanov knew better than to interrupt the brief silence that ensued. "Don't worry, I'll give you all the backing you need – although I've never had a request quite like this one before."

"Am I allowed to know why the icon is so important?" Romanov enquired.

The Chairman of the KGB frowned. "I do not have the authority to answer that question, but as Comrade Brezhnev's enthusiasm for the arts is well known you must have been able to work out that it is not the painting itself that we are after."

What secret can the painting hold? thought Romanov, and decided to press on. "I wondered if . . ."

The Chairman of the KGB shook his head firmly.

Bugs don't have eyes, thought Romanov, but you know what that something is, don't you?

The Chairman rose from his desk and walked over to the wall and tore another page from the calendar. "Only ten days left to find the damn thing," he said. "The General Secretary has taken to phoning me at one o'clock every morning."

"One o'clock in the morning?" said Romanov joining in the game.

"Yes, the poor man can't sleep, they tell me," said the Chairman, returning to his desk. "It comes to all of us in time – perhaps even you, Romanov, and maybe earlier than you expect if you don't stop asking questions." He gave his young colleague a wry smile.

Romanov left the Chairman a few minutes later and returned to his office to go over the questions that did need to be answered by the Chairman of Gosbank. He couldn't help becoming distracted by thoughts of what could possibly be the significance of such a small painting, but accepted that he must concentrate his efforts on finding it and then perhaps the secret it contained would become obvious.

Romanov reached the steps of Neglinnaya 12 at three thirty because he knew he needed more than the fifteen minutes he had been allocated if he was to get all his questions answered. He only hoped Poskonov would agree to see him immediately.

After announcing himself at the reception desk he was accompanied by a uniformed guard up the wide marble staircase to the first floor, where Poskonov's secretary was waiting to greet him. Romanov was led to an anteroom. "I will inform the Chairman of the bank that you have arrived, Comrade Romanov," the secretary said, and then disappeared back into his own office. Romanov paced up and down the small anteroom impatiently, but the secretary did not return until the hands on the clock were in a straight line. At three fifty, Romanov was ushered into the Chairman's room.

The young major was momentarily taken aback by the sheer opulence of the room. The long red velvet curtains, the marble floor and the delicate French furniture wouldn't, he imagined, have been out of place in the Governor's rooms at the Bank of England. Romanov was reminded not for the first time that money still remained the most important commodity in the world – even in the Communist world. He stared at the old stooped man with the thinning grey hair and bushy walrus moustache who controlled the nation's money. The man of whom it was said that he knew of one skeleton in everyone's cupboard. Everyone's except mine, thought Romanov. His check suit might have been made before the Revolution and would once again be considered 'with it' in London's King's Road.

"What can I do for you, Comrade Romanov?" enquired the banker with a sigh, as if addressing a tiresome customer who was seeking a small loan.

"I require one hundred million American dollars' worth of gold bullion immediately," he announced evenly.

The chairman's bored expression suddenly changed. He went scarlet and fell back into his chair. He took several short, sharp breaths before pulling open a drawer, taking out a square box and extracting a large white pill from it. It took fully a minute before he seemed calm again.

"Have you gone out of your mind, Comrade?" the old man enquired. "You ask for an appointment without giving a reason, you then charge into my office and demand that I hand over one hundred million American dollars in gold without any explanation. For what reason do you make such a preposterous suggestion?"

"That is the business of the State," said Romanov. "But, since you have enquired, I intend to deposit equal amounts in a series of numbered accounts across Switzerland."

"And on whose authority do you make such a request?" the banker asked in a level tone.

"The General Secretary of the Party."

"Strange," said Poskonov. "I see Leonid Ilyich at least once a week and he has not mentioned this to me," the chairman looked down at the pad in the middle of his desk, "that a Major Romanov, a middle-ranking" – he stressed the words – "officer from the KGB would be making such an exorbitant demand."

65

Romanov stepped forward, picked up the phone by Poskonov's side and held it out to him. "Why don't you ask Leonid Ilyich yourself and save us all a lot of time?" He pushed the phone defiantly towards the banker. Poskonov stared back at him, took the phone and placed it to his ear. Romanov sensed the sort of tension he only felt in the field.

A voice came on the line. "You called, Comrade Chairman?"

"Yes," replied the old man. "Cancel my four o'clock appointment, and see that I am not disturbed until Major Romanov leaves."

"Yes, Comrade Chairman."

Poskonov replaced the phone and, without another word, rose from behind his desk and walked around to Romanov's side. He ushered the young man into a comfortable chair on the far side of the room below a bay window and took the seat opposite him.

"I knew your grandfather," he said in a calm, matter-of-fact tone. "I was a junior commodity clerk when I first met him. I had just left school and he was very kind to me but he was just as impatient as you are. Which was why he was the best fur trader in Russia and thought to be the worst poker player."

Romanov laughed. He had never known his grandfather and the few books that referred to him had long ago been destroyed. His father talked openly of his wealth and position which had only given the authorities ammunition finally to destroy him.

"You'll forgive my curiosity, Major, but if I am to hand over one hundred million dollars in gold I should like to know what it is to be spent on. I thought only the CIA put in chits for those sort of expenses without explanation."

Romanov laughed again and explained to the Chairman how they had discovered the Tsar's icon was a fake and he had been set the task of recovering the original. When he had completed his story he handed over the names of the fourteen banks. The banker studied the list closely while Romanov outlined the course of action he proposed to take, showing how the money would be returned intact as soon as he had located the missing icon.

"But how can one small icon possibly be that important to the State?" Poskonov asked out loud, almost as if Romanov were no longer in the room.

"I have no idea," replied Romanov truthfully and then briefed him on the results of his research.

There was an exasperated grunt from the other chair when Romanov had finished. "May I be permitted to suggest an alternative to your plan?"

"Please do," said Romanov, relieved to be gaining the older man's co-operation.

"Do you smoke?" asked the banker, taking a packet of Dunhill cigarettes from his coat pocket.

"No," said Romanov, his eyebrows lifting slightly at the sight of the red box.

The old man paused as he lit a cigarette. "That suit was not tailored in Moscow either, Major," the banker said, pointing at Romanov with his cigarette. "Now, to business – and do not hesitate to correct me if I have misunderstood any of your requirements. You suspect that lodged in one of these fourteen Swiss banks" – the Chairman tapped the list with his index finger – "is the original Tsar's icon. You therefore want me to deposit large amounts of gold with each bank in the hope that it will give you immediate access to the head of the family, or chairman. You will then offer the chairman the chance to control the entire hundred million if they promise to co-operate with you?"

"Yes," said Romanov. "Bribery is surely something the West has always understood."

"I would have said 'naïve' if I hadn't known your grandfather, though to be fair it was he who ended up making millions of roubles, not me. Nevertheless, how much do you imagine is a lot of money to a major Swiss bank?"

Romanov considered the question. "Ten million, twenty million?"

"To the Moscow Narodny Bank perhaps," said Poskonov. "But every one of the banks you hope to deal with will have several customers with deposits of over a hundred million each."

Romanov was unable to hide his disbelief.

"I confess," continued the chairman, "that our revered General Secretary showed no less incredulity when I informed him of these facts some years ago."

"Then I will need a thousand million?" asked Romanov.

"No, no, no. We must approach the problem from a different standpoint. You do not catch a poacher by offering him rabbit stew."

"But if the Swiss are not moved by the offer of vast amounts of money, what *will* move them?"

"The simple suggestion that their bank has been used for criminal activity," said the chairman.

"But how . . ." began Romanov.

"Let me explain. You say that the Tsar's icon hanging in the Winter Palace is not the original but a copy. A good copy, painted by a twentieth-century court painter, but nevertheless a copy. Therefore why not explain to each of the fourteen banks privately that, after extensive research, we have reason to believe that one of the nation's most valuable treasures has been substituted with a copy and the original is thought to have been deposited in their bank? And rather than cause a diplomatic incident – the one thing every Swiss banker wishes to avoid at any cost – perhaps they would, in the interests of good relationships, consider checking in their vaults items that have not been claimed for over twenty years."

Romanov looked straight at the old man, realising why he had survived several purges. "I owe you an apology, Comrade Poskonov."

"No, no, we each have our own little skills. I am sure I would be as lost in your world as you appear to be in mine. Now, if you will allow me to contact each of the chairmen on this list and tell them no more than the truth – a commodity I am always obliged to trade in although I imagine your counterparts are not so familiar with – namely that I suspect the Tsar's icon is in *their* bank, most of them will be disinclined to hold on to the masterpiece if they believe in so doing a crime has been perpetrated against a sovereign state."

"I cannot overstress the urgency," said Romanov.

"Just like your grandfather," Poskonov repeated. "So be it. If they can be tracked down, I shall speak to every one of them today. At least that's one of the advantages of the rest of the world waking up after us. Be assured I shall be in touch with you the moment I have any news."

"Thank you," said Romanov, rising to leave. "You have been most helpful." He was about to add, as he normally did in such circumstances, I shall so inform my Chairman, but he checked himself, realising the old man wouldn't have given a damn.

The chairman of Gosbank closed the door behind him and walked over to the bay window and watched Romanov run down the steps of the bank to a waiting car. I couldn't have supplied you with the one hundred

million in gold bullion at this particular time, even if
the General Secretary had ordered me to, he thought
to himself. I doubt if I have ten million dollars' worth
of gold left in the vaults at this moment. The General
Secretary has already ordered me to fly every available
ounce to the Bank of New York – so cleverly was his
ploy disguised that the CIA had been informed about
the deposit within an hour of its arrival. It's hard to
hide over 700 million dollars in gold, even in America.
I tried to tell him. The chairman watched Romanov's
car drive away. Of course if, like your grandfather, you
read the *Washington Post* as well as *Pravda*, you would
already have known this. He returned to his desk and
checked the names of the fourteen banks.

He knew instantly which of the fourteen had to be
phoned.

Adam stepped out of Tattersalls Tavern on the corner
of Knightsbridge Green and headed past the Hyde
Park Hotel towards the Royal Thames Yacht Club. It
seemed a strange place for the Foreign Office to hold
an interview, but so far everything connected with the
application had been somewhat mysterious.

He arrived a few minutes early and asked the ex-
Royal Marines sergeant on the door where the interviews were taking place.

"Sixth floor, sir. Take the lift in the corner," he
pointed ahead of him, "and announce yourself at reception."

Adam pressed a button and waited for the lift. The
doors opened immediately and he stepped in. A rather
overweight, bespectacled man of roughly his own age
who looked as if he never turned down the third course
of any meal followed him at a more leisurely pace.
Adam touched the sixth button, but neither man spoke

on their journey up to the sixth floor. The large man stepped out of the lift in front of Adam.

"Wainwright's the name," he informed the girl on the reception desk.

"Yes, sir," said the girl, "you're a little early, but do have a seat over there." She gestured towards a chair in the corner, then her eyes moved on to Adam and she smiled.

"Scott," he informed her.

"Yes, sir," she repeated. "Could you join the other gentleman? They will be seeing you next." Adam went over and picked up a copy of *Punch* before settling down next to Wainwright, who was already filling in the *Telegraph* crossword.

Adam soon became bored with flicking through endless issues of *Punch* and took a more careful look at Wainwright. "Do you by any chance speak German?" Adam asked suddenly, turning to face the other interviewee.

"German, French, Italian and Spanish," Wainwright replied, looking up. "I assumed that was how I managed to get this far," he added somewhat smugly.

"Then perhaps you could translate a paragraph from a German letter for me?"

"Delighted, old fellow," said Adam's companion, who proceeded to remove the pair of thick-lensed glasses from his nose, and waited for Adam to extract the middle paragraph of the letter from his envelope.

"Now, let me see," Wainwright said, taking the little slip of paper and replacing the glasses. "Quite a challenge. I say, old fellow, you're not part of the interviewing team by any chance?"

"No, no," said Adam, smiling. "I'm in exactly the same position as you – except I don't speak German, French, Italian or Spanish."

Wainwright seemed to relax. "Now let me see," he repeated, as Adam took out the small notebook from his inside pocket.

"'During the past year you cannot have failed to . . . notice that I have been receiving from one of the guards a regular, regular . . . regular supply'," he said suddenly, "yes, 'supply of Havana cigars. One of the few pleasures I have been allocated' – no, 'allowed', better still 'permitted' – 'despite my . . . incarceration'. That's the nearest I can get," Wainwright added. "'The cigars themselves have also served another purpose'," Wainwright continued, obviously enjoying himself, "'as they contained tiny capsules . . .'"

"Mr Scott."

"Yes," said Adam, jumping up obediently.

"The Board will see you now," said the receptionist.

"Do you want me to finish it off while they're finishing you off, old chap?" said Wainwright.

"Thank you," Adam replied, "if it's not too much trouble."

"Far easier than the crossword," Wainwright added, leaving on one side the little unfilled half-matrix of squares.

Alex Romanov was not a patient man at the best of times, and with the General Secretary now ringing up his chief twice a day, these were not the best of times.

While he waited for results of the chairman of Gosbank's enquiries he re-read the research papers that had been left on his desk, and checked any new intelligence that had been sent back by his agents in the field. Romanov resented the scraps of information the chairman of Gosbank must have been receiving by the hour, but he made no attempt to pester the old man despite his time problem.

Then the chairman of the bank called.

On this occasion Romanov was driven straight over to the State Bank at Neglinnaya 12 and ushered up to the finely furnished room without a moment's delay. Poskonov, dressed in another of those suits with an even larger check, was standing to greet him at the door.

"You must have wondered if I had forgotten you," were Poskonov's opening words as he ushered Romanov to the comfortable chair. "But I wanted to have some positive news to give you rather than waste your time. You don't smoke, if I remember correctly," he added, taking out his packet of Dunhill cigarettes.

"No, thank you," Romanov said, wondering if the chairman's doctor realised how much the old man smoked.

The chairman's secretary entered the room and placed two empty glasses, a frosted flask and a plate of caviar in front of them.

Romanov waited in silence.

"I have, over the past two days, managed to talk to the chairmen of twelve of the banks on your original list," Poskonov began, as he poured two vodkas, "but I have avoided making contact with the remaining two."

"Avoided?" repeated Romanov.

"Patience, Comrade," said Poskonov, sounding like a benevolent uncle. "You have longer to live than I so if there is any time to be wasted it must be yours."

Romanov lowered his eyes.

"I avoided one of the chairmen," Poskonov continued, "because he is in Mexico showing President Ordaz how not to repay their loan to Chase Manhattan while at the same time borrowing even more dollars from the Bank of America. If he pulls that off I shall have to recommend to the General Secretary of the Party that he is offered my job when I retire. The second gentleman I have avoided because he is officially in Chicago, closing a major Eurobond deal with Continental Illinois, while in fact he is booked in at the St Francis Hotel in San Francisco with his mistress. I feel certain you would agree, Comrade Major, that it would not advance our cause to disturb either of these gentlemen at this precise moment. The first has enough problems to be going on with for the rest of the week, while the second may well have his phone tapped – and we wouldn't want the Americans to discover what we are searching for, would we?"

"Agreed, Comrade," said Romanov.

"Good. Anyway as they both return to Switzerland early next week we have quite enough to be going on with for now."

"Yes, but what –" Romanov began.

"It will please you to know," continued Poskonov, "that of the twelve remaining chairmen all have agreed to co-operate with us and five have already phoned back. Four to say they have run a thorough check on the possessions of customers who have been out of contact with the bank for over twenty years, but have come up with nothing that remotely resembles an icon. In fact, one of them opened a deposit box in the presence of three other directors that had not been touched since 1931 only to discover it contained nothing but a cork from a 1929 bottle of Taylor's port."

"Only a cork?" said Romanov.

"Well, 1929 was a vintage year," admitted the chairman.

"And the fifth?" enquired Romanov.

"Now that, I suspect, may be our first breakthrough," continued Poskonov, referring to the file in front of him. He adjusted his spectacles with the forefinger of his right hand before continuing. "Herr Dieter Bischoff of Bischoff et Cie" – he looked up at his guest, as if Romanov might have recognised the name – "an honourable man with whom I have dealt many times in the past – honourable, that is, by Western standards of course, Comrade," added the chairman, obviously enjoying himself. "Bischoff has come up with something that was left with the bank in 1938. It is unquestionably an icon, but he has no way of knowing if it is the one we are looking for."

Romanov leapt up from his seat in excitement. "Then I had better go and see for myself," said Romanov. "I could fly out today," he added. The chairman waved him back into his chair.

"The plane you require does not leave Sheremtyevo airport until four thirty-five. In any case, I have already booked two seats on it for you."

"Two?" enquired Romanov.

"You will obviously need an expert to accompany you, unless you know considerably more about icons than you do about banking," Poskonov added. "I also took the liberty of booking you on the Swissair flight. One should never fly Aeroflot if it can be avoided. It has managed only one aviation record consistently every year since its inception, namely that of losing the most passengers per miles flown, and a banker never believes in going against known odds. I have fixed an appointment for you to see Herr Bischoff at ten o'clock tomorrow morning – unless, of course, you have something more pressing to keep you in Moscow, Comrade?"

Romanov smiled.

"I note from your file that you have never served in Switzerland," said the old man, showing off. "So may

I also recommend that you stay at the St Gothard while you are in Zurich. Jacques Pontin will take excellent care of you. Nationality has never been a problem for the Swiss, only currency. And so that brings my little investigation up to date, and I shall be in touch again as soon as the two itinerant chairmen return to Switzerland next Monday. All I can do for the moment however, is wish you luck in Zurich."

"Thank you," said Romanov. "May I be permitted to add how much I appreciate your thoroughness."

"My pleasure, Comrade, let's just say that I still owe your grandfather a favour, and perhaps one day you will find you owe me one, and leave it at that."

Romanov tried to fathom the meaning of the old man's words. There was no clue to be found in Poskonov's expression and so he left without another word. But as Romanov walked down the wide marble staircase, he considered the banker's sentiment again and again because throw-away lines were never delivered to an officer of the KGB.

By the time Romanov had returned to Dzerzhinsky Square, his secretary informed him that Herr Bischoff's assistant had telephoned from Zurich to confirm his appointment with the chairman at ten o'clock the following morning. Romanov asked him to call the manager at the St Gothard Hotel and book two rooms. "Oh, and confirm my flight with Swissair," he added before walking up two floors to see the Chairman and brief him on the meeting he had had with the head of the National Bank.

"Thank God for that," were Zaborski's first words. "With only nine days left at least you've given me something to discuss with the General Secretary when he calls at one tomorrow morning."

Romanov smiled.

"Good luck, Comrade. Our Embassy will be alerted to your every need. Let us fervently hope that you will be able to return the masterpiece to the walls of the Winter Palace."

"If it is in that bank, it will be in your hands by tomorrow night," said Romanov, and left the Chairman smiling.

When he walked into his own office he found Petrova waiting for him.

"You called for me, Comrade?"

"Yes, we're going to Zurich." Romanov looked at his watch. "In three hours' time. The flight and the rooms are already booked."

"In the names of Herr and Frau Schmidt, no doubt," said his lover.

CHAPTER SIX

When Adam emerged from the interview he felt quietly confident. The chairman's final words had been to ask him if he would be available for a thorough medical in a week's time. Adam had told them he could think of nothing that would stop him attending. He looked forward to the opportunity of serving in the British Foreign Service.

Back in the waiting room Wainwright looked up and handed him back his piece of paper.

"Thank you very much," said Adam, trying to look casual by slipping it into his inside pocket without looking at the results.

"What was it like, old chap?" his companion asked cautiously.

"No trouble for a man who has German, French, Spanish and Italian as part of his armoury," Adam assured him. "Best of luck, anyway."

"Mr Wainwright," said the secretary, "the Board will see you now."

Adam took the lift to the ground floor and decided to walk home, stopping on the corner of Wilton Place to buy a bag of apples from a barrow boy who seemed to spend most of his time on the lookout for the police. Adam moved on, going over in his mind the Board's questions and his answers – a pointless exercise he decided, although he still felt confident the interview had gone well. He came to such a sudden halt that the pedestrian behind only just stopped himself bumping into Adam. What had attracted his attention was a sign which read: 'The German Food Centre'. An attractive girl with a cheerful smile and laughing eyes was sitting at the cash register by the doorway. Adam strode into the shop and went straight over to her without attempting to purchase a single item.

"You have not bought anything?" she enquired with a slight accent.

"No, I'm just about to," Adam assured her, "but I wondered, do you speak German?"

"Most girls from Mainz do," she replied, grinning.

"Yes, I suppose they would," said Adam, looking at the girl more carefully. She must have been in her early twenties, Adam decided, and he was immediately attracted by her friendly smile and manner. Her shiny, dark hair was done up in a pony tail with a big red bow. Her white sweater and neat pleated skirt would have made any man take a second look. Her slim legs were tucked under the chair. "I wonder if you would be kind enough to translate a short paragraph for me?"

"I try," she said, still smiling.

Adam took the envelope containing the final section of the letter out of his pocket and handed it over to her.

"The style is a bit old-fashioned," she said, looking serious. "It may take a little time."

"I'll go and do some shopping," he told her, and started walking slowly round the long stacked shelves. He selected a little salami, frankfurters, bacon, and some German mustard, looking up now and then to see how the girl was progressing. From what he could make out, she was only able to translate a few words at a time, as she was continually interrupted by customers. Nearly twenty minutes passed before he saw her put the piece of paper on one side. Adam immediately went over to the cash register and placed his purchases on the counter.

"One pound two shillings and sixpence," she said. Adam handed over two pounds and she returned his change and the little piece of paper.

"This I consider a rough translation, but I think the meaning is clear."

"I don't know how to thank you," said Adam, as an elderly woman joined him in the queue.

"You could invite me to share with you your frankfurters," she laughed.

"What a nice idea," said Adam. "Why don't you join me for dinner tonight?"

"I was not serious," she said.

"I was," smiled Adam. Another person joined the queue and the old lady immediately behind him began to look restive.

Adam grabbed a leaflet from the counter, retreated towards the back of the store, and began to scribble down his name, address and phone number. He waited for the two customers in front of him to pay, then handed over to her a 'once in a lifetime' Persil offer.

"What's this?" the girl asked innocently.

"I've put my name and address on the centre page," Adam said. "I will expect you for dinner at about eight this evening. At least you know what's on the menu."

She looked uncertain. "I really was only joking."

"I won't eat you," said Adam. "Only the sausages."

She looked at the leaflet in her hand and laughed. "I'll think about it."

Adam strolled out on to the road whistling. A bad

morning, a good afternoon and – perhaps – an even better evening.

He was back at the flat in time to watch the five forty-five news. Mrs Gandhi, the new Prime Minister of India, was facing open revolt in her cabinet and Adam wondered if Britain could ever have a woman Prime Minister. England were 117 for seven in their first innings, with the West Indies still well on top. He groaned and turned off the television. Once he had put the food in the fridge he went into his bedroom to assemble the full text of the Goering letter. After he had read through all the little slips of paper he took out his notepad and began to copy out the translations in order: first, the paragraph supplied by the girl from the YMCA, then Wainwright's handwritten words from the notepad, and finally the section of the letter translated by the lovely girl from Mainz. He read the completed draft through slowly a second time.

Nuremberg
October 15, 1946

Dear Colonel,

Over the past year, we have come to know each other quite well. You have never disguised your distaste for the National Socialist party, but you have at all times behaved with the courtesy of an officer and a gentleman.

During the year you cannot have failed to notice that I have been receiving from one of the guards a regular supply of Havana cigars – one of the few pleasures I have been permitted, despite my incarceration. The cigars themselves have also served another purpose, as each one contained a capsule with a small amount of poison. Enough to allow me to survive my trial, while ensuring that I shall cheat the executioner.

My only regret is that you, as the officer in charge of the watch during the period when I am most likely to die, may be held responsible for something to which you were never a party. To make amends for this I enclose a document in the name of one Emmanuel Rosenbaum which should help with any financial difficulties you face in the near future.

All that will be required of you –

"Anyone at home?" shouted Lawrence. Adam folded up the pieces of paper, walked quickly over to the bookcase and inserted them alongside the original letter in the Bible seconds before Lawrence put his head round the door.

"Bloody traffic," said Lawrence cheerfully. "I can't wait to be appointed chairman of the bank and be given that luxury flat on the top floor, not to mention the chauffeur and the company car."

Adam laughed. "Had another hard day at the office, darling?" he mimicked, before joining him in the kitchen. Adam started removing food from the fridge.

"Guess who's coming to dinner," said Lawrence as each new delicacy appeared.

"A rather attractive German girl, I hope," said Adam.

"What do you mean, 'hope'?"

"Well, it could hardly have been described as a formal invitation so I'm not even certain she'll turn up."

"If that's the situation I may as well hang around in case she gives you the elbow and you need someone to help you eat that lot."

"Thanks for the vote of confidence, but I think you'll

find it's your turn to be missing, presumed dead. Anyway, what about Carolyn?" said Adam.

"Carolyn was yesterday's girl, to quote the esteemed Harold Wilson. How did you come across your *gnädiges Fräulein*?"

"She was serving at a food store in Knightsbridge."

"I see. We're down to shop assistants now."

"I have no idea what she is or even what her name is, come to that," said Adam. "But I am hoping to find out tonight. As I said, your turn to disappear."

"*Natürlich*. As you see, you can rely on me·to provide a helping hand if you need anything translated."

"Just put the wine in the fridge and lay the table."

"Are there no serious jobs for a man of my accomplishments to be entrusted with?" chuckled Lawrence.

When eight o'clock chimed, the table was set and Adam had everything ready on the boil. By eight thirty both of them stopped pretending and Adam served up two plates of frankfurters, salami and lettuce with a baked potato and sauerkraut sauce. He then hung up his Goons apron behind the kitchen door and took the chair opposite Lawrence, who had begun pouring the wine.

"Oh, *mein liebes Mädchen*, you look ravishing in that Harris tweed jacket," said Lawrence, raising his glass.

Adam was just about to retaliate with the vegetable spoon when there was a loud knock on the front door. The two men stared at each other before Adam leaped to open it. Standing in the doorway was a man well over six foot with shoulders like a professional bouncer. By his side, dwarfed by him, was the girl that Adam had invited to dinner.

"This is my brother, Jochen," she explained. Adam was immediately struck by how beautiful she looked in a dark blue patterned blouse and pleated blue skirt that fell just below the knee. Her long dark hair, now hanging loose, looked as if it had just been washed and shone even under the forty watt light bulb that hung in the hall.

"Welcome," said Adam, more than a little taken aback.

"Jochen is just dropping me off."

"Yes, of course," said Adam. "Do come in and have a drink, Jochen."

"No, I thank you. I have a date as well, but I will pick up Heidi at eleven o'clock, if all right by you?"

"Fine by me," said Adam, at last learning her name.

The giant bent down and kissed his sister on both cheeks. He then shook hands with Adam before leaving them both on the doorstep.

"I am sorry to be late," said Heidi. "My brother did not get back from work until after seven."

"It was no problem," said Adam, leading her into the flat. "If you had come any earlier I wouldn't have been ready for you. By the way, this is my flatmate, Lawrence Pemberton."

"In England the men also need a chaperone?" said Heidi.

Both men laughed. "No, no," said Lawrence. "I was just on my way out. Like your brother, I already have a date. As you can see the table is only laid for two. I'll be back around eleven, Adam, just to make sure you're safe." He smiled at Heidi, put on his coat and closed the door behind him before either could object.

"I hope I don't drive him away," said Heidi.

"No, no," said Adam, as she took Lawrence's place at the table. "He's already late for his girlfriend. Charming girl called Carolyn, a social worker." He quickly topped up her wine, pretending it hadn't already been poured.

"So I am going to eat my own sausages, after all," she said, laughing. And the laughter didn't stop for the rest of the evening, as Adam learned about Heidi's life in Germany, her family and the holiday job she had taken while on vacation from Mainz University.

"My parents only allow me to come to England because my brother is already in London; it is to help my languages course. But now, Adam, I would like to know what you are doing when you are not picking up girls in food stores."

"I was in the army for nine years and I'm now hoping to join the Foreign Office."

"In what capacity, if that is the right expression?" Heidi asked.

"It's the right expression, but I'm not sure I know the right answer," said Adam.

"When someone says that about the Foreign Service it usually means they are a spy."

"I don't know what it means, to be honest, but they're going to tell me next week. In any case, I don't think I'd make a very good spy. But what are you going to do when you return to Germany?"

"Complete my final year at Mainz and then I hope to find a job as a television researcher."

"What about Jochen?" asked Adam.

"He will join my father's law practice as soon as he is arriving home."

"So how long will you be in London?" he found himself asking.

"Another two months," she said. "If I can stand the job."

"Why do you carry on with it if it's that bad?"

"There is no better way to test your English than

impatient shoppers who speak all different accents."

"I hope you stay the full two months," said Adam.

"So do I," she replied, smiling.

When Jochen arrived back punctually at eleven o'clock, he found Adam and Heidi washing the dishes.

"Thank you for a most interesting evening," she said, wiping her hands.

"Not a good word," reprimanded Jochen. "Not interesting, I think. Lovely, happy, delightful, enjoyable perhaps, but not interesting."

"It was all those things," said Adam, "but it was also interesting."

She smiled.

"May I come and buy some more sausages tomorrow?"

"I would like that," said Heidi, "but don't hold up any sour old women this time with translation demands. By the way, you never tell me why you needed the strange paragraph translated. I have been wondering who is this Rosenbaum and what it is he left to someone."

"Next time perhaps," said Adam, looking a little embarrassed.

"And next time you can bring my sister home yourself," said Jochen, as he shook Adam's hand firmly.

After Heidi had left, Adam sat down and finished off the last glass of wine, aware that he hadn't spent such a lovely, happy, delightful, enjoyable and interesting evening for a long time.

A black limousine with dark windows and unlit number plates remained parked in the VIP area of Zurich Kloten. Fastidious Swiss policemen had twice gone up to the car and checked the driver's credentials before Major Romanov and Anna Petrova emerged from the customs hall and took their places in the back of the car.

It was already dark as the driver moved off towards the neon glow of the city. When the car drew up outside the St Gothard Hotel the only words that passed between Romanov and the driver were, "I shall return to Moscow on the Tuesday morning flight."

Jacques Pontin, the manager of the hotel, was stationed at the door waiting to greet the new arrivals; he introduced himself immediately, and as soon as he had checked them both in he banged a little bell with the palm of his hand to summon a porter to assist the guests with their bags. A moment later a young man in his early twenties, dressed in green livery, appeared.

"Suite seventy-three and room seventy-four," Jacques instructed before turning back to Romanov. "I do hope your stay will prove to be worthwhile, Herr Romanov," he said. "Please do not hesitate to call upon me if there is anything you need."

"Thank you," said Romanov as he turned to join the porter who stood sentinel-like by the door of an open lift. Romanov stood to one side to allow Anna to go in first. The lift stopped at the seventh floor and the porter led the way down a long corridor to a corner suite. He turned the key in the lock and invited the two guests to go in ahead of him. The suite was as Romanov had expected, in a different league from the finest hotels he ever experienced in either Moscow or Leningrad. When he saw the array of gadgets in the marble bathroom he reflected that even prosperous travellers to Russia, if seasoned visitors, brought their own bath plugs with them.

"Your room is through there, madam," the porter informed the researcher, and unlocked an adjoining door. Although smaller in size, the room maintained the same unassuming elegance. The porter returned to Romanov, handed him his key and asked if there would be anything else he would require. Romanov assured him there was nothing and passed over a five-franc note.

Once again the porter gave a slight bow, and closing the door behind him, left Romanov to unpack while Anna Petrova went to her own room.

Romanov started to undress and then disappeared into the bathroom. He studied himself in the mirror. Although he was vain about his looks, he was even more vain about the state of his physique. At twenty-nine, despite being six feet, he still only weighed 165 pounds on Western scales, and his muscles remained hard and taut.

By the time Romanov had returned to the bedroom, he could hear the shower beating down in the adjoining bathroom. He crept over to the door and edged it open. He could see quite clearly the outline of Anna standing in the steaming shower. He smiled and noiselessly moved back across the thick carpet, slipped under the sheets and into the researcher's bed. He waited for her to turn off the steaming shower.

Adam stepped out of the freezing shower. Within minutes he was dressed and joined Lawrence in the kitchen for breakfast.

"Still unable to charge you for hot water, am I?" Lawrence said as Adam peered over his flatmate's shoulder, trying to take in the latest Test score.

"Why can't we produce any really fast fast bowlers?" he asked rhetorically.

"Can't stay and chatter to the unemployed," said Lawrence, picking up his briefcase. "Shah of Iran wants to discuss his financial problems with me. Sorry to rush off before you've had your cornflakes but I can't afford to keep His Imperial Majesty waiting."

Left on his own, Adam boiled himself an egg and burned some toast before he turned to the newspaper to learn of the latest casualties in Vietnam and President Johnson's proposed tour of the Far East. At this rate he decided he wasn't going to win the *Daily Mail*'s 'Housewife of the Year' competition. He eventually cleared away in the kitchen, made his bed and tidied up behind Lawrence – nine years of self-discipline wasn't going to change old habits that quickly – then he settled down to plan another day.

He realised he could no longer avoid making a decision. He sat once again at his desk and began to consider how to get the official document translated without arousing further suspicion.

Almost absent-mindedly he removed the Bible from the bookshelf and extracted the letter he had read the night before. The final paragraph still puzzled him. He considered Heidi's translation once again:

All that will be required of you is to present yourself at the address printed on the top right-hand corner of the enclosed document, with some proof that you are Colonel Gerald Scott. A passport should prove sufficient. You will then be given a bequest that I have left to you in the name of Emmanuel Rosenbaum.

I hope it will bring you good fortune.

Adam turned his attention to the document. He was still quite unable to discern what the bequest could possibly be, let alone whether it was of any value. Adam mused over the fact that such an evil man could involve himself in an act of kindness hours before he knew he was going to die – an act that now left him with no choice about his own involvement.

Romanov gathered the blankets together and in one movement hurled them on to the floor to expose Anna curled up like a child, knees almost touching her exposed breasts. Anna's hand groped for a corner of the sheet to cover her naked body.

"Breakfast in bed?" she murmured hopefully.

"Dressed in ten minutes, or no breakfast at all," came back the reply. Anna lowered her feet gingerly on to the thick carpet and waited for the room to stop going round in circles before heading off towards the bathroom. Romanov heard the shower burst forth its jets. "Ahhh," came the pitiful cry. Romanov smiled when he remembered that he had left the indicator locked on dark blue.

During breakfast in the dining room they mulled over the approach he intended to take with the bank if Petrova were able to confirm that the icon was in fact Rublev's original masterpiece. He kept looking up from the table and then suddenly, without warning, said, "Let's go."

"Why?" Anna asked, as she bit into another slice of toast. Romanov rose from the table and without bothering to offer an explanation strode out of the room and headed straight for the lift. Petrova caught up with her master only moments before the lift gate closed. "Why?" she asked again, but Romanov did not speak until they were both back in his suite. He then threw open the large window that overlooked the railway station.

"Ah, it's outside your room," he said, looking to his right, and quickly walked through to the adjoining bedroom. He marched past the dishevelled double bed, jerked open the nearest window, and climbed outside. Petrova stared down from the seventh floor and felt giddy. Once Romanov had reached the bottom rung of the fire escape, he ran to a passing tram. Petrova would never have made it if she hadn't been lifted bodily on to the tram by Romanov's sheer strength.

"What's going on?" she asked, still puzzled.

"I can't be sure," said Romanov, looking out of the back of the tram. "All I do know for certain is what the local CIA agent looks like."

The researcher looked back in the direction of the hotel, but all she could see was a mass of anonymous people walking up and down the pavement.

Romanov remained on the tram for about a mile before he jumped off and hailed a passing taxi going in the opposite direction.

"Bischoff et Cie," he said as he waited for his puffing assistant to join him.

The cab headed back in the direction of the hotel, winding in and out of the morning traffic, until it came to a halt in front of a large brown granite building that filled the entire block. Romanov paid off the driver and stood in front of imposing doors made of thick glass and covered in wrought iron welded to look like the branches of a tree. By the side of the doors, carved inconspicuously into the stone and inlaid with gilt, were the words 'Bischoff et Cie'. There was no other clue as to what kind of establishment lay within.

Romanov turned the heavy wrought-iron knob and the two Russians stepped into a spacious hall. On the left-hand side of the hall stood a solitary desk behind which a smartly dressed young man was seated.

"Guten Morgen, mein Herr", he said.

"Good morning," said Romanov. "We have an appointment with Herr Dieter Bischoff."

"Yes, Herr Romanov," said the receptionist, checking the list of names in front of him. "Will you please take the lift to the fifth floor where you will be met by Herr Bischoff's secretary." When the two of them stepped out of the lift they were greeted by a lady in a neat plain suit. "Will you please follow me," she said, without any trace of accent. The two Russians were escorted along a picture-lined corridor to a comfortable room which more resembled the reception room of a country house than a bank.

"Herr Bischoff will be with you in a moment," the lady said, withdrawing. Romanov remained standing while he took in the room. Three black-and-white framed photographs of sombre old men in grey suits, trying to look like sombre old men in grey suits, took up most of the far wall, while on the other walls were discreet but pleasant oils of town and country scenes of nineteenth-century Switzerland. A magnificent oval Louis XIV table with eight carved mahogany chairs surrounding it dominated the centre of the room. Romanov felt a twinge of envy at the thought that he could never hope to live in such style.

The door opened and a man in his mid-sixties, followed by three other men in dark grey suits, entered the room. One look at Herr Bischoff and Romanov knew whose photograph would eventually join that of the other three grey, sombre men.

"What an honour for our little bank, Mr Romanov," were Bischoff's first words as he bowed and shook the Russian by the hand. Romanov nodded and introduced his assistant, who received the same courteous bow and handshake. "May I in turn present my son and two of my partners, Herr Muller and Herr Weizkopf." The three men bowed in unison, but remained standing while Bischoff took his seat at the head of the table.

At his gesture both Romanov and Anna sat down beside him.

"I wonder if I might be permitted to check your passport?" asked Bischoff, as if to show that the formal business had begun. Romanov took out the little blue passport with a soft cover from his inside pocket and handed it over. Bischoff studied it closely, as a philatelist might check an old stamp, and decided it was mint. "Thank you," he said, as he returned it to its owner

Bischoff then raised his hand and one of the partners immediately left them. "It will only take a moment for my son to fetch the icon we have in safe-keeping," he confided. "Meanwhile perhaps a little coffee – Russian," he added.

Coffee appeared within moments borne by yet another smartly dressed lady.

"Thank you," said Petrova, clearly a little overawed, but Romanov didn't speak again until Herr Bischoff's son reappeared with a small box and handed it over to his father.

"You will understand that I have to treat this matter with the utmost delicacy," the old man confided. "The icon may not turn out to be the one your Government is searching for."

"I understand," said Romanov.

"This magnificent example of Russian art has been in our possession since 1938, and was deposited with the bank on behalf of a Mr Emmanuel Rosenbaum."

Both visitors looked shocked.

"*Nevozmozhno*," said Anna, turning to her master. "He would never . . ."

"I suspect that's exactly why the name was chosen in the first place," Romanov said curtly to Anna, annoyed at her indiscretion. "Can't you see? It makes perfect sense. May I see the icon now?" said Romanov, turning back to the bank's Chairman.

Herr Bischoff placed the box in the centre of the table. The three men in grey suits each took a pace forward. Romanov looked up. "Under Swiss law we must have three witnesses when opening a box in someone else's name," explained the old man.

Romanov nodded curtly.

Herr Bischoff proceeded to unlock the metal box with a key he produced from his pocket, while his son leaned over and undid a second lock with a different key. The little ceremony completed, Herr Bischoff pushed up the lid of the box and turned it round to face his guests. Romanov placed his hands into the box like an expectant child does with a Christmas stocking, and drew out the icon. He stared at the beautiful painting. A small wooden rectangle that was covered in tiny pieces of red, gold and blue making up the mosaic of a man who looked as if he had all the worries of the world on his shoulders. The face, although sad, still evoked a feeling of serenity. The painting Romanov held in his hand was quite magnificent, as fine as any he had seen at the Winter Palace. No one in the room was quite sure what would happen next as Romanov offered no opinion.

It was Anna who finally spoke.

"A masterpiece it is," she said, "and undoubtedly fifteenth century but as you can see it's not St George and the Dragon."

Romanov nodded his agreement, still unable to let go of the little painting. "But do you know the origin of this particular icon?" Romanov asked.

"Yes," Anna replied, glad to be appreciated for the first time. "It is the Icon of St Peter, you see he holds the keys . . . painted by Dionisiy in 1471, and although it is undoubtedly one of the finest examples of his work, it is not the Tsar's icon."

"But does it belong to the Russian people?" asked Romanov, still hopeful of some reward for all his trouble.

"No, Comrade Major," said the researcher emphatically. "It belongs to the Munich Gallery, from where it has been missing since the day Hitler was appointed Reichs Chancellor."

Herr Bischoff scribbled a note on a piece of paper in front of him. At least one bank in Munich was going to be happy to do business with him in the future.

Romanov reluctantly handed back the icon to Herr Bischoff, only just managing to say, "Thank you."

"Not at all," said Herr Bischoff imperturbably, replacing the icon in the box and turning his key in his lock. His son completed the same routine with his own key and then departed with the unclaimed treasure. Romanov rose, as he considered nothing more could be gained from the meeting – although he believed he had discovered Goering's alias, or one of them.

"I wonder if I might be permitted to have a word with you in private, Herr Romanov," asked the elderly banker.

"Of course."

"It is rather a delicate matter I wish to put to you," said Herr Bischoff, "so I thought you might prefer your associate to leave us."

"That won't be necessary," said Romanov, unable to think of anything Bischoff might have to say that he wouldn't later need to discuss with Petrova.

"As you wish," said Bischoff. "I am curious to discover if there was any other reason behind your request to see me."

"I don't understand what you mean," said Romanov.

"I felt perhaps I knew the real reason you had selected this bank in particular to start your enquiry."

"I didn't select you," said Romanov. "You were only one of –" he stopped himself.

"I see," said Bischoff, himself now looking somewhat bemused. "Then may I be permitted to ask you a few questions?"

"Yes, if you must," said Romanov, now impatient to get away.

"You are Alexander Petrovich Romanov?"

"You must already believe that or we would not have proceeded this far."

"The only son of Peter Nicholevich Romanov?"

"Yes."

"And grandson of Count Nicholai Alexandrovich Romanov?"

"Is this to be a history lesson on my family tree?" asked Romanov, visibly irritated.

"No, I just wanted to be sure of my facts as I am even more convinced it would be wise for your associate to leave us for a moment," the old man suggested diffidently.

"Certainly not," said Romanov. "In the Soviet Union we are all equal," he added pompously.

"Yes, of course," said Bischoff, glancing quickly at Anna before continuing. "Did your father die in 1946?"

"Yes. He did," said Romanov, beginning to feel distinctly uncomfortable.

"And you are the only surviving child?"

"I am," confirmed Romanov proudly.

"In which case this bank is in possession . . ." Bischoff hesitated as a file was put in front of him by one of the men in grey. He placed a pair of gold, half-moon spectacles on his nose, taking as long as he could over the little exercise.

"Don't say anything more," said Romanov quietly.

Bischoff looked up. "I'm sorry, but I was given every reason to believe your visit had been planned."

Petrova was now sitting on the edge of her seat, enjoying every moment of the unfolding drama. She had already anticipated exactly what was going to happen and was disappointed when Romanov turned to speak to her.

"You will wait outside," was all he said. Petrova pouted and rose reluctantly to leave them, closing the door behind her.

Bischoff waited until he was certain the door was closed, then slid the file across the table. Romanov opened it gingerly. On the top of the first page was his grandfather's name underlined three times. Below the name were printed row upon row of incomprehensible figures.

"I think you will find that we have carried out your grandfather's instructions in maintaining a conservative portfolio of investments with his funds." Bischoff leaned across and pointed to a figure showing that the bank had achieved an average increase of 6·7 per cent per annum over the previous forty-nine years.

"What does this figure at the foot of the page represent?" asked Romanov.

"The total value of your stocks, bonds and cash at nine o'clock this morning. It has been updated every Monday since your grandfather opened an account with this bank in 1916." The old man looked up proudly at the three pictures on the wall.

"*Bozhe Moi*," said Romanov, as he took in the final figure. "But what currency is it in?"

"Your grandfather only showed faith in the English pound," said Herr Bischoff.

"Bozhe Moi," Romanov repeated.

"May I presume from your comment that you are not displeased with our stewardship?"

Romanov was speechless.

"It may also interest you to know that we are in possession of several boxes, the contents of which we have no knowledge. Your father also visited us on one occasion soon after the war. He appeared satisfied and assured me that he would return, but we never heard from him again. We were saddened to learn of his death. You might also prefer in the circumstances to return and investigate the boxes at another time," the banker continued.

"Yes," said Romanov quietly. "Perhaps I could come back this afternoon?"

"The bank will always be at your service, Your Excellency," replied Herr Bischoff.

No one had addressed a Romanov by his title since the Revolution. He sat in silence for some time.

Eventually he rose and shook hands with Herr Bischoff. "I will return this afternoon," he repeated before joining his companion in the corridor.

Neither uttered a word until they were back on the street outside the bank. Romanov was still so overcome by what he had learned that he failed to notice that the man he had so deftly avoided at the hotel was now standing in a tram queue on the far side of the road.

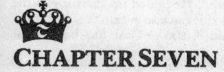

CHAPTER SEVEN

The pastor sat at the table studying the document but didn't offer an opinion for some considerable time. When he had heard Adam's request he had invited the young man into the privacy of his little office at the back of the German Lutheran Church.

It turned out to be a stark room dominated by a wooden table and several wooden chairs that didn't match. A small black crucifix was the only ornament on the blank whitewashed walls. Two of the unmatching chairs were now occupied by Adam and the pastor. Adam sat bolt upright while the man of God, clad from head to toe in a black cassock, elbows on the table and head in hands, stared down at the copy of the document.

After some considerable time, without raising his eyes, he offered, "This is a receipt, if I am not mistaken. Although I have little knowledge of such things, I am fairly confident that Roget et Cie, who must be Swiss bankers based in Geneva, have in their possession an object described herein as 'The Tsar's Icon'. If I remember my history correctly, the original can be viewed somewhere in Moscow. It appears," he continued, his eyes still fixed on the document, "that if the holder of this receipt presents himself in Geneva he will be able to claim the aforementioned icon of St George and the Dragon, deposited there by a Mr Emmanuel Rosenbaum. I confess," said the pastor, looking up for the first time, "that I've never seen anything like it before." He folded up the copy of the document and handed it back to Adam.

"Thank you," said Adam. "That has been most helpful."

"I am only sorry that my superior the Bishop is away on his annual retreat because I feel sure he would have been able to throw more light on the matter than I have."

"You have told me everything I need to know," said Adam, but couldn't resist asking, "Are icons at all valuable?"

"Once again, I must confess that I am not the best man from whom to seek such an opinion. All I can tell you is that, as with all art, the value of any object can vary from one extreme to the other without any satisfactory explanation to us normal mortals."

"Then there is no way of knowing the value of this particular icon?" asked Adam.

"I wouldn't venture an opinion, but no doubt the art auctioneers Sotheby's or Christie's might be willing to do so. After all, they claim in their advertisements that they have an expert in every field waiting to advise you."

"Then I shall put their claim to the test," said Adam, "and pay them a visit." He rose from his chair, shook hands with the pastor and said, "You have been most kind."

"Not at all," said the pastor. "I was only too pleased to assist you. It makes a change from Frau Gerber's marital problems and the size of the churchwarden's marrows."

*　　*　　*

Adam took a bus up to Hyde Park Corner and jumped off as it turned left into Knightsbridge. He walked through the subway and continued briskly down Piccadilly towards the Ritz. He had read somewhere that Sotheby's was in Bond Street, although he couldn't remember having ever seen it.

He walked another hundred yards before turning left, where he shortened his stride to check all the signs on both sides of the road. He passed Gucci's, Cartier's, Asprey's and was beginning to wonder if his memory had failed him and whether he should check in the telephone directory. He continued on past the Irish Tourist Board and Celines before he finally spotted the gold lettering above a little newspaper kiosk on the far side of the road.

He crossed the one-way street and entered the front door by the side of the kiosk. He felt like a boy on his first day at a new school, unsure of his surroundings and not certain to whom he should turn for advice. Most of the people who passed him went straight up the stairs and he was just about to follow them when he heard a voice say, "Up the stairs and straight through, madam. The auction is due to start in a few minutes."

Adam turned and saw a man in a long, green coat. The name 'Sotheby' was embroidered over his left-hand pocket.

"Where do I go if I want something valued?" Adam asked.

"Straight along the passage, sir, as far as you can go and you'll see a girl on the left-hand side in reception," barked his informant. Adam thanked him, presuming that the guide's former place of work could only have been on an Aldershot drill square . . . He walked along to the reception area. An old lady was explaining to one of the girls behind the counter that her grandmother had left the vase to her several years before and she wondered what it might be worth.

The girl only glanced at the heirloom before asking, "Can you come back in about fifteen minutes? By then our Mr Makepeace will have had time to look at it and will be able to give you an estimate."

"Thank you, my dear," said the old lady expectantly. The girl picked up the large ornate vase and carried it to a room in the back. She returned a few moments later to be faced with Adam.

"May I help you, sir?"

"I'm not sure," began Adam. "I need some advice concerning an icon."

"Have you brought the piece with you, sir?"

"No, it's still abroad at the moment."

"Do you have any details?"

"Details?"

"Artist's name, date, size. Or better still do you have a photograph of the piece?"

"No," said Adam sheepishly. "I only know its title but I do have some documentation," he added, handing over the receipt he had shown the pastor.

"Not a lot to go on," said the girl, studying the German transcript. "But I'll ask Mr Sedgwick, the head of our Russian and Greek Icon department, if he can help you."

"Thank you," said Adam, as the girl picked up the phone.

"Is Mr Sedgwick able to advise a customer?" the girl enquired. She listened for a moment then replaced the phone.

"Mr Sedgwick will be down in a few moments, if you would care to wait."

"Certainly," said Adam, feeling something of a fraud. While the girl attended to the next customer Adam waited for Mr Sedgwick and studied the pictures on the wall. There were several photos of items that had come under the auctioneer's hammer in recent sales. A large painting by Picasso called 'Trois Baigneuses' had been sold for fourteen thousand pounds. As far as Adam could make out the brightly coloured oil was of three women on a beach dancing. He felt confident they were women because they had breasts even if they weren't in the middle of their chests. Next to the Picasso was a Degas of a girl at a ballet lesson; this time there was no doubt it was a girl. But the painting that most caught Adam's eye was a large oil by an artist he had never heard of called Jackson Pollock that had come under the hammer for eleven thousand pounds. Adam wondered what sort of people could afford to spend such sums on works of art.

"Wonderful example of the artist's brushwork," said a voice behind him. Adam turned to face a tall, cadaverous figure with a ginger moustache and thinning red hair. His suit hung on him as if from a coathanger. "My name is Sedgwick," he announced in a donnish voice.

"Scott," said Adam, offering his hand.

"Well, Mr Scott, why don't we sit over here and then you can let me know how I can help you."

"I'm not sure you can," admitted Adam, taking the seat opposite him. "It's just that I have been left an icon in a will and I was hoping it might turn out to be valuable."

"A good start," said Sedgwick, unfolding a pair of spectacles which he had removed from his top pocket.

"It may not be," said Adam, "because I know

nothing about paintings and I wouldn't want to waste your time."

"You won't be wasting my time," Sedgwick assured Adam. "We sell many items for less than ten pounds, you know." Adam hadn't known and Sedgwick's gentle voice made him feel less apprehensive. "Now am I to understand you do not have a photograph of this particular icon?"

"That's right," said Adam. "The icon is still abroad, and to be honest I've never laid eyes on it."

"I see," said Sedgwick, folding up his glasses. "But can you tell me anything of its provenance?"

"A little. It is known as 'The Tsar's Icon' and the subject is St George and the Dragon."

"How strange," said Sedgwick. "Someone else was enquiring after that particular painting only last week but he wouldn't leave his name."

"Someone else wanted to know about the Tsar's icon?" said Adam.

"Yes, a Russian gentleman, if I wasn't mistaken." Sedgwick tapped his glasses on his knee. "I checked on it extensively for him but found little that wasn't already well documented. The man wondered if it had ever passed through our hands, or even if we had heard of it. I was able to explain to him that the great work by Rublev remains in the Winter Palace for all to see. One can always be certain that it's an original from the Winter Palace because the Tsar's silver crown will be embedded in the back of the frame. Since the fourteenth century many copies of Rublev's master-piece have been made and they vary greatly in quality and value; but the one he seemed interested in was a copy made for Tsar Nicholas by a court painter circa 1914. I was unable to find any trace of such an icon in any of the standard works on the subject. Do you have any documentation on your icon?" Sedgwick enquired.

"Not a lot," said Adam. "Although I do have a copy of the receipt that was left to me in the will," he added, and handed it over.

Mr Sedgwick once again unfolded his glasses before studying the paper for several moments. "Excellent, quite excellent," he said eventually. "It seems to me that, as long as Roget et Cie will release it, a copy of the Tsar's icon painted by the court painter of the time, belongs to you. But you will have to go and pick it up yourself, that's for certain."

"But is it worth all that trouble?" asked Adam. "Can you give me any idea of its value?"

"Hard to be precise without actually seeing it," Sedgwick said, returning the document.

"So what is the lowest figure I might expect to get for it?"

The older man frowned. "Ten," he said, after considerable thought. "Perhaps fifteen, but with an absolute top of twenty."

"Twenty pounds," said Adam, unable to hide his disappointment. "I'm sorry to have wasted your time, Mr Sedgwick."

"No, no, no, Mr Scott, you misunderstand me. I meant twenty *thousand* pounds."

CHAPTER EIGHT

"A little more caviar, Comrade?" enquired Petrova across the lunch table.

Romanov frowned. His pretence at 'strictly confidential information' only to be passed on at the highest level had merely elicited a knowing smile from his companion who was also not inclined to believe that her boss had a pressing appointment at the Consulate that afternoon, an appointment that he had forgotten to mention to her before.

Anna held out a spoon brimming with caviar and pushed it towards Romanov as if she was trying to feed a reluctant baby.

"Thank you – *no*," said Romanov firmly.

"Suit yourself," said the young woman before it disappeared down her own throat. Romanov called for the bill. When he was presented with the slip of paper he couldn't help thinking that for that price he could have fed a Russian family for a month. He paid without comment.

"I'll see you back in the hotel later," he said curtly.

"Of course," said Petrova, still lingering over her coffee. "What time shall I expect you?"

Romanov frowned again. "Not before seven," he replied.

"And do you have any plans for me this afternoon, Comrade Major?"

"You may do as you please," said Romanov, and left the table without further word. Once on the street, he set off in the opposite direction to the bank, but he doubted if he had fooled the researcher, who was still eyeing him suspiciously through the restaurant window; or the agent, who had waited patiently on the far side of the road for nearly two hours.

By three o'clock Romanov was once again seated in the private room on the fifth floor looked down on by the three photographs of the Herr Bischoffs, and with the fourth Herr Bischoff sitting opposite him and the fifth Herr Bischoff standing behind him.

"We are in possession of . . ." began Herr Bischoff, in the same deliberate, formal way that had dictated the pace of the morning session, ". . . five boxes which have remained unopened since your father visited us in 1945. Should it be your desire to inspect the contents . . ."

"Why else would I have returned?" asked Romanov, already made impatient by the measured voice and studied ritual.

"Indeed," said Herr Bischoff, seemingly unaware of any discourtesy. "Then all we now require is that you sign a disclaimer in order to legalise the situation under Swiss law." Romanov looked apprehensive. "It is only a formality." The Russian still didn't speak. "You can rest assured, Your Excellency, that you are not the only one of your countrymen who from time to time sits in that chair."

Herr Bischoff slid a sheet of paper across the table. There were over twenty clauses of German, all in small print. Romanov scrawled his signature between the two X's with the proffered gold pen. He made no attempt to discover what he was signing. If they hadn't stolen his grandfather's heritage already, why should they be bothering to try now, he considered.

"Perhaps you will be kind enough to accompany me," said Herr Bischoff, quickly passing the sheet of paper to his son who left immediately. He rose and led Romanov silently back to the corridor. But on this occasion they travelled down in the chairman's private lift all the way to the basement.

When the doors opened Romanov might have thought they had entered a jail had the bars not been made of highly polished steel. A man who was seated behind a desk on the far side of the bars jumped up the moment he saw the chairman and turned the lock on the steel door with a long-shafted key. Romanov followed Herr Bischoff through the open door then waited until they were both locked inside. The guard preceded them down a corridor, not unlike that of a wine cellar with temperature and humidity gauges every few yards. The light was barely bright enough to ensure that they did not lose their footing. At the end of the corridor, they found Herr Bischoff's son waiting in front of a vast circular steel door. The old man nodded and the younger Herr Bischoff placed a key in a lock and turned it. Then the chairman stepped forward and undid a second lock. Father and son pushed open the nine inch thick door but neither made any attempt to enter the vault.

"You are in possession of five boxes. Numbers 1721, 1722, 1723, 1724 . . ."

"And 1725, no doubt," interrupted Romanov.

"Precisely," said Herr Bischoff, as he removed a small package from his pocket and added, "This is

111

your envelope and the key inside it will open all five boxes." Romanov took the envelope and turned towards the open cavern. "But we must open the bank's lock first before you proceed," said Herr Bischoff. "Will you be kind enough to follow us?" Romanov nodded and both Herr Bischoffs proceeded into the vault. Romanov ducked his head and stepped in after them. Young Mr Bischoff opened the upper lock of the five boxes, three small ones above two large ones, making a perfect cube. "Once we have left, Your Excellency," said the old man, "we shall pull the door closed, and when you require it to be opened you have only to press the red button on the side wall to alert us. But I must warn you that at six o'clock the vault locks itself automatically and it cannot be reopened until nine the following morning. However, a warning alarm will sound at five forty-five." Romanov checked the clock on the wall: three seventeen. He couldn't believe he would need over two hours to find out what was in the five boxes. The two Herr Bischoffs bowed and left.

Romanov waited impatiently for the vast door to close behind him. Once alone in the Aladdin's cave he looked around the room and estimated there must have been two or three thousand boxes filling the four walls, giving them the appearance of a library of safes. He suspected there was more private wealth in that one vault than most countries on earth could call on. He checked the numbers of his own boxes and stood waiting like an orphan who has been told there will be second helpings.

He decided to start with one of the small boxes. He turned the key and heard the lock click before pulling out the stiff drawer to discover it was full of papers. He flicked through them to find they were title deeds to many large tracts of land in Bohemia and Bulgaria – once worth millions, now controlled by the Socialist State. As he checked each document, the old saying 'not worth the paper they were written on' sprang to mind. Romanov moved to the second box which he discovered contained the bond certificates of companies once managed by His Excellency Count Nicholai Alexandrovich Romanov. The last time they had declared a profit was in 1914. He cursed the system he had been born under as he moved on to the third box which contained only one document, his grandfather's will. It took only moments to discover that it had all been left to his father and therefore he was the lawful owner of everything – and nothing.

Dismayed, Romanov knelt down to study the two larger boxes, both of which looked big enough to hold a cello. He hesitated before placing his key in the lock of the first, turning it and pulling out the vast container.

He stared down in anticipation.

It was empty. He could only presume that it had been that way for over fifty years unless his father had removed everything and there was no reason to believe that. He quickly unlocked the fifth box and in desperation pulled it open.

The box was split into twelve equal compartments. He raised the lid of the first compartment and stared down in disbelief. Before him lay precious stones of such size, variety and colour that would have made anyone who was not royal gasp. Gingerly he lifted the lid off the second compartment, to find it contained pearls of such quality that one single string of them would have transformed a plain girl into a society beauty. As he opened the third box his amazement did not lessen and he understood for the first time why his grandfather had been considered one of the most enterprising merchants of the century. And now it all belonged to Alex Romanov, an impecunious Government official who was already wondering how he could possibly enjoy such riches.

It took Romanov a further hour to go through the contents of the remaining nine compartments. When he reached the last one – almost an anti-climax, in that it contained nothing but gold coins – he felt thoroughly exhausted. He checked the clock on the wall: five thirty. He began to replace the lids on each of the compartments, but during the treasure hunt he had come across one object of such magnificence that he could not resist removing it. He paused as he held up the long heavy gold chain weighted by a medallion, also made of solid gold, that hung from it. On one side was an engraved picture of his grandfather – Count Nicholai Alexandrovich Romanov, a proud, handsome man – while on the other was a profile of his grandmother, so beautiful that she surely could have worn any of the jewellery in that treasure trove with distinction.

For some time, Romanov held the chain in his hand before finally placing it over his head and letting the medallion fall from his neck. He gave the piece one last look before tucking it under his shirt. When he had replaced the lid on the last compartment he slid the box back into place and locked it.

For the second time that day Romanov's thoughts returned to his father and the decision he must have made when faced with such a fortune. He had gone back to Russia with his secret. Had he planned to rescue Alex from the life of drudgery that was all he could look forward to? His father had always assured him that he had an exciting future but there were secrets he was too young to share and he, in turn, had passed that information on to the authorities. His reward a place at the Komsomol. But his father must have taken that secret to the grave because Alex would never have learned of the fortune if it had not been for Poskonov.

His mind turned to the old banker. Had he known all along or was it just a coincidence that he had been sent by Poskonov to this bank first? Members of his chosen profession didn't survive if they believed in coincidence.

A false move and the State would not hesitate to send him to the same grave as his father and grandfather. He would have to be at his most skilful when he next came into contact with the old banker, otherwise he might not live to choose between power in his homeland or wealth in the West.

"After I have found the Tsar's icon I will make my decision," he said, quite audibly. He turned suddenly as the alarm bell's piercing sound rang out. He checked the clock and was surprised by how much time he had spent in the locked room. He walked towards the vault door and on reaching it pressed the red button without looking back. The great door swung open to reveal two anxious-looking Herr Bischoffs. The son stepped quickly into the vault, walked over to the five boxes and made safe the bank's locks.

"We were beginning to get quite worried about the time," said the old man. "I do hope you found everything to your satisfaction."

"Entirely," said Romanov. "But what happens if I am unable to return for some considerable time?"

"It's of no importance," Herr Bischoff replied. "The boxes will not be touched again until you come back, and as they are all hermetically sealed your possessions will remain in perfect condition."

"What temperature are the boxes kept at?"

"Ten degrees Celsius," said Herr Bischoff, somewhat puzzled by the question.

"Are they airtight?"

"Certainly," replied the banker. "And watertight, not that the basement has ever been flooded," he added quite seriously.

"So anything left in them is totally safe from any investigation?"

"You are only the third person to look inside those boxes in fifty years," came back the firm response.

"Excellent," said Romanov, looking down at Herr Bischoff. "Because there is just a possibility that I shall want to return tomorrow morning, with a package of my own to deposit."

"Can you put me through to Mr Pemberton, please?" said Adam.

There was a long pause. "We don't have a Mr Pemberton working here, sir."

"That is Barclays International in the City, isn't it?"

"Yes, sir."

"Mr Lawrence Pemberton. I feel certain I've got the right branch."

The silence was even longer this time. "Ah, yes," came back the eventual reply. "Now I see which department he works in. I'll find out if he's in." Adam heard the phone ringing in the background.

"He doesn't seem to be at his desk at the moment, sir, would you like to leave a message?"

"No thank you," said Adam, and replaced the receiver. He sat alone thinking, not bothering to switch on the light as it grew darker. If he was to carry through the idea he still needed some information which Lawrence as a banker should find easy to supply.

A key turned in the door and Adam watched Lawrence enter and switch the light on. He looked startled when he saw Adam seated in front of him.

"How does one open a Swiss bank account?" were Adam's first words.

"I can't imagine one would find it that easy if all you have to offer is next week's unemployment cheque," said Lawrence. "Mind you, they usually keep a code name for English customers," he added, as he put his copy of the *Evening News* on the table. "Yours could be 'pauper'."

"It may surprise you to learn that it was a serious question," said Adam.

"Well," said Lawrence, taking the question seriously, "in truth, anyone can open a Swiss bank account as long as they have a worthwhile sum to deposit. And by worthwhile I mean at least ten thousand pounds."

"Yes, but how would you go about getting the money out?"

"That can be done over the phone or in person, and in that way Swiss banks don't differ greatly from any bank in England. Few customers, however, would risk the phone, unless they're resident in a country where there are no tax laws to break. In which case why would they need the gnomes of Zurich in the first place?"

"What happens when a customer dies and the bank can't be sure who the rightful owner of the assets is?"

"They would do nothing but a claimant would have to prove that they were the person entitled to inherit any deposits the bank held. That's not a problem if you're in possession of the correct documentation such as a will and proof of identity. We deal with such matters every day."

"But you just admitted that it's illegal!"

"Not for those clients resident overseas, or when it becomes necessary to balance our gold deposits, not to mention the bank's books. But the Bank of England keeps a strict watch over every penny that goes in and out of the country."

"So, if I were entitled to a million pounds' worth of gold left to me by an Argentinian uncle deposited in a Swiss bank, and I was in possession of the right legal documents to prove I was the beneficiary, all I would have to do is go and claim it?"

"Nothing to stop you," said Lawrence. "Although under the law as it currently stands, you would have to bring it back to this country, and sell the gold to the Bank of England for the sum they deemed correct, and then pay death duty on that sum." Adam remained silent. "If you do have an Argentinian uncle who has left you all that gold in Switzerland, your best bet would be to leave it where it is. Under this Government, if you fulfilled the letter of the law, you would end up with about seven and a half per cent of its true value."

"Pity I haven't got an Argentinian uncle," said Adam.

"He doesn't have to be Argentinian," said Lawrence, watching his friend's every reaction closely.

"Thanks for the information," said Adam and disappeared into the bedroom.

The last pieces of the jigsaw were beginning to fit into place. He was in possession of Roget's receipt of the icon originally meant for his father; all he needed now was a copy of the will to show that the document had been left to him. He could then prove that he was the owner of a worthless or priceless – he still had no way of being sure which – copy of the Tsar's icon. He lay awake that night recalling the words in his father's letter. "If there is anything to be gained from the contents of this envelope I make only one request of you, namely that your mother should be the first to benefit from it without ever being told how such good fortune came about."

When Romanov returned to the hotel, via the Russian Consulate, he found Petrova in her room dressed in jeans and a bright pink jersey, sitting in a corner reading, her legs dangling over the side of the chair.

"I hope you had a fruitful afternoon?" he enquired, politely.

"I certainly did," Anna replied. "The galleries in Zurich are well worthy of a visit. But tell me about *your* afternoon. Did it also turn out to be fruitful?"

"It was a revelation, my little one, nothing less. Why don't we have a quiet supper in my room so I can tell you all about it while we celebrate in style?"

"What a magnificent idea," said the researcher. "And may I be responsible for ordering dinner?"

"Certainly," said Romanov.

Petrova dropped her book on the floor and began to concentrate on the extensive *à la carte* menu that had been left by Romanov's bedside table. She spent a considerable time selecting each dish for their banquet and even Romanov was impressed when it finally appeared.

Anna had chosen as an entrée gravad lax edged with dill sauce. Accompanying it was a half-bottle of Premier Cru Chablis 1958. Between mouthfuls Romanov told her of the contents of his family

119

inheritance and as he described each new treasure the researcher's eyes grew larger and larger.

Romanov's monologue was only once interrupted, by a waiter who wheeled in a trolley on which sat a silver salver. The waiter lifted the salver to reveal a rack of lamb surrounded by courgettes and tiny new potatoes. To accompany this particular dish, the hotel had provided a Gevrey Chambertin.

The final course, a fluffy raspberry soufflé, required in the researcher's view only the finest Château Yquem. She had selected the 'forty-nine, which only made her lapse into singing Russian folk songs which Romanov felt, given the circumstances, was somewhat inappropriate.

As she drained the last drop of wine in her glass Petrova rose and, slightly unsteady, said, "To Alex, the man I love."

Romanov nodded his acknowledgment and suggested it might be time for them to go to bed, as they had to catch the first flight back to Moscow the following morning. He wheeled the trolley out into the corridor and placed a 'Do not disturb' sign over the door knob.

"A memorable evening," smiled the researcher, as she flicked off her shoes. Romanov stopped to admire her as she began to remove her clothes, but when he unbuttoned his shirt, the researcher stopped undressing and let out a gasp of surprise.

"It's magnificent," she said in awe. Romanov held up the gold medallion. "A bauble compared with the treasures I left behind," he assured her.

"Comrade lover," Anna said in a childlike voice, pulling him towards the bed, "you realise how much I adore, admire and respect you?"

"Um," said Romanov.

"And you also know," she continued, "that I have never asked you for any favour in the past."

"But I have a feeling you are about to now," said Romanov as she lifted back the sheet.

"Only that if the gold chain is nothing more than a mere bauble, perhaps you might allow me to wear it occasionally?"

"Occasionally?" said Romanov, staring into Anna's eyes. "Why occasionally? Why not permanently, my darling?" and without another word he removed the gold chain from around his neck and placed it over the young girl's head. Anna sighed as she fingered the thick gold rings that made up the chain that Romanov didn't let go of.

"You're hurting me, Alex," she said with a little laugh. "Please let go." But Romanov only pulled the chain a little tighter. Tears began to run down her cheeks as the metal began to bite into her skin.

"I can't breathe properly," gasped the researcher. "Please stop teasing." But Romanov only continued to tighten the chain around her throat until Anna's face began to turn red as it filled with blood.

"You wouldn't tell anyone about my windfall, would you, my little one?"

"No, never, Alex. No one. You can rely on me," she choked out desperately.

"Can I feel absolutely certain?" he asked with an edge of menace now in his voice.

"Yes, yes of course, but please stop now," she piped, her delicate hands clutching desperately at her master's blond hair, but Romanov only continued to squeeze and squeeze the heavy gold chain around her neck like a rack and pinion, tighter and tighter. Romanov was not aware of the girl's hands clinging desperately to his hair, as he twisted the chain a final time. "I'm sure you understand that I must feel absolutely certain that you wouldn't share our secret – with anyone," he explained to her. But she did not hear his plea because the vertebrae in her neck had already snapped.

On his morning run along the Embankment, Adam mulled over the tasks that still needed to be carried out next.

If he took the morning flight out of Heathrow on Wednesday, he could be back in London by the same evening, or Thursday at the latest. But there were still several things that had to be organised before he could leave for Geneva.

He came to a halt on the pavement outside his block and checked his pulse, before climbing the stairs to the flat.

"Three letters for you," said Lawrence. "None for me. Mind you," he added as his flatmate joined him in the kitchen, "two of them are in buff envelopes." Adam picked up the letters and left them on the end of his bed en route to the shower. He survived five minutes of ice-cold water before towelling down. Once he was dressed he opened the letters. He began with the white one, which turned out to be a note from Heidi thanking him for dinner, and hoping she would be seeing him again some time. He smiled and tore open the first of the buff envelopes, which was yet another missive from the Foreign Office Co-ordination Staff.

Captain Scott – the rank already seemed out of place – was requested to attend a medical at 122 Harley Street at three o'clock on the following Monday, to be conducted by Dr John Vance.

Finally he opened the other brown envelope and

pulled out a letter from Lloyds, Cox and King's branch in Pall Mall, informing Dear Sir/Madam that they had been in receipt of a cheque for five hundred pounds from Holbrooke, Holbrooke and Gascoigne, and that his current account at the close of business the previous day was in credit to the sum of £272.18s.4d. When Adam checked through the account it showed that at one point he had, for the first time in his life, run up an overdraft – a situation that he knew would have been frowned upon had he still been in the army, for as little as twenty years before it was in some regiments a court-martial offence for an officer to be overdrawn.

What would his brother officers have said if he told them he was about to remove two hundred pounds from the account with no real guarantee of a return?

Once Adam had finished dressing, he rejoined Lawrence in the kitchen.

"How was the Shah of Iran?" he asked.

"Oh, very reasonable really," said Lawrence, turning a page of the *Daily Telegraph*, "considering the circumstances. Promised he would do what he could about his current financial embarrassment, but he was a bit pushed until the West allowed him to raise the price of oil."

"Where did you eventually take him to lunch?" asked Adam enjoying the game.

"I offered him a shepherd's pie at the Green Man, but the bloody fellow became quite snotty. It seems he and the Empress had to pop along to Harrods to be measured up for a new throne. Would have gone along with him, of course, but my boss wanted his wastepaper basket emptied, so I missed out on the Harrods deal as well."

"So what are you up to today?"

"I shouldn't let you in on this," said Lawrence,

Jeffrey Archer

peering at the photograph of Ted Dexter, the defeated English cricket captain, "but the Governor of the Bank of England wants my views on whether we should devalue the pound from $2.80 to $2.40."

"And what are your views?"

"I've already explained to the fellow that the only 240 I know is the bus that runs between Golders Green and Edgware, and if I don't get a move on I'll miss my beloved 14," said Lawrence, checking his watch. Adam laughed as he watched his friend slam his briefcase shut and disappear out of the door.

Lawrence had changed considerably over the years since he had left Wellington. Perhaps it was that Adam could only remember him as school captain and then leaving with the top classics scholarship to Balliol. He had seemed so serious in those days and certainly destined for greater things. No one would have thought it possible that he would end up as an investment analyst at Barclays DCO. At Oxford contemporaries half joked about him being a cabinet minister. Was it possible that one always expected too much of those idols who were only a couple of years older than oneself? On leaving school their friendship had grown. And when Adam was posted to Malaya, Lawrence never accepted the army report that posted his friend as missing presumed dead. And when Adam announced that he was leaving the army, Lawrence asked for no explanation and couldn't have been kinder about his unemployment problem. Adam hoped that he would be given the chance to repay such friendship.

Adam fried himself an egg and a couple of rashers of bacon. There wasn't much more he could do before nine thirty, although he did find time to scribble a note to his sister, enclosing a cheque for fifty pounds.

At nine thirty he made a phone call. Mr Holbrooke

– Adam wondered if he actually had a Christian name – couldn't hide his surprise at receiving a call from young Mr Scott. Now that my father is dead, *I* must be old Mr Scott, Adam wanted to tell him. And Holbrooke sounded even more surprised by his request. "No doubt connected in some way with that envelope," he muttered, but agreed to put a copy of his father's will in the post that afternoon.

Adam's other requirements could not be carried out over the phone, so he locked up the flat and jumped on a bus heading up the King's Road. He left the double-decker at Hyde Park Corner and made his way to Lloyds Bank in Pall Mall, where he joined a queue at the Foreign Exchange counter.

"May I help you?" asked a polite assistant when he finally reached the front.

"Yes," said Adam. "I would like fifty pounds in Swiss francs, fifty pounds in cash and a hundred pounds in traveller's cheques."

"What is your name?" she enquired.

"Adam Scott."

The girl entered some calculations on a large desk-top machine before cranking the handle round several times. She looked at the result, then disappeared for a few moments to return with a copy of the bank statement Adam had received in the morning post.

"The total cost, including our charges, will be £202.1s.8d. That would leave your account in credit with £70.16s.4d.," she informed him.

"Yes," said Adam, but didn't add that in truth it would only be £20.16s.4d. the moment his sister presented her cheque. He began to hope that the Foreign Office paid by the week, otherwise it would have to be another frugal month. Unless of course . . .

Adam signed the tops of the ten traveller's cheques

in the cashier's presence and she then handed over five hundred and ninety-four Swiss francs and fifty pounds in cash. It was the largest sum of money Adam had ever taken out at one time.

Another bus journey took him to the British European Airways terminal in Cromwell Road where he asked the girl to book him on a return flight to Geneva.

"First class or economy?" she asked.

"Economy," said Adam, amused by the thought that anyone might think he would want to go first class.

"That will be thirty-one pounds please, sir." Adam paid in cash and placed the ticket in his inside pocket, before returning to the flat for a light lunch. During the afternoon he called Heidi who agreed to join him for dinner at the Chelsea Kitchen at eight o'clock. There was one more thing Adam needed to be certain about before he joined Heidi for dinner.

Romanov was woken by the ringing of the phone.

"Yes," he said.

"Good morning, Comrade Romanov, it's Melinski, the Second Secretary at the Embassy."

"Good morning, Comrade, what can I do for you?"

"It's about Comrade Petrova," Romanov smiled at the thought of her now lying in the bath. "Have you come across the girl since you reported her missing?"

"No," replied Romanov. "And she didn't sleep in her bed last night."

"I see," said the Second Secretary. "Then your suspicions that she might have defected are beginning to look a serious possibility."

"I fear so," said Romanov, "and I shall have to make a full report of the situation to my superiors the moment I get back to Moscow."

"Yes, of course, Comrade Major."

"I shall also point out that you have done everything possible to assist me with this problem, Comrade Second Secretary."

"Thank you, Comrade Major."

"And brief me the moment you come up with any information that might lead us to where she is."

"Of course, Comrade Major." Romanov replaced the phone and walked across to the bathroom in the adjoining room. He stared down at the body hunched up in the bath. Anna's eyes were bulging in their sockets, her face contorted and the skin already grey. After throwing a towel over the dead researcher's head and locking the door, he went into his own bathroom for an unusually long shower.

He returned and sat on his side of the bed, only a towel around his waist, and picked up the phone. He ordered breakfast which arrived fifteen minutes later, by which time he had dressed. Once he had finished orange juice and croissants he returned to the phone trying to recall the name of the hotel's manager. It came back to him just as the receptionist said, "*Guten Morgen, mein Herr.*"

"Jacques, please," was all Romanov said. A moment later he heard the manager's voice, "Good morning, Herr Romanov."

"I have a delicate problem that I was hoping you might be able to help me with."

"I shall certainly try, sir," came back the reply.

"I am in possession of a rather valuable object that I wish to deposit with my bank and I wouldn't want . . ."

"I understand your dilemma entirely," said the manager. "And how can I be of assistance?"

"I require a large container in which to place the object."

127

"Would a laundry basket be large enough?"

"Ideal, but does it have a secure lid?"

"Oh, yes," replied Jacques. "We often have to drop them off down lift shafts."

"Perfect," said Romanov.

"Then it will be with you in a matter of moments," said Jacques. "I shall send a porter to assist you. May I also suggest that it is taken down in the freight elevator at the rear of the hotel, thus ensuring that no one will see you leaving?"

"Very considerate," said Romanov.

"Will a car be calling to collect you?"

"No," said Romanov. "I –"

"Then I shall arrange for a taxi to be waiting. When will you require it?"

"In no more than half an hour."

"You will find it parked outside the freight entrance in twenty minutes' time."

"You have been most helpful," said Romanov, before adding, "the Chairman of the State Bank did not exaggerate his praise of you."

"You are too kind, Herr Romanov," said Jacques. "Will there be anything else?"

"Perhaps you would be good enough to have my account prepared so that there will be no delay."

"Certainly."

Romanov put the phone down wishing he could export such service to Moscow. He only waited a moment before he dialled the first of two local numbers. On both occasions his wishes were immediately granted. As he replaced the phone for the third time there was a gentle tap on the door. Romanov went quickly over to answer it. A young porter stood in the corridor, a large laundry basket by his side. He smiled politely. Romanov merely nodded and pulled in the basket. "Please return as soon as the taxi has arrived," said Romanov. The porter bowed slightly, but said nothing.

As soon as the porter had left, Romanov locked the door and put the chain in place before wheeling the laundry basket into the main bedroom and leaving it by the side of the bed. He undid the tough leather straps and threw open the lid.

Next, he unlocked the bathroom door and lifted Petrova's stiff body in his arms before trying to cram it into the basket. Rigor mortis had already gripped the body; the legs refused to bend and the researcher didn't quite fit in. Romanov placed the naked Petrova on the floor. He held his fingers out straight and suddenly brought them down with such force on the right leg that it broke like a branch in a storm. He repeated the action on her left leg. Like the guillotine, it didn't require a second attempt. He then tucked the legs under her body. It amused Romanov to consider that, had it been he who had been murdered, Anna Petrova would never have been able to get him in the basket whatever she had tried to break. Romanov then wheeled the trolley into the researcher's bedroom and, after emptying all her drawers, including Anna's clothes, clean and dirty, her shoes, her toilet bag, toothbrush and even an old photograph of himself he hadn't realised she possessed he threw them in the basket on top of her. Once he had removed the gold medallion from around her neck and was certain that there was nothing of the researcher's personal belongings left, he covered up the body with a hotel bath towel, and sprayed it with a liberal amount of Chanel No. 5 that had been left courtesy of the hotel.

Finally he strapped the lid down securely and

wheeled the creaking basket out and left it by the outer door.

Romanov began to pack his own case but there was a knock on the door before he had finished.

"Wait," he said firmly. There was a muffled reply of "*Ja, mein Herr.*" A few moments later Romanov opened the door. The porter entered, nodded to him and began to tug at the laundry basket, but it took a firm shove from Romanov's foot before it got moving. The porter sweated his way down the corridor as Romanov walked by the side of the basket, carrying his suitcase. When they reached the rear of the hotel Romanov watched as the basket was wheeled safely into the freight elevator before he stepped in himself.

When the ground floor doors opened Romanov was relieved to be greeted by Jacques who was standing by a large Mercedes waiting for him with the boot already open. The taxi driver and the porter lifted up the laundry basket and wedged it into the boot, but Romanov's suitcase could not be fitted in as well so it had to be put in the front of the car alongside the driver's seat.

"Shall we forward your bill to the Consulate, *mein Herr*?" asked Jacques.

"Yes, that would be helpful . . ."

"I do hope everything has worked out to your satisfaction," said Jacques, as he held open the back door of the Mercedes for his departing guest.

"Entirely," said Romanov.

"Good, good. And will your young colleague be joining you?" asked the manager, looking back over his shoulder towards the hotel.

"No, she won't," said Romanov. "She has already gone on to the airport ahead of me."

"Of course," said Jacques, "but I am sorry to have missed her. Do please pass on my best wishes."

"I certainly will," said Romanov, "and I look forward to returning to your hotel in the near future."

"Thank you sir," the manager said as Romanov slipped into the back seat leaving Jacques to close the door behind him.

When Romanov arrived at the Swissair office his suitcase was checked in and he waited only moments before continuing on to the bank. Herr Bischoff's son, accompanied by another man, also clad in a grey suit, was waiting in the hall to greet him.

"How pleasant to see you again so soon," volunteered the young Herr Bischoff. His deep voice took Romanov by surprise. The taxi driver waited by the open boot while Herr Bischoff's companion, a man of at least six foot four and heavily built, lifted out the laundry basket as if it were a sponge cake. Romanov paid the fare and followed Herr Bischoff into the far lift.

"We are fully prepared for your deposition following your phone call," said Herr Bischoff. "My father was only sorry not to be present personally. He had a long-standing engagement with another customer and only hopes that you will understand." Romanov waved his hand.

The lift travelled straight to the ground floor where the guard, on seeing young Herr Bischoff, unlocked the great steel cage. Romanov and the two bankers proceeded at a leisurely pace down the corridor, while the giant carried the basket in their wake.

Standing with folded arms by the vault door was another of the partners Romanov recognised from the previous day. Herr Bischoff nodded and the partner placed his key in the top lock of the vault door without a word. Herr Bischoff then turned the second lock and together they pushed open the massive steel door. Herr Bischoff and his partner walked in ahead of Romanov and opened the top lock of all five of his boxes, while the guard placed the laundry basket on the floor beside them.

"Will you require any assistance?" asked Herr Bischoff as he handed his Russian client a personal sealed envelope.

"No thank you," Romanov assured him, but did not relax until he had seen the vast door close behind him and all four of his Swiss helpers left invisibly on the other side.

Once he felt certain he was alone, he stared down at the one large box he knew to be empty: it was smaller than he had recalled. Beads of sweat appeared on his forehead as he unlocked it, pulled it out and raised the airtight lid. It was going to be a tight fit. Romanov unstrapped the laundry basket and removed everything except the body. He stared down at the contorted face, the deep marks in the skin around the neck had turned to a dark blue. He bent over and lifted the researcher up by her waist, but as no part of the body moved other than her broken legs he had to drop her into the box head first. Even then he had to adjust her various limbs in order that the box could be shut: had Anna been even an inch taller the exercise would have proved pointless. He then stuffed the girl's belongings down at the sides of her body, leaving only the Chanel-covered towel behind in the laundry basket.

Romanov proceeded to replace the lid on the airtight box, before pushing it back securely in place and locking it. He then double-checked it could not be opened without his own personal key. He was relieved to find he could not budge it. He hesitated for a moment glancing at the second large box, but accepted that this was not the time to indulge himself: that would have to wait for another occasion. Satisfied that everything was back in place, he closed and strapped down the lid of the laundry basket and wheeled it back to the entrance of the vault. He pressed the little red button.

"I do hope you found everything in order," said the young Herr Bischoff once he had returned from locking the five boxes.

"Yes, thank you," said Romanov. "But would it be possible for someone to return the laundry basket to the St Gothard Hotel?"

"Of course," said the banker, who nodded towards the large man.

"And I can be assured that the boxes will not be touched in my absence?" he asked as they walked down the corridor.

"Naturally, Your Excellency," said Herr Bischoff, looking somewhat aggrieved at such a suggestion. "When you return," he continued, "you will find everything exactly as you left it."

Well, not exactly, Romanov thought to himself.

When they stepped out of the lift on the ground floor, Romanov spotted Herr Bischoff's father with another customer.

A Rolls-Royce accompanied by a police motorcycle whisked the Shah of Iran quickly away, and the chairman discreetly waved his farewell.

When they reached the entrance to the bank, the young Herr Bischoff bowed. "We shall look forward to seeing you again when you are next in Zurich, Your Excellency," he said.

"Thank you," said Romanov, who shook hands with the young man and walked out on to the pavement to find the anonymous black car waiting to take him to the airport.

He cursed. This time he *did* spot the agent he had seen earlier in the hotel.

CHAPTER NINE

"Kill him, sir," the corporal whispered in Adam's ear.

"Not much hope of that," muttered Adam as he bounced into the centre of the ring.

The lean, muscle-bound instructor stood waiting for him. "Let's have a few rounds and see how you make out, sir." Adam bobbed and weaved around the Physical Training Instructor looking for an opening.

Adam led with a left and received a tap on the nose for his trouble. "Keep your guard up," said the sergeant major. Adam led again, catching the instructor a full blow on the chest, but was punished with a sharp left jab into the side of his head. He wobbled and his ear tingled but this time he managed to keep his guard up when a right and left followed. "You're feeble, sir, that's your problem. You couldn't knock the skin off a rice pudding." Adam feinted with his right and then swung a left with such force that when it caught the sergeant major full on the chin he staggered and fell.

The corporal standing by the side of the ring smirked as the instructor remained on the floor. Eventually he managed to get back on his feet.

"I'm sorry," said Adam, his guard up and ready.

"Don't be sorry, you bloody fool . . . sir. You landed

a bloody good punch. A technical knockout, to be accurate, so I'll have to wait for a day or two to seek my revenge." Adam breathed a sigh of relief and lowered his guard. "But that doesn't mean you're off the hook. It's weight training for you now, sir. Beam work and floor exercises."

For the next hour the sergeant major chased, kicked, harried and badgered Adam until he finally collapsed in a heap on the floor, incapable of lifting an evening paper.

"Not bad, sir. I feel sure the Foreign Office will be able to find some niche for you. Mind you," he added, "as most of that lot are about as wet as a dishcloth even *you*'ll have a chance to shine."

"You are most flattering, Sergeant Major," said Adam from a supine position.

"Up, sir," the instructor bellowed. Adam unwillingly got to his feet as quickly as his tired body would allow.

"Don't tell me, Sergeant Major."

"It's the recovery that proves fitness, not the speed," they said in unison.

"Sad day when you left the army," said the instructor to Adam once they were back in the Queen's Club changing room. "Can't name a lot of officers who have put me on the floor." The instructor touched his chin tenderly. "That will teach me to underestimate a man who survived nine months of Chink food. So let's hope the Foreign Office doesn't underestimate you as well."

The sergeant major rose from the bench by his locker. "Same time Wednesday?"

"Can't make it Wednesday, Sergeant Major. I may not be back from a trip to Geneva."

"Swanning around Europe nowadays, are we?"

"I could manage Thursday morning if that suits you," Adam said, ignoring the jibe.

"Your check-up with the quack is next Monday, if I remember correctly."

"Right."

"Thursday at ten then, it will give you a little longer to think about my right-hook."

The Chairman of the KGB studied the report on the desk in front of him: something didn't ring true. He looked up at Romanov. "Your reason for visiting Bischoff et Cie was because they claimed to be in possession of a fifteenth-century icon that might have fitted the description of the one we are searching for?"

"That is correct, Comrade, and the chairman of Gosbank will confirm that he personally arranged the meeting."

"But the icon turned out to be of St Peter and not of St George and the Dragon."

"Also confirmed by Comrade Petrova in her report."

"Ah, yes, Comrade Petrova," said Zaborski, his eyes returning to the sheet of paper in front of him.

"Yes, Comrade."

"And later that evening Comrade Petrova mysteriously failed to keep an appointment with you?"

"Inexplicably," said Romanov.

"But which you reported to Comrade Melinski at the Embassy." He paused. "You were responsible for selecting Petrova yourself, were you not?"

"That is correct, Comrade Chairman."

"Does that not reveal a certain lack of judgment on your part?"

Romanov made no attempt to reply.

The Chairman's eyes returned to the file. "When

you awoke the next morning, there was still no sign of the girl?"

"She also failed to turn up to breakfast as arranged," said Romanov, "and when I went to her room all her personal belongings had gone."

"Which convinced you she had defected."

"Yes, sir," said Romanov.

"But the Swiss police," said Zaborski, "can find no trace of her. So I keep asking myself why would she want to defect? Her husband and her immediate family live in Moscow. They are all employed by the State, and it is not as if this was her first visit to the West."

Romanov didn't offer an opinion.

"Perhaps Petrova disappeared because she might have been able to tell us something you didn't want us to hear."

Still Romanov said nothing.

The Chairman's gaze once again returned to the file. "I wonder what it was that young Petrova wanted to tell us? Who else you were sleeping with that night, perhaps?" Romanov felt a shiver of fear as he wondered how much Zaborski really knew. Zaborski paused and pretended to be checking something else in the report. "Perhaps she could tell us why you felt it necessary to return to Bischoff et Cie a second time." Once again, Zaborski paused. "I think I may have to open an enquiry into the disappearance of Comrade Petrova. Because, Comrade Romanov, by the time you returned to the bank a third time," said the Chairman, his voice rising with each word, "every second-rate spy from here to Istanbul knew that we were searching for something." The Chairman paused. Romanov was still desperate to find out if Zaborski had any real evidence. Neither man spoke for some time. "You have always been a loner, Major Romanov, and I do not deny that at times your results have allowed me to overlook certain indiscretions. But I am not a loner, Comrade. I am a desk man, no longer allowed your freedom of action." He fiddled with the paperweight of Luna 9 on the desk in front of him.

"I am a file man, a paper man. I make reports in triplicate, I answer queries in quadruplicate, explain decisions in quintuplicate. Now I will have to explain the circumstances of Petrova's strange disappearance to the Politburo in multiplicate."

Romanov remained silent, something the KGB had taken several years to instil into him. He began to feel confident that Zaborski was only guessing. If he had suspected the truth the interview would have taken place in the basement where a less intellectual approach to questioning was carried out.

"In the USSR," continued Zaborski, now rising from his chair, "despite our image in the Western world, we investigate a suspicious death," he paused, "or defection more scrupulously than any other nation on earth. You, Comrade Romanov, would have found your chosen profession easier to follow had you been born in Africa, South America or even Los Angeles."

Still Romanov did not venture an opinion.

"The General Secretary informed me at one o'clock this morning that he is not impressed by your latest efforts, distinctly unimpressed were the exact words he used, especially after your excellent start. All he is interested in, however, is finding the Tsar's icon, and so, for the time being, Comrade, he has decided there will be no investigation. But if you ever act in such an irresponsible way again it will not be an enquiry you are facing, but a tribunal, and we all know what happened to the last Romanov that faced a tribunal."

He closed the file. "Against my better judgment and

because we are left with less than a week, the General Secretary has allowed you a second chance in the belief that you will indeed come up with the Tsar's icon. Do I make myself clear, Comrade?" he barked.

"Very clear, Comrade Chairman," said Romanov, and turning smartly on his heel quickly left the room.

The Chairman of the KGB waited for the door to close before his eyes settled back on the file. What was Romanov up to, Zaborski needed to know, suddenly realising that his own career might now be on the line. He flicked down a switch on the little console by his side. "Find Major Valchek," he ordered.

"I've never actually had champagne and caviar," admitted Adam, as he looked up at the beautiful girl who sat opposite him across the table. He loved the way she tied her hair, and the way she dressed, the way she laughed, but most of all the way she smiled.

"Well, don't get frightened, because I can't imagine caviar will ever find its place on this particular menu," teased Heidi. "But perhaps soon when you are the proud owner of the Tsar's icon, that is if Mr Rosenbau . . ."

Adam put a finger to his lips. "No one else knows about that, not even Lawrence."

"That may be wise," Heidi whispered. "He will only expect you to invest all the money you make from the sale in his boring bank."

"What makes you think I'd sell it?" asked Adam, trying to discover how much she had worked out.

"If you own a Rolls-Royce and you are out of work you do not then go and hire a chauffeur."

"But I've only got a motorbike."

"And you'll have to sell that as well if the icon turns out to be worthless," she said, laughing.

140

"Would you like a coffee to follow?" asked the waiter, who was already clearing their table in the hope of fitting in two more customers before the night was out.

"Yes, please. Two cappuccinos," said Adam. He turned his gaze back to Heidi. "Funnily enough," he continued as the waiter retreated, "the only time I've ever rung Lawrence at the bank the telephonist couldn't immediately locate him."

"What's so surprising about that?" asked Heidi.

"It was as if they had never heard of him," said Adam, "but perhaps I was imagining it."

"A bank that size must have over a thousand employees. You could go years without knowing everyone who worked there."

"I suppose you're right," Adam said, as two coffees were placed in front of them.

"When do you plan on going to Geneva?" Heidi asked, after she had tried a sip of the coffee and found it too hot.

"First thing Wednesday morning. I hope to be back the same evening."

"Considerate."

"What do you mean?" asked Adam.

"To choose my one day off to fly away," she said. "Not very romantic."

"Then why not come with me?" he asked, leaning across the table to take her hand.

"That might turn out to be more significant than sharing your sausages."

"I would hope so and in any case, you could be most useful."

"You do have a way with words," said Heidi.

"You know I didn't mean it that way. It's simply that I don't speak German or French and I've never

141

been to Switzerland other than on a school skiing trip — and then I kept falling over." Heidi tried her coffee again.

"Well?" said Adam, not letting go of her hand.

"The Swiss speak perfect English," she said eventually, "and should you have any problem with the bank, you can always get in touch with Lawrence."

"It would only be for the day," said Adam.

"And a waste of your money."

"Not very romantic," said Adam.

"Touché."

"Think about it," said Adam. "After the cost of your return flight I will be left with only £19,969. I don't know how I'll get by."

"You really mean it, don't you?" said Heidi, sounding serious for the first time. "But women are not impulsive creatures."

"You could always bring Jochen along with you."

Heidi laughed. "He wouldn't fit on the plane."

"Do say you'll come," said Adam.

"On one condition," said Heidi thoughtfully.

"Separate planes?" said Adam grinning.

"No, but if the icon turns out to be worthless you will let me refund the price of my ticket."

"It couldn't be worth less than thirty-one pounds, so I agree to your terms," said Adam. He leaned over and kissed Heidi on the lips. "Perhaps it will take more than one day," he said. "Then what would you say?"

"I would demand separate hotels," replied Heidi, "if it wasn't for the high cost of the Swiss franc," she added.

"You are always so reliable, Comrade Romanov. You fulfil the primary qualification for a successful banker." Romanov studied the old man carefully, looking for some sign that he knew exactly what had been awaiting him at the bank.

"And you are always so efficient, Comrade Poskonov," he paused, "the only qualification necessary in my chosen profession."

"Good heavens, we are beginning to sound like a couple of ageing commissars at an annual reunion. How was Zurich?" he asked, as he lit a cigarette.

"Like a Polish tractor. The bits that worked were fine."

"From that I assume the bits that didn't work failed to produce the Tsar's icon," the chairman said.

"Correct, but Bischoff turned out to be most helpful, as was Jacques. My every need was catered for."

"Your every need?"

"Yes," replied Romanov.

"Good man, Bischoff," said the banker. "That's why I sent you to him first." The old man slumped down into his chair.

"Was there any other reason you sent me to him first?" asked Romanov.

"Five other reasons," said Poskonov, "but we'll not bother with any of them until you have found your icon."

"Perhaps I'd like to bother now," said Romanov firmly.

"I've outlived two generations of Romanovs," said the old man raising his eyes. "I wouldn't want to outlive a third. Let's leave it at that for now, I'm sure we can come to an understanding when the spotlight is no longer on you."

Romanov nodded.

"Well, you will be pleased to learn that I have not been idle in your absence. But I fear my results also resemble a Polish tractor."

The banker waved Romanov to a seat before he reopened his file which had grown in size since he had last seen it. "Originally," the chairman began, "you presented me with a list of fourteen banks, eleven of which have now confirmed that they are not in possession of the Tsar's icon."

"I have been wondering about that – is their word to be taken at face value?" asked Romanov.

"Not necessarily," said the banker. "But on balance the Swiss prefer not to become involved rather than tell a deliberate lie. In time the liar is always found out, and I still, from this office, control the cash flow of eight nations. I may not wield what they would call financial clout but I can still put the odd spanner in the works of the capitalist monetary system."

"That still leaves us with three banks?" said Romanov.

"Correct, Comrade. The first is Bischoff et Cie, whom you have already visited. But the other two have refused to co-operate in any way."

"Why is it your influence does not extend to them?"

"The most obvious of reasons," replied Poskonov. "Other interests exert a stronger influence. If, for example, your major source of income emanates from the leading Jewish families, or alternatively the Americans, no amount of pressure will ever allow you to deal with the Soviet Union." Romanov nodded his understanding. "That being the case," continued Poskonov, "there still has to be an outside chance that one of these two banks is in possession of the Tsar's icon, and as they are never going to admit as much to Mother Russia I am not sure what I can recommend you do next."

The banker sat back and waited for Romanov to take in his news.

"You are unusually silent," Poskonov ventured, after he had lit another cigarette.

"You have given me an idea," said Romanov. "I think the Americans would describe it as a 'long shot'. But if I'm right, it will be the Russians who will get the home run."

"Baseball is a game that I've never understood but I am, however, glad to have been of some use today. Although I suspect you will still need this, whatever your long shot." Poskonov removed a single piece of paper from his file and handed it over to Romanov. On it were the words: Simon et Cie, Zurich (refused), Roget et Cie, Geneva (refused).

"No doubt you will be returning to Switzerland very soon."

Romanov stared directly at the banker.

"I wouldn't recommend you visit Bischoff et Cie on this trip, Alex. There will be time enough for that in the future."

Romanov straightened his fingers.

The old man returned his stare. "You won't find me as easy to get rid of as Anna Petrova," he added.

CHAPTER TEN

The elderly-looking man took his place at the back of the taxi queue. It was hard to estimate his height because he looked so bent and frail. A large overcoat that might have been even older than its wearer reached almost to the ground and the fingers that could only just be seen peeping through the sleeves were covered in grey woollen mittens. One hand clung on to a little leather suitcase, with the initials E.R. in black looking so worn that it might have belonged to his grandfather.

One would have had to bend down or be very short to see the old man's face – a face that was dominated by a nose that would have flattered Cyrano de Bergerac. He shuffled forward slowly until it was his turn to climb into a taxi. The operation was a slow one, and the driver was already drumming his fingers against the wheel when his passenger told him in guttural tones that he wanted to be taken to the bankers, Simon et Cie. The driver moved off without asking for further directions. Swiss taxi-drivers know the way to the banks in the same way as London cabbies can always find a theatre and New York's yellow cabs a westside bar.

When the old man arrived at his destination he took

147

some time sorting out which coins to pay with. He then pushed himself slowly out on to the pavement and stood gazing at the marble building. Its solidity made him feel safe. He was about to touch the door when a man in a smart blue uniform opened it.

"I have come to see –" he began in stilted German, but the doorman only pointed to the girl behind the reception desk. He shuffled over to her and then repeated, "I have come to see Herr Daumier. My name is Emmanuel Rosenbaum."

"Do you have an appointment?" she asked.

"I fear not."

"Herr Daumier is in conference at the moment," said the girl, "but I will find out if there is another partner available to see you." After a phone conversation in German she said, "Can you take the lift to the third floor?" Mr Rosenbaum nodded with obvious signs of reluctance, but did as he was bid. When he stepped out of the lift, only just before the door closed on him, another young woman was standing there ready to greet him. She asked him if he would be kind enough to wait in what he would have described as a cloakroom with two chairs. Some time passed before anyone came to see him, and the old man was unable to hide his surprise at the age of the boy who eventually appeared.

"I am Welfherd Praeger," said the young man, "a partner of the bank."

"Sit down, sit down," said Mr Rosenbaum. "I cannot stare up at you for so long." The young partner complied.

"My name is Emmanuel Rosenbaum. I left a package with you in 1938, and I have returned to collect it."

"Yes, of course," said the junior partner, the tone of his voice changing. "Do you have any proof of your identity, or any documentation from the bank?"

"Oh, yes," came back the reply, and the old man handed over his passport and a receipt that had been folded and unfolded so many times it was now almost in pieces.

The young man studied both documents carefully. He recognised the Israeli passport immediately. Everything seemed to be in order. The bank's receipt, too, although issued in the year of his birth, appeared authentic.

"May I leave you for a moment, sir?"

"Of course," said the old man, "after twenty-eight years I think I can wait for a few more minutes."

Shortly after the young man had left, the woman returned and invited Mr Rosenbaum to move to another room. This time it was larger and comfortably furnished. Within minutes the junior partner returned with another man, whom he introduced as Herr Daumier.

"I don't think we have ever met, Herr Rosenbaum," said the chairman courteously. "You must have dealt with my father."

"No, no," said Mr Rosenbaum. "I dealt with your grandfather, Helmut."

A look of respect came into Herr Daumier's eyes.

"I saw your father only on the one occasion, and was sad to learn of his premature death," added Rosenbaum. "He was always so considerate. You do not wear a rose in your lapel as he did."

"No, sir, a tiny rebellion."

Rosenbaum tried to laugh but only coughed.

"I wonder if you have any further proof of identity

149

other than your passport?" Herr Daumier asked politely.

Emmanuel Rosenbaum raised his head and, giving Herr Daumier a tired look, turned his wrist so that it faced upwards. The number 712910 was tattooed along the inside.

"I apologise," said Daumier, visibly embarrassed. "It will take me only a few minutes to bring your box up, if you will be kind enough to wait."

Mr Rosenbaum's eyes blinked as if he were too tired even to nod his agreement. The two men left him alone. They returned a few minutes later with a flat box about two feet square and placed it on the table in the centre of the room. Herr Daumier unlocked the top lock while the other partner acted as a witness. He then handed over a key to Rosenbaum saying, "We will now leave you, sir. Just press the button underneath the table when you wish us to return."

"Thank you," said Rosenbaum, and waited for the door to close behind them. He turned the key in the lock and pushed up the lid. Inside the box was a package in the shape of a picture, about eighteen by twelve inches, covered in muslin and tied securely. Rosenbaum placed the package carefully in his old suitcase. He then shut the box and locked it. He pressed the button under the table and within seconds Herr Daumier and the junior partner returned.

"I do hope everything was as you left it, Herr Rosenbaum," said the chairman, "it has been some considerable time."

"Yes, thank you." This time the old gentleman did manage a nod.

"May I mention a matter of no great consequence?" asked Herr Daumier.

"Pray do so," said the old man.

"Is it your intention to continue with the use of the

box? The funds you left to cover the cost have recently run out."

"No, I have no need for it any longer."

"It's just that there was a small charge outstanding. But in the circumstances we are happy to waive it."

"You are most kind." Herr Daumier bowed and the junior partner accompanied their client to the front door, helped him into a taxi and instructed the driver to take Mr Rosenbaum to Zurich airport.

At the airport, the old man took his time reaching the check-in desk, because he appeared to be frightened of the escalator, and with the suitcase now quite heavy the flight of steps was difficult to negotiate.

At the desk he produced his ticket for the girl to check and was pleased to find that the passenger lounge was almost empty. He shuffled over towards the corner and collapsed on to a comfortable sofa. He checked to be sure he was out of sight of the other passengers in the lounge.

He flicked back the little knobs on the old suitcase and the springs rose reluctantly. He pushed up the lid, pulled out the parcel and held it to his chest. His fingers wrestled with the knots for some time before they became loose. He then removed the muslin to check his prize. Mr Rosenbaum stared down at the masterpiece. 'The Cornfields' by Van Gogh – which he had no way of knowing had been missing from the Vienna National Gallery since 1938.

Emmanuel Rosenbaum swore, which was out of character. He packed the picture safely up and re-turned it to his case. He then shuffled over to the girl at the Swissair sales desk and asked her to book him on the first available flight to Geneva. With luck he could still reach Roget et Cie before they closed.

* * *

The BEA Viscount landed at Geneva airport at eleven twenty-five local time that morning, a few minutes later than scheduled. The stewardess advised passengers to put their watches forward one hour to Central European Time.

"Perfect," said Adam. "We shall be in Geneva well in time for lunch, a visit to the bank and then back to the airport for the five past five flight home."

"You're treating the whole thing like a military exercise," said Heidi, laughing.

"All except the last part," said Adam.

"The last part?" she queried.

"Our celebration dinner."

"At the Chelsea Kitchen again, no doubt."

"Wrong," said Adam. "I've booked a table for two at eight o'clock at the Coq d'Or just off Piccadilly."

"Counting your chickens before they're hatched, aren't we?" said Heidi.

"Oh, very droll," said Adam.

"Droll? I do not understand."

"I'll explain it to you when we have that dinner tonight."

"I was hoping we wouldn't make it," said Heidi.

"Why?" asked Adam.

"All I have to look forward to tomorrow is the check-out counter at the German Food Centre."

"That's not as bad as a work out with the sergeant major at ten," groaned Adam. "And by ten past I shall be flat on my back regretting I ever left Geneva."

"That will teach you to knock him out," said Heidi. "So perhaps we ought to stay put after all," she added, taking him by the arm. Adam leant down and kissed her gently on the cheek as they stood in the gangway waiting to be let off the plane. A light drizzle was falling out on the aircraft steps. Adam unbuttoned his raincoat and attempted to shelter Heidi beneath it as they ran across the tarmac to the Immigration Hall.

"Good thing I remembered this," he said.

"Not so much a raincoat, more a tent," said Heidi.

"It's my old army trenchcoat," he assured her, opening it up again. "It can hold maps, compasses, even an overnight kit."

"Adam, we're just going to be strolling around Geneva in the middle of summer, not lost in the Black Forest in the middle of winter."

He laughed. "I'll remember your sarcasm whenever it pours."

The airport bus that travelled to and from the city took only twenty minutes to reach the centre of Geneva.

The short journey took them through the outskirts of the city until they reached the magnificent still lake nestled in the hills. The bus continued alongside the lake until it came to a halt opposite the massive single-spouting fountain that shot over four hundred feet into the air.

"I'm beginning to feel like a day tripper," said Heidi, as they stepped out of the bus, pleased to find the light rain had stopped.

Both of them were immediately struck by how clean the city was as they walked along the wide litter-free pavement that ran alongside the lake. On the other side of the road neat hotels, shops and banks seemed in equal preponderance.

"First we must find out where our bank is so that we can have lunch nearby before going to pick up the booty."

"How does a military man go about such a demanding exercise?" asked Heidi.

"Simple. We drop in at the first bank we see and ask them to direct us to Roget et Cie."

"I'll bet your little arm must have been covered in initiative badges when you were a Boy Scout."

Adam burst out laughing. "Am I that bad?"

"Worse," said Heidi. "But you personify every German's image of the perfect English gentleman." Adam turned, touched her hair gently and leaning down, kissed her on the lips.

Heidi was suddenly conscious of the stares from passing strangers. "I don't think the Swiss approve of that sort of thing in public," she said. "In fact, I'm told some of them don't approve of it in private."

"Shall I go and kiss that old prune over there who is still glaring at us?" said Adam.

"Don't do that, Adam, you might turn into a frog. No, let's put your plan of campaign into action," she said, pointing to the Banque Populaire on the far side of the avenue.

When they had crossed the road Heidi enquired of the doorman the way to Roget et Cie. They followed his directions, once again admiring the great single-spouted fountain as they continued on towards the centre of the city.

Roget et Cie was not that easy to pinpoint, and they walked past it twice before Heidi spotted the discreet sign chiselled in stone by the side of a high wrought-iron and plate-glass door.

"Looks impressive," said Adam, "even when it's closed for lunch."

"What were you expecting – a small branch in the country? I know you English don't like to admit it but this is the centre of the banking world."

"Let's find that restaurant before our entente cordiale breaks down," said Adam. They retraced their steps towards the fountain and, as the sun was trying to find gaps between the clouds, they chose a pavement café overlooking the lake. Both selected a cheese salad and shared a half bottle of white wine. Adam was enjoying Heidi's company so much that he began to tell her stories of his army days. She had to stop him and point out that it was nearly two. He reluctantly called for the bill. "The time has now come to discover if the Tsar's icon really exists," he said.

When they had returned to the entrance of the bank Adam pushed open the heavy door, took a step inside and stared around the gloomy hall.

"Over there," said Heidi, pointing to a woman who was seated behind a desk.

"Good morning. My name is Adam Scott. I have come to collect something that has been left to me in a will."

The woman smiled. "Have you made an appointment with anyone in particular?" she asked, with only the slightest trace of accent.

"No," said Adam. "I didn't realise that I had to."

"I'm sure it will be all right," said the lady. She picked up a phone, dialled a single number and held a short conversation in French. Replacing the phone she asked them both to go to the fourth floor.

As Adam walked out of the lift, he was surprised to be met by someone of his own age.

"Good afternoon, my name is Pierre Neffe and I am a partner of the bank," said the young man in perfect English.

"I did warn you that I would be redundant," whispered Heidi.

"Don't speak too soon," replied Adam. "We haven't even begun to explain our problem yet."

M. Neffe led them to a small, exquisitely furnished room.

"I could settle down here," said Adam, taking off his coat, "without any trouble."

"We do like to make our customers feel at home," said M. Neffe condescendingly.

"You obviously haven't seen my home," said Adam. M. Neffe did not laugh.

"How can I help you?" was all the young partner offered by way of reply.

"My father," began Adam, "died last month and left me in his will a receipt for something I think you have had in your safe-keeping since 1938. It was a gift given to him by one of your customers." Adam hesitated. "A Mr Emmanuel Rosenbaum."

"Do you have any documentation relating to this gift?" enquired M. Neffe.

"Oh, yes," said Adam, digging into the map pocket of his trenchcoat. He passed over the Roget et Cie receipt to the young banker. M. Neffe studied it and nodded. "May I be permitted to see your passport, Mr Scott?"

"Certainly," said Adam, delving back into his trenchcoat and passing it to M. Neffe.

"If you will excuse me for one moment." M. Neffe rose, and left them on their own.

"What do you imagine they are up to now?" said Heidi.

"Checking first if they still have the icon, and second if my receipt is authentic. 1938 was rather a long time ago."

As the minutes ticked by, Adam started to feel disappointed, then depressed, and finally began to believe it was all going to turn out to be a complete waste of time.

"You could always take one of the pictures off the wall and put it in your trenchcoat," teased Heidi. "I'm sure it would fetch a good price in London. Perhaps even more than your beloved icon."

"Too late," said Adam as M. Neffe reappeared with another banker whom he introduced as M. Roget.

"Good morning," said M. Roget. "I am sorry that my father is not here to meet you, Mr Scott, but he has been held up in Chicago on business." He shook hands with both Adam and Heidi. "We have on file a letter from Mr Rosenbaum giving clear instructions to the bank that the box is not to be opened by any other than" – he looked at the piece of paper he had brought with him – "Colonel Gerald Scott, DSO, OBE, MC."

"My father," said Adam. "But as I explained to M. Neffe, he died last month and left me the gift in his will."

"I would be happy to accept what you say," said M. Roget, "if I might be allowed sight of a copy of the death certificate and of the will itself."

Adam smiled at his own foresight and once more searched in his trenchcoat before removing a large brown envelope with the words 'Holbrooke, Holbrooke and Gascoigne' printed in heavy black letters across the top. He took out copies of his father's death certificate, the will and a letter marked 'To Whom It May Concern' and passed them to M. Roget, who read all three documents slowly, then handed them to his senior partner, who after he had read them whispered in his chairman's ear.

"Would you object to us phoning Mr Holbrooke in your presence?" asked M. Roget.

"No," said Adam simply. "But I must warn you that he is rather curmudgeonly."

"Curmudgeonly?" said the banker. "A word I am not familiar with, but I think I can sense its meaning." He turned and spoke to M. Neffe, who swiftly left the room, only to return a minute later with a copy of the English Law Society Register, 1966.

Adam was impressed by the bank's thoroughness as M. Roget checked that the number and address on the letterhead corresponded with the number and address in the Year Book. "I don't think it will be necessary to call Mr Holbrooke," said M. Roget, "but we have encountered one small problem, Mr Scott."

"And what is that?" asked Adam, nervously.

"Mr Rosenbaum's position is somewhat overdrawn, and the bank's rule is that an account must be cleared before any box can be opened."

Adam's pulse raced as he assumed that he hadn't brought enough money to cover this eventuality.

"The account is only 120 francs in debit," continued M. Roget, "which is the charge for housing the box over the past two years since Mr Rosenbaum's deposit ran out."

Adam breathed a sigh of relief. He took out his wallet and signed a traveller's cheque and handed it over.

"And finally," said M. Roget, "we will need you to sign a form of indemnity for the bank."

M. Roget passed over a long form containing clause after clause in tightly printed French at which Adam only glanced before passing it over to Heidi. She studied each clause carefully. M. Roget used the time to explain to Adam that it was a standard disclaimer clearing the bank of any liability concerning what might be in the box and Adam's legal claim to it.

Heidi looked up and nodded her agreement.

Adam signed on the dotted line with a flourish.

"Excellent," said the banker. "All we have to do now is go and retrieve your box."

"I suppose it could be empty," said Adam once the two of them were left alone again.

"And it could be jam-packed with gold doubloons, you old pessimist," said Heidi.

When both men returned a few minutes later, M. Neffe was carrying a flat metal box about twelve by nine inches, and some three inches deep.

Adam was disappointed by its modest size, but didn't show his feelings. M. Roget proceeded to undo the top lock with the bank's key and then handed Adam a small faded envelope with signatures scrawled across the waxed seal. "Whatever is in the box belongs to you, Mr Scott. When you have finished, perhaps you would be kind enough to let us know. Until then we shall remain outside in the corridor."

Both men left the room.

"Come on," said Heidi, "I can't wait." Adam opened the envelope and a key fell out. He fumbled with the lock which clicked and then he pushed up the lid. Inside the box was a small flat package wrapped in muslin and tied tightly with string. The knots took some undoing and then finally an impatient Adam tore off the string before slowly removing the muslin. They both stared at the masterpiece in disbelief.

The simple beauty of the golds, reds and blues left them both speechless. Neither of them had expected the icon to be so breathtaking. St George towering over the dragon, a massive sword in hand on the point of plunging it into the heart of the beast. The fire that belched from the dragon's jaw was a deep red and made a startling contrast to the gold cloak that seemed to envelop the saint.

"It's magnificent," said Heidi, eventually finding her voice.

Adam continued to hold the tiny painting in his hand.

"Say something," said Heidi.

"I wish my father had seen it, perhaps it would have changed his whole life."

"Don't forget he wanted it to change yours," said Heidi.

Adam finally turned the icon over and found on the back a small silver crown inlaid in the wood. He stared at it, trying to recall what Mr Sedgwick of Sotheby's had said that proved.

"I wish my father had opened the letter," said Adam, turning the icon back over and once again admiring St George's triumph. "Because it was his by right."

Heidi checked there was nothing else left inside the box. She then flicked down the lid and Adam locked it again with his key. He tucked the muslin round the masterpiece, tied it up firmly and slipped the little painting into the map pocket of his trenchcoat.

Heidi smiled. "I knew you'd be able to prove that you needed that coat even if it didn't rain."

Adam walked over to the door and opened it. The two bankers immediately returned.

"I hope you found what you had been promised," said M. Roget.

"Yes, indeed," said Adam. "But I shall have no further need of the box," he added, returning the key.

"As you wish," said M. Roget, bowing, "and here is the change from your traveller's cheque, sir," he said, passing over some Swiss notes to Adam. "If you will excuse me I will now take my leave of you. Monsieur Neffe will show you out." He shook hands with Adam, bowed slightly to Heidi and added with a faint smile, "I do hope you didn't find us too cur – mud – geonly." They both laughed.

"I also hope that you will enjoy a pleasant stay in our city," said M. Neffe as the lift took its leisurely pace down.

"It will have to be very quick," said Adam. "We have to be back at the airport in just over an hour."

The lift stopped at the ground floor and M. Neffe accompanied Adam and Heidi across the hall. The door was held open for them but they both stood aside to allow an old man to shuffle past. Although most people would have stared at his nose Adam was more struck by his penetrating eyes.

When the old man eventually reached the woman at the reception desk, he announced, "I have come to see Monsieur Roget."

"I'm afraid he's in Chicago at the moment, sir, but I'll see if his son is available. What name shall I tell him?"

"Emmanuel Rosenbaum." The woman picked up the phone and held another conversation in French. When she had replaced it she asked, "Would you go to the fourth floor, Mr Rosenbaum?"

Once again he had to take the fearsome lift, and once again he only just got out before its great teeth sprang back on him. Another middle-aged woman accompanied him to the waiting room. He politely declined her offer of coffee, thumping his heart with his right hand.

"Monsieur Roget will be with you shortly," she reassured the old gentleman.

He did not have to wait long before a smiling M. Roget appeared.

"How nice to make your acquaintance, Monsieur

Rosenbaum, but I'm afraid you have just missed Mr Scott."

"Mr Scott?" the old man uttered in surprise.

"Yes. He left only a few minutes ago, but we carried out the instructions as per your letter."

"My letter?" said Mr Rosenbaum.

"Yes," said the banker, opening for the second time that morning a file which had remained untouched for over twenty years.

He handed a letter to the old man.

Emmanuel Rosenbaum removed a pair of glasses from his inside pocket, unfolded them slowly and proceeded to read a hand that he recognised. It was a bold script written in thick black ink.

> Forsthaus Haarhot
> Amsberg 14
> Vosswinnel
> Sachsen
> Germany
> September 12, 1946

Dear M. Roget,

I have left in your safe-keeping a small icon of St George and the Dragon in my box 718. I am transferring the ownership of that painting to a British army officer, Colonel Gerald Scott, DSO, OBE, MC. If Colonel Scott should come to claim the icon at any time please ensure that he receives my key without delay.

My thanks to you for your help in this matter, and I am only sorry we have never met in person.

> Yours sincerely,
> Emmanuel Rosenbaum

"And you say that Colonel Scott came to collect the contents of the box earlier today?"

"No, no, Monsieur Rosenbaum. The colonel died quite recently and left the contents of the box to his son, Adam Scott. Monsieur Neffe and I checked all the documents including the death certificate and the will, and we were left in no doubt that they were both authentic and that everything was in order. He was also in possession of your receipt." The young banker hesitated. "I do hope we did the right thing, Monsieur Rosenbaum?"

"You certainly did," said the old man. "I came only to check that my wishes had been carried out."

M. Roget smiled in relief. "I feel I ought also to mention that your account had run into a small deficit."

"How much do I owe you?" asked the old man, fumbling in his breast pocket.

"Nothing," said M. Roget. "Nothing at all. Monsieur Scott dealt with it."

"I am in debt to Mr Scott. Are you able to tell me the amount?"

"One hundred and twenty francs," said M. Roget.

"Then I must repay the sum immediately," said the old man. "Do you by any chance have an address at which I can contact him?"

"No, I'm sorry I am unable to help you there," said M. Roget. "I have no idea where he is staying in Geneva." A hand touched M. Roget's elbow, and M. Neffe bent down and whispered in his ear.

"It appears," said M. Roget, "that Mr Scott was planning to return to England shortly because he had to check in at Geneva airport by five."

The old man lifted himself up. "You have been most helpful, gentlemen, and I will not take up any more of your time."

*　　*　　*

"It's flight BE 171 and your seats are 14A and B," the man behind the check-in counter told them. "The plane's on time so you should be boarding at gate Number Nine in about twenty minutes."

"Thank you," said Adam.

"Do you have any luggage that needs checking in?"

"No," said Adam. "We only spent the day in Geneva."

"Then have a good flight, sir," said the man, handing over their boarding passes. Adam and Heidi started walking towards the escalator that would take them to the departure lounge.

"I have seven hundred and seventy Swiss francs left," said Adam, thumbing through some notes, "and while we're here I must get my mother a box of decent liqueur chocolates. When I was a boy I used to give her a minute box every Christmas. I swore when I grew up if I ever got to Switzerland I would find her the finest box available." Heidi pointed to a counter that displayed row upon row of ornate boxes. Adam walked over and selected a large, gold-wrapped box of Lindt chocolates which the girl behind the counter gift-wrapped and placed in a carrier bag.

"Why are you frowning?" asked Adam after collecting his change.

"She's just reminded me that I have to be back behind a till tomorrow morning," said Heidi.

"Well, at least we've got the Coq d'Or to look forward to tonight," said Adam. He checked his watch. "Not much else we can do now except perhaps pick up some wine in the duty free."

"I'd like to find a copy of *Der Spiegel* before we go through customs."

"Fine," said Adam. "Why don't we try the paper shop over in the corner?"

"A call for Mr Adam Scott. Will Adam Scott please return to the BEA desk on the ground floor," came booming out over the public address system.

Adam and Heidi stared at each other. "Must have given us the wrong seat allocation, I suppose," said Adam, shrugging. "Let's go back and find out."

They returned downstairs and walked over to the man who had handed them their boarding passes. "I think you put a call out for me," said Adam. "My name is Scott."

"Oh, yes," said the man. "There's an urgent message for you," he said, reading from a pad in front of him. "Please call Monsieur Roget at Roget et Cie on Geneva 271279." He ripped off the piece of paper and handed it over. "The phones are over there in the far corner behind the KLM desk, and you'll need twenty centimes."

"Thank you," said Adam, studying the message, but it gave no clue as to why M. Roget should need to speak to him.

"I wonder what he can want," said Heidi. "It's a bit late to ask for the icon back."

"Well, there's only one way I'm going to find out," said Adam, passing over the bag to her. "Hang on to that and I'll be back in a moment."

"I'll try and pick up my magazine at the same time, if I can find a newspaper shop on this floor," said Heidi as she gripped the brightly coloured bag which contained the chocolates.

"Right," said Adam. "Meet you here in a couple of minutes."

"Roget et Cie. Est-ce-que je peux vous aider?"

"I am returning Monsieur Roget's call," said Adam, making no attempt to answer in French.

"Yes, sir. Whom shall I say is calling?" asked the telephonist, immediately switching to English.

"Adam Scott."

"I'll find out if he's available, sir."

Adam swung round to see if Heidi had returned to the BEA counter, but as there was no sign of her he assumed she must still be looking for a newspaper. Then he noticed an old man shuffling across the hall. He could have sworn he had seen him somewhere before.

"Mr Scott?" Adam leaned back into the box.

"Yes, Monsieur Roget, I am returning your call."

"Returning my call?" said the banker, sounding puzzled. "I don't understand."

"There was a message left at the BEA counter asking me to phone you. Urgent."

"There must be some mistake, I didn't leave any message. But now that you have rung, it might interest you to know that just as you were leaving Mr Emmanuel Rosenbaum paid us a visit."

"Emmanuel Rosenbaum?" said Adam, "but I assumed he was . . ."

"Could you assist me, please, young lady?" Heidi looked up at the old man who had addressed her in English, but with such a strong mid-European accent. She wondered why he had taken for granted that she spoke English but decided it must be the only language he felt confident conversing in.

"I am trying to find a taxi and I am already late, but I fear my eyesight is not what it used to be."

Heidi replaced the copy of *Der Spiegel* on the shelf and said, "They're just through the double doors in the centre. Let me show you."

"How kind," he said. "But I do hope I am not putting you to too much trouble."

"Not at all," said Heidi, taking the old man by the arm and guiding him back towards the door marked 'Taxi et Autobus'.

"Are you sure it was Rosenbaum?" said Adam anxiously.

"I'm certain," replied the banker.

"And he seemed happy about me keeping the icon?"

"Oh, yes. That was not the problem. His only concern was to return your 120 francs. I think he may try and get in touch with you."

"BEA announce the departure of their flight BE 171 to London Heathrow from gate Number Nine."

"I must leave," said Adam. "My plane takes off in a few minutes."

"Have a good flight," said the banker.

"Thank you, Monsieur Roget," said Adam and replaced the receiver. He turned towards the BEA counter and was surprised to find that Heidi had not yet returned. His eyes began to search the ground floor for a paper shop as he feared she might well not have heard the departure announcement. Then he spotted her walking out through the double door, helping the old man he had noticed earlier.

Adam called out and quickened his pace. Something didn't feel quite right. When he reached the automatic door he had to check his stride to allow it to slide back. He could now see Heidi standing on the pavement in front of him, opening a taxi door for the old man.

"Heidi," he shouted. The old gentleman suddenly turned and once again Adam found himself staring at the man he could have sworn he had seen at the bank. "Mr Rosenbaum?" he questioned. Then with a movement of his arm that was so fast and powerful it took Adam by surprise, the old man threw Heidi into the back of the taxi, jumped in beside her, and pulling the taxi door closed, hollered at the top of his voice, "*Allez vite.*"

For a moment Adam was stunned but then he dashed to the side of the taxi and only just managed to touch the handle as it accelerated away from the kerb. The car's sudden momentum knocked Adam backwards on the pavement, but not before he saw the petrified look on Heidi's face. He stared at the number plate of the departing car: GE-7-1-2 – was all he could catch, but at least he recognised it was a blue Mercedes. Desperately he looked around for another taxi but the only one in sight was already being filled up with luggage.

A Volkswagen Beetle drew up on the far side of the concourse. A woman stepped out of the driver's seat and walked to the front to open the boot. A man joined her from the passenger's side and lifted out a suitcase, before she slammed the boot lid back into place.

On the kerb, the two of them embraced. As they did so, Adam sprinted across the road and opening the passenger door of the Volkswagen, leapt inside and slid into the driver's seat. The key was still in the ignition. He turned it on, threw the car into gear, slammed his foot on the accelerator and shot backwards. The embracing couple stared at him in disbelief. Adam jerked the gear lever out of reverse into what he hoped was first. The engine turned over slowly, but just fast enough for him to escape the pursuing man. It must be third, he thought, and changed down as he began to follow the signs to the centre of Geneva.

By the time he reached the first junction he had mastered the gears, but had to concentrate hard on remaining on the right-hand side of the road. "GE712 . . . GE712," he repeated to himself again and again, to be sure it was fixed in his memory. He checked the number plate and the passengers of every blue taxi he passed. After a dozen or so, he began to wonder if Heidi's taxi might have left the motorway for a minor road. He pressed the accelerator even harder – 90, 100, 110, 120 kilometres an hour. He passed three more taxis but there was still no sign of Heidi.

Then he saw a Mercedes in the outside lane some considerable distance ahead of him, its lights full on and travelling well above the speed limit. He felt confident that the Volkswagen was powerful enough to catch the Mercedes, especially if it had a diesel engine. Metre by metre he began to narrow the gap as he tried to fathom out why the old man would want to kidnap Heidi in the first place. Could it be Rosenbaum? But he had wanted him to keep the icon, or so the banker had assured him. None of it made sense, and he drove on wondering if at any moment he was going to wake up.

When they reached the outskirts of the city Adam hadn't woken up as he followed carefully the taxi's chosen route. By the next intersection only three cars divided them. "A red light, I need a red light," Adam shouted, but the first three traffic lights into the city remained stubbornly green. And when one finally turned red, a van suddenly pulled in front of him, lengthening the gap between them. Adam cursed as he leaped out of the car and started running towards the taxi, but the light changed back to green just before he could reach it and the Mercedes sped away. Adam sprinted back to the Volkswagen and only just managed to drive the car across the junction as the light turned red. His decision to get out of the car had lost him several crucial seconds and when he looked anxiously ahead he could only just spot the taxi in the distance.

When they reached the Avenue de France, running parallel with the west side of the lake, both cars weaved in and out of the traffic, until the Mercedes suddenly turned left and climbed up a slight hill. Adam threw his steering wheel over to follow it, and for several yards careered up the wrong side of the road, narrowly missing a post van meandering down towards him. He watched carefully as the taxi turned left again, and in order to keep in contact he veered in front of a bus so sharply that it was forced to slam on its brakes. Several passengers, thrown from their seats, waved their fists at him as the bus's horn blared.

The taxi was now only a couple of hundred yards ahead. Once again Adam began to pick up some ground when suddenly it swerved into the kerbside and screeched to a halt. Nothing seemed to happen for the next few seconds as Adam weaved his way towards the stationary taxi, skidding to a halt directly behind the Mercedes. He then leaped out of the car and ran towards the parked vehicle. But, without warning, the old man jumped out of the taxi on the far side of the car and sprinted off up a side-street carrying with him Heidi's airport shopping bag and a small suitcase.

Adam pulled the back door open and stared at the beautiful girl who sat motionless. "Are you all right, are you all right?" he shouted, suddenly realising how much she meant to him. Heidi did not move a muscle and made no reply. Adam put his arms on her shoulders and looked into her eyes but they showed no response. He began to stroke her hair and then without warning her head fell limply on to his shoulder like a rag doll and a small trickle of blood started to run from the corner of her mouth. Adam felt cold and sick and began to tremble uncontrollably. He looked up at the taxi-driver. His arms were loose by his side and his body slumped over the wheel. There was no sign of life in the middle-aged man.

He refused to accept that they were dead.

Adam kept holding on to Heidi as he stared beyond her: the old man had reached the top of the hill.

Why did he still think of him as an old man? He was obviously not old at all, but young and very fit. Suddenly Adam's fear turned to anger. He had a split second to make a decision. He let go of Heidi, jumped out of the car and started to sprint up the hill after her killer. Two or three onlookers had already gathered on the kerbside and were now staring at Adam and the two cars. He had to catch the man who was still running. Adam moved as fast as he could but the trenchcoat he was wearing slowed him down, and by the time he too had reached the top of the hill the killer was a clear hundred yards ahead of him, weaving his way through the main thoroughfare. Adam tried to lengthen his stride as he watched the man leap on to a passing tram, but he was too far behind to make any impression on him and could only watch the tram moving inexorably into the distance.

The man stood on the tram steps and stared back at Adam. He held up the shopping bag defiantly with one hand. The back was no longer hunched, the figure no longer frail, and even at that distance, Adam could sense the triumph in the man's stance. Adam stood for several seconds in the middle of the road helplessly watching the tram as it disappeared out of sight.

He tried to gather his thoughts. He realised that there was little hope of picking up a taxi during the rush hour. Behind him he could hear sirens of what he presumed were ambulances trying to rush to the scene of the accident. "Accident," said Adam. "They will soon discover it was murder." He tried to start sorting out in his mind the madness of the last half hour. None of it made sense. He would surely find it was all a mistake ... Then he touched the side of his coat, touched the package that held the Tsar's icon. The killer hadn't gone to all that trouble for £20,000 — murdering two innocent people who happened to have got in his way — why, why, *why*, was the icon that important? What had the Sotheby's expert said? "A Russian gentleman had enquired after the piece." Adam's mind began to whirl. If it was Emmanuel Rosenbaum and that was what he had killed for, all he had ended up with was a large box of Swiss liqueur chocolates.

When Adam heard the whistle behind him he felt relieved that help was at hand but as he turned he saw two officers with guns out of their holsters pointing towards him. He instinctively turned his jog into a run, and looking over his shoulder he saw that several police were now giving chase. He lengthened his stride again and, despite the trenchcoat, doubted if there were a member of the Swiss force who could hope to keep up the pace he set for more than a quarter of a mile. He turned into the first alley he came to and speeded up. It was narrow — not wide enough for even two bicycles to pass. Once he was beyond the alley he selected a one-way street. It was crammed with cars, and he was able swiftly and safely to move in and out of the slow-moving oncoming traffic.

In a matter of minutes he had lost the pursuing police, but he still ran on, continually switching direction until he felt he had covered at least two miles. He finally turned into a quiet street and halfway down saw a fluorescent sign advertising the Hotel Monarque. It didn't look much more than a guest house, and certainly wouldn't have qualified under the description of an hotel. He stopped in the shadows and waited, taking in great gulps of air. After about three minutes his breathing was back to normal and he marched straight into the hotel.

CHAPTER ELEVEN

He stood naked, staring at the image of Emmanuel Rosenbaum in the hotel mirror. He didn't like what he saw. First he removed the teeth, then began to click his own up and down: he had been warned that the gums would ache for days. Then painstakingly he shed each layer of his bulbous nose, admiring the skill and artistry that had gone into creating such a monstrosity. It will be too conspicuous, he had told them. They will remember nothing else, had come back the experts' reply.

When the last layer had been removed, the aristocratic one that took its place looked ridiculous in the centre of such a face. Next he began on the lined forehead that even moved when he frowned. As the lines disappeared, so the years receded. Next the flaccid red cheeks, and finally, the two chins. The Swiss bankers would have been amazed at how easily the sharp rubbing of a pumice stone removed the indelible number on the inside of his arm. Once more he studied himself in the mirror. The hair, short and greying, would take nature longer. When they had cut his hair and smeared that thick, mud-like concoction all over his scalp he realised how an Irishman must feel to be tarred and feathered. Moments later he stood under a warm shower, his fingers massaging deep into the roots of his hair. Black treacly water started to run down his face and body before finally disappearing down the plug hole. It took half a bottle of shampoo before his hair had returned to its normal colour, but he realised that it would take considerably longer before he stopped looking like a staff sergeant in the United States Marines.

In a corner of the room lay the long baggy coat, the shiny shapeless suit, the black tie, the off-white shirt, woollen mittens and the Israeli passport. Hours of preparation discarded in a matter of minutes. He longed to burn them all, but instead left them in a heap. He returned to the main room and stretched himself out on the bed like a yawning cat. His back still ached from all the bending and crouching. He stood up, then touched his toes and threw his arms high above his head fifty times. He rested for one minute before completing fifty press-ups.

He returned to the bathroom and had a second shower – cold. He was beginning to feel like a human being again. He then changed into a freshly ironed cream silk shirt and a new double-breasted suit.

Before making one phone call to London and two more to Moscow he ordered dinner in his room so that no one would see him – he had no desire to explain how the man who checked in was thirty years younger than the man eating alone in his room. Like a hungry animal he tore at the steak and gulped the wine.

He stared at the colourful carrier bag but felt no desire to finish off the meal with one of Scott's liqueur chocolates. Once again he felt anger at the thought of the Englishman getting the better of him.

His eyes then rested on the little leather suitcase that lay on the floor by the side of his bed. He opened it and took out the copy of the icon that Zaborski had ordered he should always have with him so that there could be no doubt when he came across the original of St George and the Dragon.

At a little after eleven he switched on the late-night news. They had no photograph of the suspect, only one of that stupid taxi-driver who had driven so slowly it had cost the fool his life, and the pretty German girl who had tried to fight back. It had been pathetic, one firm clean strike and her neck was broken. The television announcer said the police were searching for an unnamed Englishman. Romanov smiled at the thought of police searching for Scott while he was eating steak in a luxury hotel. Although the Swiss police had no photograph of the murderer, Romanov didn't need one. It was a face he would never forget. In any case, his contact in England had already told him a lot more about Captain Scott in one phone call than the Swiss police could hope to discover for another week.

When Romanov was told the details of Scott's military career and decorations for bravery he considered it would be a pleasure to kill such a man.

Lying motionless on a mean little bed, Adam tried to make sense of all the pieces that made up a black jigsaw. If Goering had left the icon to his father, and his alias had been Emmanuel Rosenbaum, then a real-life Emmanuel Rosenbaum didn't exist. But he *did* exist: he had even killed twice in his attempt to get his hands on the Tsar's icon. Adam leaned over, switched on the bedside light, then pulled the small package out of the pocket of his trenchcoat. He unwrapped it carefully before holding the icon under the light. St George stared back at him – no longer looking magnificent, it seemed to Adam, more accusing. Adam would have handed the icon over to Rosenbaum without a second thought if it would have stopped Heidi from sacrificing her life.

By midnight Adam had decided what had to be done, but he didn't stir from that tiny room until a few minutes after three. He lifted himself quietly off the bed, opened the door, checked the corridor, and then locked the door noiselessly behind him before creeping down the stairs. When he reached the bottom step he waited and listened. The night porter had nodded off in front of a television that now let out a dim, monotonous hum. A silver dot remained in the centre of the screen. Adam took nearly two minutes to reach the front door, stepping on a noisy floorboard just once: but the porter's snores had been enough to cover that. Once outside, Adam checked up and down the street but there was no sign of any movement. He didn't want to go far, so he stayed in the shadows by the side of the road, moving at a pace unfamiliar to him. When he reached the corner he saw what he was searching for and it was still about a hundred yards away.

There was still no one to be seen, so he quickly made his way to the phone box. He pressed a twenty centime coin into the box and waited. A voice said, "*Est-ce-que je peux vous aider?*" Adam uttered only one word, "International." A moment later another voice asked the same question.

"I want to make a reverse charge call to London," said Adam firmly. He had no desire to repeat himself.

"Yes," said the voice. "And what is your name?"

"George Cromer," replied Adam.

"And the number you are speaking from?"

"Geneva 271982." He reversed the last three digits:

he felt the police could well be listening in on all calls to England that night. He then told the girl the number in London he required.

"Can you wait for a moment, please?"

"Yes," said Adam as his eyes checked up and down the street once again, still looking for any unfamiliar movement. Only the occasional early morning car sped by. He remained absolutely motionless in the corner of the box.

He could hear the connection being put through. "Please wake up," his lips mouthed. At last the ringing stopped and Adam recognised the familiar voice which answered.

"Who is this?" Lawrence asked, sounding irritated but perfectly awake.

"Will you accept a reverse charge call from a Mr George Cromer in Geneva?"

"George Cromer, Lord Cromer, the Governor of the Bank of Eng –? Yes, I will," he said.

"It's me, Lawrence," said Adam.

"Thank God. Where are you?"

"I'm still in Geneva but I'm not sure you're going to believe what I'm about to tell you. While we were waiting to board our plane home a man pulled Heidi into a taxi and later murdered her before I could catch up with them. And the trouble is that the Swiss police think I'm the killer."

"Now just relax, Adam. I know that much. It's been on the evening news and the police have already been around to interview me. It seems Heidi's brother identified you."

"What do you mean *identified* me? I didn't do it. You know I couldn't do it. It was a man called Rosenbaum, not me, Lawrence."

"Rosenbaum? Adam, who is Rosenbaum?"

179

Adam tried to sound calm. "Heidi and I came to Geneva this morning to pick up a gift from a Swiss bank that Pa had left me in his will. It turned out to be a painting. Then when we returned to the airport, this Rosenbaum grabbed Heidi thinking she had got the painting which didn't make any sense because the damned icon's only worth £20,000."

"Icon?" said Lawrence.

"Yes, an icon of St George and the Dragon," said Adam. "That's not important. What's important is that . . ."

"Now listen and listen carefully," interrupted Lawrence, "because I'm not going to repeat myself. Keep out of sight until the morning and then give yourself up at our Consulate. Just see you get there in one piece and I'll make sure that the Consul will be expecting you. Don't arrive until eleven because London is an hour behind Geneva and I'll need every minute to arrange matters and see that the consul staff is properly organised."

Adam found himself smiling for the first time in twelve hours.

"Did the killer get what he was after?" Lawrence asked.

"No, he didn't get the icon," said Adam, "he only got my mother's chocolates . . ."

"Thank God for that and keep out of sight of the Swiss police because they are convinced it was you who killed Heidi."

"But . . ." began Adam.

"No explanations. Just be at the Consulate at eleven. Now you'd better get off the line," said Lawrence. "Eleven, and don't be late."

"Right," said Adam, "and . . ." but the phone was only giving out a long burr. Thank God for Lawrence, he thought: the Lawrence of old who didn't need to ask any questions because he already knew the answers. Christ, what had he got himself involved in? Adam checked the street once again. Still no one in sight. He quickly stole the two hundred yards back to the hotel. The front door remained unlocked, the porter asleep, the television screen still faintly humming, the silver dot in place. Adam was back on his bed by five minutes past four. He didn't sleep. Rosenbaum, Heidi, the taxi driver, the Russian gentleman at Sotheby's. So many pieces of a jigsaw, none of them fitting into place.

But the one thing that worried him most was the conversation with Lawrence – the Lawrence of old?

The two policemen arrived at the Hotel Monarque at twenty past seven that Thursday morning. They were tired, discontented and hungry. Since midnight they had visited forty-three hotels on the west side of the city, on each occasion with no success. They had checked over a thousand registration cards and woken seven innocent Englishmen who had not come anywhere near fitting the description of Adam Scott.

At eight they would be off duty and could go home to their wives and breakfasts; but they still had three more hotels to check before then. When the landlady saw them coming into the hall she waddled as quickly as possible from the inner office towards them. She loathed the police and was willing to believe anyone who told her that the Swiss pigs were even worse than the Germans. Twice in the last year she had been fined and once even threatened with jail over her failure to register every guest. If they caught her once more she knew they would take her licence away and with it her living. Her slow mind tried to recall who had booked in the previous evening. Eight people had registered but only two had paid cash – the Englishman who hardly opened his mouth, Mr Pemberton was the name he had filled in on the missing card, and Maurice who always turned up with a different girl whenever he was in Geneva. She had destroyed both their cards and pocketed the money. Maurice and the girl had left by seven and she had already made up their bed, but the Englishman was still asleep in his room.

"We need to check your registration cards for last night, madame."

"Certainly, monsieur," she replied with a warm smile, and gathered together the six remaining cards: two Frenchmen, one Italian, two nationals from Zurich and one from Basle.

"Did an Englishman stay here last night?"

"No," said the landlady firmly. "I haven't had an Englishman," she added helpfully, "for at least a month. Would you like to see the cards for last week?"

"No, that won't be necessary," said the policeman. The landlady grunted with satisfaction. "But we will still need to check your unoccupied rooms. I see from the certificate that there are twelve guest bedrooms in the hotel," the policeman continued. "So there must be six that should be empty."

"There's no one in them," said the landlady. "I've already checked them once this morning."

"We still need to see for ourselves," the other officer insisted.

The landlady picked up her pass key and waddled towards the stairs, which she proceeded to climb as if they were the final summit of Everest. She opened bedrooms five, seven, nine, ten, eleven. Maurice's room had been remade within minutes of his leaving but the old lady knew she would lose her licence the moment they entered twelve. She just stopped herself from knocking on the door before she turned the key in the lock. The two policemen walked in ahead of her while she remained in the corridor, just in case there was any trouble. Not for the first time that day she cursed the efficiency of Swiss police.

"Thank you, madame," said the first policeman as he stepped back into the corridor. "We are sorry to have troubled you," he added. He put a tick on his list next to the Hotel Monarque.

As the two policemen made their way downstairs the landlady walked into room number twelve, mystified. The bed was undisturbed, as if it had not been slept in, and there was no sign of anyone having spent the night there. She called on her tired memory. She hadn't drunk that much the previous night – she touched the fifty francs in her pocket as if to prove the point. "I wonder where he is," she muttered.

For the past hour Adam had been crouching behind a derelict coach in a railway goods yard less than half a mile from the hotel. He had a clear view for a hundred yards in every direction. He had watched the early morning commuters flooding in on every train. By twenty past eight Adam judged they were at their peak. He checked that the icon was in place and left his hideout to join the flood as they headed to work. He stopped at the kiosk to purchase a newspaper. The only English paper on sale at that time in the morning was the *Herald-Tribune*: the London papers didn't arrive until the first plane could land, but Adam had seen the *Herald-Tribune* come in on the train from Paris. He made two other purchases at the station kiosk before rejoining the scurrying crowds: a city map of Geneva and a large bar of Nestlé's chocolate.

There was still plenty of time to kill before he could present himself at the Consulate. A glance at the map confirmed that he could already see the building he had marked out as his next place of sanctuary. He steered a route towards it that allowed him to stay in contact with the largest number of people. When he arrived in the square he continued under the shop awnings round the longest route, clinging to the wall, always avoiding the open spaces. It took a considerable time but his judgment was perfect. He reached the front door as hundreds of worshippers were leaving from the early morning Communion service.

Once inside, he felt safe. Notre Dame was the main Catholic Church in the city and Adam found his bearings in a matter of moments. He made his way slowly down the side aisle towards the Lady Chapel, dropped some coins in one of the collection boxes, lit a candle and placed it in a vacant holder below a statue of the Virgin Mother. He then fell on his knees, but his eyes never closed. A lapsed Catholic, he found he no longer believed in God – except when he was ill, frightened or in an aeroplane. After about twenty minutes had passed Adam was distressed to see that there was now only a handful of people left in the cathedral. Some old ladies dressed in black filled a front pew, moving their rosary beads methodically and chanting, "*Ave Maria, gratia plena, Domine teum, Benedicta . . .*" A few tourists were craning their necks to admire the fine roof, their eyes only looking upwards.

Adam rose slowly, his eyes darting from side to side. He stretched his legs and walked over to a confessional box partly hidden behind a pillar. A small sign on the wooden support showed that the box was not in use. Adam slipped in, sat down and pulled the curtain closed.

First he took out the *Herald-Tribune* from his trench-coat pocket, and then the bar of chocolate. He tore the silver paper from the chocolate and began to munch greedily. Next he searched for the story. Only one or two items of English news were on the front page, as most of the articles were devoted to what was happening in America. "The pound still too high at $2.80?" one headline suggested. Adam's eyes passed over the smaller headlines until he saw the paragraph he was looking for. It was in the bottom left-hand corner: "Englishman sought after German girl and Swiss taxi-driver murdered." Adam read the story, and only began to tremble when he discovered they knew his name:

"Captain Adam Scott, who recently resigned his commission from the Royal Wessex Regiment, is wanted . . . please turn to page fifteen." Adam began to turn the large pages. It was not easy in the restricted space of a confessional box. ". . . for questioning by the Geneva police in connection with . . ."

"Au nom du Père, du Fils et du Saint Esprit."

Adam looked up from the paper startled and considered making a dash for it. But he allowed his long-ago training to take hold as he found himself saying automatically, "Father, bless me, for I have sinned and wish to confess."

"Good, my son, and what form has this sin taken?" asked the priest in accented but clear English.

Adam thought quickly, I must give him no clue as to who I am. He looked out through the gap in the curtain and was alarmed to see two policemen questioning another priest by the west door. He drew the curtains tight and turned to the only accent he could ever imitate with any conviction.

"I'm over from Dublin, Father, and last night I

picked up this local girl in a bar and took her back to my hotel."

"Yes, my son."

"Well, one thing led to another, Father."

"Another what, my son?"

"Well, I took her up to my room."

"Yes, my son?"

"And she started to undress."

"And then what happened?"

"She started to undress me."

"Did you try to resist, my son?"

"Yes, Father, but it got harder."

"And did intercourse take place?" asked the priest.

"I'm afraid so, Father. I couldn't stop myself. She was very beautiful," Adam added.

"And is it your intention to marry this girl, my son?"

"Oh, no, Father, I'm already married and have two lovely children, Seamus and Maureen."

"It is a night you must for ever put behind you."

"I'd like to, Father."

"Has this happened before?"

"No, Father, it's the first time I've been abroad on my own. I swear to it."

"Then let it be a lesson to you, my son, and may the Lord find it in his mercy to forgive you this abominable sin and now you must make your act of contrition."

"Oh my God . . ."

When Adam had completed the act of contrition the priest pronounced absolution and told him he must as penance say three decades of the Rosary.

"And one more thing."

"Yes, Father?"

"You will tell your wife everything the moment you return to Ireland or you cannot hope for atonement. You must promise me that, my son."

"When I see my wife, I will tell her everything that happened last night, Father," Adam promised, as he once again checked through the curtains. The police were no longer anywhere to be seen.

"Good, and continue to pray to our Blessed Lady to keep you from the evils of temptation."

Adam folded up his paper, pushed it in the trench-coat and bolted from the little box and took a seat on the end of a pew. He lowered his head and began to whisper the Lord's Prayer as he opened the map of Geneva and began to study the road plan. He had located the British Consulate on the far side of a large garden square by the time he reached 'Deliver us from evil.' He estimated that it was just over a mile away from the cathedral, but seven streets and a bridge had to be negotiated before he would be safe. He returned to the Lady Chapel and his knees. Adam checked his watch. It was too early to leave St Peter's so he remained head in hands for another thirty minutes, going over the route again and again. He watched a party of tourists as they were conducted through the cathedral. His eyes never left them as they began to move nearer and nearer to the great door at the west end of the aisle. He needed to time it to perfection.

Suddenly Adam rose and walked quickly down the side aisle reaching the porch only a yard behind the party of tourists. They shielded him out on to the square. Adam ducked under a shop awning at the side of the road, then walked round three sides of the square to avoid the one policeman on duty by the north corner. He crossed the first road as the light turned red and headed up a one-way street. He kept on the inside of the pavement, knowing he had to turn left at the end of the road. Two uniformed policemen came round the corner and walked straight towards him. He jumped into the first shop without looking and turned his back on the pavement.

"*Bonjour, monsieur,*" said a young lady to Adam. "*Vous désirez quelque chose?*" Adam looked around him. Lissome mannequins in knickers and bras with suspenders and long black nylon stockings stood all around him.

"I'm looking for a present for my wife."

The girl smiled. "Perhaps a slip?" she suggested.

"Yes," said Adam, "definitely a slip. Do you have one in burgundy?" he asked, as he half turned to watch the policemen stroll past.

"Yes, I think so, but I'll have to check in the stockroom."

Adam had reached the next street corner long before she had returned with 'just the thing'.

He managed the next few minutes walk without incident and with only two hundred yards to go could already feel his heart thumping as if it was trying to escape from his body. On the final corner there was only one policeman in sight, and he seemed intent on directing traffic. Adam kept his back to the officer as he could now see the garden square that had only shown up on the map as a tiny green blob. On the far side of the road he spotted a Union Jack hanging above a blue door.

Never run the last few yards, especially when it's open ground, his sergeant had told him many times when on patrol in the Malayan jungle. He crossed the road and stood on the edge of the small park, only fifty yards away from safety. A policeman was patrolling aimlessly up the road but Adam suspected that was only because there were several consulates standing adjacent to one another. He watched the officer carefully. It took the man two minutes to reach the end before he turned and continued his leisurely walk back. Adam ducked behind a tree in the corner of the little park and selected another tree on the far side of the road only yards from the Consulate front door that would shield him from the oncoming policeman. He estimated that by walking at a speed that wouldn't attract attention he could cover the last thirty yards in under ten seconds. He waited for the policeman to reach his farthest point.

He checked the Consulate door again, relieved to see a girl go in and a man carrying a briefcase come out on to the street. There seemed to be no guard in sight as the door remained half open. He looked up at the bay window on the first floor. He could see two men staring out at the park as if waiting expectantly for someone to arrive. Lawrence had succeeded. In moments he would be safe. Adam pulled up the collar of his trenchcoat and set off as the cathedral clock behind him struck eleven. The policeman was now a few paces from reaching his farthest point but still walking in the opposite direction. Adam crossed the road at a measured stride. When he reached the centre of the row he had to stop suddenly to let a car pass by. The policeman turned to start his journey back.

For several seconds Adam remained motionless in the broad street as he stared at the tree he had selected to shield him if the policeman turned before he could reach the front door. He took a confident pace towards the British Consulate. A tall man of athletic build, his head covered in a stubble of short fair hair, stepped out to greet him.

Adam would not have recognised him but for the eyes.

PART TWO

10 DOWNING STREET
LONDON SW1

June 17, 1966

CHAPTER TWELVE

10 DOWNING STREET, LONDON SW1 *June 17, 1966*

When Sir Morris Youngfield left the Prime Minister he still was unable to work out why the possession of any icon could be that important.

Leaving Number 10 behind him, Sir Morris marched quickly into the Foreign Office courtyard and within moments was stepping out of the lift on the seventh floor. When he walked into his office, Tessa, his secretary, was laying out some papers for him.

"I want a D4 assembled immediately," he said to the woman who had served him so loyally for fourteen years. "And ask Commander Busch to join the team."

Tessa raised her eyebrows but Sir Morris ignored her silent comment as he knew he couldn't hope to get to the bottom of this one without the co-operation of the Americans. Once more Sir Morris considered the Prime Minister's instructions. Harold Wilson hadn't needed to explain that he didn't get that many transatlantic calls from Lyndon Johnson seeking his help.

But why a Russian icon of an English saint?

*   *   *

As Romanov moved towards him, Adam took a pace backwards from the tramlines to allow the tramcar to pass between them. When the tram had passed Adam was no longer to be seen. Romanov snarled at such an amateur trick, sprinted the twenty yards necessary to catch up with the tram and to the astonishment of the passengers, leapt on. He began checking over the faces row by row.

Adam waited for the tramcar to travel another twenty yards before he emerged from behind a tree on the far side of the road. He felt confident he could reach the safety of the Consulate door long before Heidi's killer could hope to return. He checked the other side of the road and swore under his breath. The policeman patrolling was now only a few paces from the Consulate and heading relentlessly towards it. Adam looked back at the tram which had just been passed by another heading towards him. To his dismay, he saw his adversary leap from one platform to the other with the agility of a top-class gymnast. With the policeman now only yards from the Consulate door Adam was left with no choice but to retreat and sprint back up the one-way street. After fifty yards he glanced over his shoulder. The man he knew only as Rosenbaum couldn't have looked less like a helpless old man as he started running towards him.

Adam jumped between the cars and buses and dodged around the milling pedestrians as he tried to lengthen the fifty yards' distance between them. At the first crossroad he saw a plump lady coming out of a phone box a few yards away. He changed direction quickly and leapt into the empty box, crouching into the far corner. The door slowly squelched shut. Rosenbaum came hurtling round the corner and was twenty yards past the box before he realised that Adam had shot back out and down the road in the opposite direction. Adam knew he had at least five seconds before Rosenbaum could hope to see which direction he had chosen. One and two and three and four and five, he counted as he ran along the road. He then checked right, before mounting three steps and pushing through some swing doors. He found himself in front of a small counter, behind which sat a young woman holding a small wad of tickets.

"Deux francs, monsieur," said the girl. Adam looked at the little box, quickly took out two francs and made his way down the long dark passage and through another set of swing doors. He stood at the back waiting for his eyes to become accustomed to the dark. It was the first performance of the day and the cinema was nearly empty. Adam chose a seat on the end of a row that was an equal distance from both exits.

He stared at the screen, thankful that the movie had just begun, because he needed some time to formulate a plan. Whenever the screen was bright enough he checked the little red road on the map, and then using the top of his thumb as a one-inch ruler, he was able to estimate that the nearest border into France was only eight miles away at Ferney-Voltaire. From there he could travel to Paris via Dijon and be back home almost as quickly as it would take him to sit through *Exodus* a second time. Having decided on his route, the next problem for Adam was how to travel. He dismissed all forms of public transport and settled on hiring a car. He remained in his seat during the interval to double-check the routes. The moment Paul Newman reappeared on the screen, he folded up the map and left the cinema by the exit which had been least used during the past four hours.

* * *

When Sir Morris entered the room for the meeting of the 'Northern Department', he found the rest of the D4 were already assembled, and familiarising themselves with the files that had been presented to them only an hour before.

He glanced round the table at the specially selected D4, all hand-picked men but only one of them did he consider his equal. And it wasn't the old war-horse Alec Snell who had served at the Foreign Office longer than any of them and was touching his moustache nervously as he waited for Sir Morris to take his seat. Next to him sat Brian Matthews, known in the Department as the 'well-balanced man': a grammar school boy with a double first and a chip on both shoulders. Opposite him was Commander Ralph Busch, the CIA representative with a short fuse, who after five years attached to the Embassy in Grosvenor Square considered himself more British than the British, and even imitated the Foreign Office style of dress to prove it. At the far end of the table, Sir Morris's second in command, who some said was a little too young, although everyone except Tessa had forgotten that Sir Morris had held his job at the same age.

The four members of the committee stopped talking once Sir Morris had settled in his seat at the head of the table.

"Gentlemen," he began – the only lady present being Tessa, whose existence he rarely acknowledged – "the Prime Minister has given this D4 his full blessing. And he requires detailed reports to be sent to him every twelve hours, wherever he is, and at any time of the night or day if there should be any unexpected development. So, as you can see, there is no time to waste. This particular D4 has co-opted as part of its team a liaison officer from the CIA, Commander Ralph

Busch. I have worked with Commander Busch several times over the past five years and I am delighted that the American Embassy has chosen him to represent them."

. The man seated on Sir Morris's right bowed slightly. At five feet nine inches, with broad, muscular shoulders and a neat black beard, he looked every inch the sailor whom Player's cigarettes were always trying to please. Indeed, a sailor wouldn't have been a bad guess because Busch had been a commander in PT boats during the Second World War.

"From the latest reports I have received," Sir Morris continued, opening the file in front of him, "it appears that Scott never reached the Consulate this morning, despite our request for the police to have no more than a token force on duty within two hundred yards of the park.

"Since our sketchy information yesterday, BEA have confirmed," said Sir Morris consulting a note in front of him, "that Scott received a call from Roget et Cie while he was at the airport. After considerable pressure from our Ambassador and Interpol we have learned from Mr Roget that the purpose of Scott's visit to the bank was to pick up an unknown bequest from a Mr Emmanuel Rosenbaum. Further checking shows that a Mr Rosenbaum arrived in Zurich yesterday morning and travelled on to Geneva in the afternoon. He left his hotel first thing this morning and has subsequently vanished from the face of the earth. None of this would be of any great significance if Mr Rosenbaum had not boarded the aeroplane to Zurich from –" Sir Morris couldn't resist a short dramatic pause "– Moscow. I think it is not unreasonable therefore to assume that Mr Rosenbaum, whoever he is, works directly or indirectly for the KGB.

"The KGB, as we know to our cost, is well serviced in Geneva, by a large number of East Europeans working under the guise of the United Nations for ILO and WHO, all with the necessary diplomatic status they need to carry out undercover work. What still remains a mystery to me is why Mr Rosenbaum should be willing to kill two innocent people for a relatively obscure icon. That brings my report up to date. But perhaps you have come up with something new," said Sir Morris turning to his Number Two.

Lawrence Pemberton looked up from his end of the table. "Since our meeting this morning, Sir Morris," he began, "I have spoken to Scott's sister, his mother and a firm of solicitors in Appleshaw who administered his father's will. It transpires that Scott was left with nothing of any real importance in the will apart from an envelope which his mother says contained a letter from Reichsmarshal Hermann Goering." There was an immediate buzz around the table until Sir Morris tapped his knuckle on the desk.

"Do we have any idea of the contents of Goering's letter?" asked Sir Morris.

"The whole letter, no, sir. But one of our examination entrants, a Mr Nicholas Wainwright, was asked by Scott to translate what we now believe was a paragraph from the letter because later Wainwright asked the examination board if it was part of his test." Lawrence extracted a piece of paper from the file in front of him and read out the paragraph:

During the year you cannot have failed to notice that I have been receiving from one of the guards a regular supply of Havana cigars – one of the few pleasures I have been permitted, despite my incarceration. The cigars themselves have also served another purpose, as each one contained a capsule with a small amount of poison. Enough to allow me to survive my trial, while ensuring that I shall cheat the executioner.

"That's all?" said Sir Morris.

"I'm afraid so," said Lawrence, "although I believe it confirms what Scott told me last night was his reason for travelling to Geneva. There is no doubt in my mind that the package he went to pick up contained the icon of St George and the Dragon left to his father by Goering."

"St George and the Dragon," said Matthews interrupting, "but that's the icon that half of the KGB have been searching for during the past two weeks and my Department has been trying to find out why."

"And what have you come up with?" asked Sir Morris.

"Very little," admitted Matthews. "But we began to assume that it must be a decoy because the Tsar's icon of St George and the Dragon hangs in the Winter Palace at Leningrad and has done so for three hundred years."

"Anything else?" asked Sir Morris.

"Only that the section leader in search of the icon is Alex Romanov," said Matthews.

Snell gave out a low whistle. "Well, at least we know we're dealing with the First Division," he said.

There was a long silence before Sir Morris offered, "One thing is clear. We have to get to Scott first and must assume that it's Romanov we're up against. So what are we doing about it?"

"As much as we can get away with," said Lawrence. "Along with the Americans we have seventeen men operatives in Geneva, all of them trying to find Scott."

"The Swiss police have a thousand doing the same job, though heaven knows whose side they imagine they're on," added Snell.

Lawrence chipped back in. "And it's been almost impossible to convince them that Scott is not in any way responsible for the two murders. So we may have to get him out without relying on their co-operation."

"But what do you imagine would be the outcome if Romanov or this Rosenbaum, who must also be part of the KGB, manages to get to Scott before we do?" asked Matthews.

"A civilian up against one of the Russians' most ruthless agents. That's all we need," said Commander Busch.

Lawrence inclined his head towards the American. "I've known Adam for most of my life. The irony of his particular predicament is that it was I who, without his knowledge, recommended that he should be interviewed for a place in the Northern Department. It was my intention that he should join us as soon as he had completed his course as a trainee. If Romanov or any of his cohorts come face to face with Scott they'd better remember that he was awarded a Military Cross when faced with a thousand Chinese."

"But if it turned out to be Romanov," asked Snell, "would Scott be able to kill him?"

"I would have said no before Rosenbaum murdered his girlfriend," said Lawrence.

"I wouldn't be confident of his chances even then," said Busch.

"Neither would I," added Matthews.

"That's because you don't know Adam Scott," said Lawrence.

Matthews lowered his eyes in order to avoid a clash with his boss. His boss. Ten years his junior. A shortlist of two and they had chosen another Oxbridge man to be Under-Secretary. Matthews knew that as far as the Foreign Office was concerned, he had gone to the wrong school and the wrong university. He should have taken his father's advice and joined the police force. There were no class barriers there, and he would probably have been a chief superintendent by now.

Sir Morris ignored the little outburst which had become fairly common since he had selected Pemberton to leapfrog the older man.

"Are we allowed to know," interrupted Snell, looking straight at Busch, "why a relatively obscure icon is of such disproportionate importance to both Russia and the United States?"

"We are as mystified as you," said the American. "All we can add to your current information, is that two weeks ago the Russians deposited gold bullion in New York to the value of over seven hundred million dollars without any explanation. We are, of course, not certain at the moment there is any connection."

"Seven hundred million dollars?" said Sir Morris. "You could buy half the countries in the United Nations for that."

"And every icon that has ever been painted," said Matthews.

"Let's get down to what we actually know, and stop guessing at what might be," said Sir Morris turning back to his Number Two. "What's the exact IA position?"

Lawrence undid a folder with a red band around it, the words 'Immediate Action' printed across the top in black. He did not need to refer to it, but still glanced down from time to time to check he had not forgotten anything. "As I have already briefed you, we have seventeen agents in the field and the Americans are flying a further twelve into Geneva today. With the Russians and the Swiss roaming the city like knights of the round table in search of the Holy Grail, I can only believe that someone will come across Scott fairly soon. One of our biggest problems, as I explained, is that the Swiss are unwilling to co-operate. As far as they are concerned, Scott is a common criminal on the run and should they get to him first they have made it clear they will not allow him diplomatic immunity.

"We, as well as the Swiss police, and undoubtedly the Russians," continued Lawrence, "have started checking out all the obvious places: hotels, guest houses, restaurants, airports, car hire companies, even lavatories, and we remain in constant touch with every one of our agents on the ground. So if Scott suddenly appears out of nowhere we should be able to go to his aid at a moment's notice." Lawrence looked up to observe that one of the team was taking down all the details. "Added to that, the Post Office are intercepting every call made to Barclays DCO from Geneva. If Scott does try to get in contact with me again at the bank or at my flat it will be put through to this office automatically," he said.

"Is he aware that you work for the Service?" asked Snell, putting a hand through his dark hair.

"No. He, like my dear mother, still thinks I'm a bank official in the International Department of Barclays DCO. But it won't be long before he works out that that's only a front. Unlike my mother, he doesn't always believe everything I tell him and after our conversation last night he is bound to have become suspicious."

"Do we have anything else to go on?" Sir Morris asked, looking up at Lawrence.

"Not a lot more at the moment, sir. We are doing

everything possible, remembering this is not a home match; but I still anticipate that the exercise will be over one way or another within twenty-four hours. Because of that I have requested overnight facilities to be set up in the building should you feel we need them. When you return after dinner you will find beds already made up in your offices."

"No one will be going out to dinner tonight," said Sir Morris.

The cinema door opened on to the busy pavement and Adam slipped into the main stream of commuters who were now returning home for dinner. As he kept walking he made certain of as little head movement as possible but his eyes never stayed still, checking everything within 180 degrees. After he had covered three blocks, he spotted a red Avis sign swinging in the afternoon breeze on the far side of the road. He safely reconnoitred the crowded crossing, but once his foot touched the far pavement he froze on the spot. Just ahead of him in the fast, jostling crowd stood a man in a raincoat. He was continually looking around, while making no attempt to walk in either direction. Was he one of Rosenbaum's men, the police, or even British? There was no way of telling whose side he was on. Adam's eyes didn't leave the man as he took out an intercom and, putting it to his mouth, whispered into it. "Nothing to report, sir. Still no sign of our man, and I haven't seen any of the KGB either."

Adam, unable to hear the words, switched into a side road and almost knocked over a boy selling papers. '*Le soldat anglais toujours à Genève*' the headline blared. Quickly he crossed another road, where he came to a stop again, this time behind a marble statue in the centre of a small patch of grass. He stared at the building in front of him but he knew there would be no point in his trying to hide there. He started to move away as a large, empty touring coach drew up and parked in front of the block. Smart blue lettering along the side of the coach proclaimed 'The Royal Philharmonic Orchestra'. Adam watched as some musicians walked out of the front door and climbed on to the coach carrying their instrument cases of assorted lengths and widths. One was even lugging a large kettle drum which he deposited in the boot of the coach. As the musicians continued to stream out of the hotel Adam decided he wouldn't get a better opportunity. When the next group came through the double doors he walked quickly forward and stepped into the middle of them before anyone could have spotted him. He then continued on past them through the open hotel door. The first thing he spotted in the crowded lobby was a double bass leaning against the wall. He glanced at the label around the neck of the unwieldy case. 'Robin Beresford.'

Adam walked over to the counter and gestured to the clerk. "I need my room key quickly – I've left my bow upstairs and now I'm holding everyone up."

"Yes, sir. What room number?" asked the clerk.

"I think it's 312, or was that yesterday?" said Adam.

"What name, sir?"

"Beresford – Robin Beresford."

The clerk handed him key 612. His only comment was: "You were three floors out."

"Thank you," said Adam. As he left the counter, he turned to check that the receptionist was already dealing with another customer. He walked smartly over to the lift which was disgorging still more musicians. Once it had emptied he stepped in, pressed the button for the sixth floor, and waited. He felt exhilarated as the lift doors eventually slid across and he was alone for the first time in several hours. When the doors opened again he was relieved to find there was no one standing in the corridor. He made his way quickly along the passage to room 612.

As he turned the key and opened the door he said firmly in as good a French accent as he could manage, "Room service", but as no one responded, he stepped in and locked the door behind him. An unopened suitcase had been left in one corner. Adam checked the label. Obviously Mr Beresford hadn't even had time to unpack. Adam checked the room, but there was no other sign of the hotel guest apart from a piece of paper on the side table. It was a typed itinerary:

'European Tour: Geneva, Frankfurt, Berlin, Amsterdam, London.

'Geneva, Bus 5.00 to Concert Hall rehearsal 6.00, Concert performance 7.30, encores 10.00.

'Programme: Mozart's Third Horn Concerto, First Movement, Brahms's Second Symphony, Schubert's Unfinished Symphony.'

Adam looked at his watch: by the time Robin Beresford had completed the 'Unfinished Symphony' he would be over the border; but he still felt safe to remain in Room 612 until it was dark.

He picked up the phone by the bed and dialled room service. "Beresford, 612," he announced, and ordered himself some dinner before going into the bathroom. On the side of the basin was propped a little plastic bag with the words 'Compliments of the Management' printed across it. Inside Adam found soap, a tiny toothbrush, toothpaste and a plastic razor.

He had just finished shaving when he heard a knock on the door and someone calling "Room service". Adam quickly covered his face with lather again and put on a hotel dressing gown before he opened the door. The waiter set up a table without giving Adam a second look. When he had finished his task he enquired, "Will you sign the bill, please, sir?"

He handed Adam a slip of paper. He signed it 'Robin Beresford' and added a fifteen per cent tip.

"Thank you," said the waiter and left. As soon as the door closed behind him Adam's eyes settled on the feast of onion soup, rump steak with green beans and potatoes, and finally a raspberry sorbet. A bottle of house wine had been uncorked and needed only to be poured. He suddenly didn't feel that hungry.

He still couldn't accept what he had gone through. If only he hadn't pressed Heidi into joining him on this unnecessary journey. A week before she hadn't even known him and now he was responsible for her death. He would have to explain to her parents what had happened to their only daughter. But before Adam could face them he still had to come up with some explanation for the things he hadn't yet begun to understand. Not least the unimportant icon. Unimportant?

After he had half finished the meal he wheeled the trolley out into the corridor and placed the 'Do not disturb' sign on the door. Once back in the bedroom he stared out of the window over the city. The sun looked as if it had another hour allocated for Geneva. Adam lay down on the bed and began to consider what had happened in the last twenty-four hours of his life.

"Antarctic is in possession of an icon of St George and the Dragon. But we know from our files of that period that that particular icon was destroyed when the Grand Duke of Hesse's plane crashed over Belgium in 1937."

"That may well be what is written in your files," said the man on the other end of the phone. "But what if your information at Langley turns out to be wrong and the icon was found by Goering but not returned to the Grand Duke?"

"But Stalin confirmed at Yalta that the icon and its contents had been destroyed in the plane crash. He agreed to make no protest while he was not in possession of the original document. After all, that was the reason Roosevelt appeared to be gaining so little at the time while Stalin was getting so much in return. Can't you remember the fuss Churchill made?"

"I certainly can because he had worked out that it wasn't Britain who was going to benefit from such a decision."

"But if the Russians have now discovered the existence of the original icon?"

"You are suggesting they might also get their hands on the original document?"

"Precisely. So you must be sure to get to Antarctic before the Russians do, or for that matter, the Foreign Office."

"But I'm part of the Foreign Office team."

"And that's precisely what we want the Foreign Office to go on believing."

"And who's been sleeping in my bed, said Mother Bear."

Adam woke with a start. Looking down at him was a girl who held a double bass firmly by the neck with one hand and a bow in the other. She was nearly six foot and certainly weighed considerably more than Adam. She had long, gleaming red hair that was in such contrast to the rest of her that it was as if the Maker had started at the top and quickly lost interest.

She wore a white blouse and a black flowing skirt that stopped an inch above the ground.

"Who are you?" asked Adam, startled.

"I'm not Goldilocks, that's for sure," parried the girl. "More to the point, who are you?"

Adam hesitated. "If I told you, you wouldn't believe me."

"I can't imagine why not," she said. "You don't look like Prince Charles or Elvis Presley to me, so go on, try me."

"I'm Adam Scott."

"Am I meant to swoon and run to your side, or scream and run away?" she enquired.

Adam suddenly realised that the girl couldn't have watched television or read a paper for at least two days. He switched tactics. "I thought my friend Robin Beresford was meant to be booked into this room," he said confidently.

"And so did I until I saw you on my bed."

"You're Robin Beresford?"

"You're quite sharp for someone who has just woken up."

"But Robin?"

"It's not my fault my father wanted a boy," she said. "And you still haven't explained what you're doing on my bed."

"Is there any hope of you listening to me for five minutes without continually interrupting?" asked Adam.

"Yes, but don't bother with any more fairy stories," said Robin. "My father was a born liar, and by the time I was twelve I could see through him like a pane of glass."

"I should have a seat if I were you," said Adam. "This may take longer than the average double bass accompaniment."

"I'll remain on my feet, if you don't mind," said Robin. "At least until the first lie."

"Suit yourself. What would you like first? The good news or the bad news?"

"Try me on the bad news," said Robin.

"The Swiss police want to arrest me and . . ."

"What for?" interrupted Robin.

"Murder," said Scott.

"What's the good news?" she asked.

"I'm innocent."

Romanov stood in the Ambassador's office and rested his fingers on the table. "I blame myself," he said very quietly, "even more than I blame any of you. I underestimated the Englishman. He's good, and if any of you are hoping to kill him before I get to him you'll have to be *very* good." No one assembled in the Ambassador's office that night was disposed to disagree with the Comrade Major. Romanov paused to study the group of men who had been flown in from several Eastern satellites at short notice. All with long records of service to the State but only one of them, Valchek, was known to Romanov personally and he worked too closely with Zaborski to be trusted. Romanov had already faced the fact that only a few of them were acquainted with Geneva. He could only pray that the British and Americans were suffering from the same problem.

His eyes swept around the room. The Swiss police had the best chance of finding Scott and they weren't being at all helpful, he thought ruefully. However, Romanov had been pleased to learn from their head man stationed in Geneva that the Swiss had also refused to co-operate with the British or the Americans.

"Comrades," he said, the moment they had all

settled, "there is no need to remind you that we have been entrusted with a vital assignment for the Motherland." He paused to check if any of the faces registered the slightest suggestion of cynicism. Satisfied, he continued, "We will therefore maintain a tight surveillance over Geneva in case Scott is still holed up somewhere in the city. My own guess is that, like all amateurs, he is, and will wait until it's dark, perhaps even first light, before he makes a run for the nearest border. The French border will be his most obvious choice. Despite going to war against the Germans twice in the past fifty years, the English have never bothered to master the German language, although a few of them can manage to speak passable French. So he's more likely to feel safe in that country. It also offers him the opportunity to cross only one border before reaching the coast.

"If he's stupid enough to try and leave by plane he will find we have the airports covered; if by train, we have the stations manned. But my guess is still that he will try to escape by motor vehicle.

"I shall therefore take five men to the French border with me while Major Valchek will take another five to Basle to cover the German crossing point. The rest of you will remain on surveillance in Geneva. Those of you who have just arrived will relieve those agents who are in the field already. And don't expect Scott to be roaming around looking like a tourist on holiday. Study your picture of the Englishman carefully and even be prepared for him to try and get away with some amateur disguise."

Romanov paused for effect. "The man who brings me the Tsar's icon need have no fear for his future prosperity when we return home." Hopeful expressions appeared on their faces for the first time as Romanov pulled out the duplicate icon from his coat pocket and held it high above his head for all to see.

"When you find the original of this your task will be completed. Study it carefully, Comrades, because no photographs are being issued. And remember," Romanov added, "the only difference between this and Scott's icon is that his has a small silver crown embedded in the back of the frame. Once you see the crown you will know that you have found the missing masterpiece."

Romanov put the icon back in his pocket and looked down at the silent men.

"Remember that Scott is good but he's not that good."

CHAPTER THIRTEEN

"You're not bad, Scott, not bad at all," said Robin, who had remained standing by the double bass throughout Adam's story. "Either you're one hell of a liar, or I've lost my touch." Adam smiled up at the massive girl, who made the bow she was holding in her right hand look like a toothpick.

"Am I permitted to see this icon, or am I just supposed to take your word for it?"

Adam jumped off the bed and pulled out the package containing the Tsar's icon from the map pocket of his trenchcoat. Robin put her double bass up against the wall and leaving the bow propped against it, lowered herself into the only chair in the room.

Adam handed the icon over to her. For some time, she stared at the face of St George without making any comment. "It's magnificent," she said at last. "And I can understand anyone wanting to possess it. But no painting could be worth the tragedy and trouble you've had to go through."

"I agree it's inexplicable," said Adam. "But Rosenbaum or whatever his real name is has been willing to kill twice to get his hands on the piece, and he's already convinced me that as long as I am in possession of the icon then I'll be the next in line."

Robin continued to stare at the tiny pieces of gold, red, blue and yellow that made up St George and the Dragon.

"No other clues?" she asked, looking up.

"Only the letter given to my father by Goering."

Robin turned the painting over. "What does that mean?" she asked, pointing to the tiny silver crown embedded in the wood.

"That proves it was once owned by a Tsar, according to the man from Sotheby's. And greatly enhances its value, he assured me."

"Still couldn't be worth killing for," said Robin. She handed the icon back to Adam. "So what other secret is St George keeping to himself?"

Adam shrugged and frowned, having asked himself the same question again and again since Heidi's death. He returned the silent saint to his trenchcoat.

"What was to have been your plan if you had stayed awake?" asked Robin. "Other than making the bed?"

Adam smiled. "I hoped to call Lawrence again once I could be sure he had returned home and check if he had any more news for me. If he wasn't back, or couldn't help, I was going to hire a car and try to get across the Swiss border to France and then on to England. I felt sure that between Rosenbaum and his men and the Swiss police they would have had all the airports and stations fully covered."

"No doubt Rosenbaum will have also thought that much out as well, if he's half as good as you claim," said Robin. "So we'd better try and get in touch with your friend Lawrence and see if he's come up with any bright ideas." She pushed herself up out of the chair and walked across to the phone.

"You don't have to get yourself involved," said Adam hesitantly.

"I am involved," said Robin. "And I can tell you it's far more exciting than Schubert's Unfinished. Once I've got your friend on the line I'll pass him over to you and then no one will realise who's phoning." Adam told her the number of the flat and she asked the girl on the switchboard to connect her.

Adam checked his watch: eleven forty. Surely Lawrence would be home by now? The phone didn't complete its first two rings before Robin heard a man's voice on the line. She immediately handed the receiver over.

"Hello, who is that?" asked the voice. Adam was reminded how strange he always found it that Lawrence never announced his name.

"Lawrence, it's me."

"Where are you?"

"I'm still in Geneva."

"My clients were waiting for you at eleven o'clock this morning."

"So was Rosenbaum."

"Who is Rosenbaum?"

"A six-foot, fair-haired, blue-eyed monster, who seems determined to kill me."

Lawrence did not speak for some time. "And are you still in possession of our patron saint?"

"Yes, I am," said Adam. "But what can be so important about . . ."

"Put the phone down and ring me back again in three minutes."

The line went dead. Adam couldn't fathom the sudden change in his old friend's manner. What had he missed during those months he had lodged with him? He tried to recall details that he had previously considered unimportant and that Lawrence had so skilfully disguised.

"Is everything all right?" asked Robin, breaking into his thoughts.

"I think so," said Adam, a little mystified. "He wants me to ring back in three minutes. Will that be all right with you?"

"This tour's already lost eight thousand pounds of the taxpayers' money, so what difference can a few international calls make?" she said.

Three minutes later, Robin picked up the receiver and repeated the number. In one ring Lawrence was back on the line.

"Only answer my questions," said Lawrence.

"No, I will not answer your questions," said Adam, becoming increasingly annoyed with Lawrence's manner. "I want one or two of my own answered before you get anything more out of me. Do I make myself clear?"

"Yes," said a more gentle sounding Lawrence.

"Who is Rosenbaum?"

Lawrence didn't immediately reply.

"You'll get nothing further from me until you start telling the truth," said Adam.

"From your description I have every reason to believe Rosenbaum is a Russian agent whose real name is Alex Romanov."

"A Russian agent? But why should a Russian agent want to get his hands on my icon?"

"I don't know," said Lawrence. "We were rather hoping you might be able to tell us."

"Who's we?"

Another long silence.

"Who's we?" repeated Adam. "You can't really expect me to go on believing you work for Barclays DCO."

"I work at the Foreign Office," said Lawrence.

"In what capacity?"

216

"I am not at liberty . . ."

"Stop being so pompous, Lawrence. In what capacity?"

"I'm the Number Two in a small section that deals in . . ." Lawrence hesitated.

"Espionage I think is the current jargon we laymen are using," said Adam, "and if you want my icon that badly you had better get me out of this mess alive because Romanov is willing to kill for it as I am sure you are aware."

"Where are you?"

"The Richemond Hotel."

"In a public phone box?" asked Lawrence, sounding incredulous.

"No, in a private room."

"But not registered in your name?"

"No, in the name of a friend. A girlfriend."

"Is she with you now?" asked Lawrence.

"Yes," said Adam.

"Damn," said Lawrence. "Right. Don't leave that room until seven a.m., then phone on this number again. That will give me enough time to get everything in place."

"Is that the best you can do?" said Adam, but the phone had already gone dead. "It looks as if I'm stuck with you for the night," he told Robin as he replaced the phone.

"On the contrary, it is I who am stuck with you," said Robin, and disappeared into the bathroom. Adam paced around the room several times before he tested the sofa. Either he had to rest his head on a cushion, balanced on the thin wooden arm, or he had to let his legs dangle over the far end. By the time Robin had come back out clad in a pair of sky-blue pyjamas he had selected the floor as his resting place.

"Not much of a chair, is it?" said Robin. "But then British Intelligence didn't warn me to book a double room." She climbed into the bed and turned out the light. "Very comfortable," were the last words she uttered.

Adam lay down flat on the bedroom floor, using the cushion from the chair as a pillow and a hotel dressing gown as a blanket. He slept intermittently, his mind switching between why the icon could be that important, how Lawrence knew so much about it, and, most immediate, how the hell were they going to get him out of the hotel alive?

Romanov waited patiently for the phone to be picked up.

"Yes," said a voice that he recognised immediately.

"Where is he?" were the only words Romanov uttered. Four words were all he received from Mentor in reply before the phone went dead.

Adam woke with a start an hour before he was due to phone Lawrence back. For nearly forty minutes he lay on the floor with only Robin's steady breathing to remind him he was not alone. Suddenly he became aware of a strange sound coming from the corridor outside – two or three steps, a pause, then whoosh, two or three steps, a pause, another whoosh. Adam raised himself up silently from the floor and crept to the door. The rhythm of Robin's breathing never faltered. Whoosh: it now sounded closer. He picked up a heavy wooden coathanger from the table by the door. He gripped it firmly in his right hand, raised it above his head and waited. Whoosh – and a newspaper shot under the door and the steps moved on. He didn't have to bend down to see that it was his photograph that dominated the front page of the international edition of the *Herald Tribune*.

Adam took the paper into the bathroom, closed the door silently, switched on the light and read the lead article. It was yesterday's story with guarded comments from his old commanding officer and embarrassed silence from his mother. He felt helpless.

He crept up to Robin hoping she wouldn't wake. He stood over her but she didn't stir. He silently picked up the phone and dragged it to the bathroom. He could only just manage to close the door behind him. He dialled the operator and repeated the number.

When the ringing stopped, he immediately said, "Is that you, Lawrence?"

"Yes," came back the reply.

"Things have become much worse now. I'm still holed up in the hotel but my picture is on the front page of every paper."

"I know," said Lawrence. "We tried to prevent it, but yet again the Swiss wouldn't co-operate."

"Then I may as well give myself up to the Swiss," said Adam. "Damn it all, I am innocent."

"No, Adam, in Switzerland you're guilty until proven innocent and you must have worked out by now that you're involved in something far more important than a double murder."

"What could be more important than a double murder when the rest of the world thinks you're the murderer?" asked Adam angrily.

"I can understand exactly how you feel, but your only chance now is to carry out my instructions to the letter and treat with suspicion every other person with whom you come in contact."

"I'm listening," said Adam.

"Just remember everything I say because I am only going to tell you once. The Royal Philharmonic Orchestra are staying in the same hotel as you. They are going on to Frankfurt at ten o'clock this morning. Leave your room at five to ten, join the orchestra in the lobby and then make your way to the front door where you'll find their coach parked. We will have a car waiting for you on the far side of the road. The car is a black Mercedes and you will see a man in grey chauffeur's uniform holding the door open for you. We have already arranged that no other car will be able to park on that side of the road between nine thirty and ten thirty, so you can't mistake it. Just get into the back and wait. There will be another man in the back with you and you will then be driven to the safety of our Consulate. Do you need me to repeat any of that?"

"No," said Adam, "but . . ."

"Good luck," said Lawrence, and the phone went dead.

By seven-thirty he had showered, while Robin remained unrepentant in a deep sleep. Adam envied her; only a twig had to break outside and he was wide awake. Two years of living in the Malayan jungle, never knowing when the Chinese would strike, never being able to sleep for more than two or three hours at a time if one wanted to stay alive, still kept its hold on him.

Robin did not stir for another thirty minutes, during which time Adam sat on the sofa and went over Lawrence's plan in his mind. At ten to eight she finally woke, even then taking several minutes before she was fully conscious. Robin blinked at Adam and a large grin appeared on her face.

"So you didn't murder me while I slept," she said.

"I don't think you'd have noticed if I had," said Adam.

"When your father is an habitual drunk and comes home at all hours of the night, you learn to sleep through anything," she explained, placing both feet firmly on the carpet. "Aren't you meant to have phoned London by now?"

"I already have."

"And what is the master plan to be?" she asked, rubbing her eyes on her way to the bathroom.

"I will be leaving with you," said Adam.

"Most of my one-night stands don't bother to stay that long," she remarked as she closed the bathroom door behind her. He tried to read the paper while the bath was filling up.

"Does that mean we're sharing a room in Frankfurt as well?" she asked a few minutes later when the bathroom door reopened, as if the conversation had never been interrupted.

"No, as soon as we're clear of the hotel I leave you at the coach and make my own way to a car on the far side of the road."

"That sounds more like the men in my life," she said. "But at least we can have a farewell breakfast," she added, picking up the phone. "I'm nuts about kippers. How about you?"

Adam didn't answer. He had begun looking at his watch every few moments. The waiter arrived with breakfast about fifteen minutes later: Adam waited in the bathroom. When he reappeared he showed no interest in the food, so Robin ate four kippers and most of the toast. Nine o'clock passed; a porter took away the breakfast trolley and Robin began to pack. The phone rang and Adam jumped nervously as Robin picked it up.

"Yes, Stephen," she said. "No, I won't need any help with my luggage. Not this time." She put the phone down. "We depart for Frankfurt at ten."

"I know," said Adam.

"We ought to make Lawrence the orchestra manager. He seems to know everything even before it's been decided." Adam had been thinking the same thing. "Well, at least I've found someone to help with my luggage for a change," added Robin.

"I'll carry the double bass for you if you like," offered Adam.

"I'd like to see you try," said Robin. Adam walked over to the large instrument that was propped up in its case against the wall. He tried the double bass from all angles but couldn't manage to do better than hold it off the floor for a few moments. Robin joined him and with one flick she had the stem on her shoulder and the instrument balanced perfectly. She walked up and down the bedroom demonstrating her prowess.

"It's a matter of skill, my puny friend," she said. "And to think I believed all those stories last night about your outrunning half the Swiss police force to spend a night with me."

Adam tried to laugh. He picked up his trenchcoat, checking the icon was zipped up. But he couldn't stop himself shaking from a combination of fear and anticipation.

Robin looked at him. "Don't worry," she said gently. "It will all be over in a few minutes' time." Then she saw the paper on the floor. "I should sue them if I were you."

"Why?" asked Adam.

"You're a lot better looking than that." Adam smiled and walked across, and just managed to get his arms round her to give her a hug.

"Thanks for everything," he said. "But now we have to go."

"You're sounding more like one of my lovers all the time," said Robin, mournfully.

Adam picked up her suitcase while Robin jerked up the stem of the double bass onto her shoulder. She opened the door and checked the corridor: two of her colleagues from the RPO were waiting by the lift, otherwise there was nobody else in sight. Robin and Adam joined the two musicians and after "Good mornings" no one spoke until the lift doors slid open. Once the doors were closed Robin's colleagues couldn't resist taking a closer look at Adam. At first Adam was anxious they had recognised him from the newspaper. Then he realised that it was who Robin had spent the night with that fascinated them. Robin gave him a lewd wink, as if she fully intended to live off this one for a long time. For his part Adam ducked behind the double bass and remained in the corner breathing deeply in and out as the lift trundled down towards the ground floor. The doors sprang open and Robin waited for her two colleagues to leave before she shielded Adam as best she could all the way across the foyer. His eyes were now fixed on the front door. He could see the bus taking up most of the road and several members of the orchestra were already clambering on. One more minute and he should be safely away. He watched as the drums were packed carefully in the large boot.

"Oh, God, I forgot," said Robin. "I'm meant to put this in the boot at the back of the bus."

"Do it later," said Adam sharply. "Just keep going until you reach the coach door." Then he saw the car on the far side of the road. He felt light with relief, almost dizzy. The car door was being held open for him. Another man was seated in the back just as Lawrence had promised. Ten o'clock struck somewhere in the distance. The man dressed in chauffeur's uniform, hat pulled down over his forehead, stood by the open door. He turned towards the hotel in anticipation. Adam stared towards him as the man's eyes scanned the hotel entrance. The uniform wasn't a good fit.

"Into the bus," hissed Adam.

"With this thing? They'll kill me," said Robin.

"If you don't, he'll kill me."

Robin obeyed, despite the adverse comments as she lumbered down the aisle with her double bass screening Adam from the gaze of anyone on the far side of the road. He wanted to be sick.

Adam slumped into a seat next to Robin with the double bass between them.

"Which one?" she whispered.

"In the chauffeur's uniform."

Robin glanced out of the window. "He may be evil, but he's damned good looking," she said, inconsequentially.

Adam looked disbelieving. Robin smiled apologetically.

"Everybody's in," called a man from the front of the bus, "and I've double-checked and we seem to have one extra."

Oh, my God, thought Adam, he's going to throw me off the bus.

"My brother," shouted Robin from the back. "He's only travelling with us for part of the journey."

"Oh, that's okay then," said the manager. "Well, let's be on our way." He turned to the driver.

"He's started looking at the bus," said Robin.

"But I don't think he can see you. No, you're all right, he's now turned his gaze back to the hotel entrance."

"I didn't realise you had a brother," said the manager, who was suddenly standing beside them. The coach moved slowly out of the square.

"Neither did I until this morning," mumbled Robin, still looking out of the window. She turned and faced her boss. "Yes, I forgot to mention to you that he might be in Switzerland at the same time as the orchestra. I do hope it's not going to cause a problem."

"Not at all," said the manager.

"Adam, this is Stephen Grieg who, as you will already have gathered, is the orchestra's manager."

"Are you a musician as well?" asked Stephen as he shook Adam's hand.

"No, I can truthfully say that I have never been able to master any instrument," said Adam.

"He's tone deaf," butted in Robin. "Takes after my father. He's in tyres, actually," she continued, enjoying herself.

"Oh, really. Which company are you with?" enquired Stephen.

"I'm with Pirelli," said Adam, mentioning the first tyre company that came into his head.

"Pirelli, the company that produces those fabulous calendars?"

"What's so special about their calendars?" asked Robin innocently. "If you want one I'm sure Adam can get you one."

"Oh, that would be great," said Stephen. "I hope it won't put you to too much trouble."

"No trouble at all," said Robin, leaning over Adam conspiratorially. "Actually, to let you in on a little family secret there is a rumour at HQ that Adam will soon be joining the main board. The youngest member in the company's history, you know."

"How impressive," said the manager, taking a closer look at the orchestra's latest recruit.

"Where shall I send the calendar?" bleated out Adam.

"Oh, direct to the RPO. No need to tell you the address, is there?"

"In a brown envelope, no doubt," said Robin. "And don't worry about the year. It's not the dates that he gets worked up about."

"What time are we expecting to reach Frankfurt, Stephen?" shouted a voice from the front. "Must leave you now," said the manager. "Thanks for the promise of a calendar. Robin's right, of course – any year will do."

"Who taught you to spin a yarn like that?" asked Adam, as soon as he was out of earshot.

"My father," said Robin. "You should have heard him at his best. In a class of his own. The problem was my mother still believed every word."

"He would have been proud of you today."

"Now we've found out what you do for a living," said Robin, "may we learn what's next on the agenda for the youngest director of Pirelli?"

Adam smiled. "I've started trying to reason like Rosenbaum, and I think he'll stay in Geneva for at least an hour, two at the most, so with luck I'll get a fifty-mile start on him." He unfolded the map across the two seats.

His finger ran along the road the bus was travelling on, and it was Robin who spoke first.

"That means you could make Zurich airport before he has any chance of catching up with you."

"Perhaps," said Adam, "but that would be too much

of a risk. Whoever Rosenbaum is," he went on, abiding by Lawrence's request to be cautious by not letting Robin into his secret, "we now know for certain that he has a professional organisation behind him so I must expect the airports to be the first place he will have covered. And don't forget the Swiss police are still on the lookout for me as well."

"So why don't you come on to Frankfurt with us?" asked Robin. "I can't believe you'll have any trouble from Stephen."

"I've thought about that already but discounted it also as too great a risk," said Adam.

"Why?"

"Because, when Rosenbaum has had time to think about it," said Adam, "the one thing he'll remember is this bus. Once he's found out the direction we're heading in he's sure to come after us."

Robin's eyes returned to the map. "So you'll need to decide where and when to get off."

"Exactly," whispered Adam. "I can risk sixty to seventy miles, but not a lot further."

Robin's finger ran along the little road. "About here," she said, her finger stopping on a little town called Solothurn.

"Looks about the right distance."

"But once you're off the bus what will you do for transport?"

"I've little choice but to walk or thumb lifts – unless I pinch another car."

"With your luck, Rosenbaum will be the one person who stops to pick you up."

"Yes, I've thought about that as well," said Adam. "I would have to find a long stretch of road where I can see without being seen for about one hundred yards, and then thumb lifts only from British cars or cars with British number plates."

"They taught you a trick or two in the army, didn't they?" said Robin. "But how do you intend to cross the frontier with your passport?"

"That's one of the many problems I haven't yet come up with a solution for."

"If you decide to stay with us," said Robin, "it wouldn't be a problem."

"Why?" asked Adam.

"Because whenever we cross a border they only count the number of people on the bus and the number of passports, and as long as they tally the customs officials don't bother to check everyone individually. After all, why should they? The RPO is not exactly an unknown quantity. All I would have to do is add your passport to the bundle and mention it to the manager."

"It's a clever idea but it's not on. If Rosenbaum caught up with me while I'm still on this bus then I would be left with no escape route."

Robin was silent for a moment. "Once you're on your own will you contact Lawrence again?"

"Yes. I've got to let him know what happened this morning, because whoever he's dealing with must have a direct line to Rosenbaum."

"Could it be Lawrence himself?"

"Never," said Adam.

"Your loyalty is touching," said Robin, turning to look at him, "but what you actually mean is you don't want to believe it could be Lawrence."

"What are you getting at?"

"Like my mother didn't want to believe that my father was a liar and a drunk. So she turned a blind eye to his little foibles. You know even when he dropped dead of cirrhosis of the liver, her only words were, 'strange for a man who never drank'."

Adam thought about his relationship with Lawrence and wondered if you could know someone for twenty years and really not know them at all.

"Just be wary how much you let him know," advised Robin.

They sat in silence as Adam checked the map and went over all the different possible routes he could take once he had left the bus. He decided to aim for the German border and take the long route back to England, from Hamburg or Bremerhaven, rather than the shorter, more obvious route via Calais or Ostend.

"Got it," said Robin suddenly.

"Got what?" said Adam, looking up from the map.

"How we solve your passport problem," she murmured.

Adam glanced at her hopefully. "If you let me have your passport," she explained, "I'll substitute it for the member of the orchestra who most resembles you. No one will notice anything strange at our end until we're back home in Britain on Sunday night."

"Not a bad idea, if there is anyone who remotely resembles me."

"We'll have to see what we can do," said Robin. She sat bolt upright, her eyes moving slowly from person to person. By the time she had scanned all those in the bus from front to back, a small smile appeared on her face. "There are two of our lot who bear a passable resemblance to you. One is about five years older and the other is four inches shorter, but you go on working out the safest way of escape while I carry out some research. Let me have your passport," she said. Adam handed it over and then watched Robin walk up to the front and sit next to the manager. He was chatting to the driver about the most convenient place to stop for lunch.

"I need to check something in my passport," Robin broke in. "Sorry to bother you."

"No bother. You'll find them all under my seat in a plastic bag," he said, and continued his conversation with the driver.

Robin bent down and started to shuffle through the passports as if searching for her own. She picked out the two she had considered as possible substitutes and compared the photographs. The shorter man's photo looked nothing like Adam. The older man's was at least five years out of date but could have passed for Adam as long as the officials didn't study the date of birth too carefully. She bundled up the passports, placing Adam's in the middle. She then put them back in the plastic bag and returned the bag under the manager's seat.

Robin made her way back to her seat. "Take a look at yourself," she said, slipping the passport over to Adam. He studied the photo.

"Other than the moustache, not a bad likeness, and it's certainly my best chance in the circumstances. But what will happen when you return to London and they find out my passport has been substituted?"

"You'll be back in England long before us," said Robin. "So put this one in an envelope with the calendar and send it direct to the RPO in Wigmore Street, W1, and I'll see that they return yours." Adam vowed to himself that if he ever got back to London, he would become a life subscriber to the Friends of the Royal Philharmonic.

"That seems to have solved one of your problems."

"For the moment at least," said Adam. "I only wish I could take you with me for the rest of the trip."

Robin smiled. "Frankfurt, Berlin, Amsterdam – just in case you get bored. I wouldn't mind meeting up with Rosenbaum. But this time face to face."

"He might just have met his match," said Adam.

"Can I have a last look at the icon?" Robin asked, ignoring the comment.

Adam bent down to retrieve his trenchcoat and slipped the painting out of his map pocket, careful to shield it from anyone else's view. Robin stared into the eyes of St George before she spoke again. "When I lay awake last night waiting for you to ravish me, I passed the time trying to fathom out what secret the icon held."

"I thought you were asleep," said Adam smiling. "When all along we were both doing the same thing. Anyway, did you come up with any worthwhile conclusions?"

"First, I decided your taste was for male double bass players," said Robin, "or how else could you have resisted me?"

"But what about St George and the Dragon?" asked Adam, grinning.

"To begin with I wondered if the little pieces of mosaic made up a code. But the picture is so magnificently executed that the code would have to have been worked out afterwards. And that didn't seem credible."

"Good thinking, Batman."

"No, you're Batman. So I wondered if there was another painting underneath. I remembered from my schooldays that Rembrandt and Constable often painted on the top of their paintings, either because they didn't care for their original effort or because, in the case of Rembrandt, he couldn't afford another canvas."

"If that were the answer only an expert could have

carried out the task of removing every piece of paint."

"Agreed," said Robin. "So I dismissed that as well. My third idea was that the crown on the back" – she turned the icon over and stared at the little piece of silver embedded in the wood – "indicates as your expert suggested that this is the original by Rublev and not a copy as you have been led to believe."

"I had already considered that," said Adam, "during my sleepless night and although it would place a far higher value on the work, it is still not enough to explain why Rosenbaum would kill indiscriminately for it."

"Perhaps someone else needs St George every bit as much as Rosenbaum does," said Robin.

"But who and why?"

"Because it's not the icon they're after, but something else. Something hidden in or behind the painting."

"That was the first thing I checked," said Adam smugly. "And I'm convinced that it's a solid piece of wood."

"I don't agree with you," said Robin as she began tapping the wood all over like a doctor examining someone's chest. "I've worked with instruments all my life, watched them being made, played with them, even slept with them, and this icon is not solid right through, though God knows how I can prove it. If something is hidden inside it was never intended to be discovered by laymen like ourselves."

"Quite an imaginative little thing, aren't you?" said Adam.

"Comes naturally," she said as she handed the icon back to Adam. "Do let me know if you ever discover what is inside," she added.

"When I get five minutes to myself I might even

spend some time on one or two of my own theories," said Adam, returning the icon to his trenchcoat pocket.

"Two more kilometres to Solothurn," said Robin, pointing out of the window at a signpost.

Adam buttoned up his coat. "I'll see you off," she said, and they both made their way up the aisle. When Adam reached the front of the coach he asked the driver if he could drop him off just before they reached the next village.

"Sure thing," said the driver without looking back.

"Leaving us so soon?" said Stephen.

"Afraid so," said Adam. "But thanks for the lift. And I won't forget the calendar." The driver pulled into a lay-by, pressed a knob and the hydraulic doors swung back.

"Bye, Robin," said Adam, giving her a brotherly kiss on the cheek.

"Goodbye, baby brother," said Robin. "Give my love to mother if you see her before I do." She smiled and waved at him as the door swung closed and the coach returned to the highway to continue its journey on to Frankfurt.

Adam was on his own again.

CHAPTER FOURTEEN

Professor Brunweld was rarely treated with any respect. It was the fate of academics, he had long ago concluded. The 'President' was all they had said and he had wondered if he should believe it. Certainly they had got him out of bed in the middle of the night and escorted him silently to the Pentagon. They wanted Brunweld's expert opinion, they had assured him. Could it be possible? After Cuba and Dallas he'd begun to believe anything was possible.

He had once read that the Pentagon had as many floors below the ground as there were above it. He could now confirm that as an established fact.

Once they had handed him the document they left him alone. They only wanted one question answered. He studied the clauses for over an hour and then called them back. It was, he told them, in his opinion, authentic and if the Russians were still in possession of their copy, also signed in 1867, then his adopted country was – what was that awful American expression? Ah, yes – in all sorts of trouble.

He began to realise how serious it was when they told him that he would not be allowed to leave the Pentagon until Monday. That didn't surprise him once he'd seen the date on the bottom of the treaty. So it was to be three days of solitude away from his demanding students and chattering wife. He would never have a better opportunity to settle down and read the collected works of Proust.

Romanov knew he couldn't risk standing by the side of the car for much longer. He was too conspicuously dressed not to be noticed by everyone who came out of the hotel. Three minutes later he thew his grey cap on the back seat and instructed Valchek to get rid of the car and then return to the Consulate.

Valchek nodded. He had already carried out Romanov's orders to kill the two British agents as if he had been asked to fix a burst water pipe. The only thing that hadn't run to plan was when Valchek tried to button up the dead chauffeur's uniform. Romanov thought he detected the suggestion of a smirk on Valchek's face when he realised who would have to be the chauffeur.

Romanov slipped into the shadows and waited for another half hour, by which time he was sure the plan must have been aborted from the London end. He hailed a taxi and asked the driver to take him to the Soviet Consulate. He didn't notice the taxi-driver's look of disbelief at his passenger's chauffeur-clad vision.

Could he really have lost Scott twice? Had he also underestimated him? Once more and Zaborski was going to require a very convincing explanation.

On his way back to the Consulate an image kept flashing across Romanov's mind, but he couldn't make any sense of it. Something had happened outside the hotel that didn't quite fit. If he could only think clearly for a moment he felt certain it would become clear to him. He kept playing the last thirty minutes over in his mind, as if rewinding the reel of an old film; but some of the frames still remained blurred.

Once Romanov was back in the Consulate Valchek handed him a large envelope which he was informed had just arrived in the diplomatic pouch from Moscow.

Romanov read over the decoded telex a second time, still unable to fathom its possible significance.

"Information has come to light concerning the late Colonel Gerald Scott, DSO, OBE, MC, that may prove useful when you make contact with your quarry. Full documentation will be with you by morning, latest, A1."

Romanov wondered what headquarters had discovered about Scott's father that could possibly prove of interest to him. It was still his avowed intention that the son would be despatched to join the father long before any further missive from Moscow had arrived.

Romanov thought of his own father and the escape route he had made possible by leaving such a fortune, and how for the sake of advancement he had betrayed him to the State. Now, for the sake of further advancement he had to kill Scott and bring home the icon. If he failed . . . He dismissed both fathers.

"Either he's very clever or he's living on an amateur's luck," Romanov said, moving into the small office that had been made available for his use. Valchek who followed him did not comment other than to ask what he should do next.

"Tell me what you saw when we were at the hotel."

"What do you mean?" asked Valchek.

"Don't ask questions," said Romanov, changing back into his own clothes, "answer them. Tell me everything you remember seeing, from the moment we drew up outside the hotel."

"We arrived at the Richmond a few minutes before ten," began Valchek, "parked the Mercedes on the far side of the road, and waited for Scott to show up. We stayed put for a few minutes after ten but Scott never materialised."

"No, no, no. Be more specific. Don't just generalise. For instance, do you remember anything unusual taking place while we were waiting?"

"Nothing in particular," said Valchek. "People continually entering and leaving the hotel – but I'm sure Scott wasn't among them."

"You are fortunate to be so certain. What happened next?" asked Romanov.

"Next? You instructed me to go back to the Consulate and wait for you to return."

"What time was that?"

"It must have been about seven minutes past ten. I remember because I checked my watch when that coach left."

"The coach?" said Romanov.

"Yes, the one that was being loaded up with musical instruments. It left about . . ."

"Instruments, that's it," said Romanov. "Now I remember what was worrying me. Cellos, violins, and a double bass that didn't go into the boot." Valchek looked puzzled but said nothing. "Ring the hotel immediately and find out who was on that bus and where they are heading." Valchek scurried away.

Romanov checked his watch: ten fifty-five. We are going to have to move, and move quickly. He pressed the intercom by the side of the phone. "I want a fast car, and more important, a superb driver." Valchek returned as Romanov replaced the receiver. "The bus was hired by the Royal Philharmonic Orchestra, who are on a European tour . . ."

"Where are they heading next?" asked Romanov.
"Frankfurt."

He strolled away from the village, having checked everything with a professional soldier's eye. The main street was deserted but for a little boy who relentlessly kicked a plastic football into a gap in the hillside which he was using as a goal. The boy turned when he saw Adam and kicked the ball towards him. Adam kicked it back and the boy took it in his arms, a wide smile appearing on his face. The smile disappeared as he watched Adam continue quickly up the hill. There were only a few old houses on the main road. On one side was a dangerous ravine with tree-covered hills rising in the distance, while on the other side stretched green fields in which cows, bells round their necks, munched happily away. It made Adam feel hungry.

He went further up the road until he came to a sharp bend in the hill. Standing on the corner he could see down the hill for about half a mile without being seen. He tested the feasibility of his plan for several minutes and soon became expert at picking out British cars or cars with British number plates as far as two or three hundred yards away. It didn't take long to work out how few foreigners bought British.

During the next twenty minutes he thumbed optimistically at seven cars with English number plates heading towards Lausanne, but they all ignored him. He had forgotten just how easy it had been for him when he was a cadet in uniform. In those days almost everyone would stop. He checked his watch: he could only risk it for a few more minutes. Three more cars refused to pull up and when a fourth slowed down it only sped away again as Adam ran towards it.

By eleven twenty Adam decided he could no longer

chance being seen on the road. He stared down the ravine, realising there was no alternative left open to him now but to travel by foot. He shrugged and began to climb down one of the steep trails that led into the valley, in the hope of meeting up with the other road that was marked clearly on the map.

He cursed when he looked at the open ground between him and safety. If only he'd started an hour earlier.

"I fear Antarctic has become expendable."

"Why?"

"Because we now know his father was involved in helping Goering to an easy death."

"I don't understand."

"No reason why you should although it's quite simple. That patriotic stiff-upper-lipped Englishman of yours is the son of the bastard who smuggled a cyanide capsule into Goering's cell at Nuremberg. His reward for services rendered turns out to be the Tsar's icon."

"But all the members of D4 are convinced that he's our only hope."

"I don't give a damn what your D4 thinks. If the father would side with the Germans during a war, why shouldn't the son side with the Russians in peace?"

"Like father, like son."

"Precisely."

"So what am I expected to do?"

"Just keep us briefed as to what the Foreign Office is up to. Our agents in Switzerland will do the rest."

"Faster!" said Romanov, aware that it was not possible as the Ambassador's driver was proving to be a consummate professional. Not once did Romanov feel that he had missed a gap, a light, a chance to overtake. In fact another five kilometres an hour on the speedometer might well have seen them over the precipice. The moment they were on the highway, with full lights blazing and the driver's hand almost lodged on the horn, the speedometer rarely fell below 130 kilometres an hour. "We must beat them to the border," he kept repeating as he thumped his fist on the leather dashboard. After they had covered one hundred kilometres in fifty-five minutes, the three men began watching ahead of them for the coach, but it was another thirty kilometres before Valchek was able to point ahead and shout, "That must be them, about a kilometre up the hill."

"Force them off the road," said Romanov, his eyes never leaving the bus. The Embassy driver swung out to overtake and once he was in front immediately cut across, forcing the coach driver to throw on his brakes and swerve into the side. Valchek waved dictatorially at the coach driver to slow down and the man stopped the vehicle just off the road on the edge of the mountain.

"Don't either of you speak. Just leave everything to me," said Romanov, "and remain near the driver in case there's trouble." Romanov jumped out of the car and ran towards the coach, his eyes already searching for anyone who might be attempting to leave it. He banged on the door impatiently until the driver pressed a knob and the big doors swung open. Romanov leapt on, with the other two following only paces behind. He took out his passport from an inside pocket, flashed it in the frightened driver's face and shouted, "Who's in charge here?"

Stephen Grieg stood up. "I am the manager of the company, and I can . . ."

"Swiss police," said Romanov. Grieg was about to ask a question when Romanov said, "When you left your hotel in Geneva this morning, did you take on any extra passengers?"

"No," said Grieg. Romanov scowled. "Unless you count Robin Beresford's brother."

"Robin Beresford's brother?" enquired Romanov, his eyebrows raising interrogatively.

"Yes," said the manager. "Adam Beresford. But he only travelled with us as far as Solothurn. Then he got off."

"Which one of you is Robin?" said Romanov, staring around a sea of men's faces.

"I am," piped up a voice from the back. Romanov marched down the bus and saw the double bass case and then everything fitted into place. It always worried him when something was out of context. Yes, that was what hadn't rung true. Why hadn't she put the double bass in the boot with all the other large instruments? He stared down at the heavy-framed woman who now sat behind the monstrous instrument.

"Your brother is the one called Adam?"

"Yes," said Robin.

"Quite a coincidence."

"I don't understand what you mean," she said, trying not to sound nervous.

"The man I am looking for just happens to be called Adam as well."

"Common enough name," said Robin. "Perhaps you've never read the first chapter of the Bible?"

"Six foot one inch, perhaps two inches, dark hair, dark eyes, slim and fit. Not a convincing brother for you," added Romanov studying her frame.

Robin pushed back her red hair but didn't rise. Romanov could sense from the nervous expressions on the faces around him that it was Scott who had been on the bus.

"Where was your *brother*," he emphasised the word, "intending to go once he had left the coach?" Romanov asked, tapping his passport against his other hand, like a baton.

"I have no idea," said Robin, still not changing her expression from one of uninterested politeness.

"I will give you one more chance to co-operate with me. Where was your brother heading?"

"And I'll tell you once more, I don't know."

"If you refuse to answer my questions," said Romanov, "I shall have to arrest you."

"On whose authority?" asked Robin calmly.

Romanov considered showing her his passport but realised that this girl was sharper than either the driver or the manager.

"With the authority of the Swiss police," Romanov said confidently.

"Then no doubt you'll be happy to show me proof of your identity."

"Don't be insolent," Romanov said sharply. He towered over her.

"It is you who are insolent," said Robin, standing up. "You drive in front of our coach like a lunatic, nearly sending us down the mountain, then the three of you burst in like a bunch of Chicago mobsters, claiming to be Swiss police. I have no idea who you are or what you are, but I'll let you into two secrets. You touch me and there are forty men on this coach who will beat you and your two cronies to pulp. And even if you managed to get off this bus alive, we are members of the Royal Philharmonic Orchestra of Great Britain, and as such are guests of the Swiss Government. In a few moments when we cross the border, we will become guests of the West German Government, so you're about to get yourself on to every front page in the world. Single-handedly, you will bring a totally new meaning to the words 'diplomatic incident'." She leaned forward and pointing a finger at him said, "So I'm telling you, whoever you are, in as ladylike fashion as I can, 'piss off'."

Romanov stood staring at her for some moments and then backed away as Robin's eyes remained glued on him. When he reached the front he waved at Valchek and the chauffeur, indicating that they should leave the coach. Reluctantly they obeyed him. The coach driver closed the door the moment Romanov's foot touched the ground and he quickly moved into first gear and drove back on to the highway.

The entire orchestra turned round and gave Robin the kind of ovation normally reserved for the entrance of the leader of the orchestra.

It went unappreciated. Robin had collapsed back into her seat, shaking uncontrollably, only too aware that not one of the forty men on that coach would have lifted a finger against Rosenbaum.

Sir Morris Youngfield glanced round the table: everyone was in place despite the few minutes' notice the head of D4 had given them.

"Let's hear the latest report," said Sir Morris, looking up at his Number Two, who was once again seated at the far end of the table.

"Not clever, sir, I'm afraid," began Lawrence. "Two of our most experienced agents were selected to pick up Scott at the Richmond Hotel as planned and then take him to the safety of the British Consulate."

"So what happened?" asked Sir Morris.

"No one at our Geneva office can be certain. Our men certainly never turned up at the hotel and they haven't been seen since."

"What are the Swiss police saying?" asked Busch.

"They are not being very helpful," said Lawrence, turning to the American. "They are aware that we are not the only foreign power involved and as is their custom in such circumstances, they have no intention of being seen to favour either side."

"Bloody Swiss," said Snell with feeling.

"And where do we imagine Scott is now?" asked Matthews.

"We've also drawn a blank on that," said Lawrence. Matthews smiled at Lawrence's embarrassment. "We feel certain he must have got on the coach with the girl –" he looked down at the sheet of paper on the table in front of him "– Robin Beresford. But he wasn't on it when we were waiting for them at the border. The orchestra is due at their Frankfurt hotel in about one hour so we will be able to find out more then. The German police are being far more co-operative," Lawrence added.

"Meanwhile what else are *we* doing?" asked Sir Morris.

"Checking all the usual places as well as keeping a close eye on Romanov who, incidentally, turned up on the French border last night. One of our old hands recognised him despite the fact that he's cut his hair very short; doesn't suit him, apparently."

"So Scott could be anywhere by now?" said Matthews. "Do you think he's still in Switzerland, or managed to cross one of the borders?"

Lawrence hesitated. "I have no idea," he said without expression.

Sir Morris stared at him from the far end of the table but didn't comment.

"Do you think he'll contact you again?" asked Snell.

"Almost certainly, if he's still alive."

"If Romanov is still in Switzerland, Scott *must* still be alive," said Busch. "Because the moment he gets his hands on the icon he will head east."

"Agreed," said Lawrence, "and we have men stationed at the airport checking every flight out to the East. I therefore suggest we follow up any further leads and assemble again tomorrow at seven a.m. unless Scott contacts me before then."

Sir Morris nodded and rose to leave. Everyone stood.

"Thank you, gentlemen," he said, and walked towards the far end of the room. As he passed Lawrence, he murmured, "Perhaps you could come to my office when you have a moment."

Adam slipped and stumbled the last few yards down the ravine before finally landing with a bump on his backside. His hands were cut and bleeding in several places, his trousers torn and smeared with clay and earth. He sat still for about two minutes trying to get his breath back as he looked back up towards the road. He had taken just under an hour to cover what a stone could have managed in three seconds. Still, there had been one advantage: no one could have seen him from the road. He gazed across the valley ahead. Anyone would be able to see him now, but he had left himself with no alternative.

Judge by eye, check by map. The map wasn't much help but he estimated the distance to the far ridge to be about two more miles. At least the map had promised him there was a road, hidden from sight on the other side of the ridge. He studied the terrain – rolling green fields, no hedgerows to shield him, and then one wide, shallow river. He reckoned he could cover the ground to the road in about twenty minutes. He checked that the icon was securely in place and then set off at an even pace.

Romanov had hardly uttered a word since the three men had been unceremoniously removed from the coach, and Valchek and the driver certainly hadn't ventured any opinions. Romanov knew the girl had called his bluff, and he couldn't afford a further diplomatic incident which would undoubtedly be reported back to his Chairman in Moscow. But Romanov would never forget the girl with the man's name.

Solothurn was about forty kilometres back in the direction they had already travelled, and the driver could have completed the journey in about twenty minutes had Romanov not insisted on slowing down as they passed every vehicle that travelled towards them. They checked the occupants of each vehicle on the other side of the road, just in case Scott had managed to thumb a lift. It was a necessary precaution in Romanov's judgment, but it meant a total time of thirty-one minutes before they arrived back in Solothurn. At least Romanov felt confident Scott wasn't heading for the German border – unless he had been very well disguised or travelled in the boot of a car.

As soon as they reached Solothurn Romanov instructed the driver to leave the car in the middle of the town while they split up to see if they could discover any clues as to the route Scott might have taken. None of the locals whom they questioned had seen anyone resembling Scott that morning, and Romanov was beginning to wonder which border he should now head for when he saw the driver kicking a football back to a little boy. Romanov ran down the hill and was about to remonstrate with him when the boy turned and kicked the ball hard at the Russian. Romanov trapped the ball automatically and kicked it firmly past the boy and into the goal. Romanov turned towards the driver and was about to shout at him when the ball re-appeared at his feet. He picked it up in anger and was going to throw it back at the boy when he saw his hopeful smile. Romanov held the ball high above his head. The boy ran up and jumped towards the ball but however hard he tried he couldn't reach it.

"Have you seen any strangers this morning?" he asked in slow deliberate German.

"Yes, yes," said the boy. "But he didn't score a goal."

"Where did he go?" asked Romanov.

"Up the hill," said the boy. To the child's dismay, Romanov dropped the ball and began to run. Valchek and the driver followed after him.

"*Nein, nein,*" cried the little boy who followed after them. Romanov looked back to see the boy was standing on the spot where Adam had been thumbing lifts, pointing out over the ravine.

Romanov quickly turned to the driver. "Get the car, I need the glasses and the map." The driver ran back down the hill once again followed by the boy. A few minutes later the Mercedes drew up by Romanov's side. The driver jumped out and handed the glasses over to Romanov, while Valchek spread a map out on the car bonnet.

Romanov focused the binoculars and began to sweep the hills in the distance. It was several minutes before the glasses stopped and settled upon a brown speck climbing up the farthest hill.

"The rifle," were Romanov's only words.

Valchek ran to the boot of the car and took out a Dragunov sniper's rifle with telescopic sights. He assembled the long, slim weapon with its distinctive wooden skeleton stock and checked that it was loaded. He then raised it, moved it around until it felt comfortable nestled in his shoulder and swept the ground in front of him until he too focused on Scott. Romanov followed Adam's relentless stride with the binoculars. Valchek's arm moved with him, keeping the same pace. "Kill him," said Romanov. Valchek was grateful for the clear windless day as he kept the rifle sight in the middle of the Englishman's back, waited for three more strides, then slowly squeezed the trigger. Adam had almost reached the top of the ridge when the bullet tore through him. He fell to the ground with a thud. Romanov smiled and lowered the glasses.

Adam knew exactly what had ripped through his shoulder and where the shot must have come from. He instinctively rolled over until he reached the nearest tree. And then the pain began. Although the bullet had lost a lot of its power at such a distance, it still stung like an adder's bite, and blood was already beginning to seep through his trenchcoat from the torn muscle. He turned his head and gazed back behind him. He could see no one but he knew Romanov must be standing there waiting to take a second shot.

Turning with difficulty, he looked back up towards the edge of the hill. Only thirty yards to the safety of the ridge, but he would have to run over the top, remaining exposed for several vital seconds. Even if he made it Romanov would still be able to reach him by car within thirty minutes.

Nevertheless, that was his one chance. Slowly, very slowly, he crawled inch by inch up the ridge, thankful for the tree that he could still use as protection. One arm followed one leg, like a beached crab. Once he had covered ten yards he knew the angle would be against him and Romanov would have a flat, slow-moving target to aim at. He moved four more lengths of his body and stopped.

You can't hold a rifle up on your shoulder for ever, Adam thought. He counted to two hundred slowly.

"I suspect he's going to make a run for it," Romanov told Valchek as he raised the glasses, "which will give you about three seconds. I'll shout the moment he moves." Romanov kept the glasses trained on the tree. Suddenly Adam jumped up and sprinted as though it were the last twenty metres of an Olympic final. Romanov shouted "Now" and Valchek pulled the rifle up into his shoulder, focused on the moving man and squeezed the trigger as Adam threw himself over the ridge. The second bullet whistled by the side of Adam's head.

Romanov cursed, as he stared through the binoculars, knowing that Valchek had missed. He turned to the open map. The others joined him around the car as he began to consider the alternatives. "He should reach that road in about ten minutes," he said, putting his finger in the middle of a small red line that ran between Neuchâtel and the French border. "Unless the first bullet hit him, in which case it could take him longer. So how long will it take you to get to that border?" Romanov asked the driver.

The chauffeur studied the map. "About twenty-five, at most thirty minutes, Comrade Major," came back the reply.

Romanov turned and looked back towards the hills. "Thirty minutes, Scott, that's how long you've got to live."

When the car sped away, the little boy ran home as fast as he could. He quickly told his mother everything he had seen. She smiled understandingly. Only children always had such vivid imaginations.

*   *   *

250

When Adam looked up, he was relieved to see the road was only about a mile away. He jogged towards it at a steady pace, but found that the running caused him even more discomfort. He was anxious to stop and check the wound but waited till he reached the road. The bullet had torn through the outer flesh of his shoulder muscle leaving him in considerable pain. An inch lower and he would have been unable to move. He was relieved to see that the blood had only made a small stain on his trenchcoat. He folded a handkerchief in four and placed it between his shirt and the wound. He knew he daren't risk a hospital. As long as he could get to a pharmacy by nightfall, he felt he could take care of the problem himself.

Adam checked the map. He was now only a few kilometres from the French border, and decided, because of the wound, to cross into France as quickly as possible rather than keep to his original plan of going up through Basle and on to Bremerhaven.

Desperately he began to thumb at any car that passed, no longer bothering with the nationality of the number plates. He felt he was safe for about twenty minutes but after that he would have to disappear back into the hills. Unfortunately there were far fewer cars driving towards the French border than there had been on the Basle road, and they all ignored his plea. He feared that the time was fast approaching for him to return to the hills when a yellow Citroën drew into the side of the road a few yards ahead of him.

By the time Adam had reached the car the woman in the passenger seat had already wound down the window.

"Where – are – you – going?" asked Adam, pronouncing each word slowly and carefully.

The driver leant across, took a lengthy look at Adam and said in a broad Yorkshire accent, "We're on our way to Dijon. Any use to you, lad?"

"Yes, please," said Adam, relieved that his scruffy appearance had not put them off.

"Then jump in the back with my daughter."

Adam obeyed. The Citroën moved off, as Adam checked out of the back window; he was relieved to see an empty road stretching out behind him.

"Jim Hardcastle's the name," said the man, as he moved the car into third gear. Jim appeared to have a large, warm smile perpetually imprinted on his chubby red face. His dark ginger hair went straight back and was plastered down with Brylcreem. He wore a Harris tweed jacket and an open-necked shirt that revealed a little red triangle of hair. It looked to Adam as if he had given up attempts to do anything about his waistline. "And this is the wife, Betty," he said, gesturing with his elbow towards the woman in the front seat. She turned towards Adam, revealing the same ruddy cheeks and warm smile. Her hair was dyed blonde but the roots remained an obstinate black. "And sitting next to you is our Linda," Jim Hardcastle added, almost as an afterthought. "Just left school and going to work for the local council, aren't you, Linda?" Linda nodded sulkily. Adam stared at the young girl whose first experiment with make-up hadn't worked that well. The dark over-lined eye shadow and the pink lipstick did not help what Adam considered was an attractive girl probably in her late teens. "And what's your name, lad?"

"Dudley Hulme," said Adam, recalling the name on his new passport. "And are you on holiday?" he asked, trying to keep his mind off the throbbing shoulder.

"Mixing business with pleasure," said Jim. "But this part of the trip is rather special for Betty and myself. We flew to Genoa on Saturday and hired the car to tour Italy. First we travelled up through the Simplon Pass. It's a bit breathtaking after our home town of Hull."

Adam would have asked for details, but Jim didn't reckon on any interruptions. "I'm in mustard, you see. Export director for Colman's, and we're on our way to the annual conference of the IMF. You may have heard of us." Adam nodded knowingly. "International Mustard Federation," Jim added. Adam wanted to laugh, but because of the pain in his shoulder, managed to keep a straight face.

"This year they've elected me President of the IMF, the high point of my career in mustard, you might say. And, if I may be so bold as to suggest, an honour for Colman's as well, the finest mustard in the world," he added, as if he said it at least a hundred times a day. "As President I have to preside over the conference meetings and chair the annual dinner. Tonight I shall be making a speech of welcome to delegates from all over the world."

"How fascinating," winced Adam, as the car went over a pothole.

"It certainly is," said Jim. "People have no idea how many makes of mustards there are." He paused for a second and then said, "One hundred and forty-three. There's no doubt the Frogs make one or two good attempts and even the Krauts don't do too badly, but there's still nothing to beat Colman's. British is best after all, I always say. Probably the same in your line of country," said Jim. "By the way, what is your line of country?"

"I'm in the army," said Adam.

"What's a soldier doing thumbing a lift on the borders of Switzerland?"

"Can I speak to you in confidence?" asked Adam.

"Mum's the word," said Jim. "We Hardcastles know how to keep our traps shut."

In the case of Jim's wife and daughter, Adam had no proof to the contrary.

"I'm a captain in the Royal Wessex, at present on a NATO exercise," began Adam. "I was dumped off the coast at Brindisi in Italy last Sunday with a false passport and ten English pounds. I have to be back in barracks at Aldershot by midnight Saturday." When he saw the look of approbation appear on Jim's face, he felt even Robin would have been proud of him. Mrs Hardcastle turned around to take a more careful look at him.

"I knew you were an officer the moment you opened your mouth," said Jim. "You couldn't have fooled me. I was a sergeant in the Royal Army Service Corps in the last war myself. Doesn't sound much, but I did my bit for the old country." The acronym for the Corps – 'Rob All Serving Comrades' – flashed through Adam's mind. "Have you seen any action yourself, Dudley?" Jim was asking.

"A little in Malaya," said Adam.

"I missed that one," said Jim. "After the big one was over, I went back into mustard. So where's the problem in getting you back to England?"

"There are about eight of us trying to reach Aldershot, and a thousand Americans trying to stop us."

"Yanks," said Jim with disdain. "They only join wars just as we're about to win them. All medals and glory, that lot. No, I mean is there any real problem?"

"Yes, the border officials have been briefed that eight British officers are attempting to get over into

France and the Swiss love to be the ones to pull us in. Only two officers out of twelve made it back to barracks last year," said Adam, warming to his own theme. "Both were promoted within weeks."

"The Swiss," said Jim. "They're even worse than the Americans. They don't even join in a war – happy to fleece both sides at the same time. They won't pick you up, lad, believe me. I'll see to that."

"If you can get me across the border, Mr Hardcastle, I'm confident I will be able to make it all the way back to Aldershot."

"Consider it done, lad."

The fuel indicator was flashing red. "How many kilometres left when that happens?" demanded Romanov.

"About twenty, Comrade Major," said the driver.

"Then we should still make the French border?"

"Perhaps it might be safer to stop and fill up," suggested the driver.

"There is no time for safety," said Romanov. "Go faster."

"Yes, Comrade Major," said the driver, who decided it was not the occasion to point out they would run out of petrol even more quickly if he was made to push the car to its limits.

"Why didn't you fill the tank up this morning, you fool?" said Romanov.

"I thought I was only taking the Consul to lunch at the town hall today, and I had intended to fill the tank up during my lunch hour."

"Just pray for your sake that we reach the border," said Romanov. "Faster."

The Mercedes touched 140 kilometres per hour and Romanov relaxed only when he saw a sign saying they were only ten kilometres from the border. A few minutes later a smile grew on his face as they passed the five-kilometre sign, and then suddenly the engine spluttered as it tried helplessly to continue turning over at the speed the pressed-down accelerator was demanding. The indicator on the speedometer started to drop steadily as the engine continued to chug. The driver turned off the ignition and threw the gear lever into neutral. The sheer momentum of the heavy Mercedes took them another kilometre before the car slowed to a complete stop.

Romanov did not even look at the driver as he jumped out of the car and began running the last three kilometres towards the border.

"I've come up with an idea," said Jim, as they passed a signpost warning drivers that the border was only two kilometres away.

"What's that, sir?" asked Adam, who could now feel his shoulder beating like a steady tune hammered out by a child on a tin drum.

"When it comes to the time for us to present our passports, you put your arm round Linda and start cuddling her. Leave the rest to me."

Mrs Hardcastle turned round and gave Adam a much closer look as Linda went scarlet. Adam looked across at the mini-skirted pink-lipped Linda and felt embarrassed by the predicament her father had placed his daughter in. "Don't argue with me, Dudley," continued Jim confidently. "I promise you what I have in mind will work." Adam made no comment and neither did Linda. When they reached the Swiss border a few moments later, Adam could see that there were two checkpoints about one hundred yards apart. Drivers were avoiding one line of traffic in which a row was going on between a customs official and an irate lorry driver. Jim drove up straight behind the gesticulating Frenchman. "Give me your passport, Dudley," he said. Adam handed over the violinist's passport.

Why did you choose this line? Adam wanted to ask.

"I chose this line," continued Jim, "because by the time it comes for our passports to be inspected I reckon the customs officer will be only too happy to allow us through without much fuss." As if in reaction to his logic, a long queue started to form behind Jim, but still the argument raged in front of them. Adam remained alert, continually looking out of the back window, waiting for the moment when Romanov would appear. When he turned back, he was relieved to find that the lorry in front of them was being told to pull over into the side and wait.

Jim drove quickly up to the customs post. "Get necking, you two," he said.

Up until that point Adam had kept his hands hidden in his trenchcoat pocket because they were so scratched and bruised. But he obeyed Jim and took Linda in his arms and kissed her perfunctorily, one eye still open watching for Romanov. To his surprise she parted his lips and began exploring inside his mouth with her tongue. Adam thought about protesting but realised there was no way he could make it sound gallant or credible.

"The wife, the daughter and the future son-in-law," said Jim, handing over the four passports.

The customs man started to check.

"What was all the trouble about, officer?"

"Nothing for you to worry about," said the official, flicking through the passports. "I hope it hasn't inconvenienced you."

"No, no," said Jim. "They didn't even notice," he said, pointing over his shoulder and laughing.

The policeman shrugged and, handing the passports back, he said, "*Allez*," waving them on.

"Sharp as mustard Jim, that's what they call me back in Hull." He looked over his shoulder towards Adam. "You can stop that now, Dudley, thank you." Adam felt Linda release him with some reluctance.

She glanced at him shyly, then turned towards her father. "But we still have to go over the French border, don't we?"

"We have already been alerted to look out for him and I can assure you he hasn't been through this post," said the senior customs officer. "Otherwise one of my men would have spotted him. But if you want to double-check, be my guest."

Romanov went quickly from officer to officer showing them the blown-up photograph of Adam, but none of them could recall anyone resembling him. Valchek joined him a few minutes later and confirmed that Scott was not in any of the cars still waiting to be allowed over the border and that the Mercedes was being pushed into the border garage.

"Is it back to the hills, Comrade Major?" asked Valchek.

"Not yet. I want to be absolutely certain he hasn't managed to cross the border."

The senior official emerged from his post in the centre of the road. "Any luck?" he asked.

"No," said Romanov glumly. "You seem to be right."

"I thought as much. If any of my men had let the Englishman through they would have been looking for a new job by now."

Romanov nodded in acknowledgment. "Could I have missed any of your staff?"

"Doubt it – unless there's a couple of them taking a break. If so you'll find them in the bar about a hundred metres up towards the French border point."

Four customs officers and a French waitress were the only people to be found in the bar. Two of the officers were playing pool while the other two sat at a corner table, drinking coffee. Romanov took the photo out once more and showed it to the two men at the pool table. They both shook their heads in an uninterested fashion and returned to potting the multi-coloured balls.

The two Russians made their way to the bar. Valchek passed Romanov a cup of coffee and a sandwich, which he took over to the table where the other two border guards sat. One of them was telling his colleague the trouble he had had with a French lorry driver who was trying to smuggle Swiss watches over the border. Romanov pushed the photograph of Scott across the table.

"Have you seen this man today?"

Neither showed any sign of recognition and the younger one quickly returned to his story. Romanov sipped his coffee, and began to consider whether he should make a run for Basle or call for reinforcements to sweep the hills. Then he noticed that the young man's eyes kept returning to the photo. He asked once again if he had seen Scott.

"No, no," said the young officer, a little too quickly. In Moscow Romanov would have had a 'yes' out of him within minutes, but he would have to follow a more gentle approach here.

"How long ago?" Romanov asked quietly.

"What do you mean?" asked the policeman.

"How long ago?" repeated Romanov in a firmer voice.

"It wasn't him," said the officer, sweat now appearing on his forehead.

"If it wasn't him, how long ago wasn't it him?"

The officer hesitated. "Twenty minutes, maybe thirty."

"What make of vehicle?"

The young officer hesitated. "A Citroën, I think."

"Colour?"

"Yellow."

"Other passengers?"

"Three. Looked like a family. Mother, father, daughter. He was in the back with the daughter. The father said they were engaged."

Romanov had no more questions.

Jim Hardcastle managed to keep a one-sided conversation going for over an hour.

"Naturally," he said, "the IMF holds its annual conference in a different city every year. Last year it was in Denver in Colorado, and next year it'll be at Perth in Australia, so I manage to get around a bit. But as the export man you have to get used to a lot of travel."

"I'm sure you do," said Adam, trying to concentrate on his benefactor's words while his shoulder throbbed on.

"I'm only President for a year, of course," continued Jim. "But I have plans to ensure that my fellow delegates won't forget 1966 in a hurry."

"I'm sure they won't," said Adam.

"I shall point out to them that Colman's has had another record year on the export side."

"How impressive."

"Yes, but I must admit that most of our profits are left on the side of the plate," he said, laughing.

Adam laughed as well but sensed that Mrs Hardcastle and Linda might have heard the line before.

"I've been thinking, Dudley, and I'm sure the wife would agree with me, that it would be most acceptable to us if you felt able to join the presidential table for dinner tonight – as my guest, of course." Mrs Hardcastle nodded, as did Linda with enthusiasm.

"I can think of nothing that would give me greater pleasure," said Adam. "But I fear my commanding officer might not be quite as delighted to hear I had stopped on the way back to England to take in a party. I do hope you'll understand."

"If he is anything like my old CO I certainly do," said Jim. "Still, if you should ever be Hull way, look us up." He took a card out of his top pocket and passed it over his shoulder.

Adam studied the embossed letters and wondered what 'MIFT' stood for. He didn't ask.

"Where in Dijon would you like to be dropped off?" asked Jim as he drove into the outskirts of the town.

"Anywhere near the centre that's convenient for you," replied Adam.

"Just holler when it suits you then," said Jim. "Of course, I always maintain that a meal without mustard . . ."

"Can you drop me on the next corner?" said Adam suddenly.

"Oh," said Jim, sad to be losing such a good listener. And he reluctantly drew the car up alongside the kerb.

Adam kissed Linda on the cheek before getting out of the back. He then shook hands with Mr and Mrs Hardcastle.

"Nice to have made your acquaintance," said Jim. "If you change your mind you'll find us at the hotel . . . Is that blood on your shoulder, lad?"

"Just a graze from a fall – nothing to worry about. Wouldn't want the Americans to think they'd got the better of me."

"No, no, of course not," said Jim. "Well, good luck."

As the car moved off Adam stood on the pavement watching them disappear. He smiled and tried to wave, then turning, he walked quickly down a side street looking for a shopping precinct. Within moments he was in the centre of town, relieved to find that all the shops were still open. He began to search up and down the street for a green cross above a door. Adam had to walk only fifty yards before he spotted one. He entered the shop tentatively and checked the shelves.

A tall man with short fair hair, wearing a long leather coat, stood in the corner with his back to the entrance. Adam froze. Then the man turned round, frowning at the packet of tablets he wanted to purchase, while at the same time rubbing his thick Gallic moustache.

Adam walked up to the counter.

"Do you speak English, by any chance?" he asked the dispenser, trying to sound confident.

"Passable, I hope," came back the reply.

"I need some iodine, cotton wool, a bandage and heavy Elastoplast. I fell and bruised my shoulder on a rock," Adam explained.

The dispenser quickly put the order together without showing much interest.

"This is what you require but you will find that the trade names are different," explained the dispenser. "That will be twenty-three francs," he added.

"Will Swiss do?"

"Certainly."

"Is there a hotel anywhere nearby?" asked Adam.

"Around the next corner, on the other side of the square."

Adam thanked him, handed over the Swiss notes, and then left the pharmacy in search of the hotel. The Hotel Frantel was, as promised, only a short distance away. He walked across the square and up the steps into the hotel to find several people were waiting at reception to be booked in. Adam swung his trenchcoat over his blood-stained shoulder and walked past them as he checked the signs on the wall. He then strode across the entrance hall as though he were a guest of several days' standing. He followed the sign he had been looking for which took him down a flight of stairs, to come head on with three further signs. The first had the silhouette of a man on the door, the second a woman, the third a wheelchair.

He opened the third tentatively and was surprised to find behind it nothing more than a sizeable square room with a high-seated lavatory against the wall. Adam locked himself in and let his trenchcoat fall to the ground.

He rested for a few minutes before slowly stripping to the waist. He then ran a basinful of warm water.

Adam was thankful for the endless first-aid seminars every officer had to go through, never believing they would serve any purpose. Twenty minutes later the pain had subsided and he even felt comfortable.

He picked up his coat with his right hand and tried to throw it back over his shoulder. The very movement caused the icon to fall out of the map pocket and onto the tiled floor. As it hit the ground, the sound made Adam fear that it might have broken in half. He stared down anxiously and then fell to his knees.

The icon had split open like a book.

CHAPTER FIFTEEN

When Adam returned to the Hotel Frantel an hour later few guests would have recognised the man who had crept in earlier that afternoon.

He wore a new shirt, trousers, tie and a double-breasted blazer that wouldn't be fashionable in Britain for at least another year. Even the raincoat had been ditched because the icon fitted snugly into the blazer pocket. He considered the shop had probably given him a poor exchange rate for his traveller's cheques but that was not what had been occupying his mind for the past hour.

He booked himself into a single room in the name of Dudley Hulme and a few minutes later took the lift to the third floor.

Lawrence picked the phone up even before Adam heard the second ring.

"It's me," said Adam.

"Where are you?" were Lawrence's first words.

"I'll ask the questions," said Adam.

"I can understand how you feel," said Lawrence, "but . . ."

"No buts. You must be aware by now that someone on your so-called team has a direct line to the Russians because it was Romanov and his friends who were waiting for me outside the hotel in Geneva, not your lot."

"We realise that now," said Lawrence.

"We?" said Adam. "Who are we? Because I'm finding it rather hard to work out who's on my side."

"You don't believe that . . ."

"When you get your girlfriend murdered, chased across Europe by professional killers, shot at and . . ."

"Shot at?" said Lawrence.

"Yes, your friend Romanov took a shot at me today, hit me in the shoulder. Next time we meet I intend it to be the other way round and it won't be the shoulder."

"There won't be a next time," said Lawrence, "because we'll get you out safely if you'll only let me know where you are."

The memory of Robin's words, "Just be wary of how much you let him know," stopped Adam from telling Lawrence his exact location.

"Adam, for God's sake, you're on your own; if you don't trust me who can you trust? I admit it looks as if we let you down. But it won't happen again."

There was another long silence before Adam said, "I'm in Dijon."

"Why Dijon?"

"Because the only person who would give me a lift was going to a mustard conference in Dijon."

Lawrence couldn't stop himself smiling. "Give me your number and I'll phone you back within the hour."

"No," said Adam, "I'll phone *you* back in one hour."

"Adam, you've got to show some trust in me."

"Not now that I know what it is you're all after, I can't afford to trust anybody."

Adam replaced the phone and stared down at the icon which lay open on the bed. It wasn't the signature of Stoeckle or Seward that worried him. It was the date – June 20, 1966 – that read like a death warrant.

"Goodnight, sir," said the doorkeeper as the senior civil servant left Century House that evening. "Another late night for you," he added sympathetically. He acknowledged the doorman by raising his rolled umbrella a few inches. It *had* been another late night, but at least they had caught up with Scott again. He was beginning to develop quite a respect for the man. But how they failed to pick him up in Geneva still required a fuller explanation than the one Lawrence Pemberton had supplied the D4 with that afternoon.

He set off at a brisk pace towards the Old Kent Road, conspicuous in his black coat and pin-striped trousers. He tapped his umbrella nervously before hailing a passing taxi.

"Dillon's bookshop, Malet Street," he told the driver, before getting in the back. Already seven thirty, but he still wouldn't be too late and a few minutes either way wasn't going to make that much difference. Pemberton had agreed to remain at his desk until all the loose ends were tied up and he was sure that nothing could go wrong this time. He allowed himself a wry smile as he thought how they had all accepted his plan. It had the double advantage of ensuring enough time for them to get their best men into position, while keeping Scott well out of sight in a deserted hideaway. He hoped that this was the last time they would expect him to come up with an original proposal.

"Eight shillings, guv'nor," said the taxi-driver, as he drew up outside Dillon's. He handed over the money and added a sixpenny tip. He stood staring at the window of the university bookshop, watching the reflection of the taxi as it moved off. The moment the taxi had turned the corner into Gower Street he began walking away. In moments he had reached a side road into which he turned. Ridgmount Gardens was one of those streets which even London cabbies had to think about for a few moments. He had walked only a matter of yards before he disappeared down some stone steps to a basement flat. He inserted a Yale key in the front door lock, turned it quickly, stepped inside and closed the door behind him.

During the next twenty minutes he made two telephone calls – one international, one local – and then had a bath. He emerged back on Ridgmount Gardens less than an hour later dressed in a casual brown suit, pink floral open shirt and brown brogue shoes. The parting in his hair had changed sides. He returned to Dillon's on foot and hailed another taxi.

"The British Museum," he instructed the driver, as he stepped into the back. He checked his watch: nearly ten past eight. Scott would be fully briefed by now, he thought, although his associates would be already on the way back to Dijon, as his plan had allowed for a two-hour delay.

The taxi drew up outside the British Museum. He paid and walked up the twelve steps in front of the museum, admiring the Byzantine architecture as he regularly did each week, before walking back down again to hail another taxi.

"Middlesex Hospital, please," was all he said. The taxi executed a U-turn and headed west.

Poor bastard. If Scott hadn't opened that envelope in the first place the icon would have ended up with its rightful owner.

"Shall I drive up to the entrance?" asked the cabbie.

"Yes, please."

A moment later he strolled into the hospital, checked

the board on the wall as if he were looking for a certain ward, then walked back out on to the street. From the Middlesex Hospital it always took him about three minutes at a steady pace to reach Charlotte Street, where he stopped outside a house and pressed a buzzer attached to a little intercom.

"Are you a member?" enquired a voice suspiciously.

"Yes."

On the hour Adam phoned and listened carefully to all Lawrence had to say.

"I'll take one more risk," said Adam, "but if Romanov turns up this time I'll hand over the icon to him personally and with it a piece of property so valuable that no amount of money the Americans could offer would be sufficient to purchase it back."

When Adam put the phone down Lawrence and Sir Morris played the conversation back over again and again.

"I think *property*'s the key word," said Sir Morris.

"Agreed," said Lawrence, "but what piece of property could be that valuable to both the Russians and the Americans?"

Sir Morris began slowly rotating the globe that stood by the side of his desk.

"What does that buzz mean?" asked Romanov. "We are not running out of petrol again, are we?"

"No, sir," said the chauffeur. "It's the new calling device now fixed to all ambassadorial cars. It means they expect me to check in."

"Turn round and go back to that petrol station we passed a couple of miles ago," Romanov said quietly.

Romanov started tapping the dashboard impatiently as he waited for the petrol station to reappear on the horizon. The sun was going down quickly and he feared it would be dark within the hour. They had travelled about ninety kilometres beyond Dijon and neither he nor Valchek had even seen a yellow Citroën going either way.

"Fill up again while I phone Geneva," Romanov said the moment he saw the petrol station. He ran to the phone box while Valchek still kept a watchful eye on the passing traffic.

"I am answering your signal," said Romanov when he was put through to the euphemistically titled Second Secretary.

"We've had another call from Mentor," said the Second Secretary. "How far are you from Dijon?"

The member stumbled about the dimly lit room until he came across an unoccupied table wedged up against a pillar in one corner. He sat down on a little leather stool by its side. He swivelled around nervously, as he always did when waiting for someone to bring him his usual malt whisky on the rocks. When the drink was placed on the table in front of him he sipped at it, in between trying to discover if there were any new faces spread around the dark room. Not an easy task, as he refused to put on his glasses. His eyes eventually became accustomed to the dim light thrown out by the long red fluorescent bulb that stretched above the bar. All he could make out were the same old faces staring at him hopefully; but he wanted something new.

The proprietor, noticing that a regular customer had remained on his own, came out and sat opposite him on the other little stool. The member never could get himself to look the man in the eyes.

"I've got someone who's very keen to meet you," whispered the proprietor.

"Which one?" he asked, looking up once more to check the faces at the bar.

"Leaning on the juke box in the corner. The tall, slim one. And he's young," added the proprietor. He looked towards the blaring machine. A pleasing new face smiled at him. He smiled nervously back.

"Was I right?" asked the proprietor.

"Is he safe?" was all he asked.

"No trouble with this one. Upper-class lad, right out of a top-drawer public school. Just wants to earn a bit of pocket money on the side."

"Fine." The member took a sip of whisky.

The proprietor walked over to the juke box. The member watched him talking to the young man. The boy downed his drink, hesitated for a moment, then strolled across the crowded floor to take the empty stool.

"My name is Piers," the young man said.

"Mine's Jeremy," the member said.

"A gentle name," said Piers. "I've always liked the name Jeremy."

"Would you care for a drink?"

"A dry Martini, please," said Piers.

The member ordered a dry Martini and another malt whisky. The waiter hurried away. "I haven't seen you here before."

"No, it's only my second time," said Piers. "I used to work in Soho, but it's got to be so rough lately, you never know who you might end up with."

The drinks arrived and the member took a quick gulp.

"Would you like to dance?" asked Piers.

"It's an emergency," the voice said. "Is the tape on?"

"I'm listening."

271

"Antarctic is in Dijon and he's discovered what's in the icon."

"And did he give them any clue?"

"No, all he told Pemberton was that he was in possession of a piece of property so valuable that no amount of money we could offer would be sufficient to purchase it back."

"Indeed," said the voice.

"The British think the important word is property," said the caller.

"They're wrong," said the voice on the other end of the line. "It's purchase."

"How can you be so sure?"

"Because the Russian Ambassador in Washington has requested a meeting with the Secretary of State on June 20 and he's bringing with him a bullion order to the value of 712 million dollars in gold."

"So where does that leave us?"

"On our way to Dijon so that we can be sure to lay our hands on that icon before the British or the Russians. The Russians obviously feel confident that it will soon be in their possession, so my bet is that they must already be on the way."

"But I've already agreed to go along with the British plan."

"Try not to forget which side you're on, Commander."

"Yes, sir. But what are we going to do about Antarctic if we get our hands on the icon?"

"It's only the icon we're after. Once that's in our possession, Antarctic is expendable."

Adam checked his watch: a few minutes after seven.

It was time for him to leave because he had decided not to carry out Lawrence's instructions to the letter.

He intended to be waiting for *them*, and not as Lawrence had planned. He locked the bedroom door and returned to reception where he paid for the use of the room and the telephone calls he had made.

"Thank you," he said to the receptionist, and turned to leave.

"Dudley." Adam froze on the spot.

"Dudley," the voice boomed again. "I almost didn't recognise you. Did you change your mind?" A hand thumped him on the shoulder — at least it wasn't the left shoulder, he thought — as he stared down at Jim Hardcastle.

"No," said Adam, wishing he possessed the guile of Robin's father. "I think I was spotted in town so I had to get a change of clothes and keep out of sight for a few hours."

"Then why don't you come to the mustard dinner?" said Jim. "No one will see you there."

"Wish I were able to," said Adam, "but I can't afford to lose any more time."

"Anything I can do to help?" said Jim conspiratorially.

"No, I've got to get to . . . I have a rendezvous just outside the town in less than an hour."

"Wish I could take you there myself," said Jim. "Do anything to help an old soldier, but I'm a bit stuck tonight — of all nights."

"Don't give it a second thought, Jim, I'll be all right."

"I could always take him, Dad," said Linda, who had slipped up by her father's side and was listening intently.

They both turned towards Linda who was wearing a tight-fitting black crêpe dress that started as low and ended as high as it dared while her freshly washed hair now fell to her shoulders. She looked up hopefully.

"You've only just got your licence, lass. Don't be daft."

"You always treat me like a child when there's something worthwhile to do," came back her immediate response.

Jim hesitated. "How far is this rendezvous?" he asked apprehensively.

"About five, maybe six miles," said Adam, "but I'll be fine. I can get a taxi easily."

"The lass is right," said Jim, and taking his car keys out of his pocket, he turned to her and added, "but if you ever let on to your mother I'll kill you." Jim took Adam by the hand and shook it furiously.

"But I'll be just fine . . ."

"I won't hear of it, lad. Never forget, that in the end we're both on the same side, and good luck."

"Thank you, sir," said Adam reluctantly.

Jim beamed. "You'd better be getting along, lass, before your mother shows up."

Linda happily took Adam by the hand and led him away to the car park.

"Which direction?" she asked, once they were seated in the car.

"The Auxerre road," said Adam, looking down at the piece of paper on which he had written the directions Lawrence had read over the phone to him.

Linda set off at a slow pace, seeming at first to be unsure of the car, but once they had reached the outskirts of the town Adam suggested that she might go a little faster.

"I'm very nervous," she said, as she put her hand on Adam's knee.

"Yes, I can tell you are," said Adam, crossing his

legs quickly. "Don't miss the turning," he added when he noticed a signpost pointing to the left.

Linda swung down off the main road on to a country lane while Adam kept his eyes peeled for the building Lawrence had described. It was another two miles before it came into sight.

"Draw into the side," said Adam, "and turn the lights off."

"At last," said Linda, sounding more hopeful, as she brought the car to a halt.

"Thank you very much," said Adam, as he touched the door handle.

"Is that all I get for risking life and limb?" asked Linda.

"I wouldn't want you to be late for the dinner."

"That dinner will be about as exciting as a dance at the Barnsley Young Conservatives."

"But your mother will be worried about you."

"Dudley, you're so up-tight."

"I wouldn't be in normal circumstances but if you stay much longer your life could be in danger," Adam said quietly.

Linda turned ashen. "You're not joking, are you?"

"I wish I was," said Adam. "Now, when I get out of this car you must turn round and go back to the hotel and never mention this conversation to anyone, especially your mother."

"I will," Linda said, sounding nervous for the first time.

"You're a fantastic girl," said Adam, and took her in his arms and gave her the longest, warmest kiss she had ever experienced. Adam then got out of the car and watched her do a five-point turn before she headed off back in the direction of Dijon.

He checked his watch: an hour and a half still to go

before they were due, and by then it would be pitch dark. He jogged over to the airfield and studied the burnt-out buildings that ran alongside the road. It was exactly as Lawrence had described it. It was like a ghost town and Adam was confident that no one else could be there yet as they still wouldn't have had enough time to carry out Lawrence's plan.

Looking across the runway, Adam spotted the ideal place to hide while he waited to see which of the two plans he had prepared would prove necessary.

Flight Lieutenant Alan Banks was thankful that the moon shone so brightly that night. He had landed the little Beaver full of combat men in far worse conditions when a runway had been lit up like the Blackpool seafront.

Banks circled the perimeter of the airfield once and studied the two runways carefully. The airport had been out of action for such a long time that none of the aircraft manuals included a detailed ground plan.

The flight lieutenant was breaking every rule in the book, including piloting an unmarked aircraft informing the French that they would be landing in Paris; not easy to explain overshooting an airport by over a hundred miles.

"I can make a landing on the north–south runway more easily," Banks said, turning to the SAS captain, who sat crouched in the back with his five men. "How near to that hangar do you want me to go?" he said, pointing out of the window.

"Stay well clear, at least a couple of hundred yards," came back the reply. "We still don't know what to expect."

The six SAS men continued to stare cautiously out of the side windows. They had been briefed to pick up a lone Englishman called Scott who would be waiting for them, and then get out fast. It sounded easy enough but it couldn't be that easy otherwise they wouldn't have been called in.

The pilot swung the Beaver round to the south and put the nose down. He smiled when he spotted the burnt-out Spitfire that had been left derelict on the corner of the runway. Just like the ones his father used to fly during the Second World War. But this one had obviously never made it home. He descended confidently and as the little plane touched down it bounced along not because the pilot lacked experience but because the surface of the runway was so badly pitted.

Flight Lieutenant Banks brought the plane to a halt about two hundred yards from the hangar and swung the fuselage round a full circle ready for that quick getaway the captain seemed so keen to execute. He pressed the button that cut the propellers' engines and turned the lights out. The whirring slowed to an eerie whisper. They were forty-three minutes early.

Adam watched the new arrivals suspiciously from the cockpit of the Spitfire some four hundred yards away. He wasn't going to make a run for it across that open ground while the moon shone so brightly. His eyes never left the little unmarked plane as he waited for some clue as to who the occupants might be. He estimated it would be another fifteen minutes before the moon would be shielded by clouds. A few minutes more passed before Adam watched six men drop out of the blind side of the aircraft and lie flat on the tarmac on their stomachs. They were correctly dressed in SAS battle kit but Adam remained unconvinced while he still recalled Romanov's chauffeur's uniform. The six soldiers made no attempt to move. Neither did

Adam as he was still uncertain which side they were on.

All six men on the ground hated the moon and even more the open space. The captain checked his watch: thirty-six minutes to go. He raised his hand and they began to crawl towards the hangar where Pemberton had said Scott would be waiting, a journey which took them nearly twenty minutes, and with each movement they made they became more confident that Pemberton's warning of an enemy waiting for them was unjustified.

At last a mass of clouds reached the moon and a shadow was thrown across the whole airfield. The SAS captain quickly checked his watch. Five minutes to go before the rendezvous was due. He was the first to reach the door of the hangar and he pushed it open with the palm of his hand. He wriggled in through the gap. The bullet hit him in the forehead even before he had found time to raise his gun.

"Move, laddies," shouted the second in command, and the other four were up in a flash, firing in an arc in front of them and running for the protection of the building.

As soon as Adam heard the Scottish brogue, he jumped out of the cockpit and sprinted across the tarmac towards the little plane whose propellers were already beginning to turn. He jumped on the wing and climbed in by the side of the surprised pilot.

"I'm Adam Scott, the man you've come to pick up," he shouted.

"I'm Flight Lieutenant Alan Banks, old chap," said the pilot, thrusting out his hand. Only a British officer could shake hands in such a situation, thought Adam, relieved if still terrified.

They both turned and watched the battle.

"We ought to get going," said the pilot. "My orders are to see you are brought back to England in one piece."

"Not before we are certain none of your men can make it back to the plane."

"Sorry, mate. My instructions are to get you out. Their orders are to take care of themselves."

"Let's at least give them another minute," Adam said.

They waited until the propellers were rotating at full speed. Suddenly the firing stopped and Adam could hear his heart thumping in his body.

"We ought to get moving," said the pilot.

"I know," replied Adam, "but keep your eyes skinned. There's something I still need to know."

Years of night marches made it possible for Adam to see him long before the pilot.

"Get going," said Adam.

"What?" said the pilot.

"Get going."

The pilot moved the joystick forward and the plane started moving slowly down the crumbling runway.

Suddenly a dark figure was running towards them firing long bursts straight at them. The pilot looked back to see a tall man whose fair hair shone in the moonlight.

"Faster, man, faster," said Adam.

"The throttle's full out," said the pilot, as the firing began again, but this time the bullets were ripping into the fuselage. A third burst came but by then the plane was going faster than the man and Adam let out a scream of delight when it left the ground.

He looked back to see that Romanov had turned around and was now firing at someone who was not wearing an SAS uniform.

279

"They couldn't hope to hit us now unless they've got a bazooka," said Flight Lieutenant Banks.

"Well done, well done," said Adam turning back to the pilot.

"And to think my wife had wanted me to go to the cinema tonight," said the pilot laughing.

"And what were you hoping to see?" asked Adam.

"My Fair Lady."

"Isn't it time for us to be going home?" asked Piers, removing his hand from the member's leg.

"Good idea," he said. "Just let me settle the bill."

"And I'll pick up my coat and scarf," said Piers. "Join you upstairs in a few moments?"

"Fine," he said. Catching the eye of the proprietor the member scribbled his signature in the air. When the 'account' appeared – a bare figure written out on a slip of paper without explanation – it was, as always, extortionate. As always, the member paid without comment. He thanked the proprietor as he left and walked up the dusty, creaky stairs to find his companion already waiting for him on the pavement. He hailed a taxi and while Piers climbed in the back he directed the cabbie to Dillon's bookshop.

"Not in the cab," he said, as his new friend's hand began to creep up his leg.

"I can't wait," said Piers. "It's way past my bedtime."

"Way past my bedtime," his companion repeated involuntarily, and checked his watch. The die must have been cast. They would have moved in by now: surely they had caught Scott this time and, more important, the . . . ?

"Four bob," said the cabbie, flicking back the glass.

He handed over five shillings and didn't wait for any change.

"Just around the corner," he said, guiding Piers past the bookshop and into the little side street. They crept down the stone steps and Piers waited as he unlocked the door, switched on the lights, and led the young man in.

"Oh, very cosy," said Piers. "Very cosy indeed."

Flight Lieutenant Alan Banks stared out of his tiny window as the plane climbed steadily.

"Where to now?" said Adam, relief flooding through his body.

"I had hoped England but I'm afraid the answer is as far as I can manage."

"What do you mean?" said Adam anxiously.

"Look at the fuel gauge," said Alan Banks, putting his forefinger on a little white indicator that was pointing halfway between a quarter full and empty. "We had enough to get us back to Northolt in Middlesex until those bullets ripped into my fuel tank."

The little white stick kept moving towards the red patch even as Adam watched it and within moments the propellers on the left side of the aircraft spun to a halt.

"I am going to have to put her down in a field. I can't risk going on as there are no other airports anywhere nearby. Just be thankful it's a clear moonlit night."

Without warning the plane began to descend sharply. "I shall try for that field over there," said the flight lieutenant, sounding remarkably blasé as he pointed to a large expanse of land to the west of the aircraft. "Hold on tight," he said as the plane spiralled inevitably down. The large expanse of land suddenly looked very small as the plane began to approach it.

Adam found himself gripping the side of his seat and gritting his teeth.

"Relax," said the pilot. "These Beavers have landed on far worse places than this," he went on, as the wheels touched the brown earth. "Damn mud. I hadn't anticipated that," he cursed as the wheels lost their grip in the soft earth and the plane suddenly nosedived forward. A few seconds passed before Adam realised he was still alive but upside down swinging from his seat belt.

"What do I do next?" he asked the pilot but there was no reply.

Adam tried to get his bearings and began to rock his body backwards and forwards until he could touch the side of the plane with one hand while gripping the joystick with his feet. Once he was able to grab the side of the fuselage he undid the belt and collapsed onto the roof of the plane.

He picked himself up, relieved to find nothing was broken. He quickly looked around but there was still no sign of the pilot. Adam clambered out of the plane, glad to feel the safety of the ground. He scrambled around for a considerable time before he found Alan Banks some thirty yards in front of the aircraft motionless on his back.

"Are you all right?" asked the pilot before Adam could ask the same question.

"I'm fine, but how about you, Alan?"

"I'm OK. I must have been thrown clear of the aircraft. Just sorry about the landing, old chap, have to admit it wasn't up to scratch. We must try it again some time."

Adam burst out laughing as the pilot slowly sat up.

"What next?" Banks asked.

"Can you walk?"

"Yes, I think so," said Alan, gingerly lifting himself up. "Damn," he said, "it's only my ankle but it's sure going to slow me down. You'd better get going without me. That bunch back there with the arsenal can only be about thirty minutes behind us."

"But what will you do?"

"My father landed in one of these bloody fields during the Second World War and still managed to get himself back to England without being caught by the Germans. I owe you a great debt of gratitude, Adam, because if I can get back I'll be able to shut him up once and for all. Which lot are chasing us this time, by the way?"

"The Russians," said Adam who was beginning to wonder if perhaps there was a second enemy.

"The Russians — couldn't be better. Anything less and Dad wouldn't have accepted it as a fair comparison."

Adam smiled as he thought of his own father and how much he would have liked Alan Banks. He touched the icon instinctively and was relieved to find it was still in place. The pilot's words had only made him more determined to get back to England.

"Which way?" asked Adam.

The pilot looked up at the Great Bear. "I'll head east, seems appropriate, so you'd better go west, old fellow. Nice to have made your acquaintance," and with that he limped off.

"I'm not sure how much longer I can last, Comrade Major."

"You must try to hold on, Valchek. It's imperative that you try. We cannot afford to stop now," said

Romanov. "I know that plane isn't far. I saw it falling out of the sky."

"I believe you, Comrade, but at least let me die a peaceful death on the side of the road, rather than endure the agony of this car."

Romanov glanced across at his colleague who had been shot in the abdomen. Valchek's hands were covered in blood, and his shirt and trousers were already drenched as he tried helplessly to hold himself in. He continued to clutch on to his stomach like a child who is about to be sick. The driver had also been shot, but in the back while attempting to run away. If he hadn't died instantly, Romanov would have put the next bullet into the coward himself. But Valchek was a different matter. No one could have questioned his courage. He had first taken on the British flat on their stomachs and then the Americans charging in like the seventh cavalry. Romanov had Mentor to thank for ensuring that they had been there first. But he must now quickly warn him that someone else was also briefing the Americans. Romanov, however, felt some satisfaction in having tricked the Americans into turning their fire on the British while he and Valchek waited to pick off the survivors. The last survivor was an American who fired at Valchek continually as they were making their getaway.

Romanov reckoned he had a clear hour before the French, British and Americans would be explaining away several bodies on a disused airfield. Romanov's thoughts returned to Valchek when he heard his comrade groan.

"Let's turn off into this forest," he begged. "I cannot hope to last much longer now."

"Hold on, Comrade, hold on," repeated Romanov.

"We can't be far away from Scott. Think of the Motherland."

"To hell with the Motherland," said Valchek. "Just let me die in peace." Romanov looked across again and realised that he could be stuck with a dead body within a few minutes. Despite Valchek's efforts the blood was now seeping on to the floor like a tap that wouldn't stop dripping.

Romanov noticed a gap in the trees ahead of him. He switched his lights on to full beam and swung off the road on to a dirt track and drove as far as he could until the thicket became too dense. He switched off the headlights and ran round the car to open the door.

Valchek could only manage two or three steps before he slumped to the ground, still holding on to his intestines. Romanov bent down and helped him ease himself up against the trunk of a large tree.

"Leave me to die, Comrade Major. Do not waste any more of your time on me."

Romanov frowned.

"How do you wish to die, Comrade?" he asked. "Slowly and in agony, or quickly and peacefully?"

"Leave me, Comrade. Let me die slowly, but you should go while you still have Scott in your sights."

"But if the Americans were to find you, they might force you to talk."

"You know better than that, Comrade." Romanov accepted the rebuke, then rose and after a moment's thought, ran back to the car.

Valchek began to pray that once the bastard had left someone might find him. He'd never wanted this assignment in the first place, but Zaborski needed two extra eyes on Romanov and Zaborski was not a man to cross. Valchek wouldn't talk, but he still wanted to live.

The bullet from the 9mm Makarov went straight through the back of Valchek's temple and blew away one side of his head. Valchek slumped to the ground and for several seconds his body trembled and spasmed, subsiding into twitches as he emptied his bowels and bladder on to the brown earth.

Romanov stood over him until he was certain he was dead. Valchek would probably not have talked, but this was not a time for taking unnecessary risks.

When he woke the next morning he felt the same familiar guilt. Once again he swore it would be the last time. It was never as good as he had anticipated, and the regret always lingered on for several hours.

The expense of keeping up an extra flat, the taxi fares and the club bills nearly made it prohibitive. But he always returned, like a salmon to its breeding ground. "A queer fish," he murmured out loud, and then groaned at his own pun.

Piers began to wake, and for the next twenty minutes he made his companion forget those regrets. After a moment of lying in exhausted silence the older man slipped out of bed, took ten pounds out of his wallet and left it on the dresser before going to run himself a bath. He anticipated that by the time he returned the boy and the money would have gone.

He soaked himself in the bath wondering about Scott. He knew he should feel guilty about his death. A death that, like so many others before him, had been caused by his picking up a young Pole who he had thought was safe. It was now so many years ago that he couldn't even remember his name.

But Mentor had never been allowed to forget the

286

name of the young aristocratic KGB officer he had found sitting on the end of their bed when he woke the next morning, or the look of disgust he showed for them both.

CHAPTER SIXTEEN

Adam lay flat on his stomach in the bottom of the empty barge. His head propped on one side, he remained alert to the slightest unfamiliar sound.

The bargee stood behind the wheel counting the three hundred Swiss francs for a second time. It was more than he could normally hope to earn in a month. A woman standing on tiptoes was eyeing the notes happily over his shoulder.

The barge progressed at a stately pace down the canal and Adam could no longer see the crashed plane.

Suddenly, far off in the distance, he heard distinctly the report of what sounded like a gunshot. Even as he listened the woman turned and scuttled down the hatch like a frightened rat. The barge ploughed its course on slowly through the night while Adam listened anxiously for any other unnatural noises, but all he could hear was the gentle splash of the water against the barge's hull. The clouds had moved on and full moon once again lit up the bank on both sides of the river. It became abundantly clear to Adam as he watched the towpath that they were not moving very fast. He could have run quicker. But even if it had cost him the remainder of his money, he was grateful to be escaping. He lowered himself again and curled up in the bow of the boat. He touched the icon, something he found himself doing every few minutes since he had discovered its secret. He did not move for another half hour, although he doubted that the barge had covered more than five miles.

Although everything appeared absolutely serene, he still remained alert. The river was far wider now than when he had first leapt on the barge.

The bargee's eyes never left him for long. He stood gripping the wheel, his oil-covered face not much cleaner than the old dungarees he wore – which looked as if they were never taken off. Occasionally he took a hand from the wheel, but only to remove the smokeless pipe from his mouth, cough, spit and put it back again.

The man smiled, took both hands off the wheel and placed them by the side of his head to indicate that Adam should sleep. But Adam shook his head. He checked his watch. Midnight had passed and he wanted to be off the barge and away long before first light.

He stood up, stretched, and wobbled a little. His shoulder, although healing slowly, still ached relentlessly. He walked up the centre of the barge and took his place next to the wheel.

"La Seine?" he asked, pointing at the water.

The bargee shook his head, no. "Canal de Bourgogne," he grunted.

Adam then pointed in the direction they were moving. "*Quelle ville?*"

The bargee removed his pipe. "*Ville? Ce n'est pas une ville, c'est Sombernon,*" he said, and put the stem back between his teeth.

Adam returned to his place in the bow. He tried to find a more comfortable position to relax and, curling

290

up against the side of the boat, rested his head on some old rope and allowed his eyes to close.

"You know Scott better than any of us," said Sir Morris, "and you still have no feel as to where he might be now, or what he might do next, do you?"

"No, sir," admitted Lawrence. "The only thing we know for certain is that he has an appointment for a medical on Monday afternoon, but somehow I don't think he'll make it."

Sir Morris ignored the comment. "But someone was able to get to Scott, even though we didn't call D4," he continued. "That icon must hold a secret that we haven't begun to appreciate."

"And if Scott is still alive," said Lawrence, "nothing is going to convince him now that we're not to blame."

"And if we're not, who is?" asked Sir Morris. "Because someone was so desperate to discover our next move that they must have taken one hell of a risk during the last twenty-four hours. Unless, of course, it was you," said Sir Morris. The Permanent Secretary rose from his desk and turned around to look out of his window on to Horse Guards Parade.

"Even if it was me," said Lawrence, his eyes resting on a picture of the young Queen which stood on the corner of his master's desk, "it doesn't explain how the Americans got there as well."

"Oh, that's simple," said Sir Morris. "Busch has been briefing them direct. I never doubted he would from the moment he joined us. What I hadn't anticipated was how far the Americans would go without keeping us informed."

"So it was you who told Busch," said Lawrence.

"No," said Sir Morris. "You don't end up sitting behind this desk risking your own skin. I told the Prime

Minister, and politicians can always be relied on to pass on your information if they consider it will score them a point. To be fair, I knew the Prime Minister would tell the President. Otherwise I wouldn't have told him in the first place. More important: do you think Scott can still be alive?"

"Yes, I do," said Lawrence. "I have every reason to believe that the man who ran across the tarmac to our waiting plane was Scott. The French police, who incidentally have been far more co-operative than the Swiss, have informed us that our plane crashed in a field twelve miles north of Dijon but neither Scott nor the pilot were to be found at the scene of the crash."

"And if the French reports on what took place at the airport are accurate," said Sir Morris, "Romanov escaped and they must have had a couple of hours' start on us."

"Possibly," said Lawrence.

"And do you think it equally possible," asked Sir Morris, "that they have caught up with Scott and are now in possession of the icon?"

"Yes, sir, I fear that is quite possible," Lawrence said. "But I can't pretend it's conclusive. However, the BBC monitoring service at Caversham Park picked up extra signals traffic to all Soviet embassies during the night."

"That could mean anything," said Sir Morris, removing his spectacles.

"I agree, sir. But NATO reports that Russian strategic forces have been placed at a state of readiness and several Soviet Ambassadors across Europe have requested formal audiences with their Foreign Secretaries, ours included."

"That *is* more worrying," said Sir Morris. "They don't do that unless they are hoping for our support."

"Agreed, sir. But most revealing of all is that the Active Measures section of the KGB, First Chief Directorate, has booked pages of advertising space in newspapers right across Europe and, I suspect, America."

"Next you'll be telling me they hired J. Walter Thompson to write the copy," growled Sir Morris.

"They won't need them," said Lawrence. "I suspect it's a story that will make every front page."

If it hadn't been for the ceaseless throbbing in his shoulder, Adam might not have woken so quickly. The barge had suddenly swung at 90° and started heading east when Adam woke up with a start. He looked at the bargee and indicated that as the river was far wider now could he ease them nearer to the bank so he could jump off. The old man shrugged his shoulders pretending not to understand as the barge drifted aimlessly on.

Adam looked over the side and despite the lateness of the hour could see the bed of the river quite clearly. He tossed a stone over the side and watched it drop quickly to the bottom. It looked almost as if he could reach down and touch it. He looked up helplessly at the bargee who continued to stare over his head into the distance.

"Damn," said Adam, and taking the icon out of his blazer pocket held it high above his head. He stood on the edge of the barge feeling like a football manager asking the referee for permission to substitute a player. Permission was granted and Adam leaped into the water. His feet hit the canal bed with a thud and knocked the breath out of his body despite the fact that the water only came up to his waist.

Adam stood in the canal, the icon still held high above his head as the barge sailed past him. He waded to the nearest bank and clambered up on to the tow-path, turning slowly round as he tried to get some feel for direction. He was soon able to distinguish the Plough again and plot a course due west. After an hour of soggy jogging he began to make out a light in the distance which he estimated to be under a mile away. His legs were soaking and cold as he started to squelch his way across a field towards the first rays of the morning sun.

Whenever he came to a hedge or gate he climbed over or under like a Roman centurion determined to hold a straight line with his final destination. He could now see the outline of a house, which as he got nearer he realised was no more than a large cottage. He remembered the expression 'peasant farmer' from his school geography lessons. A little cobbled path led up to a half-open wooden door that looked as if it didn't need a lock. Adam tapped gently on the knocker and stood directly below the light above the doorway so that whoever answered would see him immediately.

The door was pulled back by a woman of perhaps thirty, who wore a plain black dress and a spotless white apron. Her rosy cheeks and ample waist confirmed her husband's profession.

When she saw Adam standing under the light she couldn't mask her surprise – she had been expecting the postman, but he didn't often appear in a neat navy blue blazer and soaking grey trousers.

Adam smiled. "*Anglais*," he told her, and added, "I fell in the canal."

The lady burst out laughing and beckoned Adam into her kitchen. He walked in to find a man evidently dressed for milking. The farmer looked up and when he saw Adam he joined in the laughter – a warm, friendly laugh more with Adam than against him.

When the woman saw that Adam was dripping all over her spotless floor she quickly pulled down a towel from the rack above the fire and said, "*Enlevez-moi ça,*" pointing to Adam's trousers.

Adam turned towards the farmer for guidance but his host only nodded his agreement and added with a mime of pulling down his own trousers.

"*Enlevez les, enlevez les,*" the woman repeated, pointing at him, and handed him the towel.

Adam removed his shoes and socks but the farmer's wife went on pointing until he took off his trousers, and she didn't budge before he had finally removed his shirt and underclothes and wrapped the towel around his waist. She stared at the large bandage on his shoulder but then quickly picked up everything except his blazer and took them over to the sink while he stood by the fire and dried himself.

Adam hitched up the towel around his waist, as the farmer beckoned him to join him at the table, pouring a large glass of milk for his guest and another for himself. Adam sat down next to the farmer, hanging his fashionable new blazer over the back of the chair near the fire. A delicious aroma arose from the pan where the farmer's wife was frying a thick slice of bacon which she had cut from the joint hanging in the smoky recess of the chimney.

The farmer raised his glass of milk high in the air.

"Winston Churchill," he toasted. Adam took a long gulp from his own glass and then raised it dramatically.

"Charles de Gaulle," he said, and finished off the warm milk as if it had been his first pint at the local pub.

The farmer picked up the jug once more and refilled their glasses. "*Merci,*" said Adam, turning to the farmer's wife as she placed in front of him a large plate sizzling with eggs and bacon. She nodded and handed Adam a knife and fork before saying, "*Mangez.*"

"*Merci, merci,*" Adam repeated, as she cut him a thick oval slice from the huge loaf in front of im.

Adam began to devour the freshly cooked food which was the first meal he'd managed since the dinner he'd ordered at Robin's expense.

Without warning the farmer suddenly rose from his place and thrust out his hand. Adam also got up and shook it gratefully, only to be reminded how sore his shoulder still was.

"*Je dois travailler à la laiterie,*" he explained.

Adam nodded, and remained standing as his host left the room, but the farmer waved him down with a further, "*Mangez.*"

When Adam had finished the last scrap of food – he did everything except lick the plate – he took it over to the farmer's wife who was busy removing a pot from the stove in order to pour him a large, steaming cup of hot coffee. He sat back down and began to sip at it.

Adam tapped the jacket pocket almost automatically to make sure the icon was still safely in place. He pulled it out and studied St George and the Dragon. He turned it over, hesitated and then pressed the silver crown hard. The icon split in half like a book revealing two tiny hinges on the inside.

He glanced up at the farmer's wife, who was now wringing out his socks. Adam noticed his pants had already joined the trousers on the rack above the fire. She removed an ironing board from a little alcove by the side of the stove and began to set it up, showing no interest in Adam's discovery.

Once again he stared down at the inside of the open icon which was now laid flat on the table in front of him. The true irony was that the woman pressing his trousers was able to understand every word on the parchment while at the same time unable to explain the full significance to him. The complete surface of the inside of the icon was covered by a parchment which was glued to the wood and fell only a centimetre short of the four edges. Adam swivelled it round so that he could study it more clearly. The scrawled signatures in black ink at the bottom and the seals gave it the look of a legal document. On each reading he learned something new. Adam had been surprised originally to discover it was written in French until he came to the date on the bottom – June 20, 1867 – and then he remembered from his military history lectures at Sandhurst that long after Napoleonic times most international agreements remained conducted in French. Adam began to reread the script again slowly.

His French was not good enough to translate more than a few odd words from the finely handwritten scroll. Under *Etas Unis* William Seward's bold hand was scrawled across a crest of a two-headed eagle. Next to it was the signature of Edward de Stoeckle below a crown that mirrored the silver ornament embedded in the back of the icon. Adam double-checked. It had to be some form of agreement executed between the Russians and the Americans in 1867.

He then searched for other words that would help to explain the significance of the document. On one line he identified: '*Sept millions deux cent mille dollars d'or (7.2 million)*' and on another '*Sept cent douze millions huit cent mille dollars d'or (712.8 million) le 20 juin 1966*.

His eyes rested on a calendar hanging by a nail from the wall. It was Friday, June 17, 1966. If the date in the agreement were to be believed, then in only three days the document would no longer have any legal validity. No wonder the two most powerful nations on earth seemed desperate to get their hands on it, thought Adam.

Adam read through the document line by line searching for any further clues, pondering over each word slowly.

His eyes came to a halt on the one word that would remain the same in both languages.

The one word he had not told Lawrence.

Adam wondered how the icon had ever fallen into the hands of Goering in the first place. He must have bequeathed it to his father unknowingly – for had he realised the true importance of what was hidden inside it, he would surely have been able to bargain for his own freedom with either side.

"*Voilà, voilà,*" said the farmer's wife, waving her hands as she placed warm socks, pants and trousers in front of Adam. How long had he spent engrossed in his fateful discovery? She looked down at the upside down parchment and smiled. Adam quickly snapped the icon closed and then studied the masterpiece carefully. So skilfully had the wood been cut that he could no longer see the join. He thought of the words of the letter left to him in his father's will: "But if you open it only to discover its purpose is to involve you in some dishonourable enterprise, be rid of it without a second thought." He did not need to give a second thought to how his father would have reacted in the same circumstances. The farmer's wife was now standing hands on hips, staring at him with a puzzled look.

Adam quickly replaced the icon in his jacket pocket and pulled back on his trousers.

He could think of no adequate way of thanking the farmer's wife for her hospitality, her lack of suspicion or inquisitiveness, so he simply walked over to her, took her gently by the shoulders, and kissed her on the cheek. She blushed and handed him a small plastic bag. He looked inside to find three apples, some bread and a large piece of cheese. She removed a crumb from his lip with the edge of her apron and led him to the open door.

Adam thanked her and then walked outside into his other world.

PART THREE

THE WHITE HOUSE
WASHINGTON DC

June 17, 1966

CHAPTER SEVENTEEN

THE WHITE HOUSE WASHINGTON DC *June 17, 1966*

"I don't want to be the first god-damn President in the history of the United States to hand back an American state rather than be founding one."

"I appreciate that, Mr President," said the Secretary of State. "But . . ."

"Where do we stand on this legally, Dean?"

"We don't, Mr President. Abraham Brunweld, the leading authority on documents of this period, confirms that the terms of the ninety-nine year lease are binding on both sides. The lease was signed on behalf of Russia by Edward de Stoeckle and for the US by the then Secretary of State, William Seward."

"Can this agreement still be valid today?" asked the President, turning to his chief legal officer, Nicholas Katzenbach.

"It certainly can, sir," said the Attorney General. "But only if they can produce their original. If they do, the UN and the international court at The Hague would have no choice but to support the Russian claim. Otherwise no international agreement signed

303

by us in the past or in the future would carry any credibility."

"What you're asking me to do is lie down and wag my tail like a prize labrador while the Russians shit all over us," said the President.

"I understand how you feel, Mr President," said the Attorney General, "but it remains my responsibility to make you aware of the legal position."

"God dammit, is there a precedent for this kind of stupidity by a Head of State?"

"The British," chipped in Dean Rusk, "will be facing a similar problem with the Chinese in 1999 over the New Territories of Hong Kong. They have already accepted the reality of the situation and indeed have made it clear to the Chinese Government that they are willing to come to an agreement with them."

"That's just one example," said the President, "and we all know about the British and their 'fair play' diplomacy."

"Also, in 1898," continued Rusk, "the Russians obtained a ninety-nine-year lease on Port Arthur in Northern China. The port was vital to them because, unlike Vladivostok, it is ice-free all year round."

"I had no idea the Russians *had* a port in China."

"They don't any longer, Mr President. They returned it to Mao in 1955, as an act of goodwill between fellow Communists."

"You can be damn sure the Russians won't return this piece of land to *us* as an act of goodwill," said the President. "Am I left with any alternative?"

"Short of military action to prevent the Soviets claiming what they will rightfully see as theirs, no sir," replied the Secretary of State.

"So one Johnson buys the land from the Russians in 1867 and another has to sell it back in 1966. Why did Seward and the President ever agree to such a damn cockamaney idea in the first place?"

"At the time," said the Attorney General, removing his spectacles, "the purchase price of the land in question was seven point two million dollars and inflation was then virtually unheard of. Andrew Johnson could never have imagined the Russians wanting to purchase it back at ninety-nine times its original value, or in real terms, seven hundred and twelve point eight million dollars in gold bullion. In reality, years of inflation have made the asking price cheap. And the Russians have already lodged the full amount in a New York bank to prove it."

"So we can't even hope that they won't stump up in time," said the President.

"It would seem not, sir."

"But why did Tsar Alexander want to lease the damn land in the first place? That's what beats me."

"He was having trouble with some of his senior ministers at the time over the selling off of land belonging to Russia in Eastern Asia. The Tsar thought this transaction would be more palatable to his inner circle if he presented it as nothing more than a long lease, with a buy-back clause, rather than an outright sale."

"Why didn't Congress object?"

"After Congress ratified the main treaty, the amendment was not strictly subject to approval by the House, because no further expenditure by the United States government was involved," Rusk explained. "Ironically, Seward was proud of the fact he had demanded such a high premium in the repayment clause. At the time he had every reason to believe it would be impossible to repay."

"Now it's worth that in annual oil revenue alone," said the President, looking out of the Oval Office window towards the Washington Monument. "Not to mention the military chaos it's going to create in this country if they've got their hands on their copy of the treaty. Don't ever forget that I was the President who asked Congress to spend billions of dollars putting the early warning system right across that border so the American people could sleep easy."

Neither adviser felt able to contradict their elected leader.

"So what are the British doing about all this?"

"Playing it close to the chest, as usual, Mr President. It's an English national who is thought to be in possession of the treaty at the moment and they still seem quietly confident that they will get their hands on him and the icon before the Russians, so they may yet turn out to be our saviours."

"Nice to have the British coming to *our* rescue for a change," said the President. "But have we meanwhile been sitting on our asses while they try to solve our problems for us?"

"No, sir. The CIA have been on it for over a month."

"Then it's only surprising that the Russians haven't got their hands on the icon already."

Nobody laughed.

"So what am I expected to do next? Sit and wait for the Soviets to move 712 million dollars of gold from their New York bank to the US Treasury before midnight on Monday?"

"They must also deliver their original copy of the agreement to me at the same time," said Rusk. "And they have only sixty hours left to do that."

"Where's our copy, at this moment?" asked the President.

"Somewhere deep in the vaults of the Pentagon. Only two people know the exact location. Since the

Yalta conference, our copy of the treaty has never seen the light of day."

"Why have I never been told about it before today?" asked the President. "At least I could have put a stop to so much expenditure."

"For over fifty years, we've believed the Russians' copy was destroyed at the time of the Revolution. As the years passed it became clear that the Soviets accepted this as a *fait accompli* with the final acknowledgment of this fact coming from Stalin at Yalta. Brezhnev must have come across something within the last month that convinced him that their copy had only been mislaid."

"Christ, another month and we would have had a home run."

"That is correct, sir," said the Secretary of State.

"Do you realise, Dean, that if the Russians turn up at your office before midnight on Monday with their copy, all I'll be able to do will be so much piss in a thunderstorm?"

CHAPTER EIGHTEEN

When the cottage door closed behind Adam, all he could make out was the outskirts of a small town. While it was still so early he felt safe to jog towards the '*centre ville*', but as soon as the early-morning workers began to appear on the streets, he slowed to a walk. Adam opted not to go straight into the centre of the town but to look for somewhere to hide while he considered his next move. He came to a halt outside a multi-storey car park and decided he was unlikely to find a better place to formulate a plan.

Adam walked through an exit door at ground level and came to a lift that indicated that the car park was on four floors. He ran down the steps to the lowest level, tentatively pulled back the door to the basement, and found it was badly lit and almost empty. Adam had chosen the basement as he assumed that it would be the last floor to fill up with customers. He walked around the perimeter of the floor and studied the layout. Two cars were parked in the far corner, and a thick layer of dust suggested that they had been there for some time. He crouched down behind one of them and found that he was safely out of sight to all but the most inquisitive.

He began to fantasise that someone might park a

car on that floor and leave the keys in the ignition. He checked the doors of the two cars already parked but both were securely locked. He settled back to work out a more serious plan of how he could reach the coast by nightfall.

He was deep in thought when he heard a scraping noise that made him jump. He peered round the gloomy basement, and out of the darkness a man appeared pulling behind him a plastic dustbin half full of rubbish. Adam could barely see the old man dressed in a dirty brown coat that stretched nearly to the ground and left little doubt about the height of the previous employee. He wasn't sure what he would do if the man continued to walk towards him. But as he came nearer Adam could see that he was stooped and old; the stub of a cigarette protruded from his lips. The cleaner stopped in front of him, spotted a cigarette packet, picked it up and checked to be sure it was empty before dropping it in the dustbin. After that, a sweet paper, a Pepsi-Cola can and an old copy of *Le Figaro* all found their way into the dustbin. His eyes searched slowly round the room for more rubbish, but still he didn't notice Adam tucked away behind the farthest car. Satisfied that his task was completed, he dragged the dustbin across the floor and pushed it outside the door. Adam began to relax again but after about two minutes, the old man returned, walked over to a wall and pulled open a door that Adam hadn't previously noticed. He took off the long brown coat and replaced it with a grey one that didn't look in a much better state but at least it made a more convincing fit. He then disappeared through the exit. Moments later Adam heard a door close with a bang.

The cleaner had ended his day.

Adam waited for some time before he stood up and stretched. He crept around the edge of the wall until he reached the little door. He pulled it open quietly and removed the long brown coat from its nail, then headed back to his place in the corner. He ducked down as the first of the morning cars arrived. The driver swung into the far corner in such a fluent circle that Adam felt sure it must have been a daily routine. A short dapper man with a pencil moustache, dressed in a smart pin-stripe suit, jumped out of the car carrying a briefcase. Once he had locked the car door he proceeded with fast mincing strides towards the exit. Adam waited until the heavy door swung back into place before he stood up and tried on the brown coat over his blazer. It was tight on the shoulders and a little short in the arm, but at least it made him look as if he might have worked there.

For the next hour he watched the cars as they continued to arrive at irregular intervals. Tiresomely, all the owners carefully locked their doors and checked them before disappearing through the exit with their keys.

When he heard ten o'clock strike in the distance Adam decided that there was nothing to be gained by hanging around any longer. He had crept out from behind the car that was shielding him and began to make his way across the floor towards the exit when a Rover with English registration plates swung round the corner and nearly blinded him. He jumped to one side to let the car pass but it screeched to a halt beside him and the driver wound down his window.

"All – right – park – here?" the driver asked, emphasising each word in an English accent.

"Oui, monsieur," said Adam.

"Other – floors – marked – *privé*," the man continued, as if addressing a complete moron. "Any-where?" His arm swept round the floor.

"*Oui,*" repeated Adam, "bert ay merst paak you," he added, fearing he sounded too much like Peter Sellers.

Balls, was what Adam expected to hear him reply. "Fine," was what the man actually said. He got out of the car, and handed Adam his keys and a ten franc note.

"*Merci,*" said Adam, pocketing the note and touching his forehead with his hand. "*Quelle – heure – vous – retournez?*" he asked, playing the man at his own game.

"One hour at most," said the man as he reached the door. Adam waited by the car for a few minutes but the man did not come back. He opened the passenger door and dropped the food bag on the front seat. He then walked round to the other side and climbed in the driver's seat, switched on the ignition and checked the fuel gauge: a little over half full. He revved the engine and drove the car up the ramp until he reached the first floor, where he came to a halt unable to escape. He needed a two-franc piece to make the arm swing up and let him out. The lady in the car behind him reluctantly changed his ten-franc note once she realised there was no other way of getting out.

Adam drove quickly out on to the road looking for the sign 'Toutes Directions'. Once he had found one, it was only minutes before he was clear of the town and travelling up the N6 to Paris.

Adam estimated that he had two hours at best. By then the police would surely have been informed of the theft of the car. He felt confident he had enough petrol to reach Paris; but he certainly couldn't hope to make Calais.

He remained in the centre lane of the N6 for most

of the journey, always keeping the speedometer five kilometres below the limit. By the end of the first hour Adam had covered nearly ninety kilometres. He opened the bag the farmer's wife had given him and took out an apple and a piece of cheese. His mind began to drift to Heidi, as it had so often in the past two days.

If only he had never opened the letter.

Another hour passed before he spotted him limping up a hill only a few hundred yards from the main road. A broad smile came over Romanov's face when he realised he could get to Scott long before he could hope to reach the road. When Romanov was within a few yards of him the flight lieutenant turned round and smiled at the stranger.

When Romanov left Banks thirty minutes later hidden behind a tree with a broken neck he reluctantly admitted that the young pilot officer had been as brave as Valchek – but he couldn't waste any more time trying to discover in which direction Scott was heading.

Romanov headed west.

The moment Adam heard the siren he came out of his reverie. He checked the little clock on the dashboard. He had only been driving for about an hour and a half. Could the French police be that efficient? The police car was now approaching him fast on his left but Adam maintained the same speed – except for his heartbeat, which climbed well above the approved limit – until the police car shot past him.

As the kilometres sped by, he began to wonder if it might be wiser to turn off on to a quieter road, but decided, on balance, to risk pushing on to Paris as quickly as possible.

He remained alert for further sirens as he continued to follow the signs to Paris. When he finally reached the outskirts of the city, he proceeded to the Boulevard de l'Hôpital and even felt relaxed enough to bite into another apple. In normal circumstances he would have appreciated the magnificent architecture along the banks of the Seine, but today his eyes kept returning to the rear view mirror.

Adam decided he would abandon the vehicle in a large public car park: with any luck it could be days before anyone came across it.

He turned down the Rue de Rivoli and took in at once the long colourful banners looming up in front of him. He could hardly have picked a better place, as he felt sure it would be packed with foreign cars.

Adam backed the Rover in the farthest corner of the square. He then wolfed down the last piece of cheese, and locked the car. He started walking towards the exit, but had only gone a few yards when he realised that the strolling holidàymakers were amused by his ill-fitting brown jacket which he had completely forgotten. He decided to turn back and throw the coat in the boot. He quickly took it off and folded it in a small square.

He was only a few yards away from the car when he saw the young policeman. He was checking the Rover's number plate and repeating the letters and numbers into an intercom. Adam inched slowly back, never taking his eyes from the officer. He only needed to manage another six or seven paces before he would be lost in the throng of the crowd.

Five, four, three, two, he backed, as the man continued speaking into the intercom. Just one more pace . . . *"Alors!"* hollered the lady on whose foot Adam stepped.

"I'm so sorry," said Adam, instinctively in his native

language. The policeman immediately looked up and stared at Adam, then shouted something into the intercom and began running towards him.

Adam dropped the brown coat and swung round quickly, nearly knocking the stooping lady over before sprinting off towards the exit. The car park was full of tourists who had come to enjoy the pleasures of the Louvre, and Adam found it hard to pick up any real speed through the dense crowd. By the time he reached the entrance to the car park he could hear the policeman's whistle a few paces behind him. He ran across the Rue de Rivoli, through an archway and into a large square.

By then another policeman was coming from his right, leaving him with no choice but to run up the steps in front of him. When he reached the top he turned to see at least three other policemen in close pursuit. He threw himself through the swing door and past a group of Japanese tourists who were surrounding the Rodin statue that stood in the hallway. He charged on past a startled ticket collector, and on up the long marble staircase. *"Monsieur, monsieur, votre billet?"* he heard shouted in his wake.

At the top of the staircase he turned right and ran through *The Special '66' Centuries Exhibition*, Modern – Pollock, Bacon, Hockney – into the Impressionist room – Monet, Manet, Courbet – desperately looking for any way out. On into Eighteenth Century – Fragonard, Goya, Watteau – but still no sign of an exit. Through the great arch into Seventeenth Century – Murillo, Van Dyck, Poussin – as people stopped looking at the pictures and turned their attention to what was causing such a commotion. Adam ran on into Sixteenth Century – Raphael, Caravaggio, Michelangelo – suddenly aware that there were only two centuries of paintings to go.

Right or left? He chose right, and entered a huge square room. There were three exits. He slowed momentarily to decide which would be his best bet when he became aware that the room was full of Russian icons. He came to a halt at an empty display case. '*Nous regrettons que ce tableau soit soumis à la restauration.*'

The first policeman had already entered the large room and was only a few paces behind as Adam dashed on towards the farthest exit. There were now only two exits left open for him from which to choose. He swung right, only to see another policeman bearing straight down on him. Left: two more. Ahead, yet another.

Adam came to a halt in the middle of the Icon Room at the Louvre, his hands raised above his head. He was surrounded by policemen, their guns drawn.

CHAPTER NINETEEN

Sir Morris picked up the phone on his desk.

"An urgent call from Paris, sir," said his secretary.

"Thank you, Tessa." He listened carefully as his brain quickly translated the exciting news.

"*Merci, merci,*" said Sir Morris to his opposite number at the French Foreign Ministry. "We will be back in touch with you as soon as we have made all the necessary arrangements to collect him. But for now, please don't let him out of your sight." Sir Morris listened for a few moments before he said: "And if he has any possessions on him, please keep them guarded under lock and key. Thank you once again." His secretary took down every word of the conversation in shorthand – as she had done for the past seventeen years.

Once the police had snapped the handcuffs on Adam and marched him off to a waiting car, he was surprised how relaxed, almost friendly, they became. He was yanked into the back of the car by the policeman to whom he was attached. He noticed that there was a police car in front of him and yet another behind. Two motorcycle outriders led the little motorcade away. Adam felt more like visiting royalty than a criminal who was wanted for questioning for two murders, two car thefts and travelling under false identification. Was it possible at last that someone had worked out he was innocent?

When Adam arrived at the Sûreté on the Ile de la Cité, he was immediately ordered to empty all his pockets. One wristwatch, one apple, forty pounds in traveller's cheques, eight francs, and one British passport in the name of Dudley Hulme. The station inspector asked him politely to strip to his vest and pants. It was the second time that day. Once Adam had done so, the inspector carefully checked every pocket of the blazer, even the lining. His expression left Adam in no doubt he hadn't found what he was looking for.

"Do you have anything else in your possession?" the officer asked in slow, precise English.

Damn silly question, thought Adam. You can see for yourself. "No," was all he replied. The inspector checked the blazer once again but came across nothing new. "You must be dressed," he said abruptly.

Adam put back on his shirt, jacket and trousers but the inspector kept his tie and shoelaces.

"All your things will be returned to you when you leave," the inspector explained. Adam nodded as he slipped on his shoes, which flapped uncomfortably when he walked. He was then accompanied to a small cell on the same floor, locked in and left alone. He looked around the sparsely furnished room. A small wooden table was placed in its centre, with two wooden chairs on either side. His eyes checked over a single bed in the corner which had on it an ancient horse-hair mattress. He could not have described the room properly as a cell because there were no bars, even across the one small window. He took off his jacket, hung it over the chair and lay down on the bed. At least it was an improvement over anything he had slept on for the past two nights, he reflected. Could it have only been two nights since he had slept on the floor of Robin's hotel room in Geneva?

As the minutes ticked by, he made only one decision. That when the inspector returned, he would demand to see a lawyer. "What the hell's the French for lawyer?" he asked out loud.

When an officer eventually appeared, in what Adam estimated must have been about half an hour, he was carrying a tray laden with hot soup, a roll, and what looked to Adam like a steak with all the trimmings and a plastic cup filled to the brim with red wine. He wondered if they had got the wrong man, or if this was simply his last meal before the guillotine. He followed the officer to the door.

"I demand to speak to a lawyer," he said emphatically, but the policeman only shrugged.

"*Je ne comprends pas l'anglais,*" he said, and slammed the door behind him.

Adam settled down to eat the meal that had been set before him, thankful that the French assumed good food should be served whatever the circumstances.

Sir Morris told them his news an hour later and then studied each of them round the table carefully. He would never have called the D4 if he hadn't felt sure that Adam was at last secure. Matthews continued to show no emotion. Busch was unusually silent while Snell looked almost relaxed for a change. Lawrence was the only one who seemed genuinely pleased.

"Scott is locked up in the Ministry of the Interior off the Place Beauvais," continued Sir Morris, "and I have already contacted our military attaché at the Embassy . . ."

"Colonel Pollard," interrupted Lawrence.

"Colonel Pollard," said Sir Morris, "who has been sent over in the Ambassador's car and will bring Scott back to be debriefed at our Embassy in Faubourg St Honoré. Sûreté rang a few moments ago to confirm that Colonel Pollard had arrived." Sir Morris turned towards his Number Two. "You will fly over to Paris tonight and conduct the debriefing yourself."

"Yes, sir," said Lawrence, looking up at his boss, a smile appearing on his face.

Sir Morris nodded. A cool lot, he considered, as he stared round that table, but the next half hour would surely find out which one of them it was who served two masters.

"Good. I don't think I shall need any of you again today," said Sir Morris as he rose from his chair.

Mentor smiled as Sir Morris left the room; his task had already been completed. So simple when you can read upside-down shorthand.

A black Jaguar bearing CD plates had arrived at police headquarters a few minutes earlier than expected. The traffic had not been as heavy as the colonel had anticipated. The inspector was standing on the steps as Pollard jumped out of the car. The policeman looked at the flapping Union Jack on the bonnet and considered the whole exercise was becoming rather melodramatic.

Pollard, a short, thickset man, dressed in a dark suit, regimental tie and carrying a rolled umbrella, looked like so many of those Englishmen who refuse to acknowledge that they could possibly be abroad.

The inspector took Pollard directly through to the little room where Adam had been incarcerated.

"Pollard's the name, Colonel Pollard. British Military Attaché stationed here in Paris. Sorry you've been put through this ordeal, old fellow, but a lot of paperwork had to be completed to get you out. Bloody red tape."

"I understand," said Adam, jumping off the bed and shaking the colonel by the hand. "I was in the army myself."

"I know. Royal Wessex, wasn't it?"

Adam nodded, feeling a little more confident.

"Still, the problem's been sorted out now," continued the colonel. "The French police have been most co-operative and have agreed to let you accompany me to our Embassy."

Adam looked at the colonel's tie. "Duke of York's?"

"What? Certainly not," said Pollard, his hand fingering his shirt front. "Green Jackets."

"Yes, of course," said Adam, pleased to have his mistake picked up.

"Now I think we ought to be cutting along, old fellow, I know you'll be relieved to hear that they won't be laying any charges."

The colonel didn't know just how relieved Adam did feel.

The inspector led them both back out into the hall where Adam had only to identify and sign for his personal belongings. He put them all in his pocket, except for the watch, which he slipped over his wrist, and his shoelaces, which he quickly inserted and tied. He wasn't surprised they didn't return Dudley Hulme's passport.

"Don't let's hang around too long, old fellow," said the colonel, beginning to sound a little anxious.

"I won't be a moment," said Adam. "I'm just as keen to get out of this place as you are." He checked his laces before following Colonel Pollard and the inspector out to the waiting Jaguar. He noticed for the first time that the colonel had a slight limp. A chauffeur held the door open for him; Adam laughed.

"Something funny, old fellow?" asked the colonel.

"No. It's just that the last chauffeur who offered to do that for me didn't look quite as friendly."

Adam climbed into the back of the Jaguar and the colonel slipped in beside him.

"Back to the Embassy," said Pollard, and the car moved off briskly.

Adam stared in horror at the flapping Union Jack.

CHAPTER TWENTY

When Adam awoke he was naked.

He looked around the sparse room but this time, unlike the French jail, he was unable to see what was behind him: his arms, legs and body were bound tightly by a nylon cord to a chair that had been placed in the middle of the room, and which made him all but immobile.

When he looked up from the chair all he could see was Colonel Pollard standing over him. The moment the colonel was satisfied that Adam had regained consciousness he quickly left the room.

Adam turned his head to see all his clothes laid out neatly on a bed at the far side of the cell. He tried to manoeuvre the chair, but he could barely manage to make it wobble from side to side, and after several minutes had advanced only a few inches towards the door. He switched his energies to trying to loosen the cords around his wrists, rubbing them up and down against the wood of the slats, but his arms were bound so tightly that he could only manage the slightest friction.

After struggling ineffectively for several minutes he was interrupted by the sound of the door swinging open. Adam looked up as Romanov strode through.

He decided he was no less terrifying at close quarters. He was followed by another man whom Adam didn't recognise. The second man was clutching what looked like a cigar box as he took his place somewhere behind Adam. Pollard followed him, carrying a large plastic sheet.

Romanov looked at Adam's naked body and smiled; enjoying his humiliation he came to a halt directly in front of the chair.

"My name is Alexander Petrovich Romanov," he announced with only a slight accent.

"Or Emmanuel Rosenbaum," said Adam, staring at his adversary closely.

"I am only sorry that we are unable to shake hands," he added, as he began circling the chair. "But I felt in the circumstances certain precautions were necessary. First I should like to congratulate you on having eluded me for so long, but as you will now realise my source in London can place a call every bit as quickly as yours."

"Your source?" said Adam.

"Don't be naïve, Captain. You must be painfully aware by now that you're in no position to be asking questions, only answering them."

Adam fixed his gaze on a brick in the wall in front of him, making no attempt to follow Romanov's circum-navigations.

"Pollard," said Romanov sharply, "put Captain Scott back in the centre of the room. He seems to have managed to move at least a foot in his getaway attempt."

Pollard did as he was bid, first spreading the plastic sheet on the floor, then manoeuvring Adam till the chair was on the centre of the sheet.

"Thank you," said Romanov. "I think you have

already met our Colonel Pollard," he continued. "That's not his real name, of course, and indeed he's not a real colonel either, but that's what he always wanted to be in life, so when the opportunity arose, we happily obliged.

"In fact the good colonel did serve in the British Army, but I fear he entered the service of King and country as a private soldier and eighteen years later left, still as a private soldier. And despite an injury to his leg – unfortunately not received from any known enemy of the Crown – he was unable to claim a disability pension. Which left him fairly destitute. But, as I explained, he always wanted to be a colonel," continued Romanov. "It was a good attempt of yours – 'The Duke of York's?' – but as the colonel had genuinely served with the Green Jackets it was the one tie he felt safe wearing."

Adam's eyes remained fixed on the wall. "Now I confess, our mistake over the Union Jack was lax but as it is impossible to fly the Russian flag upside down without everyone noticing, it was perhaps understandable. Although, in truth, Pollard should have spotted it immediately, we must be thankful that you did not until the car doors were safely locked."

Romanov stopped his endless circling and stared down at the nude body.

"Now I think the time has come for you to be introduced to our Dr Stavinsky who has so been looking forward to making your acquaintance because he hasn't had a lot of work to do lately and he fears he might be becoming a little rusty."

Romanov took a pace backward allowing Stavinsky to come and take his place immediately in front of Adam. The cigar box was still tucked under his arm. Adam stared at the diminutive figure who seemed to be sizing him up. Stavinsky must have been no taller than five feet and wore an open-necked grey shirt and a badly creased grey suit that made him resemble a junior clerk in a not very successful solicitor's office. A one-day bristle covered his face, leaving the impression that he hadn't expected to be working that day. His thin lips suddenly parted in a grin as if he had come to some conclusion.

"It is a pleasure to make your acquaintance, Captain Scott," began Stavinsky. "Although you are an unexpected guest of the Embassy you are most welcome. You could of course make our association very short by simply letting me have one piece of information. In truth" – he let out a small sigh – "I only require to know the whereabouts of the Tsar's icon." He paused. "Although I have a feeling it's not going to be that easy. Am I correct?"

Adam didn't reply.

"It doesn't come as a great surprise. I warned Comrade Romanov that after his laudatory description of you a simple series of questions and answers would be unlikely to suffice. However, I must follow the normal procedure in such circumstances. As you will find, the Russians go by the book every bit as much as the British. Now you may have wondered," added Stavinsky as if it were an afterthought, "why a man who never smokes should be seen carrying a Cuban cigar box."

Stavinsky waited for Adam's reply but none was forthcoming.

"Ah, no attempt at conversation. I see you have been through such an experience before. Well, then I must continue talking to myself for the moment. When I was a student at the University of Moscow my subject was chemistry, but I specialised in one particular aspect of the science."

Adam feigned no interest as he tried not to recall his worst days in the hands of the Chinese.

"What few people in the West realise is that we Russians were the first to pioneer, at university level, a Department of Scientific Interrogation with a full professorial chair and several research assistants. They are still without one at either Oxford or Cambridge I am told. But then the West continues to preserve a quixotic view of the value of life and the right of the individual. Now, as you can imagine, only certain members of the university were aware of the existence of such a department, let alone able to enrol as a student – especially as it was not on the curriculum. But as I had already been a member of the Perviyotdel it was common sense that I should add the craft of torture to my trade. Now I am basically a simple man," continued Stavinsky, "who had previously shown little interest in research but once I had been introduced to the 'cigar box' I became, overnight, an enthralled and retentive pupil. I could not wait to be let loose to experiment." He paused to see what effect he was having on Scott, and was disappointed to be met by the same impassive stare.

"Torture, of course, is an old and honourable profession," continued Stavinsky. "The Chinese have been at it for nearly three thousand years as I think you have already experienced, Captain Scott, and even you British have come a long way since the rack. But that particular instrument has proved to be rather cumbersome for carrying around in a modern world. With this in mind, my tutor at Moscow, Professor Metz, has developed something small and simple that even a man of average intelligence can master after a few lessons."

Adam was desperate to know what was in the box but his look remained impassive.

"With torture, as with making love, Captain Scott, foreplay is the all-important factor. Are you following me, Captain?" asked Stavinsky.

Adam tried to remain relaxed and calm.

"Still no response, Captain Scott, but as I explained I am in no hurry. Especially, as I suspect in your case, the whole operation may take a little longer than usual, which I confess will only add to my enjoyment. And although we are not yet in possession of the Tsar's icon I *am* at least in control of the one person who knows where it is."

Adam still made no comment.

"So I will ask you once and once only before I open the box. Where is the Tsar's icon?"

Adam spat at Stavinsky.

"Not only ill-mannered," remarked Stavinsky, "but also stupid. Because in a very short time you will be desperate for any liquid we might be kind enough to allow you. But, to be fair, you had no way of knowing that."

Stavinsky placed the box on the floor and opened it slowly.

"First, I offer you," he said, like a conjurer in front of a child, "a six-volt nickel-cadmium battery, made by EverReady." He paused. "I thought you would appreciate that touch. Second," he continued, putting his hand back in the box, "a small pulse generator." He placed the rectangular metal box next to the battery. "Third, two lengths of wire with electrodes attached to their ends. Fourth, two syringes, fifth, a tube of collodion glue and finally, a phial, of which more later. When I say 'finally', there are still two items left in the box which I shall not require unless it becomes necessary for us to progress to Stage Two in our little experiment, or even Stage Three."

Stavinsky placed everything in a straight line on the floor in front of Adam.

"Doesn't look a lot, I confess," said Stavinsky. "But with a little imagination I'm sure you will be able to work out its potential. Now. In order that Comrade Romanov and the colonel can enjoy the spectacle I am about to offer it is necessary to add a few details about the nervous system itself. I do hope you are following my every word, Captain Scott, because it is the victim's knowledge which allows him to appreciate the true genius of what is about to follow."

It didn't please Adam that Stavinsky spoke English so well. He could still vividly remember how the Chinese had told Adam what they were going to do to him in a language that he couldn't understand. With them, he had found it easier to allow his mind to drift during their diatribe but he still ended up in a fridge for four hours.

"Now to the practical," continued the grey figure. "By sending a small electrical impulse to the end of the synapse, it is possible to pass on a large electric message to thousands of other nerves within a fraction of a second. This causes a nasty sensation not unlike touching a live wire when the electrical power has been left on in one's home, more commonly known as an electric shock. Not deadly, but distinctly unpleasant. In the Moscow school this is known as Stage One and there is no necessity for you to experience this if you are now willing to tell me where I can find the Tsar's icon."

Adam remained impassive.

"I see you have not paid attention during my little

lecture so I fear we will have to move from the theoretical to the practical."

Adam began reciting to himself the thirty-seven plays of Shakespeare. How his old English master would have been delighted to know that after all those years of drumming the complete Shakespearean canon into a reluctant student, Adam could still recall them at a moment's notice.

Henry VI part one, Henry VI part two, Henry VI part three, Richard II . . .

Stavinsky picked up the tube of collodion glue, removed the cap and smeared two lumps of it on Adam's chest.

. . . *Comedy of Errors, Titus Andronicus, The Taming of the Shrew* . . .

The Russian attached the two electrodes to the glue, taking the wires back and screwing them to the six-volt battery, which in turn was connected to the tiny pulse generator.

. . . *Two Gentlemen of Verona, Love's Labour's Lost, Romeo and Juliet* . . .

Without warning, Stavinsky pressed down the handle of the generator for two seconds during which time Adam received a two-hundred-volt shock. For those seconds Adam screamed as he experienced excruciating pain as the volts forced their way to every part of his body. But the sensation was over in a moment.

"Do feel free to let us know how exactly you feel. You are in a soundproof room, and therefore you won't be disturbing anyone else in the building."

Adam ignored the comment and gripping the side of the chair, mumbled . . . *Richard III, Midsummer Night's Dream, King John* . . .

Stavinsky pressed the plunger down for another two

seconds. Adam felt the pain instantly the second time. The moment it was over he felt violently nauseated, but he managed to remain conscious.

Stavinsky waited for some time before he volunteered an opinion. "Impressive. You have definitely qualified to enter Stage Two, from which you can be released immediately by answering one simple question. Where is the Tsar's icon?"

Adam's mouth had become so dry that he couldn't speak, let alone spit.

"I did try to warn you, Captain Scott." Stavinsky turned towards the door. "Do go and fetch the captain some water, Colonel."

. . . *The Merchant of Venice, Henry IV part one, Henry IV part two* . . .

A moment later Pollard was back, and a bottle was thrust into Adam's mouth. He gulped half the contents down until it was pulled away.

"Mustn't overdo it. You might need some more later. But that won't be necessary if you let me know where the icon is."

Adam spat what was left of the water towards where his adversary was standing.

Stavinsky leapt forward and slapped Adam hard across the face with the back of his hand. Adam's head slumped.

"You give me no choice but to advance to Stage Two," said Stavinsky. He looked towards Romanov who nodded. Stavinsky's thin lips parted in another smile. "You may have wondered," he continued, "how much more harm I can do with a simple six-volt battery, and indeed having seen in numerous American gangster movies an execution by the electric chair you will know a large generator is needed to kill a man. But first it is important to remember that I don't want to kill you. Second, my science lessons didn't end at Stage One. Professor Metz's mind was also exercised by the feebleness of this stage and after a lifetime of dedicated research he came up with an ingenious solution known as 'M', which the Academy of Science named after him in his honour. If you inject 'M' into the nervous system, messages can be transmitted to all your nerves many times more efficiently, thus allowing the pain to multiply without actually proving fatal.

"I only need to multiply a few milli-amps by a suitable factor to create a far more interesting effect – so I must ask you once again, where is the Tsar's icon?"

... *Much Ado About Nothing, Henry V, Julius Caesar* ...

"I see you are determined that I should proceed," said Stavinsky, removing a syringe from the floor and jabbing the long thin needle into a phial before withdrawing the plunger until the barrel of the syringe was half full. Stavinsky held the needle in the air, pressed the knob and watched a little spray flow out like a tiny fountain. He moved behind Adam.

"I am now going to give you a lumbar puncture which if you attempt to move will paralyse you from the neck down for life. By nature I am not an honest man but on this occasion I must recommend you to trust me. I assure you that the injection will not kill you because, as you already know, that is not in our best interest."

Adam didn't move a muscle as he felt the syringe go into his back. *As You Like* ... he began. Then excruciating pain swept his body, and suddenly, blessedly, he felt nothing.

When he came round there was no way of telling how much time had passed. His eyes slowly focused on his tormentor pacing up and down the room impatiently. Seeing Adam's eyes open, the unshaven man stopped pacing, smiled, walked over to the chair and ran his fingers slowly over the large piece of sticking plaster that covered Adam's two-day-old shoulder wound. The touch appeared gentle, but to Adam it felt like a hot iron being forced across his shoulder.

"As I promised," said Stavinsky. "A far more interesting sensation is awaiting you. And now I think I'll rip the plaster off." He waited for a moment while Adam pursed his lips. Then, in one movement, he tore the plaster back. Adam screamed as if the bullet had hit him again. Romanov came forward, leaned over and studied the wound.

"I'm relieved to see my colleague didn't miss you completely," Romanov said before adding, "can you imagine what it will be like when I allow Mr Stavinsky to wire you up again and then press the little generator?"

". . . *Twelfth Night, Hamlet, The Merry Wives of Windsor* . . ." Adam said aloud for the first time.

"I see you wish to leave nothing to the imagination," said Romanov and disappeared behind him. Stavinsky checked that the wires were attached to the collodion glue on Adam's chest and then he returned to the generator. "I shall press down the handle in three seconds' time. You know what you have to do to stop me."

". . . *Troilus and Cressida, All's Well That Ends Well* . . ."

As the handle plunged down the volts seemed to find their way to every nerve-ending in his body. Adam let out such a scream that if they had not been in a soundproofed room anyone within a mile would have heard him. When the initial effect was over he was left shaking and retching uncontrollably. Stavinsky and Pollard rushed forward to the chair and quickly undid the nylon cords. Adam fell on his hands and knees, still vomiting.

"Couldn't afford to let you choke to death, could we?" said Stavinsky. "We lost one or two that way in the early days but we know better now."

As soon as the sickness subsided, Stavinsky threw Adam back up on to the chair and Pollard tied him up again.

"Where is the Tsar's icon?" shouted Stavinsky.

". . . *Measure for Measure, Othello, King Lear* . . ." Adam said, his voice now trembling.

Pollard picked up another bottle of water and thrust it at Adam's lips. Adam gulped it down but it was as a tiny oasis in a vast desert. Romanov came forward and Stavinsky took his place beside the plunger.

"You are a brave man, Scott," said Romanov, "with nothing left to prove, but this is madness. Just tell me where the icon is and I will send Stavinsky away and order the colonel to leave you on the steps of the British Embassy."

". . . *Macbeth, Antony and Cleopatra* . . ."

Romanov let out a sigh and nodded. Stavinsky pushed the plunger down once again. Even the colonel turned white as he watched Adam's reaction. The pitch of the scream was even higher and the muscles contorted visibly as Adam felt the volts reach the millions of little nerve-ends in his body. When once more he had been released, Adam lay on the floor on his hands and knees. Was there anything left in his stomach that could still possibly come up? He raised his head, only to be hurled back on to the chair and bound up again. Stavinsky stared down at him.

"Most impressive, Captain Scott, you have qualified for Stage Three."

When Lawrence arrived at Orly Airport that evening he was looking forward to a quiet dinner with his old friend at the Ambassador's residence. He was met at the barrier by Colonel Pollard.

"How is he?" were Lawrence's first words.

"I hoped you were going to tell us," said Pollard, as he took Lawrence's overnight suitcase. Lawrence stopped in his tracks and stared at the tall, thin soldier who was in the full dress uniform of the Royal Dragoon Guards.

"What do you mean?" said Lawrence.

"Simply that," said Pollard. "I followed your instructions to the letter and went to pick up Scott at the Ile de la Cité but when I arrived I was informed that he had been taken away twenty minutes earlier by someone else using my name. We contacted your office immediately but as you were already en route the Ambassador ordered me straight to the airport while he phoned Sir Morris."

Lawrence staggered and nearly fell. The colonel came quickly to his side. He didn't understand what Lawrence meant when he said, "He's bound to believe it's me."

When Adam regained consciousness, Romanov stood alone.

"Sometimes," said the Russian, continuing as if Adam had never passed out, "a man is too proud to show lack of resolution in front of the torturer or indeed one of his own countrymen, especially a traitor. That is why I have removed Stavinsky and the colonel from our presence. Now I have no desire to see Stavinsky continue his experiment to Stage Three, but I can stop him only if you will tell me where you have put the icon."

"Why should I?" said Adam belligerently. "It's legally mine."

"Not so, Captain Scott. What you picked up from the bank in Geneva is the priceless original painted by Rublev which belongs to the Union of Soviet Socialist Republics. And if that icon were to appear in any auction house or gallery in the world, we would immediately claim it as a national treasure stolen by the seller."

"But how could that be . . .?" began Adam.

"Because," said Romanov, "it is you who are now in possession of the original that the Tsar left in the safe-keeping of the Grand Duke of Hesse and for over fifty years the Soviet Union has only had a copy." Adam's eyes opened wide in disbelief as Romanov removed from the inside pocket of his overcoat an icon of St George and the Dragon. Romanov paused and then turned it over; a smile of satisfaction crossed his face as Adam's eyes registered the significance of the missing crown.

"Like you," continued Romanov, "I only have this one on loan – but you tell me where the original is and I will release you and exchange the copy for the original. No one will be any the wiser and you'll still be able to make yourself a worthwhile profit."

"Old lamps for new," said Adam with a sneer.

Romanov's eyes narrowed menacingly. "Surely you realise, Scott, that you are in possession of a priceless masterpiece that belongs to the Soviet Union. Unless you return the icon you are going to cause considerable embarrassment for your country and you will probably end up in jail. All you have to do is tell me where the icon is and you can go free."

Adam didn't even bother to shake his head.

"Then the time has obviously come to let you into some information you will be more interested in," Romanov said, extracting a single sheet of paper from an envelope he removed from his inside pocket. Adam was genuinely puzzled, quite unable to think what it could be. Romanov opened it slowly and held it up so that Adam could only see the back.

"This single sheet of paper reveals a sentence carried out in Moscow in 1946 by Judge I. T. Nikitchenko – the death sentence," continued Romanov, "pronounced on a certain Major Vladimir Kosky, the Russian guard in charge of the Soviet watch the night Reichsmarshal Hermann Goering died." He turned the paper round so Adam could see it. "As you can see, Major Kosky was found guilty of collaboration with the enemy for financial gain. It was proved he was directly responsible for smuggling cyanide into the Reichsmarshal's cell on the night he died." Adam's eyes widened. "Ah, I see I have dealt the ace of spades," said Romanov. "Now I think you will finally tell me where the icon actually is because you have an expression in England, if I recall correctly: fair exchange is no robbery. Your icon for my icon, plus the legal judgment that will finally vindicate your father's honour."

Adam closed his eyes, painfully aware for the first time that Romanov had no idea what was inside the icon.

Romanov was unable to hide his anger. He walked to the door and flung it open. "He's yours," he said.

Dr Stavinsky re-entered the room and, smiling, continued as if nothing had interrupted him. "Professor

Metz was never really satisfied with Stage Two because he found the recovery time even for an extremely brave and fit man like yourself could sometimes hold him up for hours, even days. So during his final years at the university he devoted his time to finding how he could possibly speed the whole process up. As for all geniuses the final solution was staggering in its simplicity. All he had to produce was a chemical formula that when injected into the nervous system caused an immediate recovery – a rapid analgesic. It took him twelve years and several deaths before he came up with the final solution," said Stavinsky, removing another phial from the cigar box and plunging the needle of a second syringe into the seal on the top of the phial.

"This," Stavinsky said, holding up the little phial in triumph, "when injected into your blood stream, will aid recovery so quickly that you may even wonder if you ever went through any pain in the first place. For this piece of genius Metz should have been awarded the Nobel Prize, but it was not something we felt he could share with the rest of the scientific world. But because of him I can repeat the process you have just experienced again and again, never permitting you to die. You see, I can keep this generator pumping up and down every thirty minutes for the next week if that is your desire," said Stavinsky, as he stared down at Adam's white, disbelieving face flecked with yellow specks of his vomit.

"Or I can stop immediately after I have administered the antidote the moment you let me know where the Tsar's icon is."

Stavinsky stood in front of Adam and half filled the syringe. Adam felt intensely cold, yet the shock of his torture had caused him to sweat profusely. "Sit still, Captain Scott, I have no desire to do you any permanent injury." Adam felt the needle go deep in and moments later the fluid entered his blood stream.

He could not believe how quickly he felt himself recovering. Within minutes he no longer felt sick or disorientated. The sensation in his arms and legs returned to normal while the wish never to experience Stage Two again became acute.

"Brilliant man, Professor Metz, on that I'm sure we can both agree," said Stavinsky, "and if he were still alive I feel certain he would have written a paper on your case." Slowly and carefully Stavinsky began to smear more lumps of jelly on Adam's chest. When he was satisfied with his handiwork he once again attached the electrodes to the jelly.

"*Coriolanus, Timon of Athens, Pericles.*" Stavinsky thrust his palm down and Adam hoped that he would die. He found a new level to scream at, as his body shook and shook. Seconds later he felt ice cold and, shivering uncontrollably, he started to retch.

Stavinsky was quickly by his side to release him. Adam fell to the ground and coughed up what was left in his body. When he was only spitting, Pollard placed him back in the chair.

"You must understand I can't let you die, Captain. Now where is the icon?" Stavinsky shouted.

In the Louvre, Adam wanted to scream, but his words barely came out as a whisper, the inside of his mouth feeling like sandpaper. Stavinsky proceeded to fill the second syringe again and injected Adam with the fluid. Once again it was only moments before the agony subsided and he felt completely recovered.

"Ten seconds, we go again. Nine, eight, seven . . ."

"*Cymbeline.*"

". . . six, five, four . . ."

"*The Winter's Tale.*"

". . . three, two, one."

"*The Tempest*. Aahhhh," he screamed and immediately fainted. The next thing Adam remembered was the cold water being poured over him by the colonel before he began to retch again. Once tied back in the chair Stavinsky thrust the syringe into him once more, but Adam couldn't believe he would ever recover again. He must surely die, because he wanted to die. He felt the syringe jab into his flesh again.

Romanov stepped forward and looking straight at Adam, said, "I feel Dr Stavinsky and I have earned a little supper. We did consider inviting you but felt your stomach wouldn't be up to it, but when we return fully refreshed Dr Stavinsky will repeat the entire exercise again and again until you let me know where you have hidden the icon."

Romanov and Stavinsky left as Colonel Pollard came back in. Romanov and the colonel exchanged a few sentences which Adam could not make out. Then Romanov left the room, closing the door quietly behind him.

Pollard came over to Adam and offered him the water bottle. Adam gulped it down and was genuinely surprised how quickly he was recovering. Yet although his senses were returning to normal Adam still doubted he could survive one more time.

"I'm going to throw up again," said Adam and suddenly thrust his head forward. Pollard quickly undid the knots and watched Adam slump to his hands and knees. He threw up some spit and rested before the colonel helped him gently back into the chair. As he sat down Adam gripped both sides of the chair legs firmly, then with all the strength he could muster jack-knifed forward, swung the chair over his head, and brought it crashing down on top of the unsuspecting colonel. Pollard collapsed in a heap, unconscious, on the floor in front of Adam and never heard him utter the words, "*Henry VIII* and *Two Noble Kinsmen* – I'll bet that's one you've never heard of, Colonel. Mind you, to be fair, not everyone thinks Shakespeare wrote it."

Adam remained on his knees over the colonel's body, wondering what his next move should be. He was grateful that the soundproofed room was now working in his favour. He waited for a few more seconds as he tried to measure what was left of his strength. He picked up the water bottle that had been knocked over and drained it of its last drops. He then crawled across to the bed and pulled on his pants and socks, shoes, and his not so white shirt, followed by his trousers. He was about to put on the blazer, but found the lining had been ripped to shreds. He changed his mind and stumbled like an old man back towards the colonel, removed his Harris tweed coat and slipped it on. It was large round the shoulders but short at the hips.

Adam made his way to the door, feeling almost exhilarated. He turned the handle and pulled. The door came open an inch – nothing happened – two inches – still nothing. He stared through the crack but all he could see was a dark corridor. As he pulled the door wide open the hinges sounded to Adam like racing tyres screeching. Once he was certain that no one was going to return, he ventured into the corridor.

Standing against the wall he stared up and down the thin windowless passage, waiting for his eyes to adjust to the dark. He could make out a light shining through a pebbled pane in a door at the far end of the corridor, and began to take short steps towards it. He continued on, as if he were a blind man, creeping slowly forward until he saw another beam of light coming from under a door to his right about ten yards away from the one he needed to reach. He edged cautiously on and was only a pace away from the first door when it opened abruptly and out stepped a small man in a white tunic and blue kitchen overalls. Adam froze against the wall as the kitchen hand removed a packet of cigarettes and a box of matches from his pocket and headed away in the opposite direction. When the man reached the glazed door he opened it and walked out. Adam watched the silhouette outlined against the pebbled window, a match being struck, a cigarette being lit, the first puff of smoke; he even heard a sigh.

Adam crept past what he now assumed was a kitchen and on towards the outer door. He turned the knob slowly, waiting for the silhouette to move. The outer door also possessed hinges which no one had bothered to oil for months. The smoker turned round and smiled as Adam's left hand landed firmly in his stomach. As the smoker bent over, Adam's right fist came up to the man's chin with all the force he could muster. The smoker sank in a heap on the ground, and Adam stood over him thankful that he didn't move.

He dragged the limp body across the grass, dumped it behind a bush and remained kneeling by it while he tried to work out his bearings. Adam could just make out a high wall ahead of him with a gravelled courtyard in front of it. The wall threw out a long shadow from the moon across the tiny stones. About twenty yards . . . Summoning up every ounce of energy, he ran to the wall and then clung to it like a limpet, remaining motionless in its shadow. Slowly and silently he moved round the wall, yard by yard, until he reached the front of what he now felt sure was the Russian Embassy. The great green wooden gates at the front entrance were open, and every few seconds limousines swept past him. Adam looked back up towards the front door of the Embassy and at the top of the steps he saw a massive man, medals stretching across his formal dress jacket, shaking hands with each of his departing guests. Adam assumed he was the Ambassador.

One or two of the guests were leaving by foot. There were two armed gendarmes on the gate who stood rigidly to attention and saluted as each car or guest passed by.

Adam waited until a vast BMW, the West German flag fluttering on its bonnet, slowed as it passed through the gates. Using the car to shield him, Adam walked out into the centre of the drive, then, following closely behind, walked straight between the guards towards the road.

"Bonsoir," he said lightly to the guards as the car moved forward: he was only a yard from the road. "Walk," he told himself, "don't run. Walk, walk until you are out of their sight." They saluted deferentially. "Don't look back." Another car followed him out, but he kept his eyes firmly to the front.

"Tu cherches une femme?" a voice repeated from the shadows of a recessed doorway. Adam had ended up in a badly lit one-way street. Several men of indeterminate age seemed to be walking aimlessly up and down the kerbside. He eyed them with suspicion as he moved on through the darkness.

"Wha –?" said Adam, stepping sharply into the road, his senses heightened by the unexpected sound.

"From Britain, eh? Do you search for a girl?" The voice held an unmistakable French accent.

"You speak English," said Adam, still unable to see the woman clearly.

343

"You have to know a lot of languages in my profession, *chéri*, or you'd starve."

Adam tried to think coherently. "How much for the night?"

"*Eh bien*, but it's not yet midnight," said the girl. "So I would have to charge two hundred francs."

Although he had no money Adam hoped the girl might at least lead him to safety.

"Two hundred is fine."

"*D'accord*," said the girl, at last stepping out of the shadows. Adam was surprised by how attractive she turned out to be. "Take my arm and if you pass a gendarme say only, '*Ma femme*'."

Adam stumbled forward.

"Ah, I think you drink too much, *chéri*. Never mind, you can lean on me, yes."

"No, I'm just tired," said Adam, trying hard to keep up with her pace.

"You have been to party at Embassy, *n'est-ce pas?*"

Adam was startled.

"Don't be surprised, *chéri*. I find most of my regulars from the Embassies. They can't risk to be involved in casual affairs, *tu comprends?*"

"I believe you," said Adam.

"My apartment is just round the corner," she assured him. Adam was confident he could get that far but he took a deep breath when they arrived at a block of flats and first saw the steps. He just managed to reach the front door.

"I live on the top of the house, *chéri*. Very nice view," she said matter-of-factly, "but I'm afraid – how you say – no lift."

Adam said nothing, but leaned against the outside wall, breathing deeply.

"You are *fatigué*," she said. By the time they had

reached the second floor she almost had to drag Adam up the last few steps.

"I don't see you getting it up tonight, *chéri*," she said, opening her front door and turning on the light. "Still, it's your party." She strode in, turning on other lights as she went.

Adam staggered across the floor towards the only chair in sight and collapsed into it. The girl had by this time disappeared into another room and he had to make a supreme effort not to fall asleep before she returned.

As she stood in the light of the doorway Adam was able to see her properly for the first time. Her blonde hair was short and curly and she wore a red blouse and a knee-length skin-tight black skirt. A wide white plastic belt emphasised her small waist. She wore black mesh stockings and what he could see of her legs would have normally aroused him had he been in any other condition.

She walked over to Adam with a slight swing of the hips, and knelt down in front of him. Her eyes were a surprisingly luminous green.

"Would you please give me the two hundred now?" she asked, without harshness. She ran her hand along his thigh.

"I don't have any money," said Adam quite simply.

"What?" she said, sounding angry for the first time. Placing her hand in his inside pocket she removed a wallet and asked, "Then what's this? I don't play the games," handing the thick wallet over to Adam. He opened the flap to find it was jammed full of French francs and a few English notes. Adam concluded that the colonel was obviously paid in cash for his services.

Adam extracted two one-hundred francs and dutifully handed them over.

"That's better," she said, and disappeared into the other room.

Adam checked quickly through the wallet to discover a driving licence and a couple of credit cards in the colonel's real name of Albert Tomkins. He quickly looked around: a double bed that was wedged up against the far wall took up most of the floor space. Apart from the chair he was settled in, the only other pieces of furniture were a dressing table and a tiny stool with a red velvet cushion on it. A stained blue carpet covered most of the wooden floor.

To his left was a small fireplace with logs stacked neatly in one corner. All Adam wished to do was fall asleep but with what strength was left in his body, he pushed himself up, wobbled over to the fireplace and hid the wallet between the logs. He lurched back towards the chair and fell into it as the door reopened.

Again the girl stood in the light of the doorway but this time she wore only a pink negligée, which even in his present state Adam could see right through whenever she made the slightest movement. She walked slowly across the room and once more knelt down beside him.

"How you like it, *mon cher*? Straight or the French way?"

"I need to rest," said Adam.

"For two hundred francs you sleep in any 'otel," she said in disbelief.

"I only want to be allowed to rest a few minutes," he assured her.

"*L'Anglais,*" she said, and began to try to lift Adam out of the chair and towards the bed. He stumbled and fell, landing half on and half off the corner of the mattress. She undressed him as deftly as any nurse could have done before lifting his legs up on to the bed. Adam made no effort to help or hinder her. She hesitated for a moment when she saw the shoulder wound, bewildered as to what kind of accident could have caused such a gash. She rolled him over to the far side and pulled back the top sheet and blanket. Then she walked round to the other side of the bed and rolled him back again. Finally she pushed him flat on his back and covered him with the sheet and blankets.

"I could still give you French if you like," she said. But Adam was already asleep.

CHAPTER TWENTY-ONE

When Adam eventually awoke the sun was already shining through the small window of the bedroom. He blinked as he took in his surroundings and tried to recall what had happened the night before. Then it all came back to him and suddenly he felt sick again at the memory. He sat on the edge of the bed but the moment he tried to stand he felt giddy and weak, and fell back down. At least he had escaped. He looked around the room but the girl was nowhere to be seen or heard. Then he remembered the wallet.

He sat bolt upright, gathering himself for a few moments before standing up again and trying to walk. Although he was still unsteady it was better than he had expected. It's only the recovery that counts, not the speed, he thought ironically. When he reached the fireplace he fell on his knees and searched among the logs, but the colonel's wallet was no longer there. As quickly as he could he went to the jacket hanging over the back of the chair. He checked in the inside pocket: a pen, a half-toothless comb, a passport, a driving licence, some other papers, but no wallet. He searched the outside pockets: a bunch of keys, a penknife, a few assorted coins, English and French, but that was all that was left. With a string of oaths he collapsed on to the floor. He sat there for some time and didn't move until he heard a key in the lock.

The front door of the flat swung open and the girl sauntered in carrying a shopping basket. She was dressed in a pretty floral skirt and white blouse that would have been suitable for any churchgoer on a Sunday morning. The basket was crammed with food.

"Woken up, 'ave we, *chéri*? *Est-ce-que tu prends le petit déjeuner*?"

Adam looked a little taken aback.

She returned his stare. "Even working girls need their breakfast, *n'est-ce pas*? Sometimes is the only meal I manage all day."

"Where's my wallet?" asked Adam coldly.

"On the table," said the girl, pointing.

Adam glanced across the room, to see that she had left the wallet in the most obvious place.

"It not necessary of you to 'ide it," she reprimanded him. "Because I'm a whore don't think I'm a thief." With this she strode off into the kitchen, leaving the door open.

Adam suddenly knew how big Tom Thumb felt.

"Coffee and croissants?" she shouted.

"Fantastic," said Adam. He paused. "I'm sorry. I was stupid."

"Not to think about it," she said. "*Ça n'est rien*."

"I still don't know your name," said Adam.

"My working name is Brigitte, but as you 'ave not use my services last night or this morning you can call me by my real name – Jeanne."

"Can I have a bath, Jeanne?"

"The door in the corner, but don't take too long, unless you like croissants cold." Adam made his way to the bathroom and found Jeanne had provided for everything a man might need: a razor, shaving cream, soap, flannel, clean towels – and a gross box of Durex.

After a warm bath and a shave – delights Adam had nearly forgotten – he felt almost back to normal again, if still somewhat fragile. He tucked a pink towel around his waist before joining Jeanne in the kitchen. The table was already laid and she was removing a warm croissant from the oven.

"Good body," she said, turning round and scrutinising him carefully. "Much better than I usually 'ave." She put the plate down in front of him.

"You're not so bad yourself," said Adam grinning, taking the seat opposite her.

"I am 'appy you notice," said Jeanne. "I was beginning to think about you." Adam spread the roll liberally with jam and didn't speak again for several seconds.

"When 'ave you last eat?" asked Jeanne as he devoured the final scrap left on the plate.

"Yesterday lunch. But I emptied my stomach in between."

"Sick, eh? You mustn't drink so much."

"I think 'drained' might be a better word. Tell me, Jeanne," said Adam, looking up at her, "are you still available for work?"

She checked her watch. "One of my regulars is at two this afternoon, and I must be back on the streets by five. So it would 'ave to be this morning," she said matter-of-factly.

"No, no, that's not what I meant," said Adam.

"You could quickly give a girl, how do you say in England? – a complex," said Jeanne. "You not one of those weird ones, are you?"

"No, nothing like that," said Adam, laughing. "But I would be willing to pay you another two hundred francs for your services."

351

"Is it legal?"

"Absolutely."

"*Alors*, that makes a change. 'Ow long you need me?"

"An hour, two at the most."

"It's better than the rate for my present job. What am I expected to do?"

"For one hour I want every man in Paris to fancy you. Only this time you won't be available – at any price."

"Scott has just contacted me a few minutes ago," said Lawrence to the assembled D4.

"What did he have to say?" asked an anxious Sir Morris.

"Only that he was turning back the clock."

"What do you think he meant by that?" asked Snell.

"Geneva would be my guess," said Lawrence.

"Why Geneva?" said Matthews.

"I'm not certain," said Lawrence, "but he said it had something to do with the German girl, or the bank, but I can't be sure which."

No one spoke for some time.

"Did you trace the call?" asked Busch.

"Only the area," said Lawrence, "Neuchâtel on the German–Swiss border."

"Good. Then we're in business again," said Sir Morris. "Have you informed Interpol?"

"Yes sir, and I've personally briefed the German, French and Swiss police," added Lawrence, which was the only true word he had spoken since the meeting had begun.

Jeanne took forty minutes to get herself ready and when Adam saw the result he let out a long whistle.

"No one is going to give me a second look, even if I were to empty the till in front of them," he told her.

"That is the idea, *n'est-ce pas?*" Jeanne said, grinning.

"Now, are you sure you know exactly what you have to do?"

"I know well." Jeanne checked herself once more in the long mirror. "We 'ave rehearse like military exercise four times already."

"Good," said Adam. "You sound as if you're ready to face the enemy. So let's begin with what in the army they call 'advance to contact'."

Jeanne took out a plastic bag from a drawer in the kitchen. The single word 'Céline' was printed across it. She handed it over to Adam. He folded the bag in four, and stuffed it into his jacket pocket before walking into the corridor. She then locked the flat door behind them, and they walked down the stairs together and out on to the pavement.

Adam hailed a taxi and Jeanne told the driver "Tuileries gardens". Once they had arrived, Adam paid the fare and joined Jeanne on the pavement.

"*Bonne chance,*" said Adam as he remained on the corner, allowing Jeanne to walk twenty yards ahead of him. Although he still felt unsteady he was able to keep up at her pace. The sun beat down on his face as he watched her walk in and out of the ornate flower beds. Her pink leather skirt and tight white sweater made almost every man she passed turn and take a second look. Some even stopped in their tracks and continued watching until she was out of sight.

The comments she could hear and Adam, twenty yards behind, couldn't, ranged from "*Je payerais n'importe quoi,*" which she reluctantly had to pass up, to just plain "*Putain*", which Adam had told her to ignore. Her part had to be acted out, and for two hundred francs she would just have to suffer the odd insult.

Jeanne reached the far side of the gardens and did not look back: she had been instructed not to turn around in any circumstances. Keep going forwards, Adam had told her. He was still twenty yards behind her when she reached the Quai des Tuileries. She waited for the lights to turn green before she crossed the wide road, keeping in the centre of a throng of people.

At the end of the quai she turned sharp right, and for the first time could see the Louvre straight in front of her. She had been too embarrassed to admit to him that she had never been inside the building before.

Jeanne climbed the steps to the entrance hall. By the time she had reached the swing doors, Adam was approaching the bottom step. She continued on up the marble staircase with Adam still following discreetly behind.

When Jeanne reached the top of the stairs she passed the statue of the Winged Victory of Samothrace. She proceeded into the first of the large crowded rooms and began counting to herself, noting as she passed through each gallery that there was at least one attendant on duty in each, usually standing around aimlessly near one of the exits. A group of schoolchildren were studying 'The Last Supper' by Giovanni but Jeanne ignored the masterpiece and marched straight on. After passing six attendants she arrived in the room Adam had described to her so vividly. She strode purposefully into the centre and paused for a few seconds. Some of the men began to lose interest in the paintings. Satisfied by the impact she was making, she flounced over to the guard, who straightened up his jacket and smiled at her.

"*Dans quelle direction se trouve la peinture du seizième siècle?*" Jeanne asked innocently. The guard turned to point in the direction of the relevant room. The moment he turned back, Jeanne slapped him hard across the face and shouted at him at the top of her voice: "*Quelle horreur! Pour qui est-ce que vous me prenez?*"

Only one person in the Icon Room didn't stop to stare at the spectacle. "*Je vais parler à la Direction,*" she screamed, and flounced off towards the main exit. The entire charade was over in less than thirty seconds. The bemused guard remained transfixed, staring after his assailant in bewilderment.

Jeanne continued on through three centuries more quickly than H. G. Wells. She took a left turn into the sixteenth-century room as instructed and then another left brought her back into the long corridor. A few moments later, she joined Adam at the top of the marble staircase leading down to the front entrance.

As they walked back down the steps together, Adam handed her the Céline bag and was about to set off again, when two attendants waiting on the bottom step threw out their arms indicating they should halt.

"Do you wish a run for it?" she whispered.

"Certainly not," said Adam very firmly. "Just don't say anything."

"*Madame, excusez-moi, mais je dois fouiller votre sac.*"

"*Allez-y pour tout ce que vous y trouvez!*" said Jeanne.

"Certainly you can search her bag," said Adam, returning to her side before Jeanne could say anything more. "It's an icon, quite a good one, I think. I purchased it in a shop near the Champs-Elysées only this morning."

"*Vous me permettez, monsieur?*" the senior attendant asked suspiciously.

"Why not?" said Adam. He removed the Tsar's icon

355

from the bag and handed it over to the attendant, who seemed surprised by the way things were turning out. Two more attendants rushed over and stood on each side of Adam.

The senior attendant asked in broken English if Adam would mind if one of the gallery's experts were to look at the painting.

"Only too delighted," said Adam. "It would be fascinating to have a second opinion."

The senior attendant was beginning to look unsure of himself. "*Je dois vous demander de me suivre,*" he suggested in a tone that was suddenly less hostile. He ushered them quickly through to a little room at the side of the gallery. The attendant put the Tsar's icon in the middle of a table that dominated the room. Adam sat down and Jeanne, still bemused, took the seat beside him.

"I'll only be a moment, sir." The senior attendant almost ran out while the two other attendants remained stationed near the door. Adam still did not attempt to speak to Jeanne although he could see that she was becoming more and more apprehensive. He shot her a little smile as they sat waiting.

When the door eventually opened, an elderly man with a scholarly face preceded the senior attendant.

"*Bonjour, monsieur,*" the man began, looking at Adam, the first man who did not show an overt interest in Jeanne. "I understand that you are English," and without giving either of them more than a glance, he picked up the icon.

He studied the painting carefully for some time before he spoke. Adam felt just a moment's apprehension. "Most interesting. Yes, yes." One of the attendants put a hand on his truncheon.

"Interesting," he repeated. "I would be so bold as

to suggest," he hesitated, "late nineteenth century, eighteen seventy, possibly eighty. Fascinating. Not that we have ever had anything quite like it at the Louvre," he added. "You do realise it's an inferior copy," he said as he handed the icon back to Adam. "The original Tsar's icon of St George and the Dragon hangs in the Winter Palace in Leningrad. I've seen it, you know," he added, sounding rather pleased with himself.

"You certainly have," said Adam under his breath as he placed the icon back in its plastic bag. The old man bowed low to Jeanne and said as he shuffled away, "Funnily enough, someone else was making enquiries about the Tsar's icon only a few weeks ago." Adam was the only person who didn't seem surprised.

"I was only –" began the senior attendant.

"Doing your duty," completed Adam. "A natural precaution, if I may say so," he added a little pompously. "I can only admire the way you carried out the entire exercise."

Jeanne stared at them both, quite unable to comprehend what was happening.

"You are kind, *monsieur*," said the attendant, sounding relieved. "Hope you come again," he added, smiling at Jeanne.

The attendant accompanied the two of them to the entrance of the Louvre, and when they pushed through the door he stood smartly to attention and saluted.

Adam and Jeanne walked down the steps and into the Paris sun.

"Well, now can I know what that's all about?" asked Jeanne.

"You were *magnifique*," said Adam, not attempting to explain.

"I know, I know," said Jeanne. "But why you need

Oscar-winning show by me when the picture was always yours?"

"True," agreed Adam. "But I had left it in their safe-keeping overnight. And without your bravura performance it might have taken considerably longer to convince the authorities that it belonged to me in the first place."

Adam realised from the look on her face that Jeanne had no idea what he was talking about.

"You know, that my first time in the Louvre?" said Jeanne linking her arm in Adam's.

"You're priceless," said Adam, laughing.

"That I'm not," she said, turning to face him. "Two hundred francs was our bargain even if it belongs to you or not."

"Correct," said Adam, taking out the colonel's wallet and extracting two hundred francs, to which he added another hundred. "A well-earned bonus," said Adam.

She pocketed the money gratefully. "I think I'll take an evening off," she said.

Adam held her in his arms and kissed her on both cheeks as if she was a French general.

She kissed him on the lips and smiled. "When you next in Paris, *chéri*, look me up. I owe you one – on the house."

"How can you be so sure?"

"Because Antarctic was willing to give Pemberton too many facts."

"What do you mean?"

"You told me that Pemberton said he would never phone back if you let him down again. Not only did he phone back but he peppered you with facts. Which way did he say he was going?"

"Back to Geneva. Something to do with the German girl and the bank."

"The girl's dead and the bank's closed for the week-end. He must be on his way to England."

"I would like to rent a car which I will be dropping off at the coast. I haven't decided which port yet," he told the girl behind the counter.

"Bien sûr, monsieur," said the girl. "Would you be kind enough to fill in the form, and we will also need your driving licence." Adam removed all the papers from his inside pocket and passed over the colonel's driving licence. He filled in the forms slowly, copying the signature off the back of the colonel's Playboy Club card. He handed over the full amount required in cash hoping it would speed up the trans-action.

The girl picked up the cash and counted the notes carefully before checking the back of the licence against the signature on the form. Adam was relieved that she hadn't spotted the disparity in the dates of birth. He replaced all Albert Tomkins's documents and the wallet in his inside jacket pocket, as the girl turned round and removed an ignition key from a hook on a board behind her.

"It's a red Citroën, parked on the first floor," she told him. "The registration number is stamped on the key ring."

Adam thanked her and walked quickly up to the first floor where he handed the key over to an attendant, who drove the car out of its parking space for him.

When the attendant returned the key, Adam handed him a ten-franc note. Exactly the same sum as the other man had given him to let him know if an English-

Jeffrey Archer

man who fitted Adam's description tried to hire a car.
What had he promised? Another hundred francs if he
phoned within five minutes of seeing him.

PART FOUR

THE KREMLIN
MOSCOW

June 19, 1966

CHAPTER TWENTY-TWO

THE KREMLIN, MOSCOW
June 19, 1966

Leonid Ilyich Brezhnev entered the room, hardly allowing the other four members of the inner quorum of the Defence Council enough time to stand. Their faces were grim, resolute, no different from their public image – unlike Western politicians.

The General Secretary took his place at the head of the table and nodded to his colleagues to sit.

The last time the inner quorum of the Defence Council had been summoned to a meeting at an hour's notice had been at the request of Khrushchev, who was hoping to enlist support for his Cuban adventure. Brezhnev would never forget the moment when his predecessor had uncontrollably burst into tears because they forced him to order the Soviet ships to return home. From that moment, Brezhnev knew it could only be a matter of time before he would succeed Khrushchev as the leader of the Communist world. On this occasion he had no intention of bursting into tears.

On his right sat Marshal Malinovsky, Minister of Defence: on his left Andrei Gromyko, the young

Foreign Minister. Beside him sat the Chief of the General Staff, Marshal Zakharov, and, on his left, Zaborski. Even the seating plan confirmed Brezhnev's obvious displeasure with the Chairman of the KGB.

He raised his eyes and stared up at the massive oil painting of Lenin reviewing an early military parade in Red Square: a picture no one other than members of the Politburo had seen since it disappeared from the Tretyakov in 1950.

If only Lenin had realised the icon was a fake in the first place, Brezhnev reflected ... Yet, despite the traditional Russian pastime of blaming the dead for everything that goes wrong, he knew that Vladimir Ilyich Lenin was beyond criticism. He would have to find a living scapegoat.

His eyes rested on Zaborski. "Your report, Comrade Chairman."

Zaborski fingered a file in front of him although he knew the contents almost off by heart. "The plan to locate the Tsar's icon was carried out in an exemplary fashion," he began. "When the Englishman, Adam Scott, was caught and later . . . questioned" – they all accepted the euphemism – "by Comrade Dr Stavinsky in the privacy of our Embassy in Paris, the Englishman gave no clue as to where we would find the icon. It became obvious he was a professional agent of the West. After three hours, interrogation was momentarily suspended. It was during this period that the prisoner managed to escape."

"Managed," interjected Brezhnev.

Just as he had taught his subordinates over the years, the Chairman of the KGB made no attempt to reply.

"Don't you realise," continued the General Secretary, "that we had within our grasp the opportunity to turn the very land the Americans use for their early warning system into a base for our short range missiles? If it had proved possible to retrieve our icon it would also have been possible to site those very missiles along a border less than a thousand eight hundred kilometres from Seattle – two thousand kilometres from Chicago. Not only could we have made the Americans' early warning system redundant, we could have greatly improved our ability to detect any enemy missiles while they were still thousands of kilometres from our nearest border."

The General Secretary paused to see if the Chairman of the KGB had any further explanation to offer but Zaborski kept his eyes fixed on the table in front of him. When Brezhnev began again it was almost in a whisper:

"And for such a prize we would not have had to sacrifice one life, one rocket, one tank or even one bullet – because all this was ours by right. But if we fail to locate the Tsar's icon in the next thirty-six hours we will never be given such a chance again. We will have lost our one opportunity to remove a star from the American flag."

Foreign Secretary Gromyko waited until he was certain Brezhnev had completed his statement before he enquired:

"If I may ask, Comrade Chairman, why was Major Romanov allowed to continue being involved in such a sensitive operation after it was suspected he had killed" – with this he glanced down at the papers in front of him – "Researcher Petrova?"

"Because when that situation was drawn to my attention," replied Zaborski, at last looking up, "I had only seven days left to tomorrow's deadline, and in my judgment there was *no one* who could have taken over Romanov's place at such short notice –"

There was a timid knock on the door. All the faces round the table showed surprise. The Minister of Defence had given specific orders that no one was to interrupt them.

"Come," shouted Brezhnev.

The great door inched open and a secretary appeared in the gap; the thin piece of paper in his hand shook, betraying his nervousness. The Minister of Defence waved him in as Brezhnev had no intention of turning around to see who it was. The secretary walked quickly towards them. As soon as he had deposited the telex on the table he turned, and almost ran from the room.

Brezhnev slowly unfolded his tortoise-shell glasses before picking up the missive. Once he had read through the cable, he looked up at the expectant faces in front of him. "It seems an Englishman left an icon in the Louvre and picked it back up this morning."

The blood quickly drained from Zaborski's face.

The four ministers round the table all began talking together, until Brezhnev raised the vast palm of his right hand. There was immediate silence. "I intend to continue my plans on the assumption that it will still be us who get to the Englishman first."

Brezhnev turned towards his Foreign Minister. "Alert all our Western Ambassadors to be prepared to brief the Foreign Ministers of the country in which they reside on the full implications of honouring the amendment to the treaty. Then instruct Anatoly Dobrynin in Washington to demand an official meeting with the Secretary of State to be fixed for late Monday. At the same time I want a further meeting arranged between our Ambassador at the United Nations and U Thant."

Gromyko nodded as Brezhnev turned his attention to the Chief of the General Staff. "See that our strategic forces in all zones are put at a state of readiness to coincide with the timing of the announcement of our diplomatic initiative." Malinovsky smiled. The General Secretary finally turned to the Chairman of the KGB. "Do we still have advertising space booked in every major newspaper in the West?"

"Yes, Comrade General Secretary," replied Zaborski. "But I cannot be certain they will be willing to print the statement as you have prepared it."

"Then pay every one of them in advance," said Brezhnev. "Few Western editors will withdraw a full page advertisement when they already have the money in the bank."

"But if we then don't find the icon . . ." began the Chairman of the KGB.

"Then your last duty as Chairman of State Security will be to withdraw all the advertisements," said the General Secretary of the Communist Party.

CHAPTER TWENTY-THREE

Adam wound down the car window and immediately the warm summer air flooded in. He had decided to avoid the main road to Calais in favour of the N1 to Boulogne. He still considered it possible that Romanov would have men watching at every port on the Channel coast although he doubted if Lawrence or the Americans were aware he had escaped.

Once he had cleared the outskirts of the French capital, he was confident that he could average seventy kilometres an hour the rest of the way. But what he hadn't anticipated was running into a hundred or more cyclists, daubed in their various stripes of reds, greens, blues, blacks and golds, bobbing along ahead of him. As he drifted past them Adam was able accurately to check that they were averaging 40 miles an hour.

Having followed the build-up for the forthcoming World Cup in Britain, he was also able to make out the national colours of France, Germany, Italy and even Portugal. He honked his horn loudly as he passed a group of four men quite near the front, clad in red, white and blue T-shirts with the British team van driving just ahead of them. A few moments later he had overtaken the leaders, and was able to put the car back into fourth gear.

Jeffrey Archer

He switched on the car radio and fiddled around for
some time before he tuned in to the Home Service of
the BBC. He settled back to listen to the news in
English for the first time in days. The usual reports of
long strikes, high inflation, and of England's chances
when the second Test Match at Lord's resumed after
the rest day almost made him feel he was already back
home, and then he nearly swerved off the road and
into a tree.

The news reader reported matter-of-factly that a
young RAF pilot had been found dead in a field off the
Auxerre/Dijon road after his plane had crashed in
mysterious circumstances. No more details were available at the present time. Adam cursed and slammed
his fist on the steering wheel at the thought of Alan
Banks becoming another victim of Romanov. He
tapped the icon and cursed again.

"It was foolish of you to contact me, young man," said
the old banker. "You're not exactly a hero of the Soviet
Union at the present time."

"Listen, old man, I don't have to be a hero any
longer because I may never come back to the Soviet
Union."

"Be warned: Mother Russia has extremely long
finger nails."

"And because of my grandfather's foresight, I can
afford to cut them off," the caller said, touching the
gold medallion he wore beneath his shirt. "I just need
to be sure you don't let them know where I keep the
scissors."

"Why should I remain silent?" asked Poskonov.

"Because if I haven't got my hands on St George
within the next twenty-four hours, I'll phone again with
the details of how you can hope to collect a larger golden

handshake than you could have expected from your present employers." The banker offered no comment.

The Ambassador's secretary rushed into the room without knocking. "I told you no interruptions," shouted Romanov, covering the mouthpiece with his hand.

"But we've located Scott."

Romanov slammed the phone down. In Moscow, the old Russian banker wound the tape back. Poskonov smiled and listened to Romanov's words a second time and came to the conclusion that Romanov had left him with only one choice. He booked a flight to Geneva.

"Robin?"

"Batman. Where have you got to?"

"I'm just outside Paris on my way back home," Adam said. "Are you sticking to the schedule you outlined on the bus?"

"Sure am. Why, are you still desperate to spend the night with me?"

"Sure am," said Adam, mimicking her. "But when do you get back home?"

"The orchestra is taking the ferry from Dunkerque at six thirty tonight. Can you join us?"

"No," said Adam. "I have to return by another route. But, Robin, when I reach London can you put me up for the night?"

"Sounds like an offer I can't refuse," she said, and then repeated her address to be sure he had time to write it down. "When shall I expect you?" she asked.

"Around midnight tonight."

"Do you always give a girl so much notice?"

The young KGB officer standing in the adjoining box had caught most of the conversation. He smiled when he recalled Major Romanov's words: "The man who brings me the Tsar's icon need have no fear for his future in the KGB."

Adam jumped back in the car and drove on until he reached the outskirts of Beauvais, where he decided to stop at a wayside *routier* for a quick lunch.

According to the timetable he had picked up from the Hertz counter, the ferry he wanted to catch was due to leave Boulogne at three o'clock, so he felt confident he would still make it with about an hour to spare.

He sat hidden in an alcove by the window enjoying what might have been described in any English pub as a ploughman's lunch. With each mouthful he became aware that the French ploughmen demanded far higher standards of their innkeepers than any English farm-worker was happy to settle for.

As he waited for his coffee he took out Albert Tomkins's papers from his inside pocket and began to scrutinise them carefully. He was interested to discover exactly how many weeks he had been claiming unemployment benefit.

Through the window of the inn he watched the first of the cyclists as they pedalled by. The athletes' muscles strained in their determination to remain among the leading group. As they shot through Beauvais, Adam was amused by the fact that they were all breaking the speed limit. The sight of the competitors reminded him that he was expected to attend the final part of his medical for the Foreign Office tomorrow afternoon.

Romanov read the decoded message a second time. "Scott returning Geneva. Check German girl and bank." He looked up at the senior KGB officer who had handed him the missive.

"Does Mentor think I'm that naïve?" said Romanov to his Parisian colleague. "We already know from our agent in Amsterdam that he's now on his way towards the French coast."

"Then why should Mentor want to send you in the opposite direction?"

"Because it must be him who's been briefing the Americans," said Romanov coldly.

Romanov turned to the colonel who was standing by his side. "We know it can't be Dunkerque, so how many other possibilities are we left with?"

"Cherbourg, Le Havre, Dieppe, Boulogne, or Calais," replied the colonel, looking down at the map laid out on the table in front of him. "My bet would be Calais," he added.

"Unfortunately," said Romanov, "Captain Scott is not quite *that* simple. And as the motorway takes you direct to Calais, the captain will expect us to have that part of his route well covered. I think our friend will try Boulogne or Dieppe first."

He checked the timetable the Second Secretary had supplied him with. "The first boat he could hope to catch leaves Boulogne for Dover at three, and then there's one from Dieppe to Newhaven at five."

Romanov also checked Calais and Le Havre. "Good. Calais left at twelve this morning, and as he phoned the girl after twelve he had no hope of catching that one. And Le Havre doesn't leave until seven fifteen tonight, and he won't risk leaving it that late. Assuming we can beat him to the coast, Colonel, I think Captain Scott is once again within our grasp."

* * *

Once Adam had left the *relais routier* it was only minutes before he began to catch up with the straggling cyclists as they pedalled on towards Abbeville. His thoughts reverted to Romanov. Adam suspected that his agents would have the airports, stations, autoroute and ports well covered. But even the KGB could not be in fifty places at once.

Adam took the Boulogne route out of Abbeville but had to remain in the centre of the road to avoid the bobbing cyclists. He even had to slam his brakes on once when an Italian and a British rider collided in front of him. The two men, both travelling at some speed, were thrown unceremoniously to the ground. The British rider remained ominously still on the side of the road.

Adam felt guilty about not stopping to help his fellow countryman but feared that any hold-up might prevent him catching his boat. He spotted the British team van ahead of him and speeded up until he was alongside. Adam waved at the driver to pull over.

The man behind the steering wheel looked surprised but stopped and wound down the window. Adam pulled up in front of him, leaped out of his car and ran to the van.

"One of your chaps has had an accident about a mile back," shouted Adam, pointing towards Paris.

"Thanks, mate," said the driver who turned round and sped quickly back down the road.

Adam continued to drive on at a sedate speed until he had passed all the leaders. Then, once again, he put the car into top gear. A signpost informed him that it was now only thirty-two kilometres to Boulogne: he would still make the three o'clock sailing comfortably.

He began to imagine what it might be like if he could survive beyond Monday. Would his life ever be routine again? Jogs in the park, Foreign Office interviews, workouts with the sergeant major and even the acknowledgment of the part he had played in delivering the icon into safe hands. The problem was that he hadn't yet decided who had safe hands.

A helicopter looking like a squat green bullfrog swept over him; now that would be the ideal way to get back to England, Adam considered. With help like that he could even make it to Harley Street in time for his medical for the Foreign Office.

He watched as the helicopter turned and swung back towards him. He assumed that there must be a military airport somewhere nearby, but couldn't remember one from his days in the army. A few moments later he heard the whirl of the blades as the helicopter flew across his path at a considerably lower level. Adam gripped the wheel of the car until his knuckles went white as an impossible thought crossed his mind. As he did so the helicopter swung back again, and this time flew straight towards him.

Adam wound the window up and crouching over the top of the steering wheel, stared into the sky. He could see the silhouetted outline of three figures sitting in the helicopter cockpit. He banged his fist on the steering wheel in anger as he realised how easy it must have been for them to trace a car signed for in the one name they would immediately recognise. He could sense Romanov's smile of triumph as the chopper hovered above him.

Adam saw a signpost looming up ahead of him and swung off the main road towards a village called Fleureville. He pushed the speedometer well over ninety causing the little car to skid along country lanes.

The helicopter likewise swung to the right, and dog-like followed his path.

Adam took a hard left and only just avoided colliding with a tractor coming out of a newly ploughed field. He took the next right and headed back towards the Boulogne road, desperately trying to think what he could do next. Every time he looked up the helicopter was there above him: he felt like a puppet dancing on the end of Romanov's string.

A road sign depicting a low tunnel ahead flashed past them and Adam dismissed the melodramatic idea of trying to make them crash; he didn't need reminding that it was he who was proving to be the novice.

When he first saw the tunnel he estimated it to be sixty or seventy yards in length. Although it was quite wide, a double-decker bus could not have entered it without the upstairs passengers ending up walking on the bridge.

For a brief moment Adam actually felt safe. He slammed on the little Citroën's brakes and skidded to a halt about thirty yards from the end of the tunnel. The car ended up almost scraping the side of the wall. He switched on his side lights and they flashed brightly in the darkness. For several seconds he watched as approaching cars slowed down before safely overtaking him.

At last he jumped out of the car and ran to the end of the tunnel where he pinned himself against the wall. The helicopter had travelled on some way, but was already turning back, and heading straight towards the tunnel. Adam watched it fly over his head, and moments later heard it turn again. As he waited, two hitch-hikers passed by on the other side, chatting away to themselves, oblivious to Adam's predicament.

He looked across desperately at the two young men

and shouted, "Were you hoping to thumb a lift?"

"Yes," they called back in unison. Adam staggered across the road to join them.

"Are you all right?" Adam heard one of them ask but he could hardly make out which one as his eyes had not yet become accustomed to the darkness.

"No, I'm not," Adam explained simply. "I drank too much wine at lunch and because of a cycle race the road is just crawling with police. I'm sure to be picked up if I go much further. Can either of you drive?"

"I only have my Canadian licence," said the taller of the two youths. "And in any case we are heading for Paris and your car is facing the opposite direction."

"It's a Hertz Rent-a-Car," Adam explained. "I picked it up on the Rue St Ferdinand this morning, and I have to return it by seven tonight. I don't think I can make it in my present state."

The two young men looked at him apprehensively. "I will give you both one hundred francs if you will return it safely for me. You see I can't afford to lose my licence, I'm a commercial traveller," Adam explained. Neither of them spoke. "My papers are all in order, I can assure you." Adam handed them over to the taller man who crossed back over the road and used the car lights to study Albert Tomkins's licence and insurance before carying on a conversation with his friend.

Adam could hear the helicopter blades whirling above the tunnel entrance.

"We don't need the hundred francs," the taller one said eventually. "But we will need a note from you explaining why we are returning the car to Hertz in Paris on your behalf." Adam pulled out the colonel's pen and, feeling remarkably sober, he bent over the hood of the car and scribbled on the back of the Hertz agreement.

"Do you want to come back to Paris with us?"

Adam hesitated fractionally. Couldn't they hear the noise too? "No. I have to get to Boulogne."

"We could drive you to Boulogne and still have enough time to take the car to Paris."

"No, no. That's very considerate. I can take care of myself as long as I feel confident that the car will be delivered back as soon as possible."

The taller one shrugged while his companion opened a rear door and threw their rucksacks on the back seat. Adam remained in the tunnel while they started up the engine. He could hear the purr of the helicopter blades change cadence: it had to be descending to land in a nearby field.

Go, go, for God's sake go, he wanted to shout as the car shot forward towards Boulogne. He watched them travel down the road for about a hundred yards before turning in at a farm entrance, reversing, and heading back towards the tunnel. They tooted as they passed him in the dark, disappearing in the direction of Paris. Adam sank down on to his knees with relief and was about to pick himself up and start walking towards Boulogne when he saw two figures silhouetted at the far entrance of the tunnel. Against the clear blue sky he could make out the outline of two tall, thin men. They stood peering into the tunnel. Adam didn't move a muscle, praying they hadn't spotted him.

And then suddenly one of them started walking towards him, while the other remained motionless. Adam knew he could not hope to escape again. He knelt there cursing his own stupidity. In seconds they would be able to see him clearly.

"Don't let's waste any more valuable time, Marvin, we already know that the limey bastard's heading back to Paris."

"I just thought perhaps . . ." began the one called Marvin in a Southern drawl.

"Leave the thinking to me. Now let's get back to the chopper before we lose him."

When Marvin was only twenty yards away from Adam he suddenly stopped, turned around and began running back.

Adam remained rooted to the spot for several minutes. A cold, clammy sweat had enveloped his body the moment he realised his latest pursuer was not Romanov. If one of them hadn't referred to him as a 'limey bastard', Adam would have happily given himself up. Suddenly he had become painfully aware of the difference between fact and fiction: he had been left with no friends.

Adam did not move again until he heard the helicopter rise above him. Peering out, he could see outlined against the arc of the tunnel the Americans heading back in the direction of Paris.

He staggered outside and put a hand across his eyes. The sunlight seemed much fiercer than a few minutes before. What next? He had less than an hour to catch the boat but no longer had any transport. He wasn't sure whether to thumb lifts, search for a bus stop, or simply get as far away from the main road as possible. His eyes were continually looking up into the sky. How long before they reached the car, and realised it was not him inside?

Cyclists began to pass him again as he jogged slowly towards Boulogne. He kept on moving, and even found enough strength to cheer the British competitors as they pedalled by. The British team van followed close behind and Adam gave it the thumbs-up sign. To his surprise the van came to a halt in front of him.

The driver wound down the window. "Weren't you the fellow who stopped me back in Abbeville?"

"That's right," said Adam. "Has your man recovered?"

"No, he's resting in the back – pulled ligament. What happened to your car?"

"Broke down about a mile back," said Adam, shrugging philosophically.

"Bad luck. Can I give you a lift?" the man asked. "We're only going as far as Boulogne on this stage, but jump in if it will help."

"Thank you," said Adam, with the relief of a bearded beatnik who has found the one person willing to stop to pick him up. The driver leaned across and pushed open the door for him.

Before climbing in, Adam shielded his eyes and once more looked up into the sky. The helicopter was nowhere to be seen – although he knew it couldn't be long before it returned. They would quickly work out that there was only one place where the switch could possibly have been made.

"My name's Bob," said the track-suited driver, thrusting out his free hand. "I'm the British team manager."

"Mine's Adam." He shook the other's hand warmly.

"Where are you heading?"

"Boulogne," said Adam, "and with luck I could still make my crossing by three."

"We should be there about two thirty," said Bob. "We have to be: the afternoon stage starts at three."

"Will your man be able to ride?" asked Adam, pointing over his shoulder.

"No, he won't be competing in this race again," said

the team manager. "He's pulled a ligament in the back of his leg, and they always take a couple of weeks to heal properly. I shall have to leave him in Boulogne and complete the last leg myself. You don't ride by any chance, do you?" Bob asked.

"No," said Adam. "Run a little, but haven't done a lot on wheels since my sister crashed the family tricycle."

"We're still in with a chance for the bronze," Bob said, as they overtook the British riders once more.

Adam gave them the thumbs-up sign and then looked over his shoulder through the back window. He was thankful to see that there was still no sign of the helicopter as they drove into the outskirts of Boulogne. Bob took him all the way up to the dockside. "Hope you get that bronze medal," said Adam as he jumped out of the van. "And thanks again. Good luck with the next stage."

Adam checked his watch: twenty minutes before the boat was due to sail. He wondered if it was too much time. He walked over to the booking office and waited in a short line before buying a passenger ticket. He kept looking round to check if anyone was watching him, but no one seemed to be showing the slightest interest. Once he had purchased his ticket he headed towards the ship and had just begun to start whistling a tuneless version of 'Yesterday' when a black speck appeared in the distance. There was no mistaking it – the sound was enough.

Adam looked up at the gangway which led to the deck of the ship now only yards away from him, and then back to the speck as it grew larger and larger in the sky. He checked his watch: the ship was due to leave in twelve minutes – still time enough for his pursuers to land the helicopter and get on board. If he climbed on and the Americans followed, they were bound to discover him. But if the Americans got on and he stayed off that would still give him enough time to reach Dieppe before the next sailing . . .

Adam jogged quickly back towards the large crowd that was hanging about waiting for the start of the next stage of the road race. As he did so the helicopter swept overhead and started hovering, like a kestrel that is looking for a mouse.

"I thought you said you were desperate to be on that ship."

Adam swung round, his fist clenched, only to face the British team manager now dressed in riding gear.

"Changed my mind," said Adam.

"Wouldn't care to drive the van for us on the next stage?" said Bob hopefully.

"Where does the next stage go?" Adam asked.

"Dunkerque," said the team manager.

Adam tried to remember what time Robin had said her boat left from Dunkerque.

"Six minutes," a voice said over the loudspeaker.

"Okay," said Adam.

"Good," said the team manager. "Then follow me."

Adam ran behind the team manager as he headed towards the van.

"Quatre minutes," Adam heard clearly as Bob unlocked the van and handed him the keys. He stared towards the ship. The two Americans were emerging from the ticket office.

"Deux minutes."

Adam jumped up into the driver's seat, looked over towards the boat and watched Marvin and his colleague stride up the gangplank.

"Une minute."

"Just get the van to Dunkerque and leave the keys

at the British checkpoint. We'll see you when we get there."

"Good luck," said Adam.

"Thank you," said Bob, and ran to the starting line to join his team mates who were anxiously holding his bike.

"Trente secondes."

Adam watched the gangplank being hoisted up as the starter raised his gun.

"On your marks, set . . ."

The ship's fog horn belched out a droning note and the two Americans started their journey to Dover. A second later, the gun went off as Adam put the van into second gear and headed towards Dunkerque.

CHAPTER TWENTY-FOUR

Adam sat in the little dockside café waiting for the coach to appear. The team van had been left at the checkpoint and he was now ready to board the ship but he still needed to be sure Robin was on it. The coach trundled in with only ten minutes to spare and Adam greeted her as she stepped off.

"Just couldn't keep away from me, could you?" said Robin.

Adam burst out laughing and threw his arms almost round her.

"It's good to see you," he said.

"I thought you were going back to England by some mysterious route, you know, spy rocket or something even more exotic."

"I wanted to," said Adam, "but the Americans were sitting at the controls just as I decided to climb aboard."

"The Americans?" she said.

"I'll explain everything once we're on board," said Adam. Neither of them noticed the young agent who had trailed Robin from Berlin. He sat in a phone booth on the far side of the dock and dialled an overseas number.

"I wouldn't have believed a word of it a week ago," she said, "but for two things."

"Namely?"

"First, a senior official of the Foreign Office returned Dudley Hulme's passport to him in Amsterdam. Which reminds me to give you yours back." She rummaged around in her bag for a few moments before taking out a dark blue passport and handing it to him.

"And what's the second thing?" said Adam, taking the passport gratefully.

"I had the doubtful pleasure of coming face to face with Comrade Romanov, and I have no desire to do so again."

"I intend to meet him again," said Adam.

"Why?" asked Robin.

"Because I'm going to kill him."

Romanov and Pollard arrived in Dover a few minutes before the ferry was due to dock. They waited expectantly. Romanov stationed himself so that he could look through the customs hall window and watch the ferry as it sailed into Dover harbour. He had found the perfect spot behind a coffee-vending machine from which he could observe everyone who entered or left the customs hall, while at the same time remaining hidden from view.

"Just in case he should act out of character for a change," said Romanov, "and fails to go in a straight line, you will cover the car exit and report back to me if you notice anything unusual."

The colonel left Romanov secreted behind the coffee machine while he selected a place for himself on the dockside where he could watch the cars as they entered the customs area some fifty yards from the exit gate. If Scott did leave the ferry in a car Pollard would easily have enough time to run back and warn Romanov before Scott could hope to clear customs and reach the main gate. At least this would be the one place Scott couldn't risk hiding in the trunk. Both men waited.

The captain switched on his ship-to-shore radio to channel nine and spoke clearly into the small microphone. "This is the MV *Chantilly* calling the Dover Harbour Master. Are you receiving me?" He waited for a moment, flicked up the switch in front of him and then heard: "Harbour Master to MV *Chantilly*. Receiving you loud and clear, over."

"This is the captain speaking. We have an emergency. A male passenger has fallen out of a lifeboat on to the deck and contracted multiple injuries to his arms and legs." Adam groaned as the captain continued. "I shall need an ambulance to be standing by at the quayside to take him to the nearest hospital once we have docked. Over."

"Message received and understood, Captain. An ambulance will be waiting for you when the ship docks. Over and out."

"Everything will be all right, my dear," said Robin in a gentle voice that Adam had not heard before. "As soon as we arrive, they are going to see you are taken straight to a hospital."

"I must get back to the bridge," said the captain gruffly. "I shall instruct two stewards to bring a stretcher down for your brother."

"Thank you, Captain," said Robin. "You have been most helpful."

"It's quite all right, miss. You did say your brother?"

"Yes, Captain," said Robin.

"Well, you might advise him in future that it's in

387

his best interests to drink less before he comes on board."

"I've tried," said Robin, sighing. "You couldn't believe how many times I've tried, Captain, but I'm afraid he takes after my father." Adam held on to his leg and groaned again.

"Um," said the captain, looking down at the gash across Adam's shoulder. "Let's hope it turns out not to be serious. Good luck," he added.

"Thank you again, Captain," said Robin as she watched the cabin door close behind them.

"So far, so good," said Robin. "Now let's hope the second part of the plan works. By the way, your breath smells foul."

"What do you expect after making me swirl whisky round in my mouth for twenty minutes and then forcing me to spit it out all over my own clothes?"

Adam was lifted carefully on to the stretcher, then carried out on to the deck by two stewards. They waited at the head of the gangplank and placed Adam gently on the deck while a customs officer, accompanied by an immigration officer, ran up to join them. Robin handed over his passport. The immigration officer flicked through the pages and checked the photograph.

"Quite a good likeness for a change," said Robin, "but I'm afraid they may have to include this under 'unusual scars' in the next edition." She threw back the blanket dramatically and revealed the deep gash on Adam's shoulder. Adam looked suitably crestfallen.

"Is he bringing anything in with him that needs to be declared?" asked the customs official. Adam couldn't stop himself from touching the icon.

"No, I wouldn't let him buy any more booze on this

trip. And I'll be responsible for checking his personal belongings through with mine when I leave the ship."

"Right. Thank you, miss. Better see he gets off to the hospital then," said the officer, suddenly aware that a restless mob of people were waiting at the top of the gangplank to disembark.

The two stewards carried Adam down the gangplank. An attendant was on hand to check his wound. Adam waved gamely at Robin as they placed him in the ambulance.

Romanov spotted her as she came through customs. "Now I know exactly how Captain Scott hopes to get off the ship, and we will be waiting for him when he least expects it. Go and hire a car to take us to London," he barked at the colonel.

The ambulance shot out through the customs gates with its lights full on and bells ringing. By the time they had arrived at The Royal Victoria Hospital the attendant had watched his patient's remarkable recovery en route with disbelief. He was beginning to feel that the captain might have exaggerated the scale of the emergency.

Romanov stood by the gate and smiled as he watched the coach carrying the musicians emerge from the deep black hole of the ship and take its turn in the queue for customs.

As Romanov's eyes ranged up and down the coach he quickly picked out Robin Beresford. Just as he had anticipated, the double bass was propped up by her side, making it impossible to see who was seated next to her.

"You won't pull that one on me a second time," Romanov muttered, just as the colonel appeared by his side, red in the face.

"Where's the car?" the Russian demanded, not taking his eye from the coach.

"I've booked one provisionally," said the colonel, "but they'll need your international licence. I forgot Scott has got mine, along with all my other papers."

"You stay put," said Romanov, "and make sure Scott doesn't try to get off that coach." Romanov ran to the Avis desk at the same time as Adam was being wheeled into a little cubicle to be examined by the duty registrar.

The young doctor leant over his patient for several minutes. He had never seen a wound quite like it before. He examined him carefully, before making any comment. "Nasty lacerations," he said finally, cleaning Adam's shoulder wound. "Can you circle your arm?" Adam turned the arm in a full circle and straightened it again. "Good. No break, at least." He continued to clean the wound.

"I'm going to put some iodine on the open cut and it may sting a little," said the doctor. He cleaned up both elbows before placing a plaster on them.

"That didn't happen today, did it?" he asked, staring at Adam's half-healed shoulder.

"No," said Adam, without offering any explanations.

"You have been in the wars lately. I'm going to give you an anti-tetanus injection." Adam turned white. "Funny how many grown men don't care for the sight of a needle," said the doctor. Adam groaned.

"Now that wasn't so bad, was it?" he coaxed as he placed a large bandage over the top of the shoulder. "Do you have someone to collect you?" the doctor asked finally.

"Yes, thank you," said Adam. "My wife is waiting for me."

"Good, then you can go now, but please report to your GP the moment you get back home."

Romanov sat in the driver's seat and watched the coach clear customs. He followed it out of the main gate and on to the A2 in the direction of London.

"Are we going to intercept them on the way?" asked Pollard nervously.

"Not this time," said Romanov without explanation. He never once allowed the coach out of his sight all the way into the capital.

Adam walked out of the hospital and checked to see that no one was following him. The only people in sight were a man in a blue duffle coat walking in the opposite direction, and a nurse scurrying past him, looking anxiously at her watch. Satisfied, he took a taxi to Dover Priory station and purchased a single ticket to London.

"When's the next train?" he asked.

"Should be in any moment," said the ticket collector, checking his watch. "The ship docked about forty minutes ago, but it always takes a bit of time to unload all the passengers." Adam walked on to the platform, keeping a wary eye out for anyone acting suspiciously. He didn't notice the dark-haired man in a blue duffle coat leaning against the shutters of the W. H. Smith's stall reading the *Evening Standard*.

Adam's thoughts returned to Robin getting safely home. The London train drew in, packed with passengers who had been on the boat. Adam moved out of the shadows and jumped on, selecting a carriage full of teddy-boys who were apparently returning from a day at the seaside. He thought it would be unlikely anyone else would wish to join them. He took the only seat left in the far corner and sat silently but not in silence looking out of the window.

By the time the train had pulled into Canterbury no one had entered the carriage other than the ticket collector, who discreetly ignored the fact that one of the youths only presented him with a platform ticket for his inspection. Adam felt strangely safe in the corner of that particular compartment even when he noticed a dark-haired man in a blue duffle coat pass by the compartment door and look in carefully.

Adam was jolted out of his thoughts by a noisy claim made by one of the gang who during the journey had given every appearance of being its leader.

"There's a foul smell in this compartment," he declared, sniffing loudly.

"I agree, Terry," said his mate who was sitting next to Adam and also began imitating the sniff. "And I think it's quite close to me." Adam glanced towards the young man whose black leather jacket was covered in small shiny studs. The words 'Heil Hitler' were printed right across his back. He got up and pulled open the window. "Perhaps some fresh air will help," he said as he sat back down. In moments all four of them were sniffing. "Sniff, sniff, sniff, sniff, I think the smell's getting worse," their leader concluded.

"It must be me," said Adam.

The sniffing stopped and the youths stared towards the corner in disbelief — momentarily silenced by Adam's offensive.

"I didn't have time to take a shower after my judo lesson," Adam added before any of them had found time to recover their speech.

"Any good at judo, are you?" asked the one sitting next to him.

"Passable," said Adam.

"What belt are you?" demanded Terry belligerently. "Go on, tell me, a black belt, I knew it," he added, sniggering.

"I haven't been a black belt for nearly eight years," said Adam casually, "but I've been recently awarded my second Dan."

A look of apprehension came over three of the four faces.

"I was thinkin' about taking up judo myself," continued the leader, straightening his arm. "How long does it take to get any good at it?"

"I've been working at it three hours a day for nearly twelve years and I'm still not up to Olympic standard," replied Adam as he watched the dark-haired man in the duffle coat pass by the compartment again. This time he stared directly at Adam before quickly moving on.

"Of course," continued Adam, "the only quality you really need if you are thinking of taking up judo seriously is nerve, and no one can teach you that. You've either got it or you haven't."

"I've got nerve," said Terry belligerently. "I'm not frightened of nothin'. Or nobody," he added, staring straight at Adam.

"Good," said Adam. "Because you may be given the chance to prove your claim before this journey is over."

"What're you getting at?" said the 'Heil Hitler'-clad youth. "You trying to pick a fight or somethin'?"

"No," said Adam calmly. "It's just that at this moment I'm being followed by a private detective who is hoping to catch me spending the night with his client's wife."

The four of them sat still for the first time during

the journey and stared at Adam with something approaching respect.

"And are you?" asked the leader.

Adam nodded conspiratorially.

"Nice bit of skirt when you've got it in the hay?" Terry asked, leering.

"Not bad," said Adam, "not bad at all."

"Then just point out this detective git and we'll sew him up for the night," said the leader, thrusting his left hand on his right bicep while pulling up his clenched fist with gusto.

"That might turn out to be overkill," said Adam. "But if you could delay him for a little when I get off at Waterloo East, that should at least give me enough time to warn the lady."

"Say no more, squire," said the leader. "Your friend the Peeping Tom will be delivered to Charing Cross all trussed up like a British Rail parcel."

The other three youths burst out laughing and Adam was beginning to realise that it had taken Romanov only one week to turn him into a storyteller almost in the class of Robin's late father.

"That's him," whispered Adam as the duffle-coated man passed by a third time. They all looked out into the corridor but only saw his retreating back.

"The train is due to arrive at Waterloo East in eleven minutes' time," said Adam, checking his watch. "So what I suggest we do is . . . if you still think you're up to it, that is." All four of his new-found team leaned forward in eager anticipation.

A few minutes later Adam slipped out of the compartment, leaving the door wide open. He started to walk slowly in the direction opposite to that in which the man in the blue duffle coat had last been seen going. When Adam reached the end of the carriage, he turned to find the man was now following quickly behind. As he passed the open compartment the man smiled and raised a hand to attract Adam's attention but two leather-clad arms shot out and the man disappeared inside the compartment with a muffled cry. The door was slammed and the blinds pulled quickly down.

The train drew slowly into Waterloo East station.

Robin remained tense as the bus drew into Wigmore Street and came to a halt outside the RPO headquarters. A dark green Ford had been following them for at least thirty miles, and once she had become aware of it she had not dared to move from her seat.

As she dragged her double bass off the bus she looked back to see that the Ford had stopped about fifty yards down the road and turned off its headlights. Romanov was standing on the pavement looking like a caged animal that wanted to spring. Another man that Robin did not recognise remained seated behind the wheel. Adam had warned her not to turn around at any time but to walk straight into the RPO headquarters without stopping. Even so, she couldn't resist looking Romanov in the eye and shaking her head. Romanov continued to stare impassively ahead of him.

When the last musician had left the bus Romanov and 'the Colonel' searched up and down the inside of the vehicle and then finally the trunk, despite noisy protests from the driver. Robin eyed them nervously from an upstairs window, as the two of them jumped back into the green Ford and drove off. She continued watching the car until the back lights had faded away in the darkness.

*   *   *

The colonel swung out of Wigmore Street towards Baker Street, bringing the car to a halt opposite Baker Street station. Romanov jumped out, walked into a vacant telephone booth and started thumbing through the A–D directory. Only one Robin Beresford was listed and it was the same address as the young agent had read over to him. He dialled the number and after ten unanswered rings smiled at the realisation that she lived alone. He was not surprised.

"What now?" asked the colonel, once Romanov was back at the car.

"Where's Argyle Crescent, NW3?"

"Must be out towards Hampstead," said the colonel. "But I'll first check in the London A to Z roadmap. What's the plan?"

"Rather than waiting for Miss Beresford to come out we will be waiting for her to come in," said Romanov.

Robin slipped out of the back of the RPO headquarters about thirty minutes later. She zig-zagged around Portman Square then walked as quickly as she knew how up to the corner. She kept telling herself that Romanov was not coming back, but she found it impossible to stop herself from shaking all the same. She hailed a taxi and was relieved to see one draw up to her side almost immediately. She checked the driver and the back seat, as Adam had advised her, then climbed in.

Romanov arrived at Robin's front door a few moments after she had hailed the taxi. The name holder on the side wall indicated that Miss Beresford resided on the fourth floor.

The door itself would have proved no problem to any self-respecting petty thief in Moscow and

Romanov had secured entry within moments. The colonel quickly joined him before they proceeded silently up the dark staircase to the fourth floor.

Romanov slipped the Yale lock faster than Robin could have opened it with her own key. Once inside he quickly checked the layout of the room and assured himself no one else was in the flat.

The colonel stood around fidgeting. "Settle down, Colonel. I don't expect the lady will keep us waiting too long." The colonel laughed nervously.

The taxi drew up outside the house that Robin pointed to. She then jumped out and tipped the cabbie extra because the bewitching hour had long passed and at last she felt safe. It seemed ages since she had been home. All she was looking forward to now was a hot bath and a good night's sleep.

Adam stepped off the train at Waterloo East a little after midnight and was pleased to find the underground was still running. He had avoided going on to Charing Cross, as he couldn't be sure which side would have a reception committee waiting for him. He produced a season ticket for the West Indian on the ticket barrier and waited around on the underground platform for some time before the train eventually drew in.

There were several stations between Waterloo and his destination, and even at this time of night there seemed to be a prolonged stop at every one. Several late-night revellers got in at the Embankment, more still at Leicester Square. Adam waited nervously at each station, now aware that he must have caught the last train. He only hoped Robin had carried out his instructions faithfully. He looked around the carriage he was sitting in. It was full of night people, waiters, nurses, party returners, drunks – even a traffic warden. The train eventually pulled into his station, at twelve forty.

The ticket collector was able to give him the directions he needed. It was a relief to reach his final destination so quickly because there was no one else around to ask the way at that time of night. He moved slowly towards number twenty-three. There were no lights on in the house. He opened the swinging gate and walked straight up the path, removed the bunch of keys from his pocket, putting the Chubb one in the lock. Adam pushed open the door cautiously and then closed it noiselessly behind him.

A little after twelve ten the last train from Dover pulled into Charing Cross station. As Adam was nowhere to be seen, Lawrence instructed his driver to take him back to Cheyne Walk. He couldn't understand why the agent whom he had hand-picked hadn't reported in. When Lawrence arrived back at the flat he put the key in his lock, hoping to find Adam was already waiting for him.

CHAPTER TWENTY-FIVE

He pushed open the swinging gate and made his way slowly up the path in the pitch darkness. Once he reached the corner of the house he searched for the third stone on the left. When he located the correct stone where he always left his spare key, he pulled it up with his fingers and felt around in the dirt. To his relief the key was still in place. Like a burglar he pushed it into the lock quietly.

He crept into the hall and closed the door behind him, switched on the light and began to climb the stairs. Once he had reached the landing he switched off the hall light, turned the knob of his bedroom door and pushed.

As he stepped in an arm circled his throat like a whiplash and he was thrown to the ground with tremendous force. He felt a knee pressed hard against his spine and his arm was jerked up behind his back into a half nelson. He lay on the floor, flat on his face, hardly able to move or even breathe. The light switch flashed on and the first thing Adam saw was the colonel.

"Don't kill me, Captain Scott sir, don't kill me," he implored.

"I have no intention of doing so, Mr Tomkins,"

said Adam calmly. "But first, where is your esteemed employer at this moment?"

Adam kept his knee firmly in the middle of the colonel's back and pressed his arm a few inches higher before the colonel bleated out, "He went back to the Embassy once he realised the girl wasn't going to return to the flat."

"Just as I planned," said Adam, but he didn't lessen the pressure on the colonel's arm as he described in vivid detail everything that would now be expected of him.

The colonel's face showed disbelief. "But that will be impossible," he said. "I mean, he's bound to noti – Ahhh."

The colonel felt his arm forced higher up his back. "You could carry out the whole exercise in less than ten minutes and he need never be any the wiser," said Adam. "However, I feel that it's only fair that you should be rewarded for your effort."

"Thank you, sir," said the fawning colonel.

"If you succeed in delivering the one item I require and carry out my instructions to the letter you will be given in exchange your passport, driving licence, papers, wallet and a guarantee of no prosecution for your past treachery. But if, on the other hand, you fail to turn up by nine thirty tomorrow morning with the object of my desire," said Adam, "all those documents will be placed thirty minutes later on the desk of a Mr Lawrence Pemberton of the FO, along with my report on your other sources of income which you have failed to declare on your tax return."

"You wouldn't do that to me, would you, Captain Scott?"

"As ten o'clock chimes," said Adam.

"But think what would then happen to me, Captain

Scott, sir, if you carried out such a threat," moaned the colonel.

"I have already considered that," said Adam, "and I have come to two conclusions."

"And what are they, Captain Scott?"

"Spies," continued Adam, not loosening his grip, "at the present time seem to be getting anything from eighteen to forty-two years at Her Majesty's pleasure, so you might, with good behaviour, be out before the turn of the century, just in time to collect your telegram from the Queen."

The colonel looked visibly impressed. "And the other conclusion?" he blurted out.

"Oh, simply that you could inform Romanov of my nocturnal visit and he in return would arrange for you to spend the rest of your days in a very small dacha in a suitably undesirable suburb of Moscow. Because, you see, my dear Tomkins, you are a very small spy. I personally am not sure when left with such an alternative which I would view with more horror."

"I'll get it for you, Captain Scott, you can rely on me."

"I'm sure I can, Tomkins. Because if you were to let Romanov into our little secret, you would be arrested within minutes. So at best, you could try to escape on the Aeroflot plane to Moscow. And I've checked, there isn't one until the early evening."

"I'll bring it to you by nine thirty on the dot, sir. You can be sure of that. But for God's sake have yours ready to exchange."

"I will," said Adam, "as well as all your documents, Tomkins."

Adam lifted the colonel slowly off the ground and then shoved him towards the landing. He switched on the light and then pushed the colonel on down the stairs until they reached the front door.

"The keys," said Adam.

"But you've already got my keys, Captain Scott, sir."

"The car keys, you fool."

"But it's a hire car, sir," said the colonel.

"And I'm about to hire it," said Adam.

"But how will I get myself back to London in time, sir?"

"I have no idea, but you still have the rest of the night to come up with something. You could even walk it by then. The keys," Adam repeated, jerking the colonel's arm to shoulder-blade level.

"In my left hand pocket," said the colonel, almost an octave higher.

Adam put his hand into the colonel's new jacket and pulled out the car keys.

He opened the front door, shoved the colonel on to the path, and then escorted him to the pavement.

"You will go and stand on the far side of the road," said Adam, "and you will not return to the house until I have reached the end of the road. Do I make myself clear, Tomkins?"

"Abundantly clear, Captain Scott, sir."

"Good," said Adam releasing him for the first time, "and just one more thing, Tomkins. In case you think of double-crossing me, I have already instructed the Foreign Office to place Romanov under surveillance and put two extra lookouts near the Soviet Embassy with instructions to report the moment anyone suspicious turns up or leaves before nine tomorrow morning." Adam hoped he sounded convincing.

"Thought of everything, haven't you, sir?" said the colonel mournfully.

"Yes, I think so," said Adam. "I even found time to disconnect your phone while I was waiting for you to return." Adam pushed the colonel across the road before getting into the hire car. He wound the window down. "See you at nine thirty tomorrow morning. Prompt," he added, as he put the Ford into first gear.

The colonel stood shivering on the far pavement, nursing his right shoulder, as Adam drove to the end of the road. He was still standing there when Adam took a left turn back towards the centre of London.

For the first time since Heidi's death, Adam felt it was Romanov who was on the run.

"What a great honour for our little establishment," said Herr Bischoff, delighted to see the most important banker in the East sitting in his boardroom sharing afternoon tea.

"Not at all, my dear Bischoff," said Poskonov. "After all these years the honour is entirely mine. And kind of you to be so understanding about opening the bank on a Sunday. But now to business. Did you manage to get Romanov to sign the release form?"

"Oh, yes," said Bischoff, matter-of-factly. "He did it without even reading the standard clauses, let alone the extra three you asked us to put in."

"So his inheritance automatically returns to the Russian state?"

"That is so, Mr Poskonov, and we in return . . ."

". . . will represent us in all the currency exchange transactions we carry out in the West."

"Thank you," said Herr Bischoff. "And we shall be delighted to assist you in your slightest requirement, but what happens when Romanov returns to the bank and demands to know what has become of his inheritance?" asked the chairman of the bank anxiously.

"He will not return," the Russian banker said emphatically. "You can have my word on it. Now, I would like to see what is in those boxes."

"Yes, of course," said Herr Bischoff. "Will you please accompany me?"

The two banking chairmen took the private lift to the basement and Herr Bischoff accompanied his guest to the underground vault.

"I will unlock the five boxes now in your name with the bank's key but only you can open them with your key."

"Thank you," said Poskonov, and left Herr Bischoff to open the five locks and return to the entrance of the vault.

"Do take as long as you like," said Herr Bischoff, "but at six o'clock the great door is automatically locked until nine o'clock tomorrow morning, and nothing less than a nuclear weapon would prise it open. At five forty-five, an alarm goes off to warn you that you only have fifteen minutes left."

"Excellent," said the man who through his entire banking career had never been given a fifteen-minute warning of anything.

Herr Bischoff handed Comrade Poskonov the envelope with Romanov's key inside it.

As soon as the massive steel door had been swung closed behind him the Russian checked the clock on the wall. They had left him with over two hours to sort out what could be transported to Brazil and what would have to be left behind. A state pension and the Order of Lenin (second class) hadn't seemed much of an alternative to Poskonov.

He turned the key and opened the first of the small boxes and found the deeds to lands the State had owned for decades. He growled. The second box contained the shares of companies once brilliantly successful, now shells in every sense of the word. And to Poskonov's disappointment the third of the small boxes only held a will proving everything belonged to Romanov's father and his immediate heirs. Had he waited all these years to discover the stories the old man had told him of gold, jewels and pearls were nothing but a fantasy? Or had Romanov already removed them?

Poskonov opened the first of the large boxes and stared down at the twelve little compartments. He removed the lid of the first one tentatively, and when he saw the array of gems and stones that shone in front of him his legs felt weak. He put both hands into the box and let the gems slip through his fingers like a child playing with pebbles on a beach.

The second box produced pearls and the third gold coins and medallions that could make even an old man's eyes sparkle. He hadn't realised how long it had taken him to go through the remaining boxes but when the alarm went off he was five thousand miles away already enjoying his new-found wealth. He glanced at the clock. He had easily enough time to get everything back into the compartments and then he would return the following day and remove once and for all what he had earned from fifty years of serving the State.

When the last lid had been placed back on he checked the clock on the wall: six minutes to six. Just enough time to glance in the other box and see if he could expect the same again.

He turned the key and licked his lips in anticipation as he pulled the large box out. Just a quick look, he promised himself, as he lifted the lid. When he saw the decaying body with its grey skin and eyes hanging in their sockets he reeled backwards from the sight and, falling to the floor, clutched his heart.

Both bodies were discovered at nine the next morning.

The phone rang and Adam grabbed at it before the shrill tone could deafen him a second time.

"Your alarm call, sir," said a girl's voice gently. "It's eight o'clock."

"Thank you," Adam replied and replaced the receiver. The call had proved unnecessary because he had been sitting up in bed considering the implications of his plan for nearly an hour. Adam had finally worked out exactly how he was going to finish Romanov.

He jumped out of bed, threw back the curtains and stared down at the Soviet Embassy. He wondered how long the Russian had been awake.

He returned to the side of the bed and picked up the phone to dial the number Robin had given him. The phone rang several times before it was answered by an elderly voice saying, "Mrs Beresford."

"Good morning, Mrs Beresford. My name is Adam Scott, I'm a friend of Robin's. I was just phoning to check that she reached home safely last night."

"Oh, yes, thank you," said Robin's mother. "It was a pleasant surprise to see her before the weekend. She usually spends the night in the flat when she gets back that late. I'm afraid she's still asleep. Would you like me to wake her?"

"No, no, don't disturb her," said Adam. "I only rang to fix up a lunch date. Can you tell her I'll call back later?"

"I certainly will," she replied. "Thank you for phoning, Mr Scott."

Adam replaced the receiver and smiled. Each piece of the jigsaw was fitting neatly into place but without the colonel's help he still lacked the vital corner-piece.

Adam began to put everything Tomkins needed, including his passport, personal papers and wallet into a large envelope. He removed the icon from his jacket pocket, turned it over and carefully examined the little silver crest of the Tsar. He then flicked open the colonel's penknife and began the slow and delicate task of removing the crown.

Thirty minutes later, Adam was in the lift on the way to the hotel basement. When he stepped out, he walked across to the space where he had parked the green Cortina earlier that morning. He unlocked the door and threw the colonel's old jacket on to the seat, then locked the car, checking all the doors before taking the lift back up to the ground floor.

The manager of the men's shop in the arcade had just flicked over the 'closed' sign and Adam took his time selecting a white shirt, grey flannels and a blue blazer, trying them on in their little changing room.

At nine twenty-three he settled his bill with the Royal Garden Hotel and asked the doorman to bring the green Ford up from the parking lot. He waited by the hotel entrance.

As the minutes passed, he began to fear that the colonel wouldn't turn up. If he failed to, Adam knew that the next call would have to be to Lawrence and not Romanov.

His reverie was disturbed by a honk on a car horn; the colonel's rented car had been left by the entrance.

"Your car is waiting on the ramp," said the doorman, as he returned the keys to Adam.

"Thank you," said Adam and handed over the last of the colonel's pound notes. He dropped the wallet into the large envelope, which he sealed, before checking his watch again.

He stood waiting anxiously for another two minutes

before he spotted the colonel puffing up the slope leading to the hotel entrance.

He was clinging on to a small carrier bag.

"I've done it, Captain Scott, sir, I've done it," said the colonel, before he had reached Adam's side. "But I must return immediately or he's bound to notice it's gone."

He passed the carrier bag quickly to Adam who opened the top and stared down at the object inside.

"You're a man of your word," said Adam, "and as promised you'll find everything you need in there." He passed over his own package along with the car keys without speaking. He pointed to the hire car.

The colonel ran to it, jumped in and drove quickly down the ramp of the Royal Garden Hotel before turning left into Kensington Palace Gardens.

Adam checked his watch: nine thirty-five.

"Could you call me a taxi?" he asked the doorman.

The driver pulled the window down and gave Adam an enquiring look.

"Chesham Place, SW1. A carpenter's shop."

Adam spent twenty minutes looking around the shop while the craftsman carried out his unusual request. Adam studied the result with satisfaction, paid him two half-crowns and then walked back on to King's Road, to hail another taxi.

"Where to, guv'nor?"

"The Tower of London."

Everyone was in their place for the D4 meeting at nine thirty and Busch had gone on the attack even before Lawrence had had the chance to sit down.

"How in hell did you manage to lose him this time?"

"I must take the blame myself," said Lawrence. "We had every port from Newhaven to Harwich covered, but the moment my man saw Romanov and his henchman leave the quayside at Dover and chase off down the motorway after the coach he assumed he must have seen Scott. I had already instructed the senior immigration officer at the port," he continued, "to allow Scott to disembark without a fuss. It had been my intention to take over once he passed through customs. There seemed no reason to change that plan while we had Romanov under close surveillance. Scott then proceeded to fool both Romanov and our man at Dover."

"But we were given a second chance when Scott got on the train," persisted Busch. Lawrence stared at the American, waiting to see if he would admit that his two CIA agents had also lost Scott at Dover.

"My man was on the train," said Lawrence emphatically, "but had only the one opportunity to make contact with Scott while he was on his own, and at just that moment he was grabbed and badly beaten up by a bunch of drunken louts — teenagers, apparently — who were on their way back from a day trip to the seaside."

"Perhaps we're recruiting our agents from the wrong class of person," said Matthews, staring down at his briefing papers.

Lawrence made no attempt to reply.

"So, as far as we can tell, Scott, the Tsar's icon and Romanov are still holed up somewhere in London?" said Snell.

"It looks that way," admitted Lawrence.

"Perhaps all is not lost then," suggested Snell. "Scott may still try and get in touch with you again."

"I think not," said Lawrence quietly.

"How can you be so sure?" asked Busch.

"Because Scott knows that one of us in this room is a traitor and he thinks it's me."

"Good morning. Soviet Embassy."

"My name is Adam Scott and I need to get in contact with a Major Romanov."

"Good morning, Mr Scott. We do not have a Major Romanov working at the Embassy," came back the polite reply.

"I'm sure you don't."

"But if you would like to leave your number, I will make further enquiries."

"I'll wait. Wouldn't surprise me if you find him very quickly once he knows who it is calling."

There was a long silence at the other end, and Adam only hoped the shilling he had pressed into the call box would prove to be enough. At last there was a click, and then Adam heard a voice.

"Who is this?" said the voice, unable to mask its incredulity.

"You know very well who it is," said Adam curtly. "I want to make a deal."

"A deal?" Romanov repeated, his voice changing from one of disbelief to surprise.

"I'll swap you my icon – which as you so vividly pointed out is worthless to me – in exchange for your copy, which is not. But I also require the papers that prove my father's innocence."

"How do I know you're not setting me up?"

"You don't," said Adam. "But you're the one with nothing to lose."

The pips began to sound across the line.

"Tell me your number," said Romanov.

"738–9121," said Adam.

"I'll phone you back," said Romanov as the line went dead.

"How quickly can we find out where 738–9121 is located?" Romanov asked the local KGB operative who sat opposite him.

"About ten minutes," the aide replied. "But it could be a trap."

"True, but with nineteen hours to go before the icon has to be in America I don't have a lot of choice."

Romanov turned back to the KGB agent. "What's the traffic like in London on a Friday morning?"

"One of the busiest times in the week. Why do you ask?"

"Because I'll need a motorbike and a superb driver," was all Romanov said.

Adam could do nothing about the middle-aged lady who was now occupying his phone booth. He had nervously walked out to check the bridge when she slipped in. She must have been puzzled as to why the young man didn't use the empty box that stood next to it.

He checked his watch anxiously: ten forty-five. He knew he couldn't risk waiting a minute after eleven but was confident that Romanov would have traced where he'd made the call from long before then.

The talkative woman was another twelve minutes before she eventually put the phone down. When she stepped out of the box she gave Adam a warm smile.

Three more minutes and he would have to phone Lawrence and abort his original plan. He began to watch the Beefeaters as they patrolled under Traitors' Gate. Traitors' Gate – how appropriate, Adam thought. He had chosen the spot because he could see clearly up and down the path leading to the drawbridge and felt he could not be taken by surprise. And in desperation there was always the moat that surrounded them on all sides.

For the first time in his life, Adam discovered exactly how long five minutes could be. When the phone rang, it sounded like an alarm bell. He picked it up nervously, his eyes never leaving the main road.

"Scott?"

"Yes."

"I can now see you clearly as I am less than one minute away. I will be standing at the end of Tower Bridge until the end of that minute. Be sure you're there with the icon. If you're not, I shall burn the papers that prove your father's innocence in front of you."

The phone went dead.

Adam was delighted that another piece of the jigsaw had fallen into place. He stepped out of the phone booth and checked up and down the road. A BMW motorcycle swerved to a halt at the end of the bridge. A rider dressed in a leather jacket sat astride the bike but only seemed interested in watching the flow of traffic as it passed by the Tower. It was the man seated behind him who stared directly at Adam.

Adam began to walk slowly towards the end of the bridge. He put a hand in his pocket to be sure the icon was still in its place.

He was about thirty yards from the end of the bridge when the second figure got off the bike and started walking towards him. When their eyes met, Romanov stopped in his tracks and held up a small, square frame. Adam did not respond in kind, but simply tapped the side of his pocket and continued walking. Both men advanced towards each other like knights of old until they were only a few paces apart. Almost simultaneously they stopped and faced one another.

"Let me see it," said Romanov.

Adam paused, then slowly removed the icon from his pocket and held it to his chest for his adversary to see St George stared at him.

"Turn it over," said Romanov.

Adam obeyed, and the Russian could not hide his delight when he saw the little silver crown of the Tsar embedded in the back.

"Now you," said Adam. Romanov held his icon away from his body, as if brandishing a sword. The masterpiece shone in the summer sun.

"And the documents," said Adam, forcing himself to speak calmly.

The Russian pulled out a package from within his jacket and slowly unfolded them. Adam stared at the official court verdict for a second time.

"Go to the wall," said Adam, pointing with his left hand to the side of the bridge, "and leave the icon and the documents on it."

It was Romanov who now obeyed as Adam proceeded to the wall on the other side of the bridge and placed his icon in the middle of it.

"Cross slowly," called Adam. The two men moved sideways back across the bridge, never getting closer than a couple of yards from each other until they had come to a halt at each other's icon. The moment the painting was within his reach, Romanov grabbed it, ran and jumped on to the motorcycle without looking back. Within seconds the BMW had disappeared into the dense traffic.

Adam did not move. Although it had only been out of his sight for just over an hour, he was relieved to have the original back. Adam checked the papers that would establish his father's innocence and placed them in his inside pocket. Ignoring the tourists, some of whom had stopped to stare at him, Adam began to relax when suddenly he felt a sharp prod in the middle of his back. He jumped round in fright.

A little girl was staring up at him.

"Will you and your friend be performing again this morning?"

When the BMW motorcycle drew up outside the Soviet Embassy in Kensington Palace Gardens, Romanov leapt off and ran up the steps and straight into the Ambassador's office without knocking. The Ambassador didn't need to ask if he had been successful.

"It worked out just as I planned. He was taken completely by surprise," said Romanov, as he handed the icon over to the Ambassador.

The Ambassador turned the painting over and saw the little silver crown of the Tsar. Any doubts that he might have had were also dispelled.

"I have orders to send the icon to Washington in the diplomatic pouch immediately. There is no time to be lost."

"I wish I could deliver it in person," said Romanov.

"Be satisfied, Comrade Major, that you have carried out your part of the operation in an exemplary fashion."

The Ambassador pressed a button on the side of his desk. Two men appeared immediately. One held open the diplomatic pouch while the other stood motionless by his side. The Ambassador handed over the icon and watched it being placed into the pouch. The two couriers looked as if they would have had no trouble in carrying out the Ambassador's desk as well, thought Romanov.

"There is a plane standing by at Heathrow to take

you both direct to Washington," said the Ambassador. "All the necessary documentation for customs has already been dealt with. You should touch down at National airport around five o'clock Washington time, easily giving our comrades in America enough time to fulfil their part of the contract."

The two men nodded, sealed the diplomatic pouch in the Ambassador's presence and left. Romanov walked over to the window and watched the official car drive the two men out into Kensington High Street and off in the direction of Heathrow.

"Vodka, Comrade Major?"

"Thank you," Romanov replied, not moving from the window until the car was out of sight.

The Ambassador went over to a side cabinet and took out two glasses and a bottle from the fridge before pouring Romanov a large vodka.

"It would not be exaggerating to say that you have played your part in establishing the Soviet Union as the most powerful nation on earth," he said as he handed over the drink. "Let us therefore drink to the repatriation of the people of Aleuts as full citizens of the Union of Soviet Socialist Republics."

"How is that possible?" asked Romanov.

"I think the time has come to let you know," said the Ambassador, "the significance of your achievement." He then went on to tell Romanov of the briefing he had received from Moscow that morning.

Romanov was thankful he had never known how much was at stake.

"I have made an appointment to see the Foreign Secretary at three o'clock this afternoon in order to brief him. We can be sure the British will only be interested in fair play," the Ambassador continued. "I am told he is not at all pleased as he had hoped to be in his constituency to open some fete; the British have some strange ideas about how to keep their party system going."

Romanov laughed. "To Aleuts," he said, raising his glass. "But what is happening in Washington at this moment?"

"Our Ambassador has already requested a meeting with the American Secretary of State to be scheduled for eight this evening. He is also setting up a press conference at the Embassy to follow that meeting. It may amuse you to know that President Johnson had to cancel his visit to Texas this weekend and has requested that the networks should allow him to address 'his fellow Americans' at peak time on Monday as a matter of national importance."

"And we achieved it with only hours to spare," said Romanov, pouring himself another vodka.

"Touch and go, as the English would say. Let us also be thankful for the time difference between here and the United States because without that we would never have been able to beat the deadline."

Romanov shuddered at the thought of how close it had been and downed his second vodka in one gulp.

"You must join me for lunch, Comrade. Although your orders are to return to Moscow immediately my secretary assures me that the first plane leaving Heathrow for Moscow does not depart until eight this evening. I envy you the reception you will receive when you arrive back in the Kremlin tomorrow."

"I still need the £1000 for . . ."

"Ah, yes," said the Ambassador, "I have it ready for you." He unlocked the little drawer of his desk and passed over a slim wad of notes in a small cellophane wrapper.

Romanov slipped the tiny packet in his pocket and joined the Ambassador for lunch.

Busch barged into Lawrence's office.

"Romanov's got the icon," he shouted.

Lawrence's jaw dropped. A look of desperation appeared on his face. "How can you be so sure?" he demanded.

"I've just had a message from Washington. The Russians have requested an official meeting with the Secretary of State to be arranged for eight this evening."

"I don't believe it," said Lawrence.

"I do," said Busch. "We've always known that God-damned friend of yours, like his father, was a lousy traitor. There's no other explanation."

"He could be dead," said Lawrence quietly.

"I hope he is, for his sake," said Busch.

The phone on Lawrence's desk rang. He grabbed it as if it were a lifeline. "A Dr John Vance wants a word with you, sir," said his secretary. "He said you had asked him to call."

Vance? Vance? Lawrence recalled the name but couldn't quite place it. "Put him on," he said.

"Good morning, Mr Pemberton," said a voice.

"Good morning, Dr Vance. What can I do for you?"

"You asked me to call you after I had examined Scott."

"Scott?" repeated Lawrence, not believing what he was hearing.

"Yes, Adam Scott. Surely you remember? You wanted him to complete a medical for your department."

Lawrence was speechless.

"I've given him a clean bill of health," continued

the doctor. "Some cuts and a nasty bruise, but nothing that won't heal in a few days."

"Cuts and bruises?" said Lawrence.

"That's what I said, old chap. But don't worry about Scott. He's fit enough to start work whenever you want him. That's if you still want him."

"If I still want him," repeated Lawrence. "Mr Scott isn't there with you at this moment, by any chance?"

"No," said Vance. "Left my surgery about ten minutes ago."

"He didn't happen to tell you where he was going?" asked Lawrence.

"No, he wasn't specific. Just said something about having to see a friend off at the airport."

Once the coffee had been cleared away, Romanov checked his watch. He had left easily enough time to keep the appointment and still catch his plane. He thanked the Ambassador for all his help, left him, ran down the Embassy steps and climbed into the back of the anonymous black car.

The driver moved off without speaking as he had already been briefed as to where the major wanted to go.

Neither of them spoke on the short journey, and when the driver drew into Charlotte Street he parked the car in a lay-by. Romanov stepped out, walked quickly across the road to the door he was looking for and pressed the buzzer.

"Are you a member?" said a voice through the intercom.

"Yes," said Romanov, who heard a metallic click as he pushed the door open and walked down the dark staircase. Once he had entered the club it took a few seconds for his eyes to become accustomed to the light.

But then he spotted Mentor seated on his own at a little table near a pillar in the far corner of the room.

Romanov nodded and the man got up and walked across the dance floor and straight past him. Romanov followed as the member entered the only lavatory. Once inside, Romanov checked that they were alone. Satisfied, he led them both into a little cubicle and slipped the lock to engaged. Romanov removed the thousand pounds from his pocket and handed it over to the man who sat down on the lavatory seat. Mentor greedily ripped open the packet, leaned forward and began to count. He never even saw Romanov straighten his fingers; and when the hand came down with a crushing blow on the back of Mentor's neck he slumped forward and fell to the ground in a heap.

Romanov yanked him up; it took several seconds to gather the ten-pound notes that had fallen to the floor. Once he had all hundred, he stuffed them into the member's pocket. Romanov then undid the member's fly buttons one by one and pulled down his trousers until they fell around his ankles. He lifted the lid and placed the man on the lavatory seat. The final touch was to pull his legs as wide open as the fallen trousers would allow, the feet splayed apart. Romanov then slipped under the large gap at the bottom of the door leaving the cubicle locked from the inside. He quickly checked his handiwork. All that could be seen from the outside was the splayed legs and fallen trousers.

Sixty seconds later, Romanov was back in the car on his way to Heathrow.

Adam arrived at Heathrow two hours before the Aeroflot flight was due to depart. He stationed himself with a perfect view of the forty-yard stretch Romanov would have to walk to board the Russian aircraft. He felt confident he would never reach the Aeroflot steps.

Romanov checked in at the BEA desk a little after six. He couldn't resist taking the BEA flight rather than Aeroflot even though he knew Zaborski would frown at such arrogance; he doubted if anyone would comment on this of all days.

Once he had been given his boarding card, he took the escalator to the executive lounge and sat around waiting to be called. It was always the same – the moment any operation had been completed, all he wanted to do was get home. He left his seat to pour himself some coffee and, passing a table in the centre of the room, caught the headline on the London *Evening Standard*. Exclusive. 'Johnson Texas Weekend Cancelled – Mystery.' Romanov grabbed the paper from the table and read the first paragraph but it contained no information he couldn't have already told them. None of the speculation in the paragraphs that followed even began to get near the truth.

Romanov couldn't wait to see the front page of *Pravda* the next day in which he knew the true story would be emblazoned. By Western standards it would be an exclusive.

"BEA announce the departure of their flight 117 to Moscow. Would all first class passengers now board through gate No. 23." Romanov left the lounge and walked the half mile long corridor to the plane. Romanov strolled across the tarmac to the waiting plane a few minutes after six fifty. The plane carrying the icon would be touching down in Washington in about two hours. Romanov would arrive back in Moscow well in time to see Dynamo play Spartak at the Lenin Stadium on Tuesday. He wondered if they would announce his arrival to the crowd over the loudspeakers as they always did when a member of the Politburo attended a match. Romanov walked up the steps and on board, stepping over the feet of the passenger placed next to him, thankful that he had been given the window seat.

"Would you care for a drink before take-off?" the stewardess asked.

"Just a black coffee for me," said his neighbour. Romanov nodded his agreement.

The stewardess arrived back a few minutes later with the two coffees and helped the man next to Romanov pull out his table from the armrest. Romanov flicked his over as the stewardess passed him his coffee.

He took a sip but it was too hot so he placed it on the table in front of him. He watched his neighbour take out a packet of saccharines from his pocket and flick two pellets into the steaming coffee.

Why did he bother, thought Romanov. Life was too short.

Romanov stared out of the window and watched the Aeroflot plane start to taxi out on to the runway. He smiled at the thought of how much more comfortable his own flight would be. He tried his coffee a second time: just as he liked it. He took a long gulp and began to feel a little drowsy which he didn't find that strange as he had hardly slept for the last week.

He leaned back in his seat and closed his eyes. He would now take every honour the State could offer him. With Valchek conveniently out of the way, he could even position himself to take over from Zaborski. If that failed, his grandfather had left him another alternative.

He was leaving London with only one regret: he had failed to kill Scott. But then he suspected that the

421

Americans would take care of that. For the first time in a week he didn't have to stop himself falling asleep . . .

A few moments later the passenger seated next to Romanov picked up the Russian's coffee cup and put it next to his own. He then flicked Romanov's table back into the armrest and placed a woollen blanket over Romanov's legs. He quickly slipped the BEA eye shades over the Russian's head, covering his open eyes. He looked up to find that the stewardess was standing by his side.

"Can I help?" she asked, smiling.

"No, thank you. All he said was that he did not want to be disturbed during the flight as he has had a very hard week."

"Of course, sir," said the stewardess. "We'll be taking off in a few minutes," she added, and picked up the two coffee cups and whisked them away.

The man tapped his fingers impatiently on the little table. At last the chief steward appeared at his side.

"There's been an urgent call from your office, sir. You're to return to Whitehall immediately."

"I had been half expecting it," he admitted.

Adam stared up at the Russian plane as it climbed steeply and swung in a semi-circle towards the East. He couldn't understand why Romanov hadn't boarded it. Surely he wouldn't have taken the BEA flight. Adam slipped back into the shadows the moment he saw him. He stared in disbelief. Lawrence was striding back across the tarmac, a smile of satisfaction on his face.

EPILOGUE

SOTHEBY'S
FOUNDED 1744

SOTHEBY'S
NEW BOND STREET,
LONDON W1

October 18, 1966

EPILOGUE

"Sold to the gentleman in the centre of the room for five thousand pounds.

"We now move on to Lot no. 32," said the auctioneer, looking down from the raised platform at the front of the crowded room. "An icon of St George and the Dragon," he declared as an attendant placed a little painting on the easel next to him. The auctioneer stared down at the faces of experts, amateurs and curious onlookers. "What am I bid for this magnificent example of Russian art?" he asked, expectantly.

Robin gripped Adam's hand. "I haven't felt this nervous since I came face to face with Romanov."

"Don't remind me," said Adam.

"It is, of course, not the original that hangs in the Winter Palace," continued the auctioneer, "but it is nevertheless a fine copy, probably executed by a court painter circa 1914," he added, giving the little painting an approving smile. "Do I have an opening bid? Shall I say eight thousand?" The next few seconds seemed interminable to Robin and Adam. "Thank you, sir," said the auctioneer, eventually looking towards an anonymous sign that had been given somewhere at the front of the room.

Neither Adam nor Robin were able to make out

where the bid had come from. They had spent the last hour seated at the back of the room watching the previous items coming under the hammer and had rarely been able to work out whose hands they had ended up in.

"How much did the expert say it might go for?" Robin asked again.

"Anywhere between ten and twenty thousand," Adam reminded her.

"Nine thousand," said the auctioneer, his eyes moving to a bid that appeared to come from the right-hand side of the room.

"I still think it's amazing," said Robin, "that the Russians ever agreed to the exchange in the first place."

"Why?" asked Adam. "Once the Americans had extracted the treaty, there was no harm in allowing the Russians to have their original back in exchange for the copy which rightly belonged to me. As an example of diplomatic ingenuity it was Lawrence at his most brilliant."

"Ten thousand from the front of the room. Thank you, sir," said the auctioneer.

"What are you going to do with all that money?"

"Buy a new double bass, get a wedding present for my sister and hand over the rest to my mother."

"Eleven thousand, a new bid on the centre aisle," said the auctioneer. "Thank you, madam."

"No amount of money can bring back Heidi," said Robin quietly.

Adam nodded thoughtfully.

"How did the meeting with Heidi's parents turn out?"

"The Foreign Secretary saw them personally last week. It couldn't help, but at least he was able to confirm that I had only been telling them the truth."

"Twelve thousand." The auctioneer's eye returned to the front of the room.

"Did you see the Foreign Secretary yourself?"

"Good heavens, no, I'm far too junior for that," said Adam. "I'm lucky if I get to see Lawrence, let alone the Foreign Secretary."

Robin laughed. "I consider you were *lucky* to have been offered a place at the Foreign Office at all."

"Agreed," said Adam chuckling to himself, "but a vacancy arose unexpectedly."

"What do you mean, 'unexpectedly'?" asked Robin, frustrated by how few of her questions had been answered directly in the past half hour.

"All I can tell you is that one of Lawrence's old team was 'retired early'," said Adam.

"Was that also true of Romanov?" asked Robin, still desperately trying to discover all that had taken place since they had last met.

"Thirteen thousand," said the auctioneer, his eyes returning to the lady on the centre aisle.

"After all he can't have survived for long once they discovered you had done a switch on Tower Bridge that gave the Russians back the copy while Romanov ended up presenting you with the original," said Robin.

"He's never been heard of since," admitted Adam innocently.

"And all our information leads us to believe that his boss Zaborski is soon to be replaced by someone called Yuri Andropov."

"Fourteen thousand," said the auctioneer, his eye settling on the gentleman at the front once again.

"What happened when you produced the papers proving that it was not your father who had smuggled the poison into Goering's cell?"

"Once they had been authenticated by the Russians," Adam said, "Lawrence paid an official visit to the Colonel of the Regiment and furnished him with the conclusive evidence."

"Any reaction?" probed Robin.

"They're going to hold a memorial service in Pa's memory and have commissioned some fellow called Ward to paint his portrait for the regimental mess. Mother has been invited to unveil it in the presence of all those officers who served with my father."

"Fourteen thousand for the first time then," said the auctioneer raising the little gavel a few inches in the air.

"She must have been over the moon," said Robin.

"Burst into tears," said Adam. "All she could say was 'I wish Pa could have lived to see it.' Ironic, really. If only he had opened that letter."

"Fourteen thousand for the second time," said the auctioneer, the gavel now hovering.

"How do you fancy a celebration lunch at the Ritz?" said Adam, delighted with how well the sale was turning out.

"No thank you," said Robin.

Adam looked across at his companion in surprise.

"It won't be much fun if every time I ask you a question I only get the official Foreign Office briefing."

Adam looked sheepish. "I'm sorry," he said.

"No, that wasn't fair," said Robin. "Now you're on the inside it can't be easy, so I suppose I will have to go to my grave wondering what treaty was inside that icon."

Adam looked away from the girl who had saved his life.

"Or perhaps I'll find out the truth in 1996 when the cabinet papers are released."

He turned slowly to face her.

"Alas . . ." he began as the auctioneer's hammer came down with a thud. They both looked up.

"Sold to the gentleman at the front for fourteen thousand pounds."

"Not a bad price," said Adam, smiling.

"A bargain in my opinion," replied Robin quietly.

Adam turned to her, a quizzical look on his face.

"After all," she said in a whisper, "imagine what the forty-ninth state would have fetched if it had come up for auction."

THE END

TWELVE RED HERRINGS

TWELVE MINUTES.

To Chris, Carol . . . and Alyson

Contents

* The stories indicated with an asterisk are based on known incidents (some of them embellished with considerable licence). The others are the product of my own imagination.

J.A.
July 1994

TRIAL AND ERROR

I'S HARD TO KNOW EXACTLY WHERE TO begin. But first, let me explain why I'm in jail.

The trial had lasted for eighteen days, and from the moment the judge had entered the courtroom the public benches had been filled to overflowing. The jury at Leeds Crown Court had been out for almost two days, and rumour had it that they were hopelessly divided. On the barristers' bench there was talk of hung juries and retrials, as it had been more than eight hours since Mr Justice Cartwright had told the foreman of the jury that their verdict need no longer be unanimous: a majority of ten to two would be acceptable.

Suddenly there was a buzz in the corridors, and the members of the jury filed quietly into their places. Press and public alike began to stampede back into court. All eyes were on the foreman of the jury, a fat, jolly-looking little man dressed in a double-breasted suit, striped shirt and a colourful bow tie, striving to appear solemn. He seemed the sort of fellow with whom, in normal circumstances, I would have enjoyed a pint at the local. But these were not normal circumstances.

As I climbed back up the steps into the dock, my eyes

settled on a pretty blonde who had been seated in the gallery every day of the trial. I wondered if she attended all the sensational murder trials, or if she was just fascinated by this one. She showed absolutely no interest in me, and like everyone else was concentrating her full attention on the foreman of the jury.

The clerk of the court, dressed in a wig and a long black gown, rose and read out from a card the words I suspect he knew by heart.

'Will the foreman of the jury please stand.'

The jolly little fat man rose slowly from his place.

'Please answer my next question yes or no. Members of the jury, have you reached a verdict on which at least ten of you are agreed?'

'Yes, we have.'

'Members of the jury, do you find the prisoner at the bar guilty or not guilty as charged?'

There was total silence in the courtroom.

My eyes were fixed on the foreman with the colourful bow tie. He cleared his throat and said, '. . .

I first met Jeremy Alexander in 1978, at a CBI training seminar in Bristol. Fifty-six British companies who were looking for ways to expand into Europe had come together for a briefing on Community Law. At the time that I signed up for the seminar Cooper's, the company of which I was chairman, ran 127 vehicles of varying weights and sizes, and was fast becoming one of the largest private road haulage companies in Britain.

My father had founded the firm in 1931, starting out with three vehicles — two of them pulled by horses — and an overdraft limit of ten pounds at his local Martins bank. By the time we became 'Cooper & Son' in 1967 the company had seventeen vehicles with four wheels or more, and delivered goods all over the north of England. But the old man still resolutely refused to exceed his ten-pound overdraft limit.

I once expressed the view, during a downturn in the market, that we should be looking further afield in search of new business — perhaps even as far as the Continent. But my father wouldn't hear of it. 'Not a risk worth taking,' he declared. He distrusted anyone born south of the Humber, let alone those who lived on the other side of the Channel. 'If God put a strip of water between us, he must have had good reasons for doing so,' were his final words on the subject. I would have laughed, if I hadn't realised he meant it.

When he retired in 1977 — reluctantly, at the age of seventy — I took over as chairman, and began to set in motion some ideas I'd been working on for the past decade, though I knew my father didn't approve of them. Europe was only the beginning of my plans for the company's expansion: within five years I wanted to go public. By then, I realised, we would require an overdraft facility of at least a million pounds, and would therefore have to move our account to a bank which recognised that the world stretched beyond the county boundaries of Yorkshire.

It was around this time that I heard about the CBI seminar at Bristol, and applied for a place.

The seminar began on the Friday, with an opening address from the Head of the European Directorate of the CBI. After that the delegates split into eight small working groups, each chaired by an expert on Community Law. My group was headed by Jeremy Alexander. I admired him from the moment he started speaking – in fact, it wouldn't be an exaggeration to say that I was overawed. He was totally self-assured, and as I was to learn, he could effortlessly present a convincing argument on any subject, from the superiority of the Code Napoléon to the inferiority of the English middle-order batting.

He lectured us for an hour on the fundamental differences in practice and procedure between the member states of the Community, then answered all our questions on Commercial and Company Law, even finding time to explain the significance of the Uruguay Round. Like me, the other members of our group never stopped taking notes.

We broke up for lunch a few minutes before one, and I managed to grab a place next to Jeremy. I was already beginning to think that he might be the ideal person to advise me on how to go about achieving my European ambitions.

Listening to him talk about his career over a meal of stargazy pie with red peppers, I kept thinking that, although we were about the same age, we couldn't have come from more different backgrounds. Jeremy's father, a banker by profession, had escaped from Eastern Europe only days before the outbreak of the Second World War.

He had settled in England, anglicised his name, and sent his son to Westminster. From there Jeremy had gone on to King's College, London, where he read Law, graduating with first-class honours.

My own father was a self-made man from the Yorkshire Dales who had insisted I leave school the moment I passed my O levels. 'I'll teach you more about the real world in a month than you'd learn from any of those university types in a lifetime,' he used to say. I accepted this philosophy without question, and left school a few weeks after my sixteenth birthday. The next morning I joined Cooper's as an apprentice, and spent my first three years at the depot under the watchful eye of Buster Jackson, the works manager, who taught me how to take the company's vehicles apart and, more importantly, how to put them back together again.

After graduating from the workshop, I spent two years in the invoicing department, learning how to calculate charges and collect bad debts. A few weeks after my twenty-first birthday I passed the test for my heavy goods vehicles licence, and for the next three years I zig-zagged across the north of England, delivering everything from poultry to pineapples to our far-flung customers. Jeremy spent the same period reading for a master's degree in Napoleonic Law at the Sorbonne.

When Buster Jackson retired I was moved back to the depot in Leeds to take over as works manager. Jeremy was in Hamburg, writing a doctoral thesis on international trade barriers. By the time he had finally left the world of academia and taken up his first real job, as a partner with a large firm of commercial solicitors in the City, I had been earning a working wage for eight years.

Although I was impressed by Jeremy at the seminar, I sensed, behind that surface affability, a powerful combination of ambition and intellectual snobbery that my father would have mistrusted. I felt he'd only agreed to give the lecture on the off-chance that, at some time in the future, we might be responsible for spreading some butter on his bread. I now realise that, even at our first meeting, he suspected that in my case it might be honey.

It didn't help my opinion of the man that he had a couple of inches on me in height, and a couple less around the waist. Not to mention the fact that the most attractive woman on the course that weekend ended up in his bed on the Saturday night.

We met up on the Sunday morning to play squash, when he ran me ragged, without even appearing to raise a sweat. 'We must get together again,' he said as we walked to the showers. 'If you're really thinking of expanding into Europe, you might find I'm able to help.'

My father had taught me never to make the mistake of imagining that your friends and your colleagues were necessarily the same animals (he often cited the Cabinet as an example). So, although I didn't like him, I made sure that when I left Bristol at the end of the conference I was in possession of Jeremy's numerous telephone and telex numbers.

I drove back to Leeds on the Sunday evening, and when I reached home I ran upstairs and sat on the end of the bed regaling my sleepy wife with an account of why it had turned out to be such a worthwhile weekend.

Rosemary was my second wife. My first, Helen, had been at Leeds High School for Girls at the same time that I had attended the nearby grammar school. The two schools shared a gymnasium, and I fell in love with her at the age of thirteen, while watching her play netball. After that I would find any excuse to hang around the gym, hoping to catch a glimpse of her blue knickers as she leapt to send the ball unerringly into the net. As the schools took part in various joint activities, I began to take an active interest in theatrical productions, even though I couldn't act. I attended joint debates, and never opened my mouth. I enlisted in the combined schools orchestra and ended up playing the triangle. After I had left school and gone to work at the depot, I continued to see Helen, who was studying for her A levels. Despite my passion for her, we didn't make love until we were both eighteen, and even then I wasn't certain that we had consummated anything. Six weeks later she told me, in a flood of tears, that she was pregnant. Against the wishes of her parents, who had hoped that she would go on to university, a hasty wedding was arranged, but as I never wanted to look at another girl for the rest of my life, I was secretly delighted by the outcome of our youthful indiscretion.

Helen died on the night of 14 September 1964, giving birth to our son, Tom, who himself only survived a week. I thought I would never get over it, and I'm not sure I ever have. After her death I didn't so much as

9

glance at another woman for years, putting all my energy into the company.

Following the funeral of my wife and son, my father, not a soft or sentimental man – you won't find many of those in Yorkshire – revealed a gentle side to his character that I had never seen before. He would often phone me in the evening to see how I was getting on, and insisted that I regularly joined him in the directors' box at Elland Road to watch Leeds United on Saturday afternoons. I began to understand, for the first time, why my mother still adored him after more than twenty years of marriage.

I met Rosemary about four years later at a ball given to launch the Leeds Music Festival. Not a natural habitat for me, but as Cooper's had taken a full-page advertisement in the programme, and Brigadier Kershaw, the High Sheriff of the county and Chairman of the Ball Committee, had invited us to join him as his guests, I had no choice but to dress up in my seldom-worn dinner jacket and accompany my parents to the ball.

I was placed on Table 17, next to a Miss Kershaw, who turned out to be the High Sheriff's daughter. She was elegantly dressed in a strapless blue gown that emphasised her comely figure, and had a mop of red hair and a smile that made me feel we had been friends for years. She told me over something described on the menu as 'avocado with dill' that she had just finished reading English at Durham University, and wasn't quite sure what she was going to do with her life.

'I don't want to be a teacher,' she said. 'And I'm

certainly not cut out to be a secretary.' We chatted through the second and third courses, ignoring the people seated on either side of us. After coffee she dragged me onto the dance floor, where she continued to explain the problems of contemplating any form of work while her diary was so packed with social engagements.

I felt rather flattered that the High Sheriff's daughter should show the slightest interest in me, and to be honest I didn't take it seriously when at the end of the evening, she whispered in my ear, 'Let's keep in touch.'

But a couple of days later she rang and invited me to join her and her parents for lunch that Sunday at their house in the country, 'And then perhaps we could play a little tennis afterwards. You do play tennis, I suppose?'

I drove over to Church Fenton on Sunday, and found that the Kershaws' residence was exactly what I would have expected – large and decaying, which, come to think of it, wasn't a bad description of Rosemary's father as well. But he seemed a nice enough chap. Her mother, however, wasn't quite so easy to please. She originated from somewhere in Hampshire, and was unable to mask her feeling that, although I might be good for the occasional charitable donation, I was not quite the sort of person with whom she expected to be sharing her Sunday lunch. Rosemary ignored the odd barbed comment from her, and continued to chat to me about my work.

As it rained all afternoon we never got round to playing tennis, so Rosemary used the time to seduce me in the little pavilion behind the court. At first I was nervous about making love to the High Sheriff's daughter, but I soon got used to the idea. However, as the weeks passed, I began to wonder if I was anything more to her than a 'lorry driver fantasy'. Until, that is, she started to talk about marriage. Mrs Kershaw was unable to hide her disgust at the very idea of someone like me becoming her son-in-law, but her opinion turned out to be irrelevant, as Rosemary remained implacable on the subject. We were married eighteen months later.

Over two hundred guests attended the rather grand county wedding in the parish church of St Mary's. But I confess that when I turned to watch Rosemary progressing up the aisle, my only thoughts were of my first wedding ceremony.

For a couple of years Rosemary made every effort to be a good wife. She took an interest in the company, learned the names of all the employees, even became friendly with the wives of some of the senior executives. But, as I worked all the hours God sent, I fear I may not always have given her as much attention as she needed. You see, Rosemary yearned for a life that was made up of regular visits to the Grand Theatre for Opera North, followed by dinner parties with her county friends that would run into the early hours, while I preferred to work at weekends, and to be tucked up in bed before eleven most nights. For Rosemary I wasn't turning out to be the husband in the title of the Oscar Wilde play she had recently taken me to – and it didn't help that I had fallen asleep during the second act.

After four years without producing any offspring – not that Rosemary wasn't very energetic in bed – we began to drift our separate ways. If she started having affairs (and I certainly did, when I could find the time), she was discreet about them. And then she met Jeremy Alexander.

It must have been about six weeks after the seminar in Bristol that I had occasion to phone Jeremy and seek his advice. I wanted to close a deal with a French cheese company to transport its wares to British supermarkets. The previous year I had made a large loss on a similar enterprise with a German beer company, and I couldn't afford to make the same mistake again.

'Send me all the details,' Jeremy had said. 'I'll look over the paperwork at the weekend and call you on Monday morning.'

He was as good as his word, and when he phoned me he mentioned that he had to be in York that Thursday to brief a client, and suggested we get together the following day to go over the contract. I agreed, and we spent most of that Friday closeted in the Cooper's boardroom checking over every dot and comma of the contract. It was a pleasure to watch such a professional at work, even if Jeremy did occasionally display an irritating habit of drumming his fingers on the table when I hadn't immediately understood what he was getting at.

Jeremy, it turned out, had already talked to the French

company's in-house lawyer in Toulouse about any reservations he might have. He assured me that, although Monsieur Sisley spoke no English, he had made him fully aware of our anxieties. I remember being struck by his use of the word 'our'.

After we had turned the last page of the contract, I realised that everyone else in the building had left for the weekend, so I suggested to Jeremy that he might like to join Rosemary and me for dinner. He checked his watch, considered the offer for a moment, and then said, 'Thank you, that's very kind of you. Could you drop me back at the Queen's Hotel so I can get changed?'

Rosemary, however, was not pleased to be told at the last minute that I had invited a complete stranger to dinner without warning her, even though I assured her that she would like him.

Jeremy rang our front doorbell a few minutes after eight. When I introduced him to Rosemary, he bowed slightly and kissed her hand. After that, they didn't take their eyes off each other all evening. Only a blind man could have missed what was likely to happen next, and although I might not have been blind, I certainly turned a blind eye.

Jeremy was soon finding excuses to spend more and more time in Leeds, and I am bound to admit that his sudden enthusiasm for the north of England enabled me to advance my ambitions for Cooper's far more quickly than I had originally dreamed possible. I had felt for some time that the company needed an in-house lawyer, and within a year of our first meeting I offered Jeremy a place on the board, with the remit to prepare the company for going public.

During that period I spent a great deal of my time in Madrid, Amsterdam and Brussels drumming up new contracts, and Rosemary certainly didn't discourage me. Meanwhile Jeremy skilfully guided the company through a thicket of legal and financial problems caused by our expansion. Thanks to his diligence and expertise, we were able to announce on 12 February 1980 that Cooper's would be applying for a listing on the Stock Exchange later that year. It was then that I made my first mistake: I invited Jeremy to become Deputy Chairman of the company.

Under the terms of the flotation, fifty-one per cent of the shares would be retained by Rosemary and myself. Jeremy explained to me that for tax reasons they should be divided equally between us. My accountants agreed, and at the time I didn't give it a second thought. The remaining 4,900,000 one pound shares were quickly taken up by institutions and the general public, and within days of the company being listed on the Stock Exchange their value had risen to £2.80.

My father, who had died the previous year, would never have accepted that it was possible to become worth several million pounds overnight. In fact I suspect he would have disapproved of the very idea, as he went to his deathbed still believing that a ten-pound overdraft was quite adequate to conduct a well-run business.

During the 1980s the British economy showed continual growth, and by March 1984 Cooper's shares had topped the five-pound mark, following press speculation about a possible takeover. Jeremy had advised me to accept one of the bids, but I told him that I would never allow Cooper's to be let out of the family's control. After that, we had to split the shares on three separate occasions, and by 1989 the *Sunday Times* was estimating that Rosemary and I were together worth around thirty million pounds.

I had never thought of myself as being wealthy – after all, as far as I was concerned the shares were simply pieces of paper held by Joe Ramsbottom, our company solicitor. I still lived in my father's house, drove a five-year-old Jaguar, and worked fourteen hours a day. I had never cared much for holidays, and wasn't by nature extravagant. Wealth seemed somehow irrelevant to me. I would have been happy to continue living much as I was, had I not arrived home unexpectedly one night.

I had caught the last plane back to Heathrow after a particularly long and arduous negotiation in Cologne, and had originally intended to stay overnight in London. But by then I'd had enough of hotels, and simply wanted to get home, despite the long drive. When I arrived back in Leeds a few minutes after one, I found Jeremy's white BMW parked in the driveway.

Had I phoned Rosemary earlier that day, I might never have ended up in jail.

I parked my car next to Jeremy's, and was walking towards the front door when I noticed that there was only one light on in the house – in the front room on the first floor. It wouldn't have taken Sherlock Holmes to deduce what might be taking place in that particular room.

I came to a halt, and stared up at the drawn curtains for some time. Nothing stirred, so clearly they hadn't heard the car, and were unaware of my presence. I retraced my steps and drove quietly off in the direction of the city centre. When I arrived at the Queen's Hotel I asked the duty manager if Mr Jeremy Alexander had booked a room for the night. He checked the register and confirmed that he had.

'Then I'll take his key,' I told him. 'Mr Alexander has booked himself in somewhere else for the night.' My father would have been proud of such thrifty use of the company's resources.

I lay on the hotel bed, quite unable to sleep, my anger rising as each hour passed. Although I no longer had a great deal of feeling for Rosemary, and even accepted that perhaps I never had, I now loathed Jeremy. But it wasn't until the next day that I discovered just how much I loathed him.

The following morning I rang my secretary, and told her I would be driving to the office straight from London. She reminded me that there was a board meeting scheduled for two o'clock, which Mr Alexander was pencilled in to chair. I was glad she couldn't see the smile of satisfaction that spread across my face. A quick glance at the agenda over breakfast and it had become abundantly clear why Jeremy had wanted to chair this particular meeting. But his plans didn't matter any more. I had already decided to let my fellow directors know exactly

what he was up to, and to make sure that he was dismissed from the board as soon as was practicable.

I arrived at Cooper's just after 1.30, and parked in the
space marked 'Chairman'. By the time the board meeting
was scheduled to begin I'd had just enough time to check
over my files, and became painfully aware of how many
of the company's shares were now controlled by Jeremy,
and what he and Rosemary must have been planning
for some time.

Jeremy vacated the chairman's place without comment
the moment I entered the boardroom, and showed no
particular interest in the proceedings until we reached
an item concerning a future share issue. It was at this
point that he tried to push through a seemingly innocu-
ous motion which could ultimately have resulted in
Rosemary and myself losing overall control of the company, and therefore being unable to resist any future
takeover bid. I might have fallen for it if I hadn't travelled up to Leeds the previous evening and found his car
parked in my driveway, and the bedroom light on. Just
when he thought he had succeeded in having the motion
agreed without a vote, I asked the company accountants
to prepare a full report for the next board meeting before
we came to any decision. Jeremy showed no sign of
emotion. He simply looked down at his notes and began
drumming his fingers on the boardroom table. I was
determined that the report would prove to be his downfall. If only it hadn't been for my short temper, I might,
given time, have worked out a more sensible way of
ridding myself of him.

As no one had 'any other business' to raise, I closed the meeting at 5.40, and suggested to Jeremy that he join Rosemary and me for dinner. I wanted to see them together. Jeremy didn't seem too keen, but after some bluffing from me about not fully understanding his new share proposal, and feeling that my wife ought to be brought in on it at some stage, he agreed. When I rang Rosemary to let her know that Jeremy would be coming to dinner, she seemed even less enthusiastic about the idea than he had been.

'Perhaps the two of you should go off to a restaurant together,' she suggested. 'Then Jeremy can bring you up to date on what's been going on while you've been away.' I tried not to laugh. 'We haven't got much food in at the moment,' she added. I told her that it wasn't the food I was worried about.

Jeremy was uncharacteristically late, but I had his usual whisky and soda ready the moment he walked through the door. I must say he put up a brilliant performance over dinner, though Rosemary was less convincing.

Over coffee in the sitting room, I managed to provoke the confrontation that Jeremy had so skilfully avoided at the board meeting.

'Why are you so keen to rush through this new share allocation?' I asked once he was on his second brandy. 'Surely you realise that it will take control of the company out of the hands of Rosemary and me. Can't you see that we could be taken over in no time?'

He tried a few well-rehearsed phrases. 'In the best

19

interests of the company, Richard. You must realise how quickly Cooper's is expanding. It's no longer a family firm. In the long term it has to be the most prudent course for both of you, not to mention the shareholders.' I wondered which particular shareholders he had in mind.

I was a little surprised to find Rosemary not only backing him up, but showing a remarkable grasp of the finer details of the share allocation, even after Jeremy had scowled rather too obviously at her. She seemed extremely well-versed in the arguments he had been putting forward, given the fact that she had never shown any interest in the company's transactions in the past. It was when she turned to me and said, 'We must consider our future, darling,' that I finally lost my temper.

Yorkshiremen are well known for being blunt, and my next question lived up to our county's reputation.

'Are you two having an affair, by any chance?'

Rosemary turned scarlet. Jeremy laughed a little too loudly, and then said, 'I think you've had one drink too many, Richard.'

'Not a drop,' I assured him. 'Sober as a judge. As I was when I came home late last night, and found your car parked in the driveway and the light on in the bedroom.'

For the first time since I'd met him, I had completely wrong-footed Jeremy, even if it was only for a moment. He began drumming his fingers on the glass table in front of him.

'I was simply explaining to Rosemary how the new

share issue would affect her,' he said, hardly missing a beat. 'Which is no more than is required under Stock Exchange regulations.'

'And is there a Stock Exchange regulation requiring that such explanations should take place in bed?'

'Oh, don't be absurd,' said Jeremy. 'I spent the night at the Queen's Hotel. Call the manager,' he added, picking up the telephone and offering it to me. 'He'll confirm that I was booked in to my usual room.'

'I'm sure he will,' I said. 'But he'll also confirm that it was I who spent the night in your usual bed.'

In the silence that followed I removed the hotel bedroom key from my jacket pocket, and dangled it in front of him. Jeremy immediately jumped to his feet.

I rose from my chair, rather more slowly, and faced him, wondering what his next line could possibly be.

'It's your own fault, you bloody fool,' he eventually stammered out. 'You should have taken more interest in Rosemary in the first place, and not gone off gallivanting around Europe all the time. It's no wonder you're in danger of losing the company.'

Funny, it wasn't the fact that Jeremy had been sleeping with my wife that caused me to snap, but that he had the arrogance to think he could take over my company as well. I didn't reply, but just took a pace forward and threw a punch at his clean-shaven jaw. I may have been a couple of inches shorter than he was, but after twenty years of hanging around with lorry drivers, I could still land a decent blow. Jeremy staggered first backwards and then forwards, before crumpling in front of me. As he fell, he cracked his right temple on the corner of the glass table, knocking his brandy all over the floor. He lay motionless in front of me, blood dripping onto the carpet.

I must admit I felt rather pleased with myself, especially when Rosemary rushed to his side and started screaming obscenities at me.

'Save your breath for the ex-Deputy Chairman,' I told her. 'And when he comes round, tell him not to bother with the Queen's Hotel, because I'll be sleeping in his bed again tonight.'

I strode out of the house and drove back into the city centre, leaving my Jaguar in the hotel carpark. When I walked into the Queen's the lobby was deserted, and I took the lift straight up to Jeremy's room. I lay on top of the bed, but was far too agitated to sleep.

I was just dozing off when four policemen burst into the room and pulled me off the bed. One of them told me that I was under arrest and read me my rights. Without further explanation I was marched out of the hotel and driven to Millgarth Police Station. A few minutes after five a.m., I was signed in by the custody officer and my personal possessions were taken from me and dropped into a bulky brown envelope. I was told that I had the right to make one telephone call, so I rang Joe Ramsbottom, woke his wife, and asked if Joe could join me at the station as quickly as possible. Then I was locked in a small cell and left alone.

I sat on the wooden bench and tried to fathom out why I had been arrested. I couldn't believe that Jeremy would have been foolish enough to charge me with assault. When Joe arrived about forty minutes later I told him exactly what had taken place earlier in the evening. He listened gravely, but didn't offer an opinion. When I had finished, he said he would try to find out what the police intended to charge me with.

After Joe left, I began to fear that Jeremy might have had a heart attack, or even that the blow to his head from the corner of the table might have killed him. My imagination ran riot as I considered all the worst possibilities, and I was becoming more and more desperate to learn what had happened when the cell door swung open and two plain-clothes detectives walked in. Joe was a pace behind them.

'I'm Chief Inspector Bainbridge,' said the taller of the two. 'And this is my colleague, Sergeant Harris.' Their eyes were tired and their suits crumpled. They looked as if they had been on duty all night, as both of them could have done with a shave. I felt my chin, and realised I needed one as well.

'We'd like to ask you some questions about what took place at your home earlier this evening,' said the Chief Inspector. I looked at Joe, who shook his head. 'It would help our enquiries, Mr Cooper, if you co-operated with us,' the Chief Inspector continued. 'Would you be prepared to give us a statement either in writing or as a tape recording?'

'I'm afraid my client has nothing to say at the moment, Chief Inspector,' said Joe. 'And he will have nothing to say until I have taken further instructions.'

23

I was rather impressed. I'd never seen Joe that firm with anyone other than his children.

'We would simply like to take a statement, Mr Ramsbottom,' Chief Inspector Bainbridge said to Joe, as if I didn't exist. 'We are quite happy for you to be present throughout.'

'No,' said Joe firmly. 'You either charge my client, or you leave us — and leave us immediately.'

The Chief Inspector hesitated for a moment, and then nodded to his colleague. They departed without another word.

'Charge me?' I said, once the cell door had been locked behind them. 'What with, for God's sake?'

'Murder, I suspect,' said Joe. 'After what Rosemary has been telling them.'

'Murder?' I said, almost unable to mouth the word. 'But . . .' I listened in disbelief as Joe told me what he'd been able to discover about the details of the statement my wife had given to the police during the early hours of the morning.

'But that's not what happened,' I protested. 'Surely no one would believe such an outrageous story.'

'They might when they learn the police have found a trail of blood leading from the sitting room to the spot where your car was parked in the drive,' said Joe.

'That's not possible,' I said. 'When I left Jeremy, he was still lying unconscious on the floor.'

'The police also found traces of blood in the boot of your car. They seem quite confident that it will match up with Jeremy's.'

24

'Oh, my God,' I said. 'He's clever. He's very clever. Can't you see what they've been up to?'

'No, to be honest, I can't,' Joe admitted. 'This isn't exactly all in a day's work for a company solicitor like me. But I managed to catch Sir Matthew Roberts QC on the phone before he left home this morning. He's the most eminent criminal silk on the north-eastern circuit. He's appearing in the York Crown Court today, and he's agreed to join us as soon as the court has risen. If you're innocent, Richard,' Joe said, 'with Sir Matthew defending you, there will be nothing to fear. Of that you can be certain.'

Later that afternoon I was charged with the murder of Jeremy Anatole Alexander; the police admitted to my solicitor that they still hadn't found the body, but they were confident that they would do so within a few hours. I knew they wouldn't. Joe told me the following day that they had done more digging in my garden during the past twenty-four hours than I had attempted in the past twenty-four years.

Around seven that evening the door of my cell swung open once again and Joe walked in, accompanied by a heavily-built, distinguished-looking man. Sir Matthew Roberts was about my height, but at least a couple of stone heavier. From his rubicund cheeks and warm smile he looked as if he regularly enjoyed a good bottle of wine and the company of amusing people. He had a full head of dark hair that remained modelled on the old Denis Compton Brylcreem advertisements, and he was attired in the garb of his profession, a dark three-piece suit and a silver-grey tie. I liked him from the moment he introduced himself. His first words were to express the wish that we had met in more pleasant circumstances.

I spent the rest of the evening with Sir Matthew, going over my story again and again. I could tell he didn't believe a word I was saying, but he still seemed quite happy to represent me. He and Joe left a few minutes after eleven, and I settled down to spend my first night behind bars.

I was remanded in custody until the police had processed and submitted all their evidence to the Department of Public Prosecutions. The following day a magistrate committed me to trial at Leeds Crown Court, and despite an eloquent plea from Sir Matthew, I was not granted bail.

Forty minutes later I was transferred to Armley Jail.

The hours turned into days, the days into weeks, and the weeks into months. I almost tired of telling anyone who would listen that they would never find Jeremy's body, because there was no body to find.

When the case finally reached Leeds Crown Court nine months later, the crime reporters turned up in their hordes, and followed every word of the trial with relish. A multi-millionaire, a possible adulterous affair and a missing body were too much for them to resist. The tabloids excelled themselves, describing Jeremy as the

Lord Lucan of Leeds and me as an oversexed lorry driver. I would have enjoyed every last syllable of it, if I hadn't been the accused.

In his opening address, Sir Matthew put up a magnificent fight on my behalf. Without a body, how could his client possibly be charged with murder? And how could I have disposed of the body, when I had spent the entire night in a bedroom at the Queen's Hotel? How I regretted not checking in the second time, but simply going straight up to Jeremy's room. It didn't help that the police had found me lying on the bed fully dressed.

I watched the faces of the jury at the end of the prosecution's opening speech. They were perplexed, and obviously in some doubt about my guilt. That doubt remained, until Rosemary entered the witness box. I couldn't bear to look at her, and diverted my eyes to a striking blonde who had been sitting in the front row of the public gallery on every day of the trial.

For an hour the counsel for the prosecution guided my wife gently through what had taken place that evening, up to the point when I had struck Jeremy. Until that moment, I couldn't have quarrelled with a word she had spoken.

'And then what happened, Mrs Cooper?' prodded counsel for the Crown.

'My husband bent down and checked Mr Alexander's pulse,' Rosemary whispered. 'Then he turned white, and all he said was, "He's dead. I've killed him."'

'And what did Mr Cooper do next?'

'He picked up the body, threw it over his shoulder,

and began walking towards the door. I shouted after him, "What do you think you're doing, Richard?"'

'And how did he respond?'

'He told me he intended to dispose of the body while it was still dark, and that I was to make sure that there was no sign that Jeremy had visited the house. As no one else had been in the office when they left, everyone would assume that Jeremy had returned to London earlier in the evening. "Be certain there are absolutely no traces of blood," were the last words I remember my husband saying as he left the room carrying Jeremy's body over his shoulder. That must have been when I fainted.'

Sir Matthew glanced quizzically up at me in the dock. I shook my head vigorously. He looked grim as counsel for the prosecution resumed his seat.

'Do you wish to question this witness, Sir Matthew?' the judge asked.

Sir Matthew rose slowly to his feet. 'I most certainly do, M'Lud,' he replied. He drew himself up to his full height, tugged at his gown and stared across at his adversary.

'Mrs Cooper, would you describe yourself as a friend of Mr Alexander?'

'Yes, but only in the sense that he was a colleague of my husband's,' replied Rosemary calmly.

'So you didn't ever see each other when your husband was away from Leeds, or even out of the country, on business?'

'Only at social events, when I was accompanied by

my husband, or if I dropped into the office to pick up his mail.'

'Are you certain that those were the only times you saw him, Mrs Cooper? Were there not other occasions when you spent a considerable amount of time alone with Mr Alexander? For example, on the night of 17 September 1989, before your husband returned unexpectedly from a European trip: did Mr Alexander not visit you then for several hours while you were alone in the house?'

'No. He dropped by after work to leave a document for my husband, but he didn't even have time to stay for a drink.'

'But your husband says . . .' began Sir Matthew.

'I know what my husband says,' Rosemary replied, as if she had rehearsed the line a hundred times.

'I see,' said Sir Matthew. 'Let's get to the point, shall we, Mrs Cooper? Were you having an affair with Jeremy Alexander at the time of his disappearance?'

'Is this relevant, Sir Matthew?' interrupted the judge.

'It most assuredly is, M'Lud. It goes to the very core of the case,' replied my QC in a quiet even tone.

Everyone's gaze was now fixed on Rosemary. I willed her to tell the truth.

She didn't hesitate. 'Certainly not,' she replied, 'although it wasn't the first time my husband had accused me unjustly.'

'I see,' said Sir Matthew. He paused. 'Do you love your husband, Mrs Cooper?'

'Really, Sir Matthew!' The judge was unable to

disguise his irritation. 'I must ask once again if this is relevant?'

Sir Matthew exploded. 'Relevant? It's absolutely vital, M'Lud, and I am not being assisted by your lordship's thinly veiled attempts to intervene on behalf of this witness.'

The judge was beginning to splutter with indignation when Rosemary said quietly, 'I have always been a good and faithful wife, but I cannot under any circumstances condone murder.'

The jury turned their eyes on me. Most of them looked as if they would be happy to bring back the death penalty.

'If that is the case, I am bound to ask why you waited two and a half hours to contact the police?' said Sir Matthew. 'Especially if, as you claim, you believed your husband had committed murder, and was about to dispose of the body.'

'As I explained, I fainted soon after he left the room. I phoned the police the moment I came to.'

'How convenient,' said Sir Matthew. 'Or perhaps the truth is that you made use of that time to set a trap for your husband, while allowing your lover to get clean away.' A murmur ran through the courtroom.

'Sir Matthew,' the judge said, jumping in once again. 'You are going too far.'

'Not so, M'Lud, with respect. In fact, not far enough.' He swung back round and faced my wife again.

'I put it to you, Mrs Cooper, that Jeremy Alexander was your lover, and still is, that you are perfectly aware he is alive and well, and that if you wished to, you could tell us exactly where he is now.'

Despite the judge's spluttering and the uproar in the court, Rosemary had her reply ready.

'I only wish he were,' she said, 'so that he could stand in this court and confirm that I am telling the truth.' Her voice was soft and gentle.

'But *you* already know the truth, Mrs Cooper,' said Sir Matthew, his voice gradually rising. 'The truth is that your husband left the house on his own. He then drove to the Queen's Hotel, where he spent the rest of the night, while you and your lover used that time to leave clues across the city of Leeds – clues, I might add, that were intended to incriminate your husband. But the one thing you couldn't leave was a body, because as you well know Mr Jeremy Alexander is still alive, and the two of you have together fabricated this entire bogus story, simply to further your own ends. Isn't that the truth, Mrs Cooper?'

'No, no!' Rosemary shouted, her voice cracking before she finally burst into tears.

'Oh, come, come, Mrs Cooper. Those are counterfeit tears, are they not?' said Sir Matthew quietly. 'Now you've been found out, the jury will decide if your distress is genuine.'

I glanced across at the jury. Not only had they fallen for Rosemary's performance, but they now despised me for allowing my insensitive bully of a counsel to attack such a gentle, long-suffering woman. To every one of Sir Matthew's probing questions, Rosemary proved well capable of delivering a riposte that revealed to me all the hallmarks of Jeremy Alexander's expert tuition.

When it was my turn to enter the witness box, and Sir Matthew began questioning me, I felt my story sounded far less convincing than Rosemary's, despite its being the truth.

The closing speech for the Crown was deadly dull, but nevertheless deadly. Sir Matthew's was subtle and dramatic, but I feared less convincing.

After another night in Armley Jail I returned to the dock for the judge's summing up. It was clear that he was in no doubt as to my guilt. His selection of the evidence he chose to review was unbalanced and unfair, and when he ended by reminding the jury that his opinion of the evidence should ultimately carry no weight, he only added hypocrisy to bias.

After their first full day's deliberations, the jury had to be put up overnight in a hotel – ironically the Queen's – and when the jolly little fat man in the bow tie was finally asked: 'Members of the jury, do you find the prisoner at the bar guilty or not guilty as charged?' I wasn't surprised when he said clearly for all to hear, 'Guilty, my lord.'

In fact I was amazed that the jury had failed to reach a unanimous decision. I have often wondered which two members felt convinced enough to declare my innocence. I would have liked to thank them.

The judge stared down at me. 'Richard Wilfred Cooper, you have been found guilty of the murder of Jeremy Anatole Alexander . . .'

'I did not kill him, my lord,' I interrupted in a calm voice. 'In fact, he is not dead. I can only hope that you will live long enough to realise the truth.' Sir Matthew looked up anxiously as uproar broke out in the court.

The judge called for silence, and his voice became even more harsh as he pronounced, 'You will go to prison for life. That is the sentence prescribed by law. Take him down.'

Two prison officers stepped forward, gripped me firmly by the arms and led me down the steps at the back of the dock into the cell I had occupied every morning for the eighteen days of the trial.

'Sorry, old chum,' said the policeman who had been in charge of my welfare since the case had begun. 'It was that bitch of a wife who tipped the scales against you.' He slammed the cell door closed, and turned the key in the lock before I had a chance to agree with him. A few moments later the door was unlocked again, and Sir Matthew strode in.

He stared at me for some time before uttering a word. 'A terrible injustice has been done, Mr Cooper,' he eventually said, 'and we shall immediately lodge an appeal against your conviction. Be assured, I will not rest until we have found Jeremy Alexander and he has been brought to justice.'

For the first time I realised Sir Matthew knew that I was innocent.

* * *

I was put in a cell with a petty criminal called 'Fingers' Jenkins. Can you believe, as we approach the twenty-first century, that anyone could still be called 'Fingers'? Even so, the name had been well earned. Within moments of my entering the cell, Fingers was wearing my watch. He returned it immediately I noticed it had disappeared. 'Sorry,' he said. 'Just put it down to 'abit.'

Prison might have turned out to be far worse if it hadn't been known by my fellow inmates that I was a millionaire, and was quite happy to pay a little extra for certain privileges. Every morning the *Financial Times* was delivered to my bunk, which gave me the chance to keep up with what was happening in the City. I was nearly sick when I first read about the takeover bid for Cooper's. Sick not because of the offer of £12.50 a share, which made me even wealthier, but because it became painfully obvious what Jeremy and Rosemary had been up to. Jeremy's shares would now be worth several million pounds – money he could never have realised had I been around to prevent a takeover.

I spent hours each day lying on my bunk and scouring every word of the *Financial Times*. Whenever there was a mention of Cooper's, I went over the paragraph so often that I ended up knowing it by heart. The company was eventually taken over, but not before the share price had reached £13.43. I continued to follow its activities with great interest, and I became more and more anxious about the quality of the new management when they began to sack some of my most experienced staff, including Joe Ramsbottom. A week later, I wrote and instructed my stockbrokers to sell my shares as and when the opportunity arose.

It was at the beginning of my fourth month in prison that I asked for some writing paper. I had decided the time had come to keep a record of everything that had happened to me since that night I had returned home unexpectedly. Every day the prison officer on my landing would bring me fresh sheets of blue-lined paper, and I would write out in longhand the chronicle you're now reading. An added bonus was that it helped me to plan my next move.

At my request, Fingers took a straw poll among the prisoners as to who they believed was the best detective they had ever come up against. Three days later he told me the result: Chief Superintendent Donald Hackett, known as the Don, came out top on more than half the lists. More reliable than a Gallup Poll, I told Fingers.

'What puts Hackett ahead of all the others?' I asked him.

''e's honest, 'e's fair, you can't bribe 'im. And once the bastard knows you're a villain, 'e doesn't care 'ow long it takes to get you be'ind bars.'

Hackett, I was informed, hailed from Bradford. Rumour had it among the older cons that he had turned down the job of Assistant Chief Constable for West Yorkshire. Like a barrister who doesn't want to become a judge, he preferred to remain at the coalface.

'Arrestin' criminals is 'ow 'e gets his kicks,' Fingers said, with some feeling.

'Sounds just the man I'm looking for,' I said. 'How old is he?'

Fingers paused to consider. 'Must be past fifty by now,' he replied. 'After all, 'e 'ad me put in borstal for nickin' a toolset, and that was' – he paused again – 'more than twenty years ago.'

When Sir Matthew came to visit me the following Monday, I told him what I had in mind, and asked his opinion of the Don. I wanted a professional's view.

'He's a hell of a witness to cross-examine, that's one thing I can tell you,' replied my barrister.

'Why's that?'

'He doesn't exaggerate, he won't prevaricate, and I've never known him to lie, which makes him awfully hard to trap. No, I've rarely got the better of the Chief Superintendent. I have to say, though, that I doubt if he'd agree to become involved with a convicted criminal, whatever you offered him.'

'But I'm not . . .'

'I know, Mr Cooper,' said Sir Matthew, who still didn't seem able to call me by my first name. 'But Hackett will have to be convinced of that before he even agrees to see you.'

'But how can I convince him of my innocence while I'm stuck in jail?'

'I'll try to influence him on your behalf,' Sir Matthew said after some thought. Then he added, 'Come to think of it, he does owe me a favour.'

After Sir Matthew had left that night, I requested some more lined paper and began to compose a carefully worded letter to Chief Superintendent Hackett, several versions of which ended crumpled up on the floor of my cell. My final effort read as follows:

In replying to this letter, please write on the envelope:

Number A47283   Name COOPER, R.W.

ALL INMATE CORRESPONDENCE MUST
HAVE STAMPS WITH NO AND
ADDRESS AND ENVELOPE
MAIL CANNOT BE ACCEPTED
NO NUMBER DELAYS MAIL

H.M. PRISON
ARMLEY
LEEDS LS12 2TJ

Dear Chief Superintendent,

As you can see I am currently detained at
Her Majesty's pleasure. Nevertheless, I wonder
if you would be kind enough to visit me,
as I have a private matter I would
like to discuss with you that could affect
both our futures. I can assure you that my
proposal is both legal and honest, and I am
confident that it will also appeal to your
sense of justice. It has the approval of my
barrister, Sir Matthew Roberts QC, who I understand
you have come across from time to time in your
professional capacity. Naturally I will be happy
to reimburse any expenses that this inconvenience
may cause you.
I look forward to hearing from you.

Yours sincerely

I reread the letter, corrected the spelling mistake, and scrawled my signature across the bottom.

At my request, Sir Matthew delivered the letter to Hackett by hand. The first thousand-pound-a-day postman in the history of the Royal Mail, I told him.

Sir Matthew reported back the following Monday that he had handed the letter to the Chief Superintendent in person. After Hackett had read it through a second time, his only comment was that he would have to speak to his superiors. He had promised he would let Sir Matthew know his decision within a week.

From the moment I had been sentenced, Sir Matthew had been preparing for my appeal, and although he had not at any time raised my hopes, he was unable to hide his delight at what he had discovered after paying a visit to the Probate Office.

It turned out that, in his will, Jeremy had left everything to Rosemary. This included over three million pounds' worth of Cooper's shares. But, Sir Matthew explained, the law did not allow her to dispose of them for seven years. 'An English jury may have pronounced on your guilt,' he declared, 'but the hard-headed taxmen are not so easily convinced. They won't hand over Jeremy Alexander's assets until either they have seen his body, or seven years have elapsed.'

'Do they think that Rosemary might have killed him for his money, and then disposed . . .'

'No, no,' said Sir Matthew, almost laughing at my

suggestion. 'It's simply that, as they're entitled to wait for seven years, they're going to sit on his assets and not take the risk that Alexander may still be alive. In any case, if your wife *had* killed him, she wouldn't have had a ready answer to every one of my questions when she was in the witness box, of that I'm sure.'

I smiled. For the first time in my life I was delighted to learn that the taxman had his nose in my affairs.

Sir Matthew promised he would report back if anything new came up. 'Goodnight, Richard,' he said as he left the interview room.

Another first.

It seemed that everyone else in the prison was aware that Chief Superintendent Hackett would be paying me a visit long before I was.

It was Dave Adams, an old lag from an adjoining cell, who explained why the inmates thought Hackett had agreed to see me. 'A good copper is never 'appy about anyone doin' time for somethin' 'e didn't do. 'ackett phoned the Governor last Tuesday, and 'ad a word with 'im on the Q.T., accordin' to Maurice,' Dave added mysteriously.

I would have been interested to learn how the Governor's trusty had managed to hear both sides of the conversation, but decided this was not the time for irrelevant questions.

'Even the 'ardest nuts in this place think you're innocent,' Dave continued. 'They can't wait for the day when Mr Jeremy Alexander takes over your cell. You can be sure the long termers'll give 'im a warm welcome.'

A letter from Bradford arrived the following morning. 'Dear Cooper,' the Chief Superintendent began, and went on to inform me that he intended to pay a visit to the jail at four o'clock the following Sunday. He made it clear that he would stay no longer than half an hour, and insisted on a witness being present throughout.

For the first time since I'd been locked up, I started counting the hours. Hours aren't that important when your room has been booked for a life sentence.

As I was taken from my cell that Sunday afternoon and escorted to the interview room, I received several messages from my fellow inmates to pass on to the Chief Superintendent.

'Give my best regards to the Don,' said Fingers. 'Tell 'im 'ow sorry I am not to bump into 'im this time.'

'When 'e's finished with you, ask 'im if 'e'd like to drop into my cell for a cup of char and a chat about old times.'

'Kick the bastard in the balls, and tell 'im I'll be 'appy to serve the extra time.'

One of the prisoners even suggested a question to which I already knew the answer: 'Ask 'im when 'e's going to retire, 'cause I'm not coming out till the day after.'

When I stepped into the interview room and saw the

Chief Superintendent for the first time, I thought there must have been some mistake. I had never asked Fingers what the Don looked like, and over the past few days I had built up in my mind the image of some sort of superman. But the man who stood before me was a couple of inches shorter than me, and I'm only five foot ten. He was as thin as the proverbial rake and wore pebble-lensed horn-rimmed glasses, which gave the impression that he was half-blind. All he needed was a grubby raincoat and he could have been mistaken for a debt collector.

Sir Matthew stepped forward to introduce us. I shook the policeman firmly by the hand. 'Thank you for coming to visit me, Chief Superintendent,' I began. 'Won't you have a seat?' I added, as if he had dropped into my home for a glass of sherry.

'Sir Matthew is very persuasive,' said Hackett, in a deep, gruff Yorkshire accent that didn't quite seem to go with his body. 'So tell me, Cooper, what do you imagine it is that I can do for you?' he asked as he took the chair opposite me. I detected an edge of cynicism in his voice.

He opened a notepad and placed it on the table as I was about to begin my story. 'For my use only,' he explained, 'should I need to remind myself of any relevant details at some time in the future.' Twenty minutes later, I had finished the abbreviated version of the life and times of Richard Cooper. I had already gone over the story on several occasions in my cell during the past week, to be certain I didn't take too long. I wanted to leave enough time for Hackett to ask any questions.

'If I believe your story,' he said, '– and I only say "if" – you still haven't explained what it is you think I can do for you.'

'You're due to leave the force in five months' time,' I said. 'I wondered if you had any plans once you've retired.'

He hesitated. I had obviously taken him by surprise.

'I've been offered a job with Group 4, as area manager for West Yorkshire.'

'And how much will they be paying you?' I asked bluntly.

'It won't be full time,' he said. 'Three days a week, to start with.' He hesitated again. 'Twenty thousand a year, guaranteed for three years.'

'I'll pay you a hundred thousand a year, but I'll expect you to be on the job seven days a week. I assume you'll be needing a secretary and an assistant – that Inspector Williams who's leaving at the same time as you might well fit the bill – so I'll also supply you with enough money for back-up staff, as well as the rent for an office.'

A flicker of respect appeared on the Chief Superintendent's face for the first time. He made some more notes on his pad.

'And what would you expect of me in return for such a large sum of money?' he asked.

'That's simple. I expect you to find Jeremy Alexander.'

This time he didn't hesitate. 'My God,' he said. 'You

really *are* innocent. Sir Matthew and the Governor both tried to convince me you were.'

'And if you find him within seven years,' I added, ignoring his comment, 'I'll pay a further five hundred thousand into any branch of any bank in the world that you stipulate.'

'The Midland, Bradford will suit me just fine,' he replied. 'It's only criminals who find it necessary to retire abroad. In any case, I have to be in Bradford every other Saturday afternoon, so I can be around to watch City lose.' Hackett rose from his place and looked hard at me for some time. 'One last question, Mr Cooper. Why seven years?'

'Because after that period, my wife can sell Alexander's shares, and he'll become a multi-millionaire overnight.'

The Chief Superintendent nodded his understanding. 'Thank you for asking to see me,' he said. 'It's been a long time since I enjoyed visiting anyone in jail, especially someone convicted of murder. I'll give your offer serious consideration, Mr Cooper, and let you know my decision by the end of the week.' He left without another word.

Hackett wrote to me three days later, accepting my offer.

I didn't have to wait five months for him to start working for me, because he handed in his resignation within a fortnight – though not before I had agreed to continue his pension contributions, and those of the two colleagues he wanted to leave the force and join him.

Having now disposed of all my Cooper's shares, the interest on my deposit account was earning me over four hundred thousand a year, and as I was living rent-free, Hackett's request was a minor consideration.

I would have shared with you in greater detail everything that happened to me over the following months, but during that time I was so preoccupied with briefing Hackett that I filled only three pages of my blue-lined prison paper. I should however mention that I studied several law books, to be sure that I fully understood the meaning of the legal term 'autrefois acquit'.

The next important date in the diary was my appeal hearing.

Matthew – at his request I had long ago stopped calling him 'Sir' Matthew – tried valiantly not to show that he was becoming more and more confident of the outcome, but I was getting to know him so well that he was no longer able to disguise his true feelings. He told me how delighted he was with the make-up of the reviewing panel. 'Fair and just,' he kept repeating.

Later that night he told me with great sadness that his wife Victoria had died of cancer a few weeks before. 'A long illness and a blessed release,' he called it.

I felt guilty in his presence for the first time. Over the past eighteen months, we had only ever discussed my problems.

* * *

I must have been one of the few prisoners at Armley who ever had a bespoke tailor visit him in his cell. Matthew suggested that I should be fitted with a new suit before I faced the appeal tribunal, as I had lost over a stone since I had been in jail. When the tailor had finished measuring me and began rolling up his tape, I insisted that Fingers return his cigarette lighter, although I did allow him to keep the cigarettes.

Ten days later, I was escorted from my cell at five o'clock in the morning. My fellow inmates banged their tin mugs against their locked doors, the traditional way of indicating to the prison staff that they believed the man leaving for trial was innocent. Like some great symphony, it lifted my soul.

I was driven to London in a police car accompanied by two prison officers. We didn't stop once on the entire journey, and arrived in the capital a few minutes after nine; I remember looking out of the window and watching the commuters scurrying to their offices to begin the day's work. Any one of them who'd glanced at me sitting in the back of the car in my new suit, and was unable to spot the handcuffs, might have assumed I was a Chief Inspector at least.

Matthew was waiting for me at the entrance of the Old Bailey, a mountain of papers tucked under each arm. 'I like the suit,' he said, before leading me up some stone steps to the room where my fate would be decided.

Once again I sat impassively in the dock as Sir Matthew rose from his place to address the three appeal judges. His opening statement took him nearly an hour, and by now I felt I could have delivered it quite adequately myself, though not as eloquently, and certainly nowhere near as persuasively. He made great play of how Jeremy had left all his worldly goods to Rosemary, who in turn had sold our family house in Leeds, cashed in all her Cooper's shares within months of the takeover, pushed through a quickie divorce, and then disappeared off the face of the earth with an estimated seven million pounds. I couldn't help wondering just how much of that Jeremy had already got his hands on.

Sir Matthew repeatedly reminded the panel of the police's inability to produce a body, despite the fact they now seemed to have dug up half of Leeds.

I became more hopeful with each new fact Matthew placed before the judges. But after he had finished, I still had to wait another three days to learn the outcome of their deliberations.

Appeal dismissed. Reasons reserved.

Matthew travelled up to Armley on the Friday to tell me why he thought my appeal had been turned down without explanation. He felt that the judges must have been divided, and needed more time to make it appear as if they were not.

'How much time?' I asked.

'My hunch is that they'll let you out on licence within a few months. They were obviously influenced by the police's failure to produce a body, unimpressed by the trial judge's summing up, and impressed by the strength of your case.'

46

I thanked Matthew, who, for once, left the room with a smile on his face.

You may be wondering what Chief Superintendent Hackett – or rather ex-Chief Superintendent Hackett – had been up to while all this was going on.

He had not been idle. Inspector Williams and Constable Kenwright had left the force on the same day as he had. Within a week they had opened up a small office above the Constitutional Club in Bradford and begun their investigations. The Don reported to me at four o'clock every Sunday afternoon.

Within a month he had compiled a thick file on the case, with detailed dossiers on Rosemary, Jeremy, the company and me. I spent hours reading through the information he had gathered, and was even able to help by filling in a few gaps. I quickly came to appreciate why the Don was so respected by my fellow inmates. He followed up every clue, and went down every side road, however much it looked like a cul-de-sac, because once in a while it turned out to be a highway.

On the first Sunday in October, after Hackett had been working for four months, he told me that he thought he might have located Rosemary. A woman of her description was living on a small estate in the south of France called Villa Fleur.

'How did you manage to track her down?' I asked.

'Letter posted by her mother at her local pillarbox. The postman kindly allowed me to have a look at the

47

address on the envelope before it proceeded on its way,'
Hackett said. 'Can't tell you how many hours we had
to hang around, how many letters we've had to sift
through, and how many doors we've knocked on in the
past four months, just to get this one lead. Mrs Kershaw
seems to be a compulsive letter writer, but this was the
first time she's sent one to her daughter. By the way,'
he added, 'your wife has reverted to her maiden name.
Calls herself Ms Kershaw now.'

I nodded, not wishing to interrupt him.

'Williams flew out to Cannes on Wednesday, and he's
holed up in the nearest village, posing as a tourist. He's
already been able to tell us that Ms Kershaw's house is
surrounded by a ten-foot stone wall, and she has more
guard dogs than trees. It seems the locals know even
less about her than we do. But at least it's a start.'

I felt for the first time that Jeremy Alexander might
at last have met his match, but it was to be another five
Sundays, and five more interim reports, before a thin
smile appeared on Hackett's usually tight-lipped face.

'Ms Kershaw has placed an advertisement in the local
paper,' he informed me. 'It seems she's in need of a new
butler. At first I thought we should question the old
butler at length as soon as he'd left, but as I couldn't
risk anything getting back to her, I decided Inspector
Williams would have to apply for his job instead.'

'But surely she'll realise within moments that he's
totally unqualified to do the job.'

'Not necessarily,' said Hackett, his smile broadening.
'You see, Williams won't be able to leave his present

employment with the Countess of Rutland until he's served a full month's notice, and in the meantime we've signed him up for a special six-week course at Ivor Spencer's School for Butlers. Williams has always been a quick learner.'

'But what about references?'

'By the time Rosemary Kershaw interviews him, he'll have a set of references that would impress a duchess.'

'I was told you never did anything underhand.'

'That is the case when I'm dealing with honest people, Mr Cooper. Not when I'm up against a couple of crooks like this. I'm going to get those two behind bars, if it's the last thing I do.'

This was not the time to let Hackett know that the final chapter of this story, as I plotted it, did not conclude with Jeremy ending up in jail.

Once Williams had been put on the shortlist for the position of Rosemary's butler, I played my own small part in securing him the job. Rereading over the terms of the proposed contract gave me the idea.

'Tell Williams to ask for 15,000 francs a month, and five weeks' holiday,' I suggested to Hackett when he and Matthew visited me the following Sunday.

'Why?' asked the ex-Chief Superintendent. 'She's only offering 11,000, and three weeks' holiday.'

'She can well afford to pay the difference, and with references like these,' I said, looking back down at my file, 'she might become suspicious if he asked for anything less.'

Matthew smiled and nodded.

Rosemary finally offered Williams the job at 13,000 francs a month, with four weeks' holiday a year, which after forty-eight hours' consideration Williams accepted. But he did not join her for another month, by which time he had learnt how to iron newspapers, lay place settings with a ruler, and tell the difference between a port, sherry and liqueur glass.

I suppose that from the moment Williams took up the post as Rosemary's butler, I expected instant results. But as Hackett pointed out to me Sunday after Sunday, this was hardly realistic.

'Williams has to take his time,' explained the Don. 'He needs to gain her confidence, and avoid giving her any reason for the slightest suspicion. It once took me five years to nail a drug smuggler who was only living half a mile up the road from me.'

I wanted to remind him that it was me who was stuck in jail, and that five days was more like what I had in mind, but I knew how hard they were all working on my behalf, and tried not to show my impatience.

Within a month Williams had supplied us with photographs and life histories of all the staff working on the estate, along with descriptions of everyone who visited Rosemary – even the local priest, who came hoping to collect a donation for French aid workers in Somalia.

The cook: Gabrielle Pascal – no English, excellent cuisine, came from Marseilles, family checked out. The gardener: Jacques Reni – stupid and not particularly imaginative with the rosebeds, local and well known. Rosemary's personal maid: Charlotte Merieux – spoke

a little English, crafty, sexy, came from Paris, still checking her out. All the staff had been employed by Rosemary since her arrival in the south of France, and they
appeared to have no connection with each other, or with
her past life.

'Ah,' said Hackett as he studied the picture of Rosemary's personal maid. I raised an eyebrow. 'I was just
thinking about Williams being cooped up with Charlotte
Merieux day in and day out – and more important, night
in and night in,' he explained. 'He would have made
superintendent if he hadn't fooled around so much. Still,
let's hope this time it turns out to our advantage.'

I lay on my bunk studying the pictures of the staff
for hour after hour, but they revealed nothing. I read
and reread the notes on everyone who had ever visited
Villa Fleur, but as the weeks went by, it looked more
and more as if no one from Rosemary's past, other than
her mother, knew where she was – or if they did, they
were making no attempts to contact her. There was certainly no sign of Jeremy Alexander.

I was beginning to fear that she and Jeremy might
have split up, until Williams reported that there was a
picture of a dark, handsome man on a table by the side
of Rosemary's bed. It was inscribed: 'We'll always be
together – J'.

During the weeks following my appeal hearing I was
constantly interviewed by probation officers, social
workers and even the prison psychiatrist. I struggled

to maintain the warm, sincere smile that Matthew had warned me was so necessary to lubricate the wheels of the bureaucracy.

It must have been about eleven weeks after my appeal had been turned down that the cell door was thrown open, and the senior officer on my corridor announced, 'The Governor wants to see you, Cooper.' Fingers looked suspicious. Whenever he heard those words, it inevitably meant a dose of solitary.

I could hear my heart beating as I was led down the long corridor to the Governor's office. The prison officer knocked gently on the door before opening it. The Governor rose from behind his desk, thrust out his hand and said, 'I'm delighted to be the first person to tell you the good news.'

He ushered me into a comfortable chair on the other side of his desk, and went over the terms of my release. While he was doing this I was served coffee, as if we were old friends.

There was a knock on the door, and Matthew walked in, clutching a sheaf of papers that needed to be signed. I rose as he placed them on the desk, and without warning he turned round and gave me a bearhug. Not something I expect he did every day.

After I had signed the final document Matthew asked: 'What's the first thing you'll do once they release you?'

'I'm going to buy a gun,' I told him matter-of-factly.

Matthew and the Governor burst out laughing.

* * *

The great gate of Armley Prison was thrown open for me three days later. I walked away from the building carrying only the small leather suitcase I had arrived with. I didn't look back. I hailed a taxi and asked the driver to take me to the station, as I had no desire to remain in Leeds a moment longer than was necessary. I bought a first-class ticket, phoned Hackett to warn him I was on my way, and boarded the next train for Bradford. I savoured a British Rail breakfast that wasn't served on a tin plate, and read a copy of the *Financial Times* that had been handed to me by a pretty shop assistant and not a petty criminal. No one stared at me – but then, why should they, when I was sitting in a first-class carriage and dressed in my new suit? I glanced at every woman who passed by, however she was dressed, but they had no way of knowing why.

When the train pulled into Bradford, the Don and his secretary Jenny Kenwright were waiting for me on the platform. The Chief Superintendent had rented me a small furnished flat on the outskirts of the city, and after I had unpacked – not a long job – they took me out to lunch. The moment the small talk had been dispensed with and Jenny had poured me a glass of wine, the Don asked me a question I hadn't expected.

'Now that you're free, is it still your wish that we go on looking for Jeremy Alexander?'

'Yes,' I replied, without a moment's hesitation. 'I'm even more determined, now that I can taste the freedom he's enjoyed for the past three years. Never forget, that man stole my freedom from me, along with my wife, my company, and more than half my possessions. Oh yes, Donald, I won't rest until I come face to face with Jeremy Alexander.'

'Good,' said the Don. 'Because Williams thinks Rosemary is beginning to trust him, and might even, given time, start confiding in him. It seems he has made himself indispensable.'

I found a certain irony in the thought of Williams pocketing two wage packets simultaneously, and of my being responsible for one, while Rosemary paid the other. I asked if there was any news of Jeremy.

'Nothing to speak of,' said Donald. 'She certainly never phones him from the house, and we're fairly sure he never attempts to make any direct contact with her. But Williams has told us that every Friday at midday he has to drop her off at the Majestic, the only hotel in the village. She goes inside and doesn't reappear for at least forty minutes. He daren't follow her, because she's given specific instructions that he's to stay with the car. And he can't afford to lose this job by disobeying orders.'

I nodded my agreement.

'But that hasn't stopped him having the occasional drink in the hotel bar on his evening off, and he's managed to pick up a few snippets of information. He's convinced that Rosemary uses the time when she's in the hotel to make a long-distance phone call. She often drops in at the bank before going on to the Majestic, and comes out carrying a small packet of coins. The barman has told Williams that she always uses one of the two phone boxes in the corridor opposite the reception desk. She never allows the call to be put through the hotel switch-board, always dials direct.'

'So how do we discover who she's calling?' I asked.

'We wait for Williams to find an opportunity to use some of those skills he didn't learn at butlers' school.'

'But how long might that take?'

'No way of knowing, but Williams is due for a spot of leave in a couple of weeks, so he'll be able to bring us up to date.'

When Williams arrived back in Bradford at the end of the month I began asking him questions even before he had time to put his suitcase down. He was full of interesting information about Rosemary, and even the smallest detail fascinated me.

She had put on weight. I was pleased. She seemed lonely and depressed. I was delighted. She was spending my money fast. I wasn't exactly ecstatic. But, more to the point, Williams was convinced that if Rosemary had any contact with Jeremy Alexander, it had to be when she visited the hotel every Friday and placed that direct-dial call. But he still hadn't worked out how to discover who, or where, she was phoning.

By the time Williams returned to the south of France a fortnight later I knew more about my ex-wife than I had ever done when we were married.

As happens so often in the real world, the next move came when I least expected it. It must have been about 2.30 on a Monday afternoon when the phone rang.

Donald picked up the receiver, and was surprised to hear Williams's voice on the other end of the line. He switched him on to the squawk box and said, 'All three of us are listening, so you'd better begin by telling us why you're ringing when it's not your day off.'

'I've been sacked,' were Williams's opening words.

'Playing around with the maid, were you?' was Donald's first reaction.

'I only wish, chief, but I'm afraid it's far more stupid than that. I was driving Ms Kershaw into town this morning, when I had to stop at a red light. While I was waiting for the lights to change, a man crossed the road in front of the car. He stopped and stared at me. I recognised him immediately, and prayed the lights would turn to green before he could place me. But he walked back, looked at me again, and smiled. I shook my head at him, but he came over to the driver's side, tapped on the window, and said, "How are you, Inspector Williams?"'

'Who was it?' demanded Donald.

'Neil Case. Remember him, chief?'

'Could I ever forget him? "Never-on-the-Case Neil",' said Donald. 'I might have guessed.'

'I didn't acknowledge him, of course, and as Ms Kershaw said nothing, I thought I might have got away with it. But as soon as we arrived back at the house she told me to come and see her in the study, and without even asking for an explanation she dismissed me. She ordered me to be packed and off the premises within the hour, or she'd call the local police.'

'Damn. Back to square one,' said Donald.

'Not quite,' said Williams.

'What do you mean? If you're no longer in the house, we no longer have a point of contact. Worse, we can't play the butler card again, because she's bound to be on her guard from now on.'

'I know all that, chief,' said Williams, 'but suspecting that I was a policeman caused her to panic, and she went straight to her bedroom and made a phone call. As I wasn't afraid of being found out any longer, I picked up the extension in the corridor and listened in. All I heard was a woman's voice give a Cambridge number, and then the phone went dead. I assumed Rosemary had been expecting someone else to pick up the phone, and hung up when she heard a strange voice.'

'What was the number?' Donald asked.

'6407-something-7.'

'What do you mean, "something-7"?' barked Donald as he scribbled the numbers down.

'I didn't have anything to write with, chief, so I had to rely on my memory.' I was glad Williams couldn't see the expression on the Don's face.

'Then what happened?' he demanded.

'I found a pen in a drawer and wrote what I could remember of the number on my hand. I picked up the phone again a few moments later, and heard a different woman on the line, saying, "The Director's not in at the moment, but I'm expecting him back within the hour." Then I had to hang up quickly, because I could hear someone coming along the corridor. It was Charlotte, Rosemary's maid. She wanted to know why I'd been sacked. I couldn't think of a convincing reply, until she accused me of having made a pass at the mistress. I let her think that was it, and ended up getting a slapped face for my trouble.' I burst out laughing, but the Don and Jenny showed no reaction. Then Williams asked, 'So, what do I do now, chief? Come back to England?'

'No,' said Donald. 'Stay put for the moment. Book yourself into the Majestic and watch her round the clock. Let me know if she does anything out of character. Meanwhile, we're going to Cambridge. As soon as we've booked ourselves into a hotel there I'll call you.'

'Understood, sir,' said Williams, and rang off.

'When do we go?' I asked Donald once he had replaced the receiver.

'Tonight,' he replied. 'But not before I've made a few telephone calls.'

The Don dialled ten Cambridge numbers, using the digits Williams had been able to jot down, and inserting the numbers from nought to nine in the missing slot.

0223 640707 turned out to be a school. 'Sorry, wrong number,' said Donald. 717 was a chemist's shop; 727 was a garage; 737 was answered by an elderly male voice – 'Sorry, wrong number,' Donald repeated; 747 a newsagent; 757 a local policeman's wife (I tried not to laugh, but Donald only grunted); 767 a woman's voice – 'Sorry, wrong number,' yet again; 777 was St Catharine's College; 787 a woman's voice on an answering machine; 797 a hairdresser – 'Did you want a perm, or just a trim?'

Donald checked his list. 'It has to be either 737, 767 or 787. The time has come for me to pull a few strings.'

He dialled a Bradford number, and was told that the new Deputy Chief Constable of Cambridgeshire had been transferred from the West Yorkshire Constabulary the previous year.

'Leeke. Allan Leeke,' said Donald, without needing to be prompted. He turned to me. 'He was a sergeant when I was first made up to inspector.' He thanked his Bradford contact, then rang directory enquiries to find out the number of the Cambridge Police headquarters. He dialled another 0223 number.

'Cambridge Police. How can I help you?' asked a female voice.

'Can you put me through to the Deputy Chief Constable, please?' Donald asked.

'Who shall I say is calling?'

'Donald Hackett.'

The next voice that came on the line said, 'Don, this is a pleasant surprise. Or at least I hope it's a pleasant surprise, because knowing you, it won't be a social call. Are you looking for a job, by any chance? I heard you'd left the force.'

'Yes, it's true. I've resigned, but I'm not looking for a job, Allan. I don't think the Cambridge Constabulary could quite match my present salary.'

'So, what can I do for you, Don?'

'I need a trace done on three numbers in the Cambridge area.'

'Authorised?' asked the Deputy Chief Constable.

'No, but it might well lead to an arrest on your patch,' said Donald.

'That, and the fact that it's you who's asking, is good enough for me.'

Donald read out the three numbers, and Leeke asked him to hang on for a moment. While we waited, Donald told me, 'All they have to do is press a few buttons in the control room, and the numbers will appear on a screen in front of him. Things have changed since I first joined the force. In those days we had to let our legs do the walking.'

The Deputy Chief Constable's voice came back on the line. 'Right, the first number's come up. 640737 is a Wing Commander Danvers-Smith. He's the only person registered as living in the house.' He read out an address in Great Shelford, which he explained was just to the south of Cambridge. Jenny wrote the details down.

'767 is a Professor and Mrs Balcescu, also living in Great Shelford. 787 is Dame Julia Renaud, the opera singer. She lives in Grantchester. We know her quite well. She's hardly ever at home, because of her concert commitments all over the world. Her house has been burgled three times in the last year, always when she was abroad.'

'Thank you,' said Donald. 'You've been most helpful.'

'Anything you want to tell me?' asked the Deputy Chief Constable, sounding hopeful.

'Not at the moment,' replied Donald. 'But as soon as I've finished my investigation, I promise you'll be the first person to be informed.'

'Fair enough,' came back the reply, and the line went dead.

'Right,' Donald said, turning his attention back to us. 'We leave for Cambridge in a couple of hours. That will give us enough time to pack, and for Jenny to book us into a hotel near the city centre. We'll meet back here at' – he checked his watch – 'six o'clock.' He walked out of the room without uttering another word. I remember thinking that my father would have got on well with him.

Just over two hours later, Jenny was driving us at a steady sixty-nine miles per hour down the A1.

'Now the boring part of detective work begins,' said Donald. 'Intense research, followed by hours of surveillance. I think we can safely ignore Dame Julia. Jenny, you get to work on the wing commander. I want details of his career from the day he left school to the day he retired. First thing tomorrow you can begin by contacting RAF College Cranwell, and asking for details of his service record. I'll take the professor, and make a start in the university library.'

'What do I do?' I asked.

'For the time being, Mr Cooper, you keep yourself well out of sight. It's just possible that the wing commander or the professor might lead us to Alexander, so we don't need you trampling over any suspects and frightening them off.'

I reluctantly agreed.

Later that night I settled into a suite at the Garden House Hotel – a more refined sort of prison – but despite

feather pillows and a comfortable mattress I was quite
unable to sleep. I rose early the next morning and spent
most of the day watching endless updates on Sky News,
episodes of various Australian soaps, and a 'Film of the
Week' every two hours. But my mind was continually
switching between RAF Cranwell and the university
library.

When we met up in Donald's room that evening, he
and Jenny confirmed that their initial research suggested
that both men were who they purported to be.

'I was sure one of them would turn out to be Jeremy,'
I said, unable to hide my disappointment.

'It would be nice if it was always that easy, Mr
Cooper,' said Donald. 'But it doesn't mean that one of
them won't lead us to Jeremy.' He turned to Jenny.
'First, let's go over what you found out about the wing
commander.'

'Wing Commander Danvers-Smith DFC graduated
from Cranwell in 1938, served with Number Two Squad-
ron at Binbrook in Lincolnshire during the Second World
War, and flew several missions over Germany and occupied France. He was awarded the DFC for gallantry in
1943. He was grounded in 1958, and became an instructor at RAF Cottesmore in Gloucestershire. His final
posting was as Deputy Commanding Officer at RAF
Locking in Somerset. He retired in 1977, when he and
his wife moved back to Great Shelford, where he had
grown up.'

'Why's he living on his own now?' asked Donald.

'Wife died three years ago. He has two children, Sam

and Pamela, both married, but neither living in the area. They visit him occasionally.'

I wanted to ask Jenny how she had been able to find out so much information about the wing commander in such a short time, but said nothing, as I was more interested in hearing what the Don had discovered about Professor Balcescu.

Donald picked up a pile of notes that had been lying on the floor by his feet. 'So, let me tell you the results of my research into a very distinguished professor,' he began. 'Professor Balcescu escaped from Romania in 1989, after Ceausescu had had him placed under house arrest. He was smuggled out of the country by a group of dissident students, via Bulgaria and then on into Greece. His escape was well documented in the newspapers at the time. He applied for asylum in England, and was offered a teaching post at Gonville and Caius College, Cambridge, and three years later the Chair of Eastern European Studies. He advises the government on Romanian matters, and has written a scholarly book on the subject. Last year he was awarded a CBE in the Queen's Birthday Honours.'

'How could either of these men possibly know Rosemary?' I asked. 'Williams must have made a mistake when he wrote down the number.'

'Williams doesn't make mistakes, Mr Cooper,' said the Don. 'Otherwise I wouldn't have employed him. Your wife dialled one of those numbers, and we're just going to have to find out which one. This time we'll need your assistance.'

I mumbled an apology, but remained unconvinced.

Hackett nodded curtly, and turned back to Jenny. 'How long will it take us to get to the wing commander's home?'

'About fifteen minutes, sir. He lives in a cottage in Great Shelford, just south of Cambridge.'

'Right, we'll start with him. I'll see you both in the lobby at five o'clock tomorrow morning.'

I slept fitfully again that night, now convinced that we were embarked on a wild-goose chase. But at least I was going to be allowed to join them the following day, instead of being confined to my room and yet more Australian soaps.

I didn't need my 4.30 alarm call – I was already showering when the phone went. A few minutes after five, the three of us walked out of the hotel, trying not to look as if we were hoping to leave without paying our bill. It was a chilly morning, and I shivered as I climbed into the back of the car.

Jenny drove us out of the city and onto the London road. After a mile or so she turned left and took us into a charming little village with neat, well-kept houses on either side of the road. We passed a garden centre on the left and drove another half mile, then Jenny suddenly swung the car round and reversed into a layby. She switched off the engine and pointed to a small house with an RAF-blue door. 'That's where he lives,' she said. 'Number forty-seven.' Donald focused a tiny pair of binoculars on the house.

Some early-morning risers were already leaving their

homes, cars heading towards the station for the first
commuter train to London. The paperboy turned out to
be an old lady who pushed her heavily-laden bicycle
slowly round the village, dropping off her deliveries.
The milkman was next, clattering along in his electric
van – two pints here, a pint there, the occasional half-
dozen eggs or carton of orange juice left on front door-
steps. Lights began to flick on all over the village. 'The
wing commander has had one pint of red-top milk and
a copy of the *Daily Telegraph* delivered to his front
door,' said Donald.

People had emerged from the houses on either side of
number forty-seven before a light appeared in an
upstairs room of the wing commander's home. Once
that light had been switched on Donald sat bolt upright,
his eyes never leaving the house.

I became bored, and dozed off in the back at some
point. When I woke up, I hoped we might at least be
allowed a break for breakfast, but such mundane con-
siderations didn't seem to worry the two professionals
in the front. They continued to concentrate on any
movement that took place around number forty-seven,
and hardly exchanged a word.

At 10.19 a thin, elderly man, dressed in a Harris
tweed jacket and grey flannels, emerged from number
forty-seven and marched briskly down the path. All I
could see at that distance was a huge, bushy white moustache. It looked almost as if his whole body had been
designed around it. Donald kept the glasses trained on
him.

'Ever seen him before?' he asked, passing the binoculars back to me.

I focused the glasses on the wing commander and studied him carefully. 'Never,' I said as he came to a halt by the side of a battered old Austin Allegro. 'How could anyone forget that moustache?'

'It certainly wasn't grown last week,' said Donald, as Danvers-Smith eased his car out onto the main road.

Jenny cursed. 'I thought that if he used his car, the odds would be on him heading into Cambridge.' She deftly performed a three-point turn and accelerated quickly after the wing commander. Within a few minutes she was only a couple of cars behind him.

Danvers-Smith was not proving to be the sort of fellow who habitually broke the speed limit. 'His days as a test pilot are obviously long behind him,' Donald said, as we trailed the Allegro at a safe distance into the next village. About half a mile later he pulled into a petrol station.

'Stay with him,' said Donald. Jenny followed the Allegro into the forecourt and came to a halt at the pump directly behind Danvers-Smith.

'Keep your head down, Mr Cooper,' said the Don, opening his door. 'We don't want him seeing you.'

'What are you going to do?' I asked, peeping between the front seats.

'Risk an old con's trick,' Donald replied.

He stepped out of the front seat, walked round to the back of the car, and unscrewed the petrol cap just as the wing commander slipped the nozzle of a petrol pump

66

into the tank of his Allegro. Donald began slowly topping up our already full tank, then suddenly turned to face the old man.

'Wing Commander Danvers-Smith?' he asked in a plummy voice.

The wing commander looked up immediately, and a puzzled expression came over his weather-beaten face.

'Baker, sir,' said Donald. 'Flight Lieutenant Baker. You lectured me at RAF Locking. Vulcans, if I remember.'

'Bloody good memory, Baker. Good show,' said Danvers-Smith. 'Delighted to see you, old chap,' he said, taking the nozzle out of his car and replacing it in the pump. 'What are you up to nowadays?'

Jenny stifled a laugh.

'Work for BA, sir. Grounded after I failed my eye test. Bloody desk job, I'm afraid, but it was the only offer I got.'

'Bad luck, old chap,' said the wing commander, as they headed off towards the pay booth, and out of earshot.

When they came back a few minutes later, they were chattering away like old chums, and the wing commander actually had his arm round Donald's shoulder.

When they reached his car they shook hands, and I heard Donald say 'Goodbye, sir,' before Danvers-Smith climbed into his Allegro. The old airman pulled out of the forecourt and headed back towards his home. Donald got in next to Jenny and pulled the passenger door closed.

'I'm afraid *he* won't lead us to Alexander,' the Don

said with a sigh. 'Danvers-Smith is the genuine article
– misses his wife, doesn't see his children enough, and
feels a bit lonely. Even asked if I'd like to drop in for a
bite of lunch.'

'Why didn't you accept?' I asked.

Donald paused. 'I would have done, but when I mentioned that I was from Leeds, he told me he'd only been
there once in his life, to watch a test match. No, that
man has never heard of Rosemary Cooper or Jeremy
Alexander – I'd bet my pension on it. So, now it's the
turn of the professor. Let's head back towards Cambridge, Jenny. And drive slowly. I don't want to catch
up with the wing commander, or we'll all end up having
to join him for lunch.'

Jenny swung the car across the road and into the far
lane, then headed back towards the city. After a couple
of miles Donald told her to pull into the side of the
road just past a sign announcing the Shelford Rugby
Club.

'The professor and his wife live behind that hedge,'
Donald said, pointing across the road. 'Settle back, Mr
Cooper. This might take some time.'

At 12.30 Jenny went off to get some fish and chips
from the village. I devoured them hungrily. By three I
was bored stiff again, and was beginning to wonder just
how long Donald would hang around before we were
allowed to return to the hotel. I remembered 'Happy
Days' would be on at 6.30.

'We'll sit here all night, if necessary,' Donald said, as
if he were reading my thoughts. 'Forty-nine hours is

my record without sleep. What's yours, Jenny?' he asked, never taking his eyes off the house.

'Thirty-one, sir,' she replied.

'Then this may be your chance to break that record,' he said. A moment later, a woman in a white BMW nosed out of the driveway leading to the house and stopped at the edge of the pavement. She paused, looked both ways, then turned across the road and swung right, in the direction of Cambridge. As she passed us, I caught a glimpse of a blonde with a pretty face.

'I've seen her before,' I blurted out.

'Follow her, Jenny,' Donald said sharply. 'But keep your distance.' He turned round to face me.

'Where have you seen her?' he asked, passing over the binoculars.

'I can't remember,' I said, trying to focus on the back of a mop of fair, curly hair.

'Think, man. Think. It's our best chance yet,' said Donald, trying not to sound as if he was cross-examining an old lag.

I knew I had come across that face somewhere, though I felt certain we had never met. I had to rack my brains, because it was at least five years since I had seen any woman I recognised, let alone one that striking. But my mind remained blank.

'Keep on thinking,' said the Don, 'while I try to find out something a little more simple. And Jenny – don't get too close to her. Never forget she's got a rear-view mirror. Mr Cooper may not remember her, but she may remember him.'

Donald picked up the carphone and jabbed in ten numbers. 'Let's pray he doesn't realise I've retired,' he mumbled.

'DVLA Swansea. How can I help you?'

'Sergeant Crann, please,' said Donald.

'I'll put you through.'

'Dave Crann.'

'Donald Hackett.'

'Good afternoon, Chief Superintendent. How can I help you?'

'White BMW – K273 SCE,' said Donald, staring at the car in front of him.

'Hold on please, sir, I won't be a moment.'

Donald kept his eye fixed on the BMW while he waited. It was about thirty yards ahead of us, and heading towards a green light. Jenny accelerated to make sure she wouldn't get trapped if the lights changed, and as she shot through an amber light, Sergeant Crann came back on the line,

'We've identified the car, sir,' he said. 'Registered owner Mrs Susan Balcescu, The Kendalls, High Street, Great Shelford, Cambridge. One endorsement for speeding in a built-up area, 1991, a thirty-pound fine. Otherwise nothing known.'

'Thank you, sergeant. That's most helpful.'

'My pleasure, sir.'

'Why should Rosemary want to contact the Balcescus?' Donald said as he clipped the phone back into place. 'And is she contacting just one of them, or both?' Neither of us attempted to answer.

'I think it's time to let her go,' he said a moment later. 'I need to check out several more leads before we risk coming face to face with either of them. Let's head back to the hotel and consider our next move.'

'I know it's only a coincidence,' I ventured, 'but when I knew him, Jeremy had a white BMW.'

'F173 BZK,' said Jenny. 'I remember it from the file.'

Donald swung round. 'Some people can't give up smoking, you know, others drinking. But with some, it's a particular make of car,' he said. 'Although a lot of people must drive white BMWs,' he muttered almost to himself.

Once we were back in Donald's room, he began checking through the file he had put together on Professor Balcescu. The *Times* report of his escape from Romania, he told us, was the most detailed.

PROFESSOR BALCESCU first came to prominence while still a student at the University of Bucharest, where he called for the overthrow of the elected government. The authorities seemed relieved when he was offered a place at Oxford, and must have hoped that they had seen the last of him. But he returned to Bucharest University three years later, taking up the position of tutor in Politics. The following year he led a student revolt in support of Nicolae Ceausescu, and after he became president, Balcescu was rewarded with a Cabinet post, as Minister of Education. But he soon became disillusioned with the Ceausescu regime, and within eighteen months he had resigned and returned to the university as a humble tutor. Three years later he was offered the Chair of Politics and Economics.

Professor Balcescu's growing disillusionment with the government finally turned to anger, and in 1986 he began writing a series of pamphlets denouncing Ceausescu and his puppet regime. A few weeks after a particularly vitriolic attack on the establishment, he was dismissed from his post at the university, and later placed under house arrest. A group of Oxford historians wrote a letter of protest to *The Times*, but nothing more was heard of the great scholar for several years. Then, late in 1989, he was smuggled out of Romania by a group of students, finally reaching Britain via Bulgaria and Greece.

Cambridge won the battle of the universities to tempt him with a teaching post, and he became a fellow of Gonville and Caius in September 1990. In November 1991, after the retirement of Sir Halford McKay, Balcescu took over the Chair of Eastern European Studies.

Donald looked up. 'There's a picture of him taken when he was in Greece, but it's too blurred to be of much use.'

I studied the black-and-white photograph of a bearded middle-aged man surrounded by students. He wasn't anything like Jeremy. I frowned. 'Another blind alley,' I said.

'It's beginning to look like it,' said Donald. 'Especially after what I found out yesterday. According to his secretary, Balcescu delivers his weekly lecture every Friday morning, from ten o'clock to eleven.'

'But that wouldn't stop him from taking a call from Rosemary at midday,' interrupted Jenny.

'If you'll allow me to finish,' said Hackett sharply. Jenny bowed her head, and he continued. 'At twelve o'clock he chairs a full departmental meeting in his office, attended by all members of staff. I'm sure you'll agree, Jenny, that it would be quite difficult for him to take a personal call at that time every Friday, given the circumstances.'

Donald turned to me. 'I'm sorry to say we're back where we started, unless you can remember where you've seen Mrs Balcescu.' I shook my head. 'Perhaps I was mistaken,' I admitted.

Donald and Jenny spent the next few hours going over the files, even checking every one of the ten phone numbers a second time.

'Do you remember Rosemary's second call, sir,' said Jenny, in desperation. '"The Director's not in at the moment." Might that be the clue we're looking for?'

'Possibly,' said Donald. 'If we could find out who the Director is, we might be a step nearer to Jeremy Alexander.'

I remember Jenny's last words before I left for my room. 'I wonder how many directors there are in Britain, chief.'

Over breakfast in Donald's room the following morning, he reviewed all the intelligence that had been gathered to date, but none of us felt we were any nearer to a solution.

'What about Mrs Balcescu?' I said. '*She* may be the

person taking the call every Friday at midday, because that's the one time she knows exactly where her husband is.'

'I agree. But is she simply Rosemary's messenger, or is she a friend of Jeremy's?' asked Donald.

'Perhaps we'll have to tap her phone to find out,' said Jenny.

Donald ignored her comment, and checked his watch. 'It's time to go to Balcescu's lecture.'

'Why are we bothering?' I asked. 'Surely we ought to be concentrating on Mrs Balcescu.'

'You're probably right,' said Donald. 'But we can't afford to leave any stone unturned, and as his next lecture won't be for another week, we may as well get it over with. In any case, we'll be out by eleven, and if we find Mrs Balcescu's phone is engaged between twelve and twelve thirty . . .'

After Donald had asked Jenny to bring the car round to the front of the hotel, I slipped back into my room to pick up something that had been hidden in the bottom of my suitcase for several weeks. A few minutes later I joined them, and Jenny drove us out of the hotel carpark, turning right into the main road. Donald glanced at me suspiciously in the rear-view mirror as I sat silently in the back. Did I look guilty? I wondered.

Jenny spotted a parking meter a couple of hundred yards away from the Department of European Studies, and pulled in. We got out of the car and followed the flow of students along the pavement and up the steps. No one gave us a second look. Once we had entered the building, Donald whipped off his tie and slipped it in his jacket pocket. He looked more like a Marxist revolutionary than most of the people heading towards the lecture.

The lecture theatre was clearly signposted, and we entered it by a door on the ground floor, which turned out to be the only way in or out. Donald immediately walked up the raked auditorium to the back row of seats. Jenny and I followed, and Donald instructed me to sit behind a student who looked as if he spent his Saturday afternoons playing lock forward for his college rugby team.

While we waited for Balcescu to enter the room, I began to look around. The lecture theatre was a large semi-circle, not unlike a miniature Greek amphitheatre, and I estimated that it could hold around three hundred students. By the time the clock on the front wall read 9.55 there was hardly a seat to be found. No further proof was needed of the professor's reputation.

I felt a light sweat forming on my forehead as I waited for Balcescu to make his entrance. As the clock struck ten the door of the lecture theatre opened. I was so disappointed at the sight that greeted me that I groaned aloud. He couldn't have been less like Jeremy. I leaned across to Donald. 'Wrong-coloured hair, wrong-coloured eyes, about thirty pounds too light.' The Don showed no reaction.

'So the connection has to be with Mrs Balcescu,' whispered Jenny.

'Agreed,' said Donald under his breath. 'But we're stuck here for the next hour, because we certainly can't risk drawing attention to ourselves by walking out. We'll just have to make a dash for it as soon as the lecture is over. We'll still have time to see if she's at home to take the twelve o'clock call.' He paused. 'I should have checked the layout of the building earlier.' Jenny reddened slightly, because she knew *I* meant *you*.

And then I suddenly remembered where I had seen Mrs Balcescu. I was about to tell Donald, but the room fell silent as the professor began delivering his opening words.

'This is the sixth of eight lectures,' he began, 'on recent social and economic trends in Eastern Europe.' In a thick Central European accent he launched into a discourse that sounded as if he had given it many times before. The undergraduates began scribbling away on their pads, but I became increasingly irritated by the continual drone of the professor's nasal vowels, as I was impatient to tell Hackett about Mrs Balcescu and to get back to Great Shelford as quickly as possible. I found myself glancing up at the clock on the wall every few minutes. Not unlike my own schooldays, I thought. I touched my jacket pocket. It was still there, even though on this occasion it would serve no useful purpose.

Halfway through the lecture, the lights were dimmed so the professor could illustrate some of his points with slides. I glanced at the first few graphs as they appeared on the screen, showing different income groups across Eastern Europe related to their balance of payments and export figures, but I ended up none the wiser, and not just because I had missed the first five lectures.

The assistant in charge of the projector managed to get one of the slides upside down, showing Germany bottom of the export table and Romania top, which caused a light ripple of laughter throughout the theatre. The professor scowled, and began to deliver his lecture at a faster and faster pace, which only caused the assistant more difficulty in finding the right slides to coincide with the professor's statements.

Once again I became bored, and I was relieved when, at five to eleven, Balcescu called for the final graph. The previous one was replaced by a blank screen. Everyone began looking round at the assistant, who was searching desperately for the slide. The professor became irritable as the minute hand of the clock approached eleven. Still the assistant failed to locate the missing slide. He flicked the shutter back once again, but nothing appeared on the screen, leaving the professor brightly illuminated by a beam of light. Balcescu stepped forward, and began drumming his fingers impatiently on the wooden lectern. Then he turned sideways, and I caught his profile for the first time. There was a small scar above his right eye, which must have faded over the years, but in the bright light of the beam it was clear to see.

'It's him!' I whispered to Donald as the clock struck eleven. The lights came up, and the professor quickly left the lecture theatre without another word.

I leapt over the back of my bench seat, and began charging down the gangway, but my progress was impeded by students who were already sauntering out into the aisle. I pushed my way past them until I had reached ground level, and bolted through the door by which the professor had left so abruptly. I spotted him at the end of the corridor. He was opening another door, and disappeared out of sight. I ran after him, dodging in and out of the chattering students.

When I reached the door that had just been closed behind him I looked up at the sign:

PROFESSOR BALCESCU
Director of European Studies

I threw the door open, to discover a woman sitting behind a desk checking some papers. Another door was closing behind her.

'I need to see Professor Balcescu immediately,' I shouted, knowing that if I didn't get to him before Hackett caught up with me, I might lose my resolve.

The woman stopped what she was doing and looked up at me. 'The Director is expecting an overseas call at any moment, and cannot be disturbed,' she replied. 'I'm sorry, but . . .'

I ran straight past her, pulled open the door and rushed into the room, where I came face to face with Jeremy Alexander for the first time since I had left him lying on the floor of my drawing room. He was talking animatedly on the phone, but he looked up, and recognised me immediately. When I pulled the gun from my pocket, he dropped the receiver. As I took aim, the blood suddenly drained from his face.

'Are you there, Jeremy?' asked an agitated voice on

the other end of the line. Despite the passing of time, I had no difficulty in recognising Rosemary's strident tones.

Jeremy was shouting, 'No, Richard, no! I can explain! Believe me, I can explain!' as Donald came running in. He came to an abrupt halt by the professor's desk, but showed no interest in Jeremy.

'Don't do it, Richard,' he pleaded. 'You'll only spend the rest of your life regretting it.' I remember thinking it was the first time he had ever called me Richard.

'Wrong, for a change, Donald,' I told him. 'I won't regret killing Jeremy Alexander. You see, he's already been pronounced dead once. I know, because I was sentenced to life imprisonment for his murder. I'm sure you're aware of the meaning of *"autrefois acquit"*, and will therefore know that I can't be charged a second time with a crime I've already been convicted of and sentenced for. Even though this time they will have a body.'

I moved the gun a few inches to the right, and aimed at Jeremy's heart. I squeezed the trigger just as Jenny came charging into the room. She dived at my legs.

Jeremy and I both hit the ground with a thud.

Well, as I pointed out to you at the beginning of this chronicle, I ought to explain why I'm in jail – or, to be more accurate, why I'm back in jail.

I *was* tried a second time; on this occasion for attempted murder – despite the fact that I had only grazed the bloody man's shoulder. I still blame Jenny for that.

Mind you, it was worth it just to hear Matthew's closing speech, because he certainly understood the meaning of 'autrefois acquit'. He surpassed himself with his description of Rosemary as a calculating, evil Jezebel, and Jeremy as a man motivated by malice and greed, quite willing to cynically pose as a national hero while his victim was rotting his life away in jail, put there by a wife's perjured testimony of which he had unquestionably been the mastermind. In another four years, a furious Matthew told the jury, they would have been able to pocket several more millions between them. This time the jury looked on me with considerable sympathy.

'Thou shalt not bear false witness against any man,' were Sir Matthew's closing words, his sonorous tones making him sound like an Old Testament prophet.

The tabloids always need a hero and a villain. This time they had got themselves a hero and two villains. They seemed to have forgotten everything they had printed during the previous trial about the oversexed lorry driver, and it would be foolish to suggest that the page after page devoted to every sordid detail of Jeremy and Rosemary's deception didn't influence the jury.

They found me guilty, of course, but only because they weren't given any choice. In his summing up the judge almost ordered them to do so. But the foreman expressed his fellow jurors' hope that, given the circumstances, the judge might consider a lenient sentence. Mr Justice Lampton obviously didn't read the tabloids, because he lectured me for several minutes, and then said I would be sent down for five years.

Matthew was on his feet immediately, appealing for clemency on the grounds that I had already served a long sentence. 'This man looks out on the world through a window of tears,' he told the judge. 'I beseech your lordship not to put bars across that window a second time.' The applause from the gallery was so thunderous that the judge had to instruct the bailiffs to clear the court before he could respond to Sir Matthew's plea.

'His lordship obviously needs a little time to think,' Matthew explained under his breath as he passed me in the dock. After much deliberation in his chambers, Mr Justice Lampton settled on three years. Later that day I was sent to Ford Open Prison.

After considerable press comment during the next few weeks, and what Sir Matthew described to the Court of Appeal as 'my client's unparalleled affliction and exemplary behaviour', I ended up only having to serve nine months.

Meanwhile, Jeremy had been arrested at Addenbrookes Hospital by Allan Leeke, Deputy Chief Constable of Cambridgeshire. After three days in a heavily guarded ward he was charged with conspiracy to pervert the course of public justice, and transferred to Armley Prison to await trial. He comes before the Leeds Crown Court next month, and you can be sure I'll be sitting in the gallery following the proceedings every day. By the way, Fingers and the boys gave him a very handsome welcome. I'm told he's lost even more weight than he did trooping backwards and forwards across Europe fixing up his new identity.

Rosemary has also been arrested and charged with perjury. They didn't grant her bail, and Donald informs me that French prisons, particularly the one in Marseilles, are less comfortable than Armley – one of the few disadvantages of living in the south of France. She's fighting the extradition order, of course, but I'm assured by Matthew that she has absolutely no chance of succeeding, now we've signed the Maastricht Treaty. I knew *something* good must come out of that.

As for Mrs Balcescu – I'm sure you worked out where I'd seen her long before I did.

In the case of Regina v. Alexander and Kershaw, I'm told, she will be giving evidence on behalf of the Crown. Jeremy made such a simple mistake for a normally calculating and shrewd man. In order to protect himself from being identified, he put all his worldly goods in his wife's name. So the striking blonde ended up with everything, and I have a feeling that when it comes to her cross-examination, Rosemary won't turn out to be all that helpful to Jeremy, because it slipped his mind to let her know that in between those weekly phone calls he was living with another woman.

It's been difficult to find out much more about the real Professor Balcescu, because since Ceausescu's downfall no one is quite sure what really happened to the distinguished academic. Even the Romanians believed he had escaped to Britain and begun a new life.

Bradford City have been relegated, so Donald has

bought a cottage in the West Country and settled down to watch Bath play rugby. Jenny has joined a private detective agency in London, but is already complaining about her salary and conditions. Williams has returned to Bradford and decided on an early retirement. It was he who pointed out the painfully obvious fact that when it's twelve o'clock in France, it's only eleven o'clock in Britain.

By the way, I've decided to go back to Leeds after all. Cooper's went into liquidation as I suspected they would, the new management team not proving all that effective when it came to riding out a recession. The official receiver was only too delighted to accept my offer of £250,000 for what remained of the company, because no one else was showing the slightest interest in it. Poor Jeremy will get almost nothing for his shares. Still, you should look up the new stock in the *F.T.* around the middle of next year, and buy yourself a few, because they'll be what my father would have called 'a risk worth taking'.

By the way, Matthew advises me that I've just given you what's termed as 'inside information', so please don't pass it on, as I have no desire to go back to jail for a third time.

CHEAP AT
HALF THE PRICE

WOMEN ARE NATURALLY SUPERIOR TO
men, and Mrs Consuela Rosenheim was no exception.

Victor Rosenheim, an American banker, was Consuela's third husband, and the gossip columns on both
sides of the Atlantic were suggesting that, like a chain
smoker, the former Colombian model was already
searching for her next spouse before she had extracted
the last gasp from the old one. Her first two husbands
– one an Arab, the other a Jew (Consuela showed no
racial prejudice when it came to signing marriage contracts) – had not quite left her in a position that would
guarantee her financial security once her natural beauty
had faded. But two more divorce settlements would sort
that out. With this in mind, Consuela estimated that
she only had another five years before the final vow
must be taken.

The Rosenheims flew into London from their home
in New York – or, to be more accurate, from their homes
in New York. Consuela had travelled to the airport by
chauffeur-driven car from their mansion in the Hamp-
tons, while her husband had been taken from his Wall
Street office in a second chauffeur-driven car. They met

up in the Concorde lounge at JFK. When they had landed at Heathrow another limousine transported them to the Ritz, where they were escorted to their usual suite without any suggestion of having to sign forms or book in.

The purpose of their trip was twofold. Mr Rosenheim was hoping to take over a small merchant bank that had not benefited from the recession, while Mrs Rosenheim intended to occupy her time looking for a suitable birthday present – for herself. Despite considerable research I have been unable to discover exactly which birthday Consuela would officially be celebrating.

After a sleepless night induced by jetlag, Victor Rosenheim was whisked away to an early-morning meeting in the City, while Consuela remained in bed toying with her breakfast. She managed one piece of thin unbuttered toast and a stab at a boiled egg.

Once the breakfast tray had been removed, Consuela made a couple of phone calls to confirm luncheon dates for the two days she would be in London. She then disappeared into the bathroom.

Fifty minutes later she emerged from her suite dressed in a pink Olaganie suit with a dark blue collar, her fair hair bouncing on her shoulders. Few of the men she passed between the elevator and the revolving doors failed to turn their heads, so Consuela judged that the previous fifty minutes had not been wasted. She stepped out of the hotel and into the morning sun to begin her search for the birthday present.

Consuela began her quest in New Bond Street. As in the past, she had no intention of straying more than a few blocks north, south, east or west from that comforting landmark, while a chauffeur-driven car hovered a few yards behind her.

She spent some time in Asprey's considering the latest slimline watches, a gold statue of a tiger with jade eyes, and a Fabergé egg, before moving on to Cartier, where she dismissed a crested silver salver, a platinum watch and a Louis XIV long-case clock. From there she walked another few yards to Tiffany's, which, despite a determined salesman who showed her almost everything the shop had to offer, she still left empty-handed.

Consuela stood on the pavement and checked her watch. It was 12.52, and she had to accept that it had been a fruitless morning. She instructed her chauffeur to drive her to Harry's Bar, where she found Mrs Stavros Kleanthis waiting for her at their usual table. Consuela greeted her friend with a kiss on both cheeks, and took the seat opposite her.

Mrs Kleanthis, the wife of a not unknown shipowner – the Greeks preferring one wife and several liaisons – had for the last few minutes been concentrating her attention on the menu to be sure that the restaurant served the few dishes that her latest diet would permit. Between them, the two women had read every book that had reached number one on the *New York Times* bestseller list which included the words 'youth', 'orgasm', 'slimming', 'fitness' or 'immortality' in its title.

'How's Victor?' asked Maria, once she and Consuela had ordered their meals.

Consuela paused to consider her response, and decided on the truth.

'Fast reaching his sell-by date,' she replied. 'And Stavros?'

'Well past his, I'm afraid,' said Maria. 'But as I have neither your looks nor your figure, not to mention the fact that I have three teenage children, I don't suppose I'll be returning to the market to select the latest brand.'

Consuela smiled as a salade niçoise was placed in front of her.

'So, what brings you to London – other than to have lunch with an old friend?' asked Maria.

'Victor has his eye on another bank,' replied Consuela, as if she were discussing a child who collected stamps. 'And I'm in search of a suitable birthday present.'

'And what are you expecting Victor to come up with this time?' asked Maria. 'A house in the country? A thoroughbred racehorse? Or perhaps your own Lear jet?'

'None of the above,' said Consuela, placing her fork by the half-finished salad. 'I need something that can't be bargained over at a future date, so my gift must be one that any court, in any state, will acknowledge is unquestionably mine.'

'Have you found anything appropriate yet?' asked Maria.

'Not yet,' admitted Consuela. 'Asprey's yielded nothing of interest, Cartier's cupboard was almost bare, and the only attractive thing in Tiffany's was the salesman, who was undoubtedly penniless. I shall have to continue my search this afternoon.'

The salad plates were deftly removed by a waiter whom Maria considered far too young and far too thin. Another waiter with the same problem poured them both a cup of fresh decaffeinated coffee. Consuela refused the proffered cream and sugar, though her companion was not quite so disciplined.

The two ladies grumbled on about the sacrifices they were having to make because of the recession until they were the only diners left in the room. At this point a fatter waiter presented them with the bill – an extraordinarily long ledger considering that neither of them had ordered a second course, or had requested more than Evian from the wine waiter.

On the pavement of South Audley Street they kissed again on both cheeks before going their separate ways, one to the east and the other to the west.

Consuela climbed into the back of her chauffeur-driven car in order to be returned to New Bond Street, a distance of no more than half a mile.

Once she was back on familiar territory, she began to work her way steadily down the other side of the street, stopping at Bentley's, where it appeared that they hadn't sold anything since last year, and moving rapidly on to Adler, who seemed to be suffering from much the same problem. She cursed the recession once again, and blamed it all on Bill Clinton, who Victor had assured her was the cause of most of the world's current problems.

Consuela was beginning to despair of finding anything worthwhile in Bond Street, and reluctantly began her journey back towards the Ritz, feeling she might even have to consider an expedition to Knightsbridge the following day, when she came to a sudden halt outside the House of Graff. Consuela could not recall the shop from her last visit to London some six months before, and as she knew Bond Street better than she had ever known any of her three husbands, she concluded that it must be a new establishment.

She gazed at the stunning gems in their magnificent settings, heavily protected behind the bulletproof windows. When she reached the third window her mouth opened wide, like a newborn chick demanding to be fed. From that moment she knew that no further excursions would be necessary, for there, hanging round a slender marble neck, was a peerless diamond and ruby necklace. She felt that she had seen the magnificent piece of jewellery somewhere before, but she quickly dismissed the thought from her mind, and continued to study the exquisitely set rubies surrounded by perfectly cut diamonds, making up a necklace of unparalleled beauty. Without giving a moment's thought to how much the object might cost, Consuela walked slowly towards the thick glass door at the entrance to the shop, and pressed a discreet ivory button on the wall. The House of Graff obviously had no interest in passing trade.

The door was unlocked by a security officer who needed no more than a glance at Mrs Rosenheim to know that he should usher her quickly through to the inner portals, where a second door was opened and

Consuela came face to face with a tall, imposing man in a long black coat and pinstriped trousers.

'Good afternoon, madam,' he said, bowing slightly. Consuela noticed that he surreptitiously admired her rings as he did so. 'Can I be of assistance?'

Although the room was full of treasures that might in normal circumstances have deserved hours of her attention, Consuela's mind was focused on only one object.

'Yes. I would like to study more closely the diamond and ruby necklace on display in the third window.'

'Certainly, madam,' the manager replied, pulling back a chair for his customer. He nodded almost imperceptibly to an assistant, who silently walked over to the window, unlocked a little door and extracted the necklace. The manager slipped behind the counter and pressed a concealed button. Four floors above, a slight burr sounded in the private office of Mr Laurence Graff, warning the proprietor that a customer had enquired after a particularly expensive item, and that he might wish to deal with them personally.

Laurence Graff glanced up at the television screen on the wall to his left, which showed him what was taking place on the ground floor.

'Ah,' he said, once he saw the lady in the pink suit seated at the Louis XIV table. 'Mrs Consuela Rosenheim, if I'm not mistaken.' Just as the Speaker of the House of Commons can identify every one of its 650 members, so Laurence Graff recognised the 650 customers who might be able to afford the most extravagant of his treasures. He quickly stepped from behind his desk, walked out of his office and took the waiting lift to the ground floor.

Meanwhile, the manager had laid out a black velvet cloth on the table in front of Mrs Rosenheim, and the assistant placed the necklace delicately on top of it. Consuela stared down at the object of her desire, mesmerised.

'Good afternoon, Mrs Rosenheim,' said Laurence Graff as he stepped out of the lift and walked across the thick pile carpet towards his would-be customer. 'How nice to see you again.'

He had in truth only seen her once before – at a shoulder-to-shoulder cocktail party in Manhattan. But after that, he could have spotted her at a hundred paces on a moving escalator.

'Good afternoon, Mr . . .' Consuela hesitated, feeling unsure of herself for the first time that day.

'Laurence Graff,' he said, offering his hand. 'We met at Sotheby Parke Benett last year – a charity function in aid of the Red Cross, if I remember correctly.'

'Of course,' said Mrs Rosenheim, unable to recall him, or the occasion.

Mr Graff bowed reverently towards the diamond and ruby necklace.

'The Kanemarra heirloom,' he purred, then paused, before taking the manager's place at the table. 'Fashioned in 1936 by Silvio di Larchi,' he continued. 'All the rubies were extracted from a single mine in Burma, over a period of twenty years. The diamonds were purchased

94

from De Beers by an Egyptian merchant who, after the necklace had been made up for him, offered the unique piece to King Farouk — for services rendered. When the monarch married Princess Farida he presented it to her on their wedding day, and she in return bore him four heirs, none of whom, alas, was destined to succeed to the throne.' Graff looked up from one object of beauty, and gazed on another.

'Since then it has passed through several hands before arriving at the House of Graff,' continued the proprietor. 'Its most recent owner was an actress, whose husband's oil wells unfortunately dried up.'

The flicker of a smile crossed the face of Consuela Rosenheim as she finally recalled where she had previously seen the necklace.

'Quite magnificent,' she said, giving it one final look. 'I will be back,' she added as she rose from her chair. Graff accompanied her to the door. Nine out of ten customers who make such a claim have no intention of returning, but he could always sense the tenth.

'May I ask the price?' Consuela asked indifferently as he held the door open for her.

'One million pounds, madam,' Graff replied, as casually as if she had enquired about the cost of a plastic keyring at a seaside gift shop.

Once she had reached the pavement, Consuela dismissed her chauffeur. Her mind was now working at a speed that would have impressed her husband. She slipped across the road, calling first at The White House, then Yves Saint Laurent, and finally at Chanel, emerging some two hours later with all the weapons she required for the battle that lay ahead. She did not arrive back at her suite at the Ritz until a few minutes before six.

Consuela was relieved to find that her husband had not yet returned from the bank. She used the time to take a long bath, and to contemplate how the trap should be set. Once she was dry and powdered, she dabbed a suggestion of a new scent on her neck, then slipped into some of her newly acquired clothes.

She was checking herself once again in the full-length mirror when Victor entered the room. He stopped on the spot, dropping his briefcase on the carpet. Consuela turned to face him.

'You look stunning,' he declared, with the same look of desire she had lavished on the Kanemarra heirloom a few hours before.

'Thank you, darling,' she replied. 'And how did your day go?'

'A triumph. The takeover has been agreed, and at half the price it would have cost me only a year ago.'

Consuela smiled. An unexpected bonus.

'Those of us who are still in possession of cash need have no fear of the recession,' Victor added with satisfaction.

Over a quiet supper in the Ritz's dining room, Victor described to his wife in great detail what had taken place at the bank that day. During the occasional break in this monologue Consuela indulged her husband by remarking 'How clever of you, Victor,' 'How amazing,' 'How you managed it I will never understand.' When he finally ordered a large brandy, lit a cigar and leaned back in his chair, she began to run her elegantly stockinged right foot gently along the inside of his thigh. For the first time that evening, Victor stopped thinking about the takeover.

As they left the dining room and strolled towards the lift, Victor placed an arm around his wife's slim waist. By the time the lift had reached the sixth floor he had already taken off his jacket, and his hand had slipped a few inches further down. Consuela giggled. Long before they had reached the door of their suite he had begun tugging off his tie.

When they entered the room, Consuela placed the 'Do Not Disturb' sign on the outside doorknob. For the next few minutes Victor was transfixed to the spot as he watched his slim wife slowly remove each garment she had purchased that afternoon. He quickly pulled off his own clothes, and wished once again that he had carried out his New Year's resolution.

Forty minutes later, Victor lay exhausted on the bed. After a few moments of sighing, he began to snore. Consuela pulled the sheet over their naked bodies, but her eyes remained wide open. She was already going over the next step in her plan.

Victor awoke the following morning to discover his wife's hand gently stroking the inside of his leg. He rolled over to face her, the memory of the previous night still vivid in his mind. They made love a second time, something they had not done for as long as he could recall.

It was not until he stepped out of the shower that Victor remembered it was his wife's birthday, and that he had promised to spend the morning with her selecting a gift. He only hoped that her eye had already settled on something she wanted, as he needed to spend most of the day closeted in the City with his lawyers, going over the offer document line by line.

'Happy birthday, darling,' he said as he padded back into the bedroom. 'By the way, did you have any luck finding a present?' he added as he scanned the front page of the *Financial Times*, which was already speculating on the possible takeover, describing it as a coup. A smile of satisfaction appeared on Victor's face for the second time that morning.

'Yes, my darling,' Consuela replied. 'I did come across one little bauble that I rather liked. I just hope it isn't too expensive.'

'And how much is this "little bauble"?' Victor asked. Consuela turned to face him. She was wearing only two garments, both of them black, and both of them remarkably skimpy.

Victor started to wonder if he still had the time, but then he remembered the lawyers, who had been up all night and would be waiting patiently for him at the bank.

'I didn't ask the price,' Consuela replied. 'You're so much cleverer than I am at that sort of thing,' she added, as she slipped into a navy silk blouse.

Victor glanced at his watch. 'How far away is it?' he asked.

'Just across the road, in Bond Street, my darling,' Consuela replied. 'I shouldn't have to delay you for too long.' She knew exactly what was going through her husband's mind.

'Good. Then let's go and look at this little bauble without delay,' he said as he did up the buttons on his shirt.

While Victor finished dressing, Consuela, with the help of the *Financial Times*, skilfully guided the conversation back to his triumph of the previous day. She listened once more to the details of the takeover as they left the hotel and strolled up Bond Street together arm in arm.

'Probably saved myself several million,' he told her yet again. Consuela smiled as she led him to the door of the House of Graff.

'Several million?' she gasped. 'How clever you are, Victor.'

The security guard quickly opened the door, and this time Consuela found that Mr Graff was already standing by the table waiting for her. He bowed low, then turned to Victor. 'May I offer my congratulations on your brilliant coup, Mr Rosenheim.' Victor smiled. 'How may I help you?'

'My husband would like to see the Kanemarra heirloom,' said Consuela, before Victor had a chance to reply.

'Of course, madam,' said the proprietor. He stepped behind the table and spread out the black velvet cloth. Once again the assistant removed the magnificent necklace from its stand in the third window, and carefully laid it out on the centre of the velvet cloth to show the jewels to their best advantage. Mr Graff was about to embark on the piece's history, when Victor simply said, 'How much is it?'

Mr Graff raised his head. 'This is no ordinary piece of jewellery. I feel . . .'

'How much?' repeated Victor.

'Its provenance alone warrants . . .'

'How much?'

'The sheer beauty, not to mention the craftsmanship involved . . .'

'How much?' asked Victor, his voice now rising.

'. . . the word unique would not be inappropriate.'

'You may be right, but I still need to know how much it's going to cost me,' said Victor, who was beginning to sound exasperated.

'One million pounds, sir,' Graff said in an even tone, aware that he could not risk another superlative.

'I'll settle at half a million, no more,' came back the immediate reply.

'I am sorry to say, sir,' said Graff, 'that with this particular piece, there is no room for bargaining.'

'There's always room for bargaining, whatever one is selling,' said Victor. 'I repeat my offer. Half a million.'

'I fear that in this case, sir . . .'

'I feel confident that you'll see things my way, given time,' said Victor. 'But I don't have that much time to spare this morning, so I'll write out a cheque for half a million, and leave *you* to decide whether you wish to cash it or not.'

'I fear you are wasting your time, sir,' said Graff. 'I cannot let the Kanemarra heirloom go for less than one million.'

Victor took out a chequebook from his inside pocket, unscrewed the top of his fountain pen, and wrote out the words 'Five Hundred Thousand Pounds Only' below the name of the bank that bore his name. His wife took a discreet pace backwards.

Graff was about to repeat his previous comment, when he glanced up, and observed Mrs Rosenheim silently pleading with him to accept the cheque.

A look of curiosity came over his face as Consuela continued her urgent mime.

Victor tore out the cheque and left it on the table. 'I'll give you twenty-four hours to decide,' he said. 'We return to New York tomorrow morning – with or without the Kanemarra heirloom. It's your decision.'

Graff left the cheque on the table as he accompanied Mr and Mrs Rosenheim to the front door and bowed them out onto Bond Street.

'You were brilliant, my darling,' said Consuela as the chauffeur opened the car door for his master.

'The bank,' Rosenheim instructed as he fell into the back seat. 'You'll have your little bauble, Consuela. He'll cash the cheque before the twenty-four hours are up, of that I'm sure.' The chauffeur closed the back door, and the window purred down as Victor added with a smile, 'Happy birthday, darling.'

Consuela returned his smile, and blew him a kiss as the car pulled out into the traffic and edged its way towards Piccadilly. The morning had not turned out quite as she had planned, because she felt unable to agree with her husband's judgement – but then, she still had twenty-four hours to play with.

Consuela returned to the suite at the Ritz, undressed, took a shower, opened another bottle of perfume, and slowly began to change into the second outfit she had purchased the previous day. Before she left the room she turned to the commodities section of the *Financial Times*, and checked the price of green coffee.

She emerged from the Arlington Street entrance of the Ritz wearing a double-breasted navy blue Yves Saint Laurent suit and a wide-brimmed red and white hat. Ignoring her chauffeur, she hailed a taxi, instructing the driver to take her to a small, discreet hotel in Knightsbridge. Fifteen minutes later she entered the foyer with her head bowed, and after giving the name of her host to the manager, was accompanied to a suite on the fourth floor. Her luncheon companion stood as she entered the room, walked forward, kissed her on both cheeks and wished her a happy birthday.

After an intimate lunch, and an even more intimate hour spent in the adjoining room, Consuela's companion listened to her request and, having first checked his watch, agreed to accompany her to Mayfair. He didn't mention to her that he would have to be back in his office by four o'clock to take an important call from South America. Since the downfall of the Brazilian president, coffee prices had gone through the roof.

As the car travelled down Brompton Road, Consuela's companion telephoned to check the latest spot price of green coffee in New York (only her skill in bed had managed to stop him from calling earlier). He was pleased to learn that it was up another two cents, but not as pleased as she was. Eleven minutes later, the car deposited them outside the House of Graff.

When they entered the shop together arm in arm, Mr Graff didn't so much as raise an eyebrow.

'Good afternoon, Mr Carvalho,' he said. 'I do hope that your estates yielded an abundant crop this year.'

Mr Carvalho smiled and replied, 'I cannot complain.'

'And how may I assist you?' enquired the proprietor.

'We would like to see the diamond necklace in the third window,' said Consuela, without a moment's hesitation.

'Of course, madam,' said Graff, as if he were addressing a complete stranger.

Once again the black velvet cloth was laid out on the table, and once again the assistant placed the Kanemarra heirloom in its centre.

This time Mr Graff was allowed to relate its history, before Carvalho politely enquired after the price.

'One million pounds,' said Graff.

After a moment's hesitation, Carvalho said, 'I'm willing to pay half a million.'

'This is no ordinary piece of jewellery,' replied the proprietor. 'I feel . . .'

'Possibly not, but half a million is my best offer,' said Carvalho.

'The sheer beauty, not to mention the craftsmanship involved . . .'

'Nevertheless, I am not willing to go above half a million.'

'. . . the word unique would not be inappropriate.'

'Half a million, and no more,' insisted Carvalho.

'I am sorry to say, sir,' said Graff, 'that with this particular piece there is no room for bargaining.'

'There's always room for bargaining, whatever one is selling,' the coffee grower insisted.

'I fear that is not true in this case, sir. You see . . .'

'I suspect you will come to your senses in time,' said Carvalho. 'But, regrettably, I do not have any time to spare this afternoon. I will write out a cheque for half a million pounds, and leave *you* to decide whether you wish to cash it.'

Carvalho took a chequebook from his inside pocket, unscrewed the top of his fountain pen, and wrote out the words 'Five Hundred Thousand Pounds Only'. Consuela looked silently on.

Carvalho tore out the cheque, and left it on the counter.

'I'll give you twenty-four hours to decide. I leave for Chicago on the early evening flight tomorrow. If the cheque has not been presented by the time I reach my office . . .'

Graff bowed his head slightly, and left the cheque on

the table. He accompanied them to the door, and bowed again when they stepped out onto the pavement.

'You were brilliant, my darling,' said Consuela as the chauffeur opened the car door for his employer.

'The Exchange,' said Carvalho. Turning back to face his mistress, he added, 'You'll have your necklace before the day is out, of that I'm certain, my darling.'

Consuela smiled and waved as the car disappeared in the direction of Piccadilly, and on this occasion she felt able to agree with her lover's judgement. Once the car had turned the corner, she slipped back into the House of Graff.

The proprietor smiled, and handed over the smartly wrapped gift. He bowed low and simply said, 'Happy birthday, Mrs Rosenheim.'

DOUGIE MORTIMER'S
RIGHT ARM

Robert Henry Kefford III, known to his friends as Bob, was in bed with a girl called Helen when he first heard about Dougie Mortimer's right arm.

Bob was sorry to be leaving Cambridge. He had spent three glorious years at St John's, and although he hadn't read as many books as he had done for his undergraduate degree at the University of Chicago, he had striven every bit as hard to come head of the river.

It wasn't unusual for an American to win a rowing blue in the early 1970s, but to have stroked a victorious Cambridge eight for three years in a row was acknowledged as a first.

Bob's father, Robert Henry Kefford II, known to his friends as Robert, had travelled over to England to watch his son take part in all three races from Putney to Mortlake. After Bob had stroked Cambridge to victory for the third time, his father told him that he must not return to his native Illinois without having presented a memento to the University Boat Club that they would remember him by.

'And don't forget, my boy,' declared Robert Henry Kefford II, 'the gift must not be ostentatious. Better to show that you have made an effort to present them with an object of historic value than give them something that obviously cost a great deal of money. The British appreciate that sort of thing.'

Bob spent many hours pondering his father's words, but completely failed to come up with any worthwhile ideas. After all, the Cambridge University Boat Club had more silver cups and trophies than they could possibly display.

It was on a Sunday morning that Helen first mentioned the name of Dougie Mortimer. She and Bob were lying in each other's arms, when she started prodding his biceps.

'Is this some form of ancient British foreplay that I ought to know about?' Bob asked, placing his free arm around Helen's shoulder.

'Certainly not,' Helen replied. 'I was simply trying to discover if your biceps are as big as Dougie Mortimer's.'

As Bob had never known a girl talk about another man while he was in bed with her, he was unable to think of an immediate response.

'And are they?' he eventually enquired, flexing his muscles.

'Hard to tell,' Helen replied. 'I've never actually touched Dougie's arm, only seen it at a distance.'

'And where did you come across this magnificent specimen of manhood?'

'It hangs over the bar at my dad's local, in Hull.'

'Doesn't Dougie Mortimer find that a little painful?' asked Bob, laughing.

'Doubt if he cares that much,' said Helen. 'After all, he's been dead for over sixty years.'

'And his arm still hangs above a bar?' asked Bob in disbelief. 'Hasn't it begun to smell a bit by now?'

This time it was Helen's turn to laugh. 'No, you Yankee fool. It's a bronze cast of his arm. In those days, if you were in the University crew for three years in a row, they made a cast of your arm to hang in the club-house. Not to mention a card with your picture on it in every packet of Player's cigarettes. I've never seen *your* picture in a cigarette packet, come to think of it,' said Helen as she pulled the sheet over his head.

'Did he row for Oxford or Cambridge?' asked Bob.

'No idea.'

'So, what's the name of this pub in Hull?'

'The King William,' Helen replied, as Bob took his arm from around her shoulder.

'Is this American foreplay?' she asked after a few moments.

Later that morning, after Helen had left for Newnham, Bob began searching his shelves for a book with a blue cover. He dug out his much-thumbed *History of the Boat Race* and flicked through the index, to discover that there were seven Mortimers listed. Five had rowed for Oxford, two for Cambridge. He began to pray as he checked their initials. Mortimer, A.J. (Westminster and Wadham, Oxon), Mortimer, C.K. (Uppingham and Oriel, Oxon), Mortimer, D.J.T. (Harrow and

St Catharine's, Cantab), Mortimer, E.L. (Oundle and Magdalen, Oxon). Bob turned his attention to Mortimer, D.J.T., biography page 129, and flicked the pages backwards until he reached the entry he sought. Douglas John Townsend Mortimer (St Catharine's), Cambridge 1907, −08, −09, stroke. He then read the short summary of Mortimer's rowing career.

> DOUGIE MORTIMER stroked the Cambridge boat to victory in 1907, a feat which he repeated in 1908. But in 1909, when the experts considered Cambridge to have one of the finest crews for years, the light blues lost to an Oxford boat that was regarded as the rank outsider. Although many explanations were suggested by the press at the time, the result of the race remains a mystery to this day. Mortimer died in 1914.

Bob closed the book and returned it to the shelf, assuming the great oarsman must have been killed in the First World War. He perched on the end of the bed, considering the information he now possessed. If he could bring Dougie Mortimer's right arm back to Cambridge and present it to the Club at the annual Blues' Dinner, it would surely be a prize that met his father's demanding criterion.

He dressed quickly and went downstairs to the pay phone in the corridor. Once directory enquiries had given him the four numbers he required, he set about trying to remove the next obstacle.

The first calls he made were to the King William — or, to be precise, the King Williams, because the directory had supplied him with the numbers of three pubs in Hull which bore that name. When he was put through to the first, he asked, 'Does Dougie Mortimer's right arm hang above your counter?' He couldn't quite make out every word of the broad northern accent that replied, but he was left in no doubt that it didn't.

The second call was answered by a girl who said, 'Do you mean that thing that's nailed to the wall above the bar?'

'Yes, I guess that will be it,' said Bob.

'Well then, this is the pub you're looking for.'

After Bob had taken down the address and checked the pub's opening hours, he made a third call. 'Yes, that's possible,' he was told. 'You can take the 3.17 to Peterborough, where you'll have to change and catch the 4.09 for Doncaster, then change again. You'll arrive in Hull at 6.32.'

'What about the last train back?' asked Bob.

'8.52, change at Doncaster and Peterborough. You should be back in Cambridge just after midnight.'

'Thank you,' said Bob. He strolled off to his college for lunch and took a place at the large centre table, but proved unusually poor company for those around him.

He boarded the train to Peterborough later that afternoon, still thinking about how he could possibly relieve the pub owners of their prize possession. At Peterborough he jumped out, walked across to a waiting train on platform three and climbed aboard, still deep in thought. When his train pulled into Hull a couple of hours later he was no nearer to solving the problem. He asked the first taxi on the rank to take him to the King William.

'Market Place, Harold's Corner or Percy Street?' asked the cabbie.

'Percy Street, please,' replied Bob.

'They don't open until seven, lad,' the cabbie told him once he had dropped Bob outside the front door.

Bob checked the time. Twenty minutes to kill. He walked down a side street at the back of the pub, and stopped to watch some young lads playing football. They were using the front walls of two houses on either side of the street as goals, and showed amazing accuracy in never hitting any of the windows. Bob wondered if the game would ever catch on in America.

He became so captivated by the youngsters' skill that they stopped to ask him if he wanted to join in. He said, 'No thank you,' confident that if he did play with them, he would be the one person who ended up breaking a window.

He arrived back outside the King William a few minutes after seven, and strolled into the empty pub, hoping that no one would pay much attention to him. But at six feet four inches, and dressed in a double-breasted blue blazer, grey flannels, a blue shirt and college tie, the three people behind the bar might well have wondered if he had dropped in from another planet. He stopped himself from looking above the bar, as a young blonde barmaid stepped forward and asked him what he would like.

'A half a pint of your best bitter,' Bob said, trying to

sound like one of his English friends when they ordered a drink from the college buttery.

The landlord eyed Bob suspiciously as he took his half-pint glass over to a small round table in the corner and sat down quietly on a stool. He was pleased when two other men entered the pub, so that the landlord's attention was distracted.

Bob took a sip of the dark liquid and nearly choked. When he had recovered, he allowed his eyes to glance above the bar. He tried to hide his excitement when he saw the bronze cast of a massive arm embedded in a large piece of varnished wood. He thought the object both dreadful and inspiring at the same time. His eyes moved down to the bold lettering printed in gold beneath it:

D. J. T. MORTIMER
1907–08–09
(ST CATHARINE'S, STROKE)

Bob kept his eye on the landlord as the pub began to fill up, but he soon became aware that it was his wife – everyone called her Nora – who was not only in charge, but who did most of the serving.

When he had finished his drink, he made his way over to her end of the bar.

'What can I do for you, young man?' Nora asked.

'I'll have another, thank you,' said Bob.

'An American,' she said, as she pulled the pump and began to refill his glass. 'We don't get many of you lot up 'ere, at least not since the bases closed.' She placed his half-pint on the counter in front of him. 'So, what brings you to 'ull?'

'You do,' Bob replied, ignoring his drink.

Nora looked suspiciously at the stranger, who was young enough to be her son.

Bob smiled, 'Or, to be more accurate, Dougie Mortimer does.'

'Now I've figured you out,' said Nora. 'You phoned this morning, didn't you? My Christie told me. I should 'ave guessed.'

Bob nodded. 'How did the arm end up in Hull?' he asked.

'Now, that's a long story,' said Nora. 'It was my grandfather's, wasn't it. Born in Ely 'e was, and 'e used to spend his holidays fishin' the Cam. Said it was the only catch he managed that year, which I suppose is one better than sayin' it fell off the back of a lorry. Still, when 'e died a few years back, my father wanted to throw the bloody thing out with the rest of the rubbish, but I wouldn't 'ear of it, told 'im 'e should 'ang it in the pub, didn't I? I cleaned and polished it, it came up real nice, and then I 'ung it above the bar. Still, it's a long way for you to travel just to 'ave a look at that load of old cobblers.'

Bob looked up and admired the arm once again. He held his breath. 'I didn't come just to look.'

'Then why did you come?' she asked.

'I came to buy.'

'Get a move on, Nora,' said the landlord. 'Can't you see there are customers waitin' to be served?'

Nora swung round and said, 'Just 'old your tongue, Cyril Barnsworth. This young man's come all the way up to 'ull just to see Dougie Mortimer's arm, and what's more, 'e wants to buy it.' This caused a ripple of laughter from the regulars standing nearest to the bar, but as Nora didn't join in they quickly fell silent.

'Then it's been a wasted journey, 'asn't it?' said the landlord. 'Because it's not for sale.'

'It's not yours to sell,' said Nora, placing her hands on her hips. 'Mind you, lad, 'e's right,' she said, turning back to face Bob. 'I wouldn't part with it for a 'undred quid,' said Nora. Several others in the room were beginning to show an interest in the proceedings.

'How about two hundred,' said Bob quietly. This time Nora burst out laughing, but Bob didn't even smile.

When Nora had stopped laughing, she stared directly at the strange young man. 'My God, 'e means it,' she said.

'I certainly do,' said Bob. 'I would like to see the arm returned to its rightful home in Cambridge, and I'm willing to pay two hundred pounds for the privilege.'

The landlord looked across at his wife, as if he couldn't believe what he was hearing. 'We could buy that little second-hand car I've had my eye on,' he said.

'Not to mention a summer 'oliday and a new overcoat for next winter,' Nora added, staring at Bob as if she still needed to be convinced that he wasn't from another planet. Suddenly she thrust her hand over the counter and said, 'You've got yourself a deal, young man.'

Bob ended up having to supply several rounds of

drinks for those customers who claimed to have been close personal friends of Nora's grandfather, even if some of them looked rather obviously too young. He also had to stay overnight in a local hotel, because Nora wouldn't part with her grandfather's 'heirloom', as she now kept referring to it, until her bank manager had phoned Cambridge to check that Robert Henry Kefford III was good for two hundred pounds.

Bob clung onto his treasure all the way back to Cambridge that Monday morning, and then lugged the heavy object from the station to his digs in the Grange Road, where he hid it under the bed. The following day he handed it over to a local furniture restorer, who promised to return the arm to its former glory in time for the night of the Blues' Dinner.

When, three weeks later, Bob was allowed to see the results of the restorer's efforts, he immediately felt confident that he now possessed a prize not only worthy of the C.U.B.C., but that also complied with his father's wishes. He resolved not to share his secret with anyone – not even Helen – until the night of the Blues' Dinner, although he did warn the puzzled President that he was going to make a presentation, and that he required two hooks, eighteen inches apart and eight feet from the floor, to be screwed into the wall beforehand.

The University Blues' Dinner is an annual event held in the Boat House overlooking the Cam. Any former or current rowing blue is eligible to attend, and Bob was delighted to find when he arrived that night that it was a near-record turnout. He placed the carefully wrapped brown paper parcel under his chair, and put his camera on the table in front of him.

Because it was his last Blues' Dinner before returning to America, Bob had been seated at the top table, between the Honorary Secretary and the current President of Boats. Tom Adams, the Honorary Secretary, had gained his blue some twenty years before, and was recognised as the club's walking encyclopedia, because he could name not only everyone in the room, but all the great oarsmen of the past.

Tom pointed out to Bob three Olympic medallists dotted around the room. 'The oldest is sitting on the left of the President,' he said. 'Charles Forester. He rowed at number three for the club in 1908–09, so he must be over eighty.'

'Can it be possible?' said Bob, recalling Forester's youthful picture on the clubhouse wall.

'Certainly can,' said the Secretary. 'And what's more, young man,' he added, laughing, 'you'll look like that one day too.'

'What about the man at the far end of the table?' asked Bob. 'He looks even older.'

'He is,' said the Secretary. 'That's Sidney Fisk. He was boatman from 1912 to 1945, with only a break for the First World War. Took over from his uncle at short notice, if I remember correctly.'

'So he would have known Dougie Mortimer,' said Bob wistfully.

'Now, there's a great name from the past,' said Adams. 'Mortimer, D.J.T., 1907–08–09, St Catharine's, stroke. Oh, yes, Fisk would certainly have known Mortimer, that's for sure. Come to think of it, Charles Forester must have been in the same boat as Mortimer when he was stroke.'

During the meal, Bob continued to quiz Adams about Dougie Mortimer, but he was unable to add a great deal to the entry in Bob's *History of the Boat Race*, other than to confirm that Cambridge's defeat in 1909 still remained a mystery, as the light blues demonstrably had the superior crew.

When the last course had been cleared away, the President rose to welcome his guests and to make a short speech. Bob enjoyed the parts he was able to hear above the noise made by the rowdy undergraduates, and even joined in the frenzy whenever Oxford was mentioned. The President ended with the words, 'There will be a special presentation to the club this year, by our colonial stroke Bob Kefford, which I'm sure we're all going to appreciate.'

When Bob rose from his place the cheering became even more raucous, but he spoke so softly that the noise quickly died away. He told his fellow members how he had come to discover, and later retrieve, Dougie Mortimer's right arm, leaving out only his exact location when he first learned of its whereabouts.

With a flourish, he unwrapped the parcel that had been secreted under his chair, and revealed the newly restored bronze cast. The assembled members rose to their feet and cheered. A smile of satisfaction came over Bob's face as he looked around, only wishing his father could have been present to witness their reaction.

As his eyes swept the room, Bob couldn't help noticing that the oldest blue present, Charles Forester, had remained seated, and was not even joining in the applause. Bob's gaze then settled on Sidney Fisk, the only other person who had not risen to his feet. The old boatman's lips remained fixed in a straight line, and his hands didn't move from his knees.

Bob forgot about the two old men when the President, assisted by Tom Adams, hung the bronze arm on the wall, placing it between a blade that had been pulled by one of the Olympic crew of 1908, and a zephyr worn by the only blue ever to row in a Cambridge boat that had beaten Oxford four years in a row. Bob began to take photographs of the ceremony, so that he would have a record to show his father that he had carried out his wishes.

When the hanging was over, many of the members and old blues surrounded Bob to thank and congratulate him, leaving him in no doubt that all the trouble he had taken to track down the arm had been worthwhile.

Bob was among the last to leave that night, because so many members had wanted to wish him good luck for the future. He was strolling along the footpath back to his digs, humming as he went, when he suddenly remembered that he had left his camera on the table. He decided to collect it in the morning, as he was sure that the clubhouse would be locked and deserted by now, but when he turned round to check, he saw a single light coming from the ground floor.

He turned and began walking back towards the clubhouse, still humming. When he was a few paces away, he glanced through the window, and saw that there were two figures standing in the committee room. He strode over to take a closer look, and was surprised to see the elderly blue, Charles Forester, and Sidney Fisk, the retired boatman, trying to shift a heavy table. He would have gone in to assist them if Fisk hadn't suddenly pointed up towards Dougie Mortimer's arm. Bob remained motionless as he watched the two old men drag the table inch by inch nearer to the wall, until it was directly below the plaque.

Fisk picked up a chair and placed it against the wall, and Forester used it as a step to climb onto the table. Forester then bent down and took the arm of the older man, to help him up.

Once they were both safely on the table, they held a short conversation before reaching up to the bronze cast, easing it off its hooks and slowly lowering it until it rested between their feet. Forester, with the help of the chair, stepped back down onto the floor, then turned round to assist his companion again.

Bob still didn't move, as the two old men carried Dougie Mortimer's arm across the room and out of the boathouse. Having placed it on the ground outside the door, Forester returned to switch off the lights. When he stepped back outside into the cold night air, the boatman quickly padlocked the door.

Once again the two old men held a short conversation before lifting Bob's trophy up and stumbling off with it along the towpath. They had to stop, lower the arm to the ground, rest, and start again several times. Bob followed silently in their wake, using the broad-trunked trees to conceal himself, until the elderly pair suddenly turned and made their way down the bank towards the river. They came to a halt at the water's edge, and lowered their bounty into a small rowing boat.

The old blue untied the rope, and the two men pushed the boat slowly out into the river, until the water was lapping around the knees of their evening dress trousers. Neither seemed at all concerned about the fact that they were getting soaked. Forester managed to clamber up into the little boat quite quickly, but it took Fisk several minutes to join him. Once they were both aboard, Forester took his place at the oars, while the boatman remained in the bow, clutching on to Dougie Mortimer's arm.

Forester began to row steadily towards the middle of the river. His progress was slow, but his easy rhythm revealed that he had rowed many times before. When the two men calculated that they had reached the centre of the Cam, at its deepest point, Forester stopped rowing and joined his companion in the bow. They picked up the bronze arm and, without ceremony, cast it over the side and into the river. Bob heard the splash and saw the boat rock dangerously from side to side. Fisk then took his turn at the oars; his progress back to the river-bank was even slower than Forester's. They eventually reached land, and both men stumbled out and shoved the boat up towards its mooring, the boatman finally securing the rope to a large ring.

Soaked and exhausted, their breath rising visibly in the clear night air, the two old men stood and faced each other. They shook hands like two business tycoons who had closed an important deal, before disappearing into the night.

Tom Adams, the Club's Honorary Secretary, rang Bob the following morning to tell him something he already knew. In fact he had lain awake all night thinking of little else.

Bob listened to Adams's account of the break-in. 'What's surprising is that they only took one thing.' He paused. 'Your arm – or rather, Dougie's arm. It's very strange, especially as someone had left an expensive camera on the top table.'

'Is there anything I can do to help?' asked Bob.

'No, I don't think so, old boy,' said Adams. 'The local police are making enquiries, but my bet is that whoever stole the arm will probably be halfway across the county by now.'

'I expect you're right,' said Bob. 'While you're on the line, Mr Adams, I wonder if I could ask you a question about the history of the club.'

'I'll do my best,' said Adams. 'But you must remember that it's only a hobby for me, old chap.'

'Do you by any chance know who is the oldest living

Oxford rowing blue?' There was a long silence the other end of the line. 'Are you still there?' Bob asked eventually.

'Yes. I was just trying to think if old Harold Deering is still alive. I can't remember seeing his obituary in *The Times*.'

'Deering?' said Bob.

'Yes. Radley and Keble, 1909–10–11. He became a bishop, if I remember correctly, but I'm damned if I can recall where.'

'Thank you,' said Bob, 'that's most helpful.'

'I could be wrong,' Adams pointed out. 'After all, I don't read the obituary columns every day. And I'm a bit rusty when it comes to Oxford.'

Bob thanked him once again before ringing off.

After a college lunch he didn't eat, Bob returned to his digs and rang the porter's lodge at Keble. He was answered by a curmudgeonly voice.

'Do you have any record of a Harold Deering, a former member of the college?' Bob asked.

'Deering . . . Deering . . .' said the voice. 'That's a new one on me. Let me see if he's in the college handbook.' Another long pause, during which Bob really did begin to think he'd been cut off, until the voice said, 'Good heavens, no wonder. It was just a bit before my time. Deering, Harold, 1909–11, BA 1911, MA 1916 (Theology). Became Bishop of Truro. Is that the one?'

'Yes, that's the man,' said Bob. 'Do you by any chance have an address for him?'

'I do,' said the voice. 'The Rt Revd Harold Deering,

The Stone House, Mill Road, Tewkesbury, Gloucestershire.'

'Thank you,' said Bob. 'You've been very helpful.'

Bob spent the rest of the afternoon composing a letter to the former bishop, in the hope that the old blue might agree to see him.

He was surprised to receive a call at his digs three days later from a Mrs Elliot, who turned out to be Mr Deering's daughter, with whom he was now living.

'The poor old chap can't see much beyond his nose these days,' she explained, 'so I had to read your letter out to him. But he'd be delighted to meet you, and wonders if you could call on him this Sunday at 11.30, after Matins — assuming that's not inconvenient for you.'

'That's fine,' said Bob. 'Please tell your father to expect me around 11.30.'

'It has to be in the morning,' Mrs Elliot went on to explain, 'because, you see, he has a tendency to fall asleep after lunch. I'm sure you understand. By the way, I'll send directions to your college.'

On the Sunday morning, Bob was up long before the sun rose, and started out on his journey to Tewkesbury in a car he had hired the previous day. He would have gone by train, but British Rail didn't seem willing to rise quite early enough for him to reach his destination on time. As he journeyed across the Cotswolds, he tried to remember to keep the car on the left, and couldn't help wondering how long it would be before the British started to build some highways with more than one lane.

He drove into Tewkesbury a few minutes after eleven, and thanks to Mrs Elliot's clear directions, quickly found The Stone House. He parked the car outside a little wicket gate.

A woman had opened the door of the house even before Bob was halfway up the scrub-covered path. 'It must be Mr Kefford,' she declared. 'I'm Susan Elliot.' Bob smiled and shook her hand. 'I should warn you,' Mrs Elliot explained as she led him towards the front door, 'that you'll have to speak up. Father's become rather deaf lately, and I'm afraid his memory isn't what it used to be. He can recall everything that happened to him at your age, but not even the most simple things that I told him yesterday. I've had to remind him what time you would be coming this morning,' she said as they walked through the open door. 'Three times.'

'I'm sorry to have put you to so much trouble, Mrs Elliot,' said Bob.

'No trouble at all,' said Mrs Elliot as she led him down the corridor. 'The truth is, my father's been rather excited by the thought of an American blue from Cambridge coming to visit him after all these years. He hasn't stopped talking about it for the past two days. He's also curious about why you wanted to see him in the first place,' she added conspiratorially.

She led Bob into the drawing room, where he immediately came face to face with an old man seated in a winged leather chair, wrapped in a warm plaid dressing gown and propped up on several cushions, his legs covered by a tartan blanket. Bob found it hard to believe that this frail figure had once been an Olympic oarsman.

'Is it him?' the old man asked in a loud voice.

'Yes, Father,' Mrs Elliot replied, equally loudly. 'It's Mr Kefford. He's driven over from Cambridge especially to see you.'

Bob walked forward and shook the old man's bony outstretched hand.

'Good of you to come all this way, Kefford,' said the former bishop, pulling his blanket up a little higher.

'I appreciate your seeing me, sir,' said Bob, as Mrs Elliot directed him to a comfortable chair opposite her father.

'Would you care for a cup of tea, Kefford?'

'No, thank you, sir,' said Bob. 'I really don't want anything.'

'As you wish,' said the old man. 'Now, I must warn you, Kefford, that my concentration span isn't quite what it used to be, so you'd better tell me straight away why you've come to see me.'

Bob attempted to marshal his thoughts. 'I'm doing a little research on a Cambridge blue who must have rowed around the same time as you, sir.'

'What's his name?' asked Deering. 'I can't remember them all, you know.'

Bob looked at him, fearing that this was going to turn out to be a wasted journey.

'Mortimer. Dougie Mortimer,' he said.

'D.J.T. Mortimer,' the old man responded without

hesitation. 'Now, there's someone you couldn't easily forget. One of the finest strokes Cambridge ever produced – as Oxford found out, to their cost.' The old man paused. 'You're not a journalist, by any chance?'

'No, sir. It's just a personal whim. I wanted to find out one or two things about him before I return to America.'

'Then I will certainly try to help if I can,' said the old man in a piping voice.

'Thank you,' said Bob. 'I'd actually like to begin at the end, if I may, by asking if you knew the circumstances of his death.'

There was no response for several moments. The old cleric's eyelids closed, and Bob began to wonder if he had fallen asleep.

'Not the sort of thing chaps talked about in my day,' he eventually replied. 'Especially with its being against the law at the time, don't you know.'

'Against the law?' said Bob, puzzled.

'Suicide. A bit silly, when you think about it,' the old priest continued, 'even if it is a mortal sin. Because you can't put someone in jail who's already dead, now can you? Not that it was ever confirmed, you understand.'

'Do you think it might have been connected with Cambridge losing the Boat Race in 1909, when they were such clear favourites?'

'It's possible, I suppose,' said Deering, hesitating once again. 'I must admit, the thought had crossed my mind. I took part in that race, as you may know.' He paused again, breathing heavily. 'Cambridge were the clear favourites, and we didn't give ourselves a chance. The result was never properly explained, I must admit. There were a lot of rumours doing the rounds at the time, but no proof – no proof, you understand.'

'What wasn't proved?' asked Bob. There was another long silence, during which Bob began to fear that the old man might have thought he'd gone too far.

'My turn to ask you a few questions, Kefford,' he said eventually.

'Of course, sir.'

'My daughter tells me that you've stroked the winning boat for Cambridge three years in a row.'

'That's correct, sir.'

'Congratulations, my boy. But tell me: if you had wanted to lose one of those races, could you have done so, without the rest of the crew being aware of it?'

It was Bob's turn to ponder. He realised for the first time since he had entered the room that he shouldn't assume that a frail body necessarily indicates a frail mind.

'Yes, I guess so,' he eventually said. 'You could always change the stroke rate without warning, or even catch a crab as you took the Surrey bend. Heaven knows, there's always enough flotsam on the river to make it appear unavoidable.' Bob looked the old man straight in the eye. 'But it would never have crossed my mind that anyone might do so deliberately.'

'Nor mine,' said the priest, 'had their cox not taken holy orders.'

'I'm not sure I understand, sir,' said Bob.

'No reason you should, young man. I find nowadays

that I think in non sequiturs. I'll try to be less obscure. The cox of the 1909 Cambridge boat was a chap called Bertie Partridge. He went on to become a parish priest in some outpost called Chersfield in Rutland. Probably the only place that would have him,' he chuckled. 'But when I became Bishop of Truro, he wrote and invited me to address his flock. It was such an arduous journey from Cornwall to Rutland in those days, that I could easily have made my excuses, but like you, I wanted the mystery of the 1909 race solved, and I thought this might be my only chance.'

Bob made no attempt to interrupt, fearing he might stop the old man's flow.

'Partridge was a bachelor, and bachelors get very lonely, don't you know. If you give them half a chance, they love to gossip. I stayed overnight, which gave him every chance. He told me, over a long dinner accompanied by a bottle of non-vintage wine, that it was well known that Mortimer had run up debts all over Cambridge. Not many undergraduates don't, you might say, but in Mortimer's case they far exceeded even his potential income. I think he rather hoped that his fame and popularity would stop his creditors from pressing their claims. Not unlike Disraeli when he was Prime Minister,' he added with another chuckle.

'But in Mortimer's case one particular shopkeeper, who had absolutely no interest in rowing, and even less in undergraduates, threatened to bankrupt him the week before the 1909 Boat Race. A few days after the race had been lost, Mortimer seemed, without explanation, to have cleared all his obligations, and nothing more was heard of the matter.'

Once again the old man paused as if in deep thought. Bob remained silent, still not wishing to distract him.

'The only other thing I can recall is that the bookies made a killing,' Deering said without warning. 'I know that to my personal cost, because my tutor lost a five-pound wager, and never let me forget that I had told him we didn't have a snowball's chance in hell. Mind you, I was always able to offer that as my excuse for not getting a First.' He looked up and smiled at his visitor.

Bob sat on the edge of his seat, mesmerised by the old man's recollections.

'I'm grateful for your candour, sir,' he said. 'And you can be assured of my discretion.'

'Thank you, Kefford,' said the old man, now almost whispering. 'I'm only too delighted to have been able to assist you. Is there anything else I can help you with?'

'No, thank you, sir,' said Bob. 'I think you've covered everything I needed to know.'

Bob rose from his chair, and as he turned to thank Mrs Elliot he noticed for the first time a bronze cast of an arm hanging on the far wall. Below it was printed in gold:

H. R. R. DEERING
1909–10–11
(KEBLE, BOW)

'You must have been a fine oarsman, sir.'

'No, not really,' said the old blue. 'But I was lucky enough to be in the winning boat three years in a row, which wouldn't please a Cambridge man like yourself.'

Bob laughed. 'Perhaps one last question before I leave, sir.'

'Of course, Kefford.'

'Did they ever make a bronze of Dougie Mortimer's arm?'

'They most certainly did,' replied the priest. 'But it mysteriously disappeared from your boathouse in 1912. A few weeks later the boatman was sacked without explanation — caused quite a stir at the time.'

'Was it known why he was sacked?' asked Bob.

'Partridge claimed that when the old boatman got drunk one night, he confessed to having dumped Mortimer's arm in the middle of the Cam.' The old man paused, smiled, and added, 'Best place for it, wouldn't you say, Kefford?'

Bob thought about the question for some time, wondering how his father would have reacted. He then replied simply, 'Yes, sir. Best place for it.'

DO NOT PASS GO

Hamid Zebari smiled at the thought of his wife Shereen driving him to the airport. Neither of them would have believed it possible five years before, when they had first arrived in America as political refugees. But since he had begun a new life in the States, Hamid was beginning to think anything might be possible.

'When will you be coming home, Papa?' asked Nadim, who was strapped safely in the back seat next to his sister May. She was too young to understand why Papa was going away.

'Just a fortnight, I promise. No more,' their father replied. 'And when I get back, we'll all go on holiday.'

'How long is a fortnight?' his son demanded.

'Fourteen days,' Hamid told him with a laugh.

'And fourteen nights,' said his wife as she drew into the kerb below the sign for Turkish Airways. She touched a button on the dashboard and the boot flicked up. Hamid jumped out of the car, grabbed his luggage from the boot, and put it on the pavement before climbing into the back of the car. He hugged his daughter first, and then his son. May was crying – not because he was going away, but because she always cried when the car came to a sudden halt. He allowed her to stroke his bushy moustache, which usually stopped the flow of tears.

'Fourteen days,' repeated his son. Hamid hugged his wife, and felt the small swelling of a third child between them.

'We'll be here waiting to pick you up,' Shereen called out as her husband tipped the skycap on the kerb.

Once his six empty cases had been checked in, Hamid disappeared into the terminal, and made his way to the Turkish Airlines desk. As he took the same flight twice a year, he didn't need to ask the girl at the ticket counter for directions.

After he had checked in and been presented with his boarding pass, Hamid still had an hour to wait before they would call his flight. He began the slow trek to Gate B27. It was always the same – the Turkish Airlines plane would be parked halfway back to Manhattan. As he passed the Pan Am check-in desk on B5 he observed that they would be taking off an hour earlier than him, a privilege for those who were willing to pay an extra sixty-three dollars.

When he reached the check-in area, a Turkish Airlines stewardess was slipping the sign for Flight 014, New York–London–Istanbul, onto a board. Estimated time of departure, 10.10.

The seats were beginning to fill up with the usual

cosmopolitan group of passengers: Turks going home to visit their families, those Americans taking a holiday who cared about saving sixty-three dollars, and businessmen whose bottom line was closely watched by tight-fisted accountants.

Hamid strolled over to the restaurant bar and ordered coffee and two eggs sunnyside up, with a side order of hash browns. It was the little things that reminded him daily of his new-found freedom, and of just how much he owed to America.

'Would those passengers travelling to Istanbul with young children please board the plane now,' said the stewardess over the loudspeaker.

Hamid swallowed the last mouthful of his hash browns – he hadn't yet become accustomed to the American habit of covering everything in ketchup – and took a final swig of the weak, tasteless coffee. He couldn't wait to be reunited with the thick Turkish coffee served in small bone china cups. But that was a tiny sacrifice when weighed against the privilege of living in a free land. He settled his bill and left a dollar in the little tin tray.

'Would those passengers seated in rows 35 to 41 please board the aircraft now.'

Hamid picked up his briefcase and headed for the passageway that led to Flight 014. An official from Turkish Airlines checked his boarding pass and ushered him through.

He had been allocated an aisle seat near the back of economy. Ten more trips, he told himself, and he would fly Pan Am Business Class. By then he would be able to afford it.

Whenever the wheels of his plane left the ground, Hamid would look out of the little window and watch his adopted country as it disappeared out of sight, the same thoughts always going through his mind.

It had been nearly five years since Saddam Hussein had dismissed him from the Iraqi Cabinet, after he had held the post of Minister of Agriculture for only two years. The wheat crops had been poor that autumn, and after the People's Army had taken their share, and the middlemen their cut, the Iraqi people ended up with short rations. Someone had to take the blame, and the obvious scapegoat was the Minister of Agriculture. Hamid's father, a carpet dealer, had always wanted him to join the family business, and had even warned him before he died not to accept Agriculture, the last three holders of that office having first been sacked, and later disappeared – and everyone in Iraq knew what 'disappeared' meant. But Hamid did accept the post. The first year's crop had been abundant, and after all, he convinced himself, Agriculture was only a stepping stone to greater things. In any case, had not Saddam described him in front of the whole Revolutionary Command Council as 'my good and close friend'? At thirty-two you still believe you are immortal.

Hamid's father was proved right, and Hamid's only real friend – friends melted away like snow in the morning sun when this particular president sacked you – helped him to escape.

The only precaution Hamid had taken during his days as a Cabinet Minister was to withdraw from his bank account each week a little more cash than he actually needed. He would then change the extra money into American dollars with a street trader, using a different dealer each time, and never exchanging enough to arouse suspicion. In Iraq everyone is a spy.

The day he was sacked, he checked how much was hidden under his mattress. It amounted to eleven thousand two hundred and twenty-one American dollars.

The following Thursday, the day on which the weekend begins in Baghdad, he and his pregnant wife took the bus to Erbil. He left his Mercedes conspicuously parked in the front drive of his large home in the suburbs, and they carried no luggage with them – just two passports, the roll of dollars secreted in his wife's baggy clothing, and some Iraqi dinars to get them as far as the border.

No one would be looking for them on a bus to Erbil.

Once they arrived in Erbil, Hamid and his wife took a taxi to Sulaimania, using most of the remaining dinars to pay the driver. They spent the night in a small hotel far from the city centre. Neither slept as they waited for the morning sun to come shining through the curtainless window.

Next day, another bus took them high into the hills of Kurdistan, arriving in Zakho in the early evening.

The final part of the journey was the slowest of all. They were taken up through the hills on mules, at a cost of two hundred dollars – the young Kurdish smuggler showed no interest in Iraqi dinars. He delivered the former Cabinet Minister and his wife safely over the border in the early hours of the morning, leaving them to make their way on foot to the nearest village on Turkish soil. They reached Kirmizi Renga that evening, and spent another sleepless night at the local station, waiting for the first train for Istanbul.

Hamid and Shereen slept all the way through the long train journey to the Turkish capital, and woke up the following morning as refugees. The first visit Hamid made in the city was to the Iz Bank, where he deposited ten thousand eight hundred dollars. The next was to the American Embassy, where he produced his diplomatic passport and requested political asylum. His father had once told him that a recently sacked Cabinet Minister from Iraq was always a good catch for the Americans.

The Embassy arranged accommodation for Hamid and his wife in a first-class hotel, and immediately informed Washington of their little coup. They promised Hamid that they would get back to him as quickly as possible, but gave him no clue as to how long that might take. He decided to use the time to visit the carpet bazaars on the south side of the city, so often frequented by his father.

Many of the dealers remembered Hamid's father – an honest man who liked to bargain and drink gallons of coffee, and who had often talked about his son going into politics. They were pleased to make his acquaintance, especially when they learned of what he planned to do once he had settled in the States.

The Zebaris were granted American visas within the week and flown to Washington at the government's expense, which included a charge for excess baggage of twenty-three Turkish carpets.

After five days of intensive questioning by the CIA, Hamid was thanked for his co-operation and the useful information he had supplied. He was then released to begin his new life in America. He, his pregnant wife and the twenty-three carpets boarded a train for New York.

It took Hamid six weeks to find the right shop, on the Lower East Side of Manhattan, from which to sell his carpets. Once he had signed the five-year lease, Shereen immediately set about painting their new Americanised name above the door.

Hamid didn't sell his first carpet for nearly three months, by which time his meagre savings had all but disappeared. But by the end of the first year, sixteen of the twenty-three carpets had been sold, and he realised he would soon have to travel back to Istanbul to buy more stock.

Four years had passed since then, and the Zebaris had recently moved to a larger establishment on the West Side, with a small apartment above the shop. Hamid kept telling his wife that this was only the beginning, that anything was possible in the United States. He now considered himself a fully-fledged American citizen, and not just because of the treasured blue passport that confirmed his status. He accepted that he could never return to his birthplace while Saddam remained its ruler. His home and possessions had long ago been requisitioned by the Iraqi state, and the death sentence had been passed on him in his absence. He doubted if he would ever see Baghdad again.

After the stopover in London, the plane landed at Istanbul's Ataturk Airport a few minutes ahead of schedule. Hamid booked into his usual small hotel, and planned how best to allocate his time over the next two weeks. He was happy to be back among the hustle and bustle of the Turkish capital.

There were thirty-one dealers he wanted to visit, because this time he hoped to return to New York with at least sixty carpets. That would require fourteen days of drinking thick Turkish coffee, and many hours of bargaining, as a dealer's opening price would be three times as much as Hamid was willing to pay – or what the dealer really expected to receive. But there was no short cut in the bartering process, which – like his father – Hamid secretly enjoyed.

By the end of the fortnight, Hamid had purchased fifty-seven carpets, at a cost of a little over twenty-one thousand dollars. He had been careful to select only those carpets that would be sought after by the most discerning New Yorkers, and he was confident that this latest batch would fetch almost a hundred thousand dollars in America. It had been such a successful trip that Hamid felt he would indulge himself by taking the earlier Pan Am flight back to New York. After all, he had undoubtedly earned himself the extra sixty-three dollars many times over in the course of his trip.

He was looking forward to seeing Shereen and the

children even before the plane had taken off, and the American flight attendant with her pronounced New York accent and friendly smile only added to the feeling that he was already home. After lunch had been served, and having decided he didn't want to watch the in-flight movie, Hamid dozed off and dreamt about what he could achieve in America, given time. Perhaps his son would go into politics. Would the United States be ready for an Iraqi President by the year 2025? He smiled at the thought, and fell contentedly into a deep sleep.

'Ladies and gentlemen,' a deep Southern voice boomed out over the intercom, 'this is your captain. I'm sorry to interrupt the movie, or to wake those of you who've been resting, but we've developed a small problem in an engine on our starboard wing. Nothing to worry about, folks, but Federal Aviation Authority rulings insist that we land at the nearest airport and have the problem dealt with before we continue with our journey. It shouldn't take us more than an hour at the most, and then we'll be on our way again. You can be sure that we'll try to make up as much of the lost time as possible, folks.'

Hamid was suddenly wide awake.

'We won't be disembarking from the aircraft at any time, as this is an unscheduled stop. However, you'll be able to tell the folks back home that you've visited Baghdad.'

Hamid felt his whole body go limp, and then his head rocked forward. The flight attendant rushed up to his side.

'Are you feeling all right, sir?' she asked.

He looked up and stared into her eyes. 'I must see the captain immediately. Immediately.'

The flight attendant was in no doubt of the passenger's anxiety, and quickly led him forward, up the spiral staircase into the first-class lounge and onto the flight deck.

She tapped on the door of the cockpit, opened it and said, 'Captain, one of the passengers needs to speak to you urgently.'

'Show him in,' said the Southern voice. The captain turned to face Hamid, who was now trembling uncontrollably. 'How can I be of help, sir?' he asked.

'My name is Hamid Zebari. I am an American citizen,' he began. 'If you land in Baghdad, I will be arrested, tortured and then executed.' The words tumbled out. 'I am a political refugee, and you must understand that the regime will not hesitate to kill me.'

The captain only needed to take one look at Hamid to realise he wasn't exaggerating.

'Take over, Jim,' he said to his co-pilot, 'while I have a word with Mr Zebari. Call me the moment we've been given clearance to land.'

The captain unfastened his seatbelt, and led Hamid to an empty corner of the first-class lounge.

'Take me through it slowly,' he said.

During the next few minutes Hamid explained why he had had to leave Baghdad, and how he came to be living in America. When he had reached the end of his story the captain shook his head and smiled. 'No need to panic, sir,' he assured Hamid. 'No one is going to have to leave the aircraft at any time, so the passengers'

146

passports won't even be checked. Once the engine has been attended to, we'll be back up and on our way immediately. Why don't you just stay here in first class, then you'll be able to speak to me at any time, should you feel at all anxious.'

How anxious can you feel? Hamid wondered, as the captain left him to have a word with the co-pilot. He started to tremble once more.

'It's the captain once again, folks, just bringing you up to date. We've been given clearance by Baghdad, so we've begun our descent and expect to land in about twenty minutes. We'll then be taxiing to the far end of the runway, where we'll await the engineers. Just as soon as they've dealt with our little problem, we'll be back up and on our way again.'

A collective sigh went up, while Hamid gripped the armrest and wished he hadn't eaten any lunch. He didn't stop shaking for the next twenty minutes, and almost fainted when the wheels touched down on the land of his birth.

He stared out of the porthole as the aircraft taxied past the terminal he knew so well. He could see the armed guards stationed on the roof and at the doors leading onto the tarmac. He prayed to Allah, he prayed to Jesus, he even prayed to President Reagan.

For the next fifteen minutes the silence was broken only by the sound of a van driving across the tarmac and coming to a halt under the starboard wing of the aircraft.

Hamid watched as two engineers carrying bulky

toolbags got out of the van, stepped onto a small crane and were hoisted up until they were level with the wing. They began unscrewing the outer plates of one of the engines. Forty minutes later they screwed the plates back on and were lowered to the ground. The van then headed off towards the terminal.

Hamid felt relieved, if not exactly relaxed. He fastened his seatbelt hopefully. His heartbeat fell from 180 a minute to around 110, but he knew it wouldn't return to normal until the plane lifted off and he could be sure they wouldn't turn back. Nothing happened for the next few minutes, and Hamid became anxious again. Then the door of the cockpit opened, and he saw the captain heading towards him, a grim expression on his face.

'You'd better join us on the flight deck,' the captain said in a whisper. Hamid undid his seatbelt and somehow managed to stand. He unsteadily followed the captain into the cockpit, his legs feeling like jelly. The door was closed behind them.

The captain didn't waste any words. 'The engineers can't locate the problem. The chief engineer won't be free for another hour, so we've been ordered to disembark and wait in the transit area until he's completed the job.'

'I'd rather die in a plane crash,' Hamid blurted out.

'Don't worry, Mr Zebari, we've thought of a way round your problem. We're going to put you in a spare uniform. That will make it possible for you to stay with us the whole time, and use the crew's facilities. No one will ask to see your passport.'

'But if someone recognises me . . .' began Hamid.

'Once you've got rid of that moustache, and you're wearing a flight officer's uniform, dark glasses and a peaked hat, your own mother wouldn't know you.'

With the help of scissors, followed by shaving foam, followed by a razor, Hamid removed the bushy moustache that he had been so proud of, to leave an upper lip that looked as pale as a blob of vanilla ice cream. The senior flight attendant applied some of her make-up to his skin, until the white patch blended in with the rest of his face. Hamid still wasn't convinced, but after he had changed into the co-pilot's spare uniform and studied himself in the toilet mirror, he had to admit that it would indeed be remarkable if anyone recognised him.

The passengers were the first to leave the plane, and were ferried by an airport bus to the main terminal. A smart transit van then came out to collect the crew, who left as a group and sheltered Hamid by making sure that he was surrounded at all times. Hamid became more and more nervous with each yard the van travelled towards the terminal.

The security guard showed no particular interest in the air crew as they entered the building, and they were left to find themselves seats on wooden benches in the white-walled hall. The only decoration was a massive portrait of Saddam Hussein in full uniform carrying a kalashnikov rifle. Hamid couldn't bring himself to look at the picture of his 'good and close friend'.

Another crew was also sitting around waiting to board

their aircraft, but Hamid was too frightened to start up a conversation with any of them.

'They're French,' he was informed by the senior flight attendant. 'I'm about to find out if my night classes were worth all the expense.' She took the spare place next to the captain of the French aircraft, and tried a simple opening question.

The French captain was telling her that they were bound for Singapore via New Delhi, when Hamid saw him: Saad al-Takriti, once a member of Saddam's personal guard, marched into the hall. From the insignia on his shoulder, he now appeared to be in charge of airport security.

Hamid prayed that he wouldn't look in his direction. Al-Takriti sauntered through the room, glancing at the French and American crews, his eyes lingering on the stewardesses' black-stockinged legs.

The captain touched Hamid on the shoulder, and he nearly leapt out of his skin.

'It's OK, it's OK. I just thought you'd like to know that the chief engineer is on his way out to the aircraft, so it shouldn't be too long now.'

Hamid looked beyond the Air France plane, and watched a van come to a halt under the starboard wing of the Pan Am aircraft. A man in blue overalls stepped out of the vehicle and onto the little crane.

Hamid stood up to take a closer look, and as he did so Saad al-Takriti walked back into the hall. He came to a sudden halt, and the two men stared briefly at each other, before Hamid quickly resumed his place next to the captain. Al-Takriti disappeared into a side room marked 'Do Not Enter'.

'I think he's spotted me,' said Hamid. The make-up started to run down onto his lips.

The captain leant across to his chief flight attendant and interrupted her parley with the French captain. She listened to her boss's instructions, and then tried a tougher question on the Frenchman.

Saad al-Takriti marched back out of the office and began striding towards the American captain. Hamid thought he would surely faint.

Without even glancing at Hamid, al-Takriti barked, 'Captain, I require you to show me your manifest, the number of crew you are carrying, and their passports.'

'My co-pilot has all the passports,' the captain replied. 'I'll see you get them.'

'Thank you,' said al-Takriti. 'When you have collected them, you will bring them to my office so that I can check each one. Meanwhile, please ask your crew to remain here. They are not, under any circumstances, to leave the building without my permission.'

The captain rose from his place, walked slowly over to the co-pilot, and asked for the passports. Then he issued an order which took him by surprise. The captain took the passports into the security office just as a bus drew up outside the transit area to take the French crew back to their plane.

Saad al-Takriti placed the fourteen passports in front of him on his desk. He seemed to take pleasure in checking each one of them slowly. When he had finished the task, he announced in mock surprise, 'I do believe, captain, that I counted fifteen crew wearing Pan Am uniforms.'

'You must have been mistaken,' said the captain. 'There are only fourteen of us.'

'Then I will have to make a more detailed check, won't I, captain? Please return these documents to their rightful owners. Should there happen to be anyone not in possession of a passport, they will naturally have to report to me.'

'But that is against international regulations,' said the captain, 'as I'm sure you know. We are in transit, and therefore, under UN Resolution 238, not legally in your country.'

'Save your breath, captain. We have no use for UN resolutions in Iraq. And, as you correctly point out, as far as we are concerned, you are not legally even in our country.'

The captain realised he was wasting his time, and could bluff no longer. He gathered up the passports as slowly as he could and allowed al-Takriti to lead him back into the hall. As they entered the room the Pan Am crew members who were scattered around the benches suddenly rose from their places and began walking about, continually changing direction, while at the same time talking at the top of their voices.

'Tell them to sit down,' hissed al-Takriti, as the crew zig-zagged backwards and forwards across the hall.

'What's that you're saying?' asked the captain, cupping his ear.

.'Tell them to sit down!' shouted al-Takriti.

The captain gave a half-hearted order, and within a few moments everyone was seated. But they still continued talking at the top of their voices.

'And tell them to shut up!'

The captain moved slowly round the room, asking his crew one by one to lower their voices.

Al-Takriti's eyes raked the benches of the transit hall, as the captain glanced out onto the tarmac and watched the French aircraft taxiing towards the far runway.

Al-Takriti began counting, and was annoyed to discover that there were only fourteen Pan Am crew members in the hall. He stared angrily around the room, and quickly checked once again.

'All fourteen seem to be present,' said the captain after he had finished handing back the passports to his crew.

'Where is the man who was sitting next to you?' al-Takriti demanded, jabbing a finger at the captain.

'You mean my first officer?'

'No. The one who looked like an Arab.'

'There are no Arabs on my crew,' the captain assured him.

Al-Takriti strode over to the senior flight attendant. 'He was sitting next to you. His upper lip had make-up on it that was beginning to run.'

'The captain of the French plane was sitting next to me,' the senior flight attendant said. She immediately realised her mistake.

Saad al-Takriti turned and looked out of the window

to see the Air France plane at the end of the runway preparing for take-off. He jabbed a button on his hand phone as the thrust of the jet engines started up, and barked out some orders in his native tongue. The captain didn't need to speak Arabic to get the gist of what he was saying.

By now the American crew were all staring at the French aircraft, willing it to move, while al-Takriti's voice was rising with every word he uttered.

The Air France 747 eased forward and slowly began to gather momentum. Saad al-Takriti cursed loudly, then ran out of the building and jumped into a waiting jeep. He pointed towards the plane and ordered the driver to chase after it. The jeep shot off, accelerating as it weaved its way in and out of the parked aircraft. By the time it reached the runway it must have been doing ninety miles an hour, and for the next hundred yards it sped along parallel to the French aircraft, with al-Takriti standing on the front seat, clinging onto the windscreen and waving his fist at the cockpit.

The French captain acknowledged him with a crisp salute, and as the 747's wheels lifted off, a loud cheer went up in the transit lounge.

The American captain smiled and turned to his chief flight attendant. 'That only proves my theory that the French will go to any lengths to get an extra passenger.'

Hamid Zebari landed in New Delhi six hours later, and immediately phoned his wife to let her know what had happened. Early the next morning Pan Am flew him back to New York – first class. When Hamid emerged from the airport terminal, his wife jumped out of the car and threw her arms around him.

Nadim wound the window down and declared, 'You were wrong, Papa. A fortnight turns out to be fifteen days.' Hamid grinned at his son, but his daughter burst into tears, and not because their car had come to a sudden halt. It was just that she was horrified to see her mother hugging a strange man.

HURRICANE VISION.

CHUNNEL VISION

WHENEVER I'M IN NEW YORK, I ALWAYS try to have dinner with an old friend of mine called Duncan McPherson. We are opposites, and so naturally we attract. In fact, Duncan and I have only one thing in common: we are both writers. But even then there's a difference, because Duncan specialises in screenplays, which he writes in the intervals between his occasional articles for *Newsweek* and the *New Yorker*, whereas I prefer novels and short stories.

One of the other differences between us is the fact that I have been married to the same woman for twenty-eight years, while Duncan seems to have a different girlfriend every time I visit New York – not bad going, as I average at least a couple of trips a year. The girls are always attractive, lively and bright, and there are various levels of intensity – depending on what stage the relation-ship is at. In the past I've been around at the beginning (very physical) and in the middle (starting to cool off), but this trip was to be the first time I experienced an ending.

I phoned Duncan from my hotel on Fifth Avenue to let him know I was in town to promote my new novel, and he immediately asked me over for dinner the following evening. I assumed, as in the past, that it would be at his apartment. Another opposite: unlike me, he's a quite superlative cook.

'I can't wait to see you,' he said. 'I've come up with an idea for a novel at last, and I want to try the plot out on you.'

'Delighted,' I replied. 'Look forward to hearing all about it tomorrow night. And may I ask . . .' I hesitated.

'Christabel,' he said.

'Christabel . . .' I repeated, trying to recall if I had ever met her.

'But there's no need for you to remember anything about her,' he added. 'Because she's about to be given the heave-ho, to use one of your English expressions. I've just met a new one – Karen. She's absolutely sensational. You'll adore her.'

I didn't feel this was the appropriate moment to point out to Duncan that I had adored them all. I merely asked which one was likely to be joining us for dinner.

'Depends if Christabel has finished packing,' Duncan replied. 'If she has, it will be Karen. We haven't slept together yet, and I'd been planning on that for tomorrow night. But as you're in town, it will have to be postponed.'

I laughed. 'I could wait,' I assured him. 'After all, I'm here for at least a week.'

'No, no. In any case, I must tell you about my idea for a novel. That's far more important. So why don't you come to my place tomorrow evening. Shall we say around seven thirty?'

Before I left the hotel, I wrapped up a copy of my latest book, and wrote 'Hope you enjoy it' on the outside.

Duncan lives in one of those apartment blocks on 72nd and Park, and though I've been there many times, it always takes me a few minutes to locate the entrance to the building. And, like Duncan's girlfriends, the door-man seems to change with every trip.

The new doorman grunted when I gave my name, and directed me to the elevator on the far side of the hall. I slid the grille doors across and pressed the button for the fourteenth floor. It was one of those top floors that could not be described as a penthouse even by the most imaginative of estate agents.

I pulled back the doors and stepped out onto the land-ing, rehearsing the appropriate smiles for Christabel (goodbye) and Karen (hello). As I walked towards Duncan's front door I could hear raised voices – a very British expression, born of understatement; let's be frank and admit that they were screaming at each other at the tops of their voices. I concluded that this had to be the end of Christabel, rather than the beginning of Karen.

I was already a few minutes late, so there was no turning back. I pressed the doorbell, and to my relief the voices immediately fell silent. Duncan opened the door, and although his cheeks were scarlet with rage, he still managed a casual grin. Which reminds me that I forgot to tell you about a few more opposites – the damn man has a mop of boyish dark curly hair, the rugged features of his Irish ancestors, and the build of a champion tennis player.

'Come on in,' he said. 'This is Christabel, by the way – if you hadn't already guessed.'

I'm not by nature a man who likes other people's cast-offs, but I'm bound to confess I would have been happy to make Christabel the exception. She had an oval face, deep blue eyes, and an angelic smile. She was also graced with that fine fair hair that only the Nordic races are born with, and the type of figure that slimming advertisements make their profits out of. She wore a cashmere sweater and tapered white jeans that left little to the imagination.

Christabel shook me by the hand, and apologised for looking a little scruffy. 'I've been packing all afternoon,' she explained.

The proof of her labours was there for all to see – three large suitcases and two cardboard boxes full of books standing by the door. On the top of one of the boxes lay a copy of a Dorothy L. Sayers murder mystery with a torn red dustjacket.

I was becoming acutely aware that I couldn't have chosen a worse evening for a reunion with my old friend. 'I'm afraid we're going to have to eat out for a change,' Duncan said. 'It's been' – he paused – 'a busy day. I haven't had a chance to visit the local store. Good thing, actually,' he added. 'It'll give me more time to take you through the plot of my novel.'

'Congratulations,' Christabel said.

I turned to face her.

'*Your* novel,' she said. 'Number one on the *New York Times* bestseller list, isn't it?'

'Yes, congratulations,' said Duncan. 'I haven't got round to reading it yet, so don't tell me anything about it. It wasn't on sale in Bosnia,' he added with a laugh.

I handed him my little gift.

'Thank you,' he said, and placed it on the hall table. 'I'll look forward to it.'

'I've read it,' said Christabel.

Duncan bit his lip. 'Let's go,' he said, and was about to turn and say goodbye to Christabel when she asked me, 'Would you mind if I joined you? I'm starving, and as Duncan said, there's absolutely nothing in the icebox.'

I could see that Duncan was about to protest, but by then Christabel had passed him, and was already in the corridor and heading for the elevator.

'We can walk to the restaurant,' Duncan said as we trundled down to the ground floor. 'It's only Californians who need a car to take them one block.'

As we strolled west on 72nd Street Duncan told me that he had chosen a fancy new French restaurant to take me to.

I began to protest, not just because I've never really cared for ornate French food, but I was also aware of Duncan's unpredictable pecuniary circumstances. Sometimes he was flush with money, at other times stony broke. I just hoped that he'd had an advance on the novel.

'No, like you, I normally wouldn't bother,' he said. 'But it's only just opened, and the *New York Times* gave it a rave review. In any case, whenever I'm in London, you always entertain me "right royally",' he added, in what he imagined was an English accent.

It was one of those cool evenings that make walking in New York so pleasant, and I enjoyed the stroll, as Duncan began to tell me about his recent trip to Bosnia.

'You were lucky to catch me in New York,' he was saying. 'I've only just got back after being holed up in the damned place for three months.'

'Yes, I know. I read your article in *Newsweek* on the plane coming over,' I said, and went on to tell him how fascinated I had been by his evidence that a group of UN soldiers had set up their own underground network, and felt no scruples about operating an illegal black market in whatever country they were stationed.

'Yes, that's caused quite a stir at the UN,' said Duncan. 'The *New York Times* and the *Washington Post* have both followed the story up with features on the main culprits – but without bothering to give me any credit for the original research, of course.'

I turned round to see if Christabel was still with us. She seemed to be deep in thought, and was lagging a few paces behind. I smiled a smile that I hoped said I think Duncan's a fool and you're fantastic, but I received no response.

After a few more yards I spotted a red and gold awning flapping in the breeze outside something called 'Le Manoir'. My heart sank. I've always preferred simple

food, and have long considered pretentious French cuisine to be one of the major cons of the eighties, and
one that should have been passé, if not part of culinary
history, by the nineties.

Duncan led us down a short crazy-paving path
through a heavy oak door and into a brightly lit restaurant. One look around the large, over-decorated room
and my worst fears were confirmed. The maître d'
stepped forward and said, 'Good evening, monsieur.'

'Good evening,' replied Duncan. 'I have a table
reserved in the name of McPherson.'

The maître d' checked down a long list of bookings.
'Ah, yes, a table for two.' Christabel pouted, but looked
no less beautiful.

'Can we make it three?' my host asked rather half-
heartedly.

'Of course, sir. Allow me to show you to your table.'

We were guided through a crowded room to a little
alcove in the corner which had only been set for two.

One look at the tablecloth, the massive flowered plates
with 'Le Manoir' painted in crimson all over them, and
the arrangement of lilies on the centre of the table, made
me feel even more guilty about what I had let Duncan
in for. A waiter dressed in a white open-neck shirt, black
trousers and black waistcoat with 'Le Manoir' sewn in
red on the breast pocket hurriedly supplied Christabel
with a chair, while another deftly laid a place for her.

A third waiter appeared at Duncan's side and enquired
if we would care for an aperitif. Christabel smiled sweetly
and asked if she might have a glass of champagne. I

requested some Evian water, and Duncan nodded that he would have the same.

For the next few minutes, while we waited for the menus to appear, we continued to discuss Duncan's trip to Bosnia, and the contrast between scraping one's food out of a billycan in a cold dugout accompanied by the sound of bullets, and dining off china plates in a warm restaurant, with a string quartet playing Schubert in the background.

Another waiter appeared at Duncan's side and handed us three pink menus the size of small posters. As I glanced down the list of dishes, Christabel whispered something to the waiter, who nodded and slipped quietly away.

I began to study the menu more carefully, unhappy to discover that this was one of those restaurants which allows only the host to have the bill of fare with the prices attached. I was trying to work out which would be the cheapest dishes, when another glass of champagne was placed at Christabel's side.

I decided that the clear soup was likely to be the least expensive starter, and that it would also help my feeble efforts to lose weight. The main courses had me more perplexed, and with my limited knowledge of French I finally settled on duck, as I couldn't find any sign of 'poulet'.

When the waiter returned moments later, he immediately spotted Christabel's empty glass, and asked, 'Would you care for another glass of champagne, madame?'

'Yes, please,' she replied sweetly, as the maître d' arrived to take our order. But first we had to suffer an ordeal that nowadays can be expected at every French restaurant in the world.

'Today our specialities are,' he began, in an accent that would not have impressed central casting, 'for hors d'oeuvres *Gelée de saumon sauvage et caviar impérial en aigre doux*, which is wild salmon slivers and imperial caviar in a delicate jelly with sour cream and courgettes soused in dill vinegar. Also we have *Cuisses de grenouilles à la purée d'herbes à soupe, fricassée de chanterelles et racines de persil*, which are pan-fried frogs' legs in a parsley purée, fricassee of chanterelles and parsley roots. For the main course we have *Escalope de turbot*, which is a poached fillet of turbot on a watercress purée, lemon sabayon and a Gewürztraminer sauce. And, of course, everything that is on the menu can be recommended.'

I felt full even before he had finished the descriptions.

Christabel appeared to be studying the menu with due diligence. She pointed to one of the dishes, and the maître d' smiled approvingly.

Duncan leaned across and asked if I had selected anything yet.

'Consommé and the duck will suit me just fine,' I said without hesitation.

'Thank you, sir,' said the maître d'. 'How would you like the duck? Crispy, or perhaps a little underdone?'

'Crispy,' I replied, to his evident disapproval.

'And monsieur?' he asked, turning to Duncan.

'Caesar salad and a rare steak.'

The maître d' retrieved the menus and was turning to go as Duncan said, 'Now, let me tell you all about my idea for a novel.'

'Would you care to order some wine, sir?' asked another waiter, who was carrying a large red leather book with golden grapes embossed on its cover.

'Should I do that for you?' suggested Christabel. 'Then there'll be no need to interrupt your story.'

Duncan nodded his agreement, and the waiter handed the wine list over to Christabel. She opened the red leather cover with as much eagerness as if she was about to begin a bestselling novel.

'You may be surprised,' Duncan was saying, 'that my book is set in Britain. Let me start by explaining that the timing for its publication is absolutely vital. As you know, a British and French consortium is currently building a tunnel between Folkestone and Sangatte, which is scheduled to be opened by Queen Elizabeth on 6 May 1994. In fact, *Chunnel* will be the title of my book.'

I was horrified. Another glass of champagne was placed in front of Christabel.

'The story begins in four separate locations, with four different sets of characters. Although they are all from diverse age groups, social backgrounds and countries, they have one thing in common: they have all booked on the first passenger train to travel from London to Paris via the Channel Tunnel.'

I felt a sudden pang of guilt, and wondered if I should say something, but at this point a waiter returned with a bottle of white wine, the label of which Christabel studied intently. She nodded, and the sommelier extracted the cork and poured a little into her empty glass. A sip brought the smile back to her lips. The waiter then filled our glasses.

Duncan continued: 'There will be an American family – mother, father, two teenage children – on their first visit to England; a young English couple who have just got married that morning and are about to begin their honeymoon; a Greek self-made millionaire and his French wife who booked their tickets a year before, but are now considering a divorce; and three students.'

Duncan paused as a Caesar salad was placed in front of him and a second waiter presented me with a bowl of consommé. I glanced at the dish Christabel had chosen. A plate of thinly cut smoked gravadlax with a blob of caviar in the centre. She was happily squeezing half a lemon, protected by muslin, all over it.

'Now,' said Duncan, 'in the first chapter it's important that the reader doesn't realise that the students are connected in any way, as that later becomes central to the plot. We pick up all four groups in the second chapter as they're preparing for the journey. The reader discovers their motivations for wanting to be on the train, and I build a little on the background of each of the characters involved.'

'What period of time will the plot cover?' I asked anxiously, between spoonfuls of consommé.

'Probably three days,' replied Duncan. 'The day before the journey, the day of the journey, and the day after.

But I'm still not certain – by the final draft it might all happen on the same day.'

Christabel grabbed the wine bottle from the ice-bucket and refilled her glass before the wine waiter had a chance to assist her.

'Around chapter three,' continued Duncan, 'we find the various groups arriving at Waterloo station to board "le shuttle". The Greek millionaire and his French wife will be shown to their first-class seats by a black crew member, while the others are directed to second class. Once they are all on board, some sort of ceremony to commemorate the inauguration of the tunnel will take place on the platform. Big band, fireworks, cutting of tape by royalty etc. That should prove quite adequate to cover another chapter at least.'

While I was visualising the scene and sipping my soup – the restaurant may have been pretentious, but the food was excellent – the wine waiter filled my glass and then Duncan's. I don't normally care for white wine, but I had to admit that this one was quite exceptional.

Duncan paused to eat, and I turned my attention to Christabel, who was being served a second dollop of caviar that appeared even bigger than the first.

'Chapter five,' said Duncan, 'opens as the train moves out of the station. Now the real action begins. The American family are enjoying every moment. The young bride and groom make love in the rest room. The millionaire is having another row with his wife about her continual extravagance, and the three students have met up for the first time at the bar. By now you should begin to suspect that they're not ordinary students, and that they may have known each other before they got on the train.' Duncan smiled and continued with his salad. I frowned.

Christabel winked at me, to show she knew exactly what was going on. I felt guilty at being made a part of her conspiracy, and wanted to tell Duncan what she was up to.

'It's certainly a strong plot,' I ventured as the wine waiter filled our glasses for a third time and, having managed to empty the bottle, looked towards Madame. She nodded sweetly.

'Have you started on the research yet?' I asked.

'Yes. Research is going to be the key to this project, and I'm well into it already,' said Duncan. 'I wrote to Sir Alastair Morton, the Chairman of Eurotunnel, on *Newsweek* headed paper, and his office sent me back a caseload of material. I can tell you the length of the rolling stock, the number of carriages, the diameter of the wheels, why the train can go faster on the French side than the British, even why it's necessary for them to have a different-gauge track on either side of the Channel . . .'

The pop of a cork startled me, and the wine waiter began pouring from a second bottle. Should I tell him now?

'During chapter six the plot begins to unfold,' said Duncan, warming to his theme, as one of the waiters whipped away the empty plates and another brushed a few breadcrumbs off the tablecloth into a little silver scoop. 'The trick is to keep the reader interested in all four groups at the same time.'

I nodded.

'Now we come to the point in the story when the reader discovers that the students are not really students, but terrorists, who plan to hijack the train.'

Three dishes topped by domed silver salvers were placed in front of us. On a nod from the maître d', all three domes were lifted in unison by the waiters. It would be churlish of me not to admit that the food looked quite magnificent. I turned to see what Christabel had selected: truffles with foie gras. They reminded me of a Miró painting, until she quickly smudged the canvas.

'What do you think the terrorists' motive for hijacking the train should be?' Duncan asked.

This was surely the moment to tell him – but once again I funked it. I tried to remember what point in the story we had reached. 'That would depend on whether you eventually wanted them to escape,' I suggested. 'Which might prove quite difficult, if they're stuck in the middle of a tunnel, with a police force waiting for them at either end.' The wine waiter presented Christabel with the bottle of claret she had chosen. After no more than a sniff of the cork she indicated that it was acceptable.

'I don't think they should be interested in financial reward,' said Duncan. 'They ought to be IRA, Islamic fundamentalists, Basque separatists, or whatever the latest terrorist group catching the headlines happens to be.'

I sipped the wine. It was like velvet. I had only tasted such a vintage once before, in the home of a friend who possessed a cellar of old wine put down with new money. It was a taste that had remained etched in my memory.

'In chapter seven I've come up against a block,' continued Duncan, intent on his theme. 'One of the terrorists must somehow come into contact with the newly-married couple, or at least with the bridegroom.' He paused. 'I should have told you earlier that in the character-building at the beginning of the book, one of the students turns out to be a loner, while the other two, a man and a woman, have been living together for some time.' He began digging into his steak. 'It's how I bring the loner and the bridegroom together that worries me. Any ideas?'

'That shouldn't be too hard,' I said, 'what with restaurant cars, snack bars, carriages, a corridor, not to mention a black crew member, railway staff and rest rooms.'

'Yes, but it must appear natural,' Duncan said, sounding as if he was in deep thought.

My heart sank as I noticed Christabel's empty plate being whisked away, despite the fact that Duncan and I had hardly begun our main courses.

'The chapter ends with the train suddenly coming to a halt about halfway through the tunnel,' said Duncan, staring into the distance.

'But how? And why?' I asked.

'That's the whole point. It's a false alarm. Quite innocent. The youngest child of the American family – his name's Ben – pulls the communication cord while he's sitting on the lavatory. It's such a hi-tech lavatory that he mistakes it for the chain.'

I was considering if this was plausible when a breast of quail on fondant potatoes with a garnish of smoked bacon was placed in front of Christabel. She wasted no time in attacking the fowl.

Duncan paused to take a sip of wine. Now, I felt, I had to let him know, but before I had a chance to say anything he was off again. 'Right,' he said. 'Chapter eight. The train has come to a halt several miles inside the tunnel, but not quite halfway.'

'Is that significant?' I asked feebly.

'Sure is,' said Duncan. 'The French and British have agreed the exact point inside the tunnel where French jurisdiction begins and British ends. As you'll discover, this becomes relevant later in the plot.'

The waiter began moving round the table, topping up our glasses once again with claret. I placed a hand over mine – not because the wine wasn't pure nectar, but simply because I didn't wish to give Christabel the opportunity to order another bottle. She made no attempt to exercise the same restraint, but drank her wine in generous gulps, while toying with her quail. Duncan continued with his story.

'So, the hold-up,' said Duncan, 'turns out to be nothing more than a diversion, and it's sorted out fairly quickly. Child in tears, family apologises, explanation given by the guard over the train's intercom, which relieves any anxieties the passengers might have had. A few minutes later, the train starts up again, and this time it does cross the halfway point.'

Three waiters removed our empty plates. Christabel touched the side of her lips with a napkin, and gave me a huge grin.

'So then what happens?' I asked, avoiding her eye.

'When the train stopped, the terrorists were afraid that there might be a rival group on board, with the same purpose as them. But as soon as they find out what has actually happened, they take advantage of the commotion caused by young Ben to get themselves into the cabin next to the driver's.'

'Would you care for anything from the dessert trolley, madame?' the maître d' asked Christabel. I looked on aghast as she was helped to what looked like a large spoonful of everything on offer.

'It's gripping, isn't it?' said Duncan, misunderstanding my expression for one of deep concern for those on the train. 'But there's still more to come.'

'Monsieur?'

'I'm full, thank you,' I told the maitre d'. 'Perhaps a coffee later.'

'No, nothing, thank you,' said Duncan, trying not to lose his thread. 'By the start of chapter nine the terrorists have got themselves into the driver's cabin. At gunpoint they force the chef de train and his co-driver to bring the engine to a halt for a second time. But what they don't realise is that they are now on French territory. The passengers are told by the loner over the train's intercom that this time it's not a false alarm, but the train has been taken over by whichever gang I settle on, and is going to be blown up in fifteen minutes. He tells them to get themselves off the train, into the tunnel, and as far away as they possibly can before the explosion. Naturally, some of the passengers begin to panic. Several of them leap out into the dimly lit tunnel. Many are looking frantically for their husbands, wives, children, whatever, while others begin running towards the British or French side, according to their nationality.'

I became distracted when the maître d' began wheeling yet another trolley towards our table. He paused, bowed to Christabel, and then lit a small burner. He poured some brandy into a shallow copper-bottomed pan and set about preparing a crêpe suzette.

'This is the point in the story, probably chapter ten, where the father of the American family decides to remain on the train,' said Duncan, becoming more excited than ever. 'He tells the rest of his tribe to jump off and get the hell out of it. The only other passengers who stay on board are the millionaire, his wife, and the young newly-married man. All will have strong personal reasons for wanting to remain behind, which will have been set up earlier in the plot.'

The maître d' struck a match and set light to the crêpe. A blue flame licked around the pan and shot into the air. He scooped his *pièce de résistance* onto a warm platter in one movement, and placed it in front of Christabel.

I feared we had now passed the point at which I could tell Duncan the truth.

'Right, now I have three terrorists in the cab with the chef de train. They've killed the co-driver, and there are just four passengers still left on the train, plus the black ticket collector – who may turn out to be SAS in disguise, I haven't decided yet.'

'Coffee, madame?' the maître d' asked when Duncan paused for a moment.

'Irish,' said Christabel.

'Regular, please,' I said.

'Decaff for me,' said Duncan.

'Any liqueurs or cigars?'

Only Christabel reacted.

'So, at the start of chapter eleven the terrorists open negotiations with the British police. But they say they can't deal with them because the train is no longer under their jurisdiction. This throws the terrorists completely, because none of them speaks French, and in any case their quarrel is with the British government. One of them searches the train for someone who can speak French, and comes across the Greek millionaire's wife.

'Meanwhile, the police on either side of the Channel stop all the trains going in either direction. So, our train is now stranded in the tunnel on its own – there would normally be twenty trains travelling in either direction between London and Paris at any one time.' He paused to sip his coffee.

'Is that so?' I asked, knowing the answer perfectly well.

'It certainly is,' Duncan said. 'I've done my research thoroughly.'

A glass of deep red port was being poured for Christabel. I glanced at the label: Taylor's '55. This was something I had never had the privilege of tasting. Christabel indicated that the bottle should be left on the table. The waiter nodded, and Christabel immediately poured me a glass, without asking if I wanted it. Meanwhile, the maître d' clipped a cigar for Duncan that he hadn't requested.

'In chapter twelve we discover the terrorists' purpose,' continued Duncan. 'Namely, blowing up the train as a publicity stunt, guaranteed to get their cause onto every front page in the world. But the passengers who have remained on the train, led by the American father, are planning a counter-offensive.'

The maître d' lit a match and Duncan automatically picked up the cigar and put it in his mouth. It silenced him . . .

'The self-made millionaire might feel he's the natural leader,' I suggested.

. . . but only for a moment. 'He's a Greek. If I'm going to make any money out of this project, it's the American market I have to aim for. And don't forget the film rights,' Duncan said, jabbing the air with his cigar.

I couldn't fault his logic.

'Can I have the check?' Duncan asked as the maître d' passed by our table.

'Certainly, sir,' he replied, not even breaking his stride.

'Now, my trouble is going to be the ending . . .'

began Duncan as Christabel suddenly, if somewhat unsteadily, rose from her chair.

She turned to face me and said, 'I'm afraid the time has come for me to leave. It's been a pleasure meeting you, although I have a feeling we won't be seeing each other again. I'd just like to say how much I enjoyed your latest novel. Such an original idea. It deserved to be number one.'

I stood, kissed her hand and thanked her, feeling more guilty than ever.

'Goodbye, Duncan,' she said, turning to face her former lover, but he didn't even bother to look up. 'Don't worry yourself,' she added. 'I'll be out of the apartment by the time you get back.'

She proceeded to negotiate a rather wobbly route across the restaurant, eventually reaching the door that led out onto the street. The maître d' held it open for her and bowed low.

'I can't pretend I'm sorry to see her go,' said Duncan, puffing away on his cigar. 'Fantastic body, great between the sheets, but she's totally lacking in imagination.'

The maître d' reappeared by Duncan's side, this time to place a small black leather folder in front of him.

'Well, the critics were certainly right about this place,' I commented. Duncan nodded his agreement.

The maître d' bowed, but not quite as low as before.

'Now, my trouble, as I was trying to explain before Christabel decided to make her exit,' continued Duncan, 'is that I've done the outline, completed the research, but I still don't have an ending. Any ideas?' he asked, as a middle-aged woman rose from a nearby table and began walking determinedly towards us.

Duncan flicked open the leather cover, and stared in disbelief at the bill.

The woman came to a halt beside our table. 'I just wanted to tell you how much I enjoyed your new book,' she said in a loud voice.

Other diners turned round to see what was going on.

'Thank you,' I said somewhat curtly, hoping to prevent her from adding to my discomfort.

Duncan's eyes were still fixed on the bill.

'And the ending,' she said. 'So clever! I would never have guessed how you were going to get the American family out of the tunnel alive . . .'

SHOESHINE BOY

TED BARKER WAS ONE OF THOSE MEMBERS of Parliament who never sought high office. He'd had what was described by his fellow officers as a 'good war' – in which he was awarded the Military Cross and reached the rank of major. After being demobbed in November 1945 he was happy to return to his wife Hazel and their home in Suffolk.

The family engineering business had also had a good war, under the diligent management of Ted's elder brother Ken. As soon as he arrived home, Ted was offered his old place on the board, which he happily accepted. But as the weeks passed by, the distinguished warrior became first bored and then disenchanted. There was no job for him at the factory which even remotely resembled active service.

It was around this time that he was approached by Ethel Thompson, the works convenor and – more important for the advancement of this tale – Chairman of the Wedmore branch of the North Suffolk Conservative Association. The incumbent MP, Sir Dingle Lightfoot, known in the constituency as 'Tiptoe', had made it clear that once the war was over they must look for someone to replace him.

'We don't want some clever clogs from London coming up here and telling us how to run this division,' pronounced Mrs Thompson. 'We need someone who knows the district and understands the problems of the local people.' Ted, she suggested, might be just the ticket.

Ted confessed that he had never given such an idea a moment's thought, but promised Mrs Thompson that he would take her proposal seriously, only asking for a week in which to consider his decision. He discussed the suggestion with his wife, and having received her enthusiastic support, he paid a visit to Mrs Thompson at her home the following Sunday afternoon. She was delighted to hear that Mr Barker would be pleased to allow his name to go forward for consideration as the prospective parliamentary candidate for the division of North Suffolk.

The final shortlist included two clever clogs from London – one of whom later served in a Macmillan Cabinet – and the local boy, Ted Barker. When the chairman announced the committee's decision to the local press, he said that it would be improper to reveal the number of votes each candidate had polled. In fact, Ted had comfortably outscored his two rivals put together.

Six months later the Prime Minister called a general election, and after a lively three-week campaign, Ted was returned as the Member of Parliament for North Suffolk with a majority of over seven thousand. He quickly became respected and popular with colleagues on both sides of the House, though he never pretended to be anything other than, in his own words, 'an amateur politician'.

As the years passed, Ted's popularity with his constituents grew, and he increased his majority with each succeeding general election. After fourteen years of diligent service to the party nationally and locally, the Prime Minister of the day, Harold Macmillan, recommended to the Queen that Ted should receive a knighthood.

By the end of the 1960s, Sir Ted (he was never known as Sir Edward) felt that the time was fast approaching when the division should start looking for a younger candidate, and he made it clear to the local chairman that he did not intend to stand at the next election. He and Hazel quietly prepared for a peaceful retirement in their beloved East Anglia.

Shortly after the election, Ted was surprised to receive a call from 10 Downing Street: 'The Prime Minister would like to see Sir Ted at 11.30 tomorrow morning.'

Ted couldn't imagine why Edward Heath should want to see him. Although he had of course visited Number 10 on several occasions when he was a Member of Parliament, those visits had only been for cocktail parties, receptions, and the occasional dinner for a visiting head of state. He admitted to Hazel that he was a little nervous.

Ted presented himself at the front door of Number 10 at 11.17 the next day. The duty clerk accompanied him down the long corridor on the ground floor, and asked him to take a seat in the small waiting area that adjoins the Cabinet Room. By now Ted's nervousness was turning to apprehension. He felt like an errant schoolboy about to come face to face with his head-master.

After a few minutes a private secretary appeared. 'Good morning, Sir Ted. The Prime Minister will see you now.' He accompanied Ted into the Cabinet Room, where Mr Heath stood to greet him. 'How kind of you to come at such short notice, Ted.' Ted had to suppress a smile, because he knew the Prime Minister knew that it would have taken the scurvy or a localised hurricane to stop him from answering such a summons.

'I'm hoping you can help me with a delicate matter, Ted,' continued the Prime Minister, a man not known for wasting time on small-talk. 'I'm about to appoint the next Governor of St George's, and I can't think of anyone better qualified for the job than you.'

Ted recalled the day when Mrs Thompson had asked him to think about standing for Parliament. But on this occasion he didn't require a week to consider his reply – even if he couldn't quite bring himself to admit that although he'd heard of St George's, he certainly couldn't have located it on a map. Once he'd caught his breath, he simply said, 'Thank you, Prime Minister. I'd be honoured.'

During the weeks that followed Sir Ted paid several visits to the Foreign and Colonial Office to receive briefings on various aspects of his appointment. Thereafter he assiduously read every book, pamphlet and government paper the mandarins supplied.

After a few weeks of boning up on his new subject, the Governor-in-waiting had discovered that St George's was a tiny group of islands in the middle of the North Atlantic. It had been colonised by the British in 1643, and thereafter had a long history of imperial rule, the islanders having scorned every offer of independence. They were one of Her Majesty's sovereign colonies, and that was how they wished to remain.

Even before he set out on his adventure, Ted had become used to being addressed as 'Your Excellency'. But after being fitted up by Alan Bennett of Savile Row with two different full dress uniforms, Ted feared that he looked – what was that modern expression? – O.T.T. In winter he was expected to wear an outfit of dark blue doeskin with scarlet collar and cuffs embroidered with silver oakleaves, while in the summer he was to be adorned in white cotton drill with a gold-embroidered collar and gold shoulder cords. The sight of him in either uniform caused Hazel to laugh out loud.

Ted didn't laugh when the tailors sent him the bill, especially after he learned that he would be unlikely to wear either uniform more than twice a year. 'Still, think what a hit you'll be at fancy dress parties once you've retired,' was Hazel's only comment.

The newly-appointed Governor and Commander-in-Chief of St George's and his lady flew out to take up their post on 12 January 1971. They were greeted by the Prime Minister, as the colony's first citizen, and the

Chief Justice, as the legal representative of the Queen. After the new Governor had taken the salute from six off-duty policemen standing vaguely to attention, the town band gave a rendering of the national anthem. The Union Jack was raised on the roof of the airport terminal and a light splattering of applause broke out from the assembled gathering of twenty or thirty local dignitaries.

Sir Ted and Lady Barker were then driven to the official residence in a spacious but ageing Rover that had already served the two previous Governors. When they reached Government House, the driver brought the car to a halt and leaped out to open the gates. As they continued up the drive, Ted and Hazel saw their new home for the first time.

The colonial mansion was magnificent by any standards. Obviously built at the height of the British Empire, it was vastly out of proportion to either the importance of the island or Britain's current position in the real world. But size, as the Governor and his wife were quickly to discover, didn't necessarily equate with efficiency or comfort.

The air conditioning didn't work, the plumbing was unreliable, Mrs Rogers, the daily help, was regularly off sick, and the only thing Ted's predecessor had left behind was an elderly black labrador. Worse, the Foreign Office had no funds available to deal with any of these problems, and whenever Ted mentioned them in dispatches, he was met only with suggestions for cutbacks.

After a few weeks, Ted and Hazel began to think of St George's as being rather like a great big parliamentary constituency, split into several islands, the two largest being Suffolk and Edward Island. This heartened Ted, who even wondered if that was what had given the Prime Minister the idea of offering him the post in the first place.

The Governor's duties could hardly have been described as onerous: he and Hazel spent most of their time visiting hospitals, delivering speeches at school prize-givings and judging flower shows. The highlight of the year was undoubtedly the Queen's official birthday in June, when the Governor held a garden party for local dignitaries at Government House and Suffolk played Edward Island at cricket – an opportunity for most of the colony's citizens to spend two days getting thoroughly drunk.

Ted and Hazel accepted the local *realpolitik* and settled down for five years of relaxed diplomacy among delightful people in a heavenly climate, seeing no cloud on the horizon that could disturb their blissful existence.

Until the phone call came.

It was a Thursday morning, and the Governor was in his study with that Monday's *Times*. He was putting off reading a long article on the summit meeting taking place in Washington until he had finished the crossword, and was just about to fill in the answer to 12 across – Erring herd twists to create this diversion (3,7) – when his private secretary, Charles Roberts, came rushing into his office without knocking.

Ted realised it had to be something important, because he had never known Charles to rush anywhere, and certainly he had never known him to enter the study without the courtesy of a knock.

'It's Mountbatten on the line,' Charles blurted out. He could hardly have looked more anxious had he been reporting that the Germans were about to land on the north shore of the island. The Governor raised an eyebrow. 'Admiral of the Fleet Earl Mountbatten of Burma,' said Charles, as if Ted hadn't understood.

'Then put him through,' said Ted quietly, folding up his copy of *The Times* and placing it on the desk in front of him. He had met Mountbatten three times over the past twenty years, but doubted if the great man would recall any of these encounters. Indeed, on the third occasion Ted had found it necessary to slip out of the function the Admiral was addressing, as he was feeling a little queasy. He couldn't imagine what Mountbatten would want to speak to him about, and he had no time to consider the problem, as the phone on his desk was already ringing.

As Ted picked up the receiver he was still wondering whether to call Mountbatten 'My Lord' as he was an Earl, 'Commander-in-Chief', as he was a former Chief of the Defence Staff, or 'Admiral', as Admiral of the Fleet is a life appointment. He settled for 'Good morning, sir.'

'Good morning, Your Excellency. I hope I find you well?'

'Yes, thank you, sir,' replied Ted.

'Because if I remember correctly, when we last met you were suffering from a tummy bug.'

'That's right, sir,' said the surprised Governor. He

was reasonably confident that the purpose of Mount-batten's call wasn't to enquire about his health after all these years.

'Governor, you must be curious to know why I am calling.'

'Yes, sir.'

'I am presently in Washington attending the summit, and I had originally planned to return to London tomorrow morning.'

'I understand, sir,' said Ted, not understanding at all.

'But I thought I might make a slight detour and drop in to see you. I do enjoy visiting our colonies whenever I get the chance. It gives me the opportunity to brief Her Majesty on what's happening. I hope that such a visit would not be inconvenient.'

'Not at all, sir,' said Ted. 'We would be delighted to welcome you.'

'Good,' said Mountbatten. 'Then I would be obliged if you could warn the airport authorities to expect my aircraft around four tomorrow afternoon. I would like to stay overnight, but if I'm to keep to my schedule I will need to leave you fairly early the following morning.'

'Of course, sir. Nothing could be easier. My wife and I will be at the airport to welcome you at four o'clock tomorrow afternoon.'

'That's kind of you, Governor. By the way, I'd rather things were left fairly informal. Please don't put yourself to any trouble.' The line went dead.

Once he had replaced the receiver, it was Ted's turn to run for the first time in several months. He found

Charles striding down the long corridor towards him, having obviously listened in on the extension.

'Find my wife and get yourself a notepad – and then both of you join me in my office immediately. Immediately,' Ted repeated as he scuttled back into his study.

Hazel arrived a few minutes later, clutching a bunch of dahlias, followed by the breathless private secretary.

'Why the rush, Ted? What's the panic?'

'Mountbatten's coming.'

'When?' Hazel asked quietly.

'Tomorrow afternoon. Four o'clock.'

'That *is* a good reason to panic,' Hazel admitted. She dumped the flowers in a vase on the windowsill and took a seat opposite her husband on the other side of his desk. 'Perhaps this isn't the best time to let you know that Mrs Rogers is off sick.'

'You have to admire her timing,' said Ted. 'Right, we'll just have to bluff it.'

'What *do* you mean, "bluff it"?' asked Hazel.

'Well, don't let's forget that Mountbatten's a member of the Royal Family, a former Chief of the Defence Staff and an Admiral of the Fleet. The last colonial post he held was Viceroy of India with three regiments under his command and a personal staff of over a thousand. So I can't imagine what he'll expect to find when he turns up here.'

'Then let's begin by making a list of things that will have to be done,' said Hazel briskly.

Charles removed a pen from his inside pocket, turned

over the cover of his pad, and waited to write down his master's instructions.

'If he's arriving at the airport, the first thing he will expect is a red carpet,' said Hazel.

'But we don't have a red carpet,' said Ted.

'Yes we do. There's the one that leads from the dining room to the drawing room. We'll have to use that, and hope we can get it back in place before he visits that part of the house. Charles, you will have to roll it up and take it to the airport' – she paused – 'and then bring it back.'

Charles scowled, but began writing furiously.

'And Charles, can you also see that it's cleaned by tomorrow?' interjected the Governor. 'I hadn't even realised it was red. Now, what about a guard of honour?'

'We haven't got a guard of honour,' said Hazel. 'If you remember, when we arrived on the island we were met by the Prime Minister, the Chief Justice and six off-duty policemen.'

'True,' said Ted. 'Then we'll just have to rely on the Territorial Army.'

'You mean Colonel Hodges and his band of hopeful warriors? They don't even all have matching uniforms. And as for their rifles . . .'

'Hodges will just have to get them into some sort of shape by four o'clock tomorrow afternoon. Leave that one to me,' said Ted, making a note on his pad. 'I'll phone him later this morning. Now, what about a band?'

'Well there's the town band,' said Charles. 'And, of course, the police band.'

'On this occasion they'll have to combine,' said Hazel, 'so we don't offend either of them.'

'But they only know three tunes between them,' said Ted.

'They only need to know one,' said Hazel. 'The national anthem.'

'Right,' said the Governor. 'As there are sure to be a lot of musical feathers that will need unruffling, I'll leave you to deal with them, Hazel. Our next problem is how we transport him from the airport to Government House.'

'Certainly not in the old Rover,' said Hazel. 'It's broken down three times in the last month, and it smells like a kennel.'

'Henry Bendall has a Rolls-Royce,' said Ted. 'We'll just have to commandeer that.'

'As long as no one tells Mountbatten that it's owned by the local undertaker, and what it was used for the morning before he arrived.'

'Mick Flaherty also has an old Rolls,' piped up Charles. 'A Silver Shadow, if I remember correctly.'

'But he loathes the British,' said Hazel.

'Agreed,' said Ted, 'but he'll still want to have dinner at Government House when he discovers the guest of honour is a member of the Royal Family.'

'Dinner?' said Hazel, her voice rising in horror.

'Of course we will have to give a dinner in his honour,' said Ted. 'And, worse, everyone who is anyone will expect to be invited. How many can the dining room hold?' He and Hazel turned to the private secretary.

'Sixty if pushed,' replied Charles, looking up from his notes.

'We're pushed,' said Ted.

'We certainly are,' said Hazel. 'Because we don't have sixty plates, let alone sixty coffee cups, sixty teaspoons, sixty . . .'

'We still have that Royal Worcester service presented by the late King after his visit in 1947,' said Ted. 'How many pieces of that are fit for use?'

'Enough for about fourteen settings, at the last count,' said Hazel.

'Right, then that's dealt with how many people will be at the top table.'

'What about the menu?' asked Charles.

'And, more important, who is going to cook it?' added Ted.

'We'll have to ask Dotty Cuthbert if she can spare Mrs Travis for the evening,' said Hazel. 'No one on the island is a better cook.'

'And we'll also need her butler, not to mention the rest of her staff,' added Ted.

By now Charles was onto his third page.

'You'd better deal with Lady Cuthbert, my dear,' said Ted. 'I'll try to square Mick Flaherty.'

'Our next problem will be the drink,' said Hazel. 'Don't forget, the last Governor emptied the cellar a few days before he left.'

'And the Foreign Office refuses to restock it,' Ted reminded her. 'Jonathan Fletcher has the best cellar on the island . . .'

'And, God bless him, he won't expect to be at the top table,' said Hazel.

'If we're limited to fourteen places, the top table's looking awfully crowded already,' said Ted.

'Dotty Cuthbert, the Bendalls, the Flahertys, the Hodges,' said Hazel, writing down the names. 'Not to mention the Prime Minister, the Chief Justice, the Mayor, the Chief of Police, plus their wives . . . Let's hope that some of them are indisposed or abroad.' She was beginning to sound desperate.

'Where's he going to sleep?' asked Charles innocently.

'God, I hadn't thought of him sleeping,' said Ted.

'He'll have to take our bedroom. It's the only one with a bed that doesn't sink in the middle,' said Hazel.

'We'll move into the Nelson Room for the night, and suffer those dreadful woodwormed beds and their ancient horsehair mattresses.'

'Agreed,' said Hazel. 'I'll make sure all our things are out of the Queen Victoria Room by this evening.'

'And, Charles,' said the Governor, 'phone the Foreign Office, would you, and find out Mountbatten's likes and dislikes. Food, drink, eccentric habits – anything you can discover. They're sure to have a file on him, and this is one gentleman I don't want to catch me out.'

The private secretary turned over yet another page of his pad, and continued scribbling.

For the next hour, the three of them went over any and every problem that might arise during the visit, and after a self-made sandwich lunch, departed in their different directions to spend the afternoon making begging calls all round the island.

It was Charles's idea that the Governor should appear on the local television station's early-evening news programme, to let the citizens know that a member of the Royal Family would be visiting the island the following day. Sir Ted ended his broadcast by saying that he hoped as many people as possible would be at the airport to welcome 'the great war leader' when his plane touched down at four the following afternoon.

While Hazel spent the evening cleaning every room that the great war leader might conceivably enter, Charles, with the aid of a torch, tended to the flowerbeds that lined the driveway, and Ted supervised the shuttling of plates, cutlery, food and wine from different parts of the island to Government House.

'Now, what have we forgotten?' said Ted, as he climbed into bed at two o'clock that morning.

'Heaven only knows,' Hazel said wearily before turning out the light. 'But whatever it is, let's hope Mountbatten never finds out.'

The Governor, dressed in his summer uniform, with gold piping down the sides of his white trousers, decorations and campaign medals across his chest, and a Wolsey helmet with a plume of red-over-white swan's feathers on his head, walked out onto the landing to join his wife. Hazel was wearing the green summer frock she had bought for the Governor's garden party two years before, and was checking the flowers in the entrance hall.

'Too late for that,' said Ted, as she rearranged a sprig that had strayed half an inch. 'It's time we left for the airport.'

They descended the steps of Government House to find two Rolls-Royces, one black, one white, and their old Rover standing in line. Charles followed closely behind them, carrying the red carpet, which he dropped into the boot of the Rover as his master stepped into the back of the leading Rolls-Royce.

The first thing the Governor needed to check was the chauffeur's name.

'Bill Simmons,' he was informed.

'All you have to remember, Bill, is to look as if you've been doing this job all your life.'

'Right, Guv.'

'No,' said Ted firmly. 'In front of the Admiral, you must address me as "Your Excellency", and Lord Mountbatten as "My Lord". If in any doubt, say nothing.'

'Right, Guv, Your Excellency.'

Bill started up the car and drove towards the gates at what he evidently considered was a stately pace, before turning right and taking the road to the airport. When they reached the terminal fifteen minutes later a policeman ushered the tiny motorcade out onto the tarmac, where the combined bands were playing a medley from *West Side Story* – at least, that was what Ted charitably thought it might be.

As he stepped out of the car Ted came face to face

with three ranks of soldiers from the Territorial Army standing at ease, sixty-one of them, aged from seventeen to seventy. Ted had to admit that although they weren't the Grenadier Guards, they weren't 'Dad's Army' either. And they had two advantages: a real-live Colonel in full dress uniform, and a genuine Sergeant Major, with a voice to match.

Charles had already begun rolling out the red carpet when the Governor turned his attention to the hastily-erected barriers, where he was delighted to see a larger crowd than he had ever witnessed on the island, even at the annual football derby between Suffolk and Edward Island.

Many of the islanders were waving Union Jacks, and some were holding up pictures of the Queen. Ted smiled and checked his watch. The plane was due in seventeen minutes.

The Prime Minister, the local Mayor, the Chief Justice, the Commissioner of Police and their wives were lining up at the end of the red carpet. The sun beat down from a cloudless sky. As Ted turned in a slow circle to take in the scene, he could see for himself that everyone had made a special effort.

Suddenly the sound of engines could be heard, and the crowd began to cheer. Ted looked up, shielded his eyes, and saw an Andover of the Queen's Flight descending towards the airport. It touched down on the far end of the runway at three minutes before the hour, and taxied up to the red carpet as four chimes struck on the clock above the flight control tower.

The door of the plane opened, and there stood Admiral of the Fleet the Earl Mountbatten of Burma, KG, PC, GCB, OM, GCSI, GCIE, GCVO, DSO, FRS, DCL (Hon), LLD (Hon), attired in the full dress uniform of an Admiral of the Fleet (summer wear).

'If that's what he means by "fairly informal", I suppose we should be thankful that he didn't ask us to lay on an official visit,' murmured Hazel as she and Ted walked to the bottom of the steps that had been quickly wheeled into place.

As Mountbatten slowly descended the stairway, the crowd cheered even louder. Once he stepped onto the red carpet the Governor took a pace forward, removed his plumed hat, and bowed. The Admiral saluted, and at that moment the combined bands of town and police struck up the national anthem. The crowd sang 'God Save the Queen' so lustily that the occasional uncertain note was smothered by their exuberance.

When the anthem came to an end the Governor said, 'Welcome to St George's, sir.'

'Thank you, Governor,' replied Mountbatten.

'May I present my wife, Hazel.' The Governor's wife took a pace forward, did a full curtsey, and shook hands with the Admiral.

'How good to see you again, Lady Barker. This is indeed a pleasure.'

The Governor guided his guest to the end of the red carpet and introduced him to the Prime Minister and his wife Sheila, the local mayor and his wife Caroline, the Chief Justice and his wife Janet, and the Commissioner of Police and his latest wife, whose name he couldn't remember.

'Perhaps you'd care to inspect the guard of honour before we leave for Government House,' suggested Ted, steering Mountbatten in the direction of Colonel Hodges and his men.

'Absolutely delighted,' said the Admiral, waving to the crowd as the two of them proceeded across the tarmac towards the waiting guard. When they still had some twenty yards to go, the Colonel sprang to attention, took three paces forward, saluted and said crisply, 'Guard of Honour ready for inspection, sir.'

Mountbatten came to a halt and returned a naval salute, which was a sign for the Sergeant Major, standing at attention six paces behind his Colonel, to bellow out the words, 'Commanding officer on parade! General salute, pre—sent arms!'

The front row, who were in possession of the unit's entire supply of weapons, presented arms, while the second and third rows came rigidly to attention.

Mountbatten marched dutifully up and down the ranks, as gravely as if he were inspecting a full brigade of Life Guards. When he had passed the last soldier in the back row, the Colonel came to attention and saluted once again. Mountbatten returned the salute and said, 'Thank you, Colonel. First-class effort. Well done.'

The Governor then guided Mountbatten towards the white Rolls-Royce, where Bill was standing at what he imagined was attention, while at the same time holding open the back door. Mountbatten stepped in as the Governor hurried round to the other side, opened the door for himself, and joined his guest on the back seat. Hazel and the Admiral's ADC took their places in the black Rolls-Royce, while Charles and the Admiral's secretary had to make do with the Rover. The Governor only hoped that Mountbatten hadn't seen two members of the airport staff rolling up the red carpet and placing it in the Rover's boot. Hazel was only praying that they had enough sheets left over for the bed in the Green Room. If not, the ADC would be wondering about their sleeping habits.

The island's two police motorcycles, with white-uniformed outriders, preceded the three cars as they made their way towards the exit. The crowd waved and cheered lustily as the motorcade began its short journey to Government House. So successful had Ted's television appearance the previous evening been that the ten-mile route was lined with well-wishers.

As they approached the open gates two policemen sprang to attention and saluted as the leading car passed through. In the distance Ted could see a butler, two under-butlers and several maids, all smartly clad, standing on the steps awaiting their arrival. 'Damn it,' he almost said aloud as the car came to a halt at the bottom of the steps. 'I don't know the butler's name.'

The car door was smartly opened by one of the under-butlers while the second supervised the unloading of the luggage from the boot.

The butler took a pace forward as Mountbatten stepped out of the car. 'Carruthers, m'lord,' he said, bowing. 'Welcome to the residence. If you would be kind enough to follow me, I will direct you to your quarters.' The Admiral, accompanied by the Governor and Lady Barker, climbed the steps into Government House and followed Carruthers up the main staircase.

'Magnificent, these old government residences,' said Mountbatten as they reached the top of the stairs. Carruthers opened the door to the Queen Victoria Room and stood to one side, as if he had done so a thousand times before.

'How charming,' said the Admiral, taking in the Governor's private suite. He walked over to the window and looked out onto the newly-mown lawn. 'How very pleasant. It reminds me of Broadlands, my home in Hampshire.'

Lady Barker smiled at the compliment, but didn't allow herself to relax.

'Is there anything you require, m'lord?' asked Carruthers, as an under-butler began to supervise the unpacking of the cases.

Hazel held her breath.

'No, I don't think so,' said Mountbatten. 'Everything looks just perfect.'

'Perhaps you'd care to join Hazel and me for tea in the drawing room when you're ready, sir,' suggested Ted.

'How thoughtful of you,' said the Admiral. 'I'll be down in about thirty minutes, if I may.'

The Governor and his wife left the room, closing the door quietly behind them.

'I think he suspects something,' whispered Hazel as they tiptoed down the staircase.

'You may be right,' said Ted, placing his plumed hat on the stand in the hall, 'but that's all the more reason to check we haven't forgotten anything. I'll start with the dining room. You ought to go and see how Mrs Travis is getting on in the kitchen.'

When Hazel entered the kitchen she found Mrs Travis preparing the vegetables, and one of the maids peeling a mound of potatoes. She thanked Mrs Travis for taking over at such short notice, and admitted she had never seen the kitchen so full of exotic foods, or the surfaces so immaculately clean. Even the floor was spotless. Realising that her presence was superfluous, Hazel joined her husband in the dining room, where she found him admiring the expertise of the second under-butler, who was laying out the place settings for that evening, as a maid folded napkins to look like swans.

'So far, so good,' said Hazel. They left the dining room and entered the drawing room, where Ted paced up and down, trying to think if there was anything he had forgotten while they waited for the great man to join them for tea.

A few minutes later, Mountbatten walked in. He was no longer dressed in his Admiral's uniform, but had changed into a dark grey double-breasted suit.

'Damn it,' thought Ted, immediately aware of what he'd forgotten to do.

Hazel rose to greet her guest, and guided him to a large, comfortable chair.

'I must say, Lady Barker, your butler is a splendid chap,' said Mountbatten. 'He even knew the brand of whisky I prefer. How long have you had him?'

'Not very long,' admitted Hazel.

'Well, if he ever wants a job in England, don't hesitate to let me know – though I'm bound to say, you'd be a fool to part with him,' he added, as a maid came in carrying a beautiful Wedgwood tea service that Hazel had never set eyes on before.

'Earl Grey, if I remember correctly,' said Hazel.

'What a memory you have, Lady Barker,' said the Admiral, as the maid began to pour.

'Thank God for the Foreign Office briefing,' Hazel thought, as she accepted the compliment with a smile.

'And how did the Conference go, sir?' asked Ted, as he dropped a lump of sugar – the one thing he felt might be their own – into his cup of tea.

'For the British, quite well,' said Mountbatten. 'But it would have gone better if the French hadn't been up to their usual tricks. Giscard seems to regard himself as a cross between Charlemagne and Joan of Arc.' His hosts laughed politely. 'No, the real problem we're facing at the moment, Ted, is quite simply . . .'

By the time Mountbatten had dealt with the outcome of the summit, given his undiluted views of James Callaghan and Ted Heath, covered the problem of finding a wife for Prince Charles and mulled over the long-term repercussions of Watergate, it was almost time for him to change.

'Are we dressing for dinner?'

'Yes, sir – if that meets with your approval.'

'Full decorations?' Mountbatten asked, sounding hopeful.

'I thought that would be appropriate, sir,' replied Ted, remembering the Foreign Office's advice about the Admiral's liking for dressing up at the slightest opportunity.

Mountbatten smiled as Carruthers appeared silently at the door. Ted raised an eyebrow.

'I have laid out the full dress uniform, m'lord. I took the liberty of pressing the trousers. The bedroom maid is drawing a bath for you.'

Mountbatten smiled. 'Thank you,' he said as he rose from his chair. 'Such a splendid tea,' he added turning to face his hostess. 'And such wonderful staff. Hazel, I don't know how you do it.'

'Thank you, sir,' said Hazel, trying not to blush.

'What time would you like me to come down for dinner, Ted?' Mountbatten asked.

'The first guests should be arriving for drinks at about 7.30, sir. We were hoping to serve dinner at eight, if that's convenient for you.'

'Couldn't be better,' declared Mountbatten. 'How many are you expecting?'

'Around sixty, sir. You'll find a guest list on your bedside table. Perhaps Hazel and I could come and fetch you at 7.50?'

'You run a tight ship, Ted,' said Mountbatten with approval. 'You'll find me ready the moment you appear,' he added as he followed Carruthers out of the room.

Once the door was closed behind him, Hazel said to the maid, 'Molly, can you clear away the tea things, please?' She hesitated for a moment. 'It is Molly, isn't it?'

'Yes, ma'am,' said the girl.

'I think he knows,' said Ted, looking a little anxious.

'Maybe, but we haven't time to worry about that now,' said Hazel, already on her way to carry out a further inspection of the kitchen.

The mound of potatoes had diminished to a peeled heap. Mrs Travis, who was preparing the sauces, was calling for more pepper and for some spices to be fetched from a shop in town. Aware once again that she wasn't needed in the kitchen, Hazel moved on to the dining room, where she found Ted. The top table was now fully laid with the King's dinner service, three sets of wine glasses, crested linen napkins, and a glorious centrepiece of a silver pheasant, which gave added sparkle.

'Who lent us that?' she asked.

'I have no idea,' replied Ted. 'But one thing's for certain – it will have flown home by the morning.'

'If we keep the lighting low enough,' whispered Hazel, 'he might not notice that the other tables all have different cutlery.'

'Heavens, just look at the time,' said Ted.

They left the dining room and walked quickly up the

stairs. Ted nearly barged straight into Mountbatten's room, but remembered just in time.

The Governor rather liked his dark blue doeskin uniform with the scarlet collar and cuffs. He was admiring the ensemble in the mirror when Hazel entered the room in a pink Hardy Amies outfit, which she had originally thought a waste of money because she never expected it to be given a proper outing.

'Men are so vain,' she remarked as her husband continued to inspect himself in the mirror. 'You do realise you're only meant to wear that in winter.'

'I am well aware of that,' said Ted peevishly, 'but it's the only other uniform I've got. In any case, I bet Mountbatten will outdo us both.' He flicked a piece of fluff from his trousers, which he had just finished pressing.

The Governor and his wife left the Nelson Room and walked down the main staircase just before 7.20, to find yet another under-butler stationed by the front door, and two more maids standing opposite him carrying silver trays laden with glasses of champagne. Hazel introduced herself to the three of them, and again checked the flowers in the entrance hall.

As 7.30 struck on the long-case clock in the lobby the first guest walked in.

'Henry,' said the Governor. 'Lovely to see you. Thank you so much for the use of the Rolls. And Bill, come to that,' he added in a stage whisper.

'My pleasure, Your Excellency,' Henry Bendall replied. 'I must say, I like the uniform.'

Lady Cuthbert came bustling through the front door. 'Can't stop,' she said. 'Ignore me. Just pretend I'm not here.'

'Dotty, I simply don't know what we would have done without you,' Hazel said, chasing after her across the hall.

'Delighted to lend a hand,' said Lady Cuthbert. 'I thought I'd come bang on time, so I could spend a few minutes in the kitchen with Mrs Travis. By the way, Benson is standing out in the drive, ready to rush home if you find you're still short of anything.'

'You are a saint, Dotty. I'll take you through . . .'

'No, don't worry,' said Lady Cuthbert. 'I know my way around. You just carry on greeting your guests.'

'Good evening, Mr Mayor,' said Ted, as Lady Cuthbert disappeared in the direction of the kitchen.

'Good evening, Your Excellency. How kind of you to invite us to such an auspicious occasion.'

'And what a lovely dress, Mrs Janson,' said the Governor.

'Thank you, Your Excellency,' said the Mayor's wife.

'Would you care for a glass of champagne?' said Hazel as she arrived back at her husband's side.

By 7.45 most of the guests had arrived, and Ted was chatting to Mick Flaherty when Hazel touched him on the elbow. He glanced towards her.

'I think we should go and fetch him now,' she whispered.

Ted nodded, and asked the Chief Justice to take over the welcoming of the guests. They wove a path through the chattering throng, and climbed the great staircase. When they reached the door of the Queen Victoria Room, they paused and looked at each other.

Ted checked his watch – 7.50. He leaned forward and gave a gentle tap. Carruthers immediately opened the door to reveal Mountbatten attired in his third outfit of the day: full ceremonial uniform of an Admiral of the Fleet, three stars, a gold and blue sash and eight rows of campaign decorations.

'Good evening, Your Excellency,' said Mountbatten.

'Good evening, sir,' said the Governor, star struck.

The Admiral took three paces forward and came to a halt at the top of the staircase. He stood to attention. Ted and Hazel waited on either side of him. As he didn't move, they didn't.

Carruthers proceeded slowly down the stairs in front of them, stopping on the third step. He cleared his throat and waited for the assembled guests to fall silent.

'Your Excellency, Prime Minister, Mr Mayor, ladies and gentlemen,' he announced. 'The Right Honourable the Earl Mountbatten of Burma.'

Mountbatten descended the stairs slowly as the waiting guests applauded politely. As he passed Carruthers, the butler gave a deep bow. The Governor, with Hazel on his arm, followed two paces behind.

'He must know,' whispered Hazel.

'You may be right. But does he know we know?' said Ted.

Mountbatten moved deftly around the room, as Ted introduced him to each of the guests in turn. They bowed and curtsied, listening attentively to the few words the Admiral had to say to them. The one exception was Mick Flaherty, who didn't stop talking, and remained more upright than Ted had ever seen him before.

At eight o'clock one of the under-butlers banged a gong, which until then neither the Governor nor his wife had even realised existed. As the sound died away, Carruthers announced, 'My Lord, Your Excellency, Prime Minister, Mr Mayor, ladies and gentlemen, dinner is served.'

If there was a better cook on St George's than Mrs Travis, no one at the top table had ever been fed by her, and that evening she had excelled herself.

Mountbatten chatted and smiled, making no secret of how much he was enjoying himself. He spent a long time talking to Lady Cuthbert, whose husband had served under him at Portsmouth, and to Mick Flaherty, to whom he listened with polite interest.

Each course surpassed the one before: soufflé, followed by lamb cutlets, and an apricot hazelnut meringue to complete the feast. Mountbatten remarked on every one of the wines, and even called for a second glass of port.

After dinner, he joined the guests for coffee in the drawing room, and managed to have a word with everyone, even though Colonel Hodges tried to buttonhole him about defence cuts.

The guests began to leave a few minutes before midnight, and Ted was amused to see that when Mick Flaherty bade farewell to the Admiral, he bowed low and said, 'Good night, My Lord. It has been an honour to meet you.'

Dotty was among the last to depart, and she curtsied low to the guest of honour. 'You've helped to make this such a pleasant evening, Lady Cuthbert,' Mountbatten told her.

'If you only knew just how much,' thought Hazel.

After the under-butler had closed the door on the last guest, Mountbatten turned to his hostess and said, 'Hazel, I must thank you for a truly memorable occasion. The head chef at the Savoy couldn't have produced a finer banquet. Perfect in every part.'

'You are very kind, sir. I will pass your thanks on to the staff.' She just stopped herself from saying 'my staff'. 'Is there anything else we can do for you before you retire?'

'No, thank you,' Mountbatten replied. 'It has been a long day, and with your permission, I'll turn in now.'

'And at what time would you like breakfast, sir?' asked the Governor.

'Would 7.30 be convenient?' Mountbatten asked. 'That will give me time to fly out at nine.'

'Certainly,' said Ted. 'I'll see that Carruthers brings a light breakfast up to your room at 7.30 – unless you'd like something cooked.'

'A light breakfast will be just the thing,' Mountbatten said. 'A perfect evening. Your staff could not have done more, Hazel. Good night, and thank you, my dear.'

The Governor bowed and his lady curtsied as the great

man ascended the staircase two paces behind Carruthers. When the butler closed the door of the Queen Victoria Room, Ted put his arm around his wife and said, 'He knows we know.'

'You may be right,' said Hazel. 'But does he know we know he knows?'

'I'll have to think about that,' said Ted.

Arm in arm, they returned to the kitchen, where they found Mrs Travis packing dishes into a crate under the supervision of Lady Cuthbert, the long lace sleeves of whose evening dress were now firmly rolled up.

'How did you get back in, Dotty?' asked Hazel.

'Just walked round to the back yard and came in the servants' entrance,' replied Lady Cuthbert.

'Did you spot anything that went badly wrong?' Hazel asked anxiously.

'I don't think so,' replied Lady Cuthbert. 'Not unless you count Mick Flaherty failing to get a fourth glass of Muscat de Venise.'

'Mrs Travis,' said Ted, 'the head chef at the Savoy couldn't have produced a finer banquet. Perfect in every part. I do no more than repeat Lord Mountbatten's exact words.'

'Thank you, Your Excellency,' said Mrs Travis. 'He's got a big appetite, hasn't he?' she added with a smile.

A moment later, Carruthers entered the kitchen. He checked round the room, which was spotless once again, then turned to Ted and said, 'With your permission, sir, we will take our leave.'

'Of course,' said the Governor. 'And may I thank you, Carruthers, for the role you and your amazing team have played. You all did a superb job. Lord Mountbatten never stopped remarking on it.'

'His Lordship is most kind, sir. At what time would you like us to return in the morning to prepare and serve his breakfast?'

'Well, he asked for a light breakfast in his room at 7.30.'

'Then we will be back by 6.30,' said Carruthers.

Hazel opened the kitchen door to let them all out, and they humped crates full of crockery and baskets full of food to the waiting cars. The last person to leave was Dotty, who was clutching the silver pheasant. Hazel kissed her on both cheeks as she departed.

'I don't know how you feel, but I'm exhausted,' said Ted, bolting the kitchen door.

Hazel checked her watch. It was seventeen minutes past one.

'Shattered,' she admitted. 'So, let's try and grab some sleep, because *we'll* also have to be up by seven to make sure everything is ready before he leaves for the airport.'

Ted put his arm back around his wife's waist. 'A personal triumph for you, my dear.'

They strolled into the hall and wearily began to climb the stairs, but didn't utter another word, for fear of disturbing their guest's repose. When they reached the landing, they came to an abrupt halt, and stared down in horror at the sight that greeted them. Three pairs of black leather shoes had been placed neatly in line outside the Queen Victoria Room.

'Now I'm certain he knows,' said Hazel.

Ted nodded and, turning to his wife, whispered, 'You or me?'

Hazel pointed a finger firmly at her husband. 'Definitely you, my dear,' she said sweetly, before disappearing in the direction of the Nelson Room.

Ted shrugged his shoulders, picked up the Admiral's shoes, and returned downstairs to the kitchen.

His Excellency the Governor and Commander-in-Chief of St George's spent a considerable time polishing those three pairs of shoes, as he realised that not only must they pass inspection by an Admiral of the Fleet, but they must look as if the job had been carried out by Carruthers.

When Mountbatten returned to the Admiralty in Whitehall the following Monday, he made a full written report on his visit to St George's. Copies were sent to the Queen and the Foreign Secretary.

The Admiral told the story of his visit at a family gathering that Saturday evening at Windsor Castle, and once the laughter had died down, the Queen asked him, 'When did you first become suspicious?'

'It was Carruthers who gave it away. He knew everything about Sir Ted, except which regiment he had served in. That's just not possible for an old soldier.'

The Queen had one further question: 'Do you think the Governor knew you knew?'

'I can't be certain, Lillibet,' replied Mountbatten after some thought. 'But I intend to leave him in no doubt that I did.'

The Foreign Secretary laughed uproariously when he read Mountbatten's report, and appended a note to the last sheet asking for clarification on two points:

(a) How can you be certain that the staff who served dinner were not part of the Governor's entourage?

(b) Do you think Sir Ted knew that you knew?

The Admiral replied by return:

(a) After dinner, one of the maids asked Lady Barker if she took sugar in her coffee, but a moment later she gave Lady Cuthbert two lumps, without needing to ask.

(b) Possibly not. But he certainly will on Christmas Day.

Sir Ted was pleased to receive a Christmas card from Lord Mountbatten, signed, 'Best wishes, Dickie. Thank you for a memorable stay.' It was accompanied by a gift.

Hazel unwrapped the little parcel to discover a tin of Cherry Blossom shoe polish (black). Her only comment was, 'So now we know he knew.'

'Agreed,' said Ted with a grin. 'But did he know we knew he knew? That's what I'd like to know.'

YOU'LL NEVER LIVE
TO REGRET IT

ᴀɴᴅ ꜱᴏ ɪᴛ ᴡᴀꜱ ᴀɢʀᴇᴇᴅ: ᴅᴀᴠɪᴅ ᴡᴏᴜʟᴅ leave everything to Pat. If one of them had to die, at least the other would be financially secure for the rest of their life. David felt it was the least he could do for someone who'd stood by him for so many years, especially as he was the one who had been unfaithful.

They had known each other almost all their lives, because their parents had been close friends for as long as either of them could remember. Both families had hoped David might end up marrying Pat's sister Ruth, and they were unable to hide their surprise – and in Pat's father's case his disapproval – when the two of them started living together, especially as Pat was three years older than David.

For some time David had been putting it off and hoping for a miracle cure, despite a pushy insurance broker from Geneva Life called Marvin Roebuck who had been pressing him to 'take a meeting' for the past nine months. On the first Monday of the tenth month he phoned again, and this time David reluctantly agreed to see him. He chose a date when he knew Pat would be on night duty at the hotel, and asked Roebuck to come round to their apartment – that way, he felt, it would look as if it was the broker who had done the chasing.

David was watering the scarlet *clupea harengus* on the hall table when Marvin Roebuck pressed the buzzer on the front door. Once he had poured his visitor a Budweiser, David told him he had every type of insurance he could possibly need: theft, accident, car, property, health, even holiday.

'But what about life?' asked Marvin, licking his lips.

'That's one I don't need,' said David. 'I earn a good salary, I have more than enough security, and on top of that, my parents will leave everything to me.'

'But wouldn't it be prudent to have a lump sum that comes to you automatically on your sixtieth or sixty-fifth birthday?' asked Marvin, as he continued to push at a door that he had no way of knowing was already wide open. 'After all, you can never be sure what disaster might lie around the corner.'

David knew exactly what disaster lay around the corner, but he still innocently asked, 'What sort of figure are you talking about?'

'Well, that would depend on how much you are currently earning,' said Marvin.

'$120,000 a year,' said David, trying to sound casual, as it was almost double his real income. Marvin was obviously impressed, and David remained silent as he carried out some rapid calculations in his head.

'Well,' said Marvin eventually, 'I'd suggest half a million dollars – as a ballpark figure. After all,' he added, quickly running a finger down a page of actuarial tables he had extracted from his aluminium briefcase, 'you're only twenty-seven, so the payments would be well within your means. In fact, you might even consider a larger sum if you're confident your income will continue to rise over the next few years.'

'It has done every year for the past seven,' said David, this time truthfully.

'What kind of business are you in, my friend?' asked Marvin.

'Stocks and bonds,' replied David, not offering any details of the small firm he worked for, or the junior position he held.

Marvin licked his lips again, even though they had told him not to do so on countless refresher courses, especially when going in for the kill.

'So, what amount do you think I should go for?' asked David, continuing to make sure it was always Marvin who took the lead.

'Well, a million is comfortably within your credit range,' said Marvin, once again checking his little book of tables. 'The monthly payments might seem a bit steep to begin with, but as the years go by, what with inflation and your continual salary increases, you can expect that in time they will become almost insignificant.'

'How much would I have to pay each month to end up getting a million?' asked David, attempting to give the impression he might have been hooked.

'Assuming we select your sixtieth birthday for terminating the contract, a little over a thousand dollars a month,' said Marvin, trying to make it sound a mere pittance. 'And don't forget, sixty per cent of it is tax deductible, so in real terms you'll only be paying around fifteen dollars a day, while you end up getting a million, just at the time when you most need it. And by the way, that one thousand is constant, it never goes up. In fact it's inflation-proof.' He let out a dreadful shrill laugh.

'But would I still receive the full sum, whatever happens to the market?'

'One million dollars on your sixtieth birthday,' confirmed Marvin, 'whatever happens, short of the world coming to an end. Even I can't write a policy for that,' he said, letting out another shrill laugh. 'However, my friend, if unhappily you were to die before your sixtieth birthday – which God forbid – your dependants would receive the full amount immediately.'

'I don't have any dependants,' said David, trying to look bored.

'There must be someone you care about,' said Marvin. 'A good-looking guy like you.'

'Why don't you leave the forms with me, Mr Roebuck, and I'll think about it over the weekend. I promise I'll get back to you.'

Marvin looked disappointed. He didn't need a refresher course to be told that you're supposed to nail the client to the wall at the first meeting, not let them get away, because that only gave them time to think things over. His lips felt dry.

Pat returned from the evening shift in the early hours of the morning, but David had stayed awake so he could go over what had happened at the meeting with Marvin. Pat was apprehensive and uncertain about the plan. David had always taken care of any problems they had had in the past, especially financial ones, and Pat wasn't sure how it would all work out once David was no longer around to give his advice. Thank God it was David who'd had to deal with Marvin — Pat couldn't even say no to a door-to-door brush salesman.

'So, what do we do next?' asked Pat.

'Wait.'

'But you promised Marvin you'd get back to him.'

'I know, but I have absolutely no intention of doing so,' said David, placing his arm round Pat's shoulder. 'I'd bet a hundred dollars on Marvin phoning me first thing on Monday morning. And don't forget, I still need it to look as if he's the one who's doing the pushing.'

As they climbed into bed, Pat felt an attack of asthma coming on, and decided now was not the time to ask David to go over the details again. After all, as David had explained again and again, there would never be any need for Pat to meet Marvin.

Marvin phoned at 8.30 on Monday morning.

'Hoped to catch you before you went off to sell those stocks and bonds,' he said. 'Have you come to a decision?'

'Yes, I have,' said David. 'I discussed the whole idea with my mother over the weekend, and she thinks I should go for the million, because five hundred thousand may not turn out to be such a large sum of money by the time I reach sixty.'

Marvin was glad that David couldn't see him licking his lips. 'Your mother's obviously a shrewd woman,' was his only comment.

'Can I leave you to handle all the paperwork?' asked David, trying to sound as if he didn't want to deal with any of the details.

'You bet,' said Marvin. 'Don't even think about it, my friend. Just leave all that hassle to me. I know you've made the right decision, David. I promise you, you'll never live to regret it.'

The following day, Marvin phoned again to say that the paperwork had been completed, and all that was now required was for David to have a medical – 'routine' was the word he kept repeating. But because of the size of the sum insured, it would have to be with the company's doctor in New York.

David made a fuss about having to travel to New York, adding that perhaps he'd made the wrong decision, but after more pleading from Marvin, mixed with some unctuous persuasion, he finally gave in.

Marvin brought all the forms round to the apartment the following evening after Pat had left for work.

David scribbled his signature on three separate documents between two pencilled crosses. His final act was to print Pat's name in a little box Marvin had indicated with his stubby finger. 'As your sole dependant,' the broker explained, 'should you pass away before 1 September 2027 – God forbid. Are you married to Pat?'

'No, we just live together,' replied David.

After a few more 'my friends' and even more 'you'll

never live to regret it's, Marvin left the apartment, clutching the forms.

'All you have to do now is keep your nerve,' David told Pat once he had confirmed that the paperwork had been completed. 'Just remember, no one knows me as well as you do, and once it's all over, you'll collect a million dollars.'

When they eventually went to bed that night, Pat desperately wanted to make love to David, but they both accepted it was no longer possible.

The two of them travelled down to New York together the following Monday to keep the appointment David had made with Geneva Life's senior medical consultant. They parted a block away from the insurance company's head office, as they didn't want to run the risk of being seen together. They hugged each other once again, but as they parted David was still worried about whether Pat would be able to go through with it.

A couple of minutes before twelve, he arrived at the surgery. A young woman in a long white coat smiled up at him from behind her desk.

'Good morning,' he said. 'My name is David Kravits. I have an appointment with Dr Royston.'

'Oh, yes, Mr Kravits,' said the nurse. 'Dr Royston is expecting you. Please follow me.' She led him down a long, bleak corridor to the last room on the left. A small brass plaque read 'Dr Royston'. She knocked, opened the door and said, 'Mr Kravits, doctor.'

Dr Royston turned out to be a short, elderly man with only a few strands of hair left on his shiny sunburnt head. He wore horn-rimmed spectacles, and had a look on his face which suggested that his own life insurance policy might not be far from reaching maturity. He rose from his chair, shook his patient by the hand and said, 'It's for a life insurance policy, if I remember correctly.'

'Yes, that's right.'

'Shouldn't take us too long, Mr Kravits. Fairly routine, but the company does like to be sure you're fit and well if they're going to be liable for such a large amount of money. Do have a seat,' he said, pointing to the other side of his desk.

'I thought the sum was far too high myself. I would have been happy to settle for half a million, but the broker was very persuasive . . .'

'Any serious illness during the past ten years?' the doctor asked, obviously not interested in the broker's views.

'No. The occasional cold, but nothing I'd describe as serious,' he replied.

'Good. And in your immediate family, any history of heart attacks, cancer, liver complaints?'

'Not that I'm aware of.'

'Father still alive?'

'Very much so.'

'And he's fit and well?'

'Jogs every morning, and pumps weights in the local gym at the weekend.'

'And your mother?'

'Doesn't do either, but I wouldn't be surprised if she outlives him comfortably.'

The doctor laughed. 'Any of your grandparents still living?'

'All except one. My dad's father died two years ago.'

'Do you know the cause of death?'

'He just passed away, I think. At least, that was how the priest described it at his funeral.'

'And how old was he?' the doctor asked. 'Do you remember?'

'Eighty-one, eighty-two.'

'Good,' repeated Dr Royston, ticking another little box on the form in front of him. 'Have you ever suffered from any of these?' he asked, holding up a clipboard in front of him. The list began with arthritis, and ended eighteen lines later with tuberculosis.

He ran an eye slowly down the long list before replying. 'No, none of them,' was all he said, not admitting to asthma on this occasion.

'Do you smoke?'

'Never.'

'Drink?'

'Socially – I enjoy the occasional glass of wine with dinner, but I never drink spirits.'

'Excellent,' said the doctor and ticked the last of the little boxes. 'Now, let's check your height and weight. Come over here, please, Mr Kravits, and climb onto these scales.'

The doctor had to stand on his toes in order to push the wooden marker up until it was flat across his patient's head. 'Six feet one inch,' he declared, then looked down at the weighing machine, and flicked the little weight across until it just balanced. 'A hundred and seventy-nine pounds. Not bad.' He filled in two more lines of his report. 'Perhaps just a little overweight.

'Now I need a urine sample, Mr Kravits. If you would be kind enough to take this plastic container next door, fill it about halfway up, leave it on the ledge when you've finished, and then come back to me.'

The doctor wrote out some more notes while his patient left the room. He returned a few moments later.

'I've left the container on the ledge,' was all he said.

'Good. The next thing I need is a blood sample. Could you roll up your right sleeve?' The doctor placed a rubber pad around his right bicep and pumped until the veins stood out clearly. 'A tiny prick,' he said. 'You'll hardly feel a thing.' The needle went in, and he turned away as the doctor drew his blood. Dr Royston cleaned the wound and fixed a small circular plaster over the broken skin. The doctor then bent over and placed a cold stethoscope on different parts of the patient's chest, occasionally asking him to breathe in and out.

'Good,' he kept repeating. Finally he said, 'That just about wraps it up, Mr Kravits. You'll need to spend a few minutes down the corridor with Dr Harvey, so she can take a chest x-ray, and have some fun with her electric pads, but after that you'll be through, and you can go home to' – he checked his pad – 'New Jersey. The company will be in touch in a few days, as soon as we've had the results.'

'Thank you, Dr Royston,' he said as he buttoned up his shirt. The doctor pressed a buzzer on his desk and the nurse reappeared and led him to another room, with a plaque on the door that read 'Dr Mary Harvey'. Dr Harvey, a smartly-dressed middle-aged woman with her grey hair cropped short, was waiting for him. She smiled at the tall, handsome man and asked him to take off his shirt again and to step up onto the platform and stand in front of the x-ray unit.

'Place your arms behind your back and breathe in. Thank you.' Next she asked him to lie down on the bed in the corner of the room. She leaned over his chest, smeared blodges of paste on his skin and fixed little pads to them. While he stared up at the white ceiling she flicked a switch and concentrated on a tiny television screen on the corner of her desk. Her expression gave nothing away.

After she had removed the paste with a damp flannel she said, 'You can put your shirt back on, Mr Kravits. You are now free to leave.'

Once he was fully dressed, the young man hurried out of the building and down the steps, and ran all the way to the corner where they had parted. They hugged each other again.

'Everything go all right?'

'I think so,' he said. 'They told me I'd be hearing from them in the next few days, once they've had the results of all their tests.'

'Thank God it hasn't been a problem for you.'

'I only wish it wasn't for you.'

'Don't let's even think about it,' said David, holding tightly onto the one person he loved.

Marvin rang a week later to let David know that Dr Royston had given him a clean bill of health. All he had to do now was send the first instalment of $1100 to the insurance company. David posted a cheque off to Geneva Life the following morning. Thereafter his payments were made by wire transfer on the first day of each month.

Nineteen days after the seventh payment had been cleared, David Kravits died of AIDS.

Pat tried to remember the first thing he was meant to do once the will had been read. He was to contact a Mr Levy, David's lawyer, and leave everything in his hands. David had warned him not to become involved in any way himself. Let Levy, as his executor, make the claim from the insurance company, he had said, and then pass the money on to him. If in any doubt, say nothing, was the last piece of advice David had given Pat before he died.

Ten days later, Pat received a letter from a claims representative at Geneva Life requesting an interview with the beneficiary of the policy. Pat passed the letter straight to David's lawyer. Mr Levy wrote back agreeing to an interview, which would take place, at his client's request, at the offices of Levy, Goldberg and Levy in Manhattan.

'Is there anything you haven't told me, Patrick?' Levy asked him a few minutes before the insurance company's claims representative was due to arrive. 'Because if there is, you'd better tell me now.'

'No, Mr Levy, there's nothing more to tell you,' Pat replied, carrying out David's instructions to the letter.

From the moment the meeting began, the representative of Geneva Life, his eyes continually boring into Pat's bowed head, left Mr Levy in no doubt that he was not happy about paying out on this particular claim. But the lawyer stonewalled every question, strengthened by the knowledge that eight months before, when rigorous tests had been taken, Geneva Life's doctors had found no sign of David's being HIV positive.

Levy kept repeating, 'However much noise you make, your company will have to pay up in the end.' He added for good measure, 'If I have not received the full amount due to my client within thirty days, I will immediately instigate proceedings against Geneva Life.' The claims representative asked Levy if he would consider a deal. Levy glanced at Pat, who bowed his head even lower, and replied, 'Certainly not.'

Pat arrived back at the apartment two hours later, exhausted and depressed, fearing that an attack of asthma might be coming on. He tried to prepare some supper before he went to work, but everything seemed so pointless without David. He was already wondering if he should have agreed to a settlement.

The phone rang only once during the evening. Pat rushed to pick it up, hoping it might be either his mother or his sister Ruth. It turned out to be Marvin, who bleated, 'I'm in real trouble, Pat. I'm probably going to lose my job over that policy I made out for your friend David.'

Pat said how sorry he was, but felt there was nothing he could do to help.

'Yes, there is,' insisted Marvin. 'For a start, you could take out a policy yourself. That might just save my skin.'

'I don't think that would be wise,' said Pat, wondering what David would have advised.

'Surely David wouldn't have wanted to see me fired,' Marvin pleaded. 'Have mercy on me, my friend. I just can't afford another divorce.'

'How much would it cost me?' asked Pat, desperate to find some way of getting Marvin off the line.

'You're going to get a million dollars in cash,' Marvin almost shouted, 'and you're asking me what it's going to cost? What's a thousand dollars a month to someone as rich as you?'

'But I can't be sure that I am going to get the million,' Pat protested.

'That's all been settled,' Marvin told him, his voice falling by several decibels. 'I'm not meant to let you know this, but you'll be receiving the cheque on the thirtieth of the month. The company know that your lawyer's got them by the balls . . . You wouldn't even have to make the first payment until after you'd received the million.'

'All right,' said Pat, desperate to be rid of him. 'I'll do it, but not until I've received the cheque.'

'Thank you, my friend. I'll drop round with the paper-work tomorrow night.'

'No, that's not possible,' said Pat. 'I'm working nights this month. You'd better make it tomorrow afternoon.'

'You won't be working nights once you've received that cheque, my friend,' said Marvin, letting out one of his dreadful shrill laughs. 'Lucky man,' he added before he put the phone down.

By the time Marvin came round to the apartment the following afternoon, Pat was already having second thoughts. If he had to visit Dr Royston again, they would immediately realise the truth. But once Marvin had assured him that the medical could be with any doctor of his choice, and that the first payment would be post-dated, he caved in and signed all the forms between the pencilled crosses, making Ruth his sole beneficiary. He hoped David would have approved of that decision, at least.

'Thank you, my friend. I won't be bothering you again,' promised Marvin. His final words as he closed the door behind him were, 'I promise you, you'll never live to regret it.'

Pat saw his doctor a week later. The examination didn't take long, as Pat had recently had a complete check-up. On that occasion, as the doctor recalled, Pat had appeared quite nervous, and couldn't hide his relief when he'd phoned to give him the all-clear. 'Not much wrong with you, Patrick,' he said, 'apart from the asthma, which doesn't seem to be getting any worse.'

Marvin called a week later to let Pat know that the doctor had given him a clean bill of health, and that he had held on to his job with Geneva Life.

'I'm pleased for you,' said Pat. 'But what about my cheque?'

'It will be paid out on the last day of the month. Only a matter of processing it now. Should be with you twenty-four hours before the first payment is due on your policy. Just like I said, you win both ways.'

Pat rang David's lawyer on the last day of the month to ask if he had received the cheque from Geneva Life.

'There was nothing in this morning's post,' Levy told him, 'but I'll phone the other side right now, in case it's already been issued and is on its way. If not, I'll start proceedings against them immediately.'

Pat wondered if he should tell Levy that he had signed a cheque for $1100 which was due to be cleared the following day, and that he only just had sufficient funds in his account to cover it – certainly not enough to see him through until his next pay packet. All his surplus cash had gone to help with David's monthly payments to Geneva Life. He decided not to mention it. David had repeatedly told him that if he was in any doubt, he should say nothing.

'I'll phone you at close of business tonight and let you know exactly what the position is,' said Levy.

'No, that won't be possible,' said Pat. 'I'm on night duty all this week. In fact I have to leave for work right now. Perhaps you could call me first thing tomorrow morning?'

'Will do,' promised the lawyer.

When Pat returned home from work in the early hours, he couldn't get to sleep. He tossed and turned, worrying how he would survive for the rest of the month if his cheque was presented to the bank that morning, and he still hadn't received the million dollars from Geneva Life.

His phone rang at 9.31. Pat grabbed it, and was relieved to hear Mr Levy's voice on the other end of the line.

'Patrick, I had a call from Geneva Life yesterday evening while you were at work, and I must tell you that you've broken Levy's golden rule.'

'Levy's golden rule?' asked Pat, mystified.

'Yes, Levy's golden rule. It's quite simple really, Patrick. By all means drop anything you like, on anyone you like, but don't *ever* drop it all over your own lawyer.'

'I don't understand,' said Pat.

'Your doctor has supplied Geneva Life with a sample of your blood and urine, and they just happen to be identical to the ones Dr Royston has in his laboratory in the name of David Kravits.'

Pat felt the blood draining from his head as he realised the trick Marvin must have played on him. His heart began beating faster and faster. Suddenly his legs gave way, and he collapsed on the floor, gasping for breath.

'Did you hear me, Patrick?' asked Levy. 'Are you still there?'

A paramedic team broke into the apartment twenty minutes later, but, moments before they reached him, Pat had died of a heart attack brought on by a suffocating bout of asthma.

Mr Levy did nothing until he was able to confirm with

Pat's bankers that his client's cheque for $1100 had been cleared by the insurance company.

Nineteen months later Pat's sister Ruth received a payment of one million dollars from Geneva Life, but not until they had gone through a lengthy court battle with Levy, Goldberg and Levy.

The jury finally accepted that Pat had died of natural causes, and that the insurance policy was in existence at the time of his death.

I promise you, Marvin Roebuck lived to regret it.

NEVER STOP
ON THE MOTORWAY

DIANA HAD BEEN HOPING TO GET AWAY by five, so she could be at the farm in time for dinner. She tried not to show her true feelings when at 4.37 her deputy, Phil Haskins, presented her with a complex twelve-page document that required the signature of a director before it could be sent out to the client. Haskins didn't hesitate to remind her that they had lost two similar contracts that week.

It was always the same on a Friday. The phones would go quiet in the middle of the afternoon and then, just as she thought she could slip away, an authorisation would land on her desk. One glance at this particular document and Diana knew there would be no chance of escaping before six.

The demands of being a single parent as well as a director of a small but thriving City company meant there were few moments left in any day to relax, so when it came to the one weekend in four that James and Caroline spent with her ex-husband, Diana would try to leave the office a little earlier than usual to avoid getting snarled up in the weekend traffic.

She read through the first page slowly and made a

couple of emendations, aware that any mistake made hastily on a Friday night could be regretted in the weeks to come. She glanced at the clock on her desk as she signed the final page of the document. It was just flicking over to 5.51.

Diana gathered up her bag and walked purposefully towards the door, dropping the contract on Phil's desk without bothering to suggest that he have a good weekend. She suspected that the paperwork had been on his desk since nine o'clock that morning, but that holding it until 4.37 was his only means of revenge now that she had been made head of department. Once she was safely in the lift, she pressed the button for the basement carpark, calculating that the delay would probably add an extra hour to her journey.

She stepped out of the lift, walked over to her Audi estate, unlocked the door and threw her bag onto the back seat. When she drove up onto the street the stream of twilight traffic was just about keeping pace with the pinstriped pedestrians who, like worker ants, were hurrying towards the nearest hole in the ground.

She flicked on the six o'clock news. The chimes of Big Ben rang out, before spokesmen from each of the three main political parties gave their views on the European election results. John Major was refusing to comment on his future. The Conservative Party's explanation for its poor showing was that only thirty-six per cent of the country had bothered to go to the polls. Diana felt guilty – she was among the sixty-four per cent who had failed to register their vote.

The newscaster moved on to say that the situation in Bosnia remained desperate, and that the UN was threatening dire consequences if Radovan Karadzik and the Serbs didn't come to an agreement with the other warring parties. Diana's mind began to drift – such a threat was hardly news any longer. She suspected that if she turned on the radio in a year's time they would probably be repeating it word for word.

As her car crawled round Russell Square, she began to think about the weekend ahead. It had been over a year since John had told her that he had met another woman and wanted a divorce. She still wondered why, after seven years of marriage, she hadn't been more shocked – or at least angry – at his betrayal. Since her appointment as a director, she had to admit they had spent less and less time together. And perhaps she had become anaesthetised by the fact that a third of the married couples in Britain were now divorced or separated. Her parents had been unable to hide their disappointment, but then they had been married for forty-two years.

The divorce had been amicable enough, as John, who earned less than she did – one of their problems, perhaps – had given in to most of her demands. She had kept the flat in Putney, the Audi estate and the children, to whom John was allowed access one weekend in four. He would have picked them up from school earlier that afternoon, and, as usual, he'd return them to the flat in Putney around seven on Sunday evening.

Diana would go to almost any lengths to avoid being

left on her own in Putney when they weren't around, and although she regularly grumbled about being landed with the responsibility of bringing up two children without a father, she missed them desperately the moment they were out of sight.

She hadn't taken a lover and she didn't sleep around. None of the senior staff at the office had ever gone further than asking her out to lunch. Perhaps because only three of them were unmarried – and not without reason. The one person she might have considered having a relationship with had made it abundantly clear that he only wanted to spend the night with her, not the days.

In any case, Diana had decided long ago that if she was to be taken seriously as the company's first woman director, an office affair, however casual or short-lived, could only end in tears. Men are so vain, she thought. A woman only had to make one mistake and she was immediately labelled as promiscuous. Then every other man on the premises either smirks behind your back, or treats your thigh as an extension of the arm on his chair.

Diana groaned as she came to a halt at yet another red light. In twenty minutes she hadn't covered more than a couple of miles. She opened the glove box on the passenger side and fumbled in the dark for a cassette. She found one and pressed it into the slot, hoping it would be Pavarotti, only to be greeted by the strident tones of Gloria Gaynor assuring her 'I will survive'. She smiled and thought about Daniel, as the light changed to green.

She and Daniel had read Economics at Bristol University in the early 1980s, friends but never lovers. Then Daniel met Rachael, who had come up a year after them, and from that moment he had never looked at another woman. They married the day he graduated, and after they returned from their honeymoon Daniel took over the management of his father's farm in Bedfordshire. Three children had followed in quick succession, and Diana had been proud when she was asked to be godmother to Sophie, the eldest. Daniel and Rachael had now been married for twelve years, and Diana felt confident that they wouldn't be disappointing *their* parents with any suggestion of a divorce. Although they were convinced she led an exciting and fulfilling life, Diana often envied their gentle and uncomplicated existence.

She was regularly asked to spend the weekend with them in the country, but for every two or three invitations Daniel issued, she only accepted one – not because she wouldn't have liked to join them more often, but because since her divorce she had no desire to take advantage of their hospitality.

Although she enjoyed her work, it had been a bloody week. Two contracts had fallen through, James had been dropped from the school football team, and Caroline had never stopped telling her that her father didn't mind her watching television when she ought to be doing her prep.

Another traffic light changed to red.

It took Diana nearly an hour to travel the seven miles out of the city, and when she reached the first dual carriageway, she glanced up at the A1 sign, more out of habit than to seek guidance, because she knew every yard of the road from her office to the farm. She tried to increase her speed, but it was quite impossible, as both lanes remained obstinately crowded.

'Damn.' She had forgotten to get them a present, even a decent bottle of claret. 'Damn,' she repeated: Daniel and Rachael always did the giving. She began to wonder if she could pick something up on the way, then remembered there was nothing but service stations between here and the farm. She couldn't turn up with yet another box of chocolates they'd never eat. When she reached the roundabout that led onto the A1, she managed to push the car over fifty for the first time. She began to relax, allowing her mind to drift with the music.

There was no warning. Although she immediately slammed her foot on the brakes, it was already too late. There was a dull thump from the front bumper, and a slight shudder rocked the car.

A small black creature had shot across her path, and despite her quick reactions, she hadn't been able to avoid hitting it. Diana swung onto the hard shoulder and screeched to a halt, wondering if the animal could possibly have survived. She reversed slowly back to the spot where she thought she had hit it as the traffic roared past her.

And then she saw it, lying on the grass verge – a cat that had crossed the road for the tenth time. She stepped out of the car, and walked towards the lifeless body. Suddenly Diana felt sick. She had two cats of her own, and she knew she would never be able to tell the children what she had done. She picked up the dead animal and laid it gently in the ditch by the roadside.

'I'm so sorry,' she said, feeling a little silly. She gave it one last look before walking back to her car. Ironically, she had chosen the Audi for its safety features.

She climbed back into the car and switched on the ignition to find Gloria Gaynor was still belting out her opinion of men. She turned her off, and tried to stop thinking about the cat as she waited for a gap in the traffic large enough to allow her to ease her way back into the slow lane. She eventually succeeded, but was still unable to erase the dead cat from her mind.

Diana had accelerated up to fifty again when she suddenly became aware of a pair of headlights shining through her rear windscreen. She put up her arm and waved in her rear-view mirror, but the lights continued to dazzle her. She slowed down to allow the vehicle to pass, but the driver showed no interest in doing so. Diana began to wonder if there was something wrong with her car. Was one of her lights not working? Was the exhaust billowing smoke? Was . . .

She decided to speed up and put some distance between herself and the vehicle behind, but it remained within a few yards of her bumper. She tried to snatch a look at the driver in her rear-view mirror, but it was hard to see much in the harshness of the lights. As her eyes became more accustomed to the glare, she could make out the silhouette of a large black van bearing down on her, and what looked like a young man behind the wheel. He seemed to be waving at her.

Diana slowed down again as she approached the next roundabout, giving him every chance to overtake her on the outside lane, but once again he didn't take the opportunity, and just sat on her bumper, his headlights still undimmed. She waited for a small gap in the traffic coming from her right. When one appeared she slammed her foot on the accelerator, shot across the roundabout and sped on up the A1.

She was rid of him at last. She was just beginning to relax and to think about Sophie, who always waited up so that she could read to her, when suddenly those high-beam headlights were glaring through her rear windscreen and blinding her once again. If anything, they were even closer to her than before.

She slowed down, he slowed down. She accelerated, he accelerated. She tried to think what she could do next, and began waving frantically at passing motorists as they sped by, but they remained oblivious to her predicament. She tried to think of other ways she might alert someone, and suddenly recalled that when she had joined the board of the company they had suggested she have a car phone fitted. Diana had decided it could wait until the car went in for its next service, which should have been a fortnight ago.

She brushed her hand across her forehead and removed a film of perspiration, thought for a moment, then manoeuvred her car into the fast lane. The van swung across after her, and hovered so close to her bumper that she became fearful that if she so much as touched her brakes she might unwittingly cause an enormous pile-up.

Diana took the car up to ninety, but the van wouldn't be shaken off. She pushed her foot further down on the accelerator and touched a hundred, but it still remained less than a car's length behind.

She flicked her headlights onto high-beam, turned on her hazard lights and blasted her horn at anyone who dared to remain in her path. She could only hope that the police might see her, wave her onto the hard shoulder and book her for speeding. A fine would be infinitely preferable to a crash with a young tearaway, she thought, as the Audi estate passed a hundred and ten for the first time in its life. But the black van couldn't be shaken off.

Without warning, she swerved back into the middle lane and took her foot off the accelerator, causing the van to draw level with her, which gave her a chance to look at the driver for the first time. He was wearing a black leather jacket and pointing menacingly at her. She shook her fist at him and accelerated away, but he simply swung across behind her like an Olympic runner determined not to allow his rival to break clear.

And then she remembered, and felt sick for a second time that night. 'Oh my God,' she shouted aloud in terror. In a flood, the details of the murder that had taken place on the same road a few months before came rushing back to her. A woman had been raped before having her throat cut with a knife with a serrated edge and dumped in a ditch. For weeks there had been signs posted on the A1 appealing to passing motorists to phone a certain number if they had any information that might assist the police with their enquiries. The signs had now disappeared, but the police were still searching for the killer. Diana began to tremble as she remembered their warning to all woman drivers: 'Never stop on the motorway'.

A few seconds later she saw a road sign she knew well. She had reached it far sooner than she had anticipated. In three miles she would have to leave the motorway for the sliproad that led to the farm. She began to pray that if she took her usual turning, the black-jacketed man would continue on up the A1 and she would finally be rid of him.

Diana decided that the time had come for her to speed him on his way. She swung back into the fast lane and once again put her foot down on the accelerator. She reached a hundred miles per hour for the second time as she sped past the two-mile sign. Her body was now covered in sweat, and the speedometer touched a hundred and ten. She checked her rear-view mirror, but he was still right behind her. She would have to pick the exact moment if she was to execute her plan successfully. With a mile to go, she began to look to her left, so as to be sure her timing would be perfect. She no longer needed to check in her mirror to know that he would still be there.

The next signpost showed three diagonal white lines, warning her that she ought to be on the inside lane if she intended to leave the motorway at the next junction. She kept the car in the outside lane at a hundred miles per hour until she spotted a large enough gap. Two white lines appeared by the roadside: Diana knew she would have only one chance to make her escape. As she passed the sign with a single white line on it she suddenly swung across the road at ninety miles per hour, causing cars in the middle and inside lanes to throw on their brakes and blast out their angry opinions. But Diana didn't care what they thought of her, because she was now travelling down the sliproad to safety, and the black van was speeding on up the A1.

She laughed out loud with relief. To her right, she could see the steady flow of traffic on the motorway. But then her laugh turned to a scream as she saw the black van cut sharply across the motorway in front of a lorry, mount the grass verge and career onto the sliproad, swinging from side to side. It nearly drove over the edge and into a ditch, but somehow managed to steady itself, ending up a few yards behind her, its lights once again glaring through her rear windscreen.

When she reached the top of the sliproad, Diana turned left in the direction of the farm, frantically trying to work out what she should do next. The nearest town was about twelve miles away on the main road, and the farm was only seven, but five of those miles were down a winding, unlit country lane. She checked her petrol gauge. It was nearing empty, but there should still be enough in the tank for her to consider either option. There was less than a mile to go before she reached the turning, so she had only a minute in which to make up her mind.

With a hundred yards to go, she settled on the farm. Despite the unlit lane, she knew every twist and turn, and she felt confident that her pursuer wouldn't. Once she reached the farm she could be out of the car and inside the house long before he could catch her. In any case, once he saw the farmhouse, surely he would flee.

The minute was up. Diana touched the brakes and skidded into a country road illuminated only by the moon.

Diana banged the palms of her hands on the steering wheel. Had she made the wrong decision? She glanced up at her rear-view mirror. Had he given up? Of course he hadn't. The back of a Land Rover loomed up in front of her. Diana slowed down, waiting for a corner she knew well, where the road widened slightly. She held her breath, crashed into third gear, and overtook. Would a head-on collision be preferable to a cut throat? She rounded the bend and saw an empty road ahead of her. Once again she pressed her foot down, this time managing to put a clear seventy, perhaps even a hundred, yards between her and her pursuer, but this only offered her a few moments' respite. Before long the familiar headlights came bearing down on her once again.

With each bend Diana was able to gain a little time as the van continued to lurch from side to side, unfamiliar with the road, but she never managed a clear break of more than a few seconds. She checked the mileometer. From the turn-off on the main road to the farm it was just over five miles, and she must have covered about two by now. She began to watch each tenth of a mile clicking up, terrified at the thought of the van overtaking her and forcing her into the ditch. She stuck determinedly to the centre of the road.

Another mile passed, and still he clung on to her. Suddenly she saw a car coming towards her. She switched her headlights to full beam and pressed on the horn. The other car retaliated by mimicking her actions, which caused her to slow down and brush against the hedgerow as they shot past each other. She checked the mileometer once again. Only two miles to go.

Diana would slow down and then speed up at each familiar bend in the road, making sure the van was never given enough room to pull level with her. She tried to concentrate on what she should do once the farmhouse came into sight. She reckoned that the drive leading up to the house must be about half a mile long. It was full of potholes and bumps which Daniel had often explained he couldn't afford to have repaired. But at least it was only wide enough for one car.

The gate to the driveway was usually left open for her, though on the odd rare occasion Daniel had forgotten, and she'd had to get out of the car and open it for herself. She couldn't risk that tonight. If the gate was closed, she would have to travel on to the next town and stop outside the Crimson Kipper, which was always crowded at this time on a Friday night, or, if she could find it, on the steps of the local police station. She checked her petrol gauge again. It was now touching red. 'Oh my God,' she said, realising she might not have enough petrol to reach the town.

She could only pray that Daniel had remembered to leave the gate open.

She swerved out of the next bend and speeded up, but once again she managed to gain only a few yards, and she knew that within seconds he would be back in place. He was. For the next few hundred yards they remained within feet of each other, and she felt certain he must run into the back of her. She didn't once dare to touch her brakes — if they crashed in that lane, far from any help, she would have no hope of getting away from him.

She checked her mileometer. A mile to go.

'The gate must be open. It must be open,' she prayed. As she swung round the next bend, she could make out the outline of the farmhouse in the distance. She almost screamed with relief when she saw that the lights were on in the downstairs rooms.

She shouted, 'Thank God!' then remembered the gate again, and changed her plea to 'Dear God, let it be open.' She would know what needed to be done as soon as she came round the last bend. 'Let it be open, just this once,' she pleaded. 'I'll never ask for anything again, ever.' She swung round the final bend only inches ahead of the black van. 'Please, please, please.' And then she saw the gate.

It was open.

Her clothes were now drenched in sweat. She slowed down, wrenched the gearbox into second, and threw the car between the gap and into the bumpy driveway, hitting the gatepost on her right-hand side as she careered on up towards the house. The van didn't hesitate to follow her, and was still only inches behind as she straightened up. Diana kept her hand pressed down on the horn as the car bounced and lurched over the mounds and potholes.

Flocks of startled crows flapped out of overhanging branches, screeching as they shot into the air. Diana began screaming, 'Daniel! Daniel!' Two hundred yards ahead of her, the porch light went on.

Her headlights were now shining onto the front of the house, and her hand was still pressed on the horn. With a hundred yards to go, she spotted Daniel coming out of the front door, but she didn't slow down, and neither did the van behind her. With fifty yards to go she began flashing her lights at Daniel. She could now make out the puzzled, anxious expression on his face.

With thirty yards to go she threw on her brakes. The heavy estate car skidded across the gravel in front of the house, coming to a halt in the flowerbed just below the kitchen window. She heard the screech of brakes behind her. The leather-jacketed man, unfamiliar with the terrain, had been unable to react quickly enough, and as soon as his wheels touched the gravelled forecourt he began to skid out of control. A second later the van came crashing into the back of her car, slamming it against the wall of the house and shattering the glass in the kitchen window.

Diana leapt out of the car, screaming, 'Daniel! Get a gun, get a gun!' She pointed back at the van. 'That bastard's been chasing me for the last twenty miles!'

The man jumped out of the van and began limping towards them. Diana ran into the house. Daniel followed and grabbed a shotgun, normally reserved for rabbits, that was leaning against the wall. He ran back outside to face the unwelcome visitor, who had come to a halt by the back of Diana's Audi.

Daniel raised the shotgun to his shoulder and stared straight at him. 'Don't move or I'll shoot,' he said calmly. And then he remembered the gun wasn't loaded. Diana ducked back out of the house, but remained several yards behind him.

'Not me! Not me!' shouted the leather-jacketed youth, as Rachael appeared in the doorway.

'What's going on?' she asked nervously.

'Ring for the police,' was all Daniel said, and his wife quickly disappeared back into the house.

Daniel advanced towards the terrified-looking young man, the gun aimed squarely at his chest.

'Not me! Not me!' he shouted again, pointing at the Audi. 'He's in the car!' He quickly turned to face Diana. 'I saw him get in when you were parked on the hard shoulder. What else could I have done? You just wouldn't pull over.'

Daniel advanced cautiously towards the rear door of the car and ordered the young man to open it slowly, while he kept the gun aimed at his chest.

The youth opened the door, and quickly took a pace backwards. The three of them stared down at a man crouched on the floor of the car. In his right hand he held a long-bladed knife with a serrated edge. Daniel swung the barrel of the gun down to point at him, but said nothing.

The sound of a police siren could just be heard in the distance.

NOT FOR SALE

SALLY SUMMERS WON HER SCHOOL'S senior art prize at the age of fourteen. In her last four years at St Bride's the only serious competition was for second place. When, in her final year, she was awarded the top scholarship to the Slade School of Fine Art none of her contemporaries was at all surprised. The headmistress told the assembled parents on Speech Day that she was confident Sally had a distinguished career ahead of her, and that her work would soon be exhibited in one of London's major galleries. Sally was flattered by all this unqualified praise, but still wasn't sure if she had any real talent.

By the end of her first year at the Slade, the staff and senior students were already becoming aware of Sally's work. Her drawing technique was regarded as quite exceptional, and her brushwork became bolder with each term. But, above all, it was the originality of her ideas that caused other students to stop and stare at her canvases.

In her final year, Sally won both the Mary Rischgitz Prize for oil painting and the Henry Tonks Prize for drawing: a rare double. They were presented to her by

Sir Roger de Grey, the President of the Royal Academy, and Sally was among that tiny group who were spoken of as 'having a future'. But surely, she told her parents, that could be said of the top student in any year – and most of them ended up working in the creative departments of advertising agencies, or teaching art to bored schoolchildren in far-flung parts of the kingdom.

Once she had graduated, Sally had to decide whether she too would apply for a job with an advertising agency, take up a teaching appointment, or risk everything and try to put together enough original work for a London gallery to consider her for a one-woman show.

Her parents were convinced that their daughter had real talent, but what do parents know when you're their only child? thought Sally. Especially when one of them was a music teacher and the other an accountant who were the first to admit that they didn't know much about art, but they knew what they liked. Still, they seemed quite willing to support her for another year if she wanted (to use an expression of the young) to go for it.

Sally was painfully aware that, although her parents were fairly comfortably off, another year in which she produced no income could only be a burden for them. After much soul-searching she told them, 'One year, and one year only. After that, if the paintings aren't good enough, or if no one shows any interest in exhibiting them, I'll be realistic and look for a proper job.'

For the next six months Sally worked hours that she hadn't realised existed when she'd been a student.

During that time she produced a dozen canvases. She allowed no one to see them, for fear that her parents and friends would not be frank with her. She was determined to finish her portfolio and then listen only to the toughest opinions possible, those of the professional gallery owners, and, tougher still, those of the buying public.

Sally had always been a voracious reader, and she continued to devour books and monographs on artists from Bellini to Hockney. The more she read, the more she became aware that however talented an artist might be, it was industry and dedication that ultimately marked out the few who succeeded from the many who failed. This inspired her to work still harder, and she began to turn down invitations to parties, dances, even weekends with old friends, making use of every spare moment to visit art galleries or to attend lectures on the great masters.

By the eleventh month, Sally had completed twenty-seven works, but she still wasn't sure whether they displayed any real talent. Nevertheless, she felt the time had finally come to allow others to pass judgement on them.

She looked long and hard at each of the twenty-seven paintings, and the following morning she packed six of them in a large canvas folder her parents had given her the previous Christmas, and joined the early-morning commuters on their journey from Sevenoaks into London.

Sally began her quest in Cork Street, where she came across galleries exhibiting works by Bacon, Freud,

Hockney, Dunston and Chadwick. She felt overawed at the prospect of even entering their portals, let alone submitting her own humble work to the appraisal of their proprietors. She humped her canvas folder a couple of blocks north to Conduit Street, and in the windows she recognised the works of Jones, Campbell, Wczenski, Frink and Paolozzi. She became even more discouraged and unwilling to push open any of the galleries' front doors.

Sally returned home that night exhausted, her canvas folder unopened. She understood for the first time how an author must feel after receiving a string of rejection slips. She was unable to sleep that night. But as she lay awake she came to the conclusion that she must know the truth about her work, even if it meant being humiliated.

She joined the commuters again the following morning, and this time headed for Duke Street, St James's. She didn't bother with the galleries exhibiting old masters, Dutch still lifes or English landscapes, and therefore walked straight past Johnny van Haeften and Rafael Valls. Halfway down the street she turned right, and finally came to a halt outside the Simon Bouchier Gallery, which was exhibiting the sculptures of the late Sydney Harpley and the paintings of Muriel Pemberton, whose obituary Sally had read in the *Independent* only a few days before.

It was the thought of death that made Sally settle on the Bouchier Gallery. Perhaps they would be looking for someone young, she tried to convince herself, someone who had a long career ahead of them.

She stepped inside the gallery and found herself in a large, empty room, surrounded by Muriel Pemberton's watercolours. 'Can I help you?' asked a young woman who was sitting behind a desk near the window.

'No, thank you,' Sally replied. 'I was just looking.'

The girl eyed Sally's canvas folder, but said nothing. Sally decided she would do one circuit of the room, and then make good her escape. She began to circle the gallery, studying the pictures carefully. They were good, very good – but Sally believed she could do just as well, given time. She would have liked to see Muriel Pemberton's work when *she* was her age.

When Sally reached the far end of the gallery, she became aware of an office in which a short, balding man, wearing an old tweed jacket and corduroy trousers, was closely examining a picture. He looked about the same age as her father. Also studying the picture was another man, who caused Sally to stop in her tracks. He must have been a little over six foot, with those dark Italian looks that people normally only come across in glossy magazines; and *he* was old enough to be her brother.

Was he Mr Bouchier? she wondered. She hoped so, because if he owned the gallery she might be able to summon up the courage to introduce herself to him, once the little man in the scruffy jacket had left. At that moment the young man looked up and gave her a huge grin. Sally turned quickly away and began to study the pictures on the far wall.

She was wondering if it was worth hanging around any longer when the two men suddenly strolled out of the office and began walking towards the door.

She froze, pretending to concentrate on a portrait of a young girl in pastel blues and yellows, a picture that had a Matisse-like quality about it.

'What's in there?' asked a cheeky voice. Sally turned round and came face to face with the two men. The smaller one was pointing at her canvas bag.

'Just a few pictures,' Sally stammered. 'I'm an artist.'

'Let's have a look,' said the man, 'and perhaps *I* can decide if you're an artist or not.'

Sally hesitated.

'Come on, come on,' he teased. 'I haven't got all day. As you can see, I have an important client to take to lunch,' he added, indicating the tall, well-dressed young man, who still hadn't spoken.

'Oh, are *you* Mr Bouchier?' she asked, unable to hide her disappointment.

'Yes. Now, am I going to be allowed to look at your pictures or not?'

Sally quickly unzipped her canvas bag and laid out the six paintings on the floor. Both of the men bent down and studied them for some time before either offered an opinion.

'Not bad,' said Bouchier eventually. 'Not bad at all. Leave them with me for a few days, and then let's meet again next week.' He paused. 'Say Monday, 11.30. And if you have any more examples of your recent work, bring them with you.' Sally was speechless. 'Can't see you before Monday,' he continued, 'because the RA's Summer Exhibition opens tomorrow. So for the next few days I won't have a moment to spare. Now, if you'll excuse me . . .'

The younger man was still examining Sally's pictures closely. At last he looked up at her. 'I'd like to buy the one of the interior with the black cat on the windowsill. How much is it?'

'Well,' said Sally, 'I'm not sure . . .'

'N.F.S.,' said Mr Bouchier firmly, guiding his client towards the door.

'By the way,' the taller man said, turning back, 'I am Antonio Flavelli. My friends call me Tony.' But Mr Bouchier was already pushing him out onto the street.

Sally returned home that afternoon with an empty canvas folder, and was prepared to admit to her parents that a London dealer had shown an interest in her work. But it was, she insisted, no more than an interest.

The following morning Sally decided to go to the opening day of the Royal Academy Summer Exhibition, which would give her the chance to find out just how good her rivals were. For over an hour she stood in the long queue that stretched from the front door, right across the carpark and out onto the pavement. When she eventually reached the top of the wide staircase, she wished she was six feet six tall, so that she could see over the tops of the heads of the mass of people who were crowding every room. After a couple of hours strolling round the many galleries, Sally was confident that she was already good enough to enter a couple of her pictures for next year's exhibition.

She stopped to admire a Craigie Aitchison of Christ

on the cross, and checked in her little blue catalogue to
find out the price: ten thousand pounds, more than she
could hope to earn if she were to sell every one of her
canvases. Suddenly her concentration was broken, as a
soft Italian voice behind her said, 'Hello, Sally.' She
swung round to find Tony Flavelli smiling down at
her.

'Mr Flavelli,' she said.

'Tony, please. You like Craigie Aitchison?'

'He's superb,' Sally replied. 'I know his work well –
I had the privilege of being taught by him when I was
at the Slade.'

'I can remember, not so long ago, when you could
pick up an Aitchison for two, three hundred pounds at
the most. Perhaps the same thing will happen to you
one day. Have you seen anything else you think I ought
to look at?'

Sally was flattered to have her advice sought by a
serious collector, and said, 'Yes, I think the sculpture of
"Books on a Chair" by Julie Major is very striking. She
has talent, and I'm sure she has a future.'

'So do you,' said Tony.

'Do you think so?' asked Sally.

'It's not important what I think,' said Tony. 'But
Simon Bouchier is convinced.'

'Are you teasing me?' asked Sally.

'No, I'm not, as you'll find out for yourself when you
see him next Monday. He talked of little else over lunch
yesterday – "The daring brushwork, the unusual use of
colour, the originality of ideas." I thought he was never

going to stop. Still, he's promised I can have "The Sleeping Cat that Never Moved" once you've both settled on a price.'

Sally was speechless.

'Good luck,' Tony said, turning to leave. 'Not that I think you need it.' He hesitated for a moment before swinging back to face her. 'By the way, are you going to the Hockney exhibition?'

'I didn't even know there was one,' Sally confessed.

'There's a private view this evening. Six to eight.' Looking straight into her eyes he said, 'Would you like to join me?'

She hesitated, but only for a moment. 'That would be nice.'

'Good, then why don't we meet in the Ritz Palm Court at 6.30.' Before Sally could tell him that she didn't know where the Ritz was, let alone its Palm Court, the tall, elegant man had disappeared into the crowd.

Sally suddenly felt gauche and scruffy, but then, she hadn't dressed that morning with the Ritz in mind. She looked at her watch – 12.45 – and began to wonder if she had enough time to return home, change, and be back at the Ritz by 6.30. She decided that she didn't have much choice, as she doubted if they would let her into such a grand hotel dressed in jeans and a T-shirt of Munch's 'The Scream'. She ran down the wide staircase, out onto Piccadilly, and all the way to the nearest tube station.

When she arrived back home in Sevenoaks – far earlier than her mother had expected – she rushed into the kitchen and explained that she would be going out again shortly.

'Was the Summer Exhibition any good?' her mother asked.

'Not bad,' Sally replied as she ran upstairs. But once she was out of earshot she muttered under her breath, 'Certainly didn't see a lot that worried me.'

'Will you be in for supper?' asked her mother, sticking her head out from behind the kitchen door.

'I don't think so,' shouted Sally. She disappeared into her bedroom and began flinging off her clothes before heading for the bathroom.

She crept back downstairs an hour later, having tried on and rejected several outfits. She checked her dress in the hall mirror – a little too short, perhaps, but at least it showed her legs to best advantage. She could still remember those art students who during life classes had spent more time staring at her legs than at the model they were supposed to be drawing. She only hoped Tony would be similarly captivated.

' 'Bye, Mum,' she shouted, and quickly closed the door behind her before her mother could see what she was wearing.

Sally took the next train back to Charing Cross. She stepped on to the platform unwilling to admit to any passer-by that she had no idea where the Ritz was, so she hailed a taxi, praying she could get to the hotel for four pounds, because that was all she had on her. Her eyes remained fixed on the meter as it clicked past two pounds, and then three – far too quickly, she thought –

three pounds twenty, forty, sixty, eighty . . . She was just about to ask the cabbie to stop, so she could jump out and walk the rest of the way, when he drew in to the kerb.

The door was immediately opened by a statuesque man dressed in a heavy blue trenchcoat who raised his top hat to her. Sally handed over her four pounds to the cabbie, feeling guilty about the measly twenty pence tip. She ran up the steps, through the revolving door and into the hotel foyer. She checked her watch: 6.10. She decided she had better go back outside, walk slowly around the block, and return a little later. But just as she reached the door, an elegant man in a long black coat approached her and asked, 'Can I help you, madam?'

'I'm meeting Mr Tony Flavelli,' Sally stammered, hoping he would recognise the name.

'Mr Flavelli. Of course, madam. Allow me to show you to his table in the Palm Court.'

She followed the black-coated man down the wide, deeply carpeted corridor, then up three steps to a large open area full of small circular tables, almost all of which were occupied.

Sally was directed to a table at the side, and once she was seated a waiter asked, 'Can I get you something to drink, madam? A glass of champagne, perhaps?'

'Oh, no,' said Sally. 'A coke will be just fine.'

The waiter bowed and left her. Sally gazed nervously around the beautifully furnished room. Everyone seemed so relaxed and sophisticated. The waiter returned a few moments later and placed a fine cut-glass tumbler with Coca-Cola, ice and lemon in front of her. She thanked him and began sipping her drink, checking her watch every few minutes. She pulled her dress down as far as it would go, wishing she had chosen something longer. She was becoming anxious about what would happen if Tony didn't turn up, because she didn't have any money left to pay for her drink. And then suddenly she saw him, dressed in a loose double-breasted suit and an open-neck cream shirt. He had stopped to chat to an elegant young woman on the steps. After a couple of minutes he kissed her on the cheek, and made his way over to Sally.

'I am so sorry,' he said. 'I didn't mean to keep you waiting. I do hope I'm not late.'

'No, no you're not. I arrived a few minutes early,' Sally said, flustered, as he bent down and kissed her hand.

'What did you think of the Summer Exhibition?' he asked as the waiter appeared by his side.

'Your usual, sir?' he asked.

'Yes, thank you, Michael,' he replied.

'I enjoyed it,' said Sally. 'But . . .'

'But you felt you could have done just as well yourself,' he suggested.

'I didn't mean to imply that,' she said, looking up to see if he was teasing. But the expression on his face remained serious. 'I'm sure I will enjoy the Hockney more,' she added as a glass of champagne was placed on the table.

'Then I'll have to come clean,' said Tony.

Sally put down her drink and stared at him, not knowing what he meant.

'There isn't a Hockney exhibition on at the moment,' he said. 'Unless you want to fly to Glasgow.'

Sally looked puzzled. 'But you said . . .'

'I just wanted an excuse to see you again.'

Sally felt bemused and flattered, and was uncertain how to respond.

'I'll leave the choice to you,' he said. 'We could have dinner together, or you could simply take the train back to Sevenoaks.'

'How did you know I live in Sevenoaks?'

'It was inscribed in big bold letters on the side of your canvas folder,' said Tony with a smile.

Sally laughed. 'I'll settle for dinner,' she said. Tony paid for the drinks, then guided Sally out of the hotel and a few yards down the road to a restaurant on the corner of Arlington Street.

This time Sally did try a glass of champagne, and allowed Tony to select for her from the menu. He could not have been more attentive, and seemed to know so much about so many things, even if she didn't manage to find out exactly what he did.

After Tony had called for the bill, he asked her if she would like to have coffee at 'my place'.

'I'm afraid I can't,' she said, looking at her watch. 'I'd miss the last train home.'

'Then I'll drive you to the station. We wouldn't want you to miss the last train home, would we?' he said, scrawling his signature across the bill.

This time she knew he was teasing her, and she blushed.

When Tony dropped her off at Charing Cross he asked, 'When can I see you again?'

'I have an appointment with Mr Bouchier at 11.30 . . .'

'. . . next Monday morning, if I remember correctly. So why don't we have a celebration lunch together after he's signed you up? I'll come to the gallery at about 12.30. Goodbye.' He leaned over and kissed her gently on the lips.

Sitting in a cold, smelly carriage on the last train back to Sevenoaks, Sally couldn't help wondering what coffee at Tony's place might have been like.

Sally walked into the gallery a few minutes before 11.30 the following Monday to find Simon Bouchier kneeling on the carpet, head down, studying some paintings. They weren't hers, and she hoped he felt the same way about them as she did.

Simon looked up. 'Good morning, Sally. Dreadful, aren't they? You have to look through an awful lot of rubbish before you come across someone who shows any real talent.' He rose to his feet. 'Mind you, Natasha Krasnoselyodkina does have one advantage over you.'

'What's that?' asked Sally.

'She would draw the crowds for any opening.'

'Why?'

'Because she claims to be a Russian countess. Hints

she's a direct descendant of the last tsar. Frankly, I think the Pearly Queen is about the nearest she's been to royalty, but still, she's the "in" face at the moment – a sort of "Minah Bird" of the nineties. What did Andy Warhol say – "In the future, everyone will be famous for fifteen minutes." By that standard, Natasha looks good for about thirty. I see this morning's tabloids are even hinting she's the new love in Prince Andrew's life. My bet is they've never met. But if he were to turn up at the opening, we'd be packed out, that's for sure. We wouldn't sell a picture, of course, but we'd be packed out.'

'Why wouldn't you sell anything?' asked Sally.

'Because the public are not that stupid when it comes to buying paintings. A picture is a large investment for most people, and they want to believe that they have a good eye, and that they've invested wisely. Natasha's pictures won't satisfy them on either count. With you, though, Sally, I'm beginning to feel they might be convinced on both. But first, let me see the rest of your portfolio.'

Sally unzipped her bulging folder, and laid out twenty-one paintings on the carpet.

Simon dropped to his knees, and didn't speak again for some time. When he eventually did offer an opinion, it was only to repeat the single word 'Consistent.'

'But I'll need even more, and of the same quality,' he said after he had risen to his feet. 'Another dozen canvases at least, and by October. I want you to concentrate on interiors – you're good at interiors. And they'll have to be better than good if you expect me to invest my time, expertise, and a great deal of money in you, young lady. Do you think you can manage another dozen pictures by October, Miss Summers?'

'Yes, of course,' said Sally, giving little thought to the fact that October was only five months away.

'That's good, because if you deliver, and I only say *if*, I'll risk the expense of launching you on an unsuspecting public this autumn.' He walked into his office, flicked through his diary and said, 'October the seventeenth, to be precise.'

Sally was speechless.

'I don't suppose you could manage an affair with Prince Charles lasting, say, from the end of September to the beginning of November? That would knock the Russian Countess from the Mile End Road off the front pages and guarantee us a full house on opening night.'

'I'm afraid not,' said Sally, 'especially if you expect me to produce another dozen canvases by then.'

'Pity,' said Simon, 'because if we can attract the punters to the opening, I'm confident they'll want to buy your work. The problem is always getting them to come for an unknown.' He suddenly looked over Sally's shoulder and said, 'Hello, Tony. I wasn't expecting to see you today.'

'Perhaps that's because you're not seeing me,' Tony replied. 'I've just come to whisk Sally off to what I was rather hoping might be a celebratory lunch.'

'"The Summers Exhibition",' Simon said, grinning

at his little play on words, 'will open not in June at the Royal Academy, but in October at the Bouchier Gallery. October the seventeenth is to be Sally's day of reckoning.'

'Congratulations,' said Tony, turning to Sally. 'I'll bring all my friends.'

'I'm only interested in the rich ones,' said Simon, as someone else entered the Gallery.

'Natasha,' said Simon, turning to face a slim, dark-haired woman. Sally's first reaction was that she should have been an artists' model, not an artist.

'Thanks for coming back so quickly, Natasha. Have a nice lunch, you two,' he added, smiling at Tony, who couldn't take his eyes off the new arrival.

Natasha didn't notice, as her only interest seemed to be in Sally's pictures. She was unable to conceal her envy as Tony and Sally walked out of the gallery.

'Wasn't she stunning?' said Sally.

'Was she?' said Tony. 'I didn't notice.'

'I wouldn't blame Prince Andrew if he was having an affair with her.'

'Damn,' said Tony placing a hand in his inside pocket. 'I forgot to give Simon a cheque I promised him. Don't move, I'll be back in a minute.'

Tony sprinted off in the direction of the gallery, and Sally waited on the corner for what seemed like an awfully long minute before he reappeared back on the street.

'Sorry. Simon was on the phone,' Tony explained. He took Sally's arm and led her across the road to a small Italian restaurant, where once again he seemed to have his own table.

He ordered a bottle of champagne, 'To celebrate your great triumph.' As Sally raised her glass in response, she realised for the first time just how much work she would have to do before October if she was going to keep her promise to Simon.

When Tony poured her a second glass, Sally smiled. 'It's been a memorable day. I ought to phone my parents and let them know, but I don't think they'd believe me.'

When a third glass had been filled and Sally still hadn't finished her salad, Tony took her hand, leaned across and kissed it. 'I've never met anyone as beautiful as you,' he said. 'And certainly no one as talented.'

Sally quickly took a gulp of the champagne, to hide her embarrassment. She still wasn't sure whether to believe him, but a glass of white wine, followed by two glasses of red, helped to convince her that she should.

After Tony had signed the bill, he asked her again if she would like to come back to his place for coffee. Sally had already decided that she wasn't going to be able to do any work that day, so she nodded her agreement. In any case, she felt she had earned an afternoon off.

In the taxi on the way to Chelsea, she rested her head on Tony's shoulder, and he began to kiss her gently.

When they arrived at his town house in Bywater Street, he helped her out of the taxi, up the steps and through the front door. He led her along a dimly lit corridor and into the drawing room. She curled up in a corner of the sofa, as Tony disappeared into another room. Most of the furniture, and the pictures that covered every inch of the walls, were a blur to her. Tony returned a moment later, carrying another bottle of champagne and two glasses. Sally didn't notice that he was no longer wearing his jacket, tie or shoes.

He poured her a drink, which she sipped as he sat down next to her on the sofa. His arm slipped round her shoulder and he drew her close to him. When he kissed her again, she felt a little silly dangling an empty glass in mid-air. He took it from her and placed it on a side table, then held her in his arms and began to kiss her more passionately. As she fell back, his hand slipped onto the inside of her thigh, and began moving slowly up her leg.

Every time Sally was about to stop him going any further, Tony seemed to know exactly what to do next. She had always felt in control in the past whenever an over-enthusiastic art student had started to go a little too far in the back row of a cinema, but she had never experienced anyone as subtle as Tony. When her dress fell off her shoulders, she hadn't even noticed that he had undone the twelve little buttons down the back.

They broke away for a second. Sally felt she ought to make a move to go, before it was too late. Tony smiled, and undid the buttons of his own shirt before taking her back in his arms. She felt the warmth of his chest, and he was so gentle that she did not complain when she realised that the clasp of her bra had come loose. She sank back, enjoying every second, knowing that until that moment she had never experienced what it was like to be properly seduced.

Tony finally lay back and said, 'Yes, it has been a memorable day. But I don't think I'll phone my parents to let them know.' He laughed, and Sally felt slightly ashamed. Tony was only the fourth man who had made love to her, and she had known the other three for months beforehand – in one case, years.

For the next hour they talked about many things, but all Sally really wanted to know was how Tony felt about her. He gave her no clue.

Then, once again, he took her in his arms, but this time he pulled her onto the floor and made love to her with such passion that afterwards Sally wondered if she had ever made love before.

She was just in time to catch the last train home, but she couldn't help wishing she had missed it.

Over the next few months Sally devoted herself to getting her latest ideas onto canvas. When each new painting was finished, she would take it up to London for Simon to comment on. The smile on his face became broader and broader with each new picture he saw, and the word he kept repeating now was 'Original.' Sally would tell him about her ideas for the next one, and he would bring her up to date with his plans for the opening in October.

Tony would often meet her for lunch, and afterwards they would go back to his house, where they would make love until it was time for her to catch the last train home.

Sally often wished she could spend more time with Tony. But she was always conscious of the deadline set by Simon, who warned her that the printers were already proof-reading the catalogue, and that the invitations for the opening were waiting to be sent out. Tony seemed almost as busy as she was, and lately he hadn't always been able to fit in with her expeditions to London. Sally had taken to staying overnight, and catching an early train home the following morning. Tony occasionally hinted that she might consider moving in with him. When she thought about it – and she often did – she reflected that his attic could easily be converted into a studio. But she decided that before such a move could even be contemplated, the exhibition had to be a success. Then, if the hint became an offer, she would have her answer ready.

Just two days before the exhibition was due to open, Sally completed her final canvas and handed it over to Simon. As she pulled it out of the canvas folder he threw his arms in the air, and shouted, 'Hallelujah! It's your best yet. As long as we're sensible about our prices, I think that, with a touch of luck, we should sell at least half of your pictures before the exhibition closes.'

'Only half?' said Sally, unable to hide her disappointment.

'That wouldn't be at all bad for your first attempt, young lady,' said Simon. 'I only sold one Leslie Anne

Ivory at her first exhibition, and now she sells everything in the first week.'

Sally still looked crestfallen, and Simon realised he
had perhaps been a little tactless.

'Don't worry. Any unsold ones will be put into stock,
and they'll be snapped up the moment you start getting
good reviews.'

Sally continued to pout.

'How do you feel about the frames and mounts?'
Simon asked, trying to change the subject.

Sally studied the deep golden frames and light-grey
mounts. The smile returned to her face.

'They're good, aren't they?' said Simon. 'They bring
out the colour in the canvases wonderfully.'

Sally nodded her agreement, but was now beginning
to worry about how much they must have cost, and
whether she would ever be given a second exhibition if
the first one wasn't a success.

'By the way,' Simon said, 'I have a friend at the P.A.
called Mike Sallis who . . .'

'P.A.?' said Sally.

'Press Association. Mike's a photographer – always
on the lookout for a good story. He says he'll come
round and take a picture of you standing next to one of
the pictures. Then he'll hawk the photo around Fleet
Street, and we'll just have to cross our fingers, and pray
that Natasha has taken the day off. I don't want to get
your hopes up, but someone just might bite. Our only
line at present is that it's your first exhibition since
leaving the Slade. Hardly a front-page splash.' Simon

paused, as once again Sally looked discouraged. 'It's not too late for you to have a fling with Prince Charles, you know. That would solve all our problems.'

Sally smiled. 'I don't think Tony would like that.'

Simon decided against making another tactless remark.

Sally spent that evening with Tony at his home in Chelsea. He seemed a little distracted, but she blamed herself – she was unable to hide her disappointment at Simon's estimate of how few of her pictures might be sold. After they had made love, Sally tried to raise the topic of what would happen to them once the exhibition was over, but Tony deftly changed the subject back to how much he was looking forward to the opening.

That night Sally went home on the last train from Charing Cross.

The following morning she woke up with a terrible feeling of anti-climax. Her room was bereft of canvases, and all she could do now was wait. Her mood wasn't helped by the fact that Tony had told her he would be out of London on business until the day of her opening. She lay in the bath thinking about him.

'But I'll be your first customer on the night,' he had promised. 'Don't forget, I still want to buy "The Sleeping Cat that Never Moved".'

The phone was ringing, but someone answered it before Sally could get out of the bath.

'It's for you,' shouted her mother from the bottom of the stairs.

Sally wrapped a towel around her and grabbed the phone, hoping it would be Tony.

'Hi, Sally, it's Simon. I've got some good news. Mike Sallis has just called from the P.A. He's coming round to the gallery at midday tomorrow. All the pictures should be framed by then, and he'll be the first person from the press to see them. They all want to be first. I'm trying to think up some wheeze to convince him that it's an exclusive. By the way, the catalogues have arrived, and they look fantastic.'

Sally thanked him, and was about to ring Tony to suggest that she stay overnight with him, so that they could go to the gallery together the following day, when she remembered that he was out of town. She spent the day pacing anxiously around the house, occasionally talking to her most compliant model, the sleeping cat that never moved.

The following morning Sally caught an early commuter train from Sevenoaks, so she could spend a little time checking the pictures against their catalogue entries. When she walked into the gallery, her eyes lit up: half a dozen of the paintings had already been hung, and she actually felt, for the first time, that they really weren't bad. She glanced in the direction of the office, and saw that Simon was occupied on the phone. He smiled and waved to indicate that he would be with her in a moment.

She had another look at the pictures, and then spotted a copy of the catalogue lying on the table. The cover read 'The Summers Exhibition', above a picture of an interior looking from her parents' drawing room through an open window and out onto a garden overgrown with weeds. A black cat lay asleep on the windowsill, ignoring the rain.

Sally opened the catalogue and read the introduction on the first page.

Sometimes judges feel it necessary to say: It's been hard to pick this year's winner. But from the moment one set eyes on Sally Summers' work, the task was made easy Real talent is obvious for all to see, and Sally has achieved the rare feat of winning both the Slade's major prizes, for oils and for drawing, in the same year. I much look forward to watching her career develop over the coming years.

It was an extract from Sir Roger de Grey's speech when he had presented Sally with the Mary Rischgitz and the Henry Tonks Prizes at the Slade two years before.

Sally turned the pages, seeing her works reproduced in colour for the first time. Simon's attention to detail and layout was evident on every page.

She looked back towards the office, and saw that Simon was still on the phone. She decided to go downstairs and check on the rest of her pictures, now that they had all been framed. The lower gallery was a mass of colour, and the newly framed paintings were so skilfully hung that even Sally saw them in a new light.

Once she had circled the room Sally suppressed a smile
of satisfaction before turning to make her way back
upstairs. As she passed a table in the centre of the gallery, she noticed a folder with the initials 'N.K.' printed
on it. She idly lifted the cover, to discover a pile of
undistinguished watercolours.

As she leafed through her rival's never-to-be-
exhibited efforts, Sally had to admit that the nude self-
portraits didn't do Natasha justice. She was just about
to close the folder and join Simon upstairs when she
came to a sudden halt.

Although it was clumsily executed, there was no doubt
who the man was that the half-clad Natasha was clinging
on to.

Sally felt sick. She slammed the folder shut, walked
quickly across the room and back up the stairs to the
ground floor. In the corner of the large gallery Simon
was chatting to a man who had several cameras slung
over his shoulder.

'Sally,' he said, coming towards her, 'this is
Mike . . .'

But Sally ignored them both, and started running
towards the open door, tears flooding down her cheeks.
She turned right into St James's, determined to get as
far away from the gallery as possible. But then she came
to an abrupt halt. Tony and Natasha were walking
towards her, arm in arm.

Sally stepped off the pavement and began to cross the
road, hoping to reach the other side before they spotted
her.

The screech of tyres and the sudden swerve of the van came just a moment too late, and she was thrown headlong into the middle of the road.

When Sally came to, she felt awful. She blinked her eyes, and thought she could hear voices. She blinked again, but it was several moments before she was able to focus on anything.

She was lying in a bed, but it was not her own. Her right leg was covered in plaster, and was raised high in the air, suspended from a pulley. Her other leg was under the sheet, and it felt all right. She wiggled the toes of her left foot: yes, they were fine. Then she began to try to move her arms. A nurse came up to the side of the bed.

'Welcome back to the world, Sally.'

'How long have I been like this?' she asked.

'A couple of days,' said the nurse, checking Sally's pulse. 'But you're making a remarkably quick recovery. Before you ask, it's only a broken leg, and the black eyes will have gone long before we let out. By the way,' she added, as she moved on to the next patient, 'I loved that picture of you in the morning papers. And what about those flattering remarks your friend made? So what's it like to be famous?'

Sally wanted to ask what she was talking about, but the nurse was already taking the pulse of the person in the next bed.

'Come back,' Sally wanted to say, but a second nurse

had appeared by her bedside with a mug of orange juice, which she thrust into her hand.

'Let's get you started on this,' she said. Sally obeyed, and tried to suck the liquid through a bent plastic straw.

'You've got a visitor,' the nurse told her once she'd emptied the contents of the mug. 'He's been waiting for some time. Do you think you're up to seeing him?'

'Sure,' said Sally, not particularly wanting to face Tony, but desperate to find out what had happened.

She looked towards the swing doors at the end of the ward, but had to wait for some time before Simon came bouncing through them. He walked straight up to her bed, clutching what might just about have been described as a bunch of flowers. He gave her plaster cast a big kiss.

'I'm so sorry, Simon,' Sally said, before he had even said hello. 'I know just how much trouble and expense you've been to on my behalf. And now I've let you down so badly.'

'You certainly have,' said Simon. 'It's always a let down when you sell everything off the walls on the first night. Then you haven't got anything left for your old customers, and they start grumbling.'

Sally's mouth opened wide.

'Mind you, it was a rather good photo of Natasha, even if it was an awful one of you.'

'What are you talking about, Simon?'

'Mike Sallis got his exclusive, and you got your break,' he said, patting her suspended leg. 'When Natasha bent over your body in the street, Mike began clicking away for dear life. And I couldn't have scripted her quote better myself: "The most outstanding young artist of our generation. If the world were to lose such a talent . . ."'

Sally laughed at Simon's wicked imitation of Natasha's Russian accent.

'You hit most of the next morning's front pages,' he continued. '"Brush with Death" in the *Mail*; "Still Life in St James's" in the *Express*. And you even managed "Splat!" in the *Sun*. The punters flocked into the gallery that evening. Natasha was wearing a black see-through dress and proceeded to give the press soundbite after soundbite about your genius. Not that it made any difference. We'd already sold every canvas long before their second editions hit the street. But, more important, the serious critics in the broadsheets are already acknowledging that you might actually have some talent.'

Sally smiled. 'I may have failed to have an affair with Prince Charles, but at least it seems I got something right.'

'Well, not exactly,' said Simon.

'What do you mean?' asked Sally, suddenly anxious. 'You said all the pictures have been sold.'

'True, but if you'd arranged to have the accident a few days earlier, I could have jacked up the prices by at least fifty per cent. Still, there's always next time.'

'Did Tony buy "The Sleeping Cat that Never Moved"?' Sally asked quietly.

'No, he was late as usual, I'm afraid. It was snapped up in the first half hour, by a serious collector. Which reminds me,' Simon added, as Sally's parents came through the swing doors into the ward, 'I'll need another forty canvases if we're going to hold your second show in the spring. So you'd better get back to work right away.'

'But look at me, you silly man,' Sally said, laughing. 'How do you expect me to –'

'Don't be so feeble,' said Simon, tapping her plaster cast. 'It's your leg that's out of action, not your arm.'

Sally grinned and looked up to see her parents standing at the end of the bed.

'Is this Tony?' her mother asked.

'Good heavens no, Mother,' laughed Sally. 'This is Simon. He's far more important. Mind you,' she confessed, 'I made the same mistake the first time I met him.'

TIMEO DANAOS...

ARNOLD BACON WOULD HAVE MADE A fortune if he hadn't taken his father's advice.

Arnold's occupation, as described in his passport, was 'banker'. For those of you who are pedantic about such matters, he was the branch manager of Barclays Bank in St Albans, Hertfordshire, which in banking circles is about the equivalent of being a captain in the Royal Army Pay Corps.

His passport also stated that he was born in 1937, was five feet nine inches tall, with sandy hair and no distinguishing marks – although in fact he had several lines on his forehead, which served only to prove that he frowned a great deal.

He was a member of the local Rotary Club (Hon. Treasurer), the Conservative Party (Branch Vice-Chairman), and was a past Secretary of the St Albans Festival. He had also played rugby for the Old Albanians 2nd XV in the 1960s and cricket for St Albans C.C. in the 1970s. His only exercise for the past two decades, however, had been the occasional round of golf with his opposite number from the National Westminster. Arnold did not boast a handicap.

During these excursions round the golf course Arnold would often browbeat his opponent with his conviction that he should never have been a banker in the first place. After years of handing out loans to customers who wanted to start up their own businesses, he had become painfully aware that he himself was really one of nature's born entrepreneurs. If only he hadn't listened to his father's advice and followed him into the bank, heaven knows what heights he might have reached by now.

His colleague nodded wearily, then holed a seven-foot putt, ensuring that the drinks would not be on him.

'How's Deirdre?' he asked as the two men strolled towards the clubhouse.

'Wants to buy a new dinner service,' said Arnold, which slightly puzzled his companion. 'Not that I can see what's wrong with our old Coronation set.'

When they reached the bar, Arnold checked his watch before ordering half a pint of lager for himself and a gin and tonic for the victor, as Deirdre wouldn't be expecting him back for at least an hour. He stopped pontificating only when another member began telling them the latest rumours about the club captain's wife.

Deirdre Bacon, Arnold's long-suffering wife, had come to accept that her husband was now too set in his ways for her to hope for any improvement. Although she had her own opinions on what would have happened to Arnold if he hadn't followed his father's advice, she no longer voiced them. At the time of their engagement she had considered Arnold Bacon 'quite a catch'. But as the years passed, she had become more realistic about her expectations, and after two children, one of each sex, she had settled into the life of a housewife and mother – not that anything else had ever been seriously contemplated.

The children had now grown up, Justin to become a solicitor's clerk in Chelmsford, and Virginia to marry a local boy whom Arnold described as an official with British Rail. Deirdre, more accurately, told her friends at the hairdresser's that Keith was a train driver.

For the first ten years of their marriage, the Bacons had holidayed in Bournemouth, because Arnold's parents had always done so. They only graduated to the Costa del Sol after Arnold read in the *Daily Telegraph*'s 'Sun Supplement' that that was where most bank managers were to be found during the month of August.

For many years Arnold had promised his wife that they would do 'something special' when it came to celebrating their twenty-fifth wedding anniversary, though he had never actually committed himself to defining what 'special' meant.

It was only when he read in the bank's quarterly staff magazine that Andrew Buxton, the Chairman of Barclays, would be spending his summer sailing around the Greek islands on a private yacht that Arnold began writing off to numerous cruise companies and travel agents, requesting copies of their brochures. After having studied hundreds of glossy pages, he settled on a seven-day cruise aboard the *Princess Corina*, starting out from Piraeus to sail around the Greek islands, ending up at

Mykonos. Deirdre's only contribution to the discussion was that she would rather go back to the Costa del Sol, and spend the money they saved on a new dinner service. She was delighted, however, to read in one of the brochures that the Greeks were famous for their pottery.

By the time they boarded the coach to Heathrow, Arnold's junior staff, fellow members of the Rotary Club, and even a few of his more select customers were becoming tired of being reminded of how Arnold would be spending his summer break. 'I shall be sailing around the Greek islands on a liner,' he would tell them. 'Not unlike the bank's Chairman, Andrew Buxton, you know.' If anyone asked Deirdre what she and Arnold were doing for their holidays, she said that they were going on a seven-day package tour, and that the one thing she hoped to come home with was a new dinner service.

The old 'Coronation' service that had been given to them by Deirdre's parents as a wedding gift some twenty-five years before was now sadly depleted. Several of the plates were chipped or broken, while the pattern of crowns and sceptres on the pieces that were still serviceable had almost faded away.

'I can't see what's wrong with it myself,' said Arnold when his wife raised the subject once more as they waited in the departure lounge at Heathrow. Deirdre made no effort to list its defects again.

Arnold spent most of the flight to Athens complaining that the aircraft was full of Greeks. Deirdre didn't feel it was worth pointing out to him that, if one booked a passage with Olympic Airways, that was likely to be the outcome. She also knew his reply would be, 'But it saved us twenty-four pounds.'

Once they had landed at Hellenikon International Airport, the two holidaymakers climbed aboard a bus. Arnold doubted whether it would have passed its MOT in St Albans, but nevertheless it somehow managed to transport them into the centre of Athens, where Arnold had booked them overnight into a two-star hotel (two Greek stars). Arnold quickly found the local branch of Barclays and cashed one of his travellers' cheques, explaining to his wife that there was no point in changing more, as once they were on board the liner everything had already been paid for. He was sure that was how entrepreneurs conducted themselves.

The Bacons rose early the following morning, mainly because they hadn't been able to get a great deal of sleep. Their bodies had continually rolled to the centre of the lumpy concave mattress, and their ears ached after a night resting on the brick-hard convex pillows. Even before the sun had risen, Arnold jumped out of bed and threw open the little window that looked out onto a back yard. He stretched his arms and declared he had never felt better. Deirdre didn't comment, as she was already busy packing their clothes.

Over breakfast – a meal consisting of a croissant, which Arnold felt was too sticky, and which in any case fell apart in his fingers, feta cheese, which he didn't care for the smell of, and an obstinately empty cup, because the management refused to serve tea – a long debate developed between them as to whether they should hire a taxi or take a bus to the liner. They both came to the conclusion that a taxi would be more sensible, Deirdre because she didn't want to be crammed into a hot bus with a lot of sweaty Athenians, and Arnold because he wanted to be seen arriving at the gangplank in a car.

Once Arnold had settled their bill – having checked the little row of figures presented to him three times before he was willing to part with another travellers' cheque – he hailed a taxi and instructed the driver to take them to the quayside. The longer than expected journey, in an ancient car with no air conditioning, did not put Arnold into a good humour.

When he first set eyes on the *Princess Corina*, Arnold was unable to mask his disappointment. The ship was neither as large nor as modern as it had appeared in the glossy brochure. He had a feeling his Chairman would not be experiencing the same problem.

Mr and Mrs Bacon ascended the gangplank and were escorted to their cabin, which to Arnold's dismay consisted of two bunks, a washbasin, a shower and a porthole, without even enough room between the bunks for both of them to be able to undress at the same time. Arnold pointed out to his wife that this particular cabin had certainly not been illustrated in the brochure, even if it had been described on the tariff by the encomium 'De Luxe'. The brochure must have been put together by an out-of-work estate agent, he concluded.

Arnold set out to take a turn around the deck – not a particularly lengthy excursion. On the way he bumped into a solicitor from Chester who had been innocently strolling with his wife in the opposite direction. After Arnold had established that Malcolm Jackson was a senior partner in his firm, and his wife Joan was a magistrate, he suggested they should join up for lunch.

Once they had selected their meal from the buffet, Arnold lost no time in telling his new-found friends that he was a born entrepreneur, explaining, for example, the immediate changes he would make to improve efficiency on the *Princess Corina* had he been the chairman of this particular shipping line. (The list, I fear, turned out to be far too long to include in a short story.)

The solicitor, who had not had to suffer any of Arnold's opinions before, seemed quite content to listen, while Deirdre chatted away to Joan about how she was hoping to find a new dinner service on one of the islands. 'The Greeks are famous for their pottery, you know,' she kept saying.

The conversation didn't vary a great deal when the two couples reunited over dinner that evening.

Although the Bacons were tired after their first day on board, neither of them slept for more than a few moments that night. But Arnold was unwilling to admit, as they bobbed across the Aegean in their little cabin, that given the choice he would have preferred the two-star hotel (two Greek stars), with its lumpy mattress and brick-hard pillows, to the bunks on which they were now being tossed from side to side.

After two days at sea the ship docked at Rhodes, and by then even Arnold had stopped describing it as a 'liner'. Most of the passengers piled off down the gangway, only too delighted to have the chance of spending a few hours on land.

Arnold and Malcolm beat a path to the nearest Barclays Bank to cash a travellers' cheque each, while Deirdre and Joan set off in the opposite direction in search of a dinner service. At the bank, Arnold immediately informed the manager who he was, ensuring that both he and Malcolm received a tiny improvement on the advertised rate of exchange.

Arnold smiled as they stepped out of the bank, and onto the hot, dusty, cobbled street. 'I should have gone into futures trading, you know,' he told Malcolm as they sauntered off down the hill. 'I would have made a fortune.'

Deirdre's quest for a dinner service didn't turn out to be quite so straightforward. The shops were numerous and varied in quality, and she quickly discovered that Rhodes boasted a great many potters. It was therefore necessary for her to establish which of them was the most highly regarded by the locals, and then find the shop that sold his work. This information was gained by talking to the old women dressed in black who could be found sitting silently on the street corners, about one in ten of whom, she discovered, had some broken English. While her husband was at the bank saving a few drachmas, Deirdre managed to find out all the inside information she required.

The four of them met up at a small taverna in the centre of the town for lunch. Over a plate of souvlakia

Arnold tried to convince Deirdre that as they were visiting five islands in the course of the trip, it might perhaps be wise to wait until their final port of call, so they could purchase the dinner service at the last possible moment.

'Prices will undoubtedly fall,' declared Arnold, 'the closer we get to Athens.' He spoke with the air of a true entrepreneur.

Although Deirdre had already seen a thirty-two-piece set she liked, at a price well within their budget, she reluctantly agreed to Arnold's suggestion. Her acquiescence was largely brought about by the fact that it was her husband who was in possession of all the travellers' cheques.

By the time the ship had docked at Heraklion on Crete, Arnold had vetted all the British nationals on board, and had permitted a Major (Territorial Reserve) and his spouse to join their table for lunch – but only after discovering that the fellow held an account at Barclays. A dinner invitation followed once it had been established that the Major occasionally played bridge with Arnold's area manager.

From that moment Arnold spent many happy hours at the bar explaining to the Major or to Malcolm – neither of whom actually listened any longer – why he should never have taken his father's advice and followed him into the bank, as he was after all one of nature's born entrepreneurs.

By the time the ship had weighed anchor and sailed from Santorini, Deirdre knew exactly the type of dinner service she wanted, and how to establish quickly which potter she should trade with as soon as they set foot in a new port. But Arnold continued to insist that they should wait for the bigger market as they approached Athens – 'More competition, forces prices down,' he explained for the umpteenth time. Deirdre knew there was no point in telling him that prices seemed to be rising with each sea-mile they covered on their journey back towards the Greek capital.

Páros only served as further proof of Deirdre's suspicions – if proof were still needed – as the prices there were noticeably steeper than they had been on Santorini. As the *Princess Corina* steamed on towards Mykonos, Deirdre felt that although their final port of call would probably be able to supply her with a satisfactory dinner service, it would surely no longer be at a price they could afford.

Arnold kept assuring her, with the confidence of a man who knows about such things, that all would be well. He even tapped the side of his nose with his forefinger. The Major and Malcolm had reached the stage of simply nodding at him to indicate that they were still awake.

Deirdre was among the first down the gangplank when they docked at Mykonos that Friday morning. She had told her husband that she would carry out a recce of the pottery shops while he did the same with the banks. Joan and the Major's wife were happy to accompany Deirdre, as by now she had become something of an expert on the subject of Greek pottery.

The three ladies began their search at the north end of the town, and Deirdre was relieved to find that there was a greater variety of shops in Mykonos than there had been on any of the other islands. She was also able to discover, with the help of several black-clad ladies, that the town boasted a potter of genuine fame, whose work could only be purchased from one shop, The House of Pétros.

Once Deirdre had located this establishment, she spent the rest of the morning inspecting all the dinner services they had to offer. After a couple of hours she came to the conclusion that the 'Delphi' set which was prominently displayed in the centre of the shop would be a prized possession for any housewife in St Albans. But as it was double the cost of anything she had seen on any of the other islands, she knew that Arnold would dismiss it as being out of their price range.

As the three ladies finally left the shop to join their husbands for lunch, a good-looking young man in a grubby T-shirt and torn jeans, with a couple of days' stubble on his chin, jumped out in front of them and asked, 'You English?'

Deirdre stopped and stared into his deep blue eyes for a moment, but said nothing. Her companions stepped out into the cobbled road and quickened their pace, pretending it was not them to whom the stranger had spoken. Deirdre smiled at him as he stood to one side, allowing her to continue on her way. Arnold had warned her never to engage in conversation with the natives.

When they reached ρεγγα κοκκινη, the restaurant at

which they'd arranged to meet up for lunch, the three ladies found their husbands drinking imported lager at the bar. Arnold was explaining to the Major and Malcolm why he had refused to pay his subscription to the Conservative Party that year. 'Not a penny will I part with,' he insisted, 'while they can't get their own house in order.' Deirdre suspected that his unwillingness to pay had rather more to do with his recent defeat when he had stood as Chairman of the local branch.

Arnold passed the next hour offering his views on everything from defence cuts to New Age travellers to single-parent families, all of which he was resolutely against. When the bill for lunch was finally presented, he spent some considerable time working out what each of them had eaten, and therefore how much they should contribute towards the total.

Arnold had already resigned himself to the fact that he would have to allocate part of his afternoon to bargaining on Deirdre's behalf, now that she had finally found the dinner service she had set her heart on. Everyone else had agreed to come along and watch the born entrepreneur at work.

When Arnold entered The House of Pétros, he had to admit that Deirdre seemed to have 'located the correct establishment'. He kept repeating this observation, as if to prove that he had been right all along to insist that she wait until their final port of call before the big decision was taken. He seemed blissfully unaware of how the price of pottery had increased from island to island, and Deirdre made no attempt to enlighten him.

She simply guided him over to the 'Delphi' service displayed on a large table in the centre of the room, and prayed. They all agreed it was quite magnificent, but when Arnold was told the price, he shook his head sadly. Deirdre would have protested, but she, like so many of the bank's customers over the years, had seen that look on her husband's face before. She therefore resigned herself to settling for the 'Pharos' set — excellent, but unquestionably second best, and far more expensive than comparable sets had been on any of the other four islands.

The three wives began selecting the pieces they would like to buy, while their husbands gravely reminded them how much they could afford. The choices having been made, Arnold spent a considerable time haggling with the shopkeeper. He finally managed to get a twenty per cent discount on the total. Once the figure had been established, Arnold was dispatched to find an English bank at which he could change the necessary travellers' cheques. With passports and signed cheques in hand, he left the shop to carry out his mission.

As he stepped onto the pavement, the young man who had approached Deirdre leaped into his path and asked, 'You English?'

'Naturally,' replied Arnold, sidestepping him and marching on briskly in order to avoid any further conversation with such a scruffy individual. As he had told the Major over lunch, *Timeo Danaos et dona ferentis.* It was the one snippet of Latin he could still recall from his schooldays.

When he had selected a bank, Arnold marched straight into the manager's office and changed everyone's cheques at a minutely better rate than the one displayed on the board in the window. Pleased with his saving of fifty drachmas, he headed back to The House of Pétros.

He was displeased to find the young man was still loitering on the pavement outside the shop. Arnold refused to favour the unshaven ruffian with even a glance, but he did catch the words, 'You want to save money, Englishman?'

Arnold stopped in his tracks, as any born entrepreneur would, and turned to study more closely the loutish youth who had addressed him. He was about to continue on his way when the young man said, 'I know where pottery is everything half price.'

Arnold hesitated once again, and looked through the shop window to see his companions standing around waiting for his return; on the counter stood six large packages, already wrapped up and awaiting payment.

Arnold turned back to take a closer look at the inarticulate foreigner.

'Potter comes from village called Kalafatis,' he said. 'Bus journey only half hour, then everything half price.'

While Arnold was digesting this piece of information, the young Greek's hand shot out hopefully. Arnold extracted a fifty-drachma note from the roll of money he had obtained at the bank, willing to speculate with the profit he had made on that particular transaction in exchange for the information he had just acquired – the act of a true entrepreneur, he thought as he marched triumphantly into the shop.

'I have made an important discovery,' he announced, and beckoned them all into a corner to impart his inside information.

Deirdre did not seem at all convinced, until Arnold suggested, 'Perhaps we might even be able to afford the "Delphi" set you hankered after, my dear. In any case, why pay double, when the only sacrifice you need to make is a half-hour bus journey.'

Malcolm nodded his agreement, as if listening to sage advice from senior counsel, and even the Major, though grumbling a little, finally fell into line.

'As we set sail for Athens early this evening,' declared the Major, 'we ought to take the next bus to Kalafatis.' Arnold nodded, and without another word led his little band out of the shop, not even glancing towards the packages that were left behind on the counter.

When they stepped out onto the street, Arnold was relieved to find that the young man who had given him the tip-off was no longer to be seen.

They came to a halt at the bus stop, where Arnold was a little disappointed to discover several passengers from the ship already standing in the queue, but he persuaded himself that they would not be heading for the same destination. They waited in the hot sun for another forty minutes before a bus eventually pulled up. When Arnold first saw the vehicle, his heart sank. 'Just think of how much money we'll be saving,' he said when he noticed the looks of despair on the faces of his companions.

The journey across the island to the east coast might well have taken thirty minutes had it been in a Range Rover with no reason to slow down. But as the bus driver picked up everybody he saw along the way, without regard to official stops, they eventually arrived in Kalafatis an hour and twenty minutes later. Long before they had clambered off the ancient vehicle Deirdre was exhausted, Joan was exasperated, and the Major's wife was developing a migraine.

'Bus goes no further,' said the driver as Arnold and his companions filed off. 'Leave for return journey to Khóra one hour. Last bus of the day.'

The little band gazed up at the narrow, winding track that led to the potter's workplace.

'The journey was worth it for the view alone,' gasped Arnold, as he came to a halt halfway along the path and gazed out over the Aegean. His companions didn't even bother to stop and look, let alone offer an opinion. It took them another ten minutes of determined walking before they reached their destination, and by then even Arnold had fallen silent.

As the six weary tourists finally entered the pottery, what breath they had left was taken away. They stood mesmerised by shelf after shelf of beautiful objects. Arnold felt a warm glow of triumph.

Deirdre immediately went about her business, and quickly located the 'Delphi' dinner service. It looked even more magnificent than she remembered, but when she checked a little label that hung from a soup tureen's handle she was horrified to discover that the cost was only a little less than it had been at The House of Pétros.

Deirdre came to a decision. She turned to face her husband, who was toying with a pipe stand, and declared in a clarion voice that all could hear, 'As everything is at half price, Arnold, presumably I can go ahead and buy the "Delphi"?'

The other four swung round to see how the great entrepreneur would react. Arnold seemed to hesitate for a moment before he placed the pipe stand back on the shelf and said, 'Of course, my dear. Isn't that why we came all this way in the first place?'

The three women immediately began selecting items from the shelves, finally gathering between them one dinner service, two tea sets, one coffee set, three vases, five ashtrays, two jugs and a toast rack. Arnold abandoned the pipe stand.

When the bill for Deirdre's purchases was presented to her husband he hesitated once again, but he was painfully aware that all five of his shipmates were glaring at him. He reluctantly cashed his remaining travellers' cheques, unwilling to bring himself even to glance at the disadvantageous exchange rate that was displayed in the window. Deirdre made no comment. Malcolm and the Major silently signed away their own travellers' cheques, with little appearance of triumph showing on either of their faces.

The goods having been paid for, the six tourists

emerged from the workshop, laden down with carrier bags. As they began to retrace their steps back down the winding track, the door of the pottery was closed behind them.

'We'll have to get a move on if we're not going to miss the last bus,' shouted Arnold as he stepped into the centre of the path, avoiding a large cream Mercedes that was parked outside the workshop. 'But what a worthwhile excursion,' he added as they trundled off down the track. 'You have to admit, I saved you all a fortune.'

Deirdre was the last to leave the shop. She paused to rearrange her numerous bags, and was surprised to see a number of the pottery's staff forming a queue at a table by the side of the shop. A handsome young man in a grubby T-shirt and torn jeans was presenting each of them in turn with a small brown envelope.

Deirdre couldn't take her eyes off the young man. Where had she seen him before? He looked up, and for a moment she stared into those deep blue eyes. And then she remembered. The young man shrugged his shoulders and smiled. Deirdre returned the smile, picked up her bags and set off down the path after her companions.

As they clambered onto the bus, Deirdre was just in time to hear Arnold declare: 'You know, Major, I should never have taken my father's advice and settled for the life of a banker. You see, I'm one of nature's born entre . . .'

Deirdre smiled again as she looked out of the window

and watched the good-looking young man speed past them in his large cream Mercedes.

He smiled and waved to her as the last bus began its slow journey back to Mykonos.

AN EYE FOR AN EYE

S IR MATTHEW ROBERTS QC CLOSED THE
file and placed it on the desk in front of him. He was
not a happy man. He was quite willing to defend Mary
Banks, but he was not at all confident about her plea of
not guilty.

Sir Matthew leaned back in his deep leather chair to
consider the case while he awaited the arrival of the
instructing solicitor who had briefed him, and the junior
counsel he had selected for the case. As he gazed out
over the Middle Temple courtyard, he only hoped he
had made the right decision.

On the face of it, the case of Regina v. Banks was a
simple one of murder; but after what Bruce Banks
had subjected his wife to during the eleven years of
their marriage, Sir Matthew was confident not only
that he could get the charge reduced to manslaughter,
but that if the jury was packed with women, he might
even secure an acquittal. There was, however, a
complication.

He lit a cigarette and inhaled deeply, something his
wife had always chided him for. He looked at Victoria's
photograph on the desk in front of him. It reminded

him of his youth: but then, Victoria would always be young – death had ensured that.

Reluctantly, he forced his mind back to his client and her plea of mitigation. He reopened the file. Mary Banks was claiming that she couldn't possibly have chopped her husband up with an axe and buried him under the pigsty, because at the time of his death she was not only a patient in the local hospital, but was also blind. As Sir Matthew inhaled deeply once again, there was a knock on the door.

'Come in,' he bellowed – not because he liked the sound of his own voice, but because the doors of his chambers were so thick that if he didn't holler, no one would ever hear him.

Sir Matthew's clerk opened the door and announced Mr Bernard Casson and Mr Hugh Witherington. Two very different men, thought Sir Matthew as they entered the room, but each would serve the purpose he had planned for them in this particular case.

Bernard Casson was a solicitor of the old school – formal, punctilious, and always painstakingly correct. His conservatively tailored herringbone suit never seemed to change from one year to the next; Matthew often wondered if he had purchased half a dozen such suits in a closing-down sale and wore a different one every day of the week. He peered up at Casson over his half-moon spectacles. The solicitor's thin moustache and neatly parted hair gave him an old-fashioned look that had fooled many an opponent into thinking he had a second-class mind. Sir Matthew regularly gave thanks that his friend was no orator, because if Bernard had been a barrister, Matthew would not have relished the prospect of opposing him in court.

A pace behind Casson stood his junior counsel for this brief, Hugh Witherington. The Lord must have been feeling particularly ungenerous on the day Witherington entered the world, as He had given him neither looks nor brains. If He had bestowed any other talents on him, they were yet to be revealed. After several attempts Witherington had finally been called to the Bar, but for the number of briefs he was offered, he would have had a more regular income had he signed on for the dole. Sir Matthew's clerk had raised an eyebrow when the name of Witherington had been mooted as junior counsel in the case, but Sir Matthew just smiled, and had not offered an explanation.

Sir Matthew rose, stubbed out his cigarette, and ushered the two men towards the vacant chairs on the other side of his desk. He waited for both of them to settle before he proceeded.

'Kind of you to attend chambers, Mr Casson,' he said, although they both knew that the solicitor was doing no more than holding with the traditions of the Bar.

'My pleasure, Sir Matthew,' replied the elderly solicitor, bowing slightly to show that he still appreciated the old courtesies.

'I don't think you know Hugh Witherington, my junior in this case,' said Sir Matthew, gesturing towards the undistinguished young barrister.

Witherington nervously touched the silk handkerchief in his breast pocket.

'No, I hadn't had the pleasure of Mr Witherington's acquaintance until we met in the corridor a few moments ago,' said Casson. 'May I say how delighted I am that you have been willing to take on this case, Sir Matthew?'

Matthew smiled at his friend's formality. He knew Bernard would never dream of calling him by his Christian name while junior counsel was present. 'I'm only too happy to be working with you again, Mr Casson. Even if you have presented me on this occasion with something of a challenge.'

The conventional pleasantries over, the elderly solicitor removed a brown file from his battered Gladstone bag. 'I have had a further consultation with my client since I last saw you,' he said as he opened the file, 'and I took the opportunity to pass on your opinion. But I fear Mrs Banks remains determined to plead not guilty.'

'So she is still protesting her innocence?'

'Yes, Sir Matthew. Mrs Banks emphatically claims that she couldn't have committed the murder because she had been blinded by her husband some days before he died, and in any case, at the time of his death she was registered as a patient at the local hospital.'

'The pathologist's report is singularly vague about the time of death,' Sir Matthew reminded his old friend. 'After all, they didn't discover the body for at least a couple of weeks. As I understand it, the police feel the murder could have been committed twenty-four or even forty-eight hours before Mrs Banks was taken to the hospital.'

'I have also read their report, Sir Matthew,' Casson replied, 'and informed Mrs Banks of its contents. But she remains adamant that she is innocent, and that the jury will be persuaded of it. "Especially with Sir Matthew Roberts as my defender," were the exact words she used, if I remember correctly,' he added with a smile.

'I am not seduced, Mr Casson,' said Sir Matthew, lighting another cigarette.

'You did promise Victoria —' interjected the solicitor, lowering his shield, but only for a moment.

'So, I have one last chance to convince her,' said Sir Matthew, ignoring his friend's comment.

'And Mrs Banks has one last chance to convince you,' said Mr Casson.

'Touché,' said Sir Matthew, nodding his appreciation of the solicitor's neat riposte as he stubbed out his almost untouched cigarette. He felt he was losing this fencing match with his old friend, and that the time had come to go on the attack.

He returned to the open file on his desk. 'First,' he said, looking straight at Casson, as if his colleague were in the witness box, 'when the body was dug up, there were traces of your client's blood on the collar of the dead man's shirt.'

'My client accepts that,' said Casson, calmly checking his own notes. 'But . . .'

'Second,' said Sir Matthew before Casson had a chance to reply, 'when the instrument that had been used to chop up the body, an axe, was found the following day, a hair from Mrs Banks's head was discovered lodged in its handle.'

'We won't be denying that,' said Casson.

'We don't have a lot of choice,' said Sir Matthew, rising from his seat and beginning to pace around the room. 'And third, when the spade that was used to dig the victim's grave was finally discovered, your client's fingerprints were found all over it.'

'We can explain that as well,' said Casson.

'But will the jury accept our explanation,' asked Sir Matthew, his voice rising, 'when they learn that the murdered man had a long history of violence, that your client was regularly seen in the local village either bruised, or with a black eye, sometimes bleeding from cuts around the head – once even nursing a broken arm?'

'She has always stated that those injuries were sustained when working on the farm where her husband was manager.'

'That places a strain on my credulity which it's quite unable to withstand,' said Sir Matthew, as he finished circling the room and returned to his chair. 'And we are not helped by the fact that the only person known to have visited the farm regularly was the postman. Apparently everyone else in the village refused to venture beyond the front gate.' He flicked over another page of his notes.

'That might have made it easier for someone to come in and kill Banks,' suggested Witherington.

Sir Matthew was unable to hide his surprise as he

looked across at his junior, having almost forgotten that he was in the room. 'Interesting point,' he said, unwilling to stamp on Witherington while he still had it in his power to play the one trump card in this case.

'The next problem we face,' he went on, 'is that your client claims that she went blind after her husband struck her with a hot frying pan. Rather convenient, Mr Casson, wouldn't you say?'

'The scar can still be seen clearly on the side of my client's face,' said Casson. 'And the doctor remains convinced that she is indeed blind.'

'Doctors are easier to convince than prosecuting counsels and world-weary judges, Mr Casson,' said Sir Matthew, turning another page of his file. 'Next, when samples from the body were examined – and God knows who was willing to carry out that particular task – the quantity of strychnine found in the blood would have felled a bull elephant.'

'That was only the opinion of the Crown's pathologists,' said Mr Casson.

'And one I will find hard to refute in court,' said Sir Matthew, 'because counsel for the prosecution will undoubtedly ask Mrs Banks to explain why she purchased four grams of strychnine from an agricultural supplier in Reading shortly before her husband's death. If I were in his position, I would repeat that question over and over again.'

'Possibly,' said Casson, checking his notes, 'but she has explained that they had been having a problem with rats, which had been killing the chickens, and she feared for the other animals on the farm, not to mention their nine-year-old son.'

'Ah, yes, Rupert. But he was away at boarding school at the time, was he not?' Sir Matthew paused. 'You see, Mr Casson, my problem is a simple one.' He closed his file. 'I don't believe her.'

Casson raised an eyebrow.

'Unlike her husband, Mrs Banks is a very clever woman. Witness the fact that she has already fooled several people into believing this incredible story. But I can tell you, Mr Casson, that she isn't going to fool me.'

'But what can we do, Sir Matthew, if Mrs Banks insists that this is her case, and asks us to defend her accordingly?' asked Casson.

Sir Matthew rose again and paced around the room silently, coming to a halt in front of the solicitor. 'Not a lot, I agree,' he said, reverting to a more conciliatory tone. 'But I do wish I could convince the dear lady to plead guilty to manslaughter. We'd be certain to gain the sympathy of any jury, after what she's been put through. And we can always rely on some women's group or other to picket the court throughout the hearing. Any judge who passed a harsh sentence on Mary Banks would be described as chauvinistic and sexually discriminatory by every newspaper leader writer in the land. I'd have her out of prison in a matter of weeks. No, Mr Casson, we *must* get her to change her plea.'

'But how can we hope to do that, when she remains so adamant that she is innocent?' asked Casson.

A smile flickered across Sir Matthew's face. 'Mr Witherington and I have a plan, don't we, Hugh?' he said, turning to Witherington for a second time.

'Yes, Sir Matthew,' replied the young barrister, sounding pleased to at last have his opinion sought, even in this rudimentary way. As Sir Matthew volunteered no clue as to the plan, Casson did not press the point.

'So, when do I come face to face with our client?' asked Sir Matthew, turning his attention back to the solicitor.

'Would eleven o'clock on Monday morning be convenient?' asked Casson.

'Where is she at the moment?' asked Sir Matthew, thumbing through his diary.

'Holloway,' replied Casson.

'Then we will be at Holloway at eleven on Monday morning,' said Sir Matthew. 'And to be honest with you, I can't wait to meet Mrs Mary Banks. That woman must have real guts, not to mention imagination. Mark my words, Mr Casson, she'll prove a worthy opponent for any counsel.'

When Sir Matthew entered the interviewing room of Holloway Prison and saw Mary Banks for the first time, he was momentarily taken aback. He knew from his file on the case that she was thirty-seven, but the frail, grey-haired woman who sat with her hands resting in her lap looked nearer fifty. Only when he studied her fine cheekbones and slim figure did he see that she might once have been a beautiful woman.

Sir Matthew allowed Casson to take the seat opposite her at a plain formica table in the centre of an otherwise empty, cream-painted brick room. There was a small, barred window halfway up the wall that threw a shaft of light onto their client. Sir Matthew and his junior took their places on either side of the instructing solicitor. Leading counsel noisily poured himself a cup of coffee.

'Good morning, Mrs Banks,' said Casson.

'Good morning, Mr Casson,' she replied, turning slightly to face the direction from which the voice had come. 'You have brought someone with you.'

'Yes, Mrs Banks, I am accompanied by Sir Matthew Roberts QC, who will be acting as your defence counsel.'

She gave a slight bow of the head as Sir Matthew rose from his chair, took a pace forward and said, 'Good morning, Mrs Banks,' then suddenly thrust out his right hand.

'Good morning, Sir Matthew,' she replied, without moving a muscle, still looking in Casson's direction. 'I'm delighted that you will be representing me.'

'Sir Matthew would like to ask you a few questions, Mrs Banks,' said Casson, 'so that he can decide what might be the best approach in your case. He will assume the role of counsel for the prosecution, so that you can get used to what it will be like when you go into the witness box.'

'I understand,' replied Mrs Banks. 'I shall be happy to answer any of Sir Matthew's questions. I'm sure it won't prove difficult for someone of his eminence to show that a frail, blind woman would be incapable of chopping up a vicious sixteen-stone man.'

'Not if that vicious sixteen-stone man was poisoned before he was chopped up,' said Sir Matthew quietly.

'Which would be quite an achievement for someone lying in a hospital bed five miles from where the crime was committed,' replied Mrs Banks.

'If indeed that *was* when the crime was committed,' responded Sir Matthew. 'You claim your blindness was caused by a blow to the side of your head.'

'Yes, Sir Matthew. My husband picked up the frying pan from the stove while I was cooking breakfast, and struck me with it. I ducked, but the edge of the pan caught me on the left side of my face.' She touched a scar above her left eye that looked as if it would remain with her for the rest of her life.

'And then what happened?'

'I passed out and collapsed onto the kitchen floor. When I came to I could sense someone else was in the room. But I had no idea who it was until he spoke, when I recognised the voice of Jack Pembridge, our postman. He carried me to his van and drove me to the local hospital.'

'And it was while you were in hospital that the police discovered your husband's body?'

'That is correct, Sir Matthew. After I had been in Parkmead for nearly two weeks, I asked the vicar, who had been to visit me every day, to try and find out how Bruce was coping without me.'

'Did you not think it surprising that your husband

hadn't been to see you once during the time you were in hospital?' asked Sir Matthew, who began slowly pushing his cup of coffee towards the edge of the table.

'No. I had threatened to leave him on several occasions, and I don't think . . .' The cup fell off the table and shattered noisily on the stone floor. Sir Matthew's eyes never left Mrs Banks.

She jumped nervously, but did not turn to look in the direction of the broken cup.

'Are you all right, Mr Casson?' she asked.

'My fault,' said Sir Matthew. 'How clumsy of me.'

Casson suppressed a smile. Witherington remained unmoved.

'Please continue,' said Sir Matthew as he bent down and began picking up the pieces of china scattered across the floor. 'You were saying, "I don't think . . ."'

'Oh, yes,' said Mrs Banks. 'I don't think Bruce would have cared whether I returned to the farm or not.'

'Quite so,' said Sir Matthew after he had placed the broken pieces on the table. 'But can you explain to me why the police found one of your hairs on the handle of the axe that was used to dismember your husband's body?'

'Yes, Sir Matthew, I can. I was chopping up some wood for the stove before I prepared his breakfast.'

'Then I am bound to ask why there were no finger-prints on the handle of the axe, Mrs Banks.'

'Because I was wearing gloves, Sir Matthew. If you had ever worked on a farm in mid-October, you would know only too well how cold it can be at five in the morning.'

This time Casson did allow himself to smile.

'But what about the blood found on your husband's collar? Blood that was shown by the Crown's forensic scientist to match your own.'

'You will find my blood on many things in that house, should you care to look closely, Sir Matthew.'

'And the spade, the one with your fingerprints all over it? Had you also been doing some digging before breakfast that morning?'

'No, but I would have had cause to use it every day the previous week.'

'I see,' said Sir Matthew. 'Let us now turn our attention to something I suspect you didn't do every day, namely the purchase of strychnine. First, Mrs Banks, why did you need such a large amount? And second, why did you have to travel twenty-seven miles to Reading to purchase it?'

'I shop in Reading every other Thursday,' Mrs Banks explained. 'There isn't an agricultural supplier any nearer.'

Sir Matthew frowned and rose from his chair. He began slowly to circle Mrs Banks, while Casson watched her eyes. They never moved.

When Sir Matthew was directly behind his client, he checked his watch. It was 11.17. He knew his timing had to be exact, because he had become uncomfortably aware that he was dealing not only with a clever woman, but also an extremely cunning one. Mind you, he reflected, anyone who had lived for eleven years with such a man as Bruce Banks would have had to be cunning simply to survive.

'You still haven't explained why you needed such a large amount of strychnine,' he said, remaining behind his client.

'We had been losing a lot of chickens,' Mrs Banks replied, still not moving her head. 'My husband thought it was rats, so he told me to get a large quantity of strychnine to finish them off. "Once and for all" were his exact words.'

'But as it turned out, it was he who was finished off, once and for all – and undoubtedly with the same poison,' said Sir Matthew quietly.

'I also feared for Rupert's safety,' said Mrs Banks, ignoring her counsel's sarcasm.

'But your son was away at school at the time, am I not correct?'

'Yes, you are, Sir Matthew, but he was due back for half term that weekend.'

'Have you ever used that supplier before?'

'Regularly,' said Mrs Banks, as Sir Matthew completed his circle and returned to face her once again. 'I go there at least once a month, as I'm sure the manager will confirm.' She turned her head and faced a foot or so to his right.

Sir Matthew remained silent, resisting the temptation to look at his watch. He knew it could only be a matter of seconds. A few moments later the door on the far side of the interview room swung open and a boy of about nine years of age entered. The three of them watched their client closely as the child walked silently towards her. Rupert Banks came to a halt in front of his mother and smiled, but received no response. He waited for a further ten seconds, then turned and walked back out, exactly as he had been instructed to do. Mrs Banks's eyes remained fixed somewhere between Sir Matthew and Mr Casson.

The smile on Casson's face was now almost one of triumph.

'Is there someone else in the room?' asked Mrs Banks. 'I thought I heard the door open.'

'No,' said Sir Matthew. 'Only Mr Casson and I are in the room.' Witherington still hadn't moved a muscle.

Sir Matthew began to circle Mrs Banks for what he knew had to be the last time. He had almost come to believe that he might have misjudged her. When he was directly behind her once again, he nodded to his junior, who remained seated in front of her.

Witherington removed the silk handkerchief from his breast pocket, slowly unfolded it, and laid it out flat on the table in front of him. Mrs Banks showed no reaction. Witherington stretched out the fingers of his right hand, bowed his head slightly, and paused before placing his right hand over his left eye. Without warning he plucked the eye out of its socket and placed it in the middle of the silk handkerchief. He left it on the table for a full thirty seconds, then began to polish it. Sir Matthew completed his circle, and observed beads of perspiration appearing on Mrs Banks's forehead as he sat down.

When Witherington had finished cleaning the almond-shaped glass object, he slowly raised his head until he was staring directly at her, then eased the eye back into its socket. Mrs Banks momentarily turned away. She quickly tried to compose herself, but it was too late.

Sir Matthew rose from his chair and smiled at his client. She returned the smile.

'I must confess, Mrs Banks,' he said, 'I would feel much more confident about a plea of guilty to manslaughter.'

ONE MAN'S MEAT...

COULD ANYONE BE THAT BEAUTIFUL?

I was driving round the Aldwych on my way to work when I first saw her. She was walking up the steps of the Aldwych Theatre. If I'd stared a moment longer I would have driven into the back of the car in front of me, but before I could confirm my fleeting impression she had disappeared into the throng of theatregoers.

I spotted a parking space on my left-hand side and swung into it at the last possible moment, without indicating, causing the vehicle behind me to let out several appreciative blasts. I leapt out of my car and ran back towards the theatre, realising how unlikely it was that I'd be able to find her in such a mêlée, and that even if I did, she was probably meeting a boyfriend or husband who would turn out to be about six feet tall and closely to resemble Harrison Ford.

Once I reached the foyer I scanned the chattering crowd. I slowly turned 360 degrees, but could see no sign of her. Should I try to buy a ticket? I wondered. But she could be seated anywhere – the stalls, the dress circle, even the upper circle. Perhaps I should walk up and down the aisles until I spotted her. But I realised I wouldn't be allowed into any part of the theatre unless I could produce a ticket.

And then I saw her. She was standing in a queue in front of the window marked 'Tonight's Performance', and was just one away from being attended to. There were two other customers, a young woman and a middle-aged man, waiting in line behind her. I quickly joined the queue, by which time she had reached the front. I leant forward and tried to overhear what she was saying, but I could only catch the box office manager's reply: 'Not much chance with the curtain going up in a few minutes' time, madam,' he was saying. 'But if you leave it with me, I'll see what I can do.'

She thanked him and walked off in the direction of the stalls. My first impression was confirmed. It didn't matter if you looked from the ankles up or from the head down – she was perfection. I couldn't take my eyes off her, and I noticed that she was having exactly the same effect on several other men in the foyer. I wanted to tell them all not to bother. Didn't they realise she was with me? Or rather, that she would be by the end of the evening.

After she had disappeared from view, I craned my neck to look into the booth. Her ticket had been placed to one side. I sighed with relief as the young woman two places ahead of me presented her credit card and picked up four tickets for the dress circle.

I began to pray that the man in front of me wasn't looking for a single.

'Do you have one ticket for tonight's performance?' he asked hopefully, as the three-minute bell sounded. The man in the booth smiled.

I scowled. Should I knife him in the back, kick him in the groin, or simply scream abuse at him?

'Where would you prefer to sit, sir? The dress circle or the stalls?'

'Don't say stalls,' I willed. 'Say Circle . . . Circle . . . Circle . . .'

'Stalls,' he said.

'I have one on the aisle in row H,' said the man in the box, checking the computer screen in front of him. I uttered a silent cheer as I realised that the theatre would be trying to sell off its remaining tickets before it bothered with returns handed in by members of the public. But then, I thought, how would I get around that problem?

By the time the man in front of me had bought the ticket on the end of row H, I had my lines well rehearsed, and just hoped I wouldn't need a prompt.

'Thank goodness. I thought I wasn't going to make it,' I began, trying to sound out of breath. The man in the ticket booth looked up at me, but didn't seem all that impressed by my opening line. 'It was the traffic. And then I couldn't find a parking space. My girlfriend may have given up on me. Did she by any chance hand in my ticket for resale?'

He looked unconvinced. My dialogue obviously wasn't gripping him. 'Can you describe her?' he asked suspiciously.

'Short-cropped dark hair, hazel eyes, wearing a red silk dress that . . .'

'Ah, yes. I remember her,' he said, almost sighing. He picked up the ticket by his side and handed it to me.

'Thank you,' I said, trying not to show my relief that he had come in so neatly on cue with the closing line from my first scene. As I hurried off in the direction of the stalls, I grabbed an envelope from a pile on the ledge beside the booth.

I checked the price of the ticket: twenty pounds. I extracted two ten-pound notes from my wallet, put them in the envelope, licked the flap and stuck it down.

The girl at the entrance to the stalls checked my ticket. 'F-11. Six rows from the front, on the right-hand side.'

I walked slowly down the aisle until I spotted her. She was sitting next to an empty place in the middle of the row. As I made my way over the feet of those who were already seated, she turned and smiled, obviously pleased to see that someone had purchased her spare ticket.

I returned the smile, handed over the envelope containing my twenty pounds, and sat down beside her. 'The man in the box office asked me to give you this.'

'Thank you.' She slipped the envelope into her evening bag. I was about to try the first line of my second scene on her, when the house lights faded and the curtain rose for Act One of the real performance. I suddenly realised that I had no idea what play I was about to see. I glanced across at the programme on her lap and read the words 'An Inspector Calls, by J.B. Priestley'.

I remembered that the critics had been full of praise for the production when it had originally opened at the National Theatre, and had particularly singled out the performance of Kenneth Cranham. I tried to concentrate on what was taking place on stage.

The eponymous inspector was staring into a house in which an Edwardian family were preparing for a dinner to celebrate their daughter's engagement. 'I was thinking of getting a new car,' the father was saying to his prospective son-in-law as he puffed away on his cigar.

At the mention of the word 'car', I suddenly remembered that I had abandoned mine outside the theatre. Was it on a double yellow line? Or worse? To hell with it. They could have it in part-exchange for the model sitting next to me. The audience laughed, so I joined in, if only to give the impression that I was following the plot. But what about my original plans for the evening? By now everyone would be wondering why I hadn't turned up. I realised that I wouldn't be able to leave the theatre during the interval, either to check on my car or to make a phone call to explain my absence, as that would be my one chance of developing my own plot.

The play had the rest of the audience enthralled, but I had already begun rehearsing the lines from my own script, which would have to be performed during the interval between Acts One and Two. I was painfully aware that I would be restricted to fifteen minutes, and that there would be no second night.

By the time the curtain came down at the end of the first act, I was confident of my draft text. I waited for the applause to die down before I turned towards her.

'What an original production,' I began. 'Quite modernistic.' I vaguely remembered that one of the critics had followed that line. 'I was lucky to get a seat at the last moment.'

'I was just as lucky,' she replied. I felt encouraged. 'I mean, to find someone who was looking for a single ticket at such short notice.'

I nodded. 'My name's Michael Whitaker.'

'Anna Townsend,' she said, giving me a warm smile.

'Would you like a drink?' I asked.

'Thank you,' she replied, 'that would be nice.' I stood up and led her through the packed scrum that was heading towards the stalls bar, occasionally glancing back to make sure she was still following me. I was somehow expecting her no longer to be there, but each time I turned to look she greeted me with the same radiant smile.

'What would you like?' I asked, once I could make out the bar through the crowd.

'A dry martini, please.'

'Stay here, and I'll be back in a moment,' I promised, wondering just how many precious minutes would be wasted while I had to wait at the bar. I took out a five-pound note and held it up conspicuously, in the hope that the prospect of a large tip might influence the barman's sense of direction. He spotted the money, but I still had to wait for another four customers to be served before I managed to secure the dry martini and a Scotch on the rocks for myself. The barman didn't deserve the tip I left him, but I hadn't any more time to waste waiting for the change.

I carried the drinks back to the far corner of the foyer, where Anna stood studying her programme. She was silhouetted against a window, and in that stylish red silk dress, the light emphasised her slim, elegant figure.

I handed her the dry martini, aware that my limited time had almost run out.

'Thank you,' she said, giving me another disarming smile.

'How did you come to have a spare ticket?' I asked as she took a sip from her drink.

'My partner was held up on an emergency case at the last minute,' she explained. 'Just one of the problems of being a doctor.'

'Pity. They missed a quite remarkable production,' I prompted, hoping to tease out of her whether her partner was male or female.

'Yes,' said Anna. 'I tried to book seats when it was still at the National Theatre, but they were sold out for any performances I was able to make, so when a friend offered me two tickets at the last minute, I jumped at them. After all, it's coming off in a few weeks.' She took another sip from her martini. 'What about you?' she asked as the three-minute bell sounded.

There was no such line in my script.

'Me?'

'Yes, Michael,' she said, a hint of teasing in her voice. 'How did you come to be looking for a spare seat at the last moment?'

'Sharon Stone was tied up for the evening, and at the last second Princess Diana told me that she would have loved to have come, but she was trying to keep a low profile.' Anna laughed. 'Actually, I read some of the crits, and I dropped in on the off-chance of picking up a spare ticket.'

'And you picked up a spare woman as well,' said Anna, as the two-minute bell went. I wouldn't have dared to include such a bold line in her script – or was there a hint of mockery in those hazel eyes?

'I certainly did,' I replied lightly. 'So, are you a doctor as well?'

'As well as what?' asked Anna.

'As well as your partner,' I said, not sure if she was still teasing.

'Yes. I'm a GP in Fulham. There are three of us in the practice, but I was the only one who could escape tonight. And what do you do when you're not chatting up Sharon Stone or escorting Princess Diana to the theatre?'

'I'm in the restaurant business,' I told her.

'That must be one of the few jobs with worse hours and tougher working conditions than mine,' Anna said as the one-minute bell sounded.

I looked into those hazel eyes and wanted to say – Anna, let's forget the second act: I realise the play's superb, but all I want to do is spend the rest of the evening alone with you, not jammed into a crowded auditorium with eight hundred other people.

'Wouldn't you agree?'

I tried to recall what she had just said. 'I expect we get more customer complaints than you do,' was the best I could manage.

'I doubt it,' Anna said, quite sharply. 'If you're a woman in the medical profession and you don't cure your patients within a couple of days, they immediately want to know if you're fully qualified.'

I laughed, and finished my drink as a voice boomed over the Tannoy, 'Would the audience please take their seats for the second act. The curtain is about to rise.'

'We ought to be getting back,' Anna said, placing her empty glass on the nearest window ledge.

'I suppose so,' I said reluctantly, and led her in the opposite direction to the one in which I really wanted to take her.

'Thanks for the drink,' she said as we returned to our seats.

'Small recompense,' I replied. She glanced up at me questioningly. 'For such a good ticket,' I explained.

She smiled as we made our way along the row, stepping awkwardly over more toes. I was just about to risk a further remark when the house lights dimmed.

During the second act I turned to smile in Anna's direction whenever there was laughter, and was occasionally rewarded with a warm response. But my supreme moment of triumph came towards the end of the act, when the detective showed the daughter a photograph of the dead woman. She gave a piercing scream, and the stage lights were suddenly switched off.

Anna grabbed my hand, but quickly released it and apologised.

'Not at all,' I whispered. 'I only just stopped myself from doing the same thing.' In the darkened theatre, I couldn't tell how she responded.

A moment later the phone on the stage rang. Everyone in the audience knew it must be the detective on the other end of the line, even if they couldn't be sure what he was going to say. That final scene had the whole house gripped.

After the lights dimmed for the last time, the cast returned to the stage and deservedly received a long ovation, taking several curtain calls.

When the curtain was finally lowered, Anna turned to me and said, 'What a remarkable production. I'm so glad I didn't miss it. And I'm even more pleased that I didn't have to see it alone.'

'Me too,' I told her, ignoring the fact that I'd never planned to spend the evening at the theatre in the first place.

We made our way up the aisle together as the audience flowed out of the theatre like a slow-moving river. I wasted those few precious moments discussing the merits of the cast, the power of the director's interpretation, the originality of the macabre set and even the Edwardian costumes, before we reached the double doors that led back out into the real world.

'Goodbye, Michael,' Anna said. 'Thank you for adding to my enjoyment of the evening.' She shook me by the hand.

'Goodbye,' I said, gazing once again into those hazel eyes.

She turned to go, and I wondered if I would ever see her again.

'Anna,' I said.

She glanced back in my direction.

'If you're not doing anything in particular, would you care to join me for dinner . . .'

Author's Note

At this point in the story, the reader is offered the choice of four different endings.

You might decide to read all four of them, or simply select one, and consider that your own particular ending. If you do choose to read all four, they should be taken in the order in which they have been written:

1   RARE
2   BURNT
3   OVERDONE
4   À POINT

Rare

'THANK YOU, MICHAEL. I'D LIKE THAT.'
I smiled, unable to mask my delight. 'Good. I know a little restaurant just down the road that I think you might enjoy.'

'That sounds fun,' Anna said, linking her arm in mine. I guided her through the departing throng.

As we strolled together down the Aldwych, Anna continued to chat about the play, comparing it favourably with a production she had seen at the Haymarket some years before.

When we reached the Strand I pointed to a large grey double door on the other side of the road. 'That's it,' I said. We took advantage of a red light to weave our way through the temporarily stationary traffic, and after we'd reached the far pavement I pushed one of the grey doors open to allow Anna through. It began to rain just as we stepped inside. I led her down a flight of stairs into a basement restaurant buzzing with the talk of people who had just come out of theatres, and waiters dashing, plates in both hands, from table to table.

'I'll be impressed if you can get a table here,' Anna said, eyeing a group of would-be customers who were clustered round the bar, impatiently waiting for someone to leave.

I strolled across to the reservations desk. The head waiter, who until that moment had been taking a customer's order, rushed over. 'Good evening, Mr Whitaker,' he said. 'How many are you?'

'Just the two of us.'

'Follow me, please, sir,' Mario said, leading us to my usual table in the far corner of the room.

'Another dry martini?' I asked her as we sat down.

'No, thank you,' she replied. 'I think I'll just have a glass of wine with the meal.'

I nodded my agreement, as Mario handed us our menus. Anna studied hers for a few moments before I asked if she had spotted anything she fancied.

'Yes,' she said, looking straight at me. 'But for now I think I'll settle for the fettucini, and a glass of red wine.'

'Good idea,' I said. 'I'll join you. But are you sure you won't have a starter?'

'No, thank you, Michael. I've reached that age when I can no longer order everything I'm tempted by.'

'Me too,' I confessed. 'I have to play squash three times a week to keep in shape,' I told her as Mario reappeared.

'Two fettucini,' I began, 'and a bottle of . . .'

'Half a bottle, please,' said Anna. 'I'll only have one glass. I've got an early start tomorrow morning, so I shouldn't overdo things.'

I nodded, and Mario scurried away.

I looked across the table and into Anna's eyes. 'I've always wondered about women doctors,' I said, immediately realising that the line was a bit feeble.

'You mean, you wondered if we're normal?'

'Something like that, I suppose.'

'Yes, we're normal enough, except every day we have to see a lot of men in the nude. I can assure you, Michael, most of them are overweight and fairly unattractive.'

I suddenly wished I were half a stone lighter. 'But are there many men who are brave enough to consider a woman doctor in the first place?'

'Quite a few,' said Anna, 'though most of my patients are female. But there are just about enough intelligent, sensible, uninhibited males around who can accept that a woman doctor might be just as likely to cure them as a man.'

I smiled as two bowls of fettucini were placed in front of us. Mario then showed me the label on the half-bottle he had selected. I nodded my approval. He had chosen a vintage to match Anna's pedigree.

'And what about you?' asked Anna. 'What does being "in the restaurant business" actually mean?'

'I'm on the management side,' I said, before sampling the wine. I nodded again, and Mario poured a glass for Anna and then topped up mine.

'Or at least, that's what I do nowadays. I started life as a waiter,' I said, as Anna began to sip her wine.

'What a magnificent wine,' she remarked. 'It's so good I may end up having a second glass.'

'I'm glad you like it,' I said. 'It's a Barolo.'

'You were saying, Michael? You started life as a waiter . . .'

'Yes, then I moved into the kitchens for about five years, and finally ended up on the management side. How's the fettucini?'

'It's delicious. Almost melts in your mouth.' She took another sip of her wine. 'So, if you're not cooking, and no longer a waiter, what do you do now?'

'Well, at the moment I'm running three restaurants in the West End, which means I never stop dashing from one to the other, depending on which is facing the biggest crisis on that particular day.'

'Sounds a bit like ward duty to me,' said Anna. 'So who turned out to have the biggest crisis today?'

'Today, thank heaven, was not typical,' I told her with feeling.

'That bad?' said Anna.

'Yes, I'm afraid so. We lost a chef this morning who cut off the top of his finger, and won't be back at work for at least a fortnight. My head waiter in our second restaurant is off, claiming he has 'flu, and I've just had to sack the barman in the third for fiddling the books. Barmen always fiddle the books, of course, but in this case even the customers began to notice what he was up to.' I paused. 'But I still wouldn't want to be in any other business.'

'In the circumstances, I'm amazed you were able to take the evening off.'

'I shouldn't have, really, and I wouldn't have,

except . . .' I trailed off as I leaned over and topped up Anna's glass.

'Except what?' she said.

'Do you want to hear the truth?' I asked as I poured the remains of the wine into my own glass.

'I'll try that for starters,' she said.

I placed the empty bottle on the side of the table, and hesitated, but only for a moment. 'I was driving to one of my restaurants earlier this evening, when I spotted you going into the theatre. I stared at you for so long that I nearly crashed into the back of the car in front of me. Then I swerved across the road into the nearest parking space, and the car behind almost crashed into me. I leapt out, ran all the way to the theatre, and searched everywhere until I saw you standing in the queue for the box office. I joined the line and watched you hand over your spare ticket. Once you were safely out of sight, I told the box office manager that you hadn't expected me to make it in time, and that you might have put my ticket up for resale. After I'd described you, which I was able to do in great detail, he handed it over without so much as a murmur.'

Anna put down her glass of wine and stared across at me with a look of incredulity. 'I'm glad he fell for your story,' she said. 'But should I?'

'Yes, you should. Because then I put two ten-pound notes into a theatre envelope and took the place next to you. The rest you already know.' I waited to see how she would react.

She didn't speak for some time. 'I'm flattered,' she

eventually said, and touched my hand. 'I didn't realise there were any old-fashioned romantics left in the world.' She squeezed my fingers and looked me in the eyes. 'Am I allowed to ask what you have planned for the rest of the evening?'

'Nothing has been planned so far,' I admitted. 'Which is why it's all been so refreshing.'

'You make me sound like an After Eight mint,' said Anna with a laugh.

'I can think of at least three replies to that,' I told her as Mario reappeared, looking a little disappointed at the sight of the half-empty plates.

'Was everything all right, sir?' he asked, sounding anxious.

'Couldn't have been better,' said Anna, who hadn't stopped looking at me.

'Would you like some coffee?' I asked.

'Yes,' said Anna. 'But perhaps we could have it somewhere a little less crowded.'

I was so taken by surprise that it was several moments before I recovered. I was beginning to feel that I was no longer in control. Anna rose from her place and said, 'Shall we go?' I nodded to Mario, who just smiled.

Once we were back out on the street, she linked her arm with mine as we retraced our steps along the Aldwych and past the theatre.

'It's been a wonderful evening,' she was saying as we reached the spot where I had left my car. 'Until you arrived on the scene it had been a rather dull day, but you've changed all that.'

'It hasn't actually been the best of days for me either,'
I admitted. 'But I've rarely enjoyed an evening more.
Where would you like to have coffee? Annabels? Or
why don't we try the new Dorchester Club?'

'If you don't have a wife, your place. If you do . . .'

'I don't,' I told her simply.

'Then that's settled,' she said as I opened the door of
my BMW for her. Once she was safely in I walked round
to take my seat behind the wheel, and discovered that I
had left my sidelights on and the keys in the ignition.

I turned the key, and the engine immediately purred
into life. 'This has to be my day,' I said to myself.

'Sorry?' Anna said, turning in my direction.

'We were lucky to miss the rain,' I replied, as a few
drops landed on the windscreen. I flicked on the wipers.

On our way to Pimlico, Anna told me about her child-
hood in the south of France, where her father had taught
English at a boys' school. Her account of being the only
girl among a couple of hundred teenage French boys
made me laugh again and again. I found myself becoming more and more enchanted with her company.

'Whatever made you come back to England?' I asked.

'An English mother who divorced my French father,
and the chance to study medicine at St Thomas's.'

'But don't you miss the south of France, especially on
nights like this?' I asked as a clap of thunder crackled
above us.

'Oh, I don't know,' she said. I was about to respond
when she added, 'In any case, now the English have
learnt how to cook, the place has become almost

civilised.' I smiled to myself, wondering if she was teasing me again.

I found out immediately. 'By the way,' she said, 'I assume that was one of your restaurants we had dinner at.'

'Yes, it was,' I said sheepishly.

'That explains how you got a table so easily when it was packed out, why the waiter knew it was a Barolo you wanted without your having to ask, and how you could leave without paying the bill.'

I was beginning to wonder if I would always be a yard behind her.

'Was it the missing waiter, the four-and-a-half-fingered chef, or the crooked bartender?'

'The crooked bartender,' I replied, laughing. 'But I sacked him this afternoon, and I'm afraid his deputy didn't look as if he was coping all that well,' I explained as I turned right off Millbank, and began to search for a parking space.

'And I thought you only had eyes for me,' sighed Anna, 'when all the time you were looking over my shoulder and checking on what the deputy barman was up to.'

'Not *all* the time,' I said as I manoeuvred the car into the only space left in the mews where I lived. I got out of the car and walked round to Anna's side, opened the door and guided her to the house.

As I closed the door behind us, Anna put her arms around my neck and looked up into my eyes. I leaned down and kissed her for the first time. When she broke away, all she said was, 'Don't let's bother with coffee, Michael.' I slipped off my jacket, and led her upstairs and into my bedroom, praying that it hadn't been the housekeeper's day off. When I opened the door I was relieved to find that the bed had been made and the room was tidy.

'I'll just be a moment,' I said, and disappeared into the bathroom. As I cleaned my teeth, I began to wonder if it was all a dream. When I returned to the bedroom, would I discover she didn't exist? I dropped the toothbrush into its mug and went back to the bedroom. Where was she? My eyes followed a trail of discarded clothes that led all the way to the bed. Her head was propped up on the pillow. Only a sheet covered her body.

I quickly took off my clothes, dropping them where they fell, and switched off the main lights, so that only the one by the bed remained aglow. I slid under the sheets to join her. I looked at her for several seconds before I took her in my arms. I slowly explored every part of her body, as she began to kiss me again. I couldn't believe that anyone could be that exciting, and at the same time so tender. When we finally made love, I knew I never wanted this woman to leave me.

She lay in my arms for some time before either of us spoke. Then I began talking about anything that came into my head. I confided my hopes, my dreams, even my worst anxieties, with a freedom I had never experienced with anyone before. I wanted to share everything with her.

And then she leaned across and began kissing me once again, first on the lips, then the neck and chest, and as she slowly continued down my body I thought I would explode. The last thing I remember was turning off the light by my bed as the clock on the hall table chimed one.

When I woke the following morning, the first rays of sunlight were already shining through the lace curtains, and the glorious memory of the night before was instantly revived. I turned lazily to take her in my arms, but she was no longer there.

'Anna?' I cried out, sitting bolt upright. There was no reply. I flicked on the light by the side of the bed, and glanced across at the bedside clock. It was 7.29. I was about to jump out of bed and go in search of her when I noticed a scribbled note wedged under a corner of the clock.

I picked it up, read it slowly, and smiled.

'So will I,' I said, and lay back on the pillow, thinking about what I should do next. I decided to send her a dozen roses later that morning, eleven white and one red. Then I would have a red one delivered to her on the hour, every hour, until I saw her again.

After I had showered and dressed, I roamed aimlessly around the house. I wondered how quickly I could persuade Anna to move in, and what changes she would want to make. Heaven knows, I thought as I walked through to the kitchen, clutching her note, the place could do with a woman's touch.

As I ate breakfast I looked up her number in the telephone directory, instead of reading the morning paper. There it was, just as she had said. Dr Townsend, listing a surgery number in Parsons Green Lane where she could be contacted between nine and six. There was a second number, but deep black lettering requested that it should only be used in case of emergencies.

Although I considered my state of health to be an emergency, I dialled the first number, and waited impatiently. All I wanted to say was, 'Good morning, darling. I got your note, and can we make last night the first of many?'

A matronly voice answered the phone. 'Dr Townsend's surgery.'

'Dr Townsend, please,' I said.

'Which one?' she asked. 'There are three Dr Townsends in the practice – Dr Jonathan, Dr Anna and Dr Elizabeth.'

'Dr Anna,' I replied.

'Oh, Mrs Townsend,' she said. 'I'm sorry, but she's not available at the moment. She's just taken the children off to school, and after that she has to go to the airport to pick up her husband, Dr Jonathan, who's returning this morning from a medical conference in Minneapolis. I'm not expecting her back for at least a couple of hours. Would you like to leave a message?'

There was a long silence before the matronly voice asked, 'Are you still there?' I placed the receiver back on the hook without replying, and looked sadly down at the hand-written note by the side of the phone.

Dear Michael,
I will remember tonight for the rest of my life.
Thank you.
Anna

Burnt

'THANK YOU, MICHAEL. I'D LIKE THAT.'
I smiled, unable to mask my delight.

'Hi, Anna. I thought I might have missed you.'

I turned and stared at a tall man with a mop of fair hair, who seemed unaffected by the steady flow of people trying to pass him on either side.

Anna gave him a smile that I hadn't seen until that moment.

'Hello, darling,' she said. 'This is Michael Whitaker. You're lucky – he bought your ticket, and if you hadn't turned up I was just about to accept his kind invitation to dinner. Michael, this is my husband, Jonathan – the one who was held up at the hospital. As you can see, he's now escaped.'

I couldn't think of a suitable reply.

Jonathan shook me warmly by the hand. 'Thank you for keeping my wife company,' he said. 'Won't you join us for dinner?'

'That's very kind of you,' I replied, 'but I've just remembered that I'm meant to be somewhere else right now. I'd better run.'

'That's a pity,' said Anna. 'I was rather looking

361

forward to finding out all about the restaurant business. Perhaps we'll meet again sometime, whenever my husband next leaves me in the lurch. Goodbye, Michael.'

'Goodbye, Anna.'

I watched them climb into the back of a taxi together, and wished Jonathan would drop dead in front of me. He didn't, so I began to retrace my steps back to the spot where I had abandoned my car. 'You're a lucky man, Jonathan Townsend,' was the only observation I made. But no one was listening.

The next word that came to my lips was 'Damn!' I repeated it several times, as there was a distressingly large space where I was certain I'd left my car.

I walked up and down the street in case I'd forgotten where I'd parked it, cursed again, then marched off in search of a phone box, unsure if my car had been stolen or towed away. There was a pay phone just around the corner in Kingsway. I picked up the handset and jabbed three nines into it.

'Which service do you require? Fire, Police or Ambulance,' a voice asked.

'Police,' I said, and was immediately put through to another voice.

'Charing Cross Police Station. What is the nature of your enquiry?'

'I think my car has been stolen.'

'Can you tell me the make, colour and registration number please, sir.'

'It's a red Ford Fiesta, registration H107 SHV.'

There was a long pause, during which I could hear other voices talking in the background.

'No, it hasn't been stolen, sir,' said the officer when he came back on the line. 'The car was illegally parked on a double yellow line. It's been removed and taken to the Vauxhall Bridge Pound.'

'Can I pick it up now?' I asked sulkily.

'Certainly, sir. How will you be getting there?'

'I'll take a taxi.'

'Then just ask the driver for the Vauxhall Bridge Pound. Once you get there, you'll need some form of identification, and a cheque for £105 with a banker's card — that is if you don't have the full amount in cash.'

'£105?' I repeated in disbelief.

'That's correct, sir.'

I slammed the phone down just as it started to rain. I scurried back to the corner of the Aldwych in search of a taxi, only to find that they were all being commandeered by the hordes of people still hanging around outside the theatre.

I put my collar up and nipped across the road, dodging between the slow-moving traffic. Once I had reached the far side, I continued running until I found an overhanging ledge broad enough to shield me from the blustery rain.

I shivered, and sneezed several times before an empty cab eventually came to my rescue.

'Vauxhall Bridge Pound,' I told the driver as I jumped in.

'Bad luck, mate,' said the cabbie. 'You're my second this evening.'

I frowned.

As the taxi manoeuvred its way slowly through the rainswept post-theatre traffic and across Waterloo Bridge, the driver began chattering away. I just about managed monosyllabic replies to his opinions on the weather, John Major, the England cricket team and foreign tourists. With each new topic, his forecast became ever more gloomy.

When we reached the car pound I passed him a ten-pound note and waited in the rain for my change. Then I dashed off in the direction of a little Portakabin, where I was faced by my second queue that evening. This one was considerably longer than the first, and I knew that when I eventually reached the front of it and paid for my ticket, I wouldn't be rewarded with any memorable entertainment. When my turn finally came, a burly policeman pointed to a form sellotaped to the counter.

I followed its instructions to the letter, first producing my driving licence, then writing out a cheque for £105, payable to the Metropolitan Police. I handed them both over, with my cheque card, to the policeman, who towered over me. The man's sheer bulk was the only reason I didn't suggest that perhaps he ought to have more important things to do with his time, like catching drug dealers. Or even car thieves.

'Your vehicle is in the far corner,' said the officer, pointing into the distance, over row upon row of cars.

'Of course it is,' I replied. I stepped out of the Portakabin and back into the rain, dodging puddles as I ran between the lines of cars. I didn't stop until I reached the farthest corner of the pound. It still took me several more minutes to locate my red Ford Fiesta – one disadvantage, I thought, of owning the most popular car in Britain.

I unlocked the door, squelched down onto the front seat, and sneezed again. I turned the key in the ignition, but the engine barely turned over, letting out only the occasional splutter before giving up altogether. Then I remembered I hadn't switched the sidelights off when I made my unscheduled dash for the theatre. I uttered a string of expletives that only partly expressed my true feelings.

I watched as another figure came running across the pound towards a Range Rover parked in the row in front of me. I quickly wound down my window, but he had driven off before I could shout the magic words 'jump leads'. I got out and retrieved my jump leads from the boot, walked to the front of the car, raised the bonnet, and attached the leads to the battery. I began to shiver once again as I settled down for another wait.

I couldn't get Anna out of my mind, but accepted that the only thing I'd succeeded in picking up that evening was the 'flu.

In the following forty rain-drenched minutes, three people passed by before a young black man asked, 'So what's the trouble, man?' Once I had explained my problem he manoeuvred his old van alongside my car, then raised his bonnet and attached the jump leads to his battery. When he switched on his ignition, my engine began to turn over.

'Thanks,' I shouted, rather inadequately, once I'd revved the engine several times.

'My pleasure, man,' he replied, and disappeared into the night.

As I drove out of the car pound I switched on my radio, to hear Big Ben striking twelve. It reminded me that I hadn't turned up for work that night. The first thing I needed to do, if I wanted to keep my job, was to come up with a good excuse. I sneezed again, and decided on the 'flu. Although they'd probably taken the last orders by now, Gerald wouldn't have closed the kitchens yet.

I peered through the rain, searching the pavements for a pay phone, and eventually spotted a row of three outside a post office. I stopped the car and jumped out, but a cursory inspection revealed that they'd all been vandalised. I climbed back into the car and continued my search. After dashing in and out of the rain several times, I finally spotted a single phone box on the corner of Warwick Way that looked as if it might just be in working order.

I dialled the restaurant, and waited a long time for someone to answer.

'Laguna 50,' said an Italian-sounding young girl.

'Janice, is that you? It's Mike.'

'Yes, it's me, Mike,' she whispered, reverting to her Lambeth accent. 'I'd better warn you that every time your name's been mentioned this evening, Gerald picks up the nearest meat-axe.'

'Why?' I asked. 'You've still got Nick in the kitchen to see you through.'

'Nick chopped the top off one of his fingers earlier this evening, and Gerald had to take him to hospital. I was left in charge. He's not best pleased.'

'Oh, hell,' I said. 'But I've got . . .'

'The sack,' said another voice, and this one wasn't whispering.

'Gerald, I can explain . . .'

'Why you didn't turn up for work this evening?'

I sneezed, then held my nose. 'I've got the 'flu. If I'd come in tonight I would have given it to half the customers.'

'Would you?' said Gerald. 'Well, I suppose that might have been marginally worse than giving it to the girl who was sitting next to you in the theatre.'

'What do you mean?' I asked, letting go of my nose.

'Exactly what I said, Mike. You see, unfortunately for you, a couple of our regulars were two rows behind you at the Aldwych. They enjoyed the show almost as much as you seemed to, and one of them added, for good measure, that he thought your date was "absolutely stunning".'

'He must have mistaken me for someone else,' I said, trying not to sound desperate.

'He may have done, Mike, but I haven't. You're sacked, and don't even think about coming in to collect your pay packet, because there isn't one for a head waiter who'd rather take some bimbo to the theatre than do a night's work.' The line went dead.

I hung up the phone and started muttering obscenities under my breath as I walked slowly back towards my car. I was only a dozen paces away from it when a young lad jumped into the front seat, switched on the ignition, and lurched hesitatingly into the centre of the road in what sounded horribly like third gear. I chased after the retreating car, but once the youth began to accelerate, I knew I had no hope of catching him.

I ran all the way back to the phone box, and dialled 999 once again.

'Fire, Police or Ambulance?' I was asked for a second time that night.

'Police,' I said, and a moment later I was put through to another voice.

'Belgravia Police Station. What is the nature of your enquiry?'

'I've just had my car stolen!' I shouted.

'Make, model and registration number please, sir.'

'It's a red Ford Fiesta, registration H107 SHV.'

I waited impatiently.

'It hasn't been stolen, sir. It was illegally parked on a double . . .'

'No it wasn't!' I shouted even more loudly. 'I paid £105 to get the damn thing out of the Vauxhall Bridge Pound less than half an hour ago, and I've just seen it being driven off by a joyrider while I was making a phone call.'

'Where are you, sir?'

'In a phone box on the corner of Vauxhall Bridge Road and Warwick Way.'

'And in which direction was the car travelling when you last saw it?' asked the voice.

'North up Vauxhall Bridge Road.'

'And what is your home telephone number, sir?'

'081 290 4820.'

'And at work?'

'Like the car, I don't have a job any longer.'

'Right, I'll get straight onto it, sir. We'll be in touch with you the moment we have any news.'

I put the phone down and thought about what I should do next. I hadn't been left with a great deal of choice. I hailed a taxi and asked to be taken to Victoria, and was relieved to find that this driver showed no desire to offer any opinions on anything during the short journey to the station. When he dropped me I passed him my last note, and patiently waited while he handed over every last penny of my change. He also muttered an expletive or two. I bought a ticket for Bromley with my few remaining coins, and went in search of the platform.

'You've just about made it, mate,' the ticket collector told me. 'The last train's due in at any minute.' But I still had to wait for another twenty minutes on the cold, empty platform before the last train eventually pulled into the station. By then I had memorised every advertisement in sight, from Guinness to Mates, while continuing to sneeze at regular intervals.

When the train came to a halt and the doors squelched open I took a seat in a carriage near the front. It was another ten minutes before the engine lurched into action, and another forty before it finally pulled into Bromley station.

I emerged into the Kent night a few minutes before one o'clock, and set off in the direction of my little terraced house.

Twenty-five minutes later, I staggered up the short path to my front door. I began to search for my keys, then remembered that I'd left them in the car ignition. I didn't have the energy even to swear, and began to grovel around in the dark for the spare front-door key that was always hidden under a particular stone. But which one? At last I found it, put it in the lock, turned it and pushed the door open. No sooner had I stepped inside than the phone on the hall table began to ring.

I grabbed the receiver.

'Mr Whitaker?'

'Speaking.'

'This is the Belgravia police. We've located your car, sir, and . . .'

'Thank God for that,' I said, before the officer had a chance to finish the sentence. 'Where is it?'

'At this precise moment, sir, it's on the back of a pick-up lorry somewhere in Chelsea. It seems the lad who nicked it only managed to travel a mile or so before he hit the kerb at seventy, and bounced straight into a wall. I'm sorry to have to inform you, sir, that your car's a total write-off.'

'A total write-off?' I said in disbelief.

'Yes, sir. The garage who towed it away has been given your number, and they'll be in touch with you first thing in the morning.'

I couldn't think of any comment worth making.

'The good news is we've caught the lad who nicked it,' continued the police officer. 'The bad news is that he's only fifteen, doesn't have a driver's licence, and, of course, he isn't insured.'

'That's not a problem,' I said. 'I'm fully insured myself.'

'As a matter of interest, sir, did you leave your keys in the ignition?'

'Yes, I did. I was just making a quick phone call, and thought I'd only be away from the car for a couple of minutes.'

'Then I think it's unlikely you'll be covered by your insurance, sir.'

'Not covered by my insurance? What are you talking about?'

'It's standard policy nowadays not to pay out if you leave your keys in the ignition. You'd better check, sir,' were the officer's final words before ringing off.

I put the phone down and wondered what else could possibly go wrong. I slipped off my jacket and began to climb the stairs, but came to a sudden halt when I saw my wife waiting for me on the landing.

'Maureen . . .' I began.

'You can tell me later why the car is a total write-off,' she said, 'but not until you've explained why you didn't turn up for work this evening, and just who this "classy tart" is that Gerald said you were seen with at the theatre.'

Overdone

'No, I'm not doing anything in particular,' said Anna.

I smiled, unable to mask my delight.

'Good. I know a little restaurant just down the road that I think you might enjoy.'

'That sounds just fine,' said Anna as she made her way through the dense theatre crowd. I quickly followed, having to hurry just to keep up with her.

'Which way?' she asked. I pointed towards the Strand. She began walking at a brisk pace, and we continued to talk about the play.

When we reached the Strand I pointed to a large grey double door on the other side of the road. 'That's it,' I said. I would have taken her hand as she began to cross, but she stepped off the pavement ahead of me, dodged between the stationary traffic, and waited for me on the far side.

She pushed the grey doors open, and once again I followed in her wake. We descended a flight of steps into a basement restaurant buzzing with the talk of people who had just come out of theatres, and waiters dashing, plates in both hands, from table to table.

'I don't expect you'll be able to get a table here if you haven't booked,' said Anna, eyeing a group of would-be customers who were clustered round the bar, impatiently waiting for someone to leave.

'Don't worry about that,' I said with bravado, and strode across to the reservations desk. I waved a hand imperiously at the head waiter, who was taking a customer's order. I only hoped he would recognise me.

I turned round to smile at Anna, but she didn't look too impressed.

After the waiter had taken the order, he walked slowly over to me. 'How may I help you, sir?' he asked.

'Can you manage a table for two, Victor?'

'Victor's off tonight, sir. Have you booked?'

'No, I haven't, but . . .'

The head waiter checked the list of reservations and then looked at his watch. 'I might be able to fit you in around 11.15 – 11.30 at the latest,' he said, not sounding too hopeful.

'No sooner?' I pleaded. 'I don't think we can wait that long.' Anna nodded her agreement.

'I'm afraid not, sir,' said the head waiter. 'We are fully booked until then.'

'As I expected,' said Anna, turning to leave.

Once again I had to hurry to keep up with her. As we stepped out onto the pavement I said, 'There's a little Italian restaurant I know not far from here, where I can always get a table. Shall we risk it?'

'Can't see that we've got a lot of choice,' replied Anna. 'Which direction this time?'

'Just up the road to the right,' I said as a clap of thunder heralded an imminent downpour.

'Damn,' said Anna, placing her handbag over her head for protection.

'I'm sorry,' I said, looking up at the black clouds. 'It's my fault. I should have . . .'

'Stop apologising all the time, Michael. It isn't your fault if it starts to rain.'

I took a deep breath and tried again. 'We'd better make a dash for it,' I said desperately. 'I don't expect we'll be able to pick up a taxi in this weather.'

This at least secured her ringing endorsement. I began running up the road, and Anna followed closely behind. The rain was getting heavier and heavier, and although we couldn't have had more than seventy yards to cover, we were both soaked by the time we reached the restaurant.

I sighed with relief when I opened the door and found the dining room was half-empty, although I suppose I should have been annoyed. I turned and smiled hopefully at Anna, but she was still frowning.

'Everything all right?' I asked.

'Fine. It's just that my father had a theory about restaurants that were half-empty at this time of night.'

I looked quizzically at my guest, but decided not to make any comment about her eye make-up, which was beginning to run, or her hair, which had come loose at the edges.

'I'd better carry out some repair work. I'll only be a

couple of minutes,' she said, heading for a door marked 'Signorinas'.

I waved at Mario, who was serving no one in particular. He hurried over to me.

'There was a call for you earlier, Mr Whitaker,' Mario said as he guided me across the restaurant to my usual table. 'If you came in, I was to ask you to phone Gerald urgently. He sounded pretty desperate.'

'I'm sure it can wait. But if he rings again, let me know immediately.' At that moment Anna walked over to join us. The make-up had been restored, but the hair could have done with further attention.

I rose to greet her.

'You don't have to do that,' she said, taking her seat.

'Would you like a drink?' I asked, once we were both settled.

'No, I don't think so. I have an early start tomorrow morning, so I shouldn't overdo things. I'll just have a glass of wine with my meal.'

Another waiter appeared by her side. 'And what would madam care for this evening?' he asked politely.

'I haven't had time to look at the menu yet,' Anna replied, not even bothering to look up at him.

'I can recommend the fettucini, madam,' the waiter said, pointing to a dish halfway down the list of entrées. 'It's our speciality of the day.'

'Then I suppose I might as well have that,' said Anna, handing him the menu.

I nodded, indicating 'Me too,' and asked for a half-bottle of the house red. The waiter scooped up my menu and left us.

'Do you . . . ?'

'Can I . . . ?'

'You first,' I said, attempting a smile.

'Do you always order half a bottle of the house wine on a first date?' she asked.

'I think you'll find it's pretty good,' I said, rather plaintively.

'I was only teasing, Michael. Don't take yourself so seriously.'

I took a closer look at my companion, and began to wonder if I'd made a terrible mistake. Despite her efforts in the washroom, Anna wasn't quite the same girl I'd first seen — admittedly at a distance — when I'd nearly crashed my car earlier in the evening.

Oh my God, the car. I suddenly remembered where I'd left it, and stole a glance at my watch.

'Am I boring you already, Michael?' Anna asked. 'Or is this table on a time share?'

'Yes. I mean no. I'm sorry, I've just remembered something I should have checked on before we came to dinner. Sorry,' I repeated.

Anna frowned, which stopped me saying sorry yet again.

'Is it too late?' she asked.

'Too late for what?'

'To do something about whatever it is you should have checked on before we came to dinner?'

I looked out of the window, and wasn't pleased to see

that it had stopped raining. Now my only hope was that the late-night traffic wardens might not be too vigilant.

'No, I'm sure it will be all right,' I said, trying to sound relaxed.

'Well, that's a relief,' said Anna, in a tone that bordered on the sarcastic.

'So. What's it like being a doctor?' I asked, trying to change the subject.

'Michael, it's my evening off. I'd rather not talk about my work, if you don't mind.'

For the next few moments neither of us spoke. I tried again. 'Do you have many male patients in your practice?' I asked, as the waiter reappeared with our fettucini.

'I can hardly believe I'm hearing this,' Anna said, unable to disguise the weariness in her voice. 'When are people like you going to accept that one or two of us are capable of a little more than spending our lives waiting hand and foot on the male sex.'

The waiter poured some wine into my glass.

'Yes. Of course. Absolutely. No. I didn't mean it to sound like that . . .' I sipped the wine and nodded to the waiter, who filled Anna's glass.

'Then what did you mean it to sound like?' demanded Anna as she stuck her fork firmly into the fettucini.

'Well, isn't it unusual for a man to go to a woman doctor?' I said, realising the moment I had uttered the words that I was only getting myself into even deeper water.

'Good heavens, no, Michael. We live in an enlightened age. I've probably seen more naked men than you have

380

– and it's not an attractive sight, I can assure you.' I laughed, in the hope that it would ease the tension. 'In any case,' she added, 'quite a few men are confident enough to accept the existence of women doctors, you know.'

'I'm sure that's true,' I said. 'I just thought . . .'

'You didn't think, Michael. That's the problem with so many men like you. I bet you've never even considered consulting a woman doctor.'

'No, but . . . Yes, but . . .'

'"No but, yes but" – Let's change the subject before I get really angry,' Anna said, putting her fork down. 'What do you do for a living, Michael? It doesn't sound as if you're in a profession where women are treated as equals.'

'I'm in the restaurant business,' I told her, wishing the fettucini was a little lighter.

'Ah, yes, you told me in the interval,' she said. 'But what does being "in the restaurant business" actually mean?'

'I'm on the management side. Or at least, that's what I do nowadays. I started life as a waiter, then I moved into the kitchens for about five years, and finally . . .'

'. . . found you weren't very good at either, so you took up managing everyone else.'

'Something like that,' I said, trying to make light of it. But Anna's words only reminded me that one of my other restaurants was without a chef that night, and that that was where I'd been heading before I'd allowed myself to become infatuated by Anna.

'I've lost you again,' Anna said, beginning to sound exasperated. 'You were going to tell me all about restaurant management.'

'Yes, I was, wasn't I? By the way, how's your fettucini?'

'Not bad, considering.'

'Considering?'

'Considering this place was your second choice.'

I was silenced once again.

'It's not that bad,' she said, taking another reluctant forkful.

'Perhaps you'd like something else instead? I can always . . .'

'No, thank you, Michael. After all, this was the one dish the waiter felt confident enough to recommend.'

I couldn't think of a suitable response, so I remained silent.

'Come on, Michael, you still haven't explained what restaurant management actually involves,' said Anna.

'Well, at the moment I'm running three restaurants in the West End, which means I never stop dashing from one to the other, depending on which is facing the biggest crisis on that particular day.'

'Sounds a bit like ward duty to me,' said Anna. 'So who turned out to have the biggest crisis today?'

'Today, thank heaven, was not typical,' I told her with feeling.

'That bad?' said Anna.

'Yes, I'm afraid so. We lost a chef this morning who cut off the top of his finger, and won't be back at work

382

for at least a fortnight. My head waiter in our second restaurant is off, claiming he has 'flu, and I've just had to sack the barman in the third for fiddling the books. Barmen always fiddle the books, of course, but in this case even the customers began to notice what he was up to.' I paused, wondering if I should risk another mouthful of fettucini. 'But I still wouldn't want to be in any other business.'

'In the circumstances, I'm frankly amazed you were able to take the evening off.'

'I shouldn't have, really, and wouldn't have, except . . .' I trailed off as I leaned over and topped up Anna's wine glass.

'Except what?' she said.

'Do you want to hear the truth?' I asked as I poured the remains of the wine into my own glass.

'I'll try that for starters,' she said.

I placed the empty bottle on the side of the table, and hesitated, but only for a moment. 'I was driving to one of my restaurants earlier this evening, when I spotted you going into the theatre. I stared at you for so long that I nearly crashed into the back of the car in front of me. Then I swerved across the road into the nearest parking space, and the car behind almost crashed into me. I leapt out, ran all the way to the theatre, and searched everywhere until I saw you standing in the queue for the box office. I joined the line and watched you hand over your spare ticket. Once you were safely out of sight, I told the box office manager that you hadn't expected me to make it in time, and that you might have put my ticket up for resale. Once I'd described you, which I was able to do in great detail, he handed it over without so much as a murmur.'

'More fool him,' said Anna, putting down her glass and staring at me as if I'd just been released from a lunatic asylum.

'Then I put two ten-pound notes into a theatre envelope and took the place next to you,' I continued. 'The rest you already know.' I waited, with some trepidation, to see how she would react.

'I suppose I ought to be flattered,' Anna said after a moment's consideration. 'But I don't know whether to laugh or cry. One thing's for certain; the woman I've been living with for the past ten years will think it's highly amusing, especially as you paid for her ticket.'

The waiter returned to remove the half-finished plates. 'Was everything all right, sir?' he asked, sounding anxious.

'Fine, just fine,' I said unconvincingly. Anna grimaced, but made no comment.

'Would you care for coffee, madam?'

'No, I don't think I'll risk it,' she said, looking at her watch. 'In any case, I ought to be getting back. Elizabeth will be wondering where I've got to.'

She stood up and walked towards the door. I followed a yard behind. She was just about to step onto the pavement when she turned to me and asked, 'Don't you think you ought to settle the bill?'

'That won't be necessary.'

'Why?' she asked, laughing. 'Do you own the place?'

'No. But it is one of the three restaurants I manage.'

Anna turned scarlet. 'I'm so sorry, Michael,' she said. 'That was tactless of me.' She paused for a moment before adding, 'But I'm sure you'll agree that the food wasn't exactly memorable.'

'Would you like me to drive you home?' I asked, trying not to sound too enthusiastic.

Anna looked up at the black clouds. 'That would be useful,' she replied, 'if it's not miles out of your way. Where's your car?' she said before I had a chance to ask where she lived.

'I left it just up the road.'

'Oh, yes, I remember,' said Anna. 'When you jumped out of it because you couldn't take your eyes off me. I'm afraid you picked the wrong girl this time.'

At last we had found something on which we could agree, but I made no comment as we walked towards the spot where I had abandoned my car. Anna limited her conversation to whether it was about to rain again, and how good she had thought the wine was. I was relieved to find my Volvo parked exactly where I had left it.

I was searching for my keys when I spotted a large sticker glued to the windscreen. I looked down at the front offside wheel, and saw the yellow clamp.

'It just isn't your night, is it?' said Anna. 'But don't worry about me, I'll just grab a cab.'

She raised her hand and a taxi skidded to a halt. She turned back to face me. 'Thanks for dinner,' she managed, not altogether convincingly, and added, even less convincingly, 'Perhaps we'll meet again.' Before I could respond, she had slammed the taxi door closed.

As I watched her being driven away, it started to rain.

I took one more look at my immovable car, and decided I would deal with the problem in the morning.

I was about to rush for the nearest shelter when another taxi came around the corner, its yellow light indicating that it was for hire. I waved frantically and it drew up beside my clamped car.

'Bad luck, mate,' said the cabbie, looking down at my front wheel. 'My third tonight.'

I attempted a smile.

'So, where to, guv?'

I gave him my address in Lambeth and climbed into the back.

As the taxi manoeuvred its way slowly through the rainswept post-theatre traffic and across Waterloo Bridge, the driver began chattering away. I just about managed monosyllabic replies to his opinions on the weather, John Major, the England cricket team and foreign tourists. With each new topic, his forecast became ever more gloomy.

He only stopped offering his opinions when he came to a halt outside my house in Fentiman Road. I paid him, and smiled ruefully at the thought that this would be the first time in weeks that I'd managed to get home before midnight. I walked slowly up the short path to the front door.

I turned the key in the lock and opened the door quietly, so as not to wake my wife. Once inside I went through my nightly ritual of slipping off my jacket and shoes before creeping quietly up the stairs.

Before I had reached the bedroom I began to get undressed. After years of coming in at one or two in the morning, I was able to take off all my clothes, fold and stack them, and slide under the sheets next to Judy without waking her. But just as I pulled back the cover she said drowsily, 'I didn't think you'd be home so early, with all the problems you were facing tonight.' I wondered if she was talking in her sleep. 'How much damage did the fire do?'

'The fire?' I said, standing in the nude.

'In Davies Street. Gerald phoned a few moments after you'd left to say a fire had started in the kitchen and had spread to the restaurant. He was just checking to make certain you were on your way. He'd cancelled all the bookings for the next two weeks, but he didn't think they'd be able to open again for at least a month. I told him that as you'd left just after six you'd be with him at any minute. So, just how bad is the damage?'

I was already dressed by the time Judy was awake enough to ask why I had never turned up at the restaurant. I shot down the stairs and out onto the street in search of another cab. It had started raining again.

A taxi swung round and came to a halt in front of me.

'Where to this time, guv?'

À Point

'THANK YOU, MICHAEL. I'D LIKE THAT.'
I smiled, unable to mask my delight.

'Hi, Pipsqueak. I thought I might have missed you.'

I turned and stared at a tall man with a mop of fair hair, who seemed unaffected by the steady flow of people trying to pass him on either side.

Anna gave him a smile that I hadn't seen until that moment.

'Hello, Jonathan,' she said. 'This is Michael Whitaker. You're lucky – he bought your ticket, and if you hadn't turned up I was just about to accept his kind invitation to dinner. Michael, this is my brother, Jonathan – the one who was held up at the hospital. As you can see, he's now escaped.'

I couldn't think of a suitable reply.

Jonathan shook me warmly by the hand. 'Thank you for keeping my sister company,' he said. 'Won't you join us for dinner?'

'That's kind of you,' I replied, 'but I've just remembered that I'm meant to be somewhere else right now. I'd better . . .'

'You're not meant to be anywhere else right now,'

interrupted Anna, giving me the same smile. 'Don't be so feeble.' She linked her arm in mine. 'In any case, we'd *both* like you to join us.'

'Thank you,' I said.

'There's a restaurant just down the road that I've been told is rather good,' said Jonathan, as the three of us began walking off in the direction of the Strand.

'Great. I'm famished,' said Anna.

'So, tell me all about the play,' Jonathan said as Anna linked her other arm in his.

'Every bit as good as the critics promised,' said Anna.

'You were unlucky to miss it,' I said.

'But I'm rather glad you did,' said Anna as we reached the corner of the Strand.

'I think that's the place I'm looking for,' said Jonathan, pointing to a large grey double door on the far side of the road. The three of us weaved our way through the temporarily stationary traffic.

Once we reached the other side of the road Jonathan pushed open one of the grey doors to allow us through. It started to rain just as we stepped inside. He led Anna and me down a flight of stairs into a basement restaurant buzzing with the talk of people who had just come out of theatres, and waiters dashing, plates in both hands, from table to table.

'I'll be impressed if you can get a table here,' Anna said to her brother, eyeing a group of would-be customers who were clustered round the bar, impatiently waiting for someone to leave. 'You should have booked,' she added as he began waving at the head waiter, who was fully occupied taking a customer's order.

I remained a yard or two behind them, and as Mario came across, I put a finger to my lips and nodded to him.

'I don't suppose you have a table for three?' asked Jonathan.

'Yes, of course, sir. Please follow me,' said Mario, leading us to a quiet table in the corner of the room.

'That was a bit of luck,' said Jonathan.

'It certainly was,' Anna agreed. Jonathan suggested that I take the far chair, so his sister could sit between us.

Once we had settled, Jonathan asked what I would like to drin'

'How about you?' I said, turning to Anna. 'Another dry martini?'

Jonathan looked surprised. 'You haven't had a dry martini since . . .'

Anna scowled at him and said quickly, 'I'll just have a glass of wine with the meal.'

Since when? I wondered, but only said, 'I'll have the same.'

Mario reappeared, and handed us our menus. Jonathan and Anna studied theirs in silence for some time before Jonathan asked, 'Any ideas?'

'It all looks so tempting,' Anna said. 'But I think I'll settle for the fettucini and a glass of red wine.'

'What about a starter?' asked Jonathan.

'No. I'm on first call tomorrow, if you remember – unless of course you're volunteering to take my place.'

'Not after what I've been through this evening, Pipsqueak. I'd rather go without a starter too,' he said. 'How about you, Michael? Don't let our domestic problems get in your way.'

'Fettucini and a glass of red wine would suit me just fine.'

'Three fettucini and a bottle of your best Chianti,' said Jonathan when Mario returned.

Anna leaned over to me and whispered conspiratorially, 'It's the only Italian wine he can pronounce correctly.'

'What would have happened if we'd chosen fish?' I asked her.

'He's also heard of Frascati, but he's never quite sure what he's meant to do when someone orders duck.'

'What are you two whispering about?' asked Jonathan as he handed his menu back to Mario.

'I was asking your sister about the third partner in the practice.'

'Not bad, Michael,' Anna said. 'You should have gone into politics.'

'My wife, Elizabeth, is the third partner,' Jonathan said, unaware of what Anna had been getting at. 'She, poor darling, is on call tonight.'

'You note, two women and one man,' said Anna as the wine waiter appeared by Jonathan's side.

'Yes. There used to be four of us,' said Jonathan, without explanation. He studied the label on the bottle before nodding sagely.

'You're not fooling anyone, Jonathan. Michael has

already worked out that you're no sommelier,' said Anna, sounding as if she was trying to change the subject. The waiter extracted the cork and poured a little wine into Jonathan's glass for him to taste.

'So, what do you do, Michael?' asked Jonathan after he had given a second nod to the wine waiter. 'Don't tell me you're a doctor, because I'm not looking for another man to join the practice.'

'No, he's in the restaurant business,' said Anna, as three bowls of fettucini were placed in front of us.

'I see. You two obviously swapped life histories during the interval,' said Jonathan. 'But what does being "in the restaurant business" actually mean?'

'I'm on the management side,' I explained. 'Or at least, that's what I do nowadays. I started life as a waiter, then I moved into the kitchens for about five years, and finally ended up in management.'

'But what does a restaurant manager actually do?' asked Anna.

'Obviously the interval wasn't long enough for you to go into any great detail,' said Jonathan as he jabbed his fork into some fettucini.

'Well, at the moment I'm running three restaurants in the West End, which means I never stop dashing from one to the other, depending on which is facing the biggest crisis on that particular day.'

'Sounds a bit like ward duty to me,' said Anna. 'So who turned out to have the biggest crisis today?'

'Today, thank heaven, was not typical,' I said with feeling.

'That bad?' said Jonathan.

'Yes, I'm afraid so. We lost a chef this morning who cut off the top of his finger, and won't be back at work for at least a fortnight. My head waiter in our second restaurant is off, claiming he has 'flu, and I've just had to sack the barman in the third for fiddling the books. Barmen always fiddle the books, of course, but in this case even the customers began to notice what he was up to.' I paused. 'But I still wouldn't want to be in any other . . .'

A shrill ring interrupted me. I couldn't tell where the sound was coming from until Jonathan removed a tiny cellular phone from his jacket pocket.

'Sorry about this,' he said. 'Hazard of the job.' He pressed a button and put the phone to his ear. He listened for a few seconds, and a frown appeared on his face. 'Yes, I suppose so. I'll be there as quickly as I can.' He flicked the phone closed and put it back into his pocket.

'Sorry,' he repeated. 'One of my patients has chosen this particular moment to have a relapse. I'm afraid I'm going to have to leave you.' He stood up and turned to his sister. 'How will you get home, Pipsqueak?'

'I'm a big girl now,' said Anna, 'so I'll just look around for one of those black objects on four wheels with a sign on the top that reads T-A-X-I, and then I'll wave at it.'

'Don't worry, Jonathan,' I said. 'I'll drive her home.'

'That's very kind of you,' said Jonathan, 'because if it's still pouring by the time you leave, she may not be able to find one of those black objects to wave at.'

'In any case, it's the least I can do, after I ended up getting your ticket, your dinner and your sister.'

'Fair exchange,' said Jonathan as Mario came rushing up.

'Is everything all right, sir?' he asked.

'No, it isn't. I'm on call, and have to go.' He handed over an American Express card. 'If you'd be kind enough to put this through your machine, I'll sign for it and you can fill in the amount later. And please add fifteen per cent.'

'Thank you, sir,' said Mario, and rushed away.

'Hope to see you again,' said Jonathan. I rose to shake him by the hand.

'I hope so too,' I said.

Jonathan left us, headed for the bar and signed a slip of paper. Mario handed him back his American Express card.

As Anna waved to her brother, I looked towards the bar and shook my head slightly. Mario tore up the little slip of paper and dropped the pieces into a waste-paper basket.

'It hasn't been a wonderful day for Jonathan, either,' said Anna, turning back to face me. 'And what with your problems, I'm amazed you were able to take the evening off.'

'I shouldn't have, really, and wouldn't have, except . . .' I trailed off as I leaned over and topped up Anna's glass.

'Except what?' she asked.

'Do you want to hear the truth?' I asked as I poured the remains of the wine into my own glass.

'I'll try that for starters,' she said.

I placed the empty bottle on the side of the table, and hesitated, but only for a moment. 'I was driving to one of my restaurants earlier this evening, when I spotted you going into the theatre. I stared at you for so long that I nearly crashed into the back of the car in front of me. Then I swerved across the road into the nearest parking space, and the car behind almost crashed into me. I leapt out, ran all the way to the theatre, and searched everywhere until I saw you standing in the queue for the box office. I joined the line and watched you hand over your spare ticket. Once you were safely out of sight, I told the box office manager that you hadn't expected me to make it in time, and that you might have put my ticket up for resale. After I'd described you, which I was able to do in great detail, he handed it over without so much as a murmur.'

Anna put down her glass of wine and stared across at me with a look of incredulity. 'I'm glad he fell for your story,' she said. 'But should I?'

'Yes, you should. Because then I put two ten-pound notes into a theatre envelope and took the place next to you,' I continued. 'The rest you already know.' I waited to see how she would react. She didn't speak for some time.

'I'm flattered,' she said eventually. 'I didn't realise there were any old-fashioned romantics left in the world.' She lowered her head slightly. 'Am I allowed to ask what you have planned for the rest of the evening?'

'Nothing has been planned so far,' I admitted. 'Which is why it's all been so refreshing.'

'You make me sound like an After Eight mint,' said Anna with a laugh.

'I can think of at least three replies to that,' I told her as Mario reappeared, looking a little disappointed at the sight of the half-empty plates.

'Is everything all right, sir?' he asked, sounding anxious.

'Couldn't have been better,' said Anna, who hadn't stopped looking at me.

'Would you like a coffee, madam?' Mario asked her.

'No, thank you,' said Anna firmly. 'We have to go in search of a marooned car.'

'Heaven knows if it will still be there after all this time,' I said as she rose from her place.

I took Anna's hand, led her towards the entrance, back up the stairs and out onto the street. Then I began to retrace my steps to the spot where I'd abandoned my car. As we strolled up the Aldwych and chatted away, I felt as if I was with an old friend.

'You don't have to give me a lift, Michael,' Anna was saying. 'It's probably miles out of your way, and in any case it's stopped raining, so I'll just hail a taxi.'

'I want to give you a lift,' I told her. 'That way I'll have your company for a little longer.' She smiled as we reached a distressingly large space where I had left the car.

'Damn,' I said. I quickly checked up and down the road, and returned to find Anna laughing.

'Is this another of your schemes to have more of my company?' she teased. She opened her bag and took out a mobile phone, dialled 999, and passed it over to me.

'Which service do you require? Fire, Police or Ambulance?' a voice asked.

'Police,' I said, and was immediately put through to another voice.

'Charing Cross Police Station. What is the nature of your enquiry?'

'I think my car has been stolen.'

'Can you tell me the make, colour and registration number please, sir.'

'It's a blue Rover 600, registration K857 SHV.'

There was a long pause, during which I could hear other voices talking in the background.

'No, it hasn't been stolen, sir,' said the officer who had been dealing with me when he came back on the line. 'The vehicle was illegally parked on a double yellow line. It's been removed and taken to the Vauxhall Bridge Pound.'

'Can I pick it up now?' I asked.

'Certainly, sir. How will you be getting there?'

'I'll take a taxi.'

'Then just ask the driver for the Vauxhall Bridge Pound. Once you get there, you'll need some form of identification, and a cheque for £105 with a banker's card – that is if you don't have the full amount in cash.'

'£105?' I said quietly.

'That's correct, sir.'

Anna frowned for the first time that evening.

'Worth every penny.'

'I beg your pardon, sir?'

'Nothing, officer. Goodnight.'

I handed the phone back to Anna, and said, 'The next thing I'm going to do is find you a taxi.'

'You certainly are not, Michael, because I'm staying with you. In any case, you promised my brother you'd take me home.'

I took her hand and hailed a taxi, which swung across the road and came to a halt beside us.

'Vauxhall Bridge Pound, please.'

'Bad luck, mate,' said the cabbie. 'You're my fourth this evening.'

I gave him a broad grin.

'I expect the other three also chased you into the theatre, but luckily they were behind me in the queue,' I said to Anna as I joined her on the back seat.

As the taxi manoeuvred its way slowly through the rainswept post-theatre traffic and across Waterloo Bridge, Anna said, 'Don't you think I should have been given the chance to choose between the four of you? After all, one of them might have been driving a Rolls-Royce.'

'Not possible.'

'And why not, pray?' asked Anna.

'Because you couldn't have parked a Rolls-Royce in that space.'

'But if he'd had a chauffeur, that would have solved all my problems.'

'In that case, I would simply have run him over.'

The taxi had travelled some distance before either of us spoke again.

'Can I ask you a personal question?' Anna eventually said.

'If it's what I think it is, I was about to ask you the same thing.'

'Then you go first.'

'No – I'm not married,' I said. 'Nearly, once, but she escaped.' Anna laughed. 'And you?'

'I was married,' she said quietly. 'He was the fourth doctor in the practice. He died three years ago. I spent nine months nursing him, but in the end I failed.'

'I'm so sorry,' I said, feeling a little ashamed. 'That was tactless of me. I shouldn't have raised the subject.'

'I raised it, Michael, not you. It's me who should apologise.'

Neither of us spoke again for several minutes, until Anna said, 'For the past three years, since Andrew's death, I've immersed myself in work, and I seem to spend most of my spare time boring Jonathan and Elizabeth to distraction. They couldn't have been more understanding, but they must be heartily sick of it by now. I wouldn't be surprised if Jonathan hadn't arranged an emergency for tonight, so someone else could take me to the theatre for a change. It might even give me the confidence to go out again. Heaven knows,' she added as we drove into the car pound, 'enough people have been kind enough to ask me.'

I passed the cabbie a ten-pound note and we dashed through the rain in the direction of a little Portakabin.

I walked up to the counter and read the form sellotaped

to it. I took out my wallet, extracted my driving licence, and began counting.

I only had eighty pounds in cash, and I never carry a chequebook.

Anna grinned, and took the envelope I'd presented to her earlier in the evening from her bag. She tore it open and extracted the two ten-pound notes, added a five-pound note of her own, and handed them over to me.

'Thank you,' I said, once again feeling embarrassed.

'Worth every penny,' she replied with a grin.

The policeman counted the notes slowly, placed them in a tin box, and gave me a receipt.

'It's right there, in the front row,' he said, pointing out of the window. 'And if I may say so, sir, it was perhaps unwise of you to leave your keys in the ignition. If the vehicle had been stolen, your insurance company would not have been liable to cover the claim.' He passed me my keys.

'It was my fault, officer,' said Anna. 'I should have sent him back for them, but I didn't realise what he was up to. I'll make sure he doesn't do it again.'

The officer looked up at me. I shrugged my shoulders and led Anna out of the cabin and across to my car. I opened the door to let her in, then nipped round to the driver's side as she leant over and pushed my door open. I took my place behind the wheel and turned to face her. 'I'm sorry,' I said. 'The rain has ruined your dress.' A drop of water fell off the end of her nose. 'But, you know, you're just as beautiful wet or dry.'

'Thank you, Michael,' she smiled. 'But if you don't have any objection, on balance I'd prefer to be dry.'

I laughed. 'So, where shall I take you?' I asked, suddenly aware that I didn't know where she lived.

'Fulham, please. 49 Parsons Green Lane. It's not too far.'

I pushed the key into the ignition, not caring how far it was. I turned the key and took a deep breath. The engine spluttered, but refused to start. Then I realised I had left the sidelights on.

'Don't do this to me,' I begged, as Anna began laughing again. I turned the key a second time, and the motor caught. I let out a sigh of relief.

'That was a close one,' Anna said. 'If it hadn't started, we might have ended up spending the rest of the night together. Or was that all part of your dastardly plan?'

'Nothing's gone to plan so far,' I admitted as I drove out of the pound. I paused before adding, 'Still, I suppose things might have turned out differently.'

'You mean if I hadn't been the sort of girl you were looking for?'

'Something like that.'

'I wonder what those other three men would have thought of me,' said Anna wistfully.

'Who cares? They're not going to have the chance to find out.'

'You sound very sure of yourself, Mr Whitaker.'

'If you only knew,' I said. 'But I would like to see you again, Anna. If you're willing to risk it.'

She seemed to take an eternity to reply. 'Yes, I'd like

that,' she said eventually. 'But only on condition that you pick me up at my place, so I can be certain you park your car legally, and remember to switch your lights off.'

'I accept your terms,' I told her. 'And I won't even add any conditions of my own if we can begin the agreement tomorrow evening.'

Once again Anna didn't reply immediately. 'I'm not sure I know what I'm doing tomorrow evening.'

'Neither do I,' I said. 'But I'll cancel it, whatever it is.'

'Then so will I,' said Anna as I drove into Parsons Green Lane, and began searching for number forty-nine.

'It's about a hundred yards down, on the left,' she said.

I drew up and parked outside her front door.

'Don't let's bother with the theatre this time,' said Anna. 'Come round at about eight, and I'll cook you some supper.' She leant over and kissed me on the cheek before turning back to open the car door. I jumped out and walked quickly round to her side of the car as she stepped onto the pavement.

'So, I'll see you around eight tomorrow evening,' she said.

'I'll look forward to that.' I hesitated, and then took her in my arms. 'Goodnight, Anna.'

'Goodnight, Michael,' she said as I released her. 'And thank you for buying my ticket, not to mention dinner. I'm glad my other three would-be suitors only made it as far as the car pound.'

I smiled as she pushed the key into the lock of her front door.

She turned back. 'By the way, Michael, was that the restaurant with the missing waiter, the four-and-a-half-fingered chef, or the crooked bartender?'

'The crooked bartender,' I replied with a smile.

She closed the door behind her as the clock on a nearby church struck one.